Traitors in Treblinka

Jenz and Ezekiel risk their lives to help fellow Jewish residents of the Conquered Territories avoid the horror of brutal Nazi oppression.

J.H. Ahlin

Kravitz & Sons
INNOVATORS IN PUBLISHING, MARKETING AND ADVERTISING

Kravitz and Sons LLC
204 E Arlington Blvd. Suite B
Greenville, NC 27858

Published by Kravitz and Sons LLC.

ISBN: 979-8-89639-543-0 (sc)
ISBN: 979-8-89639-544-7 (e)
ISBN: 979-8-89639-545-4 (hb)

"Spy Thriller and Political Terrorism Fiction"

Dedication

Traitors in Treblinka is dedicated to the millions of victims of Nazi oppression who had their homes, possessions, and very lives stolen. The world will never know the extent of our loss. How many composers, scientists, leaders, and inventors were lost to the crematoriums? Our tragedy is ongoing and unending.

Table of Contents

Prologue

What follows is a personal account of confronting horror. Scenes pf cruelty, suffering, and explicit sexuality may not be suitable foryoung readers.

Individual experiences in this story, in fact, reflect the degradation of an entire society, previously among civilization's most advanced. Implicit in the story, then, is the question: What brought about the collapse of values and decency within Germany? Included is the debilitating hyperinflation of the post-World War I Weimer Republic, and its undermining of the trust, civility and work ethic of the German people.

Now, in the centennial year of my life, I am remembering and recounting the time my friend Ezekiel and I had to visit the death camps in Poland. We were sent to these places of inhuman horror by our boss at the secret Army Rocket Research Facility in northern Germany near the town of Peenemünde. General Dornberger* was in charge of this secret rocket research and testing facility.

His primary concern was the health of his Jewish slave-laborer workforce, who constructed, tested, and finished the secret V-I and V-II missiles. The general was determined to know why his Jewish

---

*Major General Dr. Walter Robert Dornberger was a German artillery officer whose career spanned two wars. He was captured by the armed forces of the United States in WW I and spent almost 2 years in a French POW camp. He rose to the rank of General as the leader of the Wehrmacht secret rocket base at Peenemünde in northern Germany during WW II. After WW II, General Dornberger was brought to the United States along with 1600 other German engineers and scientists to work for the United States Government rocket development program under the secret intel code, "Operation Paperclip."

From 1950-1965 he worked for the Bell Aircraft Corporation, rising to the level of Vice President. He was a major contributor to the X-15 project and instrumental in advancing the United States space exploration. Following retirement, he returned to Germany and died on 27 July 1980 at Baden-Württemberg. He was 95 years old.

technicians and laborers were lasting only a few months before getting ill and often succumbing to sickness or exhaustion.

I remember our orders read: "Discover why our Jewish prison workers are dying of disease or exhaustion after only a few months at our facility." The General appointed Ezekiel and me to discover what was happening to our Jews in the two labor camps supplying most of our laborers: Treblinka and Auschwitz.

It has been over 8 decades since those unforgettable and horrifying visits to the death camps, and I beg the reader's forgiveness. Forgiveness for being an unwilling participant in the most corrupt criminal conspiracy ever to be perpetuated on an unsuspecting nation. My beautiful country, Germany, was brought to near-total ruin by greedy and self-serving politicians and their criminal henchmen during the 1930s and 40s.

I was an unwilling participant because I looked very Aryan. At age sixteen, I was six feet four and a half inches tall with sandy blond hair and steel blue-grey eyes. My biggest problem, and the problem that saved my life, was that I was Jewish. My mother's family was one hundred percent Jewish, and my dad was Swedish- Christian. Although I never thought too deeply about my faith growing up, I found it most interesting to be comfortable attending either church or synagogue.

I always tried to be attentive to the teachings of the Bible or the written Torah. Many of the prayers I had learned in my early years attending our synagogue and church helped me and my childhood and my life-long friend, Ezekiel Leven, get through the terribly sad and difficult years of the Holocaust.

When "Traitors in the Gestapo" was completed, I knew I had purposely left out a several-month period of time near the end of 1942-1943 when Ezekiel and I were ordered to the concentration labor camps to find an answer to General Dornberger's question. He was determined to know why his Jewish technicians and laborers were only lasting a few months before they became ill or succumbed to disease or exhaustion. These few months were painful and dangerous for Ezekiel and me. Whenever I thought about our time at Auschwitz and Treblinka, I had trouble breathing and seeing clearly through watery eyes for several years. It was the most heartbreaking period in our lives. To this day, I find myself shaking and weeping at the thought of the murder of so many children and innocent victims of the Nazi occupation forces.

My lifelong friend Ezekiel and I severely underestimated the risk these camps posed to us. We really had no idea we were heading toward imminent danger. In addition, neither of us realized the Gestapo [*] was on to us until it was almost too late. Writing about these times is very difficult, but this is our story.

---

*Gestapo is an abbreviation of the German name for Geheime Staatspolizei, translated as the (Secret State Police). On February 10th, 1936, the Nazi Reichstag passed the "Gestapo Law," which included the following statement: "Neither the instructions nor the affairs of the Gestapo will be open to review by the administrative courts." This meant the Gestapo was now above the law, and there could be no legal appeal regarding anything it did. Gestapo Headquarters on No. 8 Prinz Albrecht Strasse, Berlin, brought fear and trepidation to German citizens who could often hear the cries and screams of those unlucky enough to be questioned by the Gestapo.

Introduction

The commanding officer of Germany's very secret rocket training group Major General Walter Dornberger, had a problem. It was a simple problem but with a rather complex solution, with dire implications if handled incorrectly.

In the 1930s, before the start of World War II, the Nazi top-secret rocket program was based on the northern coast of Germany on Usedom Island in the Baltic Sea. This Army research facility was so secret most people in the German Army knew nothing about it. Even senior officers in the Wehrmacht knew nothing about what was going on in this northern outpost. The German public was completely unaware of the cutting-edge advanced research being accomplished on this military facility; most folks were not even aware there was a military base at this location.

In 1936 on April second, the German Ministry of Aviation paid 750,000DMarks to the town of Wolgast for the entire northern half of the Island of Usedom in the Baltic Sea. This peninsula became the home of the secret Army Research Center for developing rockets for military use.

The German High Command was able to investigate rocket research because this form of armament was not specifically prohibited or even contemplated by the Treaty of Versailles, which ended the Great War (WW I). This loophole in the treaty allowed the Nazis to secretly develop the V-I and V-II missiles as weapons of war without violating the Versailles Treaty.

General Dornberger's principal problem was that he didn't like or ever want to work for the head boss at SS headquarters, Reichführer Heinrich Himmler.*

The General considered Himmler and his entire SS organization a para-military organization that, at best, provided the Wehrmacht and the German people very little protection or benefit for the vast sums of money the Reich was spending on developing it. Even more concerning to the General, the SS perpetuated what seemed to be a thug-like club-like atmosphere that was only one step above the SA (Brownshirts) and the Gestapo, the National German Secret State Police.

The Schutzstaffel, or SS was originally designed in 1925 as a protective squadron or echelon for our Führer, Adolf Hitler. In the 1930s, Reichführer Himmler had set up and staffed the labor camps that supplied slave labor for rocket manufacturing at Peenemünde.

After the British bombed the secret missile development base on Peenemünde in August 1943, labor from the Dora Concentration Camp was used to build and maintain the gypsum mine in Nordhausen near the geographic center of Germany. The research and manufacturing of the V-1 and V-2 missiles were moved to the gypsum mine to avoid the range and detection of the Allied and Russian bombers.

The Dora Camp supplied slave labor to build out the gypsum mine for rocket development and manufacturing. The protective-custody leader and Commandant of the Dora Camp was a monster named SS- Obersturmführer Hans Karl Moeser. **

These labor camps were built in Germany, Poland, and all-over Eastern Europe. A particular criminal element in the SS called the SS

---

*Heinrich Luitpold Himmler, a former chicken farmer, was the main architect of the Holocaust. He became head of the SS in 1929 and developed and organized the concentration camps throughout the Third Reich. He was greatly feared by friends and foes alike. He was captured by the Russians while trying to flee the country after the war. He was turned over to the British at their headquarters in Lüneburg, Germany, in May 1945. Upon examination by a British medical doctor, Himmler kept jerking his head away when it came time for an oral examination. Under threat of a forced oral examination, Himmler took the coward's way out, crushed a potassium cyanide pill, and died in 15 minutes on 23 May 1945. The man responsible for the murder of six million Jewish, Romani, and Russian Prisoners of War and countless other men, women, and children was 45 years old.

**In December 1945, an American Military Tribunal sentenced Moeser to death. At his hanging, his last words were: "The same way, with the same pleasure, you shoot deer, I shoot a human being. When I came to the SS and had to shoot the first three persons, my food didn't taste good for three days, but now it is a pleasure. It is a joy for me."

Death's Head Division was tasked with guarding and running these labor or concentration camps.

The Rocket Research Center had to be moved from Peenemünde, on Germany's northern coast, to the gypsum mine in Thuringia, Germany. Mittelwerk (Central Works) near the town of Nordhausen was chosen because the British had discovered the research center on Peenemünde and bombed it on the 17th and 18th of August 1943. The new manufacturing and assembly plant for the rockets had to be far from the reach of the Russian and Allied bombers.

The concentration camp inmates that Himmler sent the General to the Army Research Rocket Center in Peenemünde and Mittelwerk to manufacture the rockets were very talented slave laborers. The workers included electrical engineers, mechanical engineers, teachers, electricians, jewelers, clockmakers, and all sorts of technically skilled people. The problem was that almost one hundred percent of the workers sent by Himmler from the camps were sick, malnourished, and exhausted.

By the time these skilled Jewish workers mastered the manufacturing process for the V-1 and V-2 missiles, they were literally completely spent. They rarely lasted more than two or three months. If they didn't die of diseases picked up at the camps, they died of injuries because their bodies couldn't take the rigors of rocket manufacturing and army life at the research center, even though the food and living conditions were much improved over the dire conditions that existed in the labor camps. There was speculation that many prisoners died because of the abrupt change to an improved diet.

The labor situation at Peenemünde finally reached the point where General Dornberger decided to send out two men to investigate the concentration or labor camps. He could not replace his labor force fast enough to build and test the "wonder weapons" he was developing. The general wanted to see what could be done to improve the health of the slave labor workers he was getting to assemble his rockets. He decided on one of his tall SS First Lieutenants, Jens Ramsgrund, and one newly indoctrinated Wehrmacht scientist, Vitali Carapezza. These men were to head the investigation into the nutrition, health care, and typical accommodations at the different labor or concentration camps.

The general directed the investigation to start at the camps where most of their workers were coming from: Treblinka, 60 kilometers northeast of Warsaw, and Auschwitz in southern Poland. General Dornberger had no idea the camp at Treblinka was not a labor camp at all but, indeed, a death camp built specifically to liquidate the victims of the Warsaw Ghetto in Poland. These victims had been living peacefully with the city residents until the Nazis invaded their country.

The general also didn't realize that his SS First Lieutenant had a Jewish mother, and the newly Wehrmacht indoctrinated scientist wasn't Vitali Carapezza, but the First Lieutenant's boyhood friend, who also happened to be Jewish, Ezekiel Leven.

Despite their being Jews, both men were eager to investigate the labor camps and find out what was really going on within those barbed wire walls. Jenz mentioned to Vitali when they were alone, "Zeke, we just might be the best choice the General could have made. You might say we are 'uniquely qualified' to get an 'up-front' and accurate report to General Dornberger."

Chapter 1

The School Years

My name is Jenz Ramsgrund. I was born in Düsseldorf, Germany, in 1920 on the 16 if September. My mom was a German Jew and my dad was a Swedish Christian. Although I grew up in Nazi Germany, I never considered the Nazi political party a threat to our country until my 15th birthday in 1935.

My best friend in grade school was a fellow Jew named Ezekiel Leven. We had known each other since the first day of the first grade of school in our hometown of Düsseldorf, Germany. Ezekiel changed my life. Of course, I didn't realize it then, but Zeke was to become a major influence in how we thought about and survived the coming dark days of history known as the Holocaust.

Both Zeke's parents were Jewish. His mom, Mrs. Leven, was a dear lady who kept a wonderful home in an upscale section of Düsseldorf. His father, Dr. Leven, was a prominent thoracic surgeon at the University Hospital in our city. After the Summer Olympics in 1936, the restrictions on Jews in Düsseldorf and throughout Germany became increasingly difficult for all Jewish families. There were book burnings of writings from prominent Jewish authors. Jewish physicians found it increasingly difficult to practice medicine at most hospitals in the Reich.

Even workers at my dad's plant, which had been consolidated into I. G. Farben had experienced instances of anti-Semitic activity against some of their staff members. One of my dad's colleagues had been dragged out of his office on some pretense, beaten, and was never seen again. When my father went down to the local Gestapo office in

Düsseldorf to inquire about his colleague, he was told never to come back and to never inquire about the individual again.

My dad did call back using an assumed name two weeks later. When he inquired about his colleague from Farben, there was no notice or record of him ever being arrested or held by the Gestapo. It was a very sad time for the worker's family.

I was quite large for my age. I could never seem to get enough to eat. I was always a little hungry, even at the end of a meal. In the third grade, I was almost the size of my teachers. My best friend Zeke was more normal-sized. We could always intuitively know what the other was thinking. This intuitive thinking was a great help when later in our lives, we had to outthink some of the nastiest criminals in all recorded history – the Gestapo.

While I was growing up and attending school, Zeke and I became best friends. We spent most of our time in and out of school, studying, eating meals, and attending school functions. We even went to each other's church and synagogue. Our parents also became friends. We would go on picnics together in the nearby woods.

On one occasion, our families had traveled quite deep into the forest north of Düsseldorf and were enjoying a quiet picnic near a picturesque stream It was late afternoon and the sun sent slanting spears of light through the tall pines.

We heard some noises and stomping in the nearby brush and two wild boars came charging out of the brush at us from about thirty meters away. Everyone got up and headed quickly back to the car park. I just stood there, amazed at the size and threatening noises of the grunting boars.

As one started to come at me in a loping charge, he made what sounded like a high-pitched scream, I just stood my ground and gave it a swift kick on the snout as soon as it got near me. My kick rolled the boar over. The animal seemed surprised and discouraged; both the boars waddled off into the brush.

My parents warned me never to try that trick again. Dr. Leven said the boar can become enraged and quite dangerous. "It's best to leave them alone unless you are armed with a rifle. Your large size perhaps discouraged the boars."

While in grade school, many of my classmates would make fun of me in a somewhat lighthearted teasing way because I was a little oversized. My mom was a German Jew. Although quite tall and athletic, she married someone even taller. My dad was a Swede who grew to a little over six feet five inches. They had met at a conference my father's company had in Sweden just after the Great War ended in November 1919.

Mom was always concerned with the amount of food I could consume. She was forever trying to get me to eat more whole grains and less baked goods. My problem: I was almost continuously hungry. Often, I felt I could eat another meal directly after eating lunch or dinner. If I skipped a meal or was late in eating at my normal time, I could get a little peckish. My mom was quite relieved when it seemed I had stopped growing at approximately six feet four and a half inches during my mid-teenage years.

Dad had worked for a life sciences company called Hoechst AG during the Great War. The company was trying to develop a medication that would be effective against a raging epidemic in Germany called the Spanish Flu. This disease had killed millions of people worldwide and was crippling the workforce in Germany. Mom and Dad met at a company conference devoted to recent research for this viral disease in Stockholm, Sweden, in 1919.

As I mentioned, my name is Jenz Ramsgrund. I was born in Düsseldorf, Germany, in 1920 on the 16 of September. My mom was a German Jew and my dad was a Swedish Christian. Although I grew up in Nazi Germany, I never considered the Nazi political party a problem until my 15th birthday in 1935. I'm approaching my centennial year, so I must be realistic about how much of this information I can furnish before I go to the next phase of my life or my memory fades completely.

On September 15th, 1935, the political leaders of my country passed what had become known as the Nuremberg Laws. At the time, the new laws meant nothing to me. My parents, however, reacted as if it was the end of Germany as they knew it. The laws were passed at the time I was celebrating my fifteenth birthday, on the sixteenth of September.

These new laws had two essential elements: The first element was the "Law for the Protection of German Blood and Honor." This law eliminated any possible marriages between Jews and Aryan Germans and forbade the employment of non-Jewish German women under the age of forty-five in Jewish households.

The second element of the Nuremberg Law was termed "The Reich Citizenship Law." This law stated that only Germans or of related blood could be eligible for Reich citizenship. All others, meaning Jews and Romani people (Gypsies), were to be classified as state subjects without citizenship rights.

In their "wisdom," the Reich politicians decided, for foreign policy concerns, to hold off on strict enforcement of these laws until after the Olympic Games, which were scheduled for Berlin in the summer of 1936. That was the summer I met the love of my life at a most unusual place: Hitler Youth Summer Camp.

My parents and teachers in my third year of secondary school urged me to attend Hitler Camp for two very different reasons. My teachers, especially my athletic coaches felt I had some athletic potential because of my size and quickness, I was almost six feet four and a half inches tall and had very quick reflexes. My long legs were a real benefit for running any school races in any type of track competition.

My parents, however, both thought it would be wise, if not mandatory, to attend Hitler Camp to help cover up my being Jewish. Even though I was quite tall, had sandy blond hair, and steel blue-grey eyes, they urged me to hide my strength and quickness by appearing awkward and letting others at the camp often win in any test of strength or endurance. In addition, they told me never to discuss religion or politics at camp. My dad also cautioned me never to unintentionally hurt any of my fellow campers in sporting or wrestling events. This was a curious request because my training at Hitler Camp focused on how to render the opposition helpless or dead. When I think about that training today, it was quite useful as Zeke and I got older.

After the Summer Olympics in 1936, more and more signs of antiSemitism sprouted up around our city of Düsseldorf and throughout Germany. It looked like Hitler could develop and extend his hatred and disrespect for Jews since the Olympics were over and the world's attention wasn't focused on Germany.

Ezekiel and I had to be very careful. Even walking around in downtown Düsseldorf could be dangerous. Often, Jews were accosted, searched, and beaten by the brownshirts and other unsavory elements of German society who were fervently anti-Semitic.

Fortunately, for me, Ezekiel was very smart. He had a sixth sense of dangerous situations and knew how to avoid trouble. He was kind and introspective; I was proud and honored to have him as a friend. It was almost as if my outward physical strength matched his inner steel strength.

Chapter 2

Hitler Youth Camp – Summer, 1936

Ilse and I met while swimming at a lake adjacent to our Hitler Youth Camps. After a long hike with a heavy pack, I had gone down to the lake with a fellow camper, Dieter. We were hot, drenched with sweat, tired and hungry. It was a very warm mid-summer day. Our thinking at the time was that a nice refreshing swim in the cool lake water would clean us up and help wake us up for dinner. We really didn't consider or even think about any possible repercussions from the camp counselors.

We certainly were not searching for members of the opposite sex. As I recall, most of my thoughts at Hitler Camp revolved around getting enough sleep and getting enough food. I was almost continuously hungry. If I didn't eat enough, I sometimes would get a little overzealous in some of the competitions with other campers. My dad's warning would continually remind me: "Be careful not to injure your fellow campers."

While swimming, Dieter and I were interrupted by one of the councilors from the nearby Women's Camp. When a woman came into the water fully clothed from her hiding place behind the bushes, Dieter became completely flustered by her beauty and ran back up to the camp dining hall. This was the first of several encounters I had with this very lovable and truly kind woman named Ilsa, who was a counselor at the female version of the Hitler Camp known as the Hitler Youth Camp for Young Women.

On our second "chance" meeting at the lake, Ilsa brought her friend Gretchen to meet me. At first, I was disappointed that I could not spend any private time alone with Ilsa. However, her friend Gretchen seemed very comfortable meeting me and was not at all embarrassed about making love to me, while Ilsa helped me through any discomfort I had been feeling.

If memory serves me correctly, it was on our fourth or fifth meeting down by the lake in the summer of 1936 that I was in for a complete surprise. I had skipped dinner at the Hitler Camp dining hall in order to meet Ilsa and Gretchen at our private little beach for a "swim" in the late afternoon privacy of the lake.

When I think back on those days, whenever I thought about Ilsa, I completely lost my appetite for food. Although I never shared my love life at Hitler Camp with my parents, my mother probably would have been happy that at least there was something limiting my appetite for food! Mom was always concerned about the possibility that I was eating too much. She was always worried I might get too tall or overweight.

Since I had been with Ilsa and Gretchen on other occasions, I was getting to feel quite comfortable with both beautiful women making love to me. They were both very caring and loving young women. Although they were a few years older than me, our age difference didn't mean too much to them.

Even though I had explained to both women that I was only sixteen because I was tall, they both probably felt I looked older. On this late afternoon, the sun was still quite high, but the birds were singing their evening songs in the meadow. The sky was bright blue; the air was warm, and a slight breeze rustled the carpet of flowers in the meadow. As I approached the beach in my Hitler shorts and t-shirt, I found, to my complete surprise, three women swimming in the lake.

At first, I was a little surprised, even chagrined. I knew all three of them could not be there to see me. Well, I was wrong! As I approached the beach, Gretchen called up to me. "Hello, Jenz. Isn't it a wonderful afternoon for a swim?"

Ilsa followed with, "Hi, Jenz, it is wonderful to see you again. Come on in, the water feels terrific."

Both responses from my friends made me feel more comfortable; it looked like they were there to enjoy the cool lake water on a warm summer afternoon. Then they introduced Gretchen's friend.

Gretchen spoke right up, "Jenz, this is our dear friend, Erika."

Since all three girls were mostly submerged in the lake with only their heads above water, I couldn't see them very well. As I kicked off my shoes and shirt and cautiously entered the water, all three of them stood up and walked toward me.

Ilsa volunteered, "Erika is one of the senior councilors at our camp and wanted to meet the handsome man that Gretchen and I have been meeting down here at the lake."

"Oh," was all I could say. My fear was that my voice might leave me entirely. I did manage to get out a few words.

"It... it... 's a pleasure t...to... meet you, Erika." I was starting to stammer, so I decided to keep my mouth shut and not embarrass myself further.

She came over to me and shook my hand. I was relieved when she formally greeted me... that is, until she placed her other hand on my chest and said,

"My friends told me you were a very good-looking man, but I had no idea." It seemed odd to me at the time that she hadn't let go of my hand.

Also, she seemed a little older than Gretchen and Ilsa but equally as tall and beautiful. She had shiny blue eyes that seemed to dance when she talked. I found out later that she was almost thirty years old! She then pulled me closer, and whispered in a low voice,

"It is very nice to meet you."

I looked around and thought about exiting the lake in a hurry, I hadn't even swum one stroke. I muttered something about being late for dinner if I didn't get back to the camp."

Then I stated more firmly,

"If I don't get back up to the camp for dinner, my counselors will write me up and it won't look good on my camp record."

That's when Erika re-affirmed in a low sexy voice,

"Oh, Jenz, you do not have to worry about that, we are all counselors at the woman's camp, and I am the senior counselor-in-charge."

At this point, I kept trying not to think about how her hand on my chest was affecting my insides which had somehow started to tingle. I thought to myself, *I wonder if she always talks with this low whispery voice.*

I started to slowly back out of the waist-deep water. I stopped when I realized that my privates were enlarging, and I didn't want anything showing. Ilsa could sense my unease and awkwardness and came over to reassure me.

"Oh Jenz," Ilsa cooed, please do not be bashful; Erika doesn't mean to be too forward. She is a wonderful leader and example for our Hitler Youth." *In my mind, I tried to justify how "being a wonderful leader and example for our Hitler Youth" had anything to do with my current predicament.*

Ilsa put her hands around my neck, pulled me down to her level, and kissed me on the cheek.

"And besides," she whispered in a sexy voice in my ear, "We have agreed that Erika can be first this afternoon!"

"Oh, Ilsa," I started to protest. "I will embarrass myself."

That's when she put her hand down under water and massaged my swelling privates. I was tingling all over with her kind touch. *As I got older, Ilsa's very presence in my life became magical for me.*

Ilsa held one hand and Erika the other as they directed, pulling me out of the water toward the mossy glade. Gretchen reassured me,

"Jenz, we will all be very kind to you; please do not worry about embarrassment."

As they led me to the glade, my legs felt wooden and would only go where they were leading me. Erika addressed me in her low sexy, whispery voice,

"Jenz, let's sit down and relax. Please - tell me all about yourself."

I couldn't tell her anything. I could hardly talk. Words wouldn't come to my mouth. I worried about my swelling privates and tried to look at anything other than the three beautiful girls in their bathing suits surrounding me in that wooded glen. The moss felt cool and spongy to sit on.

That's when Gretchen said, "Jenz, let's get you out of your wet Hitler shorts." She and Ilsa pulled them off as they stretched out my legs; they slipped off without a struggle. I was powerless to resist. I couldn't even say anything except in a hoarse voice… "Oh... o. okay."

Erika was rubbing my neck and back while whispering in a low voice in my ear, "Jenz, you handsome man, do you mind if I'm first?" She was kneeling behind me but then put her arms around me, rubbing and messaging my chest from behind. *At the time, I had no idea my chest was so sensitive to a woman's touch. I felt a fire glowing inside of me.*

I tried to answer her, but I could only say, "Oh...Okay, ...but I don't want to.... embarrass you." *What I meant was that I felt foolish and didn't want to embarrass myself. Here I was, completely naked on a mossy glade with three beautiful women surrounding me in their bathing suits.*

Erika probably read my thoughts. She asked in that low voice, "Do you mind if I slip out of my wet bathing suit?"

She could probably tell that I was a little uncomfortable....and nervous. I really wanted to crawl under a rock - or run up to the camp for dinner. I just couldn't move. *My chest and privates were tingling so much that I felt I should cover myself.*

She said, "Jenz, look at me."

I glanced toward her.

"Aren't I appealing to you?"

"Oh yes!" I replied quickly. *Her beauty was thrilling to me.*

"Have you ever been with an older woman?"

"I... I've only b... been with Ilsa and Gretchen," I stammered. "Although I'm tall, I'm only sixteen years.

"Please, you have to relax, and let me make sure you enjoy yourself." She whispered in that low sexy voice. *At this point, I wasn't sure if it was Erika's hands on my chest or the low sexy voice —my insides were aflame.*

"Girls, help me make Jenz relax." She then gently pushed me down into the cool spongy moss, kissing my stomach and gently pinching my chest with her thumb and forefinger.

Ilsa kissed me on the lips and cheek while whispering in my ear, "Jenz, you have to learn we are just young women trying to help you relax."

I was anything but relaxed. My privates were swelling out of control, my entire body was tingling. I was hugging and kissing Ilsa while Erika was kissing my stomach. Nobody was touching my privates, but Gretchen had removed her bathing suit and rubbed my thighs.

When I thought I couldn't take it anymore, Erika whispered, "Would you like to be inside me?"

"Y... Yesss..." was all I could say in a halting, hesitant voice.

With that, she kneeled across me and slid me into her. There was no weight on top of me. Just the wonderful feeling of gently pulling and pushing on my member. Gretchen had moved from my inner thighs to my testicles, giving them a gentle massage.

When I started to thrust, all three of them said in unison - don't move. Then Ilsa whispered, "Let us do the moving for you."

Erika was playing hard to get with me. As soon as I came close to exploding inside her, she stopped moving and told me, "Relax, Jenz, you are doing just fine. You feel great but I want you to enjoy yourself!"

After a short time, she started moaning like a wounded animal, I thought I might be hurting her. I couldn't hold back any longer; my whole body started vibrating and shaking. I thrust once... twice... and exploded into Erika. She let out a long, low, sexy whimpering noise. I wasn't sure if she was uncomfortable. I heard her girlfriends giggling as I must have blacked out.

I opened my eyes and Erika was looking directly into mine. Her eyes were dancing. She asked, "Did that help you unwind after a busy day?"

"It couldn't have been any busier," I mumbled. "But yes. I'm so relaxed, I doubt if I'll be able to move for a long time."

That's when Gretchen said, "Excellent, Jenz. I don't want you to move; let us message you until you recover. Remember, I'm next!"

"Oh... Gretchen...I don't think I will be able to move until tomorrow."

"Jenz," Gretchen volunteered, "You just don't understand the recuperative powers of young men." She grabbed me around the neck and gave me a long, luscious kiss. Her tongue was darting in and out of my mouth.

Ilsa told me, "Jenz, just relax. Let us massage your aching muscles." She proceeded to kiss me on the chest and pinch my nipples with little soft bites.

Erika was messaging my legs and kissing me on my inner thighs. She whispered in her low sultry voice, "Jenz, I know you will feel very good as I work my way up your legs."

Well, she was right. When she started licking my privates, my brain immediately snapped out of its lethargy. I began tingling all over. My privates started swelling uncontrollably. I started to get up, but Gretchen gently pushed me back into the moss.

Gretchen gave me another very loving kiss and whispered in my ear, "Darling, it's my turn; you can't go anywhere, just don't move."

As I started to protest, Gretchen got on top of me and slipped me inside of her, and whispered, "Now that's much better, isn't it, Jenz?" I couldn't say anything but nodded my head slightly to say yes. She started very slow rhythmic movements on top of me, whispering in my ear: "This is what our Führer wants for us."

Since Gretchen's head only came up to my chest, Ilsa was kissing me and whispered, "Jenz, please don't move; let us do all the moving for you. Erika was gently messaging my privates and squeezing ever so gently occasionally.

Gretchen started a little fuller rhythmic movement on top of me. She increased her movements slightly. Every time I started to thrust, Ilsa would say stop... and Gretchen would stop her movement and place her hand on my chest. As soon as I stopped thrusting, she would resume her rhythmic motion. It was pure torture for me.

After a few minutes of this torture, I got so excited that I couldn't control my body any longer. I rolled her over, so she was on the cool moss with me on top of her. I kept thrusting until I exploded into my dear friend Gretchen. I collapsed and rolled off her. She was crying.

"Oh, Gretchen, I am so sorry. I don't know what possessed me. I lost complete control of my senses. I certainly didn't mean to hurt you!"

Gretchen shook her head, "Oh...Jenz, you didn't hurt me; these are tears of joy. You felt wonderful inside of me. Thank you for your loving kindness."

I was completely out of breath. My heart was racing. I felt like I was floating on that cool bed of moss in the glade.

That's when Ilsa kneeled beside me and whispered in my ear, "I hope you haven't forgotten me, darling."

"Dearest Ilsa," I mumbled through trembling lips. "I could never forget you or the kindness of your friends. I know our Führer has encouraged lovemaking with Aryan men, but are you sure this is what our God wants for us? *I had never learned this from the teachings in our church or Schule in the synagogue.* Although I love your friends, you are the only one for me - dear Ilsa, you have my heart!"

"Oh, Jenz," She whispered in my ear. Her eyes were damp with tears. "You are the only one for me. I promise I will never share you with my girlfriends ever again. I want you, and you alone, forever."

She turned and asked her friends, "Girls, I will see you back at our camp. Jenz and I need to be alone to talk."

Gretchen and Erika slipped back into their bathing suits and left us in the glade.

Ilsa and I just held each other for the longest time. The sun was almost down; the heat had gone out of the day.

For the first time that day, I felt truly relaxed.

Ilsa apologized for her girlfriends, saying, "I'm sorry they acted so forward toward you; from now on, I want you for myself!" She then hugged me and gave me a very passionate kiss.

My insides started rumbling. I wasn't sure if my attraction for Ilsa was reigniting my passion or if I was hungry since I had skipped dinner.

Ilsa answered that question for me by whispering, "Let's hold each other forever; she then slipped me inside of her.

We just rocked back and forth and mumbled to each other. She asked if we could write to each other when the school year started. I told her I would like that. Hitler Camp was almost over. The school was starting next month. I was getting sleepy.

Ilsa kissed me awake, she was dressed in her bathing suit. She got up and disappeared up the path that led to the women's Hitler Youth Camp. I got up and dressed very slowly and limped back to the dining hall at the Hitler Camp to see if there was any left-over supper. The only light came from a half-moon and millions of stars; it was a memorable evening. I had a little trouble walking, but then started thinking that maybe my friends had taken advantage of me down by the lake. Even though I might have felt they had slightly abused me, I had a very big smile on my face all the way up the hill.

A rather strange incident occurred during the last week of Hitler Camp. I was asked to go to our camp leader's office. His office was in a little cabin across from the dining hall area. Although nervous, I showed up there right after our afternoon calisthenics program.

"Good afternoon, sergeant," was my greeting to the enlisted Wehrmacht officer. I gave the sergeant a half-hearted Hitler wave of a salute and asked, "Why have you summoned me this afternoon?"

"Come in, Jenz. You have done well here this summer. Have you considered a career in the Wehrmacht?"

"Not yet, sergeant; I'm only sixteen years old and would like to study engineering at the Technical University in Berlin. If I can get a Wehrmacht deferral, I will start my engineering classes after next year."

"Oh," remarked the sergeant. "You want to be an engineer for the Reich?"

"I would very much enjoy working where I might do the most positive good for Germany," I said quickly.

The sergeant then surprised me with, "Jenz, you seem to be Schutzstaffel * material. I am going to put you on a watch list for the SS. They could be in touch with you while you study at the university."

"Thank you, sergeant. Is there anything more for me?"

"No, Ramsgrund, but congratulations. Very few are put forward to the SS from this camp. Your marksmanship and hand combat skills have been exemplary. I'm sure you are aware of the SS* motto: 'Loyalty is my Honor.' You appear to be the Nordic racially pure type the SS is looking for to join their ranks. You should also understand the SS has to ensure you marry only a suitable woman and do not dilute our racially superior code of honor."

---

*Schutzstaffel (Abbreviated SS). Originally was established as Adolf Hitler's personal bodyguard unit. It would later become both the elite guard of the Nazi Reich and Hitler's executive force prepared to carry out all security-related duties without regard for legal restraint. The "Death's Head" division of the SS performed all the security-related duties for the concentration camps.

"Yes, sergeant. I am aware of the strict discipline in the Schutzstaffel. *My thought at the time was: I certainly did not want to dilute my race with anyone having anything to do with the Nazi Party.*

The most important lesson from my time at the Hitler Youth Camp was my enduring love for Ilsa. However, a most useful skill I was later to learn in earnest, was my ease of ending a man's life. Gestapo members who were disrespectful to my Jewish friends quickly found out how efficiently I had learned killing skills at Hitler Youth Camp.

Chapter 3

Incident on Königsalee 26, Bucherer's Jewelry Shop, Downtown Düsseldorf

Late in October 1938, Ezekiel and I had been in the central library in Düsseldorf studying for an exam in physics. Ezekiel and I always studied together for a couple of important reasons. Since Jews were not allowed in public schools in Germany at this time, Zeke stayed current in his studies by following the work I was doing in school. The second reason I am a little embarrassed and reluctant to admit was that Zeke always had a much firmer grasp than me on the concepts in mathematics and physics. He was always better at explaining how to solve difficult problems and issues; he was even more thorough than my calculus instructor.

Both of us had the ambition to be engineers for Germany. Our best hope for a premier education in engineering was in Berlin at the Technical University. Zeke's only recourse for attending any public university in Germany during those dark days of growing Nazi oppression was to become anything but Jewish. At this point in our studies, I had figured out how to make him Aryan.

Various decrees and the grave danger of personal harm from the brownshirts made it impossible for Jews to be on the streets in Germany at night. I had been able to get credentials for Ezekiel that made him Aryan. He had an Italian passport and driver's license telling the world he was Vitali Carapezza. This would allow us to study in the library and for Ezekiel to study with me at the Technical University in Berlin next year.

It was getting on toward ten O'clock in the evening, the central library closed at eleven. My brain was starting to turn to mush, and I asked Zeke, "Have you had enough?" He said, "Sure, Jenz, but I can keep going if you can."

It was late enough for me, and we still had to catch a bus to our section of Düsseldorf. My suggestion is, "Let's get a snack on the way to the bus stop."

As we left the library, a surprising number of people were milling about the city. Zeke quietly announced, "They look like 'Brownshirts'; let's use some caution." The temperature had to be near freezing; the wind had a little bite to it.

As we walked toward the bus terminal, it looked like a few of the Brownshirt thugs were vandalizing some of the shops along Königsalee Street. I exclaimed to Zeke, "It looks like someone has broken into the old jewelry shop!" Bucherer's, an old-line Jewelry shop with origins back in the 1880s, was halfway down Königsalee Street. Flash lamps danced inside and around in the back of the store. The front door was slightly ajar.

There were several alarms going off on the street, but no authorities were coming. It was difficult to determine which shops the alarms were coming from. I told Zeke, "The Brownshirts are probably intimidating to the local police."

As we approached Bucherer's, we could see movement inside the shop. In addition to the front door being ajar, someone was moving behind the counter.

Zeke whispered, "Maybe the owner is injured or in some sort of confrontation with the troublemakers."

Reluctantly, I pushed open the door. Two young Brownshirt thugs were behind the counter helping themselves to a tray of expensive watches.

"Hold it!" I yelled. "Get out of here!"

The larger of the two individuals brandished a knife and exclaimed, "What are you going to do, call the authorities?" He was tall, around five foot eleven inches, with a wiry build. His face was contorted into a sneer as he yelled at us. "Get out if you know what's good for you!" He was very angry with our interference with his criminal plans.

He came around the end of the counter, directly toward me, and held the knife in front of him in a threatening position about eighteen inches from my face. He knew the police would not interfere with the Brownshirts in the burglary of a Jewish-owned shop.

I tried to tell him, "If you leave now, you won't get hurt!"

"I'm the one holding the knife, you idiot!"

I thought to myself, he does present a good argument, but then I thought, he has no idea how fast my hand can move – especially in the dim light.

I quickly grabbed his knife hand at the wrist, then pulled and twisted his arm at the elbow. I heard an audible click! I wasn't sure if I had broken his arm or just dislocated his elbow. His knife bounced harmlessly off the floor.

"Aaaa!" he bellowed. "You broke my arm!"

His companion was shorter, probably around 5 feet 7 inches, but slightly overweight, and tried to throw a punch at my face. I grabbed his fist as it was flying at my head and gave it a sharp twist backward.

"Snap." I heard the wrist bones break. Both thieves were disabled. They held their broken arms with their good arms while moaning curses and complaints as they fled the store.

Zeke and I pulled the door shut and walked out into the frigid evening. An icy blast of wind met us as it came down Königsalee Street. No one seemed to pay any attention to us, and the goons were nowhere in sight.

As we neared the bus station, there was a distinct lack of folks out around the bus station on a bitterly cold late fall evening.

Chapter 4

My Introduction to the SS

It was almost two years later, while a student at the Technical University of Berlin when I received a note from the SS informing me of an appointment at their headquarters the next day. The note made my roommate very nervous. Vitali Carapezza and I had been boyhood friends since the first day of school in Düsseldorf. Vitali's real name was Ezekiel Leven. He was a fellow Jew, and we were life-long friends. His name change helped to cover up his Jewish heritage. Having an Italian last name and credentials allowed him to attend the Technical University in Berlin. Even though we were both Jews, I looked Aryan because although my mom was Jewish, my dad was Swedish. I used my dad's last name: Ramsgrund.

Ezekiel had developed and even improved his Italian accent and could use it whenever he had a need for it. His apprehension was evident because he asked, "Are you actually going into the SS Headquarters for this appointment?"

"I'm not sure I have much choice, Ezekiel. Not showing up could be even more dangerous for both of us. I will dress up, look presentable, and try to remember my military bearing from Hitler Camp. *Although we had eliminated several members of the Gestapo over the past two years, I don't think the Gestapo or the SS were aware of who we were.*

"Do not think about or dwell on the damage we have done to the Gestapo over the past year, Zeke. Every Gestapo member we eliminated was a traitor to a free and noble Germany. Furthermore, before they were members of the secret Gestapo police force, they were probably common criminals.

"Ever since my discussion with the sergeant at the end of my summer at Hitler Camp, I had been reading a bit about the SS or Schutzstaffel and its' leaders."

"Have you been able to find anything positive to say about the SS?" Asked Ezekiel.

"Not really," was my succinct answer. "Perhaps the SS is slightly less thuggish than the Brownshirts or Gestapo. Although I'm not sure if 'less thuggish' is a very positive trait. If the SS started out as an elite guard for our Führer, they seem to have grown into a group of enforcers for Herr Hitler, Himmler, and the rest of the dastardly scoundrels running our government.

"The SS had an interesting and checkered beginning to their history, Ezekiel. It was formed in the early 1920s to originally counter the violent and bloody actions of the Brownshirt movement. The organization initially seemed like a glorified bodyguard detail for our Führer. Hitler created the SS and had its members dress in distinctly black uniforms modeled after the Italian Fascist uniforms.

"The Gestapo and the SS share space in a building at No. 8 Prinz Albrecht Strasse near the center of Berlin. This address brings terror to the hearts and minds of most God-fearing Berliners. There has been talk of citizens being harshly questioned and even tortured in the basement chambers.

"Ezekiel, the biggest problem is the Brownshirts. Hermann Göring * has control over these thugs and has prohibited the local police from interfering with them when out on the streets.

"It is getting dangerous for Jews to be out after dark, so we have to be very cautious. We cannot afford to be stopped and searched by these criminals. Let's go directly to the bus stop, get away from the center of town, and get back to our apartment to plan how to out-wit these

---

*Hermann Wilhelm Göring, as Commander-in-Chief of the Luftwaffe, rose to become the second most powerful man in Nazi Germany. His power began to wane when his air force could not prevent the bombing of German cities by Allied bombers, and he could not adequately re-supply the Wehrmacht at Stalingrad. He died from self-ingestion of cyanide the day before he was to be hanged by the Nuremberg Court on the 15th of October 1946.

cowards. I will travel to the center of Berlin tomorrow to meet with the SS people and find out what they want.”

Toward the end of my second year of engineering school, I received orders to report for SS training at one of the many labor camps sprouting up in Germany. Since the SS was charged with overseeing and guarding the labor or concentration camps throughout the country, my first assignment led me to a camp where the prisoners were treated with utmost cruelty. Heinrich Himmler originally built the Dachau labor camp in an old munition factory in 1933. It took me exactly 24 hours to realize I could never live with myself pretending to be part of the SS organization at this or any of the labor camps.

Before my paperwork was processed, I wrote a letter to the head SS office in Berlin asking if the Reich could better utilize my engineering skills anywhere in the country. Within a week, the camp commander summoned me to his office.

“Lieutenant Ramsgrund,” he began in a harsh and quite stern voice, but then calmed down, “it appears the powers to be at SS headquarters have decided to use your skills elsewhere. Although I am not accustomed to being overridden in such matters, I am holding orders in my hand for you to be transferred to a Wehrmacht base somewhere in northern Germany. I was unaware we even had a Wehrmacht base in such a remote location, and I have no idea why we have a facility in such a desolate area. However, these orders are countersigned by Himmler’s deputy and carry the full weight of our Führer.

You are to report in a little over a week. You may stay in your quarters here until you arrange for transportation to someplace called Peenemünde.”

“Oh! Thank you, Herr Commandant, but I will leave immediately. The week will allow me to visit family and perhaps arrive early at my new duty station.”

The overweight base commander struggled to stand and returned my Hitler salute. “As you wish, Lieutenant. Good luck with your new assignment in the wilderness.” He then almost collapsed as he slumped back down into his chair.

My Hitler salute had my best effort at almost a touch of enthusiasm. Even though I was unaware of what might await me at the next duty station, it had to be better than this prison of horrors. I was thrilled to be going almost anywhere - especially to a place where I might be able to utilize my engineering skills.

I spent the next week fending off the Gestapo and visiting my family and the love of my life, Ilse. In addition, it took me a little time to figure out the location and transportation to the Wehrmacht base at Peenemünde. I had some satisfaction eliminating a Gestapo Headquarters building in Hamburg and hopefully throwing the Gestapo off my parents' trail. I was able to make the destruction of the Gestapo building look like an accidental gas explosion. It was almost as if the Gestapo had little to do but ferret out Jews, honest businessmen, or anyone who disagreed with the Nazi goals of pure German blood.

My knowledge of the German Secret State Police or Gestapo had been limited. I inherently knew they were an enemy to law-abiding Germans, but I had no realization of the depths of their depravity.

Chapter 5

Peenemünde, The Wehrmacht Secret Research Center

My trip to Peenemünde was interrupted by the Gestapo on two occasions, but fortunately, I was able to get to my duty station on time. It didn't take me long to get familiar with the important work being done at this remote army base. It was the research center for the development of secret missile weapons. Once I saw some of the problems the engineers at this army base were trying to solve, I discussed with Herr Frits Gosslau, * the chief engineer of the V-I programs, the possibility of bringing on another aeronautical engineer to help with problems with the guidance system.

"Herr Gosslau, I had an acquaintance at the Technical University in Berlin who might be able to be of service to the Reich with this particular problem."

"What are you suggesting, Lieutenant?"

"I had a classmate at the Technical University who was proficient in calculus and physics and studying aeronautical engineering. One of his areas of expertise was guidance systems for aircraft."

I wanted to whet the chief engineer's curiosity, but I had to be careful not to appear overly enthusiastic.

"Just who is this individual, Lieutenant Ramsgrund?"

"His name is Vitali Carapezza. He is originally from Italy but speaks fluent German. He is one of the top students in physics at the university."

---

*Fritz Gosslau graduated with a doctorate from the Technical University in Berlin in 1926. His Ph.D. study was on cooling piston-driven aircraft. He was the principal engineer who developed the V-1 flying bomb—the world's first guided missile. After the war, he continued to develop improvements in piston engines. He died in Bavaria in 1965 at age 67.

"Give me the spelling of his name and the name of his department head. I will have him checked out."

I felt Vitali would check out fine if it weren't for the Gestapo doing the checking.

"Yes, Sir! I will write you his contact information on an internal memo this morning."

A few days later, Dr. Gosslau came to me and ordered me to get Vitali to join the engineers at the secret Rocket Research Center. Although both of us were Jews, our cover stories were strong as long as no one looked too closely into our past. I knew Vitali would be nervous, but I figured we would both be safer hiding in the confines of the secret army base.

Two weeks later, I brought Ezekiel into the base at Peenemünde. He had to go through indoctrination, swear allegiance to our Führer, and learn how to wear a Wehrmacht Sargent's uniform.

"I feel really uncomfortable in this uniform, Jenz." Ezekiel confided in me at dinner the next evening.

My reply was rather cryptic. "Can you think of a better disguise to protect our Jewishness?"

"Well, you make a good point, Jenz. It may save us from some anti-Semitic reactions from the Brownshirts."

In the following weeks and months, Ezekiel and I did everything we could think of to slow down the development of the V-I and V-II missile systems. We had to be very careful using complex mathematical formulae and physics to come up with ways of altering the guidance systems for the V-I and V-II rocket systems. We could not afford to be discovered.

The most basic alterations of the V-I fuel and the V-II fin guidance system seem to be the least detectable and least dangerous methods of slowing down the development and effectiveness of both missiles.

One afternoon head of the Army Research Center, Dr. Walter Dornberger, came and spoke to the engineers. He expressed specific concerns about the Jewish workers who were building, testing, and improving the V-I and V-II missile systems.

At first, Ezekiel and I thought the worse. Had our subterfuge been discovered?

Had anyone discovered we were actually Jewish?

Fortunately, no. Dr. Dornberger was very concerned about the health of his Jewish workers.

"I am speaking to you this afternoon about an issue of great concern," the General began.

"This secret facility on the North Sea has been in operation for the past four years. As you know, in addition to the approximately two hundred scientists and engineers, we employ almost three hundred laborers from the labor camps in Germany and the Eastern Territories. Many of these prisoners are highly skilled. We have electrical engineers, electricians, clockmakers, jewelers, and finish carpenters.

"These prisoners are an essential part of the testing, assembly, and shipping of these missiles to our field officers. These missiles may gain increasing importance as weapons during our struggle with the Allies.

One of the air-force officers raised his hand. "Is there a problem with these prisoners? Perhaps the discipline is too lax?"

"No!" replied General Dornberger. "The problem is they are dying at an alarming rate; almost as soon as they arrive, they start getting sick. I have assured Reichsführer Himmler we are not mistreating these prisoners. They receive proper discipline and berthing and eat the same diet as our enlisted soldiers.

"They are dying from systemic or infectious diseases or exhaustion. Some of them collapse on the assembly lines, some even the first week they are here. Others cannot even lift parts as small as 10 kilograms."

"Are they infected when they arrive at our base?" asked one of the scientists.

"The Reichsführer has assured me the prisoners are reliable and healthy when they leave the camps. He has given me a list of the camps we draw from and orders for two of our staff to visit any of these camps with only one stipulation: we must maintain absolute secrecy of anything we see or hear at any of the labor camps. Violation of this order is to be met with the most severe punishment: an immediate firing squad.

I raised my hand to ask a question.

"Yes, lieutenant, what is your question?"

"Approximately how many of these camps are in our country and the conquered territories?"

"Herr Himmler has assured me there are over a thousand labor camps, six designated as extermination camps. He claims we should be able to get talented prisoners from any of them."

This was the first I had heard of 'extermination' camps and a hush fell over the room. Evidently, many of the other scientists and officers hadn't heard of these camps either.

"Are any of these facilities close to our research center here at Peenemünde?" I asked.

"Let's see," answered the General while looking at the map Himmler had provided.

"Yes. It looks like Treblinka isn't too far. It is located about 85 kilometers northeast of Warsaw. From what I understand, many of the Polish Jews from the Warsaw Ghetto are imprisoned there. Herr Himmler informed me that removing Jews from our country and the conquered territories is called 'Operation Reinhard.' * As explained to me, this operation is designed to remove Jews from German lands and relocate them to the East in conquered areas of Russia for farm work.

---

*Operation Reinhard" was named after an infamous criminal Nazi, Reinhard Heydrich. He was assassinated by the Czech underground in May 1942. Heydrich was one of the cruelest Nazis in WW II. This Nazi convened the "Wannsee Conference" near Berlin on January 20th, 1942. On this date, Heydrich informed all the relevant officers in Nazi Germany of the "Final Solution of the Jewish Question" as decided by Hitler: the deportation, murder, and extermination of all the Jews in Germany and the Conquered Territories.

Chapter 6

Our Trip to Treblinka

Thankfully, Zeke had volunteered to accompany me on the inspection of the labor camps in Poland. He was the only person I could truly trust in the Peenemünde secret Army facility. Although both of us were continually worried about being discovered as Jews, we felt our bold impersonation of the SS and Wehrmacht were our best cover. Zeke and I discussed the trauma we might experience while visiting these labor or concentration camps.

"Zeke, are you sure you will be okay visiting these appalling and disgusting prisons?"

"I'm sure I would like to know where my parents wound up. I have no illusions as to the extent of the cruelty the Nazis will exhibit toward decent Germans."

The next week the Luftwaffe provided us with a flight to Warsaw. Although our orders were thoroughly checked, a carbon copy was taken when we landed at the Warsaw-Okecie Airdrome. It was a routine flight and took only about two and a half hours. Except for the exceptional loudness of the aircraft engines, it seemed like a routine flight.

A car and SS driver, Lance Corporal Heine, met us at the plane. His second sleeve insignia indicated he had over six years of service. His uniform was crisp and well-fitted. Although the answers to our questions were glib and short, he seemed polite with good military bearing. He mentioned it would take approximately ninety minutes for the drive to the Treblinka camp.

It was a beautiful warm late spring day, so we rode with the windows down.

"Corporal," I asked very politely, "How is the progress going in the Ghetto?"

Although my question was innocent enough, it prompted a rather cryptic retort. I knew our forces were trying to remove all the Jews from the part of Warsaw known as the Jewish Ghetto.

"Lieutenant, we should have the rest of the Jewish vermin cleaned out by the Fall. Our forces have the Ghetto surrounded and we have erected a sturdy wall around the entire area. It is just a question of starving them out or carting them off to Treblinka."

Zeke and I just looked at each other. The blood was draining from our faces. My first reaction was anger, but I caught myself and replied, "Excellent, Corporal. Where are the detainees being held?"

"The ones who are strong and can be of value to the Reich are kept at the Treblinka Camp for work for a limited amount of time. All the rest are euthanized immediately. Those chosen to work at the camp are usually euthanized in three to four months.

We rode in silence for a while. Zeke finally spoke up. "How are the detainees being killed, Corporal?"

"I think many of them are dead before they even leave the transports, Sargant. Several hundred Jews, including women, children, and very old people, are packed into each cattle-transport car on the train. Often, they are left at the railroad siding at Treblinka without food or water for a full day or more. There is very little fresh air and the bodies rot and mix with the fecal material and urine since there are no bathroom facilities on the transports.

I carefully worded my next question to avoid conflict of any kind. "Corporal, what happens to the able-bodied Jews after they leave the transports?"

"Oh," replied Heine, "Some of them are even reluctant to step onto the platform and have to be whipped, beaten, and yelled at by the guards. There is usually a large barking dog present to help create confusion and panic. This helps hurry the Jewish vermin to the selection area. The whole idea is to instill a feeling of dread and terror into the prisoners."

"What is the purpose of creating all the confusion and consternation," asked Zeke.

"Compliance!" Barked the Corporal. "All the Ghetto dwellers have been informed to leave the Ghetto and board the trains in order to transport them to the east for farm work. They are told to bring only what they can carry."

"So, we are basically lying to them?" questioned Zeke.

"Of Course," emphasized the Corporal. "If the vermin knew they were going to their death, they might rebel and be even more difficult to root out of their homes. In addition, it might cause interruptions in the orderly method of euthanizing them and ridding them from the Reich."

"Do some of them complain or resist?" I asked in a nonchalant manner.

"Not usually, Lieutenant. If they do, they are whipped by the Ukrainian Guards. The dogs are trained to bark and bite the Jews. The transportees are immediately herded into the selection area."

"The dogs are actually trained to bite the Jews?" was Zeke's innocent question.

"Oh, yes!" replied the Corporal. The camp's deputy commandant, SS Oberscharführer Kurt Franz, has a personal pet. A rather ferocious hound named Bari. He is trained to lunge and bite the Jews in their genitals. He is very effective.

"In addition, there are two large signs to complete the deception. The first is as the prisoners enter the camp. The first sign proclaims in Polish and German:"

"Jews of Warsaw, Attention!

You are in a transit camp, from which you will be sent to a Labor Camp. In order to avoid epidemics, you must present your clothing and belongings for immediate disinfection. Gold, money, foreign currency, and jewelry should be deposited with the cashiers in return for a receipt. They will be returned to you later when you present the receipt. Bodily cleanliness requires that everyone bathes before continuing the journey."

"Keep in mind, Lieutenant, the entire entry area to the camp is neat and clean with flower gardens and often music to greet and calm the unwary deportees.

"The women and children are immediately sent to the undressing barrack on the left, and the men are sent to the undressing barrack on the right. They must deposit all their valuables with the cashier at the end of the shed.

"Do the Jews willingly go into the undressing barracks?" asked Zeke.

"Yes, Sargant, they do. If they hesitate, they are whipped or beaten with a metal bar or cudgel."

"It seems altogether harsh and inhumane," was all I could say.

"Oh, no, Lieutenant. You will see how well organized and orderly the entire process is handled. There is a large sign at the end of the barracks in Polish which completes the deception:

"Attention!

Fold all your clothes. Everything you have brought with you must be left where you undress except for money, valuables, documents, and shoes. Hold your money and valuables until they are collected at the window. Tie your shoes together, and leave them in the places marked. You must come to the baths and vapor room entirely nude."

I then asked a question about the willingness of the Jews to enter the gas chambers.

"Corporal, do the Jews always just walk into the death chambers without hesitation?"

"Lieutenant, I have never been allowed into the camp to witness any of the actual procedures. All my information is second-hand from escapees or SS Death Head Officers from the different camps.

"From what I understand, if the Jews show hesitation, they are whipped, or beaten with iron bars. If the men try to avoid entering the gas chambers, they are summarily shot dead on the spot."

"Corporal, this is a little concerning for me and my sergeant. We had hoped to obtain some healthy, and strong men and women workers for our facility at the Army Research Center."

"What are you working on at the facility, Lieutenant?"

"Most of the work is in conjunction with our war effort. But we require a reliable and healthy workforce."

"Well, shortly, you and your sergeant will be able to see the prisoners for yourselves. We are approaching the first guard station for entrance to the Treblinka camp. I should tell you, that most of the guards are Ukrainian and have a mean disposition. If they are at all lax or forgetful in any of their duties, they are immediately shot."

As we slowed for the guard station, the guard unshouldered his rifle and aimed it in our direction until he saw our uniforms. I showed him a copy of our orders and he waved us through.

The guard did warn us to approach the entrance with caution. "Sir, there have been some difficulties with the last transport which arrived this morning. Many of the men resisted going into the undressing barracks and had to be shot. Unfortunately, some of the women and children were also killed in the melee."

Zeke shot me a sideways glance. I thought to myself, what sort of hellhole are we about to enter? I asked the driver, "Corporal, I realize the Reich has many of these labor camps, is Treblinka any different from the others?"

"Well, yes. Treblinka has been set up as an extermination camp to rid the Jews from our precious country and the conquered territories. We indeed have three of these extermination facilities, although I believe Treblinka is the largest."

"What are the others, Corporal?"

"The SS has set up Death Camps at Belzec in the south near the town of Lublin; Sobibor in the forest near the village of Sobibor, in addition to here at Treblinka."

It was all Zeke and I could do to prevent ourselves from breaking down and showing our outrage!

Chapter 7

Entering Hell on Earth

The railroad depot at the gate to Treblinka was awash with blood and bodies. I told the driver to wait for the sergeant and me to return. I took the car keys to ensure his loyalty and our ride back to Warsaw. This was not the place for two Jews in German uniforms to be discovered.

It was late morning, and the warm sun was beating down on the railroad platform, congealing the blood and gore. The sight of the platform turned my stomach. I was surprised that both of us could keep from retching.

There was a company of slave laborers carting off the bodies and washing down the platform with buckets of water. I approached the guard who looked like he was in charge. He was wearing a Ukrainian Army uniform. He was barking orders and held a whip in his right hand. He had been whipping one of the prisoners when I approached him.

I held up my hand and motioned for him to stop. **"Guard,"** I said with some authority in my voice. **"What is going on here? You know these procedures are supposed to go smoothly."**

Many of the laborers had blue armbands designated them as Platform Workers *(Bahnhofkommando)*. These were trusted prisoners overseen by the SS. Their duty was to empty and clean the transport cars as quickly as possible and transfer the transportees to the SS man in charge.

"Yes, Lieutenant. I understand. But many of the men on the transport wouldn't go quietly into the camp's selection area and had to be shot. Unfortunately, some of the women and children were killed or wounded in the disturbance."

The SS officer in charge of the prisoner disembarkation process came over to Ezekiel and me and introduced himself as *SS Oberscharführer* Kurt Bolender. *

"All of us here at Treblinka are concerned, Lieutenant; many of the Jews and other undesirables are learning this camp is not a transit camp but the end of the line for them – a death camp.

"What can I do for you, Lieutenant?"

"We are here to see the Commandant. I have orders from Reichführer Himmler." I opened the packet which displayed our orders.

The officer glanced at them and saluted with his response. "Yes, Sir. Please follow me."

"Just a moment, Officer. I need to dismiss our driver."

I motioned for Ezekiel to follow me to the automobile. When we were away from the SS Officer, but not too close to the car, I leaned close to Zeke and cautioned him: "Zeke, this could be much worse than we ever imagined. We must be very cautious not to outwardly display any emotions. Be careful of facial expressions or any outward reactions to the horrors we may encounter."

"I hear you, Jenz. I already feel like being sick to my stomach."

"Driver," I announced as I handed the Corporal the keys. "Thanks for the ride; we will find our own way back to Warsaw."

Zeke and I followed the officer into the camp.

---

*Oberscharführer Kurt Bolender joined the SS Totenkopfstandarte, (Death's Head) unit in 1939. His initial position was in the euthanasia program, where he excelled at his duties. He was known for throwing babies, children, and the sick directly from the freight transports into the trolly with a load that went straight to the Lazarett (infirmary), where they were immediately shot or thrown into pits to be cremated. In 1961 he was recognized while working as a doorman, with false identity papers, at a German nightclub. In December 1965, before the conclusion of his trial in Hagen, West Germany, Bolender committed suicide by hanging himself in his jail cell.

As we entered the facility, Zeke and I were impressed with the cleanliness of the walkways, which were bordered by flowering plants. We both noticed an odor we couldn't quite place. It might have been a cleaning solution or a disinfectant.

"Officer, what is that odor?"

"I'm used to it, so I don't really smell it anymore. It could be a combination of the gas houses' vapors or the incineration of the dead prisoners."

"Oh," I asked naively, "do you have a lot of fatalities at this facility?"

Officer Bolender proudly answered. "Close to one hundred percent! There is no time off for good behavior." His last statement was said with a bit of a chuckle.

"However, some of the stronger or more fortunate prisoners are allowed to function on work details or in the kitchen for a short period of time."

As we walked into the camp, there were several men sweeping the area the officer called the square. It was surrounded by barbed wire. "Here is the location for the separation to take place."

"What happens here?" I asked.

"Well, let me show you to the Commandant's office. You will meet our deputy commander SS Oberscharführer Kurt Franz. Our Commanding Office SS Oberscharführer Franz Stangl is an expert in euthanasia but is away at another camp at the moment.

Officer Bolender knocked and walked into a plain stripped-down office just inside the gate. He introduced us to the deputy commanding officer, Kurt Franz.

The deputy commanding officer was nothing like I had pictured. He was cordial to Zeke and deferential to me. He had an almost cherub-like face and spoke like a well-educated officer. He was physically in excellent shape – not overweight or slovenly.

"Good morning, gentlemen. What can I do for you this beautiful day?"

"Hello, commandant. We have orders from Herr Himmler to locate and procure suitable workers for our Army Research Center in northern Germany.

I displayed our orders on his desk for him to read.

After reading our orders without comment, he exclaimed.

"Excellent, Lieutenant! You are welcome to view all parts of our operation here. I think you will find it very efficient. We had a transport come in about an hour ago and the deportees have undergone separation and are now in the undressing centers. Lieutenant Bolender will show you whatever you need to see.

"Unfortunately, some of the deportees were uncooperative and had to be shot, but for the most part everything is back to normal now." "How," I asked, "did you secure the cooperation of the deportees?"

"The Ukrainian guards usually shoot the ringleaders in the head. The rest usually submit to beating with the iron bars or the whipping. My hound, Bari here, often helps by barking and biting the Jews in the genitals." A brief smile spread across his baby-like face.

My goodness, I thought, that hound is the size of a small cow!

"Lieutenant Bolender, please show our guests our efficient method of liquidation after the deportees enter the undressing sheds."

"Yes, Sir!

"Right this way, gentlemen."

We walked right into the women's undressing shed. There was some weeping and general confusion as the women were trying to undress and reassure their crying children. Many of the women were asking questions about their circumstances but were being yelled at by the shockingly belligerent female guards.

A male Ukrainian guard was shouting at the women and children to fold their clothes neatly so they could be disinfected.

"Please keep your valuables or money. You may turn them in to the cashier and get a receipt at the end of the shed," he bellowed.

There were several hundred women and children in the overcrowded undressing area. Because of my size, I might have been intimidating to many of the women and children. They seem to duck out of the way as Zeke and I followed officer Bolender through the shed. We tried to keep our eyes looking down. Many of the women were quite beautiful.

One of the young women grabbed Zeke and asked, "What is happening to us? Are we already lost?"

A woman guard stepped out of the shadows and began whipping the young girl unmercifully.

The guard yelled, "Stop bothering the sergeant, prisoner!"

Zeke grabbed the whip and yanked it from the guard's hand, "I will take care of disciplining the prisoner, guard."

Zeke threw the whip down, turned to the female prisoner, and helped her off the floor. He grabbed her under the left arm and as he pulled her gently to her feet, he whispered, "Please stay strong young Ms. I'm afraid all Germany is lost. Please follow the others to the next station."

I could tell Zeke was shaken by the guard whipping the beautiful young woman. There was a cut where the whip had been slashed across her back. But to his credit, the expression on his face remained stoic and unchanged.

Zeke and I followed Officer Bolender to the next building. About twenty male prison workers were lined up behind several tables.

"These are the Gold Jews *(GoldJuden)*" announced Officer Bolender. "They are mostly former jewelers, watchmakers or bank clerks. They are here to sort the money, jewelry, or any valuables they can steal from the prisoners.

"Of course, when their work is finished and the transports stop coming from Warsaw, they will all be killed."

"Why is that?" offered Zeke.

Bolender shot back, "Everything we do here at this death camp is very secretive. We cannot allow everyday Germans, or the rest of the world know what is going on here. We are liquidating all the vermin and Jews from the conquered territories very efficiently."

There were several hundred women and children in this crowded room. Zeke asked, "Why are some of the women lying on the tables?"

"Oh." Replied Bolender, in a very matter-of-fact tone, "These *GoldJuden* are doing cavity searches including their genitalia for hidden valuables."

"These searches seem pretty thorough," remarked Zeke.

"You have no idea!" Bolender shot back. "Wait until you view the next couple of stations. Some of these Jews are very inventive and sneaky."

Zeke just shook his head.

I gave him a sharp look and whispered, "Zeke, remember, even though all this is overwhelming, we cannot afford to show any emotion. Just remember everything we see here today. Our first-hand visit could be important for future generations of law-abiding and decent Germans."

Zeke nodded his understanding as we walked into the next building.

This building contained almost twenty men with scissors. These men *(Friseurs)* were in the process of cutting off the women's hair.

"I asked Officer Bolender, "Why is it necessary to cut off the women's hair?"

The men were cutting off the beautiful hair of all the women, including the children and tossing the hair into large suitcases.

"This has been routine in all the camps since earlier this summer," replied Bolender. "The women are told it is to ensure the effectiveness of our de-lousing program before they are transported to their next duty in the East."

"What would the Reich possibly do with this much hair," asked Zeke.

"After the hair is cleaned," Bolender offered, "It is threaded on bobbins and converted into industrial felt. The felt product is made into slippers for submarine crews and felt stockings for the Reichsbahn. Some of the human hair is also used as upholstery for furniture.

There was a lot of screaming and crying in the building. It was truly heartbreaking to see people so utterly distressed. *I thought, if Zeke doesn't lose control, I surely would.*

Officer Bolender bragged, "All this screaming and confusion will be over shortly. As soon as this group enters the tube, there is no escape. The tube runs directly to the gas chambers. This group will all be dead in 30 minutes."

It was then I realized the hideous suffering of the victims on the journeys in the stinking, over-crowded cattle cars were nothing compared to the horrors on arrival at the Treblinka camp.

Chapter 8

Saving a Few from the Gas Chambers

Zeke took me aside as the first of the nude women were being herded and whipped to enter the tube leading to the gas chambers.

"Couldn't some of these women be of use to the general at Peenemünde? Perhaps some of them could work in the kitchens, do administrative work, assemble the rockets, or be part of a cleaning crew? They could be valuable to the Reich."

I brought Officer Bolender over after nodding my approval to Zeke. I had to talk in a loud voice to be heard over the cries, screaming, and general confusion.

"Sir," I began. "Some of these women might be useful at our research facility on Germany's north coast. Our orders from Herr Himmler read that we may transport some of the prisoners found at these camps back to Peenemünde for use to the Reich."

"Take your pick, Lieutenant! Be quick about it. Once they enter the tube, I cannot save them."

Zeke looked at me and asked, "How are we supposed to pick out those who will live?"

"Here, put my SS Uniform Jacket over the young women you picked up off the floor, take the next five people in line, and bring them over to me."

"What if they have children with them?" queried Zeke.

"Bring them along, of course." I talked loud enough so Officer Bolender would know exactly what we were doing.

Zeke took my coat with the SS designations on the collar and approached the totally nude woman who had been whipped and just had her hair cut off. She was crying softly and speaking to the female child behind her.

"What is your name, Miss?"

"I am called A…Adiya." She was startled by the attention from the Wehrmacht Sargent amid all the confusion and yelling.

"Oh," Zeke replied, "God's treasure."

"How would you know what my name meant?" replied the young woman. "Unless you are…" She looked surprised and shocked.

Zeke held up his hand for her to stop talking. He kept trying to avert his eyes by looking down, and not looking at the incredibly beautifully figured woman before him. Her breasts and everything about her were perfectly proportioned. It was difficult for him to keep looking away.

"Miss," Zeke placed my coat over the shivering young woman, "would you and the next five women in line, please come with me?"

As I covered her, I kept trying to look down or away to avert my eyes from her very full body. I felt enough shame for both of us.

You could tell this young woman really wanted to live; she was around eighteen years old and had her whole life ahead of her. Her eyes were brimming with tears.

"May my younger sister come also?" she asked in a pleading voice.

"Yes! Please hurry! Come this way."

Six women and a child around ten years old followed me around one of the tables over to Jenz and Officer Bolender. They were all frightened and whimpering.

Jenz, in a very quiet voice, told the women not to pay any attention to whatever came out of his mouth next.

In a loud voice, so others, including Bolender, could hear, Jenz started shaking his finger and shouting at the women, **"You women are enemies of the Reich! You have been chosen for a special assignment. Go with the Sargent; retrieve your clothes and belongings and prepare for a long train journey."**

"Vitali," he quietly instructed, "Take the ladies to their belongings and pass through the kitchen so they may pack some food for their journey to Peenemünde. Please accompany them on the transport train back to Warsaw and board the next available train to the rocket base. Here is some money to cover the cost of transport and here is a copy of our orders in case you are questioned. Please secure some hats or kerchiefs for the women out of the piles of clothing. I will meet you at the camp at Auschwitz in a few days."

Vitali ushered the six ladies and a young child out of the hair cutting room and back to the next building to retrieve their clothing.

One of the Ukrainian Guards stopped them. "Where are you going Sargent? These women are scheduled for the showers!"

He raised his rifle and pointed it at our small group.

With the guard's comments, the women became almost hysterical. A few started crying.

"Ladies, calm down. My name is Sargent Carapezza. Please stay close to me and show no emotion until we are out of this hellhole."

"Out of my way, Guard. These women are on special assignment for the Reich; I have orders from Reichsführer Himmler!"

Zeke was stopped again at the main gate, but he then left the camp with the women who had been scheduled for death, I said a silent prayer to myself:

Father God, watch over Ezekiel and, indeed, all the men and women in this prison of horrors. Please embrace them in your heavenly arms, ease their pain and suffering, and keep them all close to you.

As I turned around to leave the hair-cutting room, Officer Bolender approached me, "Lieutenant, would you like to see the rest of the camp and how we 'encourage' the vermin into the chambers?"

"Okay," I replied.

Chapter 9

━━━━━◦⟨✥⟩◦━━━━━

The Killing Machine

Officer Bolender and I walked outside and observed a line of very reluctant and terrified women being whipped and prodded with iron bars down a sandy pathway leading to a large, enclosed building.

"Bolender," I began, "Is all this violence necessary?"

"It depends," he answered tentatively. "Most of these women think they are going to a shower area. We even have shower heads installed in the ceilings of each gas chamber. Most of the people are relatively cooperative until the last few vermin are packed into the chamber. They start to panic when they realize they are so tightly packed into the chamber that there is no room for bathing, nor are there any drains in the floor."

"Some of the condemned have to be whipped or shot. A fresh coating of sand must be swept over the path to cover up the blood after each transport goes through. We call the path the 'pathway way to heaven.'"

"Is there any way out for these souls?"

"Never," replied Bolender. "The doors of the gas chambers are locked and hermetically sealed. The tractor engine starts immediately, and the monoxide gas is pumped directly into the chamber. Most days, we can liquidate an average of three to four thousand of the Jews daily. Some days many more of these undesirables are extinguished."

Officer Bolender seemed almost cheerful as he described how Germany was efficiently liquidating all the Jews from the Reich.

My depression was tensing all the muscles in my back and head. I tried not to clench my teeth too hard. My facial muscles were bulging. My headache was going to be massive.

The weather was now slightly overcast with a chill in the air.

The tractor engine started, and I heard muffled screams from the gas chamber. My emotions were at the breaking point.

"Would you like to watch their terror through the thick glass viewing window," asked Bolender?"

"No, Bolender. I think I have seen quite enough."

"Our mission here at Treblinka," he continued, "is to euthanize all the vermin from the conquered territories eventually. A model of this camp will be used for eventually liquidating all the Jews from the East, including Russia."

"It sounds like you folks here at Treblinka will be in business for quite a while."

I tried to speak in a conversational tone as I looked over to the gas chambers. These killing machines were murdering my Jewish friends, neighbors, and probably the intellectual elite and some of the most skilled leaders and technicians from the Reich.

I was sure these officers and guards at Treblinka and throughout the Reich had no idea of the cultural, scientific, and human resources, lost to the rest of the world these deaths would represent.

"Well." After a considerable pause, Bolender continued, "We are trying to be as efficient as possible. Our goal is to remove five to six thousand ghetto inhabitants each day. However, that requires three or four transports each day. Some of the Jews in the Warsaw ghetto are putting up some resistance as their fate is getting known."

"Does our Fürher and Herr Himmler have knowledge of the Jewish resistance in the Warsaw Ghetto?"

"Oh, yes," replied Bolender, with a touch of glee. "If the Jews don't come out peacefully, and they cannot be starved into submission, our forces just go in and shoot anyone resisting arrest. If the rabble tries to hide from our men, they are burned out of their homes and shot on the spot."

"It sounds very efficient and complete." Although I was seething inside, I tried to respond in a conversational tone. I had to raise my voice over the screams and crying of the Jewish women and children being whipped and forced into the gas chambers. The scene was brutal and heart-rendering. I was afraid at one point I might fly into a rage, or just collapse from sadness.

"Who developed this 'efficient' method of" – I paused because I almost said murdering – "eliminating the Jews?"

"Our second in command is SS Officer, Kurt Franz. * He has had extensive experience with euthanasia at other camps like Auschwitz.

"Deputy Commander Franz had originally suggested we use the strong disinfectant, Zyklon B, also known as hydrogen cyanide, to kill the Jews quickly. However, our camp commander, Franz Stangl, ** felt the monoxide gas was sufficient, even though it took longer for the Jews to die. Commander Franz had the gas chambers rebuilt in order to accommodate more Jews. Our new gas chambers are capable of liquidating twelve to fifteen thousand Jews per day."

"Have you ever had to load the gas chambers to that capacity?" I asked with some trepidation.

"We need three or more transports each day to reach our capacity. Transports arrive from all over the Reich: Holland, France, Romania,

---

*Kurt Franz epitomized the worst the SS had to offer. He was the cruelest and most feared of all the SS Guards at Treblinka. He used to ride around Treblinka on his horse and took delight in whipping and shooting the prisoners. His dog, Bari, was the size of a young cow and was trained to bite the genitals of the unfortunate detainees. Franz was recognized while working as a cook, arrested in Düsseldorf on December 2nd, 1959, and sentenced to life in prison. At his trial, witnesses agreed that not a single day passed when he did not kill someone. A search of his home found a photo album of Treblinka titled "Beautiful Years." He was released in 1993 for health reasons and died shortly afterward.

**Commander Stangl was responsible for re-organizing Treblinka into a more effective killing machine. To conceal its main purpose, he beautified the grounds with flowers and flowering bushes. He would often wear a white uniform and carry a whip. The prisoners nicknamed him the "White Death." After the war, he escaped to Brazil until he was tracked down by Nazi hunter, Simon Wiesenthal and arrested on 28 February 1967. He was sentenced to life in prison and died in Düsseldorf prison on 28 June 1971.

in addition to Germany, Poland, Czechoslovakia, and Hungry. We are starting to get more from the Eastern Territories, including Belarus, Silesia, and Russia.

"Our Führer has notified all the death camps that we should expect many more transports after the fall of Stalingrad."

"What are you expecting after Stalingrad?" I asked.

"Oh, the Jews and most of the population of the city will be eliminated. The Wehrmacht will shoot the men, and the women and children will be transported to our death camps here in Poland. Sobibor and Belzec death detention facilities will handle any surplus.

"Our Führer feels that a victory at Stalingrad will cut off the oil supplies to Russia from the oil fields in the south and ensure our total victory in the East."

"What is your interest in our workforce here, Lieutenant?"

"Our facility in northern Germany needs able-bodied skilled workers for our research facility. We need machinists, engineers, electricians, and general workers to staff our facility.

"Many of our workers at Peenemünde have not been with us long because of sickness, malnourishment, or exhaustion – or all three. I will need to screen the male detainees from your transports to find people with these skills."

"Why don't we screen the last male transportees," Officer Bolender suggested. "They will be coming out of the undressing area as soon as the gas chambers are cleaned and readied for their arrival."

"Why do the chambers need cleaning," I asked in my naiveté. I was completely clueless and shocked by Bolender's answer.

"After a gassing, the chambers are awash with feces, urine, sweat, and blood. Much of the blood comes from the prisoners. As they realize they are being gassed, they try to claw their way out by the door. This frenzied panic usually lasts eight to twenty minutes before they die.

We usually wait another few minutes in order to ensure each group is completely deceased."

"What do you do with the bodies," I asked.

"All the dead are carried to the burial pits and burned or covered with lime and sand between each layer. You must understand, we have a big job here. We have to rid the Reich of thousands of Jews and other criminals every day. Herr Himmler has required us to complete the elimination of the Jewish Ghetto in Warsaw by the end of next summer."

"Would you like to see the burial pits and 'Lazarett'?"

"You will have to tell me, what is the 'Lazarett'?" I was a little reluctant to ask because it was like the Polish word for infirmary.

"Yes. Of course. The 'Lazarett' is the execution site where unruly prisoners are stood up against a sandbag wall and shot. You never want to visit this part of our camp unaccompanied."

His comment sounded a bit like a warning. I hoped he hadn't guessed I was Jewish. I kept up my bravado with another comment.

"Let's take a look at the incoming group of male deportees and see if our facility could use any of them."

As we walked back through the reception area, another transport was pulling into the station.

I asked, "Officer Bolender, what will you do with all the folks on this train that just pulled into Treblinka?"

"We never unlock the doors of the boxcars until the group before them has been completely gassed. We cannot allow a great number of anxious prisoners to wander around the camp. We just do not have the space for them."

"Isn't there any place in the camp where they can wait to be processed?" I asked.

"Unfortunately, they have to wait in the boxcars. They are so tightly packed, no one can sit or lie down. They have to wait until we have room for them."

"How long is the average wait?"

"Oh, sometimes they have to wait in the boxcars all day. It is particularly difficult for us in the summer. The Jews are without toilet facilities or food for several hours."

"How is their waiting in the boxcars difficult for the camp?" I asked the officer.

"Ramsgrund, you wouldn't believe the smell! Particularly in the heat of the summer. The mixture of sweat, fecal material, and urine is overwhelming. The boxcar transports have very little ventilation when they are not moving. Many of the Jews are dead or near death when we can finally unlock and open the sliding doors to the railroad cars."

The entire unloading and processing of the Jews sounded horrible and unthinkable. How could anyone contemplate treating another human being with this cruelty? I wouldn't have believed it, if I hadn't seen it in person.

As I walked around the Treblinka camp, a feeling of abject loneliness crept into my very soul. The horror surrounding me was pervasive. I asked myself: Could God know about this place?

Chapter 10

Male Selection for our
Research Center in Peenemünde

Officer Bolender and I went into the men's undressing area. He kept his hand on his pistol – probably in case of difficulty. There were three Ukrainian guards in the building with rifles at the ready. No one was being whipped or disciplined, but there was considerable unrest, complaining, loud talk, and shouting.

Some men shouted, **"Where have you taken our wives and daughters?"**

The answer was always the same, shouted by the Ukrainian Guards. **"You will meet up with them shortly after the fumigation process.**

I was crying inside.

Bolender drew his Luger pistol and aimed it at the ceiling, and shouted for the men to be quiet. Without discharging his weapon, everyone quieted down. I came forward and made the announcement:

"Men of Warsaw," I began, "I'm Lieutenant Ramsgrund. Reichsführer Himmler has given me orders to bring certain qualified men back to our Wehrmacht Research Center to help with the construction of innovative weapon systems for our heroic war effort against the Allies and the Russians, and all enemies of the Reich.

"To be qualified for this work, you must have a background in engineering – either electrical or mechanical or as a master machinist or electrician. Furthermore, you must be able to demonstrate your knowledge to me before we leave this facility. If I find you are not being truthful with me, there will be consequences.

"Do I have any such qualified men here now? Please step forward and keep your clothes on until we have made a determination."

I stepped back and looked over the men. Out of two or three hundred men in the room, a handful stepped forward. I encouraged them to come with me and we found a table in the small building adjacent to the women's undressing area in the hair-cutting room. A total of fourteen men followed me into the room. I encourage them to pull up chairs around one of the tables. Officer Bolender stood in the door with his hand on his pistol.

I had to speak in a loud tone because of all the murmuring and complaining.

"Men," I started my introduction, "I have orders from the highest authority to bring qualified Jews to our Wehrmacht Research Facility in northern Germany. I am specifically looking for engineers, electricians, and machinists. You must be in excellent health and physical condition.

"If any of you have come over to this room under false assumptions or credentials, or you are in poor health, you are ordered to return to the men's undressing area, and you will receive no consequential or additional punishment."

I waited a few minutes while the group collectively made up their minds to chance to go to another facility.

One man raised his hand and tentatively stood up.

"Sir." He spoke in a halting German language with a decidedly Polish accent. Although a little hard to understand, I got the essence of what he was saying.

"My name is Horace Breitman. I am a machinist, but you addressed us as men of Warsaw. I am from Belarus. I did not want to mislead you, if you were under the impression, I was from the Warsaw Ghetto. My family lived approximately one hour east of Minsk before the German invasion of Russia. After the invasion, we moved west to the Lublin district of German-occupied Poland."

I answered as carefully as possible. "I am looking for qualified men who have a skill needed by our research facility in the north of Germany. Where you are from is not important for the needs of the Reich.

"Breitman, if you are skilled in machine parts manufacturing, assembling, and fabricating, you could be valuable for our research center.

"After I have checked on the qualifications of each man here, you all will be sent back to Warsaw on a transporter with two Ukrainian Guards. These guards will take you by train to Peenemünde, in northern Germany, and the research center.

"Breitman, you remain behind after everyone is escorted to the kitchen area and then to the transports. I would like a word with you."

Most of the color drained from Breitman's face. He looked like he might pass out. I did tower over the Polish machinist, but I didn't realize he was so nervous and fearful.

I couldn't blame him. His future was disturbingly uncertain in this horrible place.

"Have, have I done something wrong?" The poor Jew was shaking and stammering.

"Not at all, Breitman. I want to know how you wound up in the Warsaw Ghetto."

Chapter 11

Killing the Elderly and Children

When I thought nothing could be as atrocious as this hell-on-earth called Treblinka, Breitman's story led me to believe there was even more dreadful news to come.

Horace Breitman was a highly trained machinist. He had done many projects for different companies in Poland, Russia, Belarus, and the Reich.

He explained he was quite friendly with one of the local reserve police captains who had come from Hamburg, Germany, to his home in Belarus to assess the "Jewish problem."

Breitman explained, "I had become friends with one police officer. Major Wilhelm Trapp became friendly with our family because our fathers had served together in the Great War. I'm not sure he even knew I was Jewish. He never asked. My father's family was originally from just south of the Stockholm area in Sweden.

"In addition to our familial connection, I had done some minor machine work for the Major when he had trouble getting parts for some of his equipment and vehicles."

"Were you able to maintain your friendship with Major Trapp as our troops conquered and swept through the Eastern Territories?" I asked.

"For the most part, yes." Breitman answered. But then a very strange emotion started to overcome the machinist and he almost fell into a vacant chair.

"Are you going to be okay, Breitman? Tell me what is going on!" I shot back with a little force of command behind my voice. "There will be no consequence for you."

"Lieutenant, do you really want to hear my story?"

"Yes, go ahead, Breitman. Enlighten me."

"Well, the whole sad story began on a Sunday afternoon early in November 1941. Major Trapp had stopped by our home in Belarus to ask questions about the Jewish section of Slutsk, Poland. Although a reserve officer in the Hamburg police force, his detachment was assigned to the Eastern Territories to help with a solution to the Jewish question in the Central Government of German-occupied Poland."

It was a warm, late fall day, and I had all the windows open for ventilation. The major seemed upset about our conversation, and I offered him some coffee cake my wife had baked and something to drink. I offered tea, but he snapped back, "Do you have any schnaps?"

I poured about two ounces into a small glass.

"Thank you." He downed it in one gulp.

"What is troubling you, Major?" I inquired.

"It is this whole 'Operation Reinhard' business. I have had orders from Heinrich Himmler through his district commander, Odilo Globocnik, *

"I was ordered to make the Lublin district Jewdenfrei by 1943. My orders were specific to start in the town of Slutsk, south of Minsk in Belorussia."

---

*Odilo Globocnik met with Himmler on 13 October 1941 and proposed eliminating Jews in the conquered areas of Poland with assembly line efficiency in concentration camps using gas chambers. Globocnik was a violent Nazi who rose to command all the Polish extermination camps. He was so unstable that he terrorized his own concentration camp commanders. Globocnik committed suicide by biting on a cyanide capsule when tracked down and arrested by British troops on 31 May 1945. His goal was to make the entire Central Government area of German-occupied Poland free of all Jews by the end of 1943.

"There must be thousands of Jewish people living in the Lublin district and throughout the Eastern Territories," I replied. Where would they all go?" I asked.

"Please don't misunderstand me, Lieutenant. All the Jews from these areas are to be liquidated. If they couldn't be shipped to concentration camps, they were to be immediately shot."

"How does our Reichsführer or Major Trapp plan on eliminating thousands of these Jews?" I asked, hoping I wasn't going to get an answer I dreaded.

"Well, Lieutenant, the Major started to rock back and forth in his chair and tell me the details of what went on in Slutsk, south of Minsk. By the end of the Major's description of the proceedings in Slutsk, he was carrying on and crying so much I had to close the windows.

"The Major complained on the morning of 27 October 1941, a reserve Police First Lieutenant with a Battalion from Lithuania backed up by the SS came to him and ordered the Major to liquidate all the Jews in Slutsk in two days."

"What happened," I asked with trepidation.

At first, the Major said it couldn't be done. Major Trapp complained, "if all the Jewish tradesmen were liquidated, vital enterprises in the city would be immediately paralyzed."

However, the Lithuanian Commander of the reserve battalion emphasized he only could spare his men for two days. He had two days to cleanse the Jews from Slutsk before he had to move on to other villages in the area. He wanted the entire city Judenrein, or cleaned of Jews before he had to leave.

"The city of Slutsk at the time had approximately 12,000 inhabitants. One-third of these folks are Jewish," complained Major Trapp. "Most inhabitants live in peace and harmony without causing any trouble for their neighbors.

The Major then related to me what happened in a very soft, almost whimpering and crying voice:

"All the Jews were pulled out of the factories and forced from their homes at gunpoint. They were loaded onto wagons and driven out to the forest in groups of twenty to fifty men, women, and children. The Jews were then ordered to remove their clothes and valuables and lie naked face down on the earth. The auxiliary police then shot them in the back of their head."

"I am a family man," sobbed Major Trapp. "Initially, I could not bring myself to shoot innocent people, especially women and little children.

The Lithuanian Lieutenant chided me. "Major, if you do not have the stomach for this work, my men will carry out the sentence. Of course, I will have to report your lack of bravery to my superiors."

Breitman continued. "Trapp was a reserve policeman from Hamburg and had no desire or inclination for further advancement in rank."

Trapp told the Lithuanian he couldn't even watch, but he heard the screams, crying, and gunfire on his way back to the village.

"Any of the Jewish men who resisted, according to Trapp, were shot in their homes or on the street. The elderly, who couldn't walk to the wagons, were shot in their beds. Children, including very young children, and their mothers, trying to protect them, were immediately shot. Corpses were lining the streets of the Jewish Ghetto and on the city streets. There was blood all over the sidewalks. It was utter chaos. There was shooting everywhere.

"I don't think Major Trapp will ever be the same. He had never witnessed anything so cruel and inhumane, even in the Great War.

"He had a military background and said he could not bring himself to be part of this beastly action."

I then asked what I thought was a reasonable question.

"Breitman, was there any consideration for Jews who might be useful for the Reich?" My suggestion would be to save these folks for working in industries that are going to be critical for Germany to win this war.

"Lieutenant, if you were Jewish and from Slutsk, you were dead. There were also a lot of White Russian people in the city who were brutalized, clubbed, and eliminated by the execution squads."

"Does Reichsführer Himmler know of these Judenrein procedures of important workers in the Eastern Territories?" I was trying to understand the source of so much hatred and anger. Even though I had witnessed all kinds of anti-Semitism, even in Hitler Youth Camp, this seemed abominable and completely wasteful.

"The Reichsführer has to know, but perhaps not the effects of the drain of critical workers on the war with the Russians." Commented Breitman.

"I will message General Dornberger to get further workers for our research center in Peenemünde. I will want you to accompany me tomorrow to Sobibor. From there, I will need an introduction to Major Trapp.

"If you help me accomplish procuring more Jews for the research center, you will be completely free to go back to your home and family in Belarus."

"My family," Breitman replied softly, "has already been murdered in the Treblinka camp."

"Will you be able to carry on for them?" I questioned.

"I will do it for my family and the many other families in Belarus."

Chapter 12

The Sobibor Death Camp

It took Breitman and me two days to make our way to the Sobibor Concentration Camp by automobile requisitioned from the Warsaw Command. My uniform and orders from Reichsführer Himmler got us through all the checkpoints on the way to the eastern part of Poland governed by the Reich.

As we approached the camp, the area looked like a peaceful farm in the middle of a meadow. The camp area looked almost like a perfect rectangle, approximately four or five hundred by six or seven hundred meters. The buildings even had the vague look of a farm with village buildings. The only unusual look was the surrounding barbed wire fencing and watch towers. The wire perimeter fence had pine branches intertwined with the barbed wire to limit the visibility of the inside of the camp. The camp looked very peaceful as we approached.

It was a picture-perfect day with puffy clouds overhanging the probable area of the crematoria. There was no wind but a faint odor of unpleasantness in the air.

I warned Breitman. "Do not show any emotion or facial expressions displaying dissatisfaction, disbelief, or outright rage at what we might encounter at this camp facility."

"Thank you, Lieutenant. I appreciate your trust."

I wanted to trust Breitman. His background was not too dissimilar to my own. I just couldn't be sure he wouldn't let my secret be known under torture or carelessness.

We went directly to the Commandant's office. Franz Stangl, the current SS Officer in charge, was not in his office, so I presented my orders to the deputy, Oberscharführer Hermann Michel. *

This officer radiated pure evil. His deep-set eyes and expanded forehead made me think of a pre-historic relic who could possibly be only part human.

The Oberscharführer, however, was pleasant enough after he viewed Himmler's orders, and even offered us a brief tour of the facility. I introduced Breitman as my aide.

"Gentlemen," he started as we walked out of the area where the incoming Jewish prisoners were kept. "Our duty here is to euthanize as many Jews as they send us. Since Operation Barbarossa began last summer, we have had many transports from the East coming to our facility."

He grabbed a white coat as he was leaving his office. We entered the separation area and he put on his white coat and stood on a table. The white coat gave the poor Jewish prisoners the idea that he was a doctor. He spoke in a very kind and understanding voice to the captured audience:

"People, please calm down. You are all being resettled in the Ukraine. You will be doing productive farm work, which will be valuable for Germany. Please go to the undressing rooms and leave your clothing in a pile for complete disinfecting. Your valuables will be returned to you after the showers and delousing. Thank you.

He spoke in such a reassuring, gentle, and refined voice, his nickname was "The Preacher." The prisoners had no idea they were being tricked into going to the gas chambers.

"Even more concerning," he addressed us, "we are getting more and more transports from as far away as France, the Netherlands, Bulgaria, and Croatia. Our staff is working at capacity. However, we

---

*SS Oberscharführer Herman Michel worked at the Sobibor Death Camp because of his extensive experience in the T-4 Euthanasia Program. His experience was gained at the Hartheim Killing Center, where physically and mentally disabled people were killed by lethal injection or gassing. After the war, Michel fled to Egypt, where he disappeared.

have an expert in euthanasia coming soon in order to expand our gas chambers.

"Who is coming, Oberscharführer?"

"His name is Christian Wirth, * Lieutenant. He is also known by the thousands of Jews coming through the camps as 'Christian the Terrible,' 'Christian the Cruel,' and by many of us as the 'Wild Christian.' He is an expert at mass extermination of the Jews, Russian prisoners of war, and Gypsies who come to our facility."

"Wirth started out as a reserve police captain but found his calling in euthanizing people. He began by killing the weak and the handicapped by lethal injection, but gradually he found more and better ways of liquidating hundreds of Jews at one time.

"Our gas chambers here can only hold up to two hundred Jews at a time, but I hear his death chambers in Auschwitz can euthanize up to two thousand Jews at a time.

"I understand from your orders, Lieutenant, that you are looking for technically trained Jews for a research facility?"

"Correct, Oberscharführer Michel. Our facility needs machinists, electricians, and engineers. Assembly and experience working with small parts would also be helpful. Breitman here is a technical expert in machinery and is helping me with the candidates."

"What is it you are building at your facility, Lieutenant?"

"It is all top-secret weapons development work for the war effort, Oberscharführer, not to be discussed outside of the research center. Knowledge of the German language would be helpful.

"Are you experimenting on humans for the Reich, Lieutenant?"

"Never! Our interest is in weapons development. I apologize, but further discussion is not permitted."

---

*It was Wirth whose guidelines and policies toward prisoners gave the Ukrainian Guards and SS men in the camps the authority and encouragement to create a reign of terror and misery for the Jews. He epitomized the worst debasement of Nazi authority. Christian Wirth was killed in May 1944, by Yugoslav Partisans while traveling in an open car near Trieste in northeastern Italy. He was 59 years old.

"How can we at Sobibor help with your efforts at the Research Center in northern Germany?"

"It would be best for us to interview a few men and women from the transports as they come into your camp. I would like technically trained people who would prove valuable for our efforts. However, they must be in good physical health.

"Many of our current laborers at the center cannot remain healthy under the strain of weapons development because of the time constraints our Fürher has placed on our project."

"Come over to the selection area. The last transport prisoners have not yet been sent to the undressing station. You may interview prisoners directly in the separation area."

Officer Michael explained to us that the Sobibor Camp was divided into three distinct areas. The Forward area of Camp I included the unloading area for deportees, living quarters for Ukrainian Guards and SS personnel, and different shops and kitchens for maintaining the camp. The Camp II area was needed to undress and store valuables and clothing removed from the prisoners. The third part of the facility, the Camp III area, was for the gas chambers, combustion engine area for producing the monoxide lethal gas, and prisoner barracks. This area also contains the mass graves and outdoor crematoria.

"It's all designed to run very efficiently, Lieutenant. Remember, we are under pressure from Herr Himmler to euthanize thousands of deportees from all the villages, cities, and towns of the conquered territories and all over Europe."

"It sounds like an impossible task," I commented.

"Yes, Lieutenant. Let me take you over to Camp II and the collection area, where you can choose some candidates for interviewing.

"I must caution you, Lieutenant, be careful not to let on these folks know they are being led to their deaths. These Jews can get very uncooperative if they know they are about to die.

"Our purpose is to get the prisoners to hurry through the undressing and hair-cutting area in order to corral them into the gas chambers. Often, we tell them to hurry because the shower water is getting cold. Occasionally, we must whip and beat them in order to get them into the chambers – especially if they have any idea they are being led to their death.

Under my breath, I said a silent prayer for my fellow Jews who were being deceived and murdered at an alarming rate. How could I ever forgive myself if I couldn't help to bring an end to this monumental crime? What could Zeke and I do? If we were discovered, we would be shot immediately.

It was getting late in the day. Breitman and I could sense a certain tension in the air. The Oberscharführer said something about the end-of-day count was approaching and several of the SS and Ukrainian Guards were not present at their duty stations.

I asked what I thought was a comment about guard reliability.

"Where are the SS men guarding the new arrivals from the transports?"

"Many of the men," offered the Oberscharführer, "pick out the best-looking young women from the transports and suggest they trade sex for their lives."

"Are any of the women saved by these encounters?" I asked.

"Never!" The Oberscharführer spit out the words. "After the sex in the officer's quarters, they are led immediately to the gas chambers."

I said a silent prayer for these poor, completely innocent women. Not only were they being unjustly and brutally murdered but abused and debased for the pleasure of these criminals.

"However, this is very strange. Although all the Jews are within the wire enclosures; however, no Ukrainian Guards or SS men are in the selection area."

Just then, we heard gunfire from the distant part of Camp II.

"Gentlemen!" shouted the officer. Something very unusual is happening. Please leave as quickly as possible for your own safety." *

As Breitman and I started for the front gate and back to our automobile, we could look over our shoulders and see armed men coming from the entrance of Camp II.

We heard multiple gunshots from within the camp as we entered our car. Machine gun fire erupted from the guard towers.

Breitman asked, "Do you think it is an uprising of some sort?"

"I'm not sure," I answered, "but let's drive a few kilometers down the road and see what develops."

---

*On the 14th of October 1943, at 4 pm, several prisoners took part in an uprising, and hundreds of their fellow Jews escaped. Eleven SS Guards were killed. A Jewish Red Army POW, Lieutenant Alexander Pechersky, planned the uprising. After the war, Lieutenant Pechersky was not allowed to leave Russia by the Russian Government. So, he was unable to testify at the Sobibor Trial at Nuremberg or the Eichmann Trial in Israel. He died in Russia in Rostov-on-Don on the 19th of January 1990. He was 81 years old.

Chapter 13

Saving a Family

We drove until we came to a forest area and parked by the side of the road. It was a quiet and peaceful area without any thought of conflict and murder. A gentle breeze was whispering in the pines, and songbirds chirped in the adjacent meadow.

I removed my cover and talked with Breitman. "Look, Breitman, if any people from the recent transport come this way, we are going to try to save them."

"Sir." The machinist had a curt reply. "These Jews have had the most traumatic experience of their lives. They may not be totally comfortable with a uniformed SS officer offering them safety."

"Breitman," I stated firmly, "that is where you are going to be indispensable. You will have to encourage and convince whoever comes this way to let us lead them to safety. Speaking to them in their native language should help."

"Sir, I will try; but there are no guarantees. I have experienced the trauma these folks have been through. Do not be surprised if they would rather take their chances in the forest!"

We waited almost thirty minutes before a group of five men came running along the edge of the meadow.

Breitman got out of the automobile and flagged them down. However, as soon as the lead escapee got within thirty meters of the car, he recognized the SS insignia on my uniform and called out to the others.

They immediately scattered into the forest like frightened animals. "Breitman, we may have to try a little different approach. These poor souls were being whipped and beaten this morning by men wearing this identical uniform. I'm going to fold my coat and place it in the back seat."

As I was talking, a group of 40-50 escapees came running through the meadow heading for the woods.

Immediately, Breitman jumped out of the car and yelled to them. Like a herd of sheep, they headed for the car. I stepped out of the driver's side as they approached the automobile in order to greet them.

I'm not sure if I looked intimidating because of my size, or perhaps a little too Aryan with my sandy-blond hair and steel-blue eyes. Or, as they approached the car, they might have spotted my uniform coat in the back seat.

Whatever the reason, almost all the escapees scattered for the woods at the edge of the meadow. One small group stayed behind. It was a husband and wife and two small children. The little ones were probably about five to eight years old. They looked terrified and completely exhausted.

The man got on his knees and begged. "Please, sir. Have mercy on my family. My children cannot run any farther from the hell of the Sobibor Camp. We have not eaten in two days and have been beaten and whipped by the Ukrainian guards at the camp.

Breitman was translating for me as I held up my hand for the poor escapee to stop.

"Young man," I started. "What is your name?"

"My name is Jacob Wiernik; my wife is called Hanel." He was trembling and shaking. He did seem to understand my German dialect.

I asked Wiernik to stand. He had difficulty standing and seemed very unsteady on his feet. It was a bit problematic, but I still towered above him. His nervousness was evident. He could barely make it to his feet. Standing there in front of Breitman and me had to be painful for him. His wife and children looked frozen with fear.

"Look, Wiernik. You and your family are in a very precarious situation. The local Polish population consists mainly of rural farms. The farmers, for the most part, are somewhat anti-Semitic and totally terrified of their Nazi occupiers. It would be very doubtful if the local population would be at all helpful in sheltering, feeding, or hiding your family. As a matter of fact, they could well turn you in to the local police for a cash bounty or as assurance for protection.

"What am I to do?" queried Wiernik in a shaky, trembling voice.

"I will tell you that your chances in the forests are very sketchy. You could come upon militant partisans, vengeful farmers who would probably get a reward for turning you in, or bandits who could kill you and your family."

"Is there any hope for my family?" Wiernik's wife began to sob.

"Yes. But you have to trust Breitman and me."

Wiernik looked at his wife, who still shaking with fear but nodded in the affirmative.

"What would you have us do?" he asked in a quiet timorous voice.

"I will remove my uniform coat from the back seat and wear it. You and your family need to squeeze into the back seat and do exactly what we tell you."

"I will do what you ask," said Wiernik. "But you have to understand how difficult it is for my family to be in an automobile with an SS officer. I know they will be very frightened."

"I know you folks will do the best you can; if we are stopped, try not to appear frightened. There will be police, Wehrmacht soldiers, SS guards, and possible Gestapo [*] looking for all of the escapees from Sobibor."

---

*Geheime Staatspolizei, abbreviated Gestapo, was the name for the Nazi Secret State Police. It was formed in 1933 by Hermann Göring and later transferred on April 20th, 1934, to the head of the SS, Heinrich Himmler. See p. VII.

"Where will you take us?" asked Wiernik.

"Breitman and I are on our way to Auschwitz. We will stop in Warsaw, Chelm, or Krakow and procure Aryan work papers for you. This way, you can blend into the general population without fear of being sent to a concentration or death camp."

Chapter 14

⎯⎯⎯⎯⎯⎯◦⟶◦⟵◦⎯⎯⎯⎯⎯⎯

Stopped and Searched by Local Police

We had been traveling south for about twenty minutes when we came to the first roadblock obstruction. What looked initially like two local police officers had parked a motorbike and an automobile across the road blocking it entirely.

As we approached, I observed that only one of the men was dressed as a local police officer. The other man was in a civilian suit. He was tall, almost six feet, with a forehead that slanted backward and a too-short lower jaw. My guess was he was most probably Gestapo. In my mind, I thought of him as "rat-faced."

As we slowed to a stop, I pulled slightly to the right to get partially off the road. I added a warning: "Wiernik, please keep your children quiet. Do not respond, even if the authorities ask you a question. I will do all the talking. And most importantly, do not get out of the car, even if ordered to do so. I may ask you to get out of the car in a commanding voice; however, do not get out of the car under any circumstances. Is that clear?"

It was obvious. The family crammed into my back seat were terrified. I just prayed they would follow my order to remain in the automobile and stay quiet.

The police officer approached our automobile and I rolled down the window. When he saw my uniform, he stiffened and asked, "Sir, where are you headed?"

"We are on our way to Lublin, Officer; what is the problem?"

"There has been an uprising at the Sobibor Camp, Lieutenant, and several of the Jewish vermin have escaped into our beautiful country," was the police officer's comment.

"Here are my orders, officer. As you can see, we are traveling at the behest of Reichführer Himmler, and we need to get on our way."

"Of course, Lieutenant, your papers look in order; you are free to continue your journey."

"Hold on, Officer. Let me see those orders!" Rat-face had quickly approached the car and had drawn his weapon.

I politely handed him my orders and, in a quiet voice, ask if there was any problem with the Reichführer's orders. I also calmly inquired, "And who are you?"

"I am the local Gestapo agent, Lieutenant. We are hunting for escaped criminal Jews from the Sobibor Camp."

"Agent, I am really sorry; but we haven't seen any criminal Jews today."

I hadn't had anything to eat since breakfast and could feel my anger rising a notch. Perhaps my stomach was growling just a little. My mother always told me my pleasant demeanor suffered a bit if I hadn't eaten in a while. I could just imagine what was going through the minds of the folks in the back seat.

"Lieutenant, I would like to inspect your automobile. Everyone out of the back seat" commanded the rat-faced Gestapo Agent with a less-than-polite tone to his voice. However, nobody in the back seat moved.

Rat-face was getting red-blotchy skin around his neck. I could tell his blood pressure was rising. He commanded again in a brusque and much louder voice,

"Everyone out of the back seat, now!"

As he was ordering the family out of the back seat, he brandished his weapon much too close to my face.

I addressed the Gestapo agent in a very polite and almost caring tone, "Sir, let me get them out of the back seat for you. And please, do not wave your pistol near an SS Officer's face ever again."

"People, please get out of the back seat and exit the automobile."

As I was issuing the order, I turned around in the seat and winked at the frightened and terrified family behind me.

Nobody moved.

I addressed the Gestapo agent. "Sir, I will remove them from the back seat."

While talking in a quiet and calm voice, I opened my door slowly and stood up beside the automobile. The Gestapo agent seemed surprised at my height. I don't think he expected anyone imposing to challenge him. I felt it gave me a critical advantage.

As I went to open the rear door of the automobile with my left hand, I instead brought my right fist down in a swift and decisive blow on the agent's gun arm. I heard a distinct snap of a broken wrist bone; the weapon fell harmlessly to the ground.

The look of shock and surprise on the agent's blotchy face was complete. He gave a short cry of surprise and did not see the side of my clenched fist slam against his carotid body in his very red neck.

I was pretty sure I had broken his neck; his head snapped violently toward me as his body lurched in the opposite direction. He fell limply to the ground without uttering another sound.

The look of shock and alarm on the policeman's face was classic. He was aghast and started to cry out in panic.

I grabbed the officer around the neck in a chokehold and twisted his chin in a violent jerk in the opposite direction from where he was facing. He died instantly and fell to the ground in a heap with a broken neck.

I'm not sure who was more surprised. Breitman's eyes were as big as saucers. I wasn't sure the family in the back seat was even breathing.

I asked Breitman, "Would you mind helping me get this trash into the boot of their automobile?"

He came to life, jumped out of the car, and asked, "Where did you learn to fight like that?"

"Hitler Camp," was my response; Breitman looked shocked and surprised. It was difficult for me to suppress my glee with a fleeting smile.

I think the stunned family in the back seat was breathing again.

Breitman and I loaded the two very dead officers into the trunk of their car. I drove it a short distance into the woods. Breitman pushed the motorbike in behind the car and into the brush.

"Are you just going to leave them in the woods?" asked Breitman.

"I think it would be best," I replied. "The local police will probably think the escapees were to blame."

Chapter 15

Getting Aryan Papers

We had been driving south for about two hours when Breitman asked where we were headed. I got the feeling he was anxious to get back to his hometown. Although the Nazis had murdered his immediate family, he still had friends, possible relatives, and an employer who needed him.

We were blessed because we passed no police checkpoints on our journey.

I made the announcement so the frightened family in the back seat would know our intentions.

"We are headed for the city of Krakow; it is about four or five hours south of where we are now."

"In Krakow, I will go to the SS main office and message my sergeant to meet me at the Auschwitz-Birkenau Labor Camp.

"In addition, I will procure Aryan work papers for you and our friends in the back seat. The work papers should protect you from further roundups. When you find work, please stay out of the Jewish Ghettos. Remember, the local police will not be your friends. The local authorities routinely work with the local Gestapo and the SS.

"If you have questions, please ask them now."

"Sir," came from a woman's voice in the back seat. "Why is a member of the SS helping poor Jews? All the SS officers we have encountered have done nothing but torment and murder our families. When the Gestapo broke into our home, they said we would be shot if we did not comply immediately and go to the square near the railroad station. They shot several of our neighbors – even their children when they resisted. They herded us like cattle onto box cars on the transports."

"The German police packed us so tightly into the rail cars, there was no place to sit down. There were no toilet facilities or food or water. Breathing in the locked box car was difficult because only a small window, which was rimmed with barbed wire, was available for air.

"When we arrived at the Sobibor Camp, the SS men whipped us and forced us into a large, barbed wire enclosed area. Several of our neighbors, especially the elderly adults, died on the transports. Then we heard shooting, shouting, and general confusion from within the camp. That is when we ran for the forest. When you told us to get into your automobile, my children were completely spent."

"Unfortunately, Miss, your story is being repeated all over Germany, Poland, and the New Territories. Anti-Semitism has infected the German people. Many good Germans oppose anti-Semitism and the maltreatment of Jews. But if they complain to the authorities, they will find themselves in the same labor camps as their Jewish neighbors."

Hanel Wiernik then spoke up again. "Sir, you are being very kind to my family, and believe me, we owe you our lives and enduring gratitude. But why are you doing this?"

"Misses Wiernik," I started, "not all Germans are anti-Semitic. Our leaders and their followers, especially the Gestapo, are probably the world's worst criminals. The men in the SS are probably no better."

"But, Misses Wiernik persisted," Please, tell my family why you saved us.

"It is complicated, dear Wiernik family. Let me try to explain while I ask you a question.

"What is your profession?"

"I am an accountant," explained Mr. Wiernik.

"Thank you, Wiernik. How many potential accountants, physicians, engineers, scientists, and world-renowned composers, artists, and craftsmen do you suppose the Nazis crammed into those cattle cars?

"I will tell you the answer, Mr. Wiernik. The world will never know! How many people have been murdered who could have discovered medicines for curing many of the diseases that directly affect the German people or other populations in all the countries in the world?

"How many men, women, and children have been murdered who could have become wonderful leaders of their city, town, or country?

"How many children have been murdered who could have become great composers, the next Wagner or Mendelssohn?

"Or philanthropists! No, Wiernik family, the Nazis have no idea of what they are forever destroying.

"My sergeant and I have orders from our German Research Center in northern Germany to find laborers from the camps to help with our weapons research."

"Will you need any of us at the Research Center, Lieutenant?"

"No, Mr. Wiernik. I will go directly to the local command center in Krakow and get Aryan work papers for your family and Mr. Breitman. It is my strong suggestion that you disappear into the city, find meaningful work, and thank our God; he has spared us so far from the worst of the Nazi regime.

Chapter 16

Nazi Command Center, Krakow, Poland

It was late afternoon by the time we arrived in the outskirts of Krakow. Our first stop was at a small hotel where everyone could get a meal and water. I knew the children had to be quite hungry, but they were being very quiet in the back seat. I will have to admit, I wasn't in the best of humor; I'm sure Breitman was also hungry. We all had to wash up in the washroom.

The sky was a lead-gray with a chill to the brisk wind; it rather matched my mood.

Although the older woman at the hotel desk didn't look too happy to be serving an SS officer, she led us to the dining area and we had a decent meal of mushroom soup, bread, and cheese. I knew food was scarce in Poland and was grateful this rather dilapidated-looking hotel had something for us to eat.

Mrs. Wiernik asked, "Why are we going to this particular city in Poland, Lieutenant?"

"Krakow is one of the few major cities in the Central Government, under Nazi occupation, which has not been completely destroyed and flattened by the Wehrmacht."

"Is it safe to be in this particular city?" asked Breitman.

My response was stern and emphatic. "No! No cities under the occupation of the Nazis in the Central Government are safe for anyone, particularly Jews.

"Many Jews have been rounded up and cordoned off in the ghetto area south of the city of Krakow. And many have been shipped off to the Plaszow slave labor camp. Please do not think of any area in Poland safe for Jews."

"Do you have any suggestions where we should go if we can obtain our Aryan documents?" asked Mr. Wiernik.

"Stay away from the Jewish Ghetto! You may be drawn to the houses of worship, but they could be a trap for capturing unwitting Jews. I know of at least one instance where the Temple was burned to the ground with the worshipers locked inside. The brownshirts burned to death over one hundred men, women, and children in their lust to rid the town of Jews. Anyone attempting to flee the burning Temple was shot and killed. Some of the congregation hung themselves or slashed their wrists rather than suffer being burned to death."

Mr. Wiernik then asked what I thought was a very reasonable question.

"Lieutenant, there has always been a bit of anti-Semitism in Poland for as long as I can remember. When we were forced to board the transport and brought to the Sobibor Camp, we thought our journey was an extension and an escalation of this anti-Semitism. We were advised that Sobibor was a transition camp. We were told our families would be sent to the East to do farm work for the Reich. Are you telling us the SS were lying to us as they packed us on the transports?

"It is certainly not my pleasure to have to inform you, Mr. Wiernik, but Sobibor is a Totenlager! (Death Camp). You and your fellow Jews were being misled by the local police and the SS in order to gain your cooperation. Had you not broken out of the camp, your entire family would be dead by this time and cremated and buried on the premises. would be dead by this time and cremated and buried on the premises.

"I'm sure those who did not break out with you when they had a chance are already murdered and buried by now."

"Mine Gott im Himmel!" cried Mrs. Wiernik. **"Is there no place in Poland where my family can be safe and live peacefully?"**

"Hiding in the city with Aryan work papers will be the safest place for your family. The Gestapo has offered many of the farmers in the countryside rewards for turning in Jews. The Partisans are very wary of anyone they do not know personally. They would kill a Jew before they would chance hiding them and being discovered by the Wehrmacht or the Gestapo."

"I have heard of one German businessman in Krakow who, although he is a member of the Nazi Party, is somewhat sympathetic to the plight of Jews. If you have problems finding work, or if the Gestapo has approached you, consider looking him up.

"Who is this Nazi who does not persecute Jews?" asked Mr. Wiernik.

"His name is Oskar Schindler. * He makes enamelware and armaments for the Wehrmacht. Although his position as a Nazi is in military intelligence and is a member of the Abwehr, he is known in the Jewish underground as saving many Jews from the transports and the death camp at Belzec.

"He appears and has admitted to being a profit-motivated Nazi, prospering mightily off the labor of hard-working Jews. If the Gestapo is in his factory, he comes across as a hard-liner, loyal Nazi with no compassion for any Jews.

"He is known, however, for actually going into the concentration labor camps to rescue his Jewish workers from the transports and the death camps. You can trust him; he will not bring any pain or hardship to your family.

---

*Oskar Schindler was in the Abwehr section of the Nazi Party. He spent all his wealth (several million dollars in today's money) on factory renovations in order to hire more Jews. He produced enamelware and armaments for the Wehrmacht. The rest of his fortune was spent on bribes of Nazi Officials and the Gestapo so they would look the other way when it came time for rounding up Jews and sending them to the death camps. Initially, he hired Jews because their labor was cheaper and his profit greater. After seeing the atrocities inflicted on the Jews by the Nazis, Schindler did everything he could to save as many Jews as possible from the death camps. After the war, he retired penniless in West Germany, partly supported by payments from Jewish relief organizations. He died in Hildesheim, Germany, on 9 October 1974 and was buried in Jerusalem on Mount Zion. He was the only former member of the Nazi Party to be so honored; he was 66 years old.

"We are nearing the Wehrmacht Command Center. When we arrive, please stay in the automobile. Do not let anyone leave the automobile unless it is on fire!"

The Wehrmacht Command Center was in the central Krakow police station. It was a low gray building with a hint of decaying Italian architectural consideration. Dark clouds hung over the building like a veil of dread. The Nazi flag was flying over the building as a proud defiance of all reason.

Chapter 17

—◦◦◦—

A Disastrous Encounter with a Childhood Bully

I parked a little way up the street from the building and repeated my instruction for everyone to stay in the automobile. I gave Breitman a carbon of my orders in case he was questioned by authorities.

The place looked quite similar to other prisons I had "visited" in the Reich. This one had lots of battle-ship gray paint to go with the cement flooring. The prison was called Montelupich Prison, after the street of the same name.

I hadn't realized the prison had been taken over by the Geheime Staatpolizei or Gestapo until after I entered and started a conversation with the older chain-smoking woman at the front desk. She had one cigarette in her hand and another still smoldering in the ashtray.

The officious-looking, pasty-complected but pleasant gray-haired woman seemed to blend in quite naturally with her surroundings. Her German, however, was excellent and understandable, with only a hint of Polish accent. She was so thin I thought for a moment she might be an Auschwitz survivor.

"I would like to talk with the commander, Herr Ludwig Hahn." *

"Good afternoon, madam," was my pleasant greeting. "I am here under orders from Reichführer Himmler." I spread out my original copy on her counter.

---

*Ludwig Herman Karl Hahn was a cruel member of the Schutzstaffel (SS). After the war, he disguised himself as a farmworker and an insurance broker. Journalists uncovered his true identity in 1960. He was convicted of deporting Jews from the Warsaw Ghetto to Treblinka. After all his appeals, he received a life sentence in 1973. He died in Ammersbeck, near Hamburg, in 1986. He was 78 years old.

The clerk looked nervous but tried to give me a satisfactory answer. I noticed a slight tremor in her voice.

"Of course," she answered. "He…he is just finishing a meeting but will be available in just a few minutes. You may wait in the conference room just down the hall; it is the first door on the right."

As I entered the conference room, I noticed a framed letter of commendation on the wall. It praised Herr Hahn for his recent promotion to the rank of Sturmbannfürher (Major) in the SS. In addition, the letter complimented his work with the Einsatzgruppe and his position as Chief of the Sicherheitdienst (SD) or the intelligence branch of the SS, and Sicherheitpolizei (SiPo) for the occupied city of Krakow.

It made me realize that this Nazi was a very dangerous man.

As the Sturmbannfürher entered the conference room, I got up and gave him an enthusiastic Hitler salute.

He waved back and remarked, "What brings you to our city, Lieutenant?"

"I am here under orders from Reichführer Himmler, Sturmbannfürher." I spread-out my orders out on the conference table.

"I need three Aryan work permits for Jewish laborers I am taking for the secret Wehrmacht Research Center in northern Germany."

"What is going on at your research center, Lieutenant?"

I didn't want to appear disrespectful and needed cooperation to get the Aryan work permits. I decided to give him a little knowledge of what was happening in Peenemünde.

"Sir, everything I am about to disclose to you is top-secret and must not be discussed with anyone. Do you understand?"

"Of course, Lieutenant! I am no stranger of the penalties of loose talk, even among friends and colleagues."

"I can tell you this much, Sturmbannfürher. We are designing, building, and testing new weapons. These weapons have a range of several hundred kilometers and can be loaded with very powerful warheads.

"As you can tell from my orders, I am visiting some of our labor camps to find Jews with special engineering, electrical, or mechanical skills to help us in this endeavor."

"What about our own engineers and scientists?" asked the Major.

"Unfortunately," I continued, "many of our scientists have been sent to labor camps or are involved with the war effort in another capacity."

"How many Jew laborers do you need?"

"Over time, we will need several hundred. I am going to meet my sergeant at another camp next week to find out who else might be available. Today I need work permits for three individuals."

The Major brought me out to the reception area and directed the gray-haired woman he called Yael to write up the Aryan work papers.

I surmised the woman to be Jewish from her Old Testament name.

The major then asked Yael to summon one of his guards to show me the prison while she was preparing the documents.

After a couple of minutes, a smartly dressed guard called Gerhard came from a door to the rear of the reception area and introduced himself. The guard looked surprised to see me, but it was probably because of my size. I was quite tall at six feet four and a half inches.

"Gerhard," commanded the Sturmbannfürher. "Please show the Lieutenant our efficient prison, but bring him back in thirty minutes for his documents."

"Ja, sicher, jawohl, Herr Sturmbannfürher."

As Gerhard led me down the hall to a flight of stairs leading down to the prison, he gave me a rather quizzical look. His facial expression didn't make too much sense to me at the time. We went down another flight of stairs to rows of small cells lined with stone. The area was below ground, unheated, cold, and damp.

Gerhard asked, "Lieutenant, what part of Germany are you from?"

This question seemed a little personal, but I assumed he was trying to be friendly to a senior SS officer.

The guard was showing me the inside of one of the cold, damp, godforsaken cells when I answered, "Düsseldorf, Gerhard, why do you ask?"

With my reply, he stepped quickly outside the cell and slammed the barred door shut, turning the key and locking me inside.

"What are you attempting to do, guard?"

"You don't remember me, do you, Lieutenant?"

"I can't say that I do. Are you familiar with me from my hometown?"

"As a matter of fact," he shot back in a rather loud and uncultured German slang dialect, "I remember you quite distinctly from grade school. You were the tallest boy in our class. You broke all my fingers on my right hand defending one of your dirty 'Jewboy' friend. It was after I left the hospital that I learned you were also a dirty Jewboy. Now I have caught you masquerading as an SS Lieutenant!"

Locked in a Gestapo-controlled small, damp prison cell by a jailer who was a grade-school bully and enemy and confirmed anti-Semitic Nazi made my stomach growl. I couldn't tell if I was truly hungry again or chagrined at my foolishness for getting into the stone-lined cell in the first place.

I stepped over to the cell door and spoke softly in a low tone so Gerhard would have to approach the bars to hear me.

Out of caution, he didn't get too close to the bars. However, he must have forgotten about the length of my arms.

As I was speaking in a low voice. I was trying to explain to him that I hadn't had a decent meal in several hours and was less than totally polite on an empty stomach.

While trying to explain to Gerhard my need for a good meal, I quickly jabbed my arm through the bars and grabbed the evil Nazi by his uniform collar. He was a little off-balance because he was trying to take a step backward. A look of shock came over his very surprised and ugly face. I pulled him with all my force into the bars on the cell. Bang!

I could tell by the clang of his skull on the bars that the guard was totally stunned. I grabbed the key to the cell from his belt, unlocked the cell, and pulled Gerhard inside with me.

I tried to explain to Gerhard, "The 'dirty Jew-boy' you were referring to was my lifelong friend and fellow Jew, Ezekiel. Even though we were quite young, I couldn't tolerate you hurting my friend."

He was mumbling something and swearing quite loudly when I placed him in a chokehold, squeezed slowly but quite firmly on his neck, and snuffed the life out of him. He kicked and tried to scream and squirm out of my chokehold.

Alas, it was no use for him to struggle or complain. I did not enjoy killing anyone, but I adjusted my grip a little and let him breathe.

I then resumed slowly squeezing his neck until his body went limp.

Then, with some effort, I eased him up to the upper bunk of the cell, where he might not get noticed for several days. I pulled the thin blanket over the mattress, laid Herr Gerhard on the mesh springs, let the thin mattress cover him and pulled the blanket over the mattress where it draped down about a foot. He might not get noticed for several weeks with the near-freezing temperature in this cellblock.

I locked the cell behind me and intentionally worked the key back and forth until it broke off in the lock, making it impossible to access the cell in the near future. I retraced my steps to Yael's office.

"Thank you so much for the work permits, Yael. You have been very helpful."

It was clear that she was still intimidated by me and my SS uniform. Even though I did not wear my cover indoors, like so many pumped-up Nazis, she was clearly cowered by my presence.

I asked her to forward a message to Vitali Carapezza at the Research Facility in Peenemünde: *Meet me at the Auschwitz Labor Camp on the 15th of this month. SS Lieutenant Jenz Ramsgrund.*

I decided to perhaps make her feel a bit better when I leaned over and whispered in a low voice in Yiddish: There are many *schlub mamzers* (clumsy, stupid bastards) who wear this uniform.

Her look of surprise and shock was immediate. I wished her a good day and walked out of the police station.

Chapter 18

—◦⟨⟩◦—

Auschwitz, A Murderous Machine

I carefully examined the Aryan work papers for the Wiernik family and Mr. Breitman. The papers looked in order and I signed them with my name and SS rank at the bottom of each page.

We took a brief tour of Krakow. I drove them by Oskar Schindler's Enamelware plant, where cookware and arms were being produced for the Wehrmacht.

Mrs. Wiernik asked, "Is this where we should come if we cannot find employment?"

"No, Mrs. Wiernik. Come to this factory only if you are in trouble or cannot find any employment elsewhere. Your Aryan work papers should be adequate for finding employment and a home.

"I will drive you by the city housing authority, where there are probably many vacant apartments available in the city. Almost all the Jews have had to flee to the ghetto or have been transported to the labor camps under the Aktion Reinhard Operation." *

It was getting dark, and I wanted to make sure my passengers were safe for the evening. Since I had to drive north and then west to the Auschwitz Camp, I drove them to the small hotel where we had taken lunch. I paid for their dinner and two rooms for 1 week at the hotel.

---

*"Operation Reinhard" was named after a brutal Nazi, Reinhard Heydrich. This unrepentant Nazi sought all his life to suppress details of his Jewish ancestry. After being dismissed from the German Naval Service for dishonorable conduct toward a young woman, Himmler appointed him to SS Obergrupenfuhrer. Heydrich was responsible for the comprehensive draft of the "Final Solution to the Jewish Problem" presented at the Wannsee Conference in January 1942. An assassination attempt was made on his life by Czech soldiers on the 27th of May 1942. Heydrich died from a massive infection caused by the assassination attempt in a Prague hospital on 4 June 1942. He was 38 years old.

I took a room and decided to wake early for the drive to Auschwitz Camp. I bid my fellow travelers goodbye before retiring.

I told Breitman he would have the option of remaining in Krakow or continuing with me to Auschwitz and on to the Research Center. I suggested he would not be safe returning to his home until the war against the Russians was concluded.

He asked, "Would it be okay to return to the Research Center with you?

I had to inform him of my plans to get more Jews from Auschwitz for laborers to our facility in northern Germany.

"Breitman, I cannot guarantee your safety at Auschwitz. It could be very dangerous for both of us. I am planning on meeting my Sargent there tomorrow."

"I understand," was his comment. "There is really no place in Germany, Poland, or all of Europe where I would consider myself safe. I have already lost my family to the Vernichtungslager (Extermination Camp) at Treblinka, I am not worried about the Auschwitz camp.

It took us most of the next morning to get to the Auschwitz Labor Camp. Although it wasn't far from Krakow, there were many checkpoints. My orders made it easy for us to get into the camp. I hadn't realized that this concentration camp was now a death camp for the extermination of all the remaining Jews in Europe.

I signed Breitman into the concentration camp as my aid and reserved a room for him and Ezekiel under his acceptable Aryan name, Vitali Carapezza. The entire camp was huge; it was spread over several hundred acres in the town of Birkenau. The officers and enlisted quarters were not too far from the main gate.

I went into the enlisted barracks with Breitman to ensure he and Ezekiel could secure a couple of rooms for a few days. As I approached the clerk at the front counter, I removed my cover and stood in front of his desk.

For some reason, the color completely drained from the clerk's face, and he started to shake. He was shaking with such a tremor that he couldn't even log in rooms for two guests. He finally gave Breitman the log and asked him to fill in the names.

I asked the clerk, "Kapo, what is the problem?"

"Sir," he replied, "I am not a Kapo. Although I wear the green triangle, I just handle the paperwork for this facility."

"Why do you seem so frightened? You must have had paperwork from officers in the SS before."

"I'm sorry," the clerk continued; he then started weeping and shaking so much I felt embarrassed for him.

"Breitman, let's find your quarters.

We left with the clerk weeping and shaking. I felt concerned and uneasy for him but knew there must be more to his story.

As soon as we were outside, I addressed Breitman. "Horace, after you have settled in your room, I want you to return to this front desk area and find out what is going on with the clerk. Here is a copy of my orders in case you are ever questioned. Try to wring out every bit of information you can from this poor soul, he may be hiding something we should know about here at Auschwitz."

"I will give him a few minutes to compose himself," Breitman replied. "Then I will quietly ask him about his family and background.

"I will report back to you in about 1 hour at the central office."

Chapter 19

Historical Anti-Semitism

Breitman met me in the central office for the Auschwitz Camp a little over an hour later. He was carrying a small notepad with several pages of scribbled notes he had taken while talking with the extremely nervous clerk.

"Lieutenant, you may want to sit down while I give you the clerk's experience he had with his hometown police and Ukrainian Guards. This might take a few minutes. The clerk was very reluctant to discuss much of anything with me until I assured him I was also Jewish and from a small town in Poland near Warsaw. He seemed relieved we could communicate fluently in Polish."

I was gaining more confidence in Breitman's adaptability to interactions with Jews and Aryans as I got to know him. "Let's try to find a quiet table in the Officer's Mess near the back of the camp. It is only a ten-minute walk from here."

It was a wonderful spring day with a hint of the warmth of summer all around the edges. The only dark clouds were above the chimneys of the four crematoriums. The chimneys occasionally roared and spit fire into the smoke when the crematoriums were burning up the bodies of my countrymen. If the wind was wrong, the ash covered the camp.

We took some tea from the self-serve counter and settled into a small table in the back of the cafeteria. We were pretty much alone in the cafeteria at this time of day. Breitman looked somewhat reluctant to begin, so I prompted him in a low quiet voice. "Tell me, Breitman, what has our clerk so frightened he cannot function with a coherent voice?"

"His name is Samuel Eisen; he's from a small town near Buczacz, Poland. He witnessed the death of many Jews from his hometown.

"When the Ukrainian Guards came into his town to round up the Jews, they made many of the Jewish men dig a deep pit in the local cemetery. The guards placed large planks across the pit. The Jewish people caught in the round-up were ordered to strip naked and stand on the planks. Five Jews at a time were ordered and whipped to the center of the planks over the pits and murdered by machine-gun fire; they fell into the pit.

"Surviving Jews were ordered to go down into the pit and arrange the bodies next to one another, packing them in like sardines so that more bodies would fit into the pit. The pit was filled with bodies as well as urine, excrement, and blood.

"Young children were thrown into the pit alive, only to be covered up by more corpses. A Ukrainian Guard would throw young children into the pit alive by grabbing them by the neck and shouting: *'Nimm das dreck und schmeiss herein!'* 'Grab the filth and throw it in.' The children would be drowning in blood.

"After the shouting and murdering were finished, somehow, our terrified clerk was able to climb out of the pit and survive. He had jumped into the pit as soon as the firing started. He lied about his age when he arrived here at Auschwitz because he knew everyone under the age of sixteen was selected to go to the left and on to the gas chambers.

"When he saw you towering over him at the front counter, he had a flash-back to his experience in the pit and was unable to speak coherently."

"*Mine Gott im Himmel,*" Horace. "What makes people so deranged they are able to commit murder with such horrible indifference?"

"I should also tell you, Lieutenant, of another case of unimaginable cruelty."

"Horace, what could you possibly tell me…; What could be worse than children crawling out of a pit of blood and dead bodies?"

"Samuel has a friend, another Jewish survivor, who usually works with him at the front counter. He was with him while Samuel was relating his story to me. He agreed with Samuel and said everything related to me was true. But he also wanted to add his own story."

"Not another atrocity, I hope!"

"This young man's name is Jacob Heiss. He remembered the Germans coming into his town of Buczacz and singing *'Spielzeit fur die Kameraden'* (Playtime for the Comrades). That night would be filled with shouting, yelling, shooting, and cries of terror for help. The next day there would be dead bodies everywhere. Jacob was spared in the round-up because, at the time, he was visiting his mother and his new baby sister in the hospital. His mom had just given birth to a baby daughter. When the Germans came into the hospital, he hid behind a long window curtain but, unfortunately, saw everything happening in the hospital room.

"The German SS guards were going from room to room shooting anyone Jewish. When they came to his mother's room, the guard took one look at the Jewish name on the chart, yelled at his mom, and confirmed she was Jewish. He then grabbed his newborn sister by her legs, smashed her head against the cinder-block wall, and hurled her out of the thirdstory window. The guard wanted to be sure the mother witnessed what was happening to her newborn daughter. Then he shot Jacob's mother. One shot in the head. The room resembled a slaughterhouse with blood splashed everywhere."

I couldn't control myself any longer. My face was unconsciously contorted in anguish. A tear dropped into my tea. "Horace, these atrocities have to be remembered, written down, and published in a country with a free press. Even with the publication, few would believe this abhorrent cruelty.

"Unfortunately," replied Breitman, "Jacob's small town of Buczacz has a long history of cruelty and torture toward the Jewish population.

The anti-Semitism goes back centuries for Jews all over Europe."

"What history are talking about?" I asked. I have heard nothing of this sort ever happening in my hometown of Düsseldorf.

"I lived not too far from Jacob's hometown. The Jewish population in Poland was subjected to the worst torture and degradation only humans could dredge to the surface of twisted minds. The history of the Cossack and peasant uprising of the mid-sixteen hundreds documents some of the atrocities. *

"Some Jews were skinned alive with their flesh thrown to the dogs.

"The most defenseless suffered the worst: some expectant women had their babies cut out of their bellies and were beaten with the fetus. Live cats were inserted into the women and sewn up. Their hands were tied so that they couldn't remove the cats. It was a most horrible way to die.

"Some young children were skewered and roasted over a roaring fire for the mothers who were forced to watch and then eat them."

I looked at Breitman with an incredulous look on my face. "Where do you get this information, Horace?"

"Unfortunately, it is a well-documented part of our history."

"Breitman, do you believe in prayer?"

"Of course! But do you think God is in this place?"

"I think God is everywhere, even in this hellhole.

"We have to be extra careful in this camp. Do not trust anyone.

"However, in the New Testament in the Christian Bible, somewhere in Ephesians, there is a quote: *"God himself is our peace. We are no longer foreigners but fellow citizens of God's household."*

"It is hard for us to have forgiveness in our hearts for the harsh brutality we have seen all around us. I need to do what I can to select almost one hundred prisoners and their families for work at our secret facility in Peenemünde, in Northern Germany. If you can help me, I

---

*Hanover, Nathan. "The Book of Deep Mire,"

will do everything I can to ensure your immediate freedom as soon as possible after we arrive at the facility with our workers.

Sargent Carapezza should be here tomorrow. We will begin the worker selection process for our facility in Peenemünde in the morning.

Chapter 20

———◦⌒◦———

A New Transport Arrives at Auschwitz

The next morning, I met with the camp commanding officer, Rudolf Höss * in his office. He scowled while reading over my orders but was pleasant enough in his demeanor to invite me to the next selection process for the just-arrived transport. I told him I would be bringing my sergeant and an aide with me for picking out the slave workers for our facility at Peenemünde.

Although Höss was persistent in wanting to know what we were doing at the secret facility, I finally recommended he call General Dornberger if he wanted further information about our projects.

"Commandant, I need healthy technicians and their families. We require engineers, machinists, jewelers, or anyone used to working with small parts. Women prisoners can work in the housing and cafeteria facilities, and they are usually terrific in small-part assembly. We cannot accept anyone who is ill, but they must be trained in their respective technical fields."

The Commandant requested, "Meet the camp doctors at the platform for the selection process at one o'clock this afternoon."

"But, Commandant, isn't the transport already at the siding?" I asked.

---

*Höss was noted for his brutal efficiency while Commandant of the Auschwitz Concentration Camp. He was the first to use the powerful and dangerous insecticide Zyklon-B for the extermination of the prisoners. After the war, he avoided arrest by working as a farmworker until he was discovered. At his trial, he claimed he was only following orders and used care to collect gold rings and teeth for the SS and women's hair for furniture upholstery. In his autobiography, he rejected any notion that he was a sadist and claimed, "I am completely normal; I led a completely normal life." Although he repented while in prison, he was hanged by the Polish Supreme National Tribunal at the Auschwitz Camp he used to command on 16 April 1947. He was 45 years old.

"Yes. Of course, Lieutenant. But we find if we keep them waiting without food or water in a sweltering enclosed cattle car for a few hours, the prisoners are much more compliant about being led to the gas chambers."

I thought to myself: *This Nazi is completely immune to the discomfort, pain, and degradation these families must be suffering. These innocent men, women, and children are packed like sardines into a cattle railroad car with no space for toilet facilities, fresh water, or even breathable air. If I could have gotten away with squeezing the life out of this bastard's neck, I would have easily and joyfully completed the task right there in his office.*

"Commandant. Won't these prisoners be adversely affected by the lack of water?"

"Of course, Lieutenant! These vermin will be very ready to accept our orders when they are let out of the transports. You might say the prisoners become eagerly compliant."

My immediate thought was that this Nazi deserved to be tried and executed. My answer to his swagger was, "Excellent, Herr Commandant! I will be on the platform after lunch.

I met Zeke and Breitman at their quarters and they joined me near the rail siding before the first transport was unlocked.

After meeting Horace Breitman, Vitali assured me,

"Jenz, all of the women we transported to Peenemünde are secure and safe. Do you remember the young woman, Adiya? She was the one I picked up off the floor after she had been whipped by the guard. I placed your uniform jacket over her to protect her and hide her nakedness and shame after the bastards had cut off her hair."

"Of course, I remember her. Didn't she have a younger sister?"

"Yes, Jenz. Her sister's name is Chasha. I think it means 'to be merciful' from the Yiddish.

"She is working in the kitchen with three women, including her older sister. The other women have adapted to assembling hardware for the V-I bomb. One lady is working in the lab since she has some experience with chemical engineering. She is actually working on improving the gas-fuel mixture for the V-I engine."

"Excellent, Ezekiel. Thanks for delivering these women to safety.

"Now let's see if we can be successful here at the Auschwitz Camp. What we are attempting here could be extremely dangerous for all of us. We have to assume an attitude of harshness, rigidity, and utter contempt for these prisoners – while attempting to save as many as possible."

"They must be getting ready to unlock the first transport," Breitman suggested. "Many of the guards with the Totenkopfverbande patch (SSVT) or Death's Head units are congregating on the platform. A few of them have clubs or whips in their hands. One of the guards has drawn his pistol."

"One of the camp doctors is at the table by the platform. I think the selection process happens at the table," suggested Zeke.

"What legitimate physician would participate in something so heinous as the selection process?" asked Breitman.

I cautiously answered, "I believe his name is Mengele." He is an SS Hauptsturmfuhrer (Captain).

"Doesn't the selection make most women, children, and old people go directly to the gas chambers?" Vitali asked.

"Even pregnant women! Only the physically strong are permitted to live and work under slave-like conditions until they are worked to death.

"You are correct," I added. "Dr. Joseph Mengele * is infamous for his abhorrent genetic research on twins. He has even injected chemicals

---

*Joseph Mengele, also known as "The Angel of Death," escaped from Nazi Germany and fled to South America after the war. He lived in Buenos Aries. He fled to Paraguay in 1959 and then to Brazil in 1960. He suffered a stroke and drowned while swimming off the coast of Bertioga in 1979 and was buried under the false name of Wolfgang Gerhard. He was 68 years old. His remains were disinterred in 1985 and positively identified by forensic examination.

into the eyes of patients in order to change their eye color from brown to blue. Most of his experiments on prisoners are truly dangerous without regard for the health or safety of his victims. If one twin dies because of his macabre experiments, he immediately kills the other twin.

Chapter 21

The Selection Process

I briefly introduced myself and my sergeant and aide to Dr. Mengele as I spread my orders on the table for him to read. He took quite an interest in the secret Wehrmacht base in Peenemünde and wanted to know if we were furthering any experiments on our prisoners.

"Our experiments involve fuels and weapons, doctor. We leave human experiments up to clinicians much more qualified than ourselves."

"If you're interested, Lieutenant, I can show you some of our progress with experiments with twins after this selection. We are still looking for twins or mothers pregnant with twins. I'm hoping some of the work will be groundbreaking. Of course, if our experiment with the twins doesn't work out, we have to euthanize the other twin."

"Isn't it wasteful to have to have to destroy the remaining child?"

"Lieutenant, these are Jews we are talking about!

"Thank you, doctor; I'm sure your experiments are most interesting."

This officer radiated pure evil. It is a mystery why the German medical profession would let him get anywhere near patients, especially children.

The cattle car gates were unlocked, and the first hapless prisoners tumbled out onto the platform. A prisoner band was playing German marching tunes. The music portrayed an almost festive atmosphere.

Bang!

One of the SS Totenkopf guards shot an elderly gentleman in the head. Blood spattered everywhere and the old prisoner tumbled off the platform. People near the old gentleman were screaming and trying to get away from the guard.

"Doctor, why are we shooting these people even before the selection process?"

"This action is quite routine, Lieutenant, don't let it bother you. This older Jew would have been sent directly to the gas house anyway.

"However, there are three reasons for our initial harsh contact with the prisoners, Lieutenant. First, it lets the Jews know they must follow orders. This cockroach was probably complaining of the severe treatment, without food or water, given to his fellow prisoners during their time of incarceration on the transports. By shooting him in the head, it lets other prisoners know what hard treatment is all about. Second, it lets the prisoners know the consequences of any kind of resistance they might be thinking of fomenting. And third, it makes them so much more compliant when we march most of them to their eternal home in the gas house."

"Why are they being whipped and beaten as they exit the transports, doctor?"

"Sometimes, Lieutenant, they have been standing for so long in the cattle car, it takes a little prodding to get them moving. When we have several thousand each day to process, we cannot let them linger on the platform. After all, if we aren't careful, this could take hours out of our day,"

"Remember, doctor, please ask the prisoners if they have any trade or craftsman skills in engineering or machine parts. Our secret base needs at least 100 skilled men and women for our production facility."

"I will make an announcement on the speaker as soon as the transports are empty. Get ready, they will start filing by our selection table directly after the transports pull out from the platform. Have your sergeant and aide bring another table for a separate workspace for you."

"I should tell you, Doctor Mengele, because of the secret nature of our work at Peenemünde, we get the best results if entire families can be routed to our facility. Even young children are put to work under their mother's supervision."

"They don't get too emotional, Lieutenant, when you take them as a group to your northern base?" asked Mengele.

"We can get much more dedication and work from these Jews if they think they have some future by working hard at our base."

"Are you sure you want some women and children? These vermin are usually gassed right away, along with the older men.

"Also, do you want Aryan-looking Jews?"

"Our main criteria are healthy-looking families. We cannot take sick or dying Jews that may need the infirmary here at Auschwitz."

"Oh, don't worry, Lieutenant, almost all the unhealthy prisoners are sent to the gas chambers. The infirmary is only for the slave workers here at the camp. Anyone admitted to the infirmary who isn't better in two weeks is automatically killed with the gas."

"Is that method pretty efficient?" I asked.

"Very! We are now using a powerful insecticide called Zyklon-B.* It ensures most prisoners are dead within twenty to thirty minutes. With this deadly gas, our chambers can exterminate up to two thousand Jews with each cycle."

My comment was without enthusiasm. "The gas sounds very efficient, doctor."

"It is efficient, Lieutenant, but it does cause a mess. There is a lot of bleeding from the vermin's ears and mouths, plus there is a lot of feces and urine to clean after each gassing."

---

*Zyklon-B, or prussic acid was used initially by the Germans in WWI during gas warfare in the trenches. Prussic acid turns into hydrogen cyanide gas when released. This gas interferes with lung function. Death comes within 30 minutes.

By this time, Vitali, Breitman, and I were ready to lose our lunch, but I forced the comment, "Doctor, please send families over to our table for final selection. We need these workers at the Wehrmacht base in Peenemünde."

It was refreshing just to put a little distance from this evil doctor. The three of us sat at a round table about thirty meters from the elongated rectangular selection table.

It was such a peaceful, warm day. It would be a great day to take a cool swim. I was reminded of my time at Hitler Youth Camp and meeting Ilsa. I missed her terribly. I vowed to make every attempt to get some time off to see her after this assignment. Just thinking about her in my arms put me in a much better place.

Vitali broke my reverie. "Jenz, I should mention to you I feel very positively toward the woman we saved from Treblinka."

"Oh, which one?" Of course, I knew, but I was desperately trying to lighten my mood.

"The young woman the guard was whipping. She seems to have fallen in love with me."

"Are you talking about Adiya?"

"Yes. She came with her sister, Chasha."

"She seemed like a beautiful, bright, and very frightened young woman, Vitali; I am very happy for you both.

"But... how do you know she is in love with you?"

I was teasing Zeke a little. I could tell by the way she looked at him after he picked her off the floor after she had been whipped. Even though he wore his sergeant's German army uniform, you could tell there was something special between them.

"As soon as we returned to Peenemünde, she thanked me profusely for rescuing her and her little sister. She knew she was about to go to the gas chamber. I haven't confided in her yet, but I think she suspects I am Jewish."

"We have to be very careful not to confide in anyone, even Breitman or Adiya. Ilsa and I have not even discussed anything about religion. Our country is just too dangerous to be discussing political or religious beliefs."

Chapter 22

Saving a Few Families from Auschwitz

Dr. Mengele made a brief announcement about the need for skilled workers for our secret research project, which seemed to confuse the poor folks getting off the transports even more. The Jewish "prisoners" from the transports weren't sure which way to go. The selectees with families were almost always separated at the selection table but those with special skills moved to our table. Vitali had them line up and we questioned the male members of each family to get an idea of prior work-related skills.

Many of them worked in small shops as cobblers, garment manufacturers, and jewelers. One of the men had been a pharmacist and two were engineers. One of the women taught mathematics at the gymnasium.

By the time we finished with the transport, we had enough families to fill three buses.

I informed Commandant Höss we were taking the busses with the Jewish families to our base in Peenemünde, but his drivers would return with the busses immediately after dropping off the slave workers.

"Also," I mentioned as an aside to Herr Commandant Höss, "I can assure you, Commandant, these vermin will all be dealt with after our experiments are completed at our secret Wehrmacht base."

I informed Breitman in a firm tone, "I want you and Vitali to go over the ground rules and regulations with these families for the trip to Peenemünde and what they should expect once they arrive. Tell them they will be kept on the base, and under no circumstances are they to discuss our work there with anyone outside of our secret facility.

"In addition, you will add, any discussion of what transpires at this secret facility with anyone will result in an immediate one-way trip back to Auschwitz."

"Yes, Sir!" An agreement from the Sargant and Breitman came in unison.

"In addition, Sargant Carapezza, I need to interview one member of each family at random to see if we have the proper mix for our base. We cannot have anyone who is going to be disruptive, have only marginal skills, or is already ill with typhus."

"I understand, Lieutenant. I will procure the transportation while Breitman organizes the prisoners."

I wanted to find out if any of these prisoners were criminals or potential troublemakers. With so many of our workers at Peenemünde dying of illness or exhaustion, we couldn't afford to bring in outside problems to our secret rocket base.

Breitman, because of his fluency in Polish, and I started interviewing the prisoners who were lined up for the bus. We interviewed these folks back at our small round table. It was out of earshot of the rest of the general confusion, crying, and the cacophony of noise from the selection committee.

I started with one woman who appeared to be alone.

"What is your name, Miss?"

"You may call me Zivia." *

"How did you come to find yourself in this camp?" I asked.

---

*I didn't realize it at the time, but the name "Zivia" had become the secret code name for the entire resistance movement in Poland. I also had no idea this woman was one of the heroes of these brave women's resistance fighters. She died of lung cancer in 1978 at the age of 63, probably from an inveterate cigarette habit. As per her husband's request, only her first name, "Zivia," appears on her tombstone. Her son explained, "Zivia is an institution; no further words are necessary."

"Lieutenant, I mean no disrespect, but when I was told to go to the left at the selection table with all the other women, children, and old people, I started to the left and then, when the doctor and guard were looking the other way, I went directly to your table. I knew going to the left was a death sentence; I could not die like a dog in your gas house."

I then asked Breitman to ask where she was from in her native language but to reply in German so I would understand completely.

Breitman asked, "Ms., in German, can you tell us where you are from?"

"I am from the ghetto in Warsaw. The Germans surrounded our ghetto on the 18th of April, 1943. The Nazis wanted to give Hitler a little present for his birthday which was on the 20th of April.

At six in the morning, the Germans attacked in force and burned, looted, and destroyed our entire section of the city. If people wouldn't come out of their homes to be shot or sent to the transports, the Nazis would pour gasoline on their homes, put it to the torch, and shoot anyone brave enough to leave.

"I saw one mother holding and trying to protect her young child from the flames. A Nazi soldier came along and ripped this sweet young daughter from the mother's arms. He then threw the child to the ground and stomped the tiny body with his steel-toed boots. He then stabbed the writhing little broken child with his bayonet and flung her into the flames.

"This same Nazi beat the mother with his rifle butt and threw her into the street. He laughed as an approaching tank crushed her frail body under the steel treads."

"You have said your name is Zivia?"

"Yes. But truthfully, there are many named Zivia in the Polish

Underground."

"Do you have any mechanical, electrical, or machine skills?" I asked.

"Yes," was all she said.

"Will you follow our strict rules at the secret research center and not be disruptive if I ship you out of this camp?"

"Yes."

In a quiet but firm voice, I told her, "Please get on the bus before the doctor at the selection table recognizes you."

Each family's story seemed more incredible than the families before. I talked with one family member from each group before they boarded the buses. I was satisfied that our orders were fulfilled.

I asked Zeke, "Vitali, will you and Breitman be able to get these folks safely to our facility in Peenemünde?

"Of course!" Replied Zeke, but what about you; aren't you going to return with us?"

I took Zeke aside and, in a low voice not heard by anyone but him, "With our Sixth Army in trouble in the east, I'm not sure how long it might take the Russians or the Allies to discover and liberate this camp. I'm going to see whatever I can do to speed up that day."

"Be careful, Jenz. I get the feeling that nothing in this camp goes undetected. You could be in grave danger."

"I will be cautious, Zeke. I want to see Ilsa as soon as I get back to Germany. I miss her with all my heart.

"I have a feeling you are pretty anxious to see Ms. Adiya."

I gave him an affirmative nod and a quick wink and added, "I hope her little sister, Chasha, is also doing well after the trauma of their lives at Treblinka."

"Please do everything possible to make all of our new workers as comfortable and as well-nourished as you can.

"Also, let General Dornberger know about Mr. Breitman. Inform him that because of his linguistic and mechanical skills, he is our new aid for dealing with the Polish Jews. He is to be released to his home after his service to the Reich.

Chapter 23

⋯⋯⋯

Digging in at Auschwitz

The next day I met with Commandant Höss to thank him for allowing us to obtain workers for our facility in Peenemünde. I told him I was going to observe some of the work crews to get some ideas for our disciplinary staff at our base.

There was a shop at the camp where all sorts of uniform parts were traded and bartered for goods and services. I traded my uniform jacket for two black SS well-worn shirts and pants. This outfit would help camouflage my real reason for hanging around this hell-on-earth: I wanted to see if there was any possible way of getting the Allies or the Russians here sooner.

The news was seeping into Germany in the Spring of 1943 of a massive defeat of the German 6th Army at Stalingrad. General Friedrich Paulus * was encircled by the Russian Army and surrendered to the Russian General Rokossovsky, ** in February 1943.

All the prisoners in Auschwitz were very anxious to hear of any news of liberation. Most of these poor unfortunate, and completely innocent folks had been very successfully dehumanized by the Nazi System. Death Head SS guards, criminal Kapo guards, and continuous harsh labor and beatings affected even the strongest innocent prisoners.

---

*General Paulus tried in vain to get his troops out of the Stalingrad Pocket, where the Russian Army encircled them. Hitler refused to let him leave Stalingrad, resulting in the defeat of the entire German 6th Army and the loss of almost 265,000 men. Only approximately 5,000 of these defeated soldiers made it back to Germany after the war. Paulus died in Dresden on the 1st of February, 1957. He was 67 years old.

**General Konstantin Rokossovsky accepted the surrender of the German 6th Army on the 2nd of February 1943. He went on to crush the German Army Group Centre in Belarus and was on the banks of the Vistula River opposite Warsaw by mid-1944. After the war, he held various high positions in Poland and Russia. He died in Russia in August 1968 at the age of 71.

Many of these poor wretches were not even capable of uttering a complete sentence, let alone forming a complete thought.

One evening I met a group of prisoners coming back from a work detail. There must have been almost 300 men trudging back from building a road in the forest. I asked a question to the Kapo in charge of marching the men back to the camp. "Kapo, where are you working these prisoners?"

He straightened up and answered, "Lieutenant, we have been taking down trees and building a road for the Germans in the nearby forest."

"Are you returning with the same number of prisoners you left with this morning?" I asked.

"We lost two from accidents or exhaustion, Lieutenant. I don't mean to be disrespectful, sir, but why do you ask? These Jews are all to be gassed soon."

I spoke loud enough so many of the prisoners could hear. "Kapo, all these workers are valuable to the Reich.

Then I continued. "Kapo, there has been a disaster for the Reich at Stalingrad this past winter. You should realize that roads and bridges are very important to the smooth-running governing of Poland. Treat these valuable workers with respect.

I walked along with the 300 or so workers until they entered their "barracks." Their housing was more like chicken coops than barracks. A slave-workers spoke up to me as they went through the gate.

"Officer," he quietly called to me. Please do not make any changes to our routine here at this camp."

"Why do you say that, prisoner?"

"We all dread changes," he replied quietly. "There is a saying here at Auschwitz, Lieutenant: 'When things change, they change for the worse!'"

"Has something happened recently? What is your name, prisoner? There will be no trouble."

"My name is Levi, * Lieutenant. Please do not say anything. My body is just healing from my last beating."

"God be with you, Levi," I whispered to him as he entered his encampment area.

I spent the rest of the day looking for officers of my own rank with whom I could discuss disciplinary measures utilized at the camp.

I also wanted to visit the main hospital, which I understood was over on block 21 of the camp. The labor camp was huge. I got directions to the main administrative office of the hospital *(Schreibstaube)* and met with the administrator.

The administrator gave me some information on the hospital structure. "All the doctors are Jews under the direct supervision of the SS Captains. Our chief selection officer is SS Captain Joseph Mengele. He also does some research with twins and expectant mothers."

I tried to keep an open mind about most of the personnel I had met at Auschwitz, but I had never heard anything positive about Dr. Mengele. He abused his authority at the camp and abused his patients who underwent sketchy medical procedures. I put him on a list as a need for elimination if the opportunity of time and place ever became relevant.

**Primo Levi was an Italian Jew captured by the Fascist Militia in December 1943, in Turin and deported to Auschwitz. Fortunately, he survived and later wrote about his time in the camp titled "Survival in Auschwitz," published in English in 1996. Touchstone, Simon & Schuster, Inc.*

Chapter 24

A Visit to the Prisoners' Hospital
(Häftlingskrankenbau or HKB)

As I walked through the hospital, it was painfully obvious that the patients were not getting very good treatment. I asked to see the current administrator. Patients were often two to a bed. Some were lying in filth. Many were lying naked on paper pads in pools of pus, blood, excrement, and urine.

SS Sturmbannführer Kurt Uhlenbroock came out from his office and offered a wave of a Hitler salute.

"What can I do for you this morning, Lieutenant?" A cheerful greeting in such a macabre setting immediately put me on the defensive.

"Good morning, Sturmbannführer. I'm visiting from the Wehrmacht Research Center and would like to get some ideas for our infirmary in Peenemünde."

"What is going on at your research center, Lieutenant?"

"We are mostly researching various arms and fuels for the use in our war efforts against the Russians." This vague reply seemed to satisfy the Sturmbannführer.

He was still curious, but he offered to help. "I will have one of the orderlies show you around our facility. Remember, we do not have top-line equipment or medicines in this facility. In addition, we are short-staffed; most of our doctors are Jewish prisoners."

He then stopped one of the orderlies passing by. "Herr Klehr, could you please show the Lieutenant our facility?"

"Of course, Sturmbannführer."

"Where would you like to start, Lieutenant? I suggest we skip the infectious disease block; it is pretty depressing and neither of us needs a dose of typhus.

"What is your full name, Herr Klehr?"

"I am Josef Klehr, * and have been here since 1941.

"Do you work in any particular area of the hospital?"

"You might say I work in all areas – especially where patients are very sick.

"I have implemented a way of reducing the number of ill patients at our facility who might be near death anyway."

He seemed pretty proud of himself, so I asked him what I thought was a simple question.

"Oh," I inquired. "How do you accomplish a quick healing?"

"Lieutenant, you don't understand. Everyone in this facility will eventually wind up in the gas houses unless they miraculously get better. Our facility is known as 'the waiting room for the crematoria!'

"If they get better, they will go back to heavy labor in one of the camp projects."

I thought I would try one more time.

"Herr Klehr, what is your method of ridding the patients of their disease or broken bodies?"

"It is very simple, Lieutenant; I inject phenol into their heart. It is a quick and easy death for these Jews. They are deceased within five minutes."

---

*Joseph Klehr was a medical orderly at Auschwitz Prisoners Hospital from 1941 until it was overrun and liberated by the Russians in 1945. He devised sadistic methods of murdering sick patients by injecting phenol directly into the heart of his patients. His logbook indicated he had killed over 14,000 patients with these cruel methods. He was well-known for his abject cruelty.

His eyes seemed to dance at the prospect of taking more Jewish lives. His squinty-mad eyes and satin-like smile displayed the zeal he put into his work.

My immediate thought was that *I would like to choke the life out of this sadistic bastard right here in the ward.*

My reply included, "How delightful, Klehr. You seem to be following an excellent program of ridding these misfortunate Jews from the Reich."

"Yes, Lieutenant, we do our best."

"Thank you for your valuable service to the Reich, Klehr, but I do have one question."

"I am at your service, Lieutenant."

"Who is the young, very pretty Aryan-looking girl I passed near the administrator's desk as I came into this block?"

"She belongs to Commandant Höss. Replied Klehr.

"Do you mean he has his daughter here at the prison camp?"

"Oh, no, Lieutenant. When I used the word, belong, perhaps I should have used a more accurate term. She is the commandant's sex slave."

"What?

"You've got to be putting me on, Klehr. How old is she, 15 years?

"Her name is Cilka Klein, * Lieutenant. I believe she is 16 years old. The Commandant took a liking to her as soon as she was out of the transport. He happened to be at the selection desk and ordered her to come with him.

---

*Cilka Klein did have special privileges at Auschwitz. However, those privileges came at a tremendous cost. When the Russians liberated the Auschwitz Camp, Cilka was labeled a collaborator, probably by the other prisoners. She was sent to Vorkuta, a brutal Russian prison camp, where she endured ten years of further sexual assaults. Her life story is historically documented in a novel by author Heather Morris called "Cilka's Journey."

This book is viewed as a sequel to Morris's best-selling novel, "The Tattooist of Auschwitz."

"Many of the other prisoners are jealous of her because she gets extra food and warm clothes in the winter. She is housed separately from the other prisoners and has many privileges denied to the other prisoners.

"From what I hear, she is continuously rapped by the commandant whenever he likes."

All the disease and death in these infirmary wards were really getting to me.

"Are you telling me, Klehr, these 4 blocks of the infirmary, 19,20,21 and 28, are basically just instruments of annihilation?"

"Lieutenant, let's put it this way: if you come into our hospital with a disease or injury – you may get better, but that would be a true miracle!

Chapter 25

Miracle Doctors at Auschwitz

As I was leaving the infirmary block 20, I came across who I thought was a young nurse or orderly. She stiffened when I spoke to her.

"Ms., could you tell me if any prison doctors are on this block in the infirmary?"

"Yes. Although I am the only woman doctor for this woman's infirmary section, there are other doctors in the prison."

Then I asked very quietly but firmly, "Doctor, is there any place where we could talk without interruption for a few moments?"

She then beckoned me to follow her into a small office.

"This is where I write up my medical notes and make notations in the patient's charts.

"Could I ask why the SS would like to talk with me?"

"Thank you for speaking with me today, doctor. I am visiting from a research center in northern Germany. I am interested in getting information on medical centers in the Reich so I am better able to make recommendations at our facility."

She asked, "Is your facility a labor camp?"

"No. Our area of research is in developing fuels and armaments for the Reich. But we do have laborers from various camps.

"May I ask your name?"

"My name is Perl, Lieutenant, Doctor Gisella Perl. * Male prisoners threw me out of the cattle-car transport when I arrived here earlier this year. Dr. Mengele assigned me to the woman's infirmary after he learned I was a gynecologist doctor."

"Are you only catering to the needs of the woman prisoners?"

"No, Lieutenant. Many of my patients have been injured in accidents or have had their bodies ravaged and rapped by your SS, brutal Kapos, or other male prisoners."

"Tell me about the injuries to the women prisoners, doctor."

"Why would the SS have an interest in the injuries they have caused, Lieutenant?"

"Because there is always a chance I could talk with the commandant and see if conditions could be improved for the women prisoners."

"There is no chance for improvement in our conditions, Lieutenant. The commandant has even set up a block of the barracks here at Auschwitz for the very purpose of brutalizing and rapping the Jewish female and young male prisoners. A few of the female victims of these attacks become pregnant. Once their pregnancies are obvious, the women's lives are in jeopardy.

"Many of these victims," the doctor continued, "will never be able to have children. Some will never be able to have normal relationships with anyone they might care about. A few will contemplate suicide, as I have on more than one occasion."

"Dr. Perl, you must know you are very needed here. These women would be in even worse condition if there were no one to look after them. If they became pregnant, it would probably mean a one-way trip to the gas chambers for the mothers and their babies."

---

*Dr. Perl came to Auschwitz after 4 days in a cattle car transport in March 1944. Dr. Mengele had advised her to send all the pregnant prisoners to him for special nutrition and treatment. After Dr. Perl discovered the "special treatment" involved experiments on live humans, and both mother and baby wound up in the crematoria, she performed live births and terminations in order to save the mothers. She moved to the US in 1951 and was convinced by Eleanor Roosevelt to practice medicine again. She had a successful practice on Park Avenue in NYC and delivered over 3000 babies. Dr. Perl passed away in Israel on 16 December 1988. She was 81 years old.

"Why would you care?" The doctor asked a pointed question.

"Doctor, you must know… *I had to choose my words carefully…* all the men who wear this uniform are not monsters. I would encourage you… no, I would implore you to continue to help as many women as you can."

"Why should any of us here at the camp trust anything you say?"

"Because my Yiddish is as good as my German, doctor. And I will let you in on a little news."

"You speak Yiddish?" The doctor asked in complete surprise.

"Yes, I learned it well in school. But don't you want to hear some news from the front?"

"Please, Lieutenant. News at Auschwitz is not usually good news!"

"You may interpret this as you would like, but please keep it to yourself. I do not want the commandant to know its source.

"The Russians have encircled and defeated Hitler's Sixth Army at Stalingrad. I would not be surprised if the Allies or the Russians are here at this camp within a year."

"Liberation of this hell-hole by the Allies would be a dream come true," was the doctor's comment. Have you shared this information with anyone else?"

"Only one prisoner who had been recently whipped and beaten."

"Why?" I asked.

"I would like you to share it with one of my colleagues," affirmed Dr. Perl. He is another doctor here at the camp. We are only allowed to use our first names so I only know him as Victor."

"I will ask Doctor Mengele to locate him for me."

"Oh! Please don't ask Mengele," the doctor implored. "Nothing good ever comes from contact with Doctor Mengele. He could make trouble for Victor or you.

"Since you seem curious about Dr. Mengele, I will explain why you should never talk to him.

"When I first started here as a doctor to pregnant women, Mengele asked me to send all the women experiencing pregnancy to him for better nutrition and care. After about a week of sending these pregnant women to him, I was passing by Crematorium 1 and saw the SS beating the most recent pregnant women I had sent to the doctor. After the SS beat these women with clubs, the pregnant women were attacked by vicious dogs. They were then thrown into the crematorium like rag-dolls - while still alive!

"Does this example give you enough reason to avoid the evil doctor?"

"Yes, Doctor Perl. I appreciate you talking freely to me. I will take your suggestion."

Although my depression deepened, I spent the rest of the day going through the wards or blocks of medical buildings. Even to the untrained eye, conditions in this particular hellhole were deplorable.

In one ward, I discovered rats just starting to eat a poor prisoner's toes. The patient was too ill to object or even care. I chased the rats out of the ward and placed a soiled blanket over the prisoner's lower body.

I noticed several of the cots had two prisoners on a single bed frame.

The spread of infectious diseases must kill many of these poor folks.

The last bed I came to was empty. But the patient was curled in a ball on the floor and definitely deceased. It looked like he had shrunk to about half the size of a normal adult prisoner. I could tell by his facial hair; he was not a child.

I looked throughout the block for another doctor or block nurse, but no one was around. I thought, *tomorrow I will look up Victor to see if there were any more physicians working in this very sad excuse for an infirmary.*

It was getting dark outside. The only bright lights in the distance were around the camp's perimeter. The breeze from the east brought the distinct odor of burning flesh from the crematoriums. After walking through the sad excuse for a hospital, I could barely place one foot in front of another. I was living my own depression. Thoughts of Ilsa were the only future I could contemplate to fight my sadness.

Chapter 26

Physicians Who Heal

Although I was up early the next morning, there were several groups of prisoners marching off to labor projects either within the camp or just outside in the nearby forests. The sky was light with a promise of the approaching dawn. Fog hung in the gullies like grey vails in the camp.

The men in the prison labor groups resembled shadows in deplorable shapes against a background of gray. My heart went out to them. Their work-day began at 4:30 in the summertime, one hour later in the winter. Almost all prisoner work was mind-numbing and back-breaking.

I even felt guilty eating at the officer's cafeteria. I know these hardworking prisoners were getting barely sustenance nutrition. Their food resembled something I wouldn't have fed to animals.

Before going out on a day-labor detail, the prisoners were given a half liter of coffee substitute or herbal tea but no food. No wonder most of the prisoners looked like a collection of skin and bones.

The midday ration for most prisoners consisted of three-quarters of a liter of watery, often foul-smelling soup, which had a very small portion of meat, four days per week, and some vegetables, mainly potatoes or rutabaga, three days per week.

In the evening, most prisoners were given 300 grams of often moldy bread along with a tablespoon of cheese or jelly. Occasionally, 25 grams of margarine or sausage were included, especially for prisoners assigned to hard labor. Many of the prisoners kept part of their ration for the morning meal in the hope that it would not get stolen overnight.

On my way to the medical blocks, I headed across an expanse of a trampled field overgrown with tired weeds. It was hot for this early in the morning. The sun was just up and burning off the dampness of the evening's dew. Admittedly, I wasn't in the best of moods after seeing the prisoner patients in the medical blocks yesterday. The low mist that hung in the air did nothing to improve my attitude.

I missed Ilse. Even the thought of her and her tender touch brought a bit of a smile to my face as I entered medical block 28. The first orderly I came across suggested I look in block 19 for the doctor called Victor.

I backtracked a bit down a clay and weed-infested road and found block 19. There was a small green cross on the door but no other notification that it was a medical building.

I went to what I guessed was the admitting desk and asked, "Is there a doctor Victor here in this ward?"

The orderly prisoner jumped to attention when he looked up and saw my SS Lieutenant bars.

"Yes. Of course, Lieutenant. Please wait here and I will bring him over."

A few minutes later, a wizened prisoner in what I guessed was somewhere in his 30s showed up at the front desk. His stature had been humbled by many months of prison food and humiliation by the Kapos and guards.

"I am Victor.* What can I do for you, Lieutenant?"

There was no fear in his speech or demeanor. His gaze was steady as he looked me in the eye.

---

*Victor Frankl was an Austrian neurologist who spent three years in 4 different concentration camps. While in the camps, he developed an existential analysis, Logotherapy, based on man's search for meaning in life. After the liberation of the Auschwitz camp, he was appointed head of neurology at the Polyclinic Hospital in Vienna, where he wrote his most famous work, "Man's Search for Meaning," in nine days. He died of heart failure on the 2nd of September 1997 in Vienna. He was 92 years old.

"Victor, I am Lieutenant Ramsgrund. I am visiting here from a research center in northern Germany. Is there a quiet place we may talk for a few minutes?"

"Yes. Can the SS Lieutenant tell me what this is about?

"Of course. I would rather we were in a more private area."

He led me down a quiet corridor to what looked like a closet tucked in the back of block 19. The small room contained an overhead bulb dangling on a cord and a board across two small saw-horses, which served as a cramped desk. There was a modest stool and a wooden box.

Victor grabbed the wooden box and motioned me to sit on the three-legged wooden stool.

"You will have to pardon the accommodations, Lieutenant. I do not get too many SS officers here in the infirmary. As a matter of fact, you are probably the first."

"You do not have to apologize for accommodations in this hellhole, Victor. What kind of a doctor are you?"

After a considerable pause, he answered. "My area of specialization is in neurology."

"Where is your home?"

"My wife and I lived in Vienna before we were sent to the Theresienstadt concentration camp in 1942. My family has all been killed in the camps. My wife might still be alive, but I have no way of knowing; I do know I will see her again."

"I have to acknowledge, doctor, your attitude seems to be quite positive, considering the conditions here at Auschwitz."

"If I could trust the SS Lieutenant, I would confide in you how I have survived. But I do not trust anyone who wears your uniform."

"Doctor, if I confided in you something that might convince you to trust me, could you keep it very confidential?"

"I don't know, Lieutenant. I have been here long enough to trust very few people. My background in psychiatry, however, has taught me to keep serious private conversations very private."

"I am about to divulge information to you that could get us both killed, is that serious enough for you?"

"I would never," the doctor replied, "acknowledge to anyone that you are Jewish."

"How would you know my religion, doctor?"

"In all my dealings with the SS lieutenant, I have never met any who has described this camp as a 'hellhole.' I will keep your private life, private. I assume there must be other reasons for you to wear our enemies' uniform. Do you care to trust me and tell me why you have joined the SS?"

"Well, if I can trust you not to acknowledge my sacred religion, I will explain the rest of my story:

"My parents sent me to Hitler Youth Camp when I was sixteen years in order to hide my Jewishness. My father is Swedish, and the SS seemed to like my Nordic features and recruited me from the Technical Institute in Berlin for engineering studies.

"I obtained Italian citizenship papers for my lifelong Jewish friend and we were both recruited to a secret Wehrmacht base in Northern Germany. The base at Peenemünde is being used to develop secret weapons systems that could turn the tide of war for the Reich."

"What sort of weapons are being developed at this secret base, lieutenant?"

"The army is developing long-range missile technology and warheads which could bring catastrophic destruction to the cities of our enemies.

"But now, doctor, please tell me how have you been able to survive in this place for so long?"

"I listen, lieutenant.

"One day, one of the meanest guards, a Kapo, came to me with a minor injury. These Kapos were even more brutal than the SS guards. They liked to demonstrate their brutality in order to curry favor with the uniform you wear.

"I sewed up his face and told him it would leave only a hair-line, almost invisible white-line scar.

"One day, I was on my way to a work detail in another section of the camp, and the same Kapo started talking to me about his love life and matrimonial troubles. He really poured out his troubles to me.

"All I did, at first, was listen. Then I gave him an assessment of his character and some psychotherapeutic advice for his marriage.

"Evidently, he was grateful. Whenever he was in charge of doling out our meager rations, he would make sure I received a full measure or slightly more. In this camp, even slightly more, like a few more peas in your soup, can mean the difference between starvation and survival."

"Is this how you are surviving, doctor?" I asked because I felt there must be more than a bit of food to help these poor souls survive.

"Yes, Lieutenant. You must do a couple of other things to survive this camp. You must always stay fit to work. You cannot get sick or lame. If you start to limp, you could get on a list to be gassed."

"Is that all of what it takes to survive in this brutal hell, doctor?" I asked in order to pass on survival techniques to others here and at our research center in Peenemünde.

"Underlying everything, Lieutenant, is the individual's attitude and his faith in God. The prisoners must realize they have to take personal responsibility for their lives. And that each prisoner is unique and has a special contribution to make – not only in this camp but in their own lives.

"I only pray this war ends before all of us are snuffed out in the harsh brutality that is Auschwitz."

Chapter 27

Surviving Auschwitz

After the first week of being at the Auschwitz camp, I was beginning to grasp the enormity of this killing machine. Commandant Höss explained to me that the total capacity of the camp was approximately 140,000 people. This number included having the crematoriums run continuously 24 hours each day of the week, including Sundays. There was a total of four crematorium complexes. Each crematorium could "process" up to 2000 people at a time.

The crematoriums seemed to create hug billowing clouds of black smoke that belched fire and gave the camp a shower of white ash if the wind was blowing back toward the barracks. It made me inconsolably sad to think this ash was the remains of European Jewry.

I told the commandant of my desire to learn more about the elimination process for all the undesirable people in the conquered areas. He told me to get in touch with one of the camp doctors, Dr. Nyiszli, * who was an assistant to Dr. Mengele.

I introduced myself to one of the SS guards outside of crematory # 1, he led me to Dr. Nyiszli in the office beside the crematory.

"Good morning, doctor. I'm Lieutenant Ramsgrund from the Army base near Peenemünde in Northern Germany."

"What can I do for you, Lieutenant?"

---

*Dr. Miklos Nyiszli, a physician, found himself at Auschwitz in 1944 when all the Jews from Hungry were sent to the camps after the Nazi invasion. He worked as a forensic pathologist for the Reich and lived next to crematorium #1. He was an admitted collaborator who helped Dr. Joseph Mengele with his medical experiments on twins and dwarfs by performing autopsies. He was liberated from the camps and continued to practice medicine, although he vowed never to lift a scalpel again. He died at age 54 in Romania in September 1985.

"I need to bring back some ideas on your methods of liquidation of such vast numbers of prisoners in your facility and a little information on your medical experiments here in Auschwitz. I find it incredible that you can eliminate trainloads of thousands of people daily in this one facility."

Dr. Nyiszli did not seem frightened or cowered by my presence. He looked me in the eyes when he talked.

"Lieutenant, would you like to see our operation?" "First, I would rather you tell me about your procedures."

"Of course, Lieutenant.

"All the prisoners who have been directed to the left at the sorting tables are marched directly to the crematoriums. Most prisoners are dead within the hour they arrive here. Men and women in good physical health, along with mothers with twins and dwarfs, are directed to the right."

Something puzzled me and I asked:

"Why are the twins and dwarfs selected out of the extermination line?"

"Dr. Mengele is conducting some minor experiments on these individuals for important scientific studies."

"Are you helping Dr. Mengele with these experimental studies, doctor?"

"Lieutenant, we have several hundred sonderkommando who are all Jewish prisoners here who care for the bodies after being gassed. Many of them get injured or have medical problems. Basically, I take care of these prisoners and see that their medical problems are well-treated."

"Excellent, doctor. But you haven't answered my question. What role do you play with the aid you are giving to Dr. Mengele?"

"It is a little difficult to explain, Lieutenant, but I shall try.

"After the experimental patients are euthanized, I do a complete autopsy with careful analysis of the findings and report these findings to the doctor.

"So far, Dr. Mengele has been favorably impressed with my work here as a forensic pathologist. I have done post-mortems on several prisoners,

"SS officers, and anyone whom the doctor has ordered me to examine."

"How are your circumstances here, doctor?"

"Our housing, food, clothing, and medical supplies are as good as anywhere in the Reich. The problem is that all the sonderkommandos, including myself, will be killed at the end of our term."

"Why is that, doctor?"

"Because the world in general, and European Jewry in particular, must never know what is going on in this place.

"If Jews were aware of their fate before they arrived, it would be almost impossible for your SS organization to herd the Jews into these efficient killing machines.

"The sonderkommandos are only vaguely aware of their fate. After three or four months, the 400-500 sonderkommandos are told to report to the courtyard for resettlement at a rest camp. Once they are lined up in the courtyard, the SS machine guns them all. Their bodies are summarily burned in the crematoriums and the ash is dumped in the Vistula. Some of the prisoner's ash is processed into soaps and fertilizer."

"It sounds very efficient, doctor."

"Would you like to view the crematorium complex # 1, Lieutenant?"

Chapter 28

A Tour of Crematorium # One at Auschwitz

"Thanks for showing me your laboratory, doctor Nyiszli; it looks very well-equipped."

"You are entirely welcome, Lieutenant. As I am showing you around Crematorium # 1, I would like to comment on the only mistake our sonderkommando force has committed as long as I have been here. The error and surrounding issues have been cleared up, but I would appreciate confidentiality. Dr. Mengele is unaccustomed to any slip-ups concerning the liquidation of our prisoners.

"All of us who work in these crematoriums realize our days are numbered. I have lasted more than the usual three-month period, but I could be killed for even slight infractions."

"I will keep our conversations private, doctor. Thank you for entrusting me with the information on the crematoriums."

"Lieutenant, this incident took place three weeks ago. I still have difficulty sleeping because I lived through it.

"This room we are in now is the undressing room.

"As you can see, there are hundreds of hooks on the wall for the prisoners to place their clothing after they undress. They are told they must be completely nude before they go into the showers. They are told to remember the number on the hook so they may retrieve their clothing after the shower."

"The room is cavernous, doctor. How many prisoners come through here at one time?"

"Each undressing room can hold up to two thousand prisoners. Often, they are reluctant to get completely undressed, so the sonderkommandos have to beat a few with rubber truncheons; then, they get more cooperative.

"Remember, we must process up to eight to ten thousand people daily. Our crematoriums are functioning day and night. The only time we halt the cremation procedure occurs when Allied or Russian planes are in the vicinity.

"The prisoners go directly from this room into the gas chamber. The prisoners are told they are going into the shower room. They don't seem to panic until the last few are crowded into the room and they realize it is far too crowded for bathing.

"The Cyclon B * gas is dropped down the four tubes in the center of the chamber as crystals. The gas is immediately released and fills the lungs with cyanide poison.

"The victims do everything they can to avoid inhaling the poisonous vapors. The prisoners climb on top of one another to try to reach the ceiling to catch a fresh breath of air. Within a few minutes, the nude bodies make a hideous pyramid of corpses to be cremated by the sonderkommandos."

"Isn't this form of liquidation pretty-much standard throughout the concentration camps in the Reich?" I asked.

The doctor held up one finger as if he had a further comment. "Lieutenant, shortly after the chamber was ventilated, a sonderkommando came running into my laboratory without knocking."

"He was so out of breath; I felt the gas must have gotten to him. He almost broke the hinges off the door as he rushed into my lab."

"Doctor!" he yelled. "We found a young girl alive at the bottom of the corpses!"

---

*The I. G. Farben Company developed two types of Cyclon products during the Second World War. The name Cyclon came from the essential ingredients: cyanide, chlorine, and nitrogen. The two products outside canisters were identical, except Cyclon A was a disinfectant; Cyclon B killed millions of people.

I shouted. "Bring her here to my laboratory and place her on the table!"

"This sonderkommando was very excited to see one of his fellow Jews had survived the gassing. She was found at the bottom of the corps pile with her face pressed into the damp cement floor. Cyclon B does not react in the presence of humidity, and the gas did not kill the girl.

"I rushed into the gas chamber and found the girl coughing and vomiting. The gas commando men were in a state of panic. Nothing like this had ever happened in the gas chambers before. I carried her back to my table and administered a small amount of stimulant to support her heart and circulation.

"Then the kommando men brought her soup and warm tea. They were treating her as if she was their own child. She was starting to sit up and the color was coming back to her skin. She said her name was Herta, and she was eighteen years old. She told us her story.

"You have to understand, Lieutenant, this was something extraordinary for our crematoriums here at Auschwitz. No one had ever survived the gas chambers.

"As she told her story, my eyes filled with water. I knew her sad story was happening all over Germany and Poland and indeed all over the conquered territories under the command of the Reich."

"What was her story, doctor?"

Chapter 29

Herta's Story

"Herta, our first and only gas chamber survivor," the doctor began, "was from Upper Silesia. * She was studying nursing. When the Nazis came to power in 1933, her family knew anxiety and fear from the Aryan German population. Gradually her family was forced to give up their clothing business. Little by little, all their rights were taken away. Herta said her family was forced out of their home and had to live in two small rooms in the Jewish Ghetto.

"Her family had to give up most of their possessions, including their radio, silverware, clothing, and anything of value. She could no longer attend school, walk in the parks, or use trolley cars or railroad trains. She said park benches bore signs in large white lettering: 'STRICTLY OFF LIMITS FOR JEWS.' Even store signs proclaimed in large letters: 'JEWS WILL NOT BE SERVED' or 'GOODS WILL NOT BE SOLD TO JEWS.'

"Herta told us her family's ration cards were restricted, so meat, vegetables, fruit, fats, and even clothing were forbidden. Since their Jewish Temples had been burned down, they had to hold religious services in make-shift locations; but even then, Hitler Youth would often throw stones through the windows and disrupt their services.

"Herta related to us that she was one of the fortunate Jews because she worked in a hospital. She cried and whimpered while telling us that many of her neighbors were marched out into the forest and made to dig their own graves. She told us how after digging their own graves,

---

*Upper Silesia, now part of Poland, was an early target of Nazi oppression of the Jewish population. The total population of approximately 100,000 Jews were rounded up, forced into ghettos, sent to concentration and death camps, or murdered by the Einsatzgruppen death squads.

the neighbors and children were told to march past the ditches while the SS or the Einsatzgruppen * units would shoot the men, women, and children, and the poor slaughtered folks would tumble into the ditch which served as their grave. Often, the people were not killed at once but only wounded, so the Nazis would just bury them alive.

"Herta spoke of being lucky as a hospital worker because her food and lodging at the hospital were somewhat better than the Jews living in the ghetto. She was the nurse in charge of the children's ward, or *Stionsschwester,* until early one morning.

"It was about five o'clock in the early morning on 23 February 1942." Herta told us, "A commotion and gunfire outside the hospital awakened me. As I looked out the window, the police were threatening all our Jewish hospital workers with rifles.

"I immediately asked one of the policemen what was going on, but he lied to us by saying we were being transported to a work camp, and not to worry.

"A few days later, we arrived at Auschwitz. None of us," Herta continued, "had any idea of what to expect. The SS guards in charge of our filthy barracks kept beating us with cudgels. Even the smallest children were not exempt from the cudgel."

I interrupted the doctor relating Herta's story by asking, "Even the children are beaten?"

"Oh yes, Lieutenant, especially if they are crying. Hungry children cry a lot. These children are quick fuel for the crematoriums. The younger children are usually thrown in first and used for kindling for the larger children and adults.

"Herta complained that the clothing provided by the guards at Auschwitz was crawling with flees and lice. The swarming insects tormented the prisoners and caused them to break out in pussy sores and bleeding scabs.

---

*Einsatzgruppen units were paramilitary or SS Special Action Groups organized by Himmler and Heydrich in 1939. These units would follow the German armies into Poland, murdering national leaders and rounding up Jews for 'resettlement' - which meant murdering them in the forests!

"Herta told us one of her close friends, a nurse from the hospital, fell during one of their forced labor projects. The guard came up to her, placed his heavy boot on her chest, and asked: 'Miss, do you want to lie there and feel sick?' The guard then put all his weight on my friend's chest and stomped her with his steel-toed boot. You could hear her ribs breaking; blood flowed from her mouth. She died almost instantly."

"So," I asked, "you brought Herta back to life?"

"Yes, with the help of the sonderkommandos, Lieutenant."

"How did she escape the crematorium complex, doctor?"

"Lieutenant, this sad story is about to get even more difficult."

"How much more difficult could it possibly get, doctor?"

"About the time we had Herta rescued and back to life, the Oberscharführer, our SS overseer of the crematorium complex, entered my office and saw the young woman on my table.

"He would frequently come into my office to look over my work. He was the supervising SS officer for the Jewish Sonderkommando unit in the crematoriums.

"When Oberscharführer Muhsfeldt * came into my office and saw the young woman on the table, he shouted, 'What is she doing here!'

"It took me a minute to collect my thoughts, but I figured it would be best to tell him the whole story.

"When I asked if Herta could be brought back to the camp by the women who come and collect the clothing of the recently gassed prisoners, he again shouted,

'Are you crazy? The minute she returned to the main camp; she would tell the first person she met what goes on in this place. We would pay for that information leak with our lives!'

---

*Eric Muhsfeldt was a German war criminal. He served as a non-commissioned member of the SS at the Auschwitz concentration camp as leader of the Sonder-commando unit that would bring the gassed corpses of the prisoners to the crematoria. He was captured after the war, tried and convicted in Krakow, and hanged on the 24th of January 1948.

"The Oberscharführer then had some of the sonderkommando men carry the young girl to the hallway of the crematorium. Since Muhsfeldt didn't have the fortitude to kill her, he commanded one of the sonderkommando Jews to take care of the problem. I heard a loud bang report of a pistol. Herta was executed with a bullet to the back of her neck and tossed into the cremation oven."

Chapter 30

⚬◦⟡◦⚬

A Snag in Getting Out of Auschwitz

All of the concentration camps Ezekiel and I have visited have been terrible experiences. These killing machines have been the source of continuing nightmares. Auschwitz has been the worst because we have seen thousands of men, women, and children wasting away on rotten food, harsh labor, and continuous beatings with rubber truncheons and whips.

I sent a message to General Dornberger in order to let him know Sargent Vitali and I had completed our mission and to see if he had an adequate workforce from the slave labor we had provided to date. I also gave him a quick summary of what we had witnessed at Treblinka, Sobibor, and Auschwitz.

I gave the General a few graphic details so he could understand what we had witnessed firsthand.

His immediate reply was quite simple and predictable: "What you are telling me is not to be believed!"

I was working out of a small office in the administrative block of the camp in a building near the commandant's office. As I was getting ready to arrange transportation back to Peenemünde, there was a knock at the door.

"Come in!" I called through the door.

A tall man dressed in civilian clothes and a fedora entered my makeshift office. He looked like Gestapo, but it had only been an hour since my message to General Dornberger.

He introduced himself. "Good afternoon, Lieutenant. I am Agent Burk from our Nordhausen office. Perhaps you don't remember me?"

My immediate thought was — how was it possible for the Gestapo to read military message mail?

"I remember you very well, Agent Burk. You and your fellow agent tried to arrest me and my colleague, Dr. Carapezza, because you lost a couple of Gestapo agents and their automobile somewhere near the secret rocket plant in Thuringia near Nordhausen."

"Yes, Lieutenant. We have not located Dr. Carapezza, but the agents and their automobile were found in the woods near the rocket center. Both agents had been murdered and buried near their automobile.

"The long arm of the Gestapo has been following you to Denmark, Sweden, and all over Poland for the past few months. I am here to arrest you for their murder."

"Agent Burk, I would suggest you look elsewhere for your criminal."

"I need to place you in handcuffs!"

"If you remember, Agent Burk, when your lead agent, Agent Rikker, tried to place me in handcuffs, it did not go well for him. Since it is late afternoon and I did not get a very excellent lunch, I would suggest you forgo the handcuffs. We should walk over to the Commandant's office and see if we can sort this out."

"Very well, Lieutenant. But remember, we are in the middle of a very secure prison here at Auschwitz."

"Yes, of course, Agent Burk. I intend on being very cooperative. How long have you been in this camp?"

"I just arrived this morning and have not had a chance to get my bearings. The secretary in the commandant's office directed me here."

"Excellent! It is only a short walk over to the commandant's office. We will have to go between a couple of the prisoner's barracks, but it should only take fifteen or twenty minutes to get there. This camp is very secure, so you do not have to worry about any attempts for escape. The camp is crawling with guards and SS.

My hope was that Agent Burk was not familiar enough with the Auschwitz Camp to know his way around. I was also counting on his not being familiar with the electric fence between the barracks.

"Right this way, Agent Burk. We will go between the prisoner's barracks in order to get directly to the commandant's office."

I took a chance and grabbed my right-hand glove out of my desk drawer on the way out and placed it in my pocket.

While walking between the prisoner barracks and the electric fence, I could see an occasional prisoner making a trip to the latrine about twenty meters from the back end of the building.

It was cloudy with a slight mist in the air.

As we were traversing between the next building and the fence, I engaged Burk in conversation:

"Tell me, Agent Burk. Has the Gestapo still been recruiting criminals for most of their dirty work?"

As I was talking and walking along, I put my hand in my pocket and slipped on my right glove.

"Of course not, Lieutenant! Whatever gave you such an outlandish idea?"

"I guess it just seemed to come naturally. Most of us in the SS consider the Gestapo a criminal organization that prays on law-abiding German citizens."

"Just wait until you are under detention with Gestapo jurisdiction, Lieutenant. You will see how the Gestapo can obtain almost any necessary information from you. You will be very sorry you have disrespected me. I will have the commandant of this camp place you in one of these prisoner barracks. You will be denied food and water for several days. Then we shall see how brave you talk!

I had just about enough of this fool. I saw a stick of wood in the weeds up ahead. I looked around to see if anyone was watching and brought my clenched fist down on the back of the agent's neck. His legs shot out from under him like a pithed frog. He went down like a sack of sand. I wasn't sure if he was dead, so I tossed him up against the electric fence and held him there with the stick I found in the weeds. His metal belt buccal sparked Burk to do a little jumping dance against the fence. I held him on the fence until I was sure he was gone.

No guards came, so I called out to the prisoner who had just entered the latrine. The prisoner reluctantly approached the electric fence.

"Prisoner," I addressed him politely. "Could you help me with this gentleman?"

"I will try, Lieutenant; what can I do?"

"I am going to drag his corps to your barrack. I would like you to strip him of his clothing and any belongings. These items will be yours to keep. Please destroy any items of identification. He is Gestapo.

"When is the next time for the selection truck to make a trip for the crematoria?"

"They come for selections every night," was the prisoner's response.

"Fine. Make sure his body is tossed into the next selection truck. The crematorium is actually too good a place for him. Make sure all identification is destroyed in the latrine."

Chapter 31

Missing Ilsa

It was becoming obvious to me that the Gestapo might be reading military messaging. If they could read military secrets, regular mail, and phone conversations were never going to be confidential. I had to assume all my communications with Ilse were going to be compromised. So, I decided to send her an innocuous letter that she would have to interpret.

Dearest Ilsa,

It has been too long since I have seen you. I hope you are well. I have been visiting some of the reconstruction camps in Germany and in the Conquered Territories. Our office is learning a lot about techniques for handling large crowds of people and medical procedures.

It would be a joy for me to be able to see you in the upcoming weeks; I look forward to seeing you safely as soon as I can arrange leave.

Lovingly,

Jenz

If there was any censoring of the mail, it was my hope that this would reach her in Hannover within a week or two. I really missed the love of my life.

My next step was to leave Auschwitz with as little notice as possible. Even though the majority of the missile construction was now taking place in a limestone-constructed factory underground near

Nordhausen, General Dornberger and some support and administrative staff were still in Peenemünde. *

I went directly to the Commandant's office. His administrative assistant was at her desk.

"The Commandant has an appointment in about twenty minutes," supplied the administrative assistant. "If you are here for a short visit, he may be able to see you now."

"Thank you, Ms. I won't be but a few minutes. I just wanted to thank him for his kindness and hospitality toward me."

"I will see if he is available"

The assistant pressed a speaker button and announced I was in the outer office.

Commandant Höss came out of his office and asked, "What can I do for you Lieutenant?"

This was a very dangerous man and I wanted to show him every military courtesy while still keeping a neutral or pleasant expression on my face.

"Good afternoon, Herr Commandant. I will be leaving this afternoon after I can arrange transportation to the train station and would like to thank you and your very efficient staff here at Auschwitz for your hospitality. General Dornberger sends his regards and thanks for the Jew laborers we were able to send to him from this camp."

"I'm happy to help our war effort in any way possible."

"Oh, by the way, Lieutenant. Did Agent Burk get ahold of you?"

My quick response was, "No, Commandant. But if he is looking for me, I will be at our secret Wehrmacht base in northern Germany." "Excellent, Lieutenant. I will have my assistant, Rebecca, arrange for you to get a ride to the train station for your trip north. It is strange; however, the agent seemed anxious to contact you."

---

*The British had discovered the secret rocket base and bombed it on the night of 17-18 August 1943.

"Thanks again, Commandant!"

I could tell by his assistant's Old Testament name; she was most likely Jewish. She would be an outright knock-out with a little effort and a bit of style in her clothing.

The Commandant's assistant asked me, "Lieutenant, I could arrange a ride for you to the train station in Krakow for early tomorrow morning, would that be all right? There is a 9:30 am train to Warsaw for your trip north.

"Yes, Rebecca. An early morning ride would be most gracious of you. Tell me, does your name mean 'servant of God'?"

Surprisingly, she answered in Yiddish, "How would you know what my name means?"

So, I answered her in Yiddish, "My German education wouldn't have been complete without a knowledge of the Old Testament."

The surprised expression on her face gave me hope that I would soon be on my way to see and hold my beloved Ilsa. Her absence from my life these past few months had been painful.

I thanked Rebecca and told her I would be in front of the officer's barrack # 11 at 7 am.

Chapter 32

Getting Back to Peenemünde

My trip back to Peenemünde went smoothly and without incident. However, our train had to travel part of the time at night because of Russian raids on moving trains in eastern Poland. These areas were designated as Conquered Territories, but no one really knew how long they would remain under German control.

It was a pleasure to see my colleagues again, especially Ezekiel. We had dinner off the base on my first full day back and discussed many of the atrocities we had witnessed in the camps.

"Zeke, we have to remember exactly what we witnessed and write everything down. We have to include names, dates, conversations, and even our impressions of the lives of these poor, suffering people.

"We have to be very careful where we keep any of our records, notes, and descriptions of the camp conditions. If these writings were to fall into the wrong hands, it could go very badly for us with the Gestapo.

"I certainly understand," replied Ezekiel. "I'm pretty sure, I will never get over what we witnessed in Treblinka.

"I know Adiya and her sister, Chasha, will never be the same," said Zeke with some emotion in his voice.

"Adiya knew they were close to being put to death, but she has kept that knowledge from her sister until she is older or whenever this war is over.

"Jenz, I should tell you General Dornberger has ordered all officers to be at an all-command required meeting with Hitler's War Minister tomorrow morning. I'm not sure why he is coming to our remote base, but I hope he isn't making more demands on our staff. The General mentioned parade dress uniforms are required."

"Wonderful," I replied. "My guess is he would like to have the V-ll operational sooner, rather than later. We have to be especially careful with any interaction with this officer, he could be very dangerous. And, we have to be doubly careful with our efforts to slow down V-ll development.

"Any idea, Zeke, of the officer's background or name?"

"I believe his name is Speer. * And, you may find this hard to believe, I think he is an architectural designer. He is also known to be close to our Fürher."

"He sounds like trouble, Zeke. I suppose there is no way we could avoid the meeting?"

"No, we have to make sure we are there. General Dornberger may have some pointed questions for us about the quality of life in the camps," emphasized Zeke. How will we be able to answer those questions truthfully?"

My answer was a little convoluted, but I know Zeke got the idea. "We have to be direct and clear in our answers, but very careful not to show any bias toward the Jews or particular conditions at the camps. Perhaps, he won't ask difficult questions or he might ask us in private. If he knows or suspects what is going on in the concentration camps, he will probably ask us in private."

While we were finishing dinner, two well-dressed men came and sat down at a nearby table. Although they didn't appear to pay any

---

*Albert Speer was a trained and gifted architect. First, he became Hitler's architect, then, over time, Hitler came to trust his judgment. Of all the Führer's interactions with his officers, Speer was the only one who could be considered a friend of Adolf Hitler. Albert Speer certainly knew how the Jews were suffering under the Nazis. However, he was the only prisoner at the Nuremberg Trials after the war that showed any remorse and apologized for his actions. He also did not protest as too harsh the 20-year sentence he served at Spandau Prison. Speer was released from Spandau Prison in 1966. He died of a stroke in London on September 1ˢᵗ,1981.

He was 76 years old.

attention to us, my first thought, which I whispered to Zeke, "The two men who just came in and sat a few tables away, certainly could pass for Gestapo. Don't look over there, but they glanced at us when they sat down.

"You would think we would be used to these creeps by now, Jenz. After Treblinka, I don't think anything will really bother me too much again."

"Get ready to look relaxed, Zeke. The creeps are heading this way."

Chapter 33

The Gestapo Catches Up with Us

It was an interesting arrest. Both agents were pretty beefy and at least six feet in height. Their suits looked stuffed with plenty of muscle mass. One of the agents headed for our table, and the other went and stood at the only exit. As the agent approached, he unbuttoned his sport jacket, allowing us to see his rather intimidating Luger pistol in a shoulder holster.

"Good evening, gentlemen. I'm sorry to interrupt your meal, but I am Agent Krauthammer and must ask for some identification."

"We will be happy to show you an identity card, agent. But first," retorted Zeke, "could you please let us know why you need to know whom we are while dining here?"

"We have it on good authority, gentlemen, you are two individuals the Gestapo has been looking for throughout the Reich. Are you, by chance, Lieutenant Ramsgrund and Sargent Carapezza?"

"Yes," Vitali replied. "We have been working at this Wehrmacht base for over a year. If you wanted to contact us, you just had to call our boss, General Dornberger, and he would let you know you were trying to reach us."

"Two agents were sent here last year, shot back Agent Krauthammer, but they had an automobile accident and subsequent fire; they were lost in the fire."

I looked at Zeke and replied, "We are both very sorry to hear about your agents. But how can we help you now?"

"Lieutenant," the Gestapo agent declared, "We have also sent an agent from our Nordhausen office to speak to you while you were visiting the Auschwitz camp. However, he seems to have disappeared."

"I'm sure the sergeant and I are both sorry to hear about the loss or disappearance of your valuable agents, but how can we help? As you may know, the Auschwitz camp is a very dangerous place for anyone who isn't Wehrmacht or SS."

"I am sorry, Lieutenant, but the Gestapo has arrest warrants for you both. Agent Grinnell is waiting for us at the door, and two other agents are waiting for us in the van."

Fortunately, we had finished most of our dinner and I was still in a rather upbeat mood. Zeke, however, wasn't quite so pleasant. A flash of fear, then anger, registered in his eyes. He pointed directly at the agent and responded with a firmness that I hadn't heard from Zeke: "Agent Krauthammer, give us a minute to finish and pay our bill. We will then walk peaceably to your van without causing any commotion. You may wait at the door, our only exit, with Agent Grinnell."

Zeke seemed to have the situation well in hand. After seeing what we saw at Treblinka, I think nothing would bother him too much anymore.

Zeke's direct toughness seemed to placate the agent and he went and stood by the only exit to the dining facility.

Vitali immediately asked me, "What happened to the agent at the Auschwitz camp?"

"He was the same agent, Burk, from their Nordhausen office. He was giving me a bit of trouble, so he 'accidentally' bumped into an electric fence separating the barracks at the prison compound. I instructed a prisoner to strip his body of all clothing and identification and place him in the pickup truck for a trip to Crematorium One at the camp. As the captured prisoners like to say in their gallows humor, he has probably escaped 'up the chimney' by now."

"Wonderful!" remarked Zeke. But do you have any suggestions for our current situation? Now they have four agents here to make sure we are taken into custody. It looks like they intend to place us in the back of a van and take us to the nearest Gestapo facility on the mainland."

"We will do our best not to be thrown in a Gestapo prison, but I think we should go peacefully to the van. Do you have any suggestions?

"Well," replied Zeke. Even though we are wearing civilian clothes, you know, as a sergeant in the Wehrmacht, I am required to carry a firearm."

"But Zeke," I queried, "neither one of us was prepared for this!"

"Let's quietly pay our bill, said Zeke. My Walther pistol is in my ankle sock as a precautionary measure."

Zeke was obviously a very different man after our trip to the concentration camps. Perhaps it was because of him finding the love of his life. I wasn't sure, but very grateful for his forethought.

We paid our bill and walked slowly toward the two agents at the entrance to the dining establishment.

Chapter 34

A Horrifying Trip in a Gestapo Van

The Gestapo's Mercedes van was directly outside the entrance to the restaurant. It was parked as if the agents expected us to make a run for freedom. One of the agents standing outside near the passenger door actually had his pistol out and was waving it in our direction. He was yelling at us while making crude comments:

"You Jews get in the back of the van. Sit on the floor. The two seats are for the agents!

I whispered to Zeke, *"Let's wait until we are outside the gate before we make any moves. These idiots seem pretty serious."*

Zeke looked down at his left leg, where an imperceptible bulge was near the cuff. "Aren't you glad I thought to bring a little insurance to dinner?"

As a gesture of compliance and to show we were not hiding anything, we took off our jackets and put them on the floor to sit on.

The two agents in the front seat didn't even introduce themselves. I thought it might be good to judge their commitment to this arrest by whispering in the ear of the agent on the driver's side before I climbed into the van: *"The crematoria would be too good for you folks."*

It generated the desired response.

The agent became infuriated, got red-faced, and slapped me quite hard across the face. I sensed the reaction and bent slightly out of the way and let the blow sound much harsher than it was.

Although I was going to have a welt on my left cheek, I responded in a quiet, but firm and measured tone. "Agent, you have just made a careerending error. You must never again raise your hand or your voice to an SS officer."

"You swine!" was the driver's comment. He raised his hand for another blow. I grabbed his fist as it flew toward my face and held it while he finished his diatribe. **"You Jews will see how the Gestapo treats you when we get to our headquarters near Greifswald."**

I replied in a calm and measured tone, "Agent, I will have to include this incident in my report."

This infuriated the driver even more and he responded, **"I think you Jews are fortunate we haven't beaten you to a bloody pulp before we take you in for interrogation."**

I could tell Zeke was getting tired of being treated like swine, I saw him brush his cuff over his Walther PPK in his sock.

My response was meant to calm the driver down. I didn't want him to escalate the situation further. "Your future actions toward the Sargent and myself will dictate what I will include in my report."

The driver's comment was pretty cryptic but delivered in a much calmer, almost subdued voice. "You Jewish swine can put anything you want in your reports. That is if you can still write after our colleagues finish questioning you at headquarters."

Zeke and I refrained from further comments or talking until we had traversed across the base and through the gate.

In a conversational tone, I suggested to Zeke we should return to the area we were traveling so we could take in the views from the bluff overlooking the ocean. Of course, there was no bluff at the time, but the comment let Zeke know the exact location we were looking to put an end to this madness.

I thought a little conversation with Agent Krauthammer might lighten the mood for us in the back of the van.

"Agent," I started, "I am not sure you realize it, but the sergeant and I have a meeting tomorrow morning with Herr Hitler's Minister of War and Armaments. It is a 'command performance' meeting which we cannot miss."

"Lieutenant," the agent responded in a calm although measured and strained tone, "You are both going to be under detention by the Gestapo for several days, perhaps weeks. I will send a message to your superior outlining the charges against you both. This message will serve as your excuse for missing your meeting with the Minister.

Then Agent Krauthammer decided to be a little more forceful; he announced in a rather loud and almost belligerent voice, **"The Gestapo has discovered you men are traitors to the Nazi Party and to our Aryan ideals. You will be held in detention and interrogated until you tell us everything about your Jew families and where they are hiding."**

I mentioned to Zeke, "It looks like we are coming up to a beautiful stretch of scenery on the right overlooking the North Sea."

That was all Zeke needed. In one smooth motion, he bent over, grabbed his PKK Walther from his sock, and squeezed off a round that went right through Agent Krauthammer's throat. **Bang!**

The agent looked up, coughed once, and slumped over in his seat toward Agent Grinnell. Blood was spurting from a neck wound. Agent Grinnell was completely surprised when Zeke's second shot followed his first by less than two seconds.

As Agent Grinnell turned to look at Agent Krauthammer, Zeke's second shot caught him directly between his eyes in the middle of his forehead. **Bang!** His head snapped back and clunked against the inside wall of the van. His eyes were fixed and wide open with surprise. There was a blood splotch on the wall of the van where his brains exited his skull.

The agent in the passenger seat turned in his seat and was reaching for his Luger in his shoulder holster.

Zeke placed the barrel of the Walther up against the back of the passenger seat and fired two quick rounds into the agent through the seat. **Bang-Bang!** The force of the 7.65 mm. slugs threw the agent into the dash and to the floor.

The sound and smoke from the heavy slugs panicked the driver. He slammed on the brakes and turned the van onto the unpaved roadside. He was reaching for his Luger when Zeke interrupted his thoughts with two quick shots in succession.

From a kneeling position, Zeke pumped his remaining two slugs into the driver through the back of his seat. Bang-Bang! The force of the slugs hitting him in the back of the head, forced the driver's face, or what was left of it, into the windshield. The entire dashboard was awash with blood, tissue, and fragments of brains.

The emotion that stuck with me most at the time and seemed truly amazing to me: Zeke was very calm and methodical. His facial expression was close to no reaction whatsoever. His facial features remained the same as in normal conversation. My thought at the time was that the camps, especially Treblinka, had hardened this mild-tempered man, who would never harm anyone. Here Zeke had committed the murder of four Gestapo thugs in lightning-quick action without so much as a moment's hesitation.

"Zeke," I asked. "Are you okay?"

"Never better, Jenz. These thugs got exactly what they deserved. I didn't like the derogatory way they spoke to us about being Jewish. It is this hateful and demeaning speech that is fomenting a lot of this antiSemitism. I'm glad our boss, General Dornberger, isn't an anti-Semite."

"You picked up pretty quick on the code word 'bluff 'after we traversed and exited the base."

"Of course, Jenz! I'm not quite ready to read your thoughts, but your suggestion was pretty clear to me.

"Now, how do we get rid of the van with four deceased Gestapo thugs inside?"

"This should be quite interesting, Zeke. We are very near the height of the next tide here on the North Sea. As you know, the tides are quite strong on the coast. If we weigh the deceased Gestapo agents with rocks and leave all the doors and windows open, the tide should take the van on the outgoing tide. By leaving the doors open, this refuse will probably wash out and sink out to the bottom of the ocean."

"Let's find some small rocks and weigh them down," exclaimed Zeke, almost enthusiastically. The wind was quite blustery, with the surf crashing on the rocks below and against the cliff.

We weighted down the agents with rocks in their pockets and inside of their shirts.

We placed a fairly heavy rock on the accelerator pedal. I held on to Zeke as he threw the van into gear, and I pulled him clear of the van as it rolled toward the bluff overlooking the North Sea.

Chapter 35

A Meeting with the Minister of War Production

It was quite a walk back to the base. The wind always blows strong on this northern peninsula. It was almost midnight but I don't believe we were noticed by any of the local population. The only lights were at the entrance to the base. The guards initially challenged us but put up no resistance once they read over the copy of our orders which I kept with me at all times in my cover.

I know the tides and storms are very strong in the North Sea. It was my hope and prayer that the waves and current would take the van with the dead Gestapo agents far out to sea. We had opened all the doors, gas tank, and hood before driving it over the bluff overlooking the sea.

The next morning, I met Zeke in the conference room at 9:45. We were both apprehensive about the meeting with War Minister Speer. We didn't have too long to wait. The room filled up with about 80 officers and technicians; the quiet buzz stopped immediately when General Dornberger got up to introduce the Minister of Armaments and War.

"Gentlemen, good morning to you all. This morning I have the pleasure of introducing one of the Reich's brightest and hardest-working leaders.

"War Minister Speer is responsible for the development and production of all the armaments in the Reich, including the army, navy, and air-force services. It is an honor to have him here today to brief us on the progress of the war and our response to our enemies. Let me remind all of you, this is a top-secret briefing. Failure to keep the proceedings of this briefing one hundred percent confidential would require immediate incarceration in a concentration labor camp under difficult conditions.

"War Minister Speer, the microphone is yours."

Enthusiastic clapping broke out from all the officers present.

When the applause tapered off, a youngish-looking, slightly balding tall gentleman sitting in the front row got up to speak.

"Good morning, and Heil Hitler. It is a pleasure to bring you an up-to-date briefing from our Führer. I met with him yesterday, so this information is quite fresh and reliable.

"First, Herr Hitler is not totally in agreement with your amazing work here in Peenemünde. He feels our resources could be better directed on more tanks, artillery shells, and bombs. I do not totally agree with him, but I will lay out his thoughts for you.

"Here, I will go into some detail.

"A new bomb is being developed under very secret orders from our Führer. This bomb is so powerful that one detonation can level an entire city. The power of this bomb comes from the splitting of uranium atoms. Our projection for the development of this destructive bomb is probably 1947 at the earliest, almost 5 years away. Unfortunately, the Gestapo has imprisoned many of our top scientists; other key personnel have fled the country to go to our enemies. In addition, some of our Wehrmacht recruiters have deemed it necessary to send many of our key technicians and scientists to the Eastern Front to confront the Russians.

"I have met recently with General Friedrich Fromm, [*] Otto Hahn, [**] and Werner Heisenberg [***] who briefed me on German

---

[*] General Fredrich Fromm was Chief of the Army and friend of the War Minister, Speer. He was executed by firing squad by the Nazis on 12 March 1945 for turning a "blind eye" on the conspirators after the assignation attempt on Hitler on 20 July 1944. His last words were: "I always wanted the best for Germany."

[**] Otto Hahn, is well known as the "Father of the Atomic Age, was a German scientist who discovered nuclear fission. He won the Nobel Prize in Chemistry in 1944. He died at age 89 in Gottingen, W. Germany, in 1968.

[***] Werner Karl Heisenberg was a German Physicist involved with the development of Nuclear Research. He died of kidney cancer at his home in Germany on February 1st, 1976, at age 75.

atomic research. The major stumbling block to the development of this armament is the use of a cyclotron. This machine is not available yet in Germany. The only cyclotron is in Paris. The problem of security might be too big to overcome.

"If the A-4 rocket being developed here could be operational, our Fürher would be greatly encouraged. This rocket could be used to deliver this bomb to the heart of our enemies.

"Are there any questions so far?" Asked the war minister.

General Dornberger stood and announced: "Our A-4 rocket currently under development will be ready for widespread use by 1944 as long as our current funding is maintained."

"If your technicians could make a movie of an A-4 launch, it might help our Führer to consider further funding for your project here, General. I witnessed the launch of the A-4 on the 13th of June 1942, along with Field Marshal Milch and General Fromm. We were very impressed by this technological development."

General Dornberger announced, "Consider it done, Minister Speer."

"I would like to enlighten you, gentlemen, on three other recent developments which would directly involve your research here at Peenemünde.

"The first takes the V-1 weapon and incorporates the propulsion mechanism into an aircraft for the Luftwaffe. Our air force has fought bravely against the 8th air force stationed in England for almost two years. Our jet aircraft, the Me-262 * fighter plane, is slated for mass production in 1944. It flies almost two times faster than the Allied bombers and can shoot them down in large numbers.

"The second defense against the constant bombing raids by the Allies is a surface-to-air missile being developed under the code name 'Waterfall.' This is a rocket approximately 25 feet in length, capable of

---

*The Me-262 fighter aircraft was the first in the world jet aircraft. Nicknamed *Schwalbe* (Swallow), it was fully operational by the end of the war. Unfortunately for the Luftwaffe, the jet aircraft's development came too late to affect the outcome of World War II.

carrying over six-hundred pounds of explosives. It follows a directional beam up to a maximum altitude of fifty thousand feet and hits the enemy bombers with exceptional accuracy. It is still on the drawing boards, but the prototype works almost 100 percent of the time. It is unaffected by day or night, clouds, cold, or fog. I have encouraged Herr Hitler to put it into production immediately.

"In addition, we are developing a torpedo for the Kriegsmarine with tracking capabilities for the sound of enemy ships. This torpedo will follow their zig-zag motions for ensured destruction.

"These are some of the recent developments in armament production or proposals in our department."

"Please, I would be happy to take your questions."

I raised my hand after a short delay. Many of the technicians seemed reluctant to be noticed.

"Sir," I asked, "how long will it take to mass-produce the Me-262?"

"A good question, Lieutenant. We are waiting for the funding from Herr Hitler. He is very reluctant to fund anything looking like advanced technology. Sometimes I think he is stuck in the Great War Generation (WW I), which believes more artillery shells and bullets will win this war.

"It is a fact, however, unless something is done about the constant bombing of our factories and cities by the British and American bombers, our capability to wage war will be greatly diminished.

Chapter 36

A Report to General Dornberger

A few days after the meeting with the Minister of War, Speer, I was surprised in the laboratory early in the morning by a visit from General Dornberger's adjunct, Sargent Albrecht. I was still on my first cup of what was being passed around as coffee.

"Lieutenant, could you come with me to General Dornberger's office for a few moments? He would like a word with you."

"Of Course, sergeant. I will need just to cover my confidential information. Lead the way.

The sergeant led me down a long corridor to a spacious, but modestly furnished office near the back of the complex. He had me sit in a comfortable chair opposite the General's desk.

In a moment, the General came in from a small room adjacent to his office; I stood and he offered his hand for shaking hands. There was no Hitler Salute.

"Good morning, Lieutenant. Thanks for coming in this morning.

"I wanted to especially thank you and your Sargent for providing us with almost three hundred new workers from the camps. There has only been one who does not feel comfortable here and may not fit into our rigorous schedule. Perhaps you would like to talk with her before she is sent back to the Auschwitz Camp."

"Who is that, General?"

"I believe her administrative officer said her name was Zivia. However, I'm unsure if that is her first or last name.

"I will have a talk with her, General, as soon as I can later this morning."

"The prisoners you have sent us from Treblinka and Auschwitz have been hard-working and driven, Lieutenant, and equally important, healthy. I would like to thank you and your sergeant for finding terrific workers. The idea of sending families together seems to be working out quite well. The workers seem much more content. I did have a couple of questions about your report, however."

"Is there something I did not explain in the report, General?"

"Lieutenant, you have reported that all the prisoners at Treblinka are whipped, beaten, raped, and killed by gas. Did you mean they are all killed or just the unruly prisoners?"

"General, some of them are allowed to live for a short period of time to work in the kitchen, cleaning the gas chambers, or cleaning the transports that bring the prisoners into the camp. But, in the end, the thousands of people from the ghetto in Warsaw are packed into cattle cars and murdered in the first hours of their arrival at the camp."

"Certainly, Lieutenant, your report cannot be correct. There must be some sort of screening process to pick out the educated scientists, technicians, and inventors?"

"Unfortunately, no. My sergeant and I did the only screening for technical people. Some of the young, pretty women were weeded out so the guards and officers could rape and defile them, but after the guards had their way with them, they were immediately sent to the gas chambers."

"What you are telling me in this written report is barbaric, Lieutenant. Were the conditions any better at the Auschwitz camp?"

"The conditions at Auschwitz were actually worse, General. Almost all the women, even pregnant women, children, and older people, were immediately sent to the gas chambers and crematoriums.

All their life-long possessions were stolen. The men and women who looked like they could work were sent to filthy, lice-ridden barracks and fed a barely subsistent diet of thin soup.

"Defenseless pregnant women who were expecting twins were subject to experiments by a doctor named Mengele. He also experimented on handicapped children, although I'm not sure what was the nature of his experiments."

"Lieutenant, this all sounds absolutely inhumane! Can your sergeant substantiate all this material in your report?"

"Of course, General. The Sargent and I were diligent and very accurate in every aspect of our reporting."

"Lieutenant, what has become of God-fearing Germans? Although I cannot put the blame on any one person, my belief is that Reichführer Himmler has had something to do with the decrepit condition of the camps.

"I don't feel comfortable sending this report to his office. He has always wanted to worm his way into our research here at Peenemünde. This report could give him the excuse he needs to make mischief for us. For now, this report will go no higher. It will remain on a shelf in my safe.

"You are dismissed, Lieutenant, and thank you for your candor."

I returned to my desk and looked over the plans for the A-4 rocket (later known as the V-II). Zeke buzzed me on the intercom and ask if I had any arrangements for lunch.

"Vitali," I started, "I would like you to look up one of the prisoners from the Auschwitz Camp who came up on one of the buses with you. Her name is Zivia; however, I'm not sure if that is her first name or surname. I would like her to meet with both of us outside of the detainee's cafeteria in one hour. We can take our lunch after we meet with her.

Zivia and Vitali were out near the entrance of the cafeteria, where the enlisted men and detainees took their lunch. I pointed to them both and motioned them to follow me to the next building, where I knew there was a small conference room where we would have some privacy.

As soon as we sat down, Zivia started being difficult.

"And what does the SS want with me now?" she barked.

I held up my hand, palm side out, for her to stop talking.

But she persisted. **"Is it time for some sort of SS gang rape, or are you just going to slap me around until I break down?"**

At that point, slapping her around a bit did come to mind. However, I asked Vitali to speak up by pointing to him.

"Miss," Vitali started in a very reasonable and quiet tone. "Everyone who wears this uniform is not a monster. We brought you here in an effort to save your life.

"Both the Lieutenant and I know you would like to get back to your native Poland and locate your friends and family. But you have to understand Poland is a very dangerous place right now. All of Germany, indeed, most of Europe, is not safe for Jews."

Then I spoke up. "Zivia, I put you on the bus to this secret rocket base because you led me to believe you had something to contribute. Now you have a choice. You can work to improve the conditions and work at this base or you can be returned to the Auschwitz Camp. Your time there would apt to be very short and end up with you being murdered by gas and being cremated. No one would know of your existence."

Finally, Zivia spoke in a normal tone of voice. "It is just very difficult to work for a regime that has destroyed my family, my city, and my country."

"Both of us," Vitali spoke up, "have lost friends and neighbors to the Gestapo. We are well aware of what this regime is capable of inflicting on decent Germans and the Polish population. All we are asking you is to work with a certain attitude and know this war cannot go on forever. The Nazi forces in the East have had a change of circumstances. Until this war is over, your chances of survival and reuniting with your friends and family, are much better here, working for the enemy.

"Please, Zivia, go take your mid-day meal; and believe me when I say this. Your food here at this Nazi army base is considerably better for you than anything you would ever see in the Auschwitz Camp.

"In addition, and this is not meant as a threat, your attitude and behavior have been noticed at the highest level at this Wehrmacht base. If you are not fully aware of the danger you are in, let me assure you, if you continue with a lot of negative social behavior, within one week, you will be escorted back to the death camp."

Chapter 37

A Chance to See the Love of My Life

I desperately wanted to see Ilsa before the Christmas holidays. I knew it would be almost impossible to get leave at this stage of the war, especially since I had a pretty good idea of what was happening to General Paulus and the Sixth Army in Stalingrad. I wrote to my dear Ilsa to see if she could come to Peenemünde. I discussed the situation with my immediate superior and it was arranged to get Ilsa lodging in the married officer's quarters. There would be no cost for the lodging, but she would have to pay for her own transportation to and from our rocket base.

Ilse arrived at the end of November. It was wonderful to be able to spend some time with her after work. Zeke, Ilse, and I would take lunch and most dinners together. I didn't trust the Gestapo, so we kept most conversations very general and quiet in our room and in the officer's dining area.

When we were alone, we talked about how most of our manufacturing facilities had moved to the Nordhausen area to avoid further attacks from the British. I told Ilse Zeke that I would have to move to the new facilities there next month.

We also discussed the progress of the war and our plans for after the war. Ilse said that because of the Allied bombing of the major cities in Northern Germany, including the airplane manufacturing facilities in Hanover, living near the city was dangerous and unnerving.

Although Ilse's family home was outside the city, the bombs were often too close for comfortable living. If it were a cloudy or rainy nighttime raid, often the bombs would fall outside of their designated drop area. In addition, the wind would sometimes carry the bombs far from their intended target.

Ilsa talked about one raid on the 9th of October 1943, just last month. This raid brought terror and destruction to Hanover's airplane and rubber manufacturing plants.

"Over 700 planes attacked the industrial areas of our city. The oil refineries, gun manufacturers, and metal-fabricating plants were targeted. The raid lasted from one in the morning until just before two O'clock. Almost an hour of continuous terror bombing of Hanover. My parents and I stayed in the cellar all night; the house was continuously shaking.

"The next day was as dark as night, even though the sun was an orange ball in the sky." Ilsa continued. "My parents are considering moving to my grandmother's summer home in Denmark just to escape the bombing and smoke."

I tried to comfort Ilsa with calming words and caresses. Talking about the end of the war seemed to make her feel better. She also brought up the topic of having a family. I told her, "Germany might not be the safest place to bring up children after the war, but I very much want to spend the rest of my life with my dearest friend and if God blesses us, children would be a wonderful gift."

The conversation seemed to calm her down because she started undressing me slowly. I wanted to make sure the room was secure, so in addition to locking the door, I pulled a heavy chest of drawers in front of it.

When she was about halfway finished undressing me, I suggested we finish undressing and get into bed.

"I'm sorry, Jenz," she replied. "It has been many months since we have been together, I have to get used to your wonderful body again."

She did give my privates a brief squeeze as she pulled off my trousers.

She could tell I was getting a little excited.

I went to start unbuttoning her shirt. She stopped me, saying, "I can undress myself, once I get you into bed."

She then stripped off my underwear and, in a firm, but friendly voice, declared, "Now you, sir, get into bed."

She started to undress herself at a slow, almost glacial, pace. She bent over, put her hand on my chest, kissed my stomach, and pinched my nipple very gently, but firmly. I was on fire.

"Please hurry," I stammered. "It has been a long time since I have held you!"

Her retort, "It has been a long time since I have held you, and I'm looking forward to being in your arms all night."

She kept finding little things to do. After folding her clothing, she looked at her nails, brushed her hair, and rearranged her shoes. I kept moving around on the bed and she recognized I might be going over the edge.

She finally said, "Relax, darling; aren't I worth waiting for?"

I knew what she was doing. She knew she was driving me crazy with desire.

She very slowly pulled back the covers and slipped in beside me. She could tell I was very excited.

"I love holding you, Ilsa. It seems like it has been such a long time. This last assignment has taken Zeke and me to places which have been difficult to describe and even more difficult to understand."

"I know these past few months have been difficult for everyone in Germany, but tonight let's just talk about us, cooed Ilsa.

She was shaking a little, perhaps because of the coolness of the room, or because of a little nervousness about being together again. My entire body was quivering. My dear Ilsa was trembling as she said, "Dearest Jenz, I want to be with you forever. I am so sorry I shared you with my friends while you were at Hitler Camp. I never wanted to; my friends talked me into it."

I ran my hand down her back to her backside. She whimpered slightly, then moaned, "Oh Jenz, it is so good to be back in your arms."

Chapter 38

A Knock on the Door

Ilsa and I were sleeping deeply and soundly. I was in dreamland, thinking about what a wonderful woman Ilsa had been for me. She seemed to be able to anticipate my every thought. We were both very happy.

All of a sudden, my eyes were instantly opened. Something had awakened me. I listened for a while and heard nothing. I lay there quietly, wondering what could have disturbed my sleep. The room was pitch-black, with just a sliver of light coming from underneath the door.

Then I heard it. Someone was trying to quietly turn a key in the door. Was it an intruder? I quietly slipped out of bed. There was a definite chill in the room. Ilsa was sleepily awakening and asked, "Jenz, what is it?"

I put my finger to my lips and whispered in her ear, "Darling, someone is at the door. Please do not move or make any noise. Quietly get up and slip under the bed from the side away from the door. I want whoever is there to think we are still sleeping."

I dressed quietly, including my officer's coat, boots, and leather gloves. I had no idea who was on the other side of the door, but I wanted to be ready no matter who it was. The Gestapo usually knocked loudly late at night. And yet, there it was…

Knock, Knock, Knock, in quick secession. It sounded like something metallic was hitting the door. My immediate thought was … the barrel of a firearm!

The metallic sound on the door was somewhat unnerving, but nothing compared to what happened next.

There was a crash against the door, and the door flew open!

But only a few inches, because the bureau blocked the entry.

Two burly men, one of whom was rather beefy looking, eventually forced their way into our room. After sliding the bureau to one side, they both looked angry. Light filtered into the room from the corridor. The one with a pistol in his hand was almost awkward looking, tall and ugly; the other wasn't too tall, perhaps five and a half feet or so, but had hands the size of dinner plates.

The one with the pistol was closer to six feet. He declared as he pointed his weapon at me, "You are under arrest. We are from the Greifswald Gestapo office. We demand to know what happened to our agents and their vehicle. They were sent here a few days ago to arrest you and Sargent Carapezza."

I spoke up in a calm and almost soothing voice. "Agent, I am not sure what you are talking about. Furthermore, I have no idea where your agents could be located now."

The ugly agent cocked his pistol and aimed it at my face.

I should explain myself. There are two predicaments that can get me a little peeved. The first is a drop in my blood sugar. Supper had been a little on the light side because I wanted to be over with it and alone with Ilse. I would have been fine, had the agents not interrupted our sleep.

Although I was a little annoyed about being awakened in the middle of the night, nothing makes me angrier than a cocked pistol thrust in my face.

Agent Ugly had three things going against him at this moment: First, he had awakened us in the middle of the night, exacerbating my problem with my good humor and low blood sugar. Second, he made the mistake of pointing a loaded and cocked firearm at me. And third, he was being extremely impolite toward me and my best friend in the world, hiding under the bed.

"Agent," I advised him, "I would suggest you never point a loaded weapon in the direction of any SS officer in uniform. Your actions here this evening could be a career-ending mistake. Furthermore, I am a little on the hungry side; it is best not to disturb me when I'm hungry."

Then dinner-plate hands started to raise his voice and stutter. **"You, …you, Lieutenant, are the one who has made a career-ending error. You Jews have done something with our agents and their vehicle. We need to know where they are, NOW!**

I came to the conclusion that there was no sense in debating these two despicable pieces of trash any longer. I did not want their yelling to disturb other guests sleeping in the barrack. If I grabbed for his weapon, it could discharge.

I certainly did not want to take the chance of a stray bullet going anywhere near my dear friend and the love of my life.

"Sirs," I started, "let me try to explain something to you."

I thought it best to keep them talking in a subdued voice while a distraction came to my mind.

"Gentlemen," I said in a low, very calm voice. "You know speakers monitor these rooms through the phones. The conversation goes directly to the duty officer at the front desk."

Dinner plate shot back, **"There was no one at the front desk when we came into the quarters."**

He was still much too loud and I knew I had to do something to shut them up.

I decided to raise their blood pressure and anger them so they wouldn't think through what I was about to do.

In a demeaning tone, I responded. "The night duty officer makes rounds around the officer's quarters specifically to keep out creeps like you two. Right after that little soliloquy, I nudged the door shut with my shoulder and stepped a little closer to Agent Ugly.

As I closed the gap between us, the agent raised the pistol and waved it in my face. He had underestimated my reach, however.

I quickly grabbed his pistol by placing my thumb behind the trigger with my left hand. My right elbow came up and slammed into his left cheek. I could hear the crunch of his infraorbital bone below his eye.

With my left hand and arm, I brought his pistol under my right armpit with the muzzle facing in back of me. I then wheeled on my right foot so the muzzle was aimed at Agent Dinner Plates.

I released my thumb guard hold on Agent Ugly's trigger and placed my forefinger over Agent Ugly's trigger finger, and fired two quick slugs into Agent Dinner Plates.

The first slug went through the agent's throat, approximately in the vicinity of his Adam's Apple, directly through his larynx. The second slug caught him under his jaw as his head snapped back from the first chunk of lead and did not exit his cranium.

By placing the firearm under my armpit, the sound was muffled somewhat to sound like two quick coughs, but still annoyingly loud.

As Agent Ugly dropped his pistol, my arm went around his neck. I squeezed hard, heard his vertebrae snap, his temporal bone being crushed, and then proceeded to squeeze his breath and life out of him.

Poor Ilsa was terrified. Her head popped up from the other side of the bed when she heard the firearm discharge.

"Are you okay, Jenz?" She asked.

"Let's just say I'm a lot better than the two creeps on the floor."

Ilsa stood and viewed the two very dead Gestapo agents beside the bed.

"Mine Gott im Himmel, Jenz, what happened?"

"They came here looking for trouble, and they found it!"

"What will we do with them, Jenz? Do we have to call anyone?"

"First, we will crack the window to get rid of the gunpowder odor. Then we will wait a few minutes to see if the noise aroused any interest from our neighbors. Hopefully, most of the folks in the quarters here are sound sleepers. After about a one-hour wait, we will load them one at a time into their automobile trunk and drive them to a drop-off spot. I think I know of a good place."

We quietly opened the door and brought Agent Ugly out to his car wrapped in a sheet. Agent Dinner Plates had the keys in his pocket. We took him out to the trunk of their car and placed him on top of the other agent.

I drove the agent's automobile out the back gate with Ilsa following me. This would allow less suspicion when we came back in just one automobile through the front gate quite early the next morning.

We drove to the bluff, where the van and the four agents had disappeared into the froth below..

I put both agents in the front seat, weighted down their bodies with rocks in their pockets, lowered the windows, and put the car in gear for the short trip over the edge.

"Will the car ever be found?" asked Ilsa.

"I don't think so," I replied. "But it might be a good idea for you and your family to move to your grandmother's summer home in Denmark because of the constant bombing."

I put my love on a bus the next day to start her journey back to Hanover.

Chapter 39

A Surprise Note from the Commanding Officer

The morning when Ezekiel and I were notified that the General, who was in charge of the entire base at Peenemünde, Major General Walter Dornberger, wanted to see the both of us together, we couldn't help but get nervous. Zeke was almost apoplectic. He thought we would be arrested and just executed by firing squad if we were lucky.

I have to admit, the firing squad was a distinct possibility. But then Zeke cautioned, "Let's at least go to the meeting with an open mind. We can always prepare for the worst. However, I would like to see Adiya again before we meet him."

I wasn't sure if Treblinka or Adiya had changed Zeke; either way, he was a changed man. His attitude was even better than mine.

I admit, it was a grey overcast day; even at midday, the amount of daylight here in northern Germany was limited. Perhaps the gloom was affecting my mood.

"Zeke, we have to face up to the fact, the general might have discovered our cover. The Gestapo has probably been investigating us for a while now. It would not be unusual for them to contact the leadership of this base to get additional information on the scientists and personnel who are working here."

Later in the morning, we received our second shock. The general's sergeant came to my work desk with a hand-written envelope and said, "Lieutenant, the General would request you and Sargent Carapezza meet him at the address in the enclosed sealed envelope this evening. Both of our names were on the outside of the envelope with a note under our names: *Hand Deliver.* Please notify your sergeant because he wasn't at his desk when I entered his office.

I immediately rang Sargent Carapezza on the inter-office phone, but there was no answer. Then I remembered he was interested in seeing Adiya before meeting the general, so I immediately opened the envelope.

The note from the General read: *Lieutenant Ramsgrund, Sargent*

Carapezza: Please be advised to meet me this evening @ 6 pm inside the entrance to the Klinikum der Universität, Universitätsumedizen, Ferdinand-Sauerbruch-Strasse, 17489, Greifswald. Civilian Dress. Gen. Dornberger.

When I located Zeke, he was talking quietly with Adiya in the antiroom in front of the cafeteria. They were the only two people in the room.

Adiya was stunningly beautiful, even in her work clothes. I didn't have to fantasize about how she looked without her clothes; I had already seen her without her clothes at Treblinka. I immediately felt a little ashamed of myself and greeted them with a warm hello.

I was probably the only person on the planet who wouldn't get a perturbed look from either of them while they were in deep conversation. They both offered me a chair. "Please join us, Jenz," said Ezekiel.

"Here, sit between us," chimed in Adiya.

I apologized for interrupting them but handed Zeke the note as I sat down.

Zeke studied the note for about a minute. His comment, "What do you think this means, Jenz?"

"I wish I knew, Vitali."

"Do you mind if Adiya reads it? She knows we have a meeting."

"Not at all. But please, Adiya, keep the contents confidential. It will be much safer for all of us if this is kept very secret."

"What is your best guess, Jenz?"

"It is a little worrisome that the General wants to see us in such a short time period. It is encouraging that the meeting is off-base and in civilian attire. There will probably be no listening devices in the hospital.

"However, and I certainly do not want to alarm either of you, but, if he wants us arrested and gone forever from the secret rocket center and the Wehrmacht, this might be an opportune time and place to be rid of us forever."

Zeke had a more positive opinion. "First, we have little choice but to attend the meeting, no matter the consequences. And, second, although the general always seems to make each decision 'by the book,' he has also had an almost paternalistic attitude toward his scientists and officers under his command.

"We should make ourselves ready to catch the 3 O'clock bus to Greifswald!"

"Vitali, I am going to leave you two alone for a while. I'm going to wrap up my work for the day and change into a suit for the meeting.

"I will meet you at the front gate for the 3 pm. bus for Greifswald."

Chapter 40

A Curious Meeting at the Hospital in Greifswald

Zeke and I were not only apprehensive and worried about meeting with the commanding officer but also resigned – because there was nothing we could do to affect the outcome of a face-to-face meeting with the general.

We took a bus from the base to Berthold-Beitz-Platz in Greifswald. The bus let us off directly in front of the main city library. Since the bus ride only took a little less than an hour, we decided to go into the library to think out exactly what we were going to say to the general based on what he wanted to talk about.

We went to one of the library conference rooms, but our conversations only enhanced our sense of foreboding. We had no idea exactly what General Dornberger wanted, or if we were going to be arrested. We decided it would be better just to respond as best we could to any accusations or predicaments we might run into.

We walked the three-and-a-half blocks to the Klinikum main entrance. During our walk, we were met by some icy stares from citizens not used to seeing military-age men walking around in civilian clothing. We saw no evidence of Allied or Russian bombings; the streets were clean and well-kept.

Inside the entrance to the Klinikum, we introduced ourselves to an older woman at the desk; she told us to wait, and that someone would be with us shortly. She directed us to sit in a waiting area off to the right of the main desk area. The pleasant surroundings and plush chairs did little to ease our discomfort.

The hospital had a mixture of odors that did nothing to allay our sense of trepidation and unease. There was a whiff of cleaning products mixed with a distinct medicine smell. We were almost 15 minutes early, so we sat down to wait for something to happen.

After a few minutes, a middle-aged man in a white clinic coat appeared at the front desk. The woman at the desk pointed in our direction. Zeke whispered to me in an almost too-loud breath, "My Gott, Jenz, they are going to do medical experiments on us!"

My retort was, "relax, Zeke. This isn't Auschwitz." *I just wished I was one hundred percent convinced of my response.* I knew this meeting posed a danger to Zeke and me, but I had no idea how to avoid the whole problem. Were we about to meet the Gestapo, Doctor Mengele, or something even more dire?

The White Coat took us to a bank of elevators, extended his arm for us to enter first, and pushed the top button. Unfortunately, I could tell what Zeke was thinking: *Great, they are going to throw us off the top floor and claim an accident!*

White Coat again extended his arm for us to get off ahead of him and led us down a corridor with lights gleaming off the polished tile floor. It was a little like being led into an operating theater. Zeke and I looked at each other; our facial expressions showed uncertainty and dread. The situation was a little disconcerting because White Coat never uttered even one word.

White Coat stopped in front of a room with a sign announcing the Executive Dining Room. He opened the door and White Coat ushered us in with a wave of his arm. The door made an audible click as it closed behind us. Part of me wanted to immediately turn around and check if the door had been locked; White Coat had disappeared.

The room appeared empty. The subdued lighting, plush carpeting, and beautifully appointed walls with elegant spotlighted paintings were in stark contrast with the rest of the almost too-clean hospital. It took a moment for our eyes to adjust to the subdued light.

The handsome furniture was polished to a mirror-like shine that exuded opulence in an age of scarcity in the Reich. The lavishly appointed seating was plush and comfortable looking. Only one person was seated back to us in the middle of the room at a table with a white linen tablecloth covering the highly polished surface.

Major General Walter Dornberger rose to greet us as we walked over to him. He extended his arm and shook hands with Zeke and me. There was no Hitler salute and no Heil Hitler greeting.

He offered, "Gentlemen, thanks for coming. My apologies for the meeting space. My colleague is in charge of this hospital and assured me there were no listening devices or other interruptions that would disturb our meeting. He was the one who ushered you here.

"I will get right to the point. As you know, we lost one of our eminent scientists during the air-raid bombing the night of August 17th- 18th * last summer. This raid, by the British, is forcing our now not-so-secret facility to move to an underground gypsum mine near Nordhausen, Germany. Reichsführer Himmler tells me the facility and base office housing should be ready next month on the 1st.

"Unfortunately, the British air raid also killed Dr. Thiel ** and his family. They were taking shelter during the raid in a slit trench in front of their home in Karlshagen. The bomb explosion killed the doctor, his wife, and their two children.

"The loss of Dr. Walter Thiel will be difficult to replace. He and other scientists were the driving force in our space exploration program with the A-4 rocket motor. Although we have had many launch failures, the rocket is becoming more reliable.

"Now that the motor for the A-4 is becoming better tested and more predictable, Reichsführer Himmler seems to want a more prominent role in our rocket development as a war weapon. Dr. Thiel

---

*The raid by the Royal Air Force, on the night of the 17th-18th August 1943, destroyed much of the launching and testing facilities at the secret rocket facilities at the Wehrmacht base at Peenemünde. The army moved the base out of the reach of the Russian and Allied bombers to the geographic center of Germany near the town of Nordhausen.

**Dr. Thiel was a key scientist at the secret rocket base in Peenemünde, Northern Germany. He was one of the first space exploration pioneers to be inducted into the International Space Hall of Fame in Alamogordo, New Mexico, USA, in 1976.

disagreed with the Reichsführer, and tried to resign from the program the day before he was killed."

I decided to ask a question by raising a finger with the query. "General, who do you think can replace Doctor Thiel?"

"A good question, Lieutenant. Dr. Thiel and I were not getting along too well with the Reichsführer. Dr. Thiel complained Himmler was spending too much time trying to direct our research, and his presence actually was slowing down our progress."

Chapter 41

Avoiding Disaster

"General, surely there is a scientist in all the Reich, who could replace the expertise of one of our key personnel," I asked.

"Yes, Lieutenant, but many of our scientists have fled to other countries because of the programs our Führer and Reichsführer Himmler set in place. I have asked Dr. von Braun * whom he would suggest. His comment, 'It would be wonderful if we could get Dr. Einstein ** back from America.

"Our best guess is that with Einstein leading our nuclear program, our possession of an atomic bomb would be sometime in 1947. Our Führer and Himmler are so anti-Semitic that it is a little like the prosecution of a war with one hand tied behind our back. Many of our best scientists are Jewish and among the missing. Himmler has basically run them out of the country or imprisoned them.

"Himmler even placed von Braun under arrest earlier this year, when I was off the base, just because he felt he was too invested in space travel and not in weaponizing the A-4 rocket. In addition, now the A-4 rocket is being perfected with successive excellent test results, Himmler seems to want to take credit for our progress."

*Wernher von Braun was the co-designer of the V-2 Rocket. He defected to America at the end of WW II along with several of his fellow scientists under a code-named "Operation Paperclip." This group of rocket engineers and scientists developed the US Space program and the Saturn V Rocket responsible for the US moon landing on the 16th of July, 1969. Dr. von Braun retired as a vice-president of Fairchild Industries in January 1977, and died from pancreatic cancer on 16 June 1977 in Alexandria, Virginia. He was 65 years old.

**Dr. Albert Einstein was a German-born theoretical physicist. He was visiting the United States in 1933 when the new German (Nazi) government was elected. Since Einstein disagreed with the newly-elected German government, he decided to stay in the United States. Although he objected to the use of nuclear weapons, he alerted President Roosevelt of the German progress in developing an atomic bomb in 1940 and encouraged nuclear research in America.

"What could we do, General Dornberger, to help ensure Himmler does not slow the development of the testing of the A-4 rocket motor?"

Vitali looked at me as I asked the question because he knew we were doing everything we could to slow down or delay the rocket's actual launch date.

The General responded in a serious tone. "Please, gentlemen, avoid contact with our Reichsführer. He is an extremely dangerous man."

Then he hit Vitali and me right between the eyes with his next statement.

"Because of all the Gestapo inquiries at our base, he may suspect you are both Jewish!"

A look of abject terror flashed across our faces before the General raised his hand off the table, palm out and interjected. "I don't care about your religion. I do care that you help run our base and the new facility near Nordhausen with professionalism and efficiency."

Both Vitali and I assured the General that we would do our best to keep our departments running smoothly. But then I asked a simple question. "Sir, how did you come to know Vitali and I were Jewish?"

General Dornberger then announced, "I have several Jewish officers and scientists working for the Wehrmacht. None have been disloyal to the Reich.

"I consider the Gestapo organization, as it has evolved, to basically be a criminal organization. Each time these criminals have enquired about you two individuals, nothing has come of it. The agents of this organization seem to disappear or lose interest in pursuing either of you. Their interest was my first clue, you were probably Jewish.

"I will confide one piece of information to you, gentlemen, of which you may not be aware. I was taken prisoner in the Great War in France. It was two Jewish young men, much like yourselves, who saved me from execution and helped me survive those difficult years. Ever since that time, probably before you were born, I have felt a family's religion is a private matter between the family and God.

"The second definitive clue was your report on the labor camps in Poland. I thought at the time I read over your report that nothing like this could be happening in our country. So, I called the commandant of each camp and asked some pointed questions. I was wrong. Your report was, unfortunately, right on target. Innocent Germans and Poles are being murdered in alarming numbers. A corrupt and debased country does not deserve a world leadership position, let alone to win a major war.

"The defeat of the Sixth Army at Stalingrad last winter was the defining blow for the Reich. Our Führer would not allow General Paulus to withdraw in a timely manner after being surrounded. The result was a loss of almost two hundred and fifty thousand men with all their equipment.

"Many divisions from our western and southern front have been shifted to counter the Russian threat, leaving our entire country vulnerable."

With this rather shocking statement, the General pointed to the kitchen door. A waiter in the window immediately came toward our table with covered trays containing heaping plates of hot food and asked us for our drink order.

As soon as the waiter departed, the General warned us. "I think it is now obvious why I wanted an off-base meeting. Nothing about this meeting or its' contents can ever be discussed with anyone at any time. Is that clear?"

In unison, Zeke and I ensured in a quiet, but firm tone, "Yes, Sir."

Chapter 42

The War Comes Closer to the Reich

As Zeke, myself, and most of the rest of the personnel at the Rocket Center had moved to the Nordhausen area, it was pretty clear the Russians had gained a foothold on the Eastern Front. Operation Barbarossa * had come to a complete and utter halt with the defeat of the Sixth Army during the cruel and brutally cold winter at Stalingrad in late January of 1943.

Everyone in senior leadership involved in the development and manufacturing of the V-I and V-II missiles at the gypsum mine near Nordhausen was even more nervous when the German Army led by von Manstein ** was defeated at Kursk *** in a famous battle of artillery and tanks beginning on the fifth of July, 1943 to August first, approximately 280 miles south-west of Moscow. The battle represented the first successful summer battle by the Red Army.

---

*Operation Barbarossa was the code name for the German invasion of the Soviet Union. It began on the 22nd of June 1941.

**Eduard von Manstein was a German Field Marshall who commanded the Wehrmacht on the Eastern Front. He disagreed with Hitler on many strategic orders for the war effort and, at one point, was quoted as saying, "Can't someone fire five bullets into that man's mouth?" He was convicted of war crimes in 1949 but only served 4 years of an 18-year sentence. He passed away in Munich in 1973. He was 85 years old.

***Kursk was a decisive victory for the Russian Army. They deployed 1.3 million men and women, 3600 tanks, 20,000 artillery pieces, and 2792 aircraft. The German response was hampered by the Allied bombing of its major cities, the Allied invasion of Italy, and the threat of Allied landings in France. It was a decisive Red (Russian) Army victory, beginning their final march into Berlin in the spring of 1945 and ending with the unconditional surrender of all German forces.

In June of 1943, I remember Ezekiel asking me an important question. "Jenz, in your estimation, how long will it take for the Red Army to get to the Vistula?" *

"That's an excellent question, Zeke. It depends on developing our defenses and probably using advanced weapons, like the V-II. ** We have done everything possible to slow the development and production of these weapons, and we have to be cautious in our new center here in Mittelwerk.

"My further concern is the development of the Atom Bomb discussed with us by our Minister of War, Speer. The combination of the V-II missile and this particular bomb would be a war-winning combination for the Reich, but an absolute catastrophe for the rest of the world. We must do whatever is necessary to make sure we can slow or halt the further development and testing of the missile."

"Jenz, be very careful. Between the Gestapo and the scientists at our new location, we have to really be on our guard. I'm reasonably sure the Gestapo has an office somewhere near Nordhausen, and could well be watching us, or listening to our every word.

There was a bit of "war hysteria" in the air. The civilian population of nearby Nordhausen was very aware of the pain the Red Army was capable of inflicting on our citizens if they invaded our country.

One late fall evening Zeke and I thought we would try a little break from our routine of taking dinner at the cafeteria mess hall. The food wasn't nearly as good as the on-base cafeteria in Peenemünde. We were out walking to our automobile and away from any possible eavesdropping by the Gestapo when Zeke said something that made me ponder our efforts. "Jenz, I think we have done all we can to ensure the Vengeance Weapons are not the deciding factor in a victory for the

---

*The Vistula River, although in Poland, was considered by Germans at this time as part of the Reich. The battle of the Vistula, in January 1945 was another decisive victory for the Red Army. The German Army was outnumbered 5-1. In another 15 days, the Red Army had advanced to the Odor River, a mere 43 miles from undefended Berlin.

**The development of the V-II rocket-powered missile, the world's first long-range ballistic missile, was fully operational by the summer of 1944. Over 3000 of these missiles were launched against the Allies, primarily London, and Antwerp, before the end of the war, killing an estimated 9000 civilian and military personnel.

However, over 12,000 Jewish forced laborers died while testing and manufacturing these missiles.

Reich or for the Nazis. Although the V-II is a monster weapon at over 5 stories tall, von Braun initially developed it for space travel."

"Yes, Zeke, but it can travel over 200 miles in five minutes without detection and it is indefensible. And, the Reich is building over 3000 of these super-sonic weapons."

"I agree, Jenz, it is a very dangerous weapon, but it cannot carry enough destructive power to justify the expense of the rocket – unless you factor in the possibility of the atom bomb being secretly developed and made ready to ride this monster."

"I believe your correct, Zeke. Our 'improvements' with the electrical system and fuel mix have made the rockets less accurate and more complicated. We can hope the development of the atom bomb is only a pipe dream for the twisted Nazi mind!"

"There is one thing we could do, Zeke, but I agree, it is too dangerous now to try to alter the fuel or electrical systems."

"What do you suggest, Jenz?"

"I think we have a working relationship with General Dornberger. I am going to send him a memo proposing we move some of the V-II missiles to our base in northern Denmark at Aalborg. Simply altering the range of these monsters would put them in an ideal position for targeting London or Moscow. Our enemies would never know where the missiles came from or what sort of weapon actually caused the destruction.

"In addition, you and I could get a few of these monsters out of circulation, by somehow making them non-functioning once we get them to the Nazi base at Aalborg."

"Let's discuss possible actions over dinner in Nordhausen."

Chapter 43

⟡

The Gestapo Follows us to Nordhausen

"Zeke, I hate to bring this to your attention but a black sedan has been following us for the past few miles since we left the base. Don't turn around, but get a look in the mirror."

"You might think it has Gestapo written all over it, Jenz. Should we try to lose them?"

"I'm pretty sure they would just harass us at dinner or in some other public place, Zeke. Although we are in civilian clothes, did you bring your insurance weapon?"

"I did happen to load it and pack it in my sock."

"Terrific; let's pull over on a desolate stretch of road in a wooded area and see if they stop with us or just keep going. There could be a logical explanation for them being behind us."

As we pulled to the side of the road, it looked like the black sedan was going to drive right by us. However, as it was passing us, the driver slammed on the brakes and pulled directly in front of our automobile.

Four men got out of the car!

One was carrying a long gun. Zeke said, "I think it might be a shotgun." The other three had drawn pistols. It was getting dusk and the shadows made it difficult to recognize anyone or determine the type or model of the long-gun.

Zeke leaned toward me and, in an attempt at humor, said, "This might be difficult to explain to the General."

"With four of them in the automobile," Jenz continued, "I'm not sure if they want to take us into custody or just murder us on this lonely stretch of roadway. Let's err on the side of caution and not let these criminals shackle us in any way. I will get out of the car first and talk with them. Perhaps you could stay in the car until they make their intentions clear.

"I will stay with you in the car as long as possible. Please cock your pistol, but keep it out of sight until the last minute. I would recommend taking out the long-gun criminal first."

"Be careful, Jenz; they don't look at all friendly.

As I looked back on this incident, it reminded me of a movie I had seen later in the States. I had a "Bonnie and Clyde" moment, even though at that time I had never even heard of those bank robbers. I certainly didn't want Zeke and I too mirror their outcome and demise!

Zeke had placed his hat in his hand and it neatly concealed his pistol.

I got out of the car and asked in a firm voice, **"What can I do for you gentlemen?"**

Trying to be friendly was an obvious mistake.

The tallest criminal, probably their leader, cocked his pistol, aimed it at my face and yelled, "get down on the ground and don't move!"

My mother had always warned me not to try to make friends while I was hungry. This unfortunate idiot was trying to arrest me while I had an empty stomach. I was going to try to explain to him I always get a little testy when I'm hungry, but he looked like he might not understand.

So, I pointed to the flat ground out on the road and took a step closer to the tallish Gestapo agent with the cocked pistol. This put me within reach of his firearm.

"Would you like me to lie down on the paved road?" I said while pointing to the road behind the Gestapo agent.

Ezekiel sensed what I was doing and exited the automobile holding his firearm in his right hand covered with his hat.

"Fine," he yelled. **"Just get down on your knees and then flat on the ground!"**

He glanced at the flat road behind him as he was yelling at me. He must have considered how close he was to me because he started to step back while yelling.

His backward glance was all the time I needed.

My right hand flew to his firearm, and my little finger lodged between the firing hammer pin and the bullet. He pulled the trigger, but my finger wouldn't allow a discharge of the firearm.

I shoved the barrel of the pistol under his chin, re-cocked the pistol, and squeezed his finger holding the trigger.

Bang!

A large chunk of the back of his head flew off.

During this commotion, the criminal with the long gun started to swing the weapon in my direction. Zeke put a chunk of lead from his "insurance weapon" directly into the Long Gun's left temple. The sudden jolt to the head caused a discharge from his firearm. The explosion of the shotgun took the lower part of the right leg off one of the other agents from the knee down.

That agent was down and writhing on the ground.

I pulled the sidearm from the agent who had yelled at me while he was headed to the deck in a heap.

I placed one quick round into the chest of the last agent standing and then carefully placed a lead bullet into his brain and another round into the back of the head of the agent writhing, whimpering, and pleading on the ground. At the time, I was thinking of just putting him out of his misery. If I had waited another couple of minutes, he would have bled out through what was left of his lower right leg.

We placed all the dead agents in the trunk of their automobile and drove it deep into the woods. After covering it with some brush, we headed back to our car on the side of the road.

As we drove slowly through Nordhausen, very few people were about. Although it was still early evening, none of the restaurants or shops seemed open. It was a cool fall evening, but not cold enough to keep everyone inside. We went back to the small eatery where we had eaten lunch in the spring, but the small sign for the "Gashouse Restaurant" was no longer in the window. We decided to try knocking on the door.

Chapter 44

⟿∘⟳∘⟾

A Surprising Dinner in Nordhausen

A prolonged but gentle knocking brought the owner's very pretty sixteen-year-old daughter to the door. I'm not sure she recognized us at first; we were out of uniform. She started to tell us they were closed at night. Ezekiel and I enjoyed a wonderful, if meager, lunch there last spring.

The daughter's name was Greta. On our first visit to her father's restaurant, she had begged us to take her with her because of the family's fear of the Russians invading their country. Everyone in the little town had by now heard about the disastrous battle at Kursk and knew the Russians, led by Marshal Georgy Zhukov [*] and Marshal Ivan Konev, [**] were almost to the Vistula River and on the march to Berlin.

The Wehrmacht (German Army) had a total of 450,000 men who were defending against the Red Army of 2,203,000 men and women hungry for revenge. The Red Army also had almost 14,000 heavy artillery pieces and over 2000 Katyusha Rocket Launchers (also called Stalin's Organs) against the German Army's approximately 4000 artillery pieces.

Zeke asked a question in a very gentle voice. "Are you Greta?"

A look of surprise and astonishment came over her face. At first, she looked confused, and then asked: "Do I know you?"

---

[*]Marshal Georgy Konstantinovich Zhukov, was the general leading the Red Army to the 1ˢᵗ Belorussia Front in the Warsaw area of Poland.

[**]Marshal Ivan Stepanovich Konev, was the general leading the Red Army to the 1ˢᵗ Ukrainian Front in the south.

"Greta," Zeke replied in a caring but quiet voice, "we had lunch here last spring when you and your dad were working the restaurant. Remember, when we were talking about escaping the Reich, you asked us to take you with us?"

"Oh!" she cried. "Of course. I recognize you now. One of you was wearing the SS uniform at the time. Have you come to take me with you?"

"Greta," I emphasized with some quiet firmness. "We came to try to get a little dinner at a local restaurant. It would be impossible for us to take you with us, but we do have some information for you and your family to escape before the Red Army arrives in Nordhausen.

"Why," I asked, "are all the eating establishments closed at this hour?"

"Please come in." Greta opened the door wide for us and we entered what was once a cozy dining room.

"Very few places are open for eating now because no one can afford to eat out at a restaurant. And many of the local townspeople are trying to make a way to flee ahead of the Russian invasion into our country.

"I will talk with my father and see if we can prepare a light supper for you both. **But, please tell me, why is there so much fear about the Russian Army?**"

There was no meat in the thin vegetable soup, but we did enjoy a hard, dark bread for dinner. When we soaked the bread in the soup, it was quite delicious. We were grateful Greta and her father could provide us with a meal.

I then tried to explain why it would be a good idea for the families to move ahead of a Red Army invasion. It was obvious, Greta, her father, and probably most of the townspeople or German citizens hadn't heard of the Einsatzgruppen [*] groups that terrorized Poland, Belorussia,

---

[*]Einsatzgruppen were "Special Action Groups," first organized by Himmler and Heydrich in 1939. They were to follow the German Army into Poland and round up Jews and force them into ghettos; in addition, they were to murder any local and national leaders. When the Nazis invaded Russia, the Einsatzgruppen were used to "resettle" (exterminate and murder) Jewish men, women, and children, by forcing them into mass graves and shooting them. Also, see page 132.

Upper Silesia, Czechoslovakia, Hungry, and all the population on the Eastern Front in Russia.

"About two years ago, when the German forces were invading Russia," I explained to Greta and her father, "there were two very antisemitic Nazi leaders who were instrumental in setting up what were called 'Special Action Groups.' These groups would force any Jews living in the conquered areas, mostly cities, to move into usually the poorest areas of a city and confine them to a Jewish Ghetto. These ghettos were the most cramped, cold, and least desirable living spaces in the cities. The Jewish population had to give up their homes, possessions, and health and safety when forced to move into these cramped and undesirable quarters. Then the local Nazi victors would attempt to starve them to death.

"Your description of these 'Special Action Groups' makes them sound absolutely inhumane!" chimed in Greta's father.

"That's absolutely horrible!" shouted Greta.

"When starving the Jews to death wasn't too effective, because this form of brutality would take time, the Nazis forced the Jews out of the ghettos and onto cattle car rail-road transports. The transports took them to death camps where they were killed by gas. I'm talking about completely innocent men, women, children, and the elderly. In addition, many prisoners of war from the Russian Army and people from all over Eastern Europe were similarly killed by gas. Then their bodies were burned in the crematoriums or buried and covered with lime."

"How could people do these things to other human beings?" Cried, Greta.

"Zeke and I have discovered two specific horrific instances where the Russian vengeance and reprisals would be understandable, and in some cases perhaps even justified."

"You have to remember," Zeke reminded Greta and her father, "Russians in general, and the Red Army in particular, have an extremely disorganized society. Not only is their army undisciplined, but also terrified and fearful of their leadership.

"Their army comes from a society that has nothing: no education, no property, and incredible poverty. Fear of their officers' retribution rules their actions.

"For ninety-nine percent of the men and women in the Red Army, stealing a watch from a dead Wehrmacht soldier would give the aggressor more value than any possession he could have accumulated in his lifetime in Russia.

"Please, let me give you two appalling examples of why the Russian Army is thirsty for revenge."

Chapter 45

Horror at Babi Yar

"In the fall of 1941," I began, "as the Wehrmacht swept into the Ukraine, they came to Kyiv, a thriving city in the southern part of Russia. The city had a large Jewish population, Greta, which stood in the way of the Nazi idea of an Aryan utopia for the Conquered Territories.

"The Nazis conquered Kyiv on the 19th of September, 1941. On the 29th and 30th of that same month, the Jews living in Kyiv were rounded up and taken to a ravine on the northern edge of the city. Included in this mass round-up were teenagers like yourself, Greta, and many younger children, as well as adults and the elderly Jewish residents of Kyiv. If the elderly were too ill to walk, they were shot in their beds.

"The Jewish residents were brought into the ravine called Babi Yar. * In this ravine, they were executed, shot, and murdered by the SS, Einsatzgruppen, and the local police."

Greta's father asked, "How many people were killed in this ravine, sir?"

"An accurate accounting of how many Russians and Ukrainians were put to death is difficult to ascertain. However, during those two days in September 1941, the body count of the innocent men, women, and children of Jewish residents was in excess of 33,000. Over the next two years, the Nazis used this ravine as a killing zone or execution place for Russian prisoners of war, gypsies, and anyone else from the area they deemed undesirable.

---

*The Babi Yar Ravine became the killing zone for the Jews and many Red Army soldiers of Kyiv.

"An additional massacre occurred in another Russian city, Odessa[*] a little later in the fall. However, I should emphasize that Kyiv and Odessa were only two of many cities and towns throughout Eastern Europe brutalized with mass killings by the Nazi war machine.

"In Odessa, the mass murder of the Jewish population occurred in the late fall of 1941 and the winter of 1942. Before the war began, Greta, the city's Jewish population, was over 200,000 people. All of these Russian Jews were living in harmony and at peace with the rest of the Russian population.

"In response to a Red Army bomb explosion, which killed the Romanian occupying general, the occupying force of the SS and Einsatzgruppen began the execution of Jews and anyone else suspected in the act of sabotage.

Over the next few months, the German and Romanian occupiers of Odessa broke into the homes and apartments of the Jewish population and hanged or shot to death anyone found in the residence, even women and children. Some estimates indicate that up to 22,000 city residents were murdered that fall and winter.

"Does this massacre of so many innocent people, Greta, give you some idea why the Red Army may not feel too kindly toward the German population living in the area?"

"Of course!" emphasized Greta and her father in unison. Then Greta's father asked a question. "Is there anyone in the Reich who could lead us out of this horrible war and secure peace with our neighbors?"

Zeke responded with a quick answer. "The Wehrmacht has several generals who could end this madness. The only one I would completely trust is General Rommel. [**]

---

[*]Odessa, Per Order of the Occupying Nazi Command 7 November 1941: All men of Jewish origin between the ages of 18 – 50 years, report to the city prison within forty-eight hours. All residents of Odessa and its' suburbs are required to notify the authorities of any Jews or men of Jewish origin. Failure to notify authorities would require the residents to face the immediate penalty of death.

[**]Irwin Rommel had a unique leadership style. He was sympathetic to the plight of the Jews and civilians in Germany. He fought on the front lines right along with his men. Toward the end of the war, he saw the need to eliminate Hitler. For his part in the plot to assassinate the Fürher, he was given the choice of suicide by cyanide or a trial and death and humiliation of his family. He was forced by Hitler to choose suicide. The story, perpetuated throughout Germany, was that Rommel was killed by strafing from an Allied fighter plane while riding in his jeep.

"From what I understand, he is a skilled tactician, fearless warrior, and has a sympathetic heart." Continued Zeke. He is known for protecting civilians – including Jews – from the horrors of the Nazi idea of placing undesirable populations, who might disagree with Hitler's philosophy, into concentration camps. As far as I know, he has never joined the Nazi party. He could lead Germany to peace.

"Do you think General Rommel could lead us out of this war?" asked Greta's father.

My reply was rather simple. "If it were not for the Gestapo, Rommel might have a chance. However, Hitler and his henchmen used the Gestapo to quell any dissent. Sadly, Rommel would never have a chance to save his beloved country."

"But what will happen to our family? Greta and I only have each other. Her mom died from the typhus last year."

Zeke spoke up. "We would recommend you both leave and head west toward the Allied lines at least 1 month before the Red Army comes into Nordhausen."

Just at that moment, there was a loud banging on the door.

Chapter 46

Knowledge of the Real Enemy

"Who could it be at this time of night?" Greta exclaimed. We are not expecting anyone!

Zeke and I had the same instant thought. "It could well be the Gestapo," whispered Zeke.

Greta's dad jumped to his feet. "Quick. Take your plates and hide in the kitchen. There is a back door if you have to flee, or there is a root cellar off to the right with stairs down to an enclosed dirt storage area."

Zeke and I quickly gathered our dinnerware and crept into the kitchen.

Greta's father called out, "Just a minute, I am coming." There was another knock at the door, louder than the first.

Bang. Bang-Bang!

Greta's father proclaimed, "Please do not break down my door," as he opened it to a pair of brutish men who barged into the room.

"We are here on official business," proclaimed the first oaf. He was a bit overweight with close-cropped hair starting to gray around the temples. He flashed a wallet with a badge attached.

The second churlish official, who was nearly bald, pointed a finger at Greta's dad and shouted, "We are from the Gestapo. We have had a report of two strangers entering this house about an hour ago. We are looking for two men who might have something to do with the disappearance of a team of missing Gestapo agents. Tell us immediately where they are, or things will not go well for you.

Greta spoke up. "We have had no strangers visiting us at this address. Please, feel free to look around as much as you would like!"

The churlish agent, who came in second, was quite muscular. He slapped Greta's dad hard across the face and threw him into a chair. The chair and Greta's father sprawled and crashed onto the floor.

Greta let out a scream. Stop! She cried out. Why are you hitting my father? We are law-abiding German citizens; we have done nothing wrong!"

The taller agent then pulled out his pistol and waved it at Greta and her father. "Tell us immediately where the two strangers are hiding, or we will have other ways to convince you to tell us."

The bald agent started searching the house. He returned after a few minutes proclaiming, "They are not here!"

"Then we will have to force you to tell us right away what you know about the two men who entered this address within the past hour," shouted the balding agent.

The two Gestapo agents proceeded to tie the wrists and ankles of Greta's father to a sturdy chair. Then they tied Greta's hands behind her back and threw her onto the couch with the warning, "If you make a sound, you will both be killed."

Greta started to protest, **"You cannot do this to law-abiding German citizens!"**

Slap!

The overweight taller agent put some muscle behind his open hand and struck Greta across her face.

"Take that, you pretty one!"

She was crying softly on the couch. Her face was already swelling, her nose was bleeding, and her eye was swelling shut.

"What are you planning to do to us," she whimpered.

"After we cut off your clothes, we shall each rape you in front of your father," offered the balding agent as he produced a knife and held it in front of Greta's face.

Zeke and I were hiding on the stairway going down to the root cellar. I asked Zeke if his insurance pistol was loaded. He nodded in the affirmative.

I slipped out the back door and came around to the front of the home.

I could hear muffled voices inside and heard the slap to Greta's face. I wanted to burst into the room, but I wasn't sure Zeke was in place.

Greta screamed as her shirt and skirt were cut and torn off her body. Her father was crying.

I knocked softly on the front door.

Chapter 47

Epiphany

It was pitch black outside; it took me a few minutes to find my way around the house to the front door. I hesitated a few moments until I was relatively sure Zeke was in position.

I could hear Greta being pushed around and threatened as her clothes were being torn off. I tried desperately not to let my emotions get control of me, but I was getting enraged.

I knocked softly on the front door.

Knock, knock…knock, knock.

"Hello. It's your neighbor. I thought I heard a woman screaming. Are you folks okay in there?"

I started to rattle the front latch and feign entering the home.

A male voice yelled out to me. **"Do not come in, this is official business!"**

The bald agent had started to molest Greta, I could hear her crying. I didn't burst in because I wanted Zeke to take out the larger of the two agents with his "insurance firearm."

In the meantime, Zeke had crept into the dining room. He took careful aim at the pistol-waving agent and placed a lead round directly behind his ear.

Bang!

That was my signal.

I burst into the room and grabbed 'Baldy' off Greta as his fellow agent tumbled very dead to the floor.

The bald agent was stronger than I first estimated, and he squirmed away from me. Now, after seeing his fellow agent dead on the floor, he panicked and tried to scuttle away from me and find his pistol.

Unfortunately for him, it was hard for him to get too far too fast with his trousers around his ankles.

As he toppled over, my boot caught him under his chin. The kick might have ended his life, but I didn't want to take a chance of him becoming a future problem. I stood him up and placed him in a choke-hold. I could hear his neck and lower jaw breaking as I squeezed any remaining life out of him.

I put my jacket over Greta; she was whimpering uncontrollably. Zeke found a sharp knife in the kitchen and was cutting her restraints off her wrists.

He then shifted his attention to Greta's father, who was also so traumatized he couldn't speak for several moments.

I went to the kitchen to see if I could find anything to warm up for them to drink. I couldn't find any tea or coffee, but there was a little soup left in a pan. I heated it with a little water and brought it to Greta and her father. It seemed to settle them a little.

As he calmed down and stopped whimpering, Greta's father asked a question. "Is this what law-abiding Germans have to suffer during this conflict?"

Zeke spoke up. "Unfortunately, sir, this is just the tip of a large iceberg for our beautiful country. Many of our citizens have had their homes, all their possessions, and their lives lost to Nazi brutality."

"Is the war responsible for all this destruction of our society?" asked Greta's father.

"The war is a symptom of our Fuhrer's greed. Our leaders have brought destruction and pain to our country because they are greedy and are not looking out for citizens' rights and concerns," was Zeke's comment.

Greta spoke up. "Thank you so much for riding our home from these terrible agents. What do we do with them now?"

"It would be expedient," I suggested, "to bury them in your root cellar, but I'm afraid more agents might come looking for them.

"Zeke and I will take them in our automobile, it is parked at the end of the block. We will dispose of them on our way back to our base near the gypsum mine."

I wasn't sure where the agents had left their automobile, I didn't see it when I drove our car back to Greta's home.

After loading the two dead agents in the trunk of our automobile, I felt I should warn our hosts.

"Greta, you and your father should make arrangements to leave this place and make it to the Allies' lines as soon as possible. You will have a much better time being under the American-controlled section of German and away from the Russian-controlled areas.

"What Zeke and I have uncovered, by eliminating some of the Gestapo agents, is a network of terrorists who have infected Germany. Once the German people discover that hoodlums have taken over the government, the tide of this war should turn.

"It is quite obvious now that the Gestapo is looking hard for the two of us. We hope we can outmaneuver them until we can do one more project for the Reich."

I certainly could not let Greta or her father know I was in the process of getting permission from the general of our research center to ferry some of the very dangerous V-2 missiles out of Germany to a Nazi base in Denmark.

"However, you and your father now know the real enemy of the German people. Unfortunately, you have met them in your own home. "Once the majority of God-fearing Germans come to the realization of the exact nature of the enemy, this conflict will be over."

Zeke and I thanked Greta and her father and gave them all the money and firearms from the dead agents.

We still had to make it back to the research center without the trash in the back of our automobile.

There was a complete black-out in Germany by this time in the fall. Most of the leaves were off the trees and there was a distinct chill of the approaching winter. Fortunately, we were able to bury the dead Gestapo agents off the road under some rocks, brush, and leaves.

When we returned to the research center, we got word that the Allies had formed a decent foothold in Normandy and most of France.

Chapter 48

⋙∘⟨⟩∘⋘

A Plan to Exit the Reich

Zeke and I thought long and hard about finding a way out of Nazi Germany while still performing helpful service for the secret rocket research center. We felt a loyalty to the center and the scientists, especially Dr. von Braun and General Dornberger.

In the fall of 1943, I received orders to investigate the Nazi air base in Aalborg, Denmark. These orders were issued because Hitler had read my report, which discussed the advantages of utilizing the air base in northern Denmark as a missile launching site for the V-2 ballistic missile. My report had gone up the chain of command from our Chief of Operations, Herr Frits Gosslau [*] then to Dr. Ernst Steinhoff, [**] from the Guidance and Telemetering Devices Laboratory, and on to General Walter Dornberger, who discussed the proposal with Hitler.

Operation Paperclip was the secret code name that brought 1600 Nazi scientists and aeronautical engineers to America after the war to aid with the U.S. space program.

Although General Dornberger thought enough of the plan to bring it to Hitler's attention, Vitali and I only had two goals. First, we wanted to get as many of these monster missiles as possible out of the Reich. We thought we could render them incapable of firing if we

---

[*]Dr. Frits Gosslau received his Ph.D. in Aeronautical Engineering from the Technical University in Berlin in 1926. He was involved in the development of the V-I and V-II missile programs for the Reich. He died in Bavaria at age 67. See p. 37.

[**]Dr. Ernst Steinhoff graduated from the Technische Universität Darmstadt in 1940 as an aeronautical engineer. He was a member of the von Braun rocket team that developed the V-I and V-II rockets. He surrendered to the Americans after WW II and came to America under "Operation Paperclip." In 1958 he was awarded the Decoration for Exceptional Civilian Service to the U.S. Rocket Program. In 1979 he was inducted into the New Mexico Space Hall of Fame.

could get them away from the watchful eyes of Nazi technicians. And second, both Zeke and I thought our chances of exiting the Reich and getting into neutral Sweden were much better from Denmark.

Fuel for the V-2 missiles was a combination of an alcohol-water mixed with liquid oxygen. The propulsion laboratory had discovered that this combination could produce the most explosive controlled thrust of 55,000 lbs. to lift the rocket to a height of 50 -60 kilometers before guiding it toward its target.

Our plan was to get the missiles out of the Reich. Perhaps the fuel for the propellant or the warheads would be difficult to get up to northern Denmark, we were not too concerned about the warheads. This was going to be our final trip to Denmark, and we hadn't planned on returning to the Nordhausen rocket facility. Of course, plan disruption is rather the norm in the military.

While Ezekiel and I were discussing our exit plans, there was a gentle knock on the door. It wasn't a hard knock like the Gestapo uses in the middle of the night to wake up and disorient its victims. It was a soft, almost gentle knock.

Ilsa and I married during my last trip to Denmark and Sweden, but I couldn't convince Ezekiel to stay with my relatives in the Stockholm area. Before answering the door, I whispered to Zeke, "I hope this isn't the convincing argument I should have used to insist you stay out of the Reich and with my uncle in Sweden."

Knock, Knock...**Knock!**

There it was again. A soft but persistent knock at our laboratory door.

Zeke and I had drawings and computations all over the laboratory. Since we were the only two working in these make-shift quarters, we thought nothing of leaving the top-secret designs of the V-2 rocket motor out while we were working.

I called out to the door, **"Come in, Sergeant!"**

Instead of our tall sergeant coming through the door, the door opened only halfway.

There standing in the half-opened doorway was a shy sixteen-year-old girl from the restaurant in Nordhausen.

"*Ach, Mine Gott im Himmel,* Greta! How did you get into this secret base?"

"My father drove me here and told the guard it was imperative that his daughter see her father, Lieutenant Ramsgrund."

"Oh, my dear Greta! Do you have any idea how dangerous it is to come onto a German Wehrmacht base without prior authorization?"

"How could your father let this happen to you?"

"It broke my father's heart to bring me here. But he brought me here because he loves me. He felt I would be safer here than anywhere near the Red Army. He said we would contact each other after the war if we survived."

"Lieutenant, I really have no idea how dangerous this base is for me. But…I do know it is a lot safer here than being raped multiple times by uncouth, undisciplined, and disgusting Red Army infantry soldiers. My father knew I would be safer with you two men.

"Besides, I am a law-abiding German citizen; what could happen to me on a secure German army base?"

"Well," Zeke spoke up. "We could all be shot for treason, breach of secrecy, or some other made-up charge. You must understand, Greta, that the Gestapo does not need to follow German law. The Gestapo can arrest, torture, and shoot us in the back of our heads for any reason they could make up. Most law-abiding Germans who are arrested and detained by the Gestapo at # 8 Prinz Albrecht Strasse in Berlin are never seen again.

Although you may not have heard of Gestapo tactics, even the mention of the address of # 8 Prinz Albrecht Strasse * brings abject fear and trepidation to most law-abiding Berliners.

Remember, Greta, the SD ** are everywhere. Often, they could be your neighbors, friends, or acquaintances. This 'intelligent' arm of the SS would provide the SiPo *** with almost any information to have you arrested.

"Well, here I am," announced Greta. "My father told me to work with you both and do whatever you want me to do in order to secure safe passage out of the Reich and to stay with you until after the war is over.

"I will do whatever you want me to do, including getting you meals, running errands, and moving items for you. Many high-ranking officers have aides, I'm sure. I will be yours."

---

*Gestapo Headquarters in Berlin. At any time of the day or night, a passerby could hear the shrieks and moans of German citizens being "questioned." The torture techniques included electric shock to the genitals, rape, burning with cigarettes or blow torch, removing fingers, one at a time, and, near-drowning experiences.

**SD, or Sicherheitdienst, was the intelligence agency of the SS.

***SiPo, or Sicherheitpolizei, was the security police with unlimited power to arrest anyone in Germany or the Conquered Territories during the Nazi era; they did not require a valid reason.

Chapter 49

A Small Complication Leaving the Reich

"Greta," I addressed her sternly. "The Wehrmacht does not indoctrinate sixteen-year-old girls into the military as aides!"

"Then," she answered quietly but with firmness, "I will become an eighteen-year-old male aide for you and Mr. Zeke."

"And just how do you propose to change your gender and feminine looks?"

"I will cut and color my hair and darken my complexion. If you get me a small male uniform from army supply, I will make it into a uniform for an eighteen-year-old male soldier. I will wear tight underwear to flatten my breasts."

"Zeke," I said with some exasperation. "Will you talk to her and explain how crazy this entire scheme of hers is for her long-term health?"

Zeke took me aside and asked in a quiet tone: "Is this request any crazier than what we are attempting? Do you recommend she try to play 'nice' with the Red Army?"

"Zeke! You're not making our decision any easier. How are we going to get this past the general?"

"Well," ...Zeke hesitated for a few seconds, "We shall have to tell General Dornberger the truth: We have decided to hire an aide, in addition to our technical sergeant, to help us with some of the technical and social issues for transferring the missiles to the Aalborg Luftwaffe Base in Denmark."

"I'm not sure," I cautiously replied, "I could tell the general anything like that without making some incriminating facial gestures or just breaking out laughing."

"I will inform the general, Jenz, and pick up a small uniform this afternoon. We will have to keep her hidden away somewhere until we have the missiles loaded on the train."

My immediate thought was exasperation. I could see us all lined up against a wall and being shot. But then I reluctantly acquiesced, saying, "She will have to stay in the office here or sleep on the floor of my officer's quarters. We will wait to see how her gender transformation goes before we can let her into the dining area."

"Zeke, while you are looking for a small male uniform, see if you can pick up some dark dye for her face and hair. Greta is going to be a significant complication to our smooth exit from the Reich, but we will have to act as if she or he is a normal part of our plans."

Later that evening, I found Greta in our back office diligently cutting apart and sewing while actually remaking an enlisted Wehrmacht uniform into her size. She was wearing very tight male undershirt which helped to flatten and disguise her developing breasts.

She had finished taking in and shortening the trousers and they looked like a pretty good fit. Her hair had gone from light blond to dark brown and her complexion was about three shades darker. I almost didn't recognize her.

"Greta," I remarked with surprise, "Your transformation is quite convincing!"

"Thanks, Lieutenant. I still have a way to go, but I'm getting there. I am going to fix my shoes to make me appear a little taller. Are there any specific insignias for military aides?

"By the way, please address me as George, my male name, from now on. I want to get comfortable using it."

"Okay, George. You might also try speaking in a little deeper voice, if you can do it without sounding ridiculous."

Zeke and I spent the next three days solidifying our orders and getting the missiles ready for transportation to the Aalborg Luftwaffe Base.

We had to make one more trip to the gypsum mine to inspect the final construction and packaging for the transport of the missiles; and to check on the living conditions of the slave workers.

As I was explaining to Zeke the hazards of another visit to the manufacturing facility, Greta, or George, as she wanted to be called, interrupted our discussion.

"Lieutenant," she chimed in, "I think it would be important for your aide to go with you on this inspection visit."

"Absolutely not!" I shot back. "The visit and inspection are dangerous enough for Zeke and me. You would complicate our safety; the mine is a very dangerous place. In addition, I cannot let you react poorly to the trauma the prisoners could be experiencing and the horror they are going through."

"Lieutenant, I promise I would not say a word. I will take notes on what we observe and write down anything you think is important. I will keep a good record of our visit for future reference.

Since I was unsure of the placement of Gestapo listening devices, I suggested we take a break from the back office and take a walk around the base. It was getting late in the afternoon and I was thinking it might be time to test out Greta's disguise in the cafeteria. In addition, the off-green walls were starting to close in on us.

I had a lot of thoughts going through my mind. In addition to our safety in the gypsum mine factory, there were reports of German losses in Africa * and the Allied invasion of Sicily. ** Many of us in the

---

*The German campaign in Africa collapsed in May 1943 with the encirclement of several hundred thousand Italian and German troops in northern Tunisia. The British had broken the Nazi secret code which proved critical in the Allied victory.

**Sicily was attacked by the Allies under the command of Lt. General George S. Patton and General Bernard Montgomery on 10 July 1943. The campaign ended in an Allied victory on the 17th of August, 1943.

Wehrmacht wondered why bad news on the battlefield took several months to reach us. With Allied victories in North Africa and Sicily, all of us wondered what was going on after the Allies had landed in Italy. *

While out walking, I felt a bit out numbered. Zeke and Greta wanted to try eating in the cafeteria for the evening meal. If the dining experience went without problems, I agreed to let Greta accompany Zeke and me to the assembly tunnel in the gypsum mine.

I didn't think the Gestapo had listening devices out in the paths around the buildings at the new facilities for the rocket base, but we still kept our voices subdued.

There was a light mist falling from clouds darkened by wind and rain. It looked like a possible storm coming off the Hartz Mountains to our east.

---

*Italy underwent an Allied invasion on the 3rd of September 1943 under the command of British General Montgomery. Later that day the Italian government agreed to an armistice with the Allies. The Germans, however, were determined to defend Italy without Italian assistance.

Chapter 50

Camouflaging the Missiles on the Train

It took the help of over two dozen technicians to get the missiles painted with camouflage paint and trucked and loaded on the train. The missiles were heavy (just over 25 tons fully loaded) and quite large, over five stories tall. Three of the monsters would just fit in one open railroad transport car. The stabilizing fin sections had to be loaded separately. Two crane loaders were used for each missile.

In addition, heavy green and brown camouflage tarps were placed over the missiles to keep the secret load safe and away from the prying eyes of the Allied bombers all the way into our Denmark Luftwaffe base at Aalborg.

Each missile was a destructive monster. The detonation of one warhead would leave a crater 20 meters (66 feet) wide and 8 meters (26 feet) deep and eject almost 3000 tons of shrapnel into the air.

I had strongly suggested Zeke stay in Sweden on our last trip, but he persisted. "If you need to go back to the rocket base to make sur the missiles are transported safely to our base in Denmark, then I will help you. I will meet you in Nordhausen in a few days."

Many of the rail lines had been smashed by Allied bombs and many rail cars and engines had been abandoned. Also, we had to travel through most of Germany at night because of the constant threat of Allied or Red Army aircraft strafing attacks. We stopped during the day in the forests for rest and to eat our cold food packed for us by the rocket base cafeteria.

As we neared Hamburg, we could see the red glow in the sky from the frequent bombings. Occasionally, the sky would light up like a lightning strike from an explosion. Our country was being ground to dust by stupid and stubborn politicians who couldn't understand that further resistance was useless.

Sometimes we could hear the Allied bombers as they raced toward their targets in the interior of our country. Industrial cities of Hamburg, Dresden, Frankfort, Schweinfurt, Bremen, and Munich were certainly on the list of cities to incur Allied and Red Army wrath.

Now that the Allies had developed fighter aircraft that could accompany the Flying Fortresses * on their bombing runs, most of Germany was unprotected at this stage of the war.

The Allies had what we Germans called *der Gabelschwanz-Teufel* (Fork-Tailed Devil) or P-38 ** fighter aircraft which was more maneuverable than our *Würger,* (Shrike in English) or *Focke-Wulf 190****

Occasionally, we would spot dogfights over the countryside as German and Allied aircraft tried to knock each other out of the sky. We could hear the distant droning of the heavy bombers; they were only specks in the sky at 30,000 feet. But their presence spelled doom to any heavy industry involved in the war effort.

Our progress north toward Denmark was halting, and even though the days were short and the nights were long, our progress was agonizingly slow. Sergeant Albert, our rocket technician was getting frustrated with traveling at night only. I told him we could speed the progress after we were in Denmark. We wouldn't have to take so many detours and we could travel by day.

---

*The Flying Fortress, otherwise known as the B-17, was developed as a heavy bomber by the Boeing Aircraft Company for the US Army Air Force in the 1930s. In the early part of the German bombing campaign, Allied fighter aircraft did not have the range to accompany the giant bombers on their missions deep into German territory. The B-17 was heavily armed with 30 and 50 caliber machine guns.

**The P-38 Lightning fighter aircraft, developed by the Lockheed Corporation, had twin tails bridged by a central boom. It was fast (over 400 mph) and highly maneuverable. The twin turbo supercharged engines turned out 1000 hp each.

***The *Focke-Wulf 190* was the German premier fighter aircraft. This aircraft became the backbone of the *Jagdwaffe* (fighter force) for the *Luftwaffe* during WW II. The top speed of the *F-W 190* was over 450 mph but diminished maneuverability at high altitudes (above 20,000 feet) limited its effectiveness against the Allied high flying heavy bombers.

Our train had seven open cars for the missiles and stabilizing fins and two cars for our food and supplies. We slept in one of the supply cars. We also carried two armed guards, and of course, our aide, Greta. I will say Greta, or George, as she now preferred, was unobtrusive and for the most part, stayed out of everyone's way.

Dawn was breaking to our east. We were traversing farmland and looking for a forest or secluded area to spend the daylight hours. We were about 40-50 kilometers south of Hamburg.

I was filling out some tedious paperwork forms when we heard an explosion in the air somewhere high above us. There was dense cloud cover, so visibility was limited. However, we could hear the desperate whine of a large aircraft with engines clawing and biting the atmosphere for survival.

Ezekiel shouted, Jenz, look behind us!"

There, low on the horizon was an obviously seriously injured B-17. One engine was missing along with about a third of one wing. Fire was blazing out of the engine next to the cockpit.

The aircraft was laboring to stay at tree-top level and it looked like the pilot was trying for a crash landing on the farmland we were traversing. The aircraft was on fire and coming directly at us. It looked like a ball of fire coming across the horizon just above the land.

Shepherding the wounded Flying Fortress was a smaller fighter plane, the P-38 Lightning. This aircraft could be extremely dangerous.*

The Lightning must have been out of ammunition. It looked like it might make a strafing run on our train, but it only buzzed us at close range.As it flew overhead, the Flying Fortress crash landed in a huge explosion spraying farmland, dirt, and flame in all directions. The aircraft landed with the one good wing touching first and spun the aircraft into a wide circle.

---

*The P-38 carried four 50-caliber machine guns as well as a 20-mm cannon in the nose housing. Both guns were accurate and could hit targets up to 1000 yards away.

The B-17 must have been out of fuel because there was no secondary explosion on impact. We could see some of the crew hastily exiting the burning aircraft.

213

Chapter 51

Saving an Allied Bomber Crew

"Ezekiel," I shouted, "Let's see if we can save any of the crew. Bring the fire extinguisher, I'll grab a couple of blankets!"

Our guards for the missiles were already ahead of us brandishing their rifles and shouting at the crew escaping from what was now a flaming inferno.

By the time Ezekiel and I got to the crash site, our two guards riding with us on the train had the crew face-down in the dirt. The guards had fired a couple of rounds from their rifles into the air. The aircraft had thrown up a five-foot deep furrow of dirt and debris around what was left of the burning aircraft.

I shouted to the guards who looked like they were about to execute the American air crew. ***What are you doing?***

The first guard shouted back, **"Lieutenant, we have to shoot these *Terrorfliegers* (terrorist flyers). They are baby killers and child murderers!"**

"Sergeant," I said with some authority behind my voice. **"These airmen are now the responsibility of the Reich. They will not be harmed. They could well prove valuable to our country. Get your fingers away from the trigger mechanisms!"**

"But, Sir!" Complained the guard. **"These men have been bombing our homeland and killing our people."**

"I am Lieutenant Ramsgrund of the *SS*. Stand down or accept the most severe consequences!"

Both guards seem to hesitate a bit but then lowered their rifles.

"George and Vitali, please see if any of the flyers are injured."

The co-pilot was severely injured when the port engine exploded and shattered the canopy. He was also badly burned. The pilot had some burns and shrapnel wounds, but could move about. One of the waist gunners was dead and the turret gunner beneath the plane had to be dead. There was no way out for that unfortunate soul.

We collected the survivors into a circle. Unfortunately, the aircraft was a mass of fire and black smoke. The whole area was too hot and dangerous to try to extinguish with a hand-held fire extinguisher. Zeke sprayed some of the flame-retardant powder on the smoldering co-pilot's clothing, then helped him out of his flight jacket.

The black smoke was my most immediate concern. Within ten minutes the engulfed plane and smoke brought a small open caravan of two trucks from one of the Hamburg suburbs with four Wehrmacht soldiers. They stopped about 50 meters from the burning aircraft near our circle of wounded airmen.

The sergeant in charge informed me he would take the prisoners to a prison camp deep in Germany. I inquired, "Where would you take these men, Sergeant?"

"They will be incarcerated at the Buchenwald Camp * Lieutenant."

My immediate thought was that the Buchenwald Camp would be a death sentence for these captured flyers.

I spoke in a firm, but moderate tone to the sergeant in charge of the 'rescue party.'

"Sergeant, these men are enemy combatants. They are under my protection and control. They will be taken prisoner and transported by our train to a prison camp in northern Germany."

---

*Bucenwald Concentration Camp, established in July 1937, was one of the largest slave-labor camps within the borders of Germany. It eventually held almost 280,000 prisoners. The well-written book by Tom Clavin, *Lightning Down,* St. Martin's Press, 2021, provides an excellent description of the horrendous conditions for Allied Army Air Force personnel imprisoned at Buchenwald during World War II.

"But, Sir," the sergeant protested, "Shouldn't these men face the ultimate penalty for their actions against our homeland?"

"Yes!" I replied in a firm and more assertive tone. **"These men are now under the control of the *SS*, Sergeant, and I would strongly advise you to alert your superiors of this fact!"**

Our technical sergeant in charge of arming the missiles came over to me and in a quiet conversational tone asked me, "Sir, we are on a secret mission. Does it make any sese to bring along a group of Allied prisoners to our base in Aalborg?"

"Can you think of a better bargaining chip with the Allies, Sergeant?"

After loading up the prisoners on the last car on the train, we did our best to tend to their injuries. We spread sulfa powder on the burn victims and bandaged up their most serious wounds.

Greta and Zeke were terrific in calming the prisoners and looking after their needs. They required water, and we shared some of the dark bread we had on hand. Zeke's English was more than acceptable.

The pilot addressed me after the guards had left. "Lieutenant, what are you planning to do with us?"

"Captain, it is important for you and your men to listen to me very carefully," I spoke to them in English as best I could.

"Your crew is now under the protection and control and prisoners of the SS. As you can see, you will be treated fairly and in accordance with the Geneva Convention."

I looked around the transport rail car to ensure no one else was listening before continuing.

"I realize it is your duty to try to escape from this train as we progress through northern Germany. I would strongly suggest that escape would be foolhardy in this area near Hamburg. You would likely be shot on sight or turned over to the Gestapo.

"Our destination is northern Denmark. As you know, Denmark is now a German state. However, if you were to escape in Denmark, your chances of success would be much greater. In addition. If you wait a bit, you might be able to take your wounded with you.

"It is my suggestion that you wait for escape when your wounded men are feeling up to traveling, and we get into a more favorable country for your survival. Our train can make a stop in the country or just outside of a Danish city, where your wounded can be treated at a hospital. From Denmark, you should be able to make it to neutral Sweden.

"However, if you try to escape in Germany, I will not be able to help you, and our own guards or the local population will probably shoot you.

"We, unfortunately, only carry mild pain-relieving medication. But I can assure you, circumstances would be much worse for your wounded men if you attempt an escape in this area of Germany."

"Sir," the pilot asked, "I understand and appreciate your adherence to the Geneva Convention, but your uniform and demeanor, you are a member of the feared SS. Why are you being kind to us and suggesting we escape at a more favorable time?"

"Captain," I informed him, "We are on a special mission for the Fatherland. Your aircrew is not our priority. We will continue our mission without interruption, as long as your crew is cooperative. Any further interruption in our mission from your crew would not be looked on favorably by my guards.

"Is my English clear enough for you and your crew?"

"Yes, Lieutenant, I think we understand."

Chapter 52

Crossing into Denmark

Our crossing into Denmark wasn't as smooth as I had originally predicted. Much of the Wehrmacht was on high alert since the Wehrmacht's incursion into the Ardennes * had not had the hoped-for result for our Führer.

As long as the inclement weather continued, our tanks and troops were successful. The moment the weather improved, our troops and armament were exposed to Allied aircraft and continuous strafing and bombing.

The weather had cleared and was decidedly colder as we entered Denmark in January 1945. The Wehrmacht went through our train and I had to let them look under the tarps. The guards were amazed at the size of the missiles. One guard commented quite loudly, "Mein Gott, we must be winning this war with weapons like this!"

I had to mention to the Wehrmacht inspector, "Sergeant, any mention of our secret mission or these missiles, would make you immediately eligible for the firing squad."

We had placed the flyers in rope restraints to assure the border guards that the prisoners were under the control of the SS. I actually gave the pilot several lengths of rope and instructed the flight crew: "Please make the ties look convincing to the Nazi border guards, but be careful of your injured crewmen."

---

*The Ardennes Counteroffensive occurred from the 16th of December 1944 until the 25th of January 1945, also known as the Battle of the Bulge. This incursion into the Allies' position was the German Army's attempt to capture Antwerp and drive a wedge between the British and American forces.

The border guards questioned me extensively about the prisoners at the crossing near Flensburg, Germany, just before we crossed the border into Denmark. The weather had turned bitter cold with a stiff wind under clear blue skies.

The border guards gave me a bit of trouble with the prisoners. "Lieutenant, these criminals should be in the custody of the Gestapo for extensive questioning!"

I assured the guards, "These prisoners are under the control of the SS, and I will deal with them appropriately as soon as I complete the Führer's orders.

The border guards were extended every courtesy from Zeke, Greta, and me while they were poking around on the train. They left with a reminder. "Be careful, Lieutenant; these terrorist flyers can be very difficult, be sure to keep them restrained.

After we had crossed the border and were on our way into Denmark, I untied the Allied flight crew. One of their members, I think he was the navigator, had a broken arm. We hadn't realized his injury but he complained of considerable pain while being restrained. Freeing the aviators from their rope restraints did wonders for their trust in Ezekiel, Greta, and me.

As we were passing through the city of Haderslev, I told the flight crew we would pull into a railroad siding outside the town of Kolding or the nearby city of Federicia. I informed the pilot and crew not to travel as a group but to go in small groups of two or three men. I suggested that the wounded travel by bus to the hospital at Fredericia. Ezekiel gave them some German money and told them not to speak English or use American money while in the German state of Denmark.

If stopped by the authorities, I suggested they have a story about how the plane came down in Denmark and warned them never to mention our transportation by train out of Germany.

My English wasn't the best, but I think I got my points across to the flight crew. One of the crew asked me a question in German.

"Where might we go where we could avoid the chance of meeting with the Gestapo?"

"It is a relief," I continued, "To hear one of your crew speaks German quite fluently. The German language might help get you through any checkpoints for traveling to the hospital and the city of Odense on your way to Copenhagen and Sweden.

"Keep in mind, Copenhagen has the central office for the Gestapo. After everyone has healed up some, you should be able to get past the Gestapo and over to Malmo, Sweden.

"Anyone dressed in a dark suit with a fedora could well be Gestapo. To be safe, trust as few people as possible. Anyone looking to curry favor with the German authorities could turn you over to the Wehrmacht."

I quietly informed the pilot, as we came to a railroad siding in Kolding, that the back door of the rail car would be unlocked for a period of half an hour after nightfall while we refueled and while I was instructing the engineer on our future progress to Aalborg.

The pilot asked me again about our kindness in letting his crew escape into Denmark. "Lieutenant, I want to thank you and your men for saving our aircrew from certain death from your guards."

"Captain," I spoke in as clear English as I could muster, "Landing your plane with survivors in a burning aircraft with half its engines inoperable was a very professional and brave act of flying. Killing your aircrew would do nothing to shorten this foolish war.

"I would like your full name and call number of your aircraft in case I am ever asked about this incident after the hostilities have ceased."

"Certainly, Lieutenant. I am Phillip Oskar Johnson of the 5th Army Air Force. My plane is, or was, the 'Flying Betty' named after a famous movie actress, Betty Grable."

"Thank you, Captain. I will briefly update you on the war and its progress."

I informed him about the Allies being close to crossing the Rhine River and the Red Army with General Zhukov located at the Lower Oder River in the East.

"In addition," I commented, "The SOE * has done an excellent job of interfering with the Nazi plans to build a superbomb."

"What superbomb?" replied the pilot. And what is the SOE?"

"You will have to ask your SOE people, Captain. Their information will be much more accurate than anything I could tell you."

"Captain, this ridiculous war cannot last another year. Our Wehrmacht has made many mistakes in the East, including an attempt to invade Russia in the winter months. However, our biggest mistake is letting a small minority of Nazi political goons take over our country.

"This political group of Nazi thugs has imprisoned, killed, or caused to flee our country many of our most prominent scientists, political and cultural leaders, innovators, church leaders, and anyone who disagrees with the Nazi philosophy of a 'Master Race.'

"The extent of what the Nazis have done to their own people and the innocent population in the Conquered Territories may never be known. We have lost an entire generation to this war and the crematoriums. What is worse, we will never know or probably understand the full extent of our loss.

"Sergeant Carapezza, my aide George, and I hope your crew finds your way to safety and to your home and families without too much further delay."

"Thank you, Lieutenant. Our flight crew will be forever grateful to you."

---

*SOE or Special Operations Executive was the highly secret British spy organization begun on 22 July 1940. This group of spies was responsible for destroying the Nazi Heavy Water plant in Norway and ending the Nazi hope for developing the Atomic Bomb.

Chapter 53

The Gestapo at the Aalborg Luftwaffe Base

It took Sergeant Albert, our rocket technician, almost three days to get the missiles unloaded and properly stored in a facility within the Luftwaffe base at Aalborg. When the unloading and storage were complete, I strongly suggested to Sergeant Albert that we would fire the missiles toward the preselected targets on my orders, and only if absolutely imperative.

"Sergeant," I reaffirmed in forceful language. "Let me make a couple of points very clear. **You are to keep the firing codes and launch mechanisms separate and out of the hands of anyone else associated with these armaments.**

"If the guards ask about the prisoners, they are with the Danish authorities. I want the guards to return on the train back to Germany. Please inform either Sergeant Carapezza or me if there are any inquiries from individuals in or associated with the Gestapo.

"You have orders to stay with the missiles until you are needed to activate and fire them. Be aware there are no warheads loaded into the missiles at this time. Under no circumstances should you let these armaments fall into the hands of the Red Army.

"If the Allies arrive here first, you may be assured they would capture the technology but not use these weapons against us. If you have to surrender, surrender to the Allied Army, not the Red Army."

"Lieutenant," the sergeant spoke up, "Do you really feel our defeat is inevitable?"

"I'm not really sure, Sergeant. But I do know our political leadership is morally bankrupt, stubborn, and not very bright. These traits are a bad combination for victory. Our Fuhrer had had several attempts on his life, one is pretty widely known. Unfortunately, Hitler has purged many of our best officers, including General Rommel.

"One of the heroes of the African campaign, Oberst Clause von Stauffenberg, * was shot by a firing squad shortly after his attempt on our Führer's life at Wolf's Lair last July.

"The Führer has used this assassination attempt to purge thousands of people he feared might disagree with him. Included in the purge were two of the von Stauffenberg brothers.

"Unfortunately, this purge of high-ranking officers will decimate the leadership and morale of the Wehrmacht. Excellent leadership is required for a good outcome in times of war.

"Our nation should have made peace with the Allies before invading Russia. However, Sergeant Albert, all of our nation's mistakes cannot be blamed on our leaders. It is the German people who never should have brought war to our beautiful country. Too many of our citizens are living in fear of the Gestapo and the SS.

"What are we to do now, Lieutenant?"

"All of us should work toward the day thatthese missiles are never fired. Peace and healing will eventually come to our nation.

"However, Albert, notify Sergeant Carapezza or me if the Gestapo starts to ask any questions."

"Yes, Sir!"

Everything seemed to be going smoothly at the Aalborg Luftwaffe Base until late one evening.

---

*Clas von Stauffenberg earned the German Cross in Gold for his courage in the African Campaign in Tunisia on 8 May 1943. In this battle action he lost his left eye, his right hand, and two fingers on his left hand. He was killed by firing squad shortly after his attempt to assassinate Adolf Hitler during operation Valkyrie on 20 July, 1944.

I was going over reports on the war progress when I heard the outside door of our officers' housing residence fly open with a bang. With a howling wind coming across the base, it wasn't inconceivable that the wind could have slammed the door open. The only other explanation possible was the typical late-night visit of the feared Gestapo.

My immediate concern was Ezekiel. I called him on the phone two rooms away.

"Zeke!" We may have a visit from our 'friends' in the Gestapo."

"I heard the door bang," Replied Zeke.

"Let's prepare for the worst, Zeke. Pack your 'insurance' weapon in your sock and prepare to meet any intruders who may show up here late this evening. Please leave your phone line open so we can easily tell if either one of us has unexpected visitors."

Almost immediately, I heard a loud knock-on Zeke's door with a metal object.

Bang, Bang...Bang seemed to echo down the hall and over the open line.

Chapter 54

Gestapo Intimidation

I could hear the Gestapo bursting into Zeke's room and yelling at him to give them information on my location.

Slap!

I could hear them strike Ezekiel. That did it for me. I finished dressing in my uniform, including my boots and leather gloves; I left my officer's hat on my dresser.

I quietly left my room and quickly walked down the hall to Zeke's room. The door was still partially open, so I could see the goons starting to slap Zeke around. There were two of them.

The one working Zeke over was beefy and around six feet tall. He had bushy hair greying around the temples and looked to be somewhere in his forties.

The second agent looked to be younger, perhaps in his early thirties. He was about the same height as 'Bushy Hair' but with a thinner build. He was pretty much completely bald except for some whispery strands of hair around his ears. I smiled inwardly because he almost looked like a cartoon character.

I pushed the door fully open and filled the opening with my six-foot four-inch frame, and asked a simple question in a commanding voice.

"May I help you, Gentlemen?"

'Bushy Hair' snapped his head around and commanded, **"Lieutenant, come in and sit down. We have been looking for you two."**

Every drop of blood seemed to drain from 'Baldy's' face, but he was the agent holding the pistol.

As 'Baldy' turned toward me, his pistol swung around and pointed in my direction.

I reached out, grabbed the barrel of the Lugar, and directed his aim toward the bed.

Bang!

'Baldy' had squeezed the trigger as I deflected his aim. I immediately wrenched his wrist backward, taking the pistol from his hand while breaking his trigger finger in the process.

'Ow, you broke my finger," He shrieked in pain.

The other agent looked like he was ready to charge me, so I aimed the Lugar at his head. He immediately backed off but started spouting his authority.

"Do you realize we are the Gestapo?" 'Bushy Hair' sounded pretty high and mighty, almost confident, even though I was holding the pistol.

"Yes." I tried to sound calm and collected.

"When I entered the room, I asked how we could help you. Then, you turned and leveled a firearm at me. Let me ask you again. How can we help you?"

"Baldy,' you sit on the bed, or I will break more than your finger."

'Bushy Hair started to spout how the Gestapo was in charge and not restrained by German law.

"You both are in big trouble," 'Bushy Hair' continued spouting off in a voice much too loud for my liking. **"Our department has**

been looking for you both all over Germany, Poland and now in Denmark. We need to question you both about the loss of some of our agents.” “Unfortunately,” I replied, “Sergeant Carapezza and I do not have time for your ridiculous questions. We have been on a mission from our Führer and need to return to Germany.”

“Sergeant, please relieve these men of their handcuffs and any other firearms they may possess and secure their hands snugly behind their backs.

‘Bushy Hair’ started to protest. **“You cannot order us around; we are the Gestapo and have jurisdiction here!”**

I pressed the barrel of the pistol to his forehead and asked Zeke to make sure the handcuffs were nice and snug on both of these criminals.

In a firm voice, I reminded him, **“Look, you idiot, you are not in charge here anymore. You are both under detention by the SS. You will be taken back to Germany for trial.”**

‘Bushy Hair’ cried out, **“You cannot put us on trial; we are above the law in Germany!”**

“Unfortunately,” Zeke reminded mister ‘Bushy Hair,’ “You are not in Germany anymore.

“Zeke, let’s get them comfortable in the boot of their automobile. I will get a blanket for warmth for these two criminals.”

“You can’t put us in the trunk of an automobile,” argued ‘Baldy.’ “We would be frozen by the time you got into Germany!”

I leveled the Lugar at eye level with the balding criminal on the bed.

“You’re both either in the boot, or your brains are scattered around this room. Who’s first?”

Fortunately, neither criminal gave us too much trouble as Zeke and I squeezed them into the boot of their automobile. I threw in a blanket, but I knew it would be useless to keep them from freezing to death.

My comment to Zeke was, "Let's get Greta out of bed and packed for a journey out of the Reich."

Ezekiel asked, "Jenz, are we going to have trouble crossing the border into Sweden?"

"We will have o dispose of the frozen criminals in the back of the automobile somewhere in Denmark, well before the border, Zeke.

"If we are stopped by the authorities on the Danish side of the border, we can use our orders to hopefully justify a visit into Sweden.

"Let's get Greta and head for the border."

"Do we have a target destination for this evening?" asked Zeke.

"We should be able to pass Randers and Aarhus this evening and be in the Vejle area by early morning. A lot depends on the roads not being too icy. There is a deep fjord in the city of Vejle where we can say goodbye to the rubbish in our boot.

"The next day, we should be able to pass Fredericia and get over to Odense and to Nyborg. I believe there is a causeway or ferry to Halsskov.

From there, we should be able to get a bus to Copenhagen.

Chapter 55

Some Difficulty Leaving the Reich for Sweden

Zeke was pretty tired from driving most of the night, so I told him I would drive the rest of the way. We were stopped in a beautiful park in Vejle, Denmark. The sun was just brightening the horizon into a beautiful red-orange glow. I think the sunrise was around 9:30 am. At this time of year.

The rubbish in our trunk was frozen solid. We filled their pockets with small rocks, placed larger rocks underneath their shirts, and gently floated them into the canal. The outgoing tide would take them to their final resting place.

The act of getting rid of two Gestapo agents didn't seem to bother Greta. She had experienced enough trauma from the two agents who invaded and terrorized her at her home for a lifetime of discomfort whenever the Gestapo or SiPo were mentioned.

Our next stop was Fredericia. We were all getting a little hungry, so we stopped at a small hotel on Krügersvej Street in Sanddal, just south of the city. The hotel was able to serve us breakfast, and before long, we were on our way to Odense. The roads were clear, so the traveling was relatively smooth.

We arrived in Copenhagen just after four in the afternoon. It was completely dark, and we were all tired from our drive from Aalborg. Zeke had a suggestion.

"Perhaps it would be best to avoid any interaction with the authorities this late in the day. We could catch the ferry to Malmo, Sweden, in the morning."

"Good suggestion, Zeke. Let's see what we can find for lodging for the evening.

My SS uniform and Ezekiel's Wehrmacht uniform raised some eyebrows in Copenhagen, but we were able to get two rooms at a hotel in the Kastrup section of Copenhagen on Englandsvej Street. It was quite obvious to us that most Danes were not thrilled with the Nazis occupying their country.

The next morning, we drove to the landing where the ferries left for Malmo, Sweden. We had debated leaving our automobile in the lot because the Gestapo would eventually find it and trace it to us in neutral Sweden. In the end, we left the car in the far corner of the lot. We decided the Gestapo would have trouble finding us as civilians in the Stockholm area.

That morning, we had an interesting interaction with the German authorities at the ferry landing.

At the disembarkation desk, we were confronted by German authorities in uniform.

"Lieutenant, what is the nature of your visit to Sweden?"

"We are traveling to visit relatives after completing a mission for our Führer, Constable."

I spread out our orders for the official to read.

After reading over the orders, the official signaled another police officer over to secure his opinion of our orders.

The name on his badge read 'Ahlbrecht.' He seemed quite officious and puffed up with his own self-importance.

"What is going on with the three of you?"

His tone of voice helped me to understand where he was coming from. He was an official who intended on giving us trouble.

In a very smooth voice, I replied calmly. "Herr Ahlbrecht, my sergeant and aide, will be going to visit relatives in the Stockholm area since we have completed our mission for the Führer. We will then be returning to the Reich in one week."

I couldn't have been any nicer to this bumbling idiot. I even handed him a copy of our orders for confirmation.

Officer Ahlbrecht's next sentence placed me and Zeke on high alert.

"These orders look legitimate enough, Lieutenant, but how do I know you are not just fleeing the Reich to avoid disaster if the Russians continue their advance."

"Officer Ahlbrecht! You should know that the SS does not tolerate this kind of defeatist talk."

Ahlbrecht seemed ready for a fight. I decided not to challenge him further until he asked, "Lieutenant, I will need to question you individually about your travel. I will need to start with your aide."

Much of the blood drained from Greta's face, but she stepped forward to answer any questions.

"No, Lieutenant. I will need to take each of you to an interrogation room in order to record your responses. If you are cleared to my satisfaction, you may proceed to the gate for ticketing and boarding."

"Unfortunately, Agent Ahlbrecht, my aide, cannot be isolated from my sergeant or me." I pointed to my head to indicate that George might have diminished mental capacity.

"However, we will not interrupt or comment on your questions to him during your interview."

Ahlbrecht seemed to relent and replied in an officious tone, **"Fine, the three of you follow me."**

He led us down a wide corridor with rooms for interviews branching off from both sides.

We entered an interrogation or interview room about twelve by fourteen feet with a tile floor and a suspended ceiling. The lighting was harsh fluorescent and glared off the pale-green walls. A table and two sturdy wooden chairs were in the center of the room. The room looked a little intimidating.

The constable took a chair and told George to sit in the other available chair. He motioned for Zeke and me to stand off to the side, up against the wall.

Immediately, the official started with an aggressive tone.

"So, young man, what have you been doing in this protectorate of Denmark since you entered?"

I have been helping the lieutenant and the sergeant on their secret mission for our Führer, Sir."

"I'm sorry, corporal, but I don't for a minute believe you. How old are you?"

"I have just turned eighteen years, sir. I assume you have read my orders?"

"Of course, I have read your orders! After some consideration, I have judged them to be completely bogus and false!"

Slap!

The official stood up and struck Greta across the face so hard he knocked her off the chair. She went sprawling onto the tile floor.

Zeke took a step forward, but I held up one finger as a 'wait signal.' Zeke stepped back to the wall with me.

This official had obviously learned some Gestapo tactics and smoothly drew his pistol while waving it at Zeke and me.

His warning, "Stay against the wall if you know what's good for you!"

Zeke and I said nothing while Greta was getting back on her feet and into her chair.

My father's words about avoiding fighting flooded back into my mind.

In a soft and kind voice, I then asked the official, "Sir, would you like to read a cover letter from our Führer that might help clear up our intentions here in Copenhagen?"

The official growled in an unfriendly voice, **"Let's have it, Lieutenant, it's probably bogus also.**

I slowly walked over to the bombastic official while opening my uniform jacket to get papers for the idiot to look over. As soon as I was within an easy distance of him, I dropped the papers on his shoes.

As Ahlbrecht looked down, I brought my fist in sharp contact with the back of his neck as hard as I was able.

Crack!

I could hear his cervical vertebrae break as I brought my weight on my closed-gloved fist down on the back of the swine's neck. His head snapped up, and he looked at me with incredulous and dying eyes. I then picked him up and squeezed his neck in a chokehold to make sure he was done bothering us. I could hear his facial bones, mandible, and hyoid bones crack as I applied continuous pressure for over a minute.

Zeke had immediately latched the door to avoid any interruption.

Greta then asked a reasonable question without a hint of panic. "Lieutenant, what are we supposed to do with this individual now?"

There were no closets or hiding places in the interrogation room. I didn't feel we could just leave him in a corner.

"Zeke, quick. Stand on the table and see if the hung ceiling will support his weight."

The wires suspending the ceiling looked too light to support this overweight bureaucrat. However, the pipes above the ceiling looked pretty sturdy. I hoped they would be strong enough to hold the weight of this bloated criminal.

"What we need to do, Zeke is loop my belt over the strongest-looking pipe. We can then loop my belt through his belt and buckle it after we hoist him above the ceiling."

The whole operation took us less than eight minutes to get Ahlbrecht up above the ceiling, suspend him securely to the pipes, and replace the ceiling tiles. It did take both Zeke and me to hoist the corpulent idiot up to the rafters.

I leaned over and whispered to Greta, "This is how we make bad men disappear."

She smiled and unlocked the door.

We proceeded to the ticketing booth and boarded the ferry for Malmo, Sweden. The bus trip to my relatives in Stockholm went smoothly. We slept most of the way intermittently.

We stayed with my relatives in the Stockholm area until April, except for my one brief return to the gypsum mine, near Nordhausen to check on conditions and food for the prisoners.

Hostilities throughout the Reich ended in May 1945.

Chapter 56

Observations from Small- Town America

When my wife, Ilsa, and I first came to America, the freedoms we found were a little difficult to understand. For the first time in our lives, no government agency seemed to care about any financial transactions we were contemplating. The Gestapo wasn't questioning our neighbors about our religion. No one seemed to care about our religious affiliation. Ilsa and I both attended synagogue and church, depending on our plans each week.

Our impression of America was a collection of small towns with the occasional city. The sky was pure blue. There was no haze or smoke from burning cities or recent bombings. The people seemed genuinely happy.

Our stepdaughter, Greta, had come with us to America. As we were blessed with our own children, we brought them to our local Methodist Church in Sudbury Center and the local synagogue. I'm not sure they ever enjoyed it either, but they never complained too much. I wanted them to realize how important freedom to worship was in their lives. We wanted both children to get the most out of each religion, just as Zeke and I had growing up.

Firearms and ammunition were available at the local hardware store, or you could purchase them directly from catalogs.

In Germany, the Nazis confiscated all firearms. Jews were not even allowed into the stores that use to carry firearms. Having a firearm in your home or possession was an extreme offense. You could be arrested, fined, and, if you were Jewish, sent to a concentration camp.

There were many cities, towns, and villages in America where having a firearm in the household was encouraged. In Kennesaw, Georgia, it is in the city charter: every household has to own a firearm.

Our family enjoyed the freedom of walking around the town center or hiking through the woods and pastures in the back of our home. We would fish in a small stream at the bottom of our hill. Pantry Brook would yield pickerel and small trout.

None of the park benches in town had signs restricting Jews from sitting on them.

Not only were the local residents friendly and helpful, no one even commented on our accents or asked questions about our origins.

I will admit I never made too much of my former position in the SS or my dealings with the Gestapo. Ilsa, Greta, and Zeke's family thought it would be better not to discuss what we did in the war. We wanted the Nazi nightmare behind us.

After Ilsa and I got married in a Lutheran church in Stockholm, Greta wrote to her father and said she was going with us to America. This was news to Ilsa and me.

We never actually adopted her, but Greta's last name was the same as ours on all her papers when we entered America. Ilsa and I thought of her as a little sister. Zeke and Adiya actually had a little sister. Zeke had rescued Adiya and her sister, Chasha, from certain death at the crematorium at Treblinka.

Zeke finished his engineering studies in Berlin at the Technical Institute and married the love of his life, Adiya. He adopted Adiya's sister, Chasha, and eventually moved to Marlboro, Massachusetts.

I still shudder and tear up when I think about how close Adiya and Chasha came to the gas chamber at Treblinka.

Whenever we had a chance, we would meet at the Wayside Inn in Sudbury on Sunday afternoons for a relaxing dinner. Ilsa and I eventually had two boys in addition to Greta. One son wanted to join the Merchant Marine and eventually became a captain sailing for Maersk Shipping Lines.

Ezekiel, Adiya, Ilsa, and I often used these Sunday afternoon gettogethers to discuss and pray for our gratefulness for living in a free and independent nation. The contrasts and similarities of some of the nightmares of the Holocaust were discussed in somewhat hushed tones and never where we could be overheard. The Nazi political deeds and cruelty of the 1930s and 40s would cause nightmares for all of us.

Chapter 57

⟶•◦❦◦•⟵

The Nazi Nightmare in America

Ezekiel and I would often discuss some of the similarities we lived through in Düsseldorf with some of the tragedies we witnessed or heard about in America.

Almost every night, there was some bit of news about an anti-Semitic comment or incident in America. Compared to what Zeke and I lived through in Düsseldorf, most of these anti-Semitic incidents were of minor concern. There were no late-night 'knocks on the door' from the Gestapo or visits from the SiPo authorities.

However, on the 27th of October 2018, a deranged anti-Semite went into a synagogue in Pittsburg, Pennsylvania, and murdered eleven worshipers and wounded six other people. Several of the killed and wounded at the Tree of Life Synagogue were Holocaust survivors. This shooting was probably the worst anti-Semitic incident I had heard about since coming to America. The U.S. president, President Trump, and some of his family who were Jewish went to the synagogue to express their horror and condolences to the congregation.

In the months and years that followed the shooting in Pittsburgh, other anti-Semitic problems were evident in America, Europe, and Australia.

In our state of Massachusetts, at least some in the state government were doing something to limit the exposure of houses of worship to terrorism and hate crimes. * The $2.9 million grant went to thirty

---

*"Synagogues Get Money to Increase Security," by Christian Wade, Statehouse reporter for; the North of Boston Media, 11 October 2021.surveillance cameras, lighting, fencing, and new locks.

Jewish nonprofits and other houses of worship as part of the money to defray the cost of metal detectors,

When I talked with the American Jewish Committee in 2022, their comment was, "Close to 25% of American Jews had experienced some form of anti-Semitic behavior in the past year."

There also seemed to be quite a bit of anti-Asian discrimination, with some serious crimes against the American-Asian community. In general, there seemed to be a rise in crime all over America.

Ezekiel and I would discuss how the political situation in America compared with the different political climates we lived through growing up in Düsseldorf in the 1920s and 1930s. Many of these comparisons gave us concern that America was losing some of its democratic and inalienable rights (rights that cannot be transferred or taken away by legislation).

It was almost like our new country was developing habits we had fled from in Germany. America seemed to become more socialistic. It was disturbing that America was becoming a country of takers.

Ezekiel and I saw the rise in the call for universal health care or a single-payer system, the call for universal fee college, and universal regulated income in order to equalize income, regardless of skill or educational level. All of these programs called for big government solutions, not too unlike what we experienced in Nazi Germany.

The Covid-19 pandemic that swept across America and the world only seemed to deepen the central government's hold on the American people. The rise in lawlessness, riots and looting in some of America's largest cities, border insecurity, and prejudice against people of different backgrounds were all deeply concerning to Ezekiel and me.

A recent, rather dramatic incident occurred in New York City. A college psychology student approached a family of young children playing in their own neighborhood. This 21-year-old female adult college student spit at an eight-year-old child and yelled at him and his two siblings, **"Hitler should have killed you all! I know where you live. And we'll make sure we get you all next time."**

The female perpetrator of this hate crime has on her Facebook account that she is studying to be a guidance counselor! [*]

It is hard to understand how a well-educated female could attack small children in such a hateful, malevolent, and vicious tome while actually spitting on her victims. The incident illustrates that hate is not too far from the surface for many normal-appearing people in this country.

We had seen what rapid inflation had done to Germany when Zeke and I were quite young. In the early 1900s, as late as 1914, the value of the German Mark was approximately 4.2 marks to 1 U.S. dollar. Less than 10 years later, the German Mark was worth 4.2 trillion Marks to 1 U.S. dollar.

Rising inflation, a rising homeless population on American city streets, and armed violence against police, minority groups, and Americans in general were topics of great concern for Zeke and me. We talked about the night in 1938 when we interrupted the thieves in Bucherer's jewelry store in Düsseldorf. We both hoped the small businesses in our hometown and all over Germany had survived the Nazis.

When Zeke and I tried to assess the problem of inflation for our families, we saw nothing very encouraging. The current president seemed to be following an agenda that included something euphemistically called "The Green New Deal."

This "Green Deal" looked to Zeke and me like it could cost trillions of dollars, wreak havoc on many industries, and flood the country with cheap dollars. Both of us were very concerned that the increased taxes and government printing of extra dollars could result in runaway inflation, severe recession, or depression for our adopted country. This is what happened in Germany. It resulted in the rise of the Nazi political party, with Adolf Hitler leading our country to ruin.

---

[*]The Hate Crime perpetrator, reported by the Daily Mail on 29 January 2022, was a student at a local college. She has been arrested for endangering and menacing the life of a child.

Both Ezekiel and I are getting on in years. However, if our discussions are put on paper, our joint notes and efforts will be included in another story, "Traitors in America." Ezekiel and I hope this new effort will become completely unnecessary with an improving economic and political climate.

Chapter 58

Author's Personal Notes

The reader should understand that the contents of "Traitors in the Gestapo" and this sequel, "Traitors in Treblinka," are works of fiction. The characters were real, except for the protagonists and their families. Some of the ancillary characters, especially those in the Gestapo, are fictitious examples of real-life criminals. Some of the heroes and survivors of the Holocaust have been 'fit' into the storyline.

For example, Zivia was a true heroine of the Polish underground, but she did not work or take part in the rocket development at Peenemünde. She was a symbol of hope and encouragement for many victims of Nazi criminal behavior during the Holocaust in her country.

Many of the physicians who survived horrible conditions during their illegal and unlawful incarceration during the Holocaust. Doctors Victor Frankl and Gisella Perl, represent true heroes of their professions. Working under conditions so dire they are almost impossible to accurately describe, these clinicians prevailed and went on to lead productive, influential, principled, and even decorous lives.

Both "Traitors in the Gestapo" and this sequel, "Traitors in Treblinka," contain scenes of sexual content and violence and may not be suitable for younger readers. Including sexual content and violence is a way for the reader to get an idea of what it was like growing up in Nazi Germany in the 1930s.

The violence is used to describe the Gestapo as probably the greatest criminal enterprise in all the world's history. The Nazis, including the Gestapo and the SS, have committed crimes that affect all of us, including future generations. As I indicated in the dedication, our tragedy is ongoing and unending.

The sexual content is a little more difficult to understand without the knowledge of a program instituted on the 12th of December 1935 called

'Lebensborn' * This program was originally instituted in order to improve the falling birth rate in Germany and provide SS wives with encouragement for having more "racially pure and healthy children." The program screened for healthy women who could prove their "racial purity."

The Nazis felt those personal character traits like loyalty and bravery were inheritable and could be promoted through a process of selected breeding. This abominable program was the way the SS hoped to raise a population of "racially elite" German population to conquer and populate the rest of Europe and eventually dominate the world.

Of course, the whole plan, devised by the head of the SS, Heinrich Himmler, a former chicken farmer, was based on very shaky or no science.

The 'Lebensborn' program was based on whimsical wishes. The entire program eventually degenerated into the kidnapping of "Aryan-looking" children from the conquered territories and placing them in "good" German households.

In addition, Himmler's Aryanization program was shown to be completely ridiculous and absurd when a black American, Jesse Owens, excelled and won four gold medals at the 1936 Olympics.

The Lebensborn children were initiated into the SS and led a cushy life of good food and excellent education. They were told they were elite human beings and that they were going to inherit the world. **

---

*Lebensborn, meaning "Fountain of Life,' was a program initiated to promote the Growth of Germany's Aryan population.

**Anni-Frid, one of the singers from the very popular "ABBA" band, was a Lebensborn child. Anni-Frid Lyngstad achieved monumental success. At the height of the band's popularity, they were earning more than the Swedish automobile company, Volvo. She was fortunate because her mother moved to Sweden when Anni-Frid was young (Norway didn't want these "Nazi rats"). The tolerance of Lebensborn children was much better in neutral Sweden. Later in life, she met her biological German father, Wehrmacht Sergeant Alfred Haase.

The 'baptism' of the Lebensborn children by the SS included a ritual of holding a silver dagger over the child, next to a Swastika Flag and candlestick made at the Dachau concentration camp. The dagger was held over the baby's head while the mother pledged her allegiance to Hitler for herself and her child. This bazaar ritual was for the "perfect" Aryan children.

If the Lebensborn children were deformed in any way, the less-than perfect children were killed or sent to concentration camps. Unfortunately, even today, it is not routine for babies with known defects in the womb to make it to full term in Germany and many other countries.

The total number of Lebensborn children in Norway and Germany numbered approximately 20,000. However, another approximately 200,000 Aryan-looking children were kidnapped from conquered counties all over Europe and placed in "good" or "normal" German homes.

The Yiddish word for father is "Abba." It is the author's speculation that the bandleader may have chosen to honor our Father in heaven or to remember the father she never had, in addition to the first initial of the band members' first names.

The Nazis didn't care about marriage or courtship as long as they produced Aryan children for the Reich. This was the atmosphere Jenz lived through when he met young girls and women at Hitler Youth Camp in 1936.

This Lebensborn program may help the reader understand what Jenz, a rather naïve, tall, Aryan-looking male sixteen-year-old was up against during the summer of 1936 at Hitler Youth Camp. The fact that he was actually Jewish may not have mattered to any of the women he met.

This novel is not meant as a voyeuristic view of the Gestapo or the SS. Everyone should understand that the Gestapo was a criminal organization praying on innocent Germans and anyone disagreeing with Nazi doctrine.

The SS was a group of "elite" Hitler henchmen who will go down in history books as misguided, depraved, and disgraced killers.

"Traitors in Treblinka" is meant as a snapshot of history in a readable form for contemporary individuals to get some feeling for the horror, deprivation, and revulsion of Nazi acts during the Holocaust.

Stealing a family's possessions and homes wasn't enough for these criminals; they had to kill whole families together so parents would witness the suffering and destruction of their own children. Children had to witness the suffering and horrible demise of their own parents and loved ones. This is probably the cruelest form of genocide.

Healing may take centuries.

Chapter 59

The Author's Family History

In the 1870s, the author's Swedish ancestors traveled to America and settled in Massachusetts. The reason they chose to live in New England were two-fold. The coast mimicked much of the country they had left: rock-strewn coastlines with occasional beautiful beaches. Also, they were assured of employment at a Norwegian-owned factory near Worcester, Massachusetts, that employed many men from Sweden. The Iver Johnson Arms and Cycle Works was expanding and had moved to Fitchburg, Massachusetts. The company needed more extensive facilities to meet the demand for reliable, safe, and inexpensive handguns and classic well-engineered bicycles.

The three Swedish men who came over together were Misters Rehnquist, Ramsgrund, and Ahlin. There was a reason they came across as a family group. These three men had married three sisters from Stockholm, Sweden. Mr. Ramsgrund had a son who was the grandfather of the main fictional character in this novel. A branch of the Ahlin family became interested in dry-goods marketing in 1899. Today, under different ownership, these department stores are still active in Sweden.

The author served two tours in Vietnam as a U.S. Navy dentist on the USS Kitty Hawk from 1969-1971. "Traitors in Treblinka," the sequel to "Traitors in the Gestapo," is his third novel. His first novel, "Overrun, The Battle for Firebase 14," was about some of the author's experiences in the Gulf of Tonkin and in the country of South Vietnam in 1969. His first two books were dental textbooks. "Maxillofacial Orthopedics, A Clinical Approach for the Growing Child," Quintessence Books, 1984, and "An Atlas of Dentofacial

Orthopedics," with Dr. Marc Saadia, 1999, were both published while the author was teaching at Harvard University, School of Dental Medicine.

The author's son, Konrad, is a senior research engineer at Georgia Tech Research. Konrad and his wife Katie and son Keayon live in Georgia. The author's daughter, Verity, and her husband, Harry, are living in Virginia. Verity has her Master's degree and is working for a small business incubator company. Harry has earned a Ph.D. in Pharmacology. Dr. Ahlin has practiced dentistry for over 50 years in Gloucester, Massachusetts.

Chapter 60

Credits to Very Deserving Authors

My thanks to the many authors cited in this work for their in-depth research and detailed explanation of some of the horror and paralyzing pain inflicted on innocent men, women, and children during the Holocaust. Without these authors' astute research and testimony, this novel would never have come to fruition.

I would also like to thank U. S. Naval Officer Michael David Rubin for his many comments on this work. His inciteful perceptions are very appreciated.

My deep appreciation to Ms. Martha Maas for her expert editing of the manuscript. Any errors or omissions belong to the author.

J.H. Ahlin, DDS

Gloucester, Massachusetts

Spring, 2025

Welcome to MANSFIELD

The Austen Chronicles book 1

4 Horsemen
Publications, Inc.

A.R. Farina

*For Lea
who always believed in me
and Jane Austen
I hope I made you both proud*

*A special thanks to Chris Pusateri
for making me a better writer*

TABLE OF CONTENTS

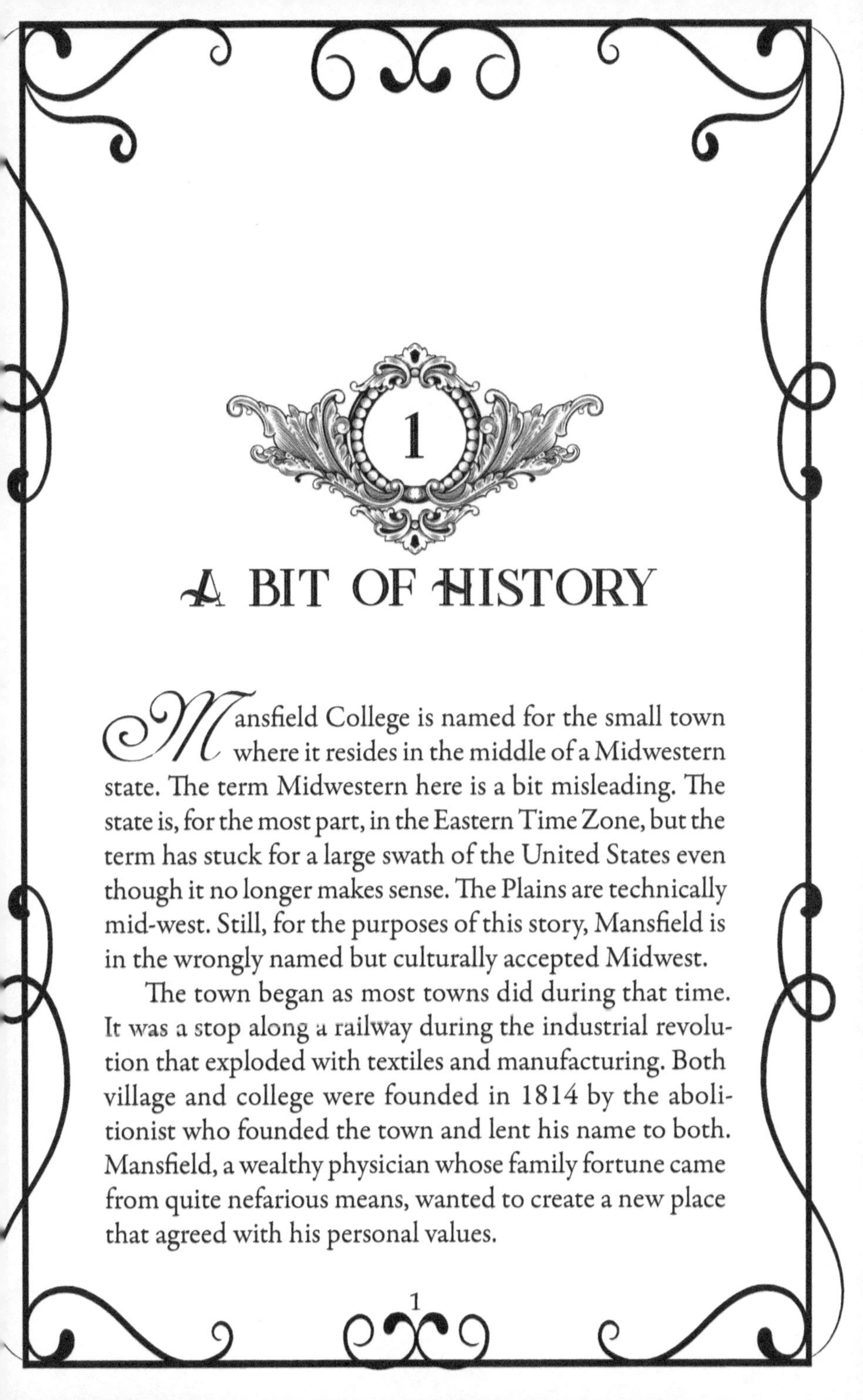

1

A BIT OF HISTORY

Mansfield College is named for the small town where it resides in the middle of a Midwestern state. The term Midwestern here is a bit misleading. The state is, for the most part, in the Eastern Time Zone, but the term has stuck for a large swath of the United States even though it no longer makes sense. The Plains are technically mid-west. Still, for the purposes of this story, Mansfield is in the wrongly named but culturally accepted Midwest.

The town began as most towns did during that time. It was a stop along a railway during the industrial revolution that exploded with textiles and manufacturing. Both village and college were founded in 1814 by the abolitionist who founded the town and lent his name to both. Mansfield, a wealthy physician whose family fortune came from quite nefarious means, wanted to create a new place that agreed with his personal values.

At the northernmost point of town was situated The Park, the familial home in which much of this tale will take place. The Park is four square acres, although it is not actually square at all. The front property edge is a straight line, but the rest of the property is rounded. From the air, The Park looks like a capital D. It is surrounded by a six-foot-tall black iron fence. The main gate faces due south. There is a public walking path around the entire property. The road leading south from The Park is called Main Street. The road crossing in front of The Park, thereby creating the straight line, which runs from east to west, is called Mansfield Parkway. To the west lies Mansfield College. To the east lies Sotherton, the Rushworth estate. More to come in due course on that estate and the family that resides therein. The road that encompasses the property is called Mansfield Circle. No one ever accused Dr. Mansfield of modesty.

Mansfield College broke with tradition at the time and enrolled worthy scholars of all races and genders. It has stood for over 200 years as a bastion of liberal arts education. Because Dr. Mansfield understood the value of education and felt everyone had the right to try, he created an open-enrollment institution with a limited number of seats. Essentially, if one applied on time, if one was willing to work harder than one has ever worked before, and most importantly, if one could afford it, the gates of Mansfield College were open to all. Once the last seat was full, the enrollment period closed.

Mansfield College has, to this day, never taken a single federal dollar. Unlike other schools that make this claim yet gleefully allow students to rack up Federal Student Loans, public student loans are simply not accepted at Mansfield.

There is no office of financial aid. At its founding, tuition was a mere 100 dollars per semester. Of course, that was a small fortune at the time; suitably adjusted for inflation, the tuition remains a small fortune to this day. Graduates of Mansfield College both then and now knew that a degree that garnered the Mansfield Crest opened doors around the world that would have been quite closed had the degree crest been any different.

Dr. Mansfield, however, understood that not all otherwise deserving, willing, and able students would be able to afford said tuition. Therefore, he set up an academic contest called the Mansfield Gift. Five students a year who agreed to come to Mansfield College without a declared major were selected from a pool of students who would, after a rigorous application and interview process, be allowed to attend Mansfield College tuition-free.

The winners of these five coveted spots all went on to achieve amazing professional success. Some members of this exclusive club have walked in space, commanded aircraft carriers, worked on cures for diseases, argued before the Supreme Court, and served as members of Congress. The Mansfield Gift was a precursor to most assured success. Unlike Skull and Bones, another precursor to assured success, the Mansfield Gift did not require anyone to keep horrible secrets or do unspeakable acts. The only requirement was the student come to Mansfield College, major undeclared, and be open to a wide range of courses for the first two years. At that time, the students would select a major and study that subject exclusively for their remaining two years at the prestigious institution. Dr. Mansfield believed that an open mind was the cure for nearly all the problems in the world.

Thanks to the prestige of this unique college, it has continued to thrive even though the town has not. Many of the factories in Mansfield closed due to various financial disasters and adverse political decisions over the years, which left a rather large hole in certain parts of town. Those who did not leave town became part of the college economy. As of this writing, three out of every five residents of Mansfield work for, or make money directly from, businesses that serve the college. The other two either work for, or make money from, the Rushworth organization.

The campus itself is still situated in the same location, only slightly expanding in size to accommodate athletics. Because there are no scholarships for athletics, all teams are clubs. That is not to say that they do not take competition seriously. On the contrary, the clubs often beat the other Division II and III schools in the surrounding areas. Those schools often claim they do not take it seriously since the games are considered scrimmages, but everyone knows that they are simply making excuses.

The homes in the immediate vicinity surrounding the campus are almost all historical buildings protected by either the federal or the state government. Most of these homes are owned by descendants of the Mansfield family or wealthy graduates who keep a home near campus to have a place to stay when they return for festivities. In an effort to keep faculty salaries down, the college provides faculty housing in well-kept single-family homes built in the early 1900s for exactly this purpose. Each home is maintained by the college at no cost to the faculty. Mansfield College maintains zero adjunct faculty. Although there is little to no pressure to publish after being hired, no previously unpublished faculty has ever been hired. Even though the nearest major city is two hours away, much like the Mansfield Gift, thousands of faculty members from all around the world apply for openings each year.

Two hundred and six years after the awarding of the first Mansfield Gift, five letters embossed with gold lettering are sent out to five addresses across the globe. One to a young woman in Exeter, England. One to a young woman in Seoul, South Korea. One letter is sent to a young man in Tacoma, Washington. Somewhere in Texarkana, Arkansas, a young man gets a letter. All of these recipients will accept the offer immediately and prepare to matriculate to Mansfield College in the fall, having sufficient funds for room and board already procured.

Each of these young people will come and go from this tale, yet only one will affect the outcome. We can be sure that each of these four people will go on to do great things. The woman from Seoul, in particular, will be quite memorable. However, it is not on them where we shine our spotlight. Instead, we will follow the trajectory of the final letter, sent to a girl, not a young woman, who lives in an unincorporated area in the Deep South.

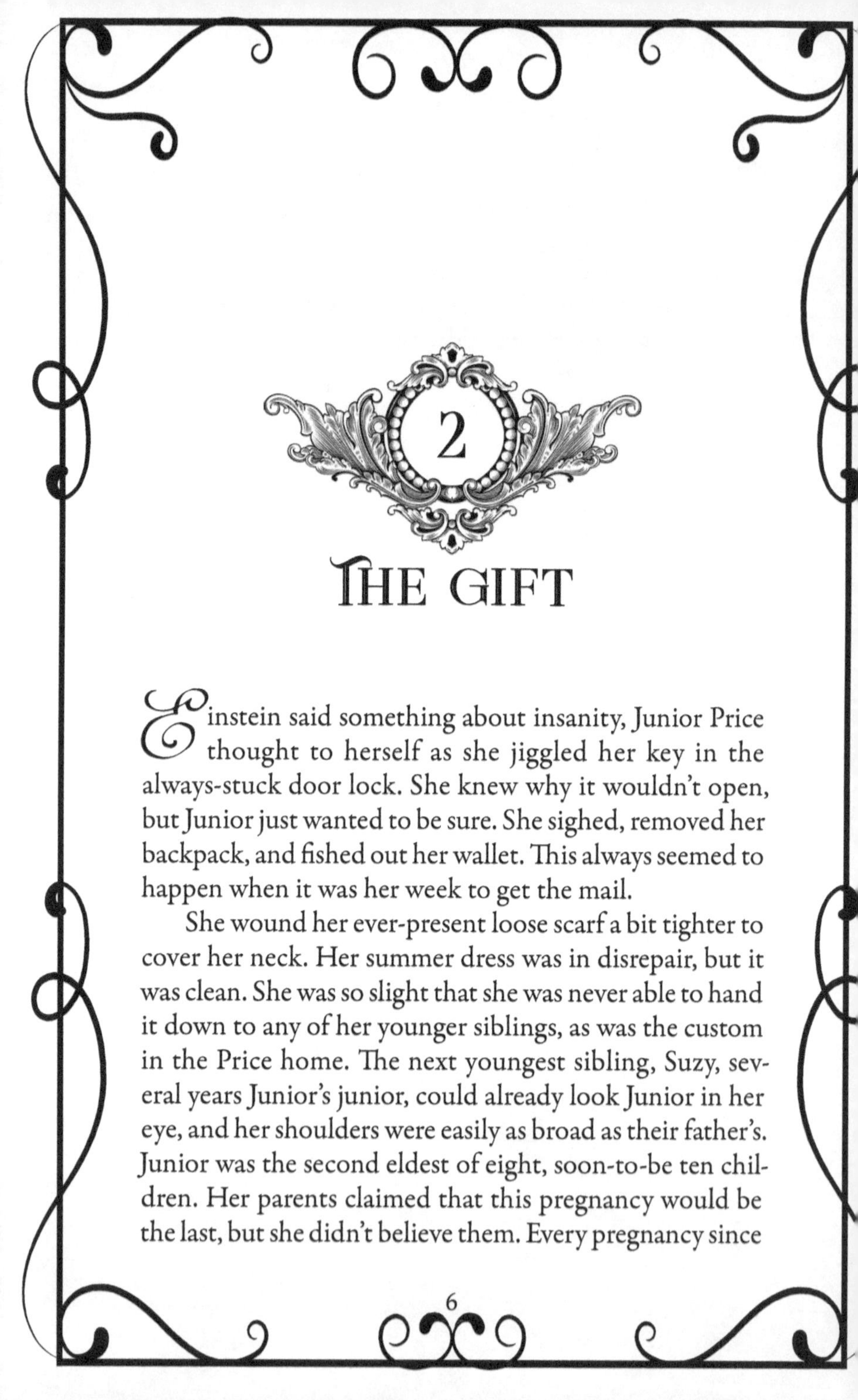

2

THE GIFT

Einstein said something about insanity, Junior Price thought to herself as she jiggled her key in the always-stuck door lock. She knew why it wouldn't open, but Junior just wanted to be sure. She sighed, removed her backpack, and fished out her wallet. This always seemed to happen when it was her week to get the mail.

She wound her ever-present loose scarf a bit tighter to cover her neck. Her summer dress was in disrepair, but it was clean. She was so slight that she was never able to hand it down to any of her younger siblings, as was the custom in the Price home. The next youngest sibling, Suzy, several years Junior's junior, could already look Junior in her eye, and her shoulders were easily as broad as their father's. Junior was the second eldest of eight, soon-to-be ten children. Her parents claimed that this pregnancy would be the last, but she didn't believe them. Every pregnancy since the fourth of the Price children was proclaimed to be the last in the line. Only the eldest three were planned, and yet, like clockwork, every two years for 18 years, in the fall, a new Price child was born.

She pulled open the doors to the main office of the tiny rural post office, and the chill of the air conditioning hit her like a gale. The sweat on her arms and on the back of her neck dried up, and she felt goosebumps form. The customer side of the counter was small and had room for maybe three people. The town gossip, Stuart, was leaning on the counter, keeping Ms. Grayson from her work. The rural postmaster, Ms. Grayson, furrowed her brows and looked as though she was hanging on every word Stuart was saying. She looked up at Junior, her facial pucker relaxed, and she smiled.

"Stuart, I have to help Ms. Price here. I will need you to give me a minute," she said, cutting him off mid-sentence as he was explaining something about someone's backyard garden and the apparent illegality of said garden.

Stuart, never one to take a hint, slid aside just enough for Junior to approach the counter. "Hi, Ms. Grayson," Junior said with a smile.

"Hiya, Junior."

"How behind?" Junior asked, avoiding all pleasantries. She was pretty sure she knew the answer, but since she didn't always get the mail, the delinquent notices did not always pass through her hands.

"Just a sec." Ms. Grayson walked over to the postal box and pulled the weeks' worth of uncollected mail out that she had bound in a rubber band and pulled out the notice. She read it and held up three fingers, indicating they were three months behind on the box rental.

Junior opened her wallet and saw five twenty-dollar bills. It was her tutoring money from the past two weeks. She sighed. Three months' rent was fifty bucks. She held up the money and nodded to Ms. Grayson, who smiled with a grimace and reached in and removed the lock from the inside. She brought the bundled mail.

"Sorry, Junior." She plucked the money from Junior's left hand and plopped the bundle into her right. "At least now you'll be paid up through summer."

"Well, that is something isn't it?" The end of summer would mean, hopefully, escape from Unincorporated Nowhere. She wished and she prayed. Of course, you, Dear Reader, already know that the bundle contains the answers to her wishes and prayers, but Junior Price did not. Had she known, she would not have thrown the bundle of mail and her wallet into her backpack and started the three-mile walk back home. She would have danced and sang and been twirled around by strangers. Instead, she was preoccupied with how to ask her mother if there was any way she could get some of her money back.

The walk back to the Price's homestead involved only one turn, and so Junior made it without having to concentrate too hard. The main road into the town that held the county post office was paved, and Junior could generally walk along the side of the road with relative safety. The traffic was usually light. Even so, she never wore headphones on the walk, just to be safe and to set a good example for the rest of the Price children.

After about two and a half miles, she turned into the long driveway that led to the smattering of living quarters that made up the Price Ranch. It was not a ranch in the sense that there were horses or cattle or anything that may grow on a ranch. It was the name Mr. Price gave the area because he thought "compound" sounded a bit "culty." It is common knowledge that by that time everyone in the area knew the family could field its own baseball team with the children alone, and the neighbors openly start calling it a cult.

Price Ranch was approximately a 1-mile square of mostly untouched trees and hills. At the center of it sat a relatively new 3-bedroom 2.5 bath doublewide mobile home. The parents lived there with the youngest three children, and the entire family dined there. The living, kitchen, and dining area was open, and so there was more than enough room for two dining tables. Upon the sudden death of Mr. Price's father five years prior, the family used the small inheritance to purchase this home. The grass that had been dug up to lay the foundation and run the electricity and water had never been replaced. What survived of the lawn after many a children's game of soccer and kickball consisted entirely of weeds and thorns.

Set back 20 yards on either side of the main house sat two identically square brick homes, built from a kit purchased in the Sears and Roebucks catalog back when that was a thing one could do. Many people, including Junior's recent ancestors, did just that. The taller two-story one, built by Mrs. Price's grandfather Emanuel Ward, housed the eldest boy Bill, aged eighteen. He watched over his two next youngest brothers. They were aged twelve and ten. In the other, built by Emanuel Ward for his son, Mrs. Price's father, lived Junior and Suzy. The arrangement raised eyebrows, but the Prices had very little choice. The small home was always eventually going to be a home for the older children just as it was for the Ward family. Once

the children reached a certain age, they moved out to learn responsibility, but not too far away that they could get in too much trouble.

The big house was connected to Bill and the boys' house with a breezeway that came off the back of the garage and connected to the front porch. There was another covered walkway between the original two homes. If one wished, and one rarely wished, one could go from house to house to house without ever being exposed to the elements. This allowed the Prices to have just one electric bill and pay property taxes on only one home.

Junior was never any trouble and was, by all accounts, an excellent influence on all of the children in the family. It is uncertain how or why things like this happen, but Junior Price was born with an uncanny sense of right and wrong. She was the only child in her entire graduating class at Unincorporated Nowhere to never once be called to the principal's office for anything. She was never called for disciplinary problems, nor was she called because she was named student of the week, month, or year. Granted, she started school early and skipped a grade, and she was only 16 at the time she earned her diploma, so leaving no indelible mark on her community could be explained that way. However, the real reason Junior was never called to the principal's office was that she never drew any attention to herself in any way.

She didn't speak up in class, but she always answered when called upon. She never offered her opinion in a debate but always gave one when asked. She never told anyone who was not her younger sibling what to do, and even then, she only made suggestions. She never ever told anyone not to do anything. She never felt it was her place to comment on how others chose to live. To that end, she never stopped a friend from going to a party where there would be drinking, nor did she turn anyone in for cheating on a test. She never went to a party that had drinking, nor had she ever cheated on a test, nor let anyone cheat off her test. By keeping herself to herself, she created a cloak of invisibility. Even her scarves, her only recognizable definable feature, were not enough of a branding mark to allow her to stand out. Everyone knew her name, as was the way of living in Unincorporated Nowhere, but no one knew much else. She was often described as the oldest daughter of that cult that lived a few miles out of town. She never corrected anyone on this, and that was that.

Junior walked past the big house and waved at her three youngest siblings. Two boys, their names not important enough to mention here, and a girl called Betsy. They called her Little Bit because she looked like a miniature version of her mother and was just a little bit like their father in that she had his hair color. They were having "tea" on the porch. They waved back. Betsy blew her a kiss, which she caught and brought to her heart. She entered her home through the screen door and dropped her bag on the small table where she and Suzy ate breakfast each day and lunch in the summer and on weekends. She unwound her scarf and hung it over the back of her chair. She pulled the cold-brewed coffee she mixed the night before out of the small apartment refrigerator and poured herself a cup. She dropped in two miniature ice cubes and a dash of French vanilla creamer and sat down to sort the mail.

She pulled her phone out of her pocket and unwound the earbuds from around the phone. She pushed them into her ears and hit play on her classic rock playlist. Because she earned her own money as a math and writing tutor after school, she had her own phone. She splurged and paid for an unlimited streaming service because there was no Wi-Fi at The Ranch. The internet was hard-wired. Her unlimited service allowed her to make playlists when she was at school or in town, and then listen to them offline at home. She could afford an unlimited data plan, but she didn't see the need.

As Eddie Van Halen wailed away, Junior separated the mail into three piles, one for each house. Ms. Grayson wrapped the mail inside the magazines, so Junior pulled the rubber band off and watched the tube open and unfurl. She placed her right hand on the letter from the local community college addressed to Bill as they were desperate to get him to come there instead of joining the Air Force, and with her left on the back of the last magazine, flipped the pile over. She took a sip of her iced coffee and then she got up, went to the junk drawer, and pulled out two more rubber bands. She wrapped up each house's mail using the same method as Postmaster Grayson.

National Geographic was hers; she put it down to the right. The three magazines for maternity clothing were most assuredly her mother's. She put those in the middle. *Nat Geo Kids* was for her brothers. She earned a free subscription when she renewed. She set it to the left. Van Halen made way for the Black Crowes. She found herself bopping her head along as Chris Robinson belted out his lyrics. She was in a rhythm. She knew what bills looked like, she knew what college recruiting letters looked like, she knew what Air Force recruiting letters looked like, and so she filtered them out without having to think.

Just as Robinson belted out the recurrence of jealousy one last time, she flipped over a thick, cream-colored envelope. Brian Setzer's opening strum of Stray Cats' "Rock This Town" started up, and Junior saw her name, in gold embossed writing:

Ms. Frances J. Price Jr.

The return address was Mansfield College. She dropped the envelope as Mr. Setzer described his date as looking so right. Junior pulled the earbuds out of her ears, allowing the Stray Cats to possibly get into a fight without her auditory intrusion.

She felt the heat run through her entire body. She stood up and sat down. She did it again. She looked down at the envelope on the table. She knew what it was. She knew what it meant. She started sweating from every pore. She could feel the heat rising in her body. When she became embarrassed or excited, red blotches would crawl up her neck. They made her look like she was coming down with or recovering from some kind of pox. Dissipation took much longer than the appearance of these temporary but telltale blotches.

Junior was often full of emotions that caused the nervous condition but never the explosive emotional outbursts that would let anyone know she was feeling any anxiety over keeping all her thoughts to herself. The scarves were not simply ornamental; they served a clear function. She picked up the envelope and could see it shaking. She picked up her mug and gulped the coffee in one big gulp. Had she been more clearheaded, she would have remembered what happened to her when she had too much caffeine at once.

She slammed her cup down and picked the envelope up. She flipped it over and slid her finger under the flap. She slid it down to the point in the middle, carefully keeping the entire thing intact so she could possibly frame it one day. She slid her finger up the other side and the flap came up. Inside were four sheets of paper folded in thirds. She opened them up. The first one was a handwritten letter on extremely expensive, ink-absorbing paper.

Dear Ms. Price,

On behalf of Mansfield College, it is my honor to present to you one of the five annual Mansfield Gifts. As you know, this gift is the most prestigious honor that can be bestowed on any student at Mansfield College. Every year, thousands of applicants from all around the world compete for one of these five spots. Clearly, your hard work and dedication have been rewarded.

Enclosed are the documents you will need to send back to accept The Gift and begin your registration for Fall Classes.

Congratulations.
Welcome to the Mansfield Family,

Dr. M. Bennet, President

3

ROOM AND BOARD

Junior burst into the big house, ignoring her youngest three siblings' cries to stop and have tea. She was shouting "MOM!" before the door was even open. Her father was asleep in the recliner, and he jolted when the door banged against the wall. His quick movement slammed his feet down as the foot of the chair locked into place. He swore then grimaced. "Oh Dad, I'm sorry." Junior ran over to him to see how she could help him, temporarily forgetting her mission.

He had been medically discharged from the Navy after an accident on an aircraft carrier deck left him with permanent damage in his right foot. Because he served 10 years, he was eligible for a disability severance package and VA permanent disability. This allowed for a small stipend for the rest of his life, but it also meant he could not take any other work or do much of anything that involved being on his feet for long.

There was debate among the people of Unincorporated Nowhere if Mr. Price's injuries were really so severe that permanent disability was the answer. He was still a young man in his 30s when the accident happened, and surely, one would not wish to do nothing forever. Mr. Price, being not of sound body, but of sound mind, knew that his wife owned the land on which they lived and the homes that stood there, that he and his family could live comfortably on the money the Navy offered him. Of course, at that time, they had four children with one on the way, and he was most assuredly going to be the last child, so he took the offer and retired young.

While his pride did not stand in the way of him taking the money from the Navy as he felt they destroyed him, and thus owed him the money, it did keep him from using any other government assistance. With each new child, and with each new batch of responsibilities dumped on one of his own children, Mr. Price dug in deeper. He would say that it wasn't the government's fault that Fran was so fertile. Even Fran felt that there was no need to take the government's help. She always said, "We have enough help right here" as she gave her older children meaningful looks. The line was a mantra, and eventually, they all believed it.

"I'm fine." He waved her off as she came over to him. He pulled the handle up and his feet rose again. He exhaled a breath he didn't know he was holding. He scanned his eldest daughter, and noticing the scarfless, blotchy neck, knew something important was happening. "What's the screaming and door slamming about?"

Realizing the conversation was being turned back to her, Junior held the envelope out to him. She wanted to see his face as he read the news. He opened it up without looking at the front and unfolded the paper with much less care than she would have liked. His eyes scanned the hand-written note from Dr. Bennet. He looked up at her and back down at it. The information was coming together. His mouth smiled, but his face did not. This made her nervous.

She convinced herself he would change his mind about all of this once he found out the news. He argued against her applying for The Gift. He argued that just because she was so smart and could graduate high school early, it didn't mean she was ready to go off to some northern college. It didn't matter that her mother went there and knew members of the founding Mansfield family.

Junior agreed that if she did not win The Gift, she would stay at home and attend the community college. She would take Bill's car as he wouldn't need it in the Air Force. Mr. Price agreed to these terms because he ever expected that college would take the daughter of a graduate who, as he put it, "never once used her grand education for anything other than figuring out nap schedules and crunching a family budget."

He flipped to the next page, which she knew was the course selections. He read through the options there, and he nodded, keeping the smile plastered on his face. The next page was a roommate preference/personality test. The smile continued. The final page was a bill for 11,000 dollars, the cost of one year's room and board. They could make payments over the summer, but they would have to pay in full before she matriculated in the fall. His fake smile faltered and Junior thought she saw, for just a second, a smirk, before he returned to his resting disinterested face. She was not expecting that. She had her half of the money in the bank as was part of the deal. He folded everything back up and stuck it back in the envelope. He held it back to her. "I don't know where your mother is. I was actually resting before you barged in. Check the laundry room." He picked up the remote control and turned on the TV.

Junior was disheartened but not defeated. Her father hadn't said anything for sure, but he hadn't said "No" either. He did not object. He neither ranted nor raved. That smirk made her uncomfortable though. Her father was one to scheme and obfuscate, while Junior found schemes abhorrent and obfuscation a waste of good time that could be spent doing something productive. Other than her love for what the family called "his music" and unwavering love for Mrs. Price, he and Junior had nothing in common. There are only so many conversations a father and daughter can have about the deep cuts on Def Leppard's *Pyromania* album, although they did have more than the rest of the family cared to hear.

Junior nodded at her father and turned to walk to the laundry room. It was located off the kitchen and doubled as the entry room from the garage. Her mother always did laundry with the door closed to keep the youngest from coming in and touching something clean with a filthy hand.

Junior opened the door and found her mother folding clothes and putting them into individual baskets. She did laundry for the youngest five, herself, and her husband. Laundry day was every day at The Ranch. Mrs. Price wore over-the-ear headphones attached to a turn-of-the-century Discman. She did not care for downloadable music. She was still convinced that CD sound quality was best. It was a hotly debated topic over many dinners at the "adult" table. So as not to scare her, Junior flicked the lights on and off. Her mother pulled the headphones off her head and turned around. She had a fake smile plastered on her face. It morphed into an actual smile when she realized she was not going to be told that she had to change a diaper or make a sandwich.

"What a pleasant surprise." She pulled her namesake into a hug. She was not due until the fall, all the kids were born in the fall, but she was showing already. She was having twins. She thought that it would be the same as having all the rest of them, but she discovered that was simply untrue. Junior kept her hips pulled back out of consideration of her new siblings' cramped quarters.

"It's a big surprise," Junior said as she held out the envelope with the gold writing facing up.

Mrs. Price brought both of her hands to her mouth as she gasped. She started doing what Junior called her happy dance. It consisted of fists in front of her face being pumped up and down while shaking her hips back and forth. Junior, never one to miss a good happy dance, joined in. After 30 seconds, they grasped each other in a tight hug, new siblings be damned. "Let's go to my office and look it all over."

They clasped hands, and Frances Sr. led Frances Jr. silently, as to not wake her husband who had already fallen back to sleep or who was faking sleep to avoid further conversations about the contents of that envelope, to the master bedroom, stopping on the way to peek out at the youngest children's tea party. Suzy had joined them, so everything was well under control. The "office" was really just one corner of the room where Mrs. Price kept her desk. She managed everything in the household, so she needed space to do it. Mr. Price kept out most of the day, so she could go in and close the door without fear of being interrupted.

Mrs. Price sat in her office chair, and Junior sat on the edge of the bed. Her mother, as carefully as Junior had, opened the envelope and removed the papers. She read the first note from Dr. Bennet and tears fell. "Oh, baby." She got up and pulled Junior up into another hug. "I'm so proud of you."

Junior, who had until that moment not fully realized that she was waiting to hear those words from her father, only to be soundly disappointed, started crying as well. "Thank you." Time ceased as they hugged and cried tears of joy. Eventually, Mrs. Price pushed back and wiped Junior's face and then her own.

"OK, let's see what else is in there." She sat back down at her desk. She moved to page two.

"I was hoping we could talk through that. They didn't include course descriptions. First-years don't have a lot of choices as you know, but I wanted to talk through the whole rotation as best we can. Things haven't changed much, and the core classes are all the same."

Mrs. Price nodded. "Of course, baby. That will be so fun." She slid the second page to the back of the stack and looked at the roommate preference form. "This could be fun too. We should get Suzy in on this."

"I was thinking the same thing." Junior kept her spirits under control because the look on her father's face was still on display in her mind.

When her mother slid out the final page, her smile cracked. She sighed deeply. "Whoa. Eleven thousand dollars is a lot."

"I know, but you don't need to have all of it, Mom. I have my half in the bank. Remember the deal?" she asked rhetorically.

Mrs. Price nodded and looked down and rubbed her belly. She looked back up, and the tears were back, but they were not joyous.

Junior knew what it meant. She took a deep breath and was ready to say something, anything, tears pouring down her cheeks.

Mrs. Price said, "Oh baby... I'm..." and before she could finish, her eyes brightened. She smiled. "I have an idea." She bobbed her eyebrows up and down. Junior knew that meant it was a good idea. She exhaled her big, angry breath and nodded, waiting to see what the solution would be.

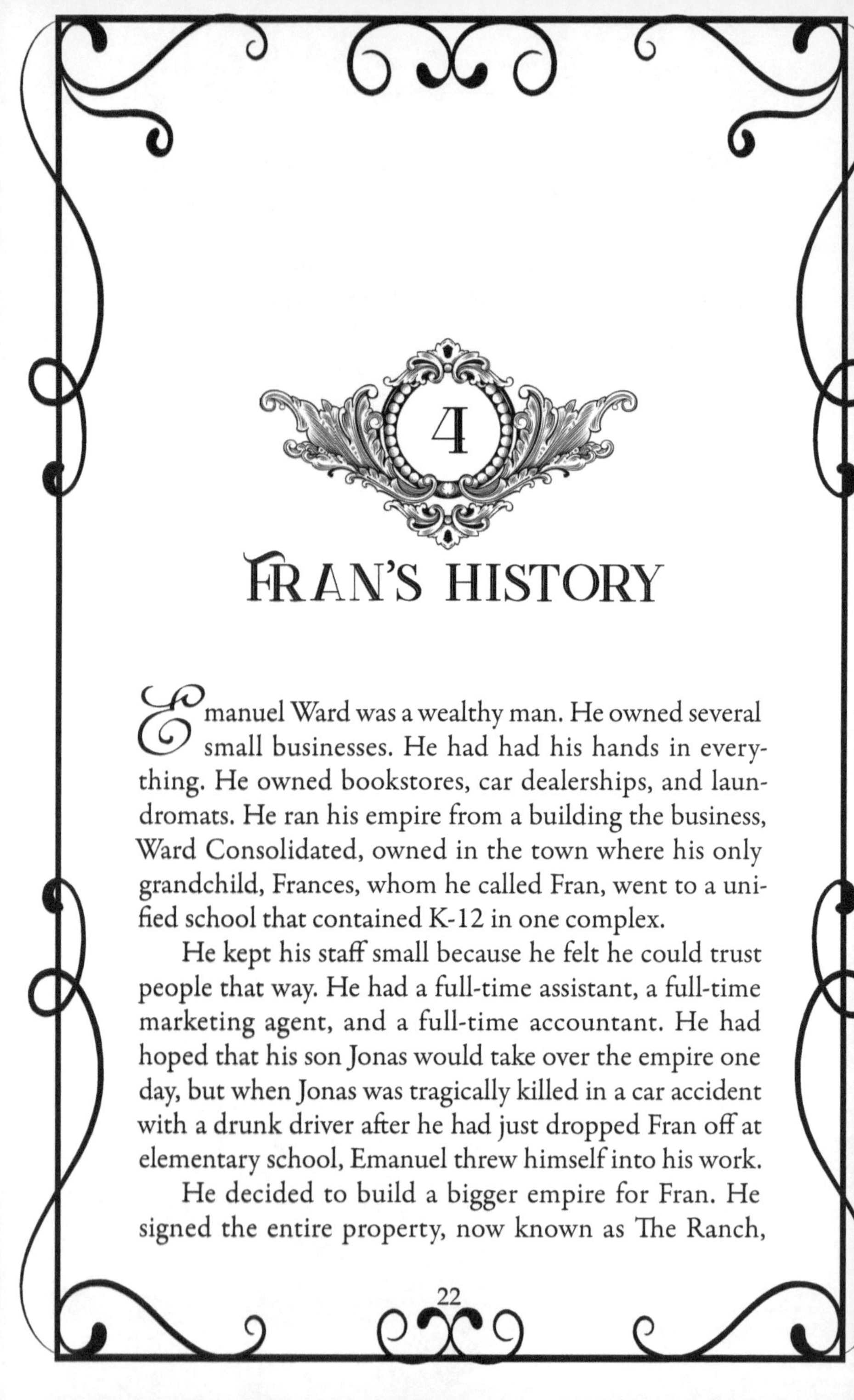

4

FRAN'S HISTORY

*E*manuel Ward was a wealthy man. He owned several small businesses. He had had his hands in everything. He owned bookstores, car dealerships, and laundromats. He ran his empire from a building the business, Ward Consolidated, owned in the town where his only grandchild, Frances, whom he called Fran, went to a unified school that contained K-12 in one complex.

He kept his staff small because he felt he could trust people that way. He had a full-time assistant, a full-time marketing agent, and a full-time accountant. He had hoped that his son Jonas would take over the empire one day, but when Jonas was tragically killed in a car accident with a drunk driver after he had just dropped Fran off at elementary school, Emanuel threw himself into his work.

He decided to build a bigger empire for Fran. He signed the entire property, now known as The Ranch, over to Fran with her mother, his daughter-in-law, as executor until such time as Fran graduated from college or if another tragedy befell the family. Fran's mother agreed to these terms if and only if Emanuel stayed on the property with them in his own home. Emanuel, long since a widower, readily agreed. The three of them lived there happily for some time.

When his only grandchild was accepted into a northern college that only accepted cash, he wrote a check. He did not, as you might expect, write a check to the college, but to Fran. The check was for the full amount of the bill for tuition and room and board, plus living expenses for four full years.

He explained, "I'm giving you this money, and I trust you to do the right thing. If you do the right thing, the Ward Empire will be waiting for you when you are done up there. If you choose to, one day, sell it all and move away, that will be up to you."

She deposited it into a checking account. Strings were pulled at the bank to ensure she would not need anyone else's name on the account, and she wrote her first of four checks to Mansfield College. Her grandfather was right to trust her. She was good with money.

She worked small jobs and saved every cent she could. She had money left over in the account after she graduated. She majored in economics and accounting. Unfortunately for him, his granddaughter had not quite earned her degree in accounting soon enough. His own accountant had secretly been "cooking the books" for years. During Fran's second year at Mansfield, the fraud was discovered. Upon realizing the betrayal, the shock of not merely finding all his money gone but all of his businesses and possessions under threat of seizure and liquidation due to unpaid debts and taxes, Emanuel dropped dead of a heart attack in his office.

The news devastated Fran who almost did not return to Mansfield after her bereavement leave. However, after words of encouragement from her mother and pleading from her sorority sisters, she returned. Her mother did stay in her home until Fran's graduation and return from Mansfield. She remarried a widower named Jarvis, and they currently live quite happily on an island off the coast of Maine. She claims she had had "enough of the humidity, but not enough of the nowhere."

However, before all of that happened, but shortly after Fran wrote the first check, she arrived on campus for first-year orientation. Mansfield was the first recorded college to drop the typical naming of grades that coincide with high school names of Freshman, Sophomore, Junior, and Senior. All students are classified by the number of years since they first attended the college. Most people graduate as fourth-years, but there have been some occasions of students leaving only to come back years later to finalize degrees. The current record is 27 years.

Fran was, and still is, quite Spartan in habit. She arrived with one suitcase on wheels and one backpack. She opted to take the train because she wanted to see the country and also thanks to the excellent planning of Dr. Mansfield, who placed the Mansfield train station a mere three-block walk from campus all those years prior.

The weather was fine, and Fran did not break a sweat walking to campus. She memorized the route before she left by using the campus and town maps that had been mailed to her after she made her payment. She walked as confidently as any first-year has ever walked into Angeline Hall. Angeline Hall, named for Dr. Mansfield's eldest daughter and first female college president, was the first-year co-educational dorm. It was situated just at the edge of campus, across the road from the chapel and living quarters for the campus minister and his or her family. Essentially, the first-years were sequestered from campus by a major thoroughfare and near the church to keep their minds, bodies, and souls safe.

Fran did not think to memorize the door layout, so after checking in and getting her room keys, she wandered about the warrenous building which seemed to have no end of tunnels and hallways. She passed door number 54 four times but could not manage to find the door that had 65, the room that would be her room for the next year after seemingly walking for miles. She arrived at her door after fifteen solid minutes and saw it was already open.

The room was fully decorated in bright yellow. The overhead light bounced off the yellow comforter, yellow wall hangings, and yellow curtains in such a way that the room seemed to be glowing. On her travels through the warren, she had peeked into several rooms. Some had bunks and others did not. Her room did not have bunks, but sliding day beds sat directly across from each other. Her roommate lay on her bed with her eyes closed against the sunny glare. She seemed to be oblivious to the hustle and bustle of the noise in the hallway. She looked long and strong. She wore short shorts that showed her sculpted legs. She had her shirt hiked up to show her bare midriff. Her long, straight black hair splayed out on her pillow like a fan. Fran didn't want to disturb her, but she wanted to get off her feet. The walk from the bus hadn't caused her to sweat, but wandering around the building had cranked up her internal thermostat, and her clothes were stuck to her. She knocked and stepped in.

Her roommate's eyes popped open. She sat up as if her body was on a hinge at the waist, smiling a genuine smile. "Hi." She fully unfolded and towered over Fran by at least a foot. "I'm Norris."

Fran extended her hand. "Fran." They shook. Norris had a firm, serious grip.

"Sorry that I picked a side and unpacked all my stuff. If it's too much, I can put some of it in storage."

Fran shook her head. "Nope. I don't mind. I don't have much." She pointed at the bag at her feet, and she swung her backpack off. "This is it. It's kind of nice to not have to worry about decorating."

"Really?" Norris leaned forward.

"Really and truly." She held up her hand, making what she thought was the Boy Scout salute but which was in fact the Star Trek "live long and prosper" Vulcan salute gesture. It is unclear as of this writing whether Norris knew this and said nothing, or if she was equally unaware of this science fiction faux pas.

"You're an angel sent from heaven, I swear it. Do you need any help unpacking?"

"No thanks, I really only have this. It shouldn't take long. I want to shower and then eat. Is the cafeteria open tonight?"

"It is, but you need not worry about that. My cousin Candy, who is also a first-year, but who is living at home, has invited us to dinner. My uncle, her dad, a Mansfield proper, pulled some strings to get me in early, which is why

I'm all unpacked. They told me to wait for my roommate and bring her to dinner."

"That sounds wonderful." Fran pulled her bed out from its couch position and unzipped her suitcase. She dumped everything out on the unmade bed, then eyed her pile and looked for a dresser.

"The dressers are in the closet," Norris said.

Fran nodded and got to work without another word. She unpacked, called her mother, made her bed, and showered all within 20 minutes. After she pulled her curly brown hair up into a ponytail without checking the mirror at all, she turned to Norris and said, "I'm starving. Let's go."

The two walked and Norris talked. It would take pages and pages to fit in everything that Norris said, and this flashback is already quite long, thank you very much. Besides, this is not her story, not really, although she will show up later, so we will cut to the chase. Norris explained that she and her cousin Candy were descendants of the Mansfields. In fact, Candy's last name was still Mansfield, and she lived in a Mansfield family home, called The Park, at the edge of campus.

Norris, whose first name is not up for discussion here, did not live in a Mansfield home with or without a name. Her mother married "out" of the family, and Norris was doing everything she could do to get back in. While Candy planned to major in whatever struck her fancy, Norris planned to eventually major in theology with the express intent of going to seminary, becoming ordained so she could be the one who would shepherd the young flock at Mansfield College one day. A Mansfield descendant had never once held that post, and Norris planned to be the first.

Candy Mansfield's birth name was Maria Mansfield. Her father, who thought she was so cute in the way that only parents think their children are cute, called her his little M&M, and thus, the nickname Candy took root. Candy was a pretty, vacuous, and spoiled girl who did not know she was pretty or spoiled. Had she not been born a Mansfield, her future would have been quite different. Candy's family home was a mansion. It was immaculately kept by an army of servants who, like their parents, served the Mansfield family. Candy was an only child and thus had the West Wing of the home to herself. She had a suite of rooms that once acted as a nursery and schoolroom for the Mansfields of years past. As time progressed, the learning in the education wing diminished to almost nothing until Candy's children took up residence. More on that later.

Candy and Norris grew up to be as close as two people whose ambition wouldn't even be invited to the same party could be. Being born Mansfields threw them together. As we will learn, they stayed in each other's orbit forever. It was a random act of roommate selection by a student intern in the Office of Residential Life that introduced Fran into their lives, and yet she too, first through the Alpha Tau Nu sorority and later Facebook and financial circumstances, stayed in their lives as well.

However, before they joined the sorority or friended each other on Facebook, not that Facebook even existed then, they all met in the suite of rooms that Candy called her own. Norris never knocked when she arrived, and so she and Fran simply walked in with no preamble and began a lifelong friendship. Candy said, "Well, hello there" to Fran. She walked over and gave her a hug simply because it seemed like the right thing to do. Fran, without realizing she did it, hugged her back and felt something she had never known: sisterhood. It was Candy's easy-going nature, Fran's kindness, and Norris' unwavering drive, which some mistook for bossiness and that later became outright meddling, which kept them together for four years.

Fran and Norris remained roommates in the dorm and later in the sorority house. Candy, having only known one home, stayed in her wing of The Park for the duration of her career at Mansfield. She majored in visual arts. She met a man called Thomas Bertram, who majored in aeronautics, at a sorority/fraternity mixer during their third year. They became attached and quickly married. They moved into The Cottage at The Park. Their first child, Tommy, was born just a few days after graduation.

Thomas went on to flight school and became a successful commercial pilot. He was gone quite often, which didn't upset Candy much. She missed him, but generally, by the time she was starting to miss him terribly, he would be back home. They lived in The Cottage on the back of the property until Candy's father, Marcus Mansfield, unexpectedly passed.

While death is always a tragedy, it was excellent timing for the Bertrams, who had four children. With Tommy, Ed, Mariah, and Julia all running around The Cottage, having more room than the name implied accommodated them just fine as it was a six-bedroom colonial home and not a cottage at all. The children still seemed always to be underfoot, and they gave the nanny and private tutors a lot of trouble.

Norris, as promised, became the first and only family member to become the campus minister at Mansfield. She was given a rectory much too large for one person since it was built for a family. She kept most of the doors closed and dined most nights at The Park or in the student dining hall where she held prayer meals and theological study circles several times a week.

Fran met William Price in her second year. He was a local boy who was still in high school. He had big dreams of joining the Navy. He stayed around in Mansfield until Fran's graduation. You already know the rest of that story.

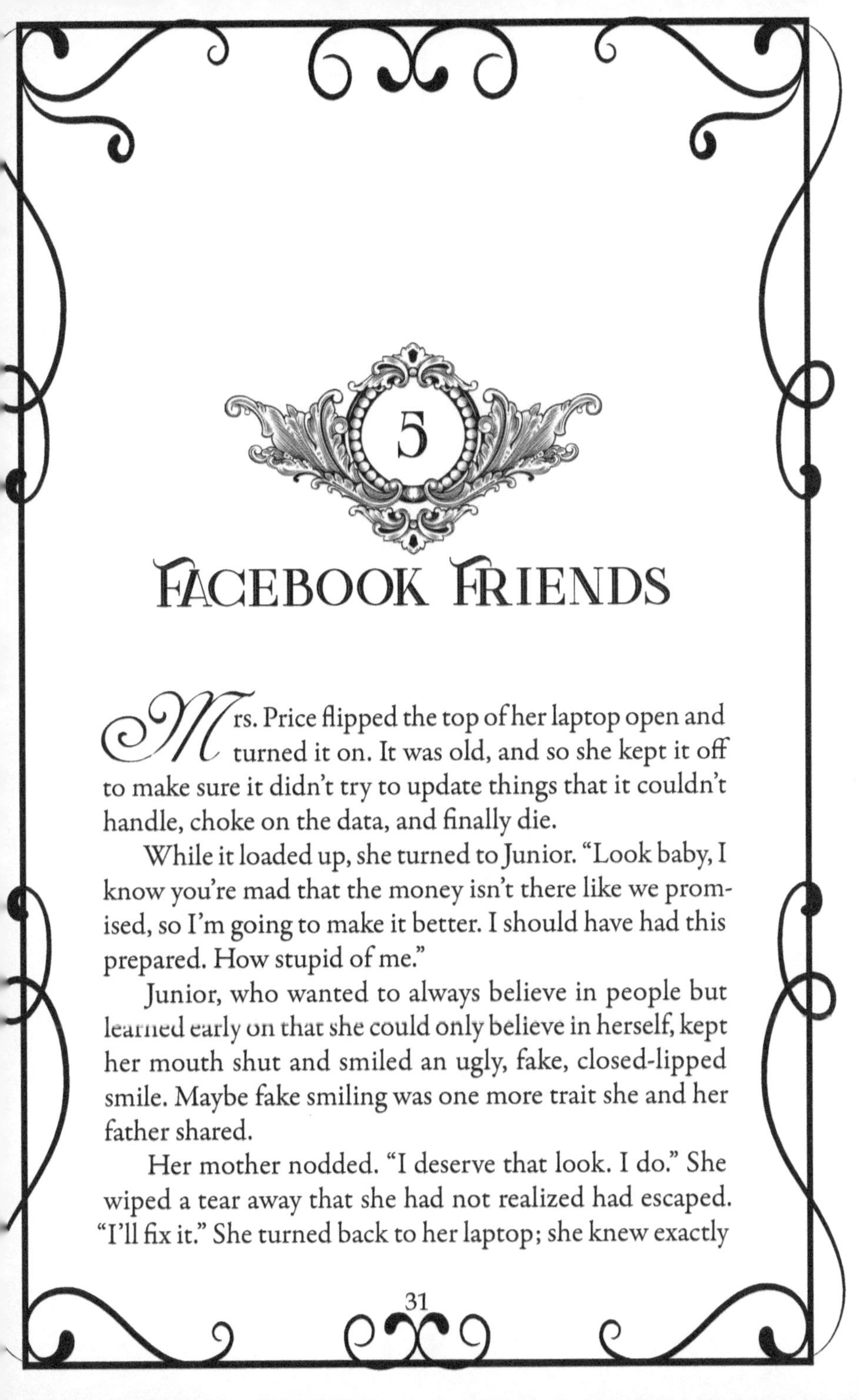

5

FACEBOOK FRIENDS

Mrs. Price flipped the top of her laptop open and turned it on. It was old, and so she kept it off to make sure it didn't try to update things that it couldn't handle, choke on the data, and finally die.

While it loaded up, she turned to Junior. "Look baby, I know you're mad that the money isn't there like we promised, so I'm going to make it better. I should have had this prepared. How stupid of me."

Junior, who wanted to always believe in people but learned early on that she could only believe in herself, kept her mouth shut and smiled an ugly, fake, closed-lipped smile. Maybe fake smiling was one more trait she and her father shared.

Her mother nodded. "I deserve that look. I do." She wiped a tear away that she had not realized had escaped. "I'll fix it." She turned back to her laptop; she knew exactly how long it took to boot up and how long to let it sit after it booted up before the update notifications could pop up and ask for permission to install new software. She clicked those into oblivion, or wherever data goes when it is clicked away, and logged into Facebook.

"How's Facebook going to help? Are you going to start a GoFundMe?" Junior asked, then calmed her voice again. She did not want to go that route, but she would if she must.

"Not exactly," her mother said without looking. She typed quickly and navigated the desktop version of Facebook the way that only Gen Xers can. She opened her direct messages and found a two-person group chat that remained dormant for some time, and she started writing.

Candy Bertram's phone pinged. She was napping on her couch in The Lounge of the same mansion where she was raised. The phone rested on the end table that was behind her head. Her pug, whom she cleverly named Pug, snored on her chest.

Pugs, while small in stature, are weighty. Candy struggled to sit up and could not. The phone pinged again, reminding her she had missed the first ping. She blindly reached over the arm of the couch but knocked the phone onto the ground. She whispered a curse to herself. She looked at Pug, whose nap had not been disturbed in the slightest. The phone made a chirp indicating that this was a text from her cousin Reverend Norris. It chirped again. She inhaled deeply and exhaled loudly to try to jostle Pug awake, but Pug remained stoic.

Finally, she softly poked Pug in the ribs. "Pug, darling, get up. Mommy needs to get up."

Pug opened her eyes and ran her tongue over her own face. She did not seem inclined to believe her "mommy." She closed her eyes again.

"Pug, get up this instant, or I will be forced to move you." Candy poked her again and this, combined with the tone of her voice, finally convinced Pug to scramble down off Candy's chest and, just to show how she felt about the entire affair, off the couch and out of the room without even looking back over her shoulder. Candy sighed and rolled off the couch with as little grace as possible onto the floor to find her phone.

She splayed herself flat on the ground and slid her torso under the couch to reach the phone that had unceremoniously bounced underneath. She pulled it out, and while still lying on the ground, she checked her notifications. There was a Facebook notification and a missed text from Norris. Knowing she would see Norris later that day, they saw each other almost every day, she opened the Facebook notifications to see a message that was addressed to both her and Norris from their long-lost sorority sister. It was quite long but worth including in its entirety here. Fear not, it is not as long as the previous flashback.

"Hello Sisters, it has been far too long. I know, I know. I have just been so busy. I have some amazing news, and I wanted to share it with you and ask for some assistance. My eldest daughter, Frances, whom you may remember we call Junior, has not only been accepted at our glorious alma mater, but she won the coveted Mansfield Gift!!! We never expected a girl who graduated high school a year early would be venturing out into the world just before her 17th birthday, but that seems to be the reality of the situation.

"Unfortunately, The Gift only covers tuition and with the other blessed news that I'm due to have twins this fall as well, we simply do not have the ability to pay the 11,000 dollars for room and board. Junior saved up 5,500 dollars and is willing to use it to cover part of her room and board costs. I'm sure there are plenty of inexpensive apartments or rooms to rent in Mansfield proper as I know the town itself has gone through quite a rough patch and housing prices are low. However, I hoped that maybe one of you, my closest Alpha Tau Nu sisters, might be able to help. Reverend Norris, I know you have that entire rectory to yourself and that there are several unused bedrooms. Candy, I know that Tommy has graduated and Ed is living on campus, and so I wondered if there was space for Junior there.

"The money she has will be more than enough to pay for her own food for the year, and she is willing to take a job on campus or in town to make sure she is not a burden. If you can't, I totally understand, and we shall start searching Craigslist.

"Thank you, sisters. I hope you are well. I miss you and love you.

Fran."

Lying there on the floor of her lounge, Candy Bertram replied immediately.

"Of course. Of course. Yes! I will talk to Tom. I'm sure we can figure something out. ☺ 👍 ♥ "

Feeling self-satisfied, she opened the text from Norris to see what she wanted. It read, "DO NOT RESPOND TO FRAN UNTIL WE TALK!" Candy laughed aloud to herself. She knew that there would be some chastisement from Norris later. There was nothing left to do about it, so she got up to go find Pug.

Later that evening, the Bertram family dinner was cleared from the table. Tommy and Yates, his business and romantic partner, more on him later, headed back to the converted movie theater they shared as a home. Ed returned to his dorm room. Mariah and Julia returned to their suite, which used to be their mother's suite. The adults sat around the table to have cocktails and discuss the Prices' predicament.

Here is a bit about the three adults' current station in life before we continue our tale. Candy Bertram was still pretty, vacuous, and spoiled. Tom Bertram had grown older gracefully much like his wife. No one who looked at them ever believed them when they said they had four children, and they were more shocked when they learned that during the events of this story, the youngest child was 16 years old. After Candy's full inheritance kicked in, they purchased a small flight company that specialized in cargo and charters. Because Tom loved the air, he put himself on the payroll and still often captained flights.

After they moved into the big house, Candy had the idea that she would breed dogs. She got so far as to purchase a prized pug who was the daughter of a world champion. After she found out what breeding dogs meant, she reconsidered the idea. Having birthed four children herself, she didn't like the idea of Pug going through that. She was far too small in Candy's opinion to carry one puppy, let alone an entire litter.

Norris, who was fast approaching her 20th year as the campus minister at Mansfield, had bad news of her own. When her ancestor created the position of the campus minister, it was ordained that no one person could hold the position for more than 20 years in order to make sure that the "spiritual well-being of the student body stayed current with the church teachings."

Dr. Bennet did not care much for Norris and was hopeful that this news would finally see Norris retire to live in The Cottage at The Park that was waiting for her. Norris, however, had thus far managed to sufficiently leverage her family lineage's connections to arrange to stay on as minister emeritus. She transitioned from the day-to-day duties of the church to a teaching position in the theology department, complete with faculty housing. Dr. Bennet knew it was better to relent than to fight a Mansfield. Against her better judgment, she agreed. She filed the proper paperwork and went on with her business of running the college while she still could.

Tom took a swallow of his scotch, and he lobbed the first volley. "I understand that Junior needs this help, but my concern is that we have a young, single teenage boy who technically doesn't live here, but who does spend a lot of time in this house. I wouldn't want anyone to talk, nor would I want him to have any untoward ideas about her."

Candy, who thought it would be fun to have another girl in the house, hadn't considered this point of view and found herself nodding along. "That is an excellent point, dear." She took a big swig of her red wine and finished off her glass. She reached for more and said, "Maybe Junior could stay with you, Norris. You have that whole place to yourself. I could talk to Dr. Bennet if there is a concern about it. Junior is practically family, and family is technically allowed to live there with you."

Norris, who was drinking a wine spritzer, took a small sip and nodded at the suggestion to make her cousin think it was a great idea. "That is obviously one option, but I would like to address Thomas' concerns."

Norris never called him Tom. She tried to remain as formal as possible with him, which was disconcerting as she was a woman who went exclusively by one name. She would only refer to Candy and Fran by their nicknames.

"I can see how some folks may think it untoward, but you must see it from a different lens. If young Frances is as beguiling as her mother, bringing her here would make perfect sense. She is a young woman with a lot of brains but not much sense, being raised in the middle of the compound in such a fashion. A young, smart, beautiful girl who is easily swayed is just the kind of devil's candy that might tempt young Edmund. However, if you were to bring her here and allow her to celebrate her 17th birthday in The Park, he would see a tender-aged girl who would feel like a sister and not a suitor." She took another sip and licked her lips.

Candy, pouring yet another glass of wine, found herself nodding along again. "Yes, dear, Norris makes an excellent point. We could put her in the wing with the girls. She and Mariah will both be first-years, and Julia could use another positive influence in her life."

"Exactly," said Reverend Norris, having expertly navigated away from the talk about her own living situation. "Although I wouldn't put her *IN* the suite with the girls, perhaps you could open up the old school room that they used as a playroom and put her in there? It is in their wing but not in their space. Keep in mind, darling, that young Frances is not a Mansfield and should not be seen as a threat to Mariah and Julia. You wouldn't want them to think they were being replaced. They need to know that this is an act of charity, and young Frances needs to know it is charity as well. You may even want to take her up on her offer of paying rent."

Tom snorted at that. "Are you suggesting, *Reverend*," he emphasized the word the same way that Norris had emphasized the word "*IN*," "that we make her pay *rent* when we clearly have the vacant room that you suggest? The Park has more than enough room for one more. She is used to living with a whole pack of children, so she will fit right in, and that is that." He gulped the remainder of his scotch and slammed the glass down on the table. Norris nodded. Candy was already on her phone sending the news back to Fran. It was settled.

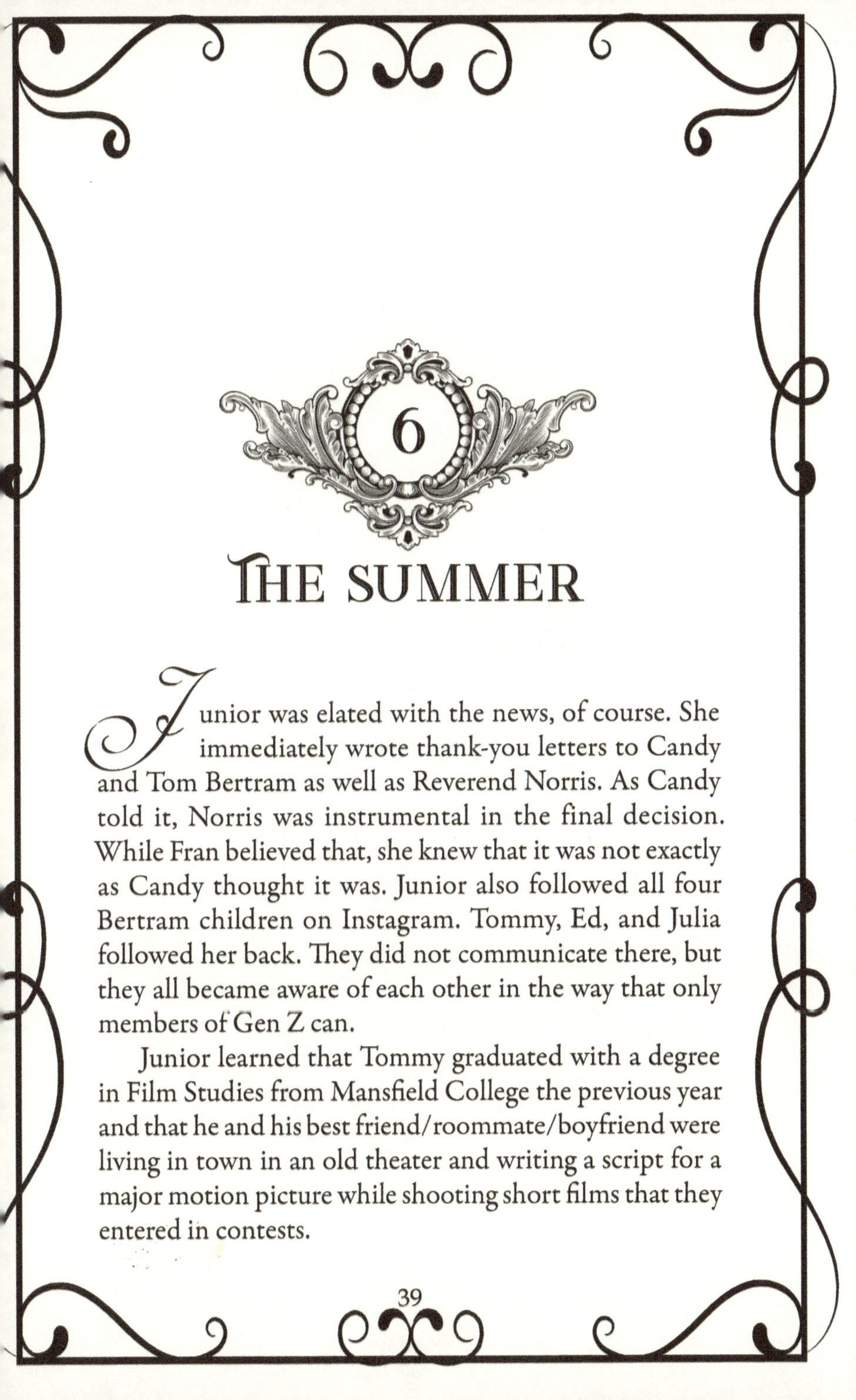

6

THE SUMMER

Junior was elated with the news, of course. She immediately wrote thank-you letters to Candy and Tom Bertram as well as Reverend Norris. As Candy told it, Norris was instrumental in the final decision. While Fran believed that, she knew that it was not exactly as Candy thought it was. Junior also followed all four Bertram children on Instagram. Tommy, Ed, and Julia followed her back. They did not communicate there, but they all became aware of each other in the way that only members of Gen Z can.

Junior learned that Tommy graduated with a degree in Film Studies from Mansfield College the previous year and that he and his best friend/roommate/boyfriend were living in town in an old theater and writing a script for a major motion picture while shooting short films that they entered in contests.

She learned that Ed was going into his third year at Mansfield College although he was not yet 19. He lived on campus instead of staying in The Park. He graduated from Mansfield Public High School as the youngest member of his class. He enrolled at Mansfield College over the summer semester and therefore was on track, as a year-round student, to graduate at the end of his third year at the age of 19. He was majoring in Religious Studies and History.

Julia, the youngest Bertram, was only two months younger than Junior. She was entering her junior year at the private Rushworth Academy where she dabbled in acting. She was good enough to have appeared in many of Tommy and Yates' short films. She was a renowned athlete as well, both running cross country and playing field hockey. It was her prowess on the field hockey field that would eventually let her follow her own path.

Mariah did not accept the request from Junior but based on what she gathered from the feeds of the Bertram siblings, Junior knew that she and Mariah would both be first-years in the fall and both would be living at The Park. Mariah seemed to have a relationship with James Rushworth, or at the very least, he went to a fancy ball as Mariah's date. Julia's date was unimportant enough, even to Julia, that he was not tagged in the photos.

James Rushworth's Instagram account was public and so a quick perusal of it confirmed Junior's suspicion that James and Mariah were in some sort of relationship. James, who appeared to be the same age as Ed, did not go to Mansfield College. Instead, he attended a large, public, nationally recognized state school, whose reputation is built upon the success of the men's sports teams and not upon any academic merit although the two are often conflated in polite society. That is not to say that there were not some excellent programs there.

While Junior learned all she could about her new foster family, Mr. Price was taking the upcoming changes terribly. He was not prepared to lose both of his eldest children at the same time. It would be wrong to suggest that Mr. Price was only worried about missing them. While one would think that would be ranked first on his list of reasons why he was against Junior going to Mansfield and Bill joining the Air Force, the fact that the oldest remaining child, Suzy, would turn 15 in the summer was extremely problematic. He would no longer have a child on the property who could drive. It was disconcerting for him because he had grown to rely on Bill and Junior as chauffeurs, personal shoppers, and nannies, as well as a plethora of other duties as assigned.

In an effort to combat the inevitable tide, he tried to convince Bill to defer his basic training and go to college first. It was the more obvious path, but this was pointless. Bill was so desperate to join the Air Force and get up in the sky that he would have dropped out of school on his 18th birthday and joined without graduating high school. His recruiter advised against it as that would preclude him from ever becoming a pilot as he would eventually have to earn a degree to earn his wings. Bill planned on serving four years, then enrolling in a distance learning program while on active duty. This way, after eight years of service, he would both have his degree and could apply for officer training school.

Mr. Price was right that if Bill wanted to earn his wings, then going to school and joining the ROTC program was a more direct path, but Bill also knew that his father was not thinking about Bill's best interest even though his logic was sound. In fact, by mid-summer, Bill would admit to anyone who asked that he would rather never fly than spend another year on The Ranch. Because one of the people who asked was Mr. Price, that tactic was eventually dropped, and Junior became the object of Mr. Price's schemes.

Fortunately, Junior did not have to deal with his schemes for long as Mrs. Price wouldn't stand for them. She parried every one of his thrusts, and the realization set in that he would have to watch his eldest daughter climb aboard a train and roll away from him, possibly forever. In an effort to ignore the coming changes in his family dynamic, he took to spending time out of the house. No one asked where he went, and because his absences made no real difference in the daily functioning of The Ranch, no one really noticed.

On the last day of July, Mrs. Price announced that Suzy and Bill would be swapping rooms. The house that Junior and Suzy shared would be shut down for the next year. When Suzy turned 16, she would move back into the small house, and by then Betsy would be old enough to move in with her. That would make room in the big house for the new babies, who by that point would no longer need to sleep in a crib in the master bedroom. She wanted Suzy and the boys to have a chance to grow accustomed to the new arrangement while the elder children were still there to help. When a family has that many sets of hands and feet, a move like that happens quickly.

On the first day of August, Bill and Junior sat on the porch of their home in Adirondack chairs, the official porch chair of Unincorporated Nowhere, and drank sweet tea, the official drink of Unincorporated Nowhere. "Do you think Dad is going to be OK?" Bill asked.

Junior took a sip and cocked her head back so she could look up and consider the question. "Define OK."

"Will he be able to let Suzy have a life? Will he let Mom care for the new babies and give them some attention of his own? Will he stop going wherever he is going?'

She nodded in understanding and thought about it for a while. She took a sip and then finally said, "I'm not sure."

"Does it give you pause?"

Junior held up her hands and looked down. "Nope, no paws, still hands." It was an old joke that existed only between them. He swatted her and she chuckled. "It doesn't, actually. Mom wants this for both of us. I want this for both of us. I don't really want this for Suzy, but we learned so much running our own houses. She's ready. I'm ready. You've been ready. Dad was never going to want this for any of us. When it's Suzy's turn, he will do the same thing, and then he will do it for each and every one of them until we are all gone, and it is just him and Mom in the big house."

Bill got up to get the pitcher to refill the tea. After he was done and the pitcher was returned to the fridge, he asked, as though there had been no interruption, "What will happen to Mom then?"

"She'll be fine. Besides, there is a good chance some of us will be living in these houses with grandkids."

"What if there isn't? Mom's whole life has been dedicated to being someone else's something. When has she ever been her own person?"

"When she was at Mansfield. That's why she wants this for us. She wants us to get out there so we can live and make our own mistakes and figure things out. She wants us to live for her. Not in a weird possessive way though. I think she will be genuinely thrilled to know we are out there doing anything that makes us happy. I think she's really happy being a mom, but she knows it isn't for everyone. She wasn't totally sure what her life would be, and while I don't know if she totally loves being a wife, she really does love being a mom."

Bill nodded at the sage wisdom of his little sister. "How did you get to be like this? What did you do that makes you know so much? How do you stay so clear-headed?"

She shrugged. "I don't try to be anything, Bill. I just listen to the voice in my head. I'm just me. I don't try at all. It allows me to see everything as it is, not as I hope it can be. Mom must be happy, right? I mean, if she didn't want this for us, she would tell us. If she wanted to leave Dad, she would have kicked him out a long time ago. The Ranch is hers remember."

Bill nodded. "Yeah. I guess so."

"I know so." She put her hand out in the space between the chairs and made a fist. He did the same and punched it. "It will have to be OK. It's not our problem anymore." She said it with such conviction that even she almost believed it.

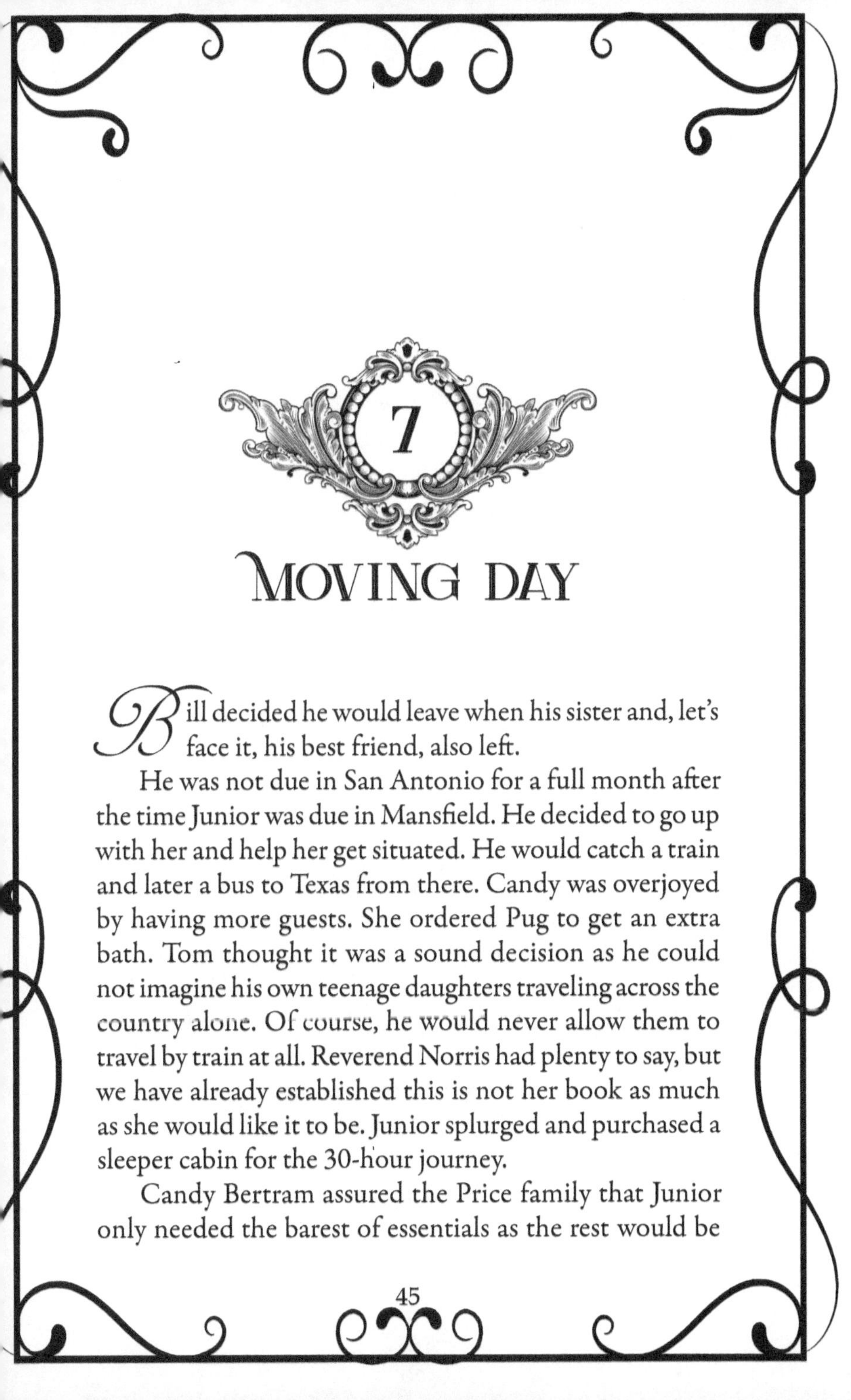

7

MOVING DAY

*B*ill decided he would leave when his sister and, let's face it, his best friend, also left.

He was not due in San Antonio for a full month after the time Junior was due in Mansfield. He decided to go up with her and help her get situated. He would catch a train and later a bus to Texas from there. Candy was overjoyed by having more guests. She ordered Pug to get an extra bath. Tom thought it was a sound decision as he could not imagine his own teenage daughters traveling across the country alone. Of course, he would never allow them to travel by train at all. Reverend Norris had plenty to say, but we have already established this is not her book as much as she would like it to be. Junior splurged and purchased a sleeper cabin for the 30-hour journey.

Candy Bertram assured the Price family that Junior only needed the barest of essentials as the rest would be provided. She would have only brought the barest of essentials anyway. Much like her namesake, Junior was Spartan. Just like her mother before her, Junior headed up north with one rolling suitcase and a backpack.

The backpack, which was designed for trekking across the tundra, not the campus of a rural liberal arts college, was deceptively roomy. It contained all the technological wonders a student would need. The contents: a refurbished laptop, refurbished tablet, and portable hard drive with digital versions of her father's entire music collection. This was his graduation present and the only acknowledgment that his oldest daughter had done anything at all. She also had three chargers, two flash drives, a digital picture frame full of hundreds of family photos, two extra sets of headphones, Bluetooth speakers, pens, notebooks, and a collected edition of *His Dark Materials*.

All of the clothes she planned to take to college, including her new coat, fit into the suitcase due to her liberal use of space bags. Fran insisted on a new winter jacket. She could not insist enough on this necessity. She reminded her namesake that the north is cold for everyone and twice as cold for southerners. Fran bought one that first year at what she decided was an exorbitant cost. As we learned, it turned out the money was not an issue in the end, but 18-year-old Fran could not have known that.

Bill, too, took only one bag. He was prepared to wear Government Issue clothes as much as possible. Other than his phone and his charger, he carried nothing of any value.

The goodbyes were pretty much what one expects from a family that lived in separate houses on a compound in the middle of the woods in Unincorporated Nowhere. The littlies handed out hugs and accepted kisses because they were told to do so. They did not really understand that Junior and Bill were not coming back, nor did they really notice for some time after they were gone. The boys, who until recently lived with Bill, had as far as they were concerned already said goodbye to him, and they knew very little about Junior. She was, to them, a nice but usually strict schoolmarm whose lessons were valuable but seemingly made no lasting impressions.

Mr. Price pretended to be too busy putting together the entertainment center that had sat untouched in its box for two months to see the kids off, letting his very pregnant wife and soon-to-be 15-year-old daughter escort his eldest two children to the train station. He shook Bill's hand, clapped him on the shoulder, and said, "Don't be stupid." He gave Junior a side-armed hug, having stopped hugging her the normal way once she turned 12, and said, "Don't get knocked up."

The eldest Price children both answered, "OK, Dad."

At the train station, Suzy was inconsolable. She had kept her brave face until then. She drove them to the station using her newly gained driver's permit. At one point, a stranger asked if she needed to call 911 because it seemed to outsiders that Suzy was in anaphylactic shock.

Eventually, after Junior promised to text every day and video chat every Wednesday and Sunday, she was able to hug Junior so tightly that she felt her back crack. Suzy whispered, "Don't leave me" over and over like a spell until it lost all meaning. Her histrionics forced Mrs. Price's own goodbye to seem less meaningful due to its brevity. However, neither of her children felt that way. They both knew everything they needed to know about their mother's feelings before they ever stood on the train platform.

She hugged both of her children tightly and whispered advice into their ears. To Bill, she said, "I'm so proud of you. Be safe and come home and visit me one day." To Junior, she said, "I'm so proud of you. Be safe and I hope you let me come see you one day. I miss Mansfield so much." Neither sibling shared what their mother said to the other, but it seems important enough to include here.

They boarded the train and found their sleeper car, called a roomette, meaning a small room. Of course, "-ette" also is used to designate the feminine, here also meaning smaller or inferior. Junior was too excited to be annoyed by this at the moment but was quite upset later. She kept it to herself, as was her wont. Being a small person, she took offense to anyone thinking it made her inferior in some way. The roomette consisted of a couch that pulled into a bed, a sink, a private, but incredibly small toilet with shower, and a pull-down loft mattress. Several meals were included as was priority access to the room and access to lounges in select stations during layovers. They dropped their bags and sat on the couch, excited about their first real trip out of Unincorporated Nowhere. Neither of them counted trips into "town" as somewhere.

The train eventually pulled away from the station. Mrs. Price did not allow Suzy the chance to wave goodbye, worried that she might fling herself on board or perhaps onto the tracks. She promised her ice cream, which has a 97 percent success rate for Mrs. Price when trying to bribe her children.

Bill watched the station become smaller as Junior set up her laptop and speakers so they could have music. "Def Leppard or Tesla?" she asked.

Bill never bonded with his father over anything and was actively not a classic rock fan, but he understood that his options were limited, and he didn't hate either choice. "Five Man," he said, referring to Tesla's 1990 live album *Five Man Acoustical Jam.*

Junior hit play and settled back onto the couch. She looked over at Bill. "Should I have stayed for Suzy?"

"No way" was his almost immediate response. He knew she was going to ask some form of this question, and his response was locked and loaded. "I mean, I know it sucks for Suzy, but it has sucked for all of us. She'll be OK."

Junior wrinkled up her face. "How can you be sure?"

"We're OK, aren't we?"

Junior nodded, not totally sure if that were true. "I suppose. She had us though."

"Exactly, we taught her well. I wish I could save them all, but I can't. All I can do is what is best for me and lead by example. Between us, we have shown the rest of them two distinct paths, either the Service or college. Maybe Suzy will follow our example, or maybe she will show them littlies a third way. We didn't have anyone like us, and we're still here. No matter what, we have to go when it is our time to go. We didn't invent our lives, sister. We just have to survive them. OK? Just survive."

Junior nodded and took it in. She didn't always respond right away, or at all, but Bill knew she heard every word and would take it all to heart. She pulled out her phone and sent a heart emoticon to Suzy. That felt like all she could do in that moment. She knew she would find a way to make this up to her; she just didn't know what it was yet. Bill was right, she decided. She had to be a beacon for the rest of them to follow.

Bill reached into his bag and pulled out a small box with a bow on it. "I got you this."

Junior, unaccustomed to gifts, put her hand over her heart. Many people, when they do this action, are being sarcastic. Junior was rarely if ever sarcastic and never in the face of a kind gesture. "Oh, Bill."

"You don't even know what it is. It could be a turd in a box."

"As if." She smiled and reached for the box and pulled the bow until it fell apart. She opened the box. Inside she found a black banded, silver watch with roman numerals on the face. "Oh, Bill," she said again. She wiped the tears away with her left hand and reached for the watch with her right. "You shouldn't have."

"Well, I did. I know you're going to have a busy schedule, and I know how you hate checking your phone for the time because you think it's rude. I thought this would be good. It winds up, so you will never lose power. I wound it this morning and set it, so it is good to go."

She put the face up to her ear so she could hear the ticking. "It's perfect. Thank you." She hugged him tight, and he hugged her back.

He felt the tears well up in his eyes, so he decided to change the subject. He asked, "Cards?" He reached back into his bag and pulled out a deck before she could answer. They had been playing one game of Gin Rummy for 10 years. They kept score in a 200-page notebook. He pulled that out as well.

"Deal." She did not specify if she was answering his OK from earlier or his question about cards or both. It didn't matter.

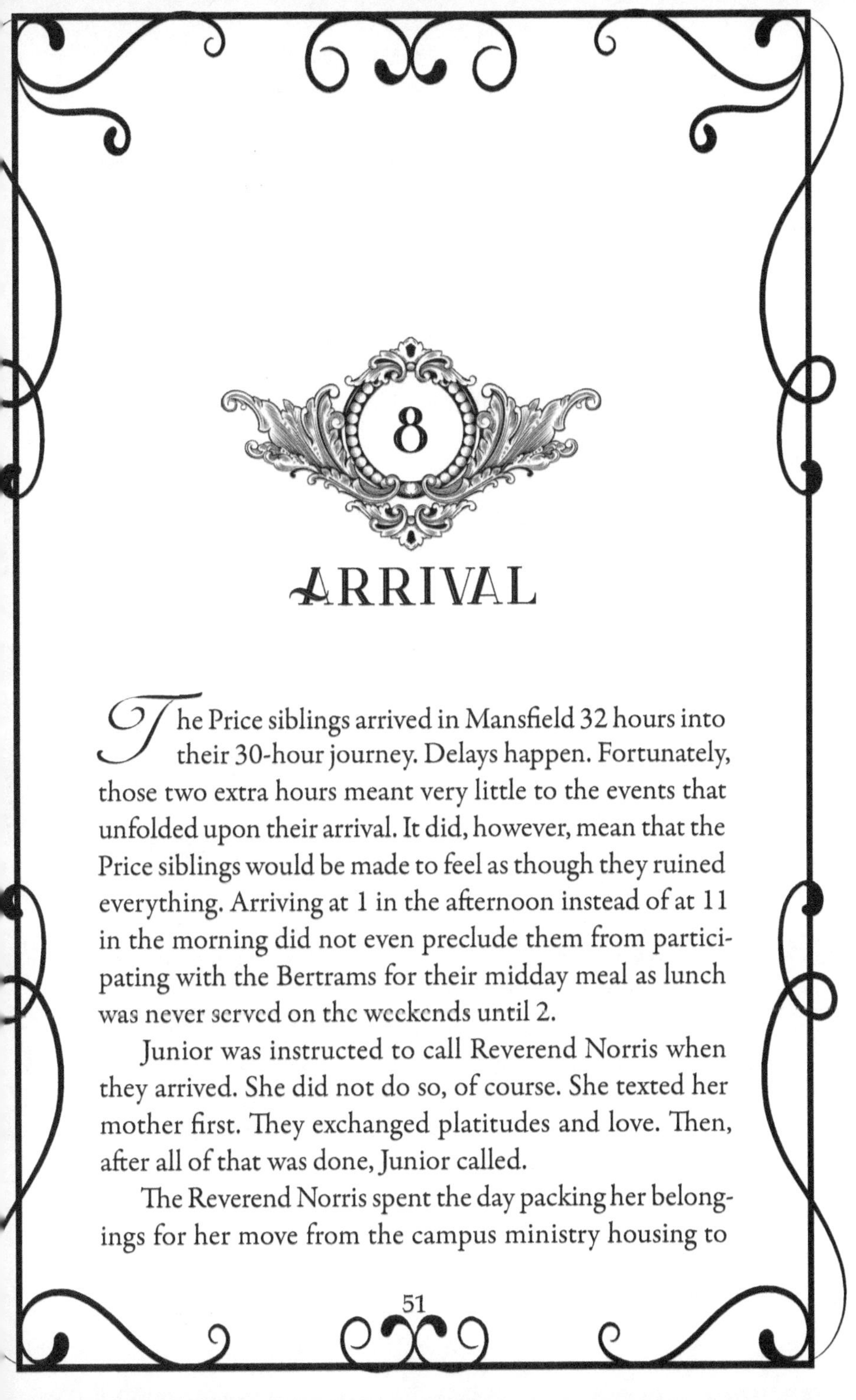

8

ARRIVAL

The Price siblings arrived in Mansfield 32 hours into their 30-hour journey. Delays happen. Fortunately, those two extra hours meant very little to the events that unfolded upon their arrival. It did, however, mean that the Price siblings would be made to feel as though they ruined everything. Arriving at 1 in the afternoon instead of at 11 in the morning did not even preclude them from participating with the Bertrams for their midday meal as lunch was never served on the weekends until 2.

Junior was instructed to call Reverend Norris when they arrived. She did not do so, of course. She texted her mother first. They exchanged platitudes and love. Then, after all of that was done, Junior called.

The Reverend Norris spent the day packing her belongings for her move from the campus ministry housing to campus faculty housing. She promised to keep her ringer on full blast, and she kept her promise.

She answered Junior's call on the third ring. "Norris," she said as dryly as she could, almost affecting a droll British accent.

"Hi, Reverend Norris. This is Junior."

"I have been expecting your call," she said as though it was some sort of inconvenience when it was nothing of the sort.

"Sorry, Reverend. I just..."

"Please, call me Norris. Your mother and the Bertram children just call me by that one name. You may do so as well."

Junior was taken aback. She was unsure what any of this had to do with the explanation as to why they were late and why she didn't call. "Thank you. Norris, I apologize for not calling and making you wait around. The signal was bad on the train. I have a pay-as-you-go plan, and my service is bad. We were delayed several times."

"Yes, well, you can't make the trains run on time. You are not a dictator, after all." She snickered, thinking her joke both clever and above Junior's head.

Junior burst out laughing. "Mussolini I am not."

Norris immediately stopped her snickering. "No one likes a know-it-all, Frances."

"Yes, Ma'am," Junior said without even realizing her tone had changed. Southern respect of elders beats northern snark every time. "Again, I apologize for our late arrival time. I sure hope we have not inconvenienced anyone. We can just walk to the Bertrams if you're..."

"The Park."

"I'm sorry?"

"The name of the residence is The Park. Please refer to it as such. I'm sure your mother told you as much."

"No, *Reverend* Norris, she most assuredly did not. You may know my mother is very busy with all the kids."

"Yes, well... It is not necessary for you to walk. I shall fetch you and William directly." Norris hung up without a salutation as was her habit.

"Hello? Reverend? Norris?" Junior pulled the phone away from her face and looked to Bill, who had been only half listening. He was taking in the sights. Buildings were over 30 feet tall. There were cars parked everywhere and almost no one was walking anywhere. The people on the train platform were avoiding eye contact with anyone else. All of this seemed like science fiction to Bill. While Mansfield is barely a town, it seemed like a metropolis to a young person from Unincorporated Nowhere.

"All good?" he asked.

"I suppose. She said she was on her way. Let's go sit over there." Junior pointed at a bench with her chin. They sat, and for the first time, she took in all the things that her brother noticed immediately. "It is something different, isn't it?"

He nodded.

She asked, "What will San Antonio be like?"

"I can't begin to imagine. I looked it up, but I still can't imagine."

"You'll send me pictures?"

"Of course. You'll send me pictures?"

"I will." She reached out her fist and he tapped it with his own.

"Deal."

They sat in an amicable silence shared only by people who truly like each other. If you don't recognize this kind of silence, you may want to evaluate your life choices. They were quite content to sit and wait and people-watch. So much so that they did not realize that it took Norris 30 full minutes to arrive.

She meant it as a slight. She wanted them to have to wait for her as she felt she had to wait for them. However, when you come from Unincorporated Nowhere, everything takes a long time, so even if they had been clock-watching, which they were not, they would have just assumed Norris lived quite far away. Having read this far and having a rudimentary understanding of Mansfield, we all know this is not the case. The Price siblings were about to learn that information. Before that though, they had to meet Norris in person.

She pulled up in her college-issued vehicle. She only would be in possession of it until her move was complete. Campus ministry has a budget for vehicles. Faculty does not. Norris wanted to get every last mile she felt she deserved before being, as she thought of it, forcibly removed from her residence. The blue mini van had the Mansfield crest on the driver's side door and a cross on the passenger door.

She spotted them immediately. She knew what they both looked like from her time on Facebook, and even if she had not, they stuck out. They were the only people on the platform looking up. Every other person's nose was buried deep into a device of some sort. Even the young children waiting to be collected were touching or staring at a screen. She would have to write a sermon about... She caught herself. She should have written a sermon about that. Well, she would at least sermonize about it later to someone.

Norris was within shouting distance of the Price siblings, so that is just what she did. She rolled down her window and pushed the button to raise the tailgate and the other to open the sliding back door. "FRANCES!" she shouted. Yes, one wonders about the paradoxical behavior of Norris. She only used birth names of those she feels are either beneath her for formality's sake but was willing to shout in public and cause a scene.

Junior was as accustomed to reacting to her birth name as anyone who primarily goes by a nickname. She jumped to her feet and looked for the sound. Norris waved a hand out of the window. Junior waved back. Bill slung his one bag over his shoulder and picked up Junior's suitcase in the other.

"Where are the rest of your bags?" was the first thing she said to them as they approached. "Are you having them shipped?"

The siblings shared a sideways glance. Bill raised his eyebrows and walked around to the back to put the bags in, leaving his sister to say whatever she wanted to say. "Well, Reverend, this is all we have." She climbed into the back of the van and slid across the bench seat to make room for Bill. "It is lovely to meet you finally. We have heard so much about you."

Norris harrumphed, ignoring the warm greeting as she was wont to do. "Just like your mother."

"Excuse me?" the Price siblings said in indignant unison. There are few things that can bring the Price siblings together quicker than anyone making derogatory comments about their mother.

Norris missed the tone completely. "Your mother arrived at this storied institution with hardly anything either, and she accumulated very little either. I suppose it is noble to live in such a way." Feeling satisfied with her commentary, Norris nodded to herself. "Seatbelts, children," Norris said, even though the car was already rolling backward.

Bill leaned forward to say something, but Junior put her arm on his shoulder to stop him. When he turned to look at her, she put both her hands up and shook her head. She mouthed the word "Please." He knew that "Please" meant not to rock the boat. He was leaving, she was staying, she didn't need the trouble, and it wasn't so bad. He huffed as he sat back on the bench and buckled in.

"Please take time to orient yourself, Frances. I will not always be available to chauffeur you around town. Your feet will be put to good use," Norris said, seemingly forgetting that Junior had offered to walk herself to The Park less than 30 minutes prior. Of course, she had not forgotten, but gaslighting was one of her favorite pastimes. "From the train station, you simply head due north, and you will run directly into The Park. Main Street dead ends at The Park's gates. When walking, do not walk through the main gate as that is for motor traffic only. It is unsafe. Although, the younger Thomas and that *friend* of his, Johnathan, tempt fate each time they arrive. I have expressed my concern, but they both seem not to care, and his parents simply shrug. I implore you, Frances, to follow the example of Edmund, Mariah, and Julia, and walk through the side gate, which was designed for human traffic."

"Yes, Ma'am."

"Good. That side gate faces campus, so of course, it will be more convenient, but when you need to come to town, you will be tempted to take the direct route. I assure you that it will be better to take a few extra minutes. Your generation is always in a hurry and rarely pays attention to your surroundings." She nodded at that comment, making a mental note to incorporate it into the sermon.

"I walk all the time from The Ranch to town down a country road, and I never wear my headphones just to be safe."

"Yes, well, this is not Unincorporated Nowhere, Frances. We have sidewalks here, so it is much safer."

Bill opened his mouth to point out the contradiction, but before he could, Norris announced their arrival. In as much time as it took one to read about the trip from the train station to The Park, they arrived. All told, it was half a mile up the road. Had the bench on which the Price siblings sat been situated on the north side of the train station instead of the south side, they would have been able to see The Park's gates.

They sat at the stop sign directly across from the gates of The Park. "If you go that way," Norris pointed west, "you will end up on campus, the rectory and faculty housing. If you go that way," Norris pointed east, "you will end up nowhere you wish to go. The side gate is that way." She pointed to the west again. "The sidewalk around The Park is open to the public, and so there is only one gate for residential access. You need a key. You will get that today. I reminded the staff to have one made for you. Should you ever have a car or need to enter here, again, by car, never on foot like young Thomas and that *friend* of his. The code is 121675. Can you remember that? I suspect the staff will have it written down for you just in case. You are not to tell anyone the code nor are you to give the key to anyone. You are not to bring guests over without first asking for and receiving permission from the Bertrams. You are to behave as though you are a member of the Bertram family, while never acting as though you are a Mansfield. Is that understood?"

"Yes, Ma'am," Junior replied meekly.

"You too, William."

"I'm not living here, Reverend, but I promise not to tell anyone the secret code that I have already forgotten, nor will I masquerade as a member of the cultural elite."

"I happen to know you have quite the head for numbers just like your mother, young man. There is no need to take that tone with me."

"Yes, Ma'am."

Feeling self-satisfied, she pulled across the street and pushed in the code. "Remember, you will be living here at The Park, but this is not your home."

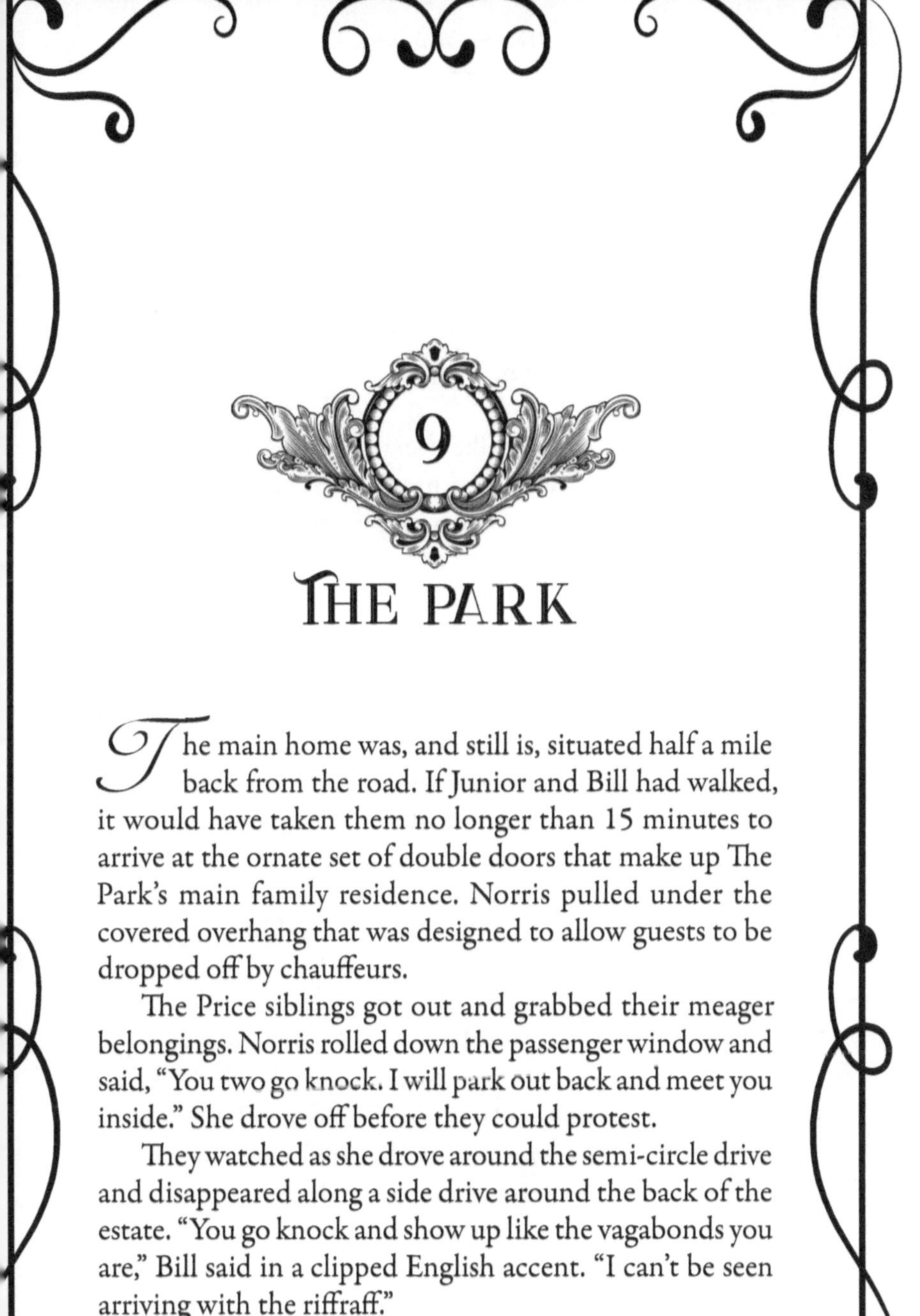

9

THE PARK

The main home was, and still is, situated half a mile back from the road. If Junior and Bill had walked, it would have taken them no longer than 15 minutes to arrive at the ornate set of double doors that make up The Park's main family residence. Norris pulled under the covered overhang that was designed to allow guests to be dropped off by chauffeurs.

The Price siblings got out and grabbed their meager belongings. Norris rolled down the passenger window and said, "You two go knock. I will park out back and meet you inside." She drove off before they could protest.

They watched as she drove around the semi-circle drive and disappeared along a side drive around the back of the estate. "You go knock and show up like the vagabonds you are," Bill said in a clipped English accent. "I can't be seen arriving with the riffraff."

Junior held in her laugh. It was wrong to make fun of a woman she barely knew or a woman she knew well. She punched him in the arm. "Stop. I have to live here."

"Yeah, but not with her."

"Seems like she's here a lot. Mom said that Norris is pretty bossy and that pretty much everyone lets her do it."

"You're not everyone."

"Yes, I am."

"No, you just seem like everyone. It's an act. I know it. Mom knows it. Suzy knows it. Sheesh, even Dad knows it. Clearly, the admission people here knew it too. You won The Gift. You are not everyone. You are Junior freaking Price."

She was starting to blush, which meant she would start to break out in red blotches soon. She did not want her first impression to be that of a blotchy, emotional wreck, but the more she thought about it, the more she could feel the heat rising up from her collarbones. Before she rang the bell, she wrapped her scarf around a few more times and ensured that her neck was covered.

"Sorry, I didn't mean to..."

She waved him off. "It's fine. I should have done it sooner anyway. I mean, I knew I would be nervous meeting everyone anyway."

"OK." He nodded. He knew that Junior never lied, and so this was not an attempt to make him feel better. "Ready?"

"I suppose." She held out a fist. He bumped it. She rang the bell. The *bing-bong* sounded like the chimes of a grandfather clock. They were loud as though they were just on the other side of the door. They repeated and faded away as the sound traveled throughout the estate and alerted everyone, in every wing, that someone was there.

This invention of the late Dr. Mansfield was not necessary as there has yet to be a time in recorded history when a member of the Mansfield family answered the bell. One could argue that one may ring the bell late at night, and thus, a Mansfield would have to answer the door, but in those cases, the person must first get through the gate, so by the time that happened, a servant would be alerted as well.

The Price siblings turned their backs on the door as they waited and took in The Park and all of its opulence. Bill said, "If there was a perfect opposite of The Ranch, this would be it."

Junior felt herself nodding. Before she could reply, they heard the door open behind them. They turned around to see an older man, dressed in the finest suit either of them had ever seen, with bright white horseshoe hair surrounding his gleaming bald head. "You must be the Price children. We've been expecting you." He spoke with his teeth clamped together.

"Yes, Sir. I'm..." Junior started but was interrupted.

"You do not call me Sir, Miss. You call me Portsmouth. I am here to serve you. I shall call you either Miss, Miss Frances, or Miss Price. You, Sir, I shall currently address as Sir or Mr. Price until you return with a rank from the United States Air Force, at such time, I shall refer to you by that rank."

Flummoxed, Junior said nothing. Twice in less than an hour, she was corrected about giving respect to her elders. She looked to Bill, who saw her vexation.

"Thank you, Portsmouth."

"You are quite welcome, Sir. Now, as I was saying. We've been expecting you. I have your quarters dressed and prepared. Miss Price's quarters are in the West Wing. For you, Mr. Price, I have a guest room arranged in the East Wing."

Portsmouth stepped back, letting the Prices enter. As they did, he reached over and pulled a cord that hung from the ceiling. Before the door was fully closed behind them, a younger man appeared from a side door dressed in an equally fine suit. Portsmouth indicated with a little bow.

"This is Hoffs, Mr. Price. He will take you to your room. I shall accompany Miss Price to her quarters. Lunch is served at two. You shall be reunited then."

He turned and started walking in one direction out of the foyer; Hoffs headed the other way. Junior and Bill, not knowing what else to do, nodded at each other, and they each chased after their respective guide.

As she caught up to him, Junior asked, "What is it you do here, Mr. Portsmouth?"

"It's just Portsmouth, Miss," he replied without looking at her. "I run the house. If so required, I arrange the schedule of the staff and the family. It is often required. If you need any help in that regard, you come to me, and I will either help you myself or have another member of the staff assist you. My office is located at the bottom of the stairs that you will find behind the door from which Hoffs appeared. If I am not in my office, there is a buzzer on my desk. You push it, and I shall be there within 10 minutes. I am the person on whom the family relies the most. It is my honor to be of service to the Mansfields. Both my mother and my grandfather served before me and it was an honor for them as well."

"So, you're like Alfred?"

"Miss?" This made him stop and turn to look at her. He had to look down at her. She was used to it. Fully grown at just over five feet tall meant most adults look down at her, but they could rarely look down on her. His eyes were not kind, but they were not vicious. He seemed almost robotic.

"Like in Batman."

Portsmouth nodded once and a small smile broke on his lips. "Correct, Miss. Like Alfred. You will find I am equally good at keeping family secrets." His stern expression broke for just a moment and he smiled.

"Me too." She smiled back.

"Excellent, Miss Frances. You will find that there are many secrets to keep."

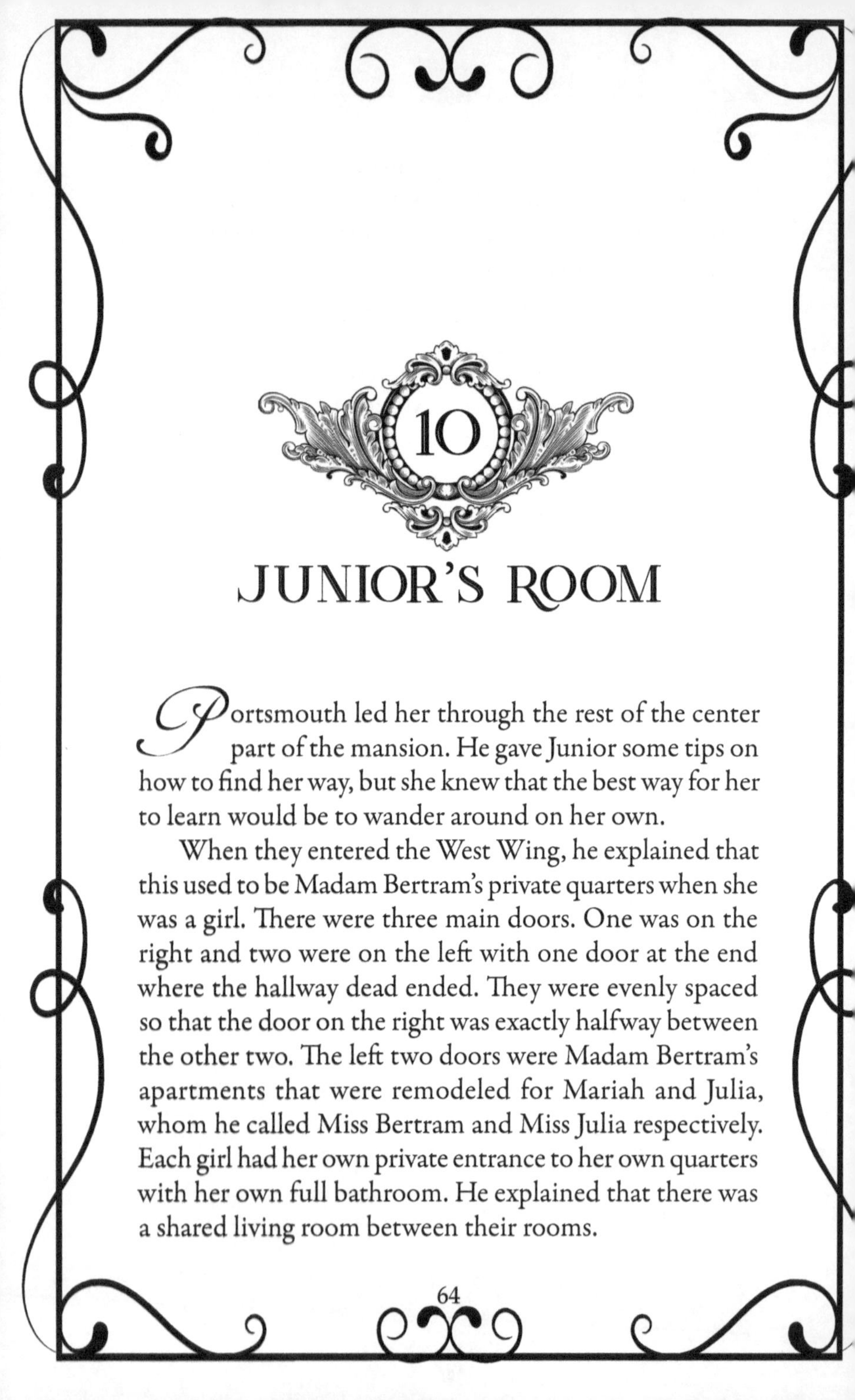

10

JUNIOR'S ROOM

Portsmouth led her through the rest of the center part of the mansion. He gave Junior some tips on how to find her way, but she knew that the best way for her to learn would be to wander around on her own.

When they entered the West Wing, he explained that this used to be Madam Bertram's private quarters when she was a girl. There were three main doors. One was on the right and two were on the left with one door at the end where the hallway dead ended. They were evenly spaced so that the door on the right was exactly halfway between the other two. The left two doors were Madam Bertram's apartments that were remodeled for Mariah and Julia, whom he called Miss Bertram and Miss Julia respectively. Each girl had her own private entrance to her own quarters with her own full bathroom. He explained that there was a shared living room between their rooms.

The door on the right led to a room that used to be a playroom for Mariah and Julia when they were younger. Before that, it was the same for Candy when she was a young girl. Farther back, it was a classroom for the older generations of Mansfields. This would be Junior's room.

He opened the door for her but did not enter. He explained that he never entered a young lady's room, and that if she ever needed anything, one of the female servants would oblige. Depending on the time of day, it would either be Miss Taylor or Mrs. Reynolds. They are both attentive and discreet. The room would be cleaned every Monday, which was also laundry day. It was always laundry day on The Ranch, so Junior could not imagine how big the machine was here to be able to do all the laundry on one day.

There were switches by the door that turned on the overhead light and ceiling fan. The room had only one small window almost directly opposite the door. It was made of frosted glass, so it did not need to have curtains. It offered little light. There was a fireplace, though. As Portsmouth explained, each room had a working fireplace; while some had been converted to gas, others were still wood burning. Her room was converted to gas, and if she wanted to use it, she could do so at any time by simply using the switch on the wall next to the mantle.

The fireplace stood in the far-right corner at an angle with the chimney running up the corner and into the ceiling. In front of it sat a small coffee table and two yellow high-backed upholstered chairs. In between the chairs sat a table with an antique-looking reading lamp. Upon further inspection, it was directly wired through the center of the table and the cord was connected straight into the floor, making it seem as though it was an oil lamp instead of an electric one.

The door opened directly in the middle of the room. They placed a four-poster canopy bed in the left corner. It was fully made up with enough pillows that she and the littlies could have pillow fought for centuries. The duvet was yellow, the canopy was yellow, the pillowcases were yellow. She suspected that when she pulled back the top, she would find yellow. She liked yellow just fine. It did add brightness.

In the near right corner was the door to her own private bathroom. It had a stand-up shower with a walk-in glass door that went all the way up to the ceiling where there hung a shower head that was 12 inches across. The stand-up shower she and Suzy shared was designed to be a basement shower. It had no top and had a plastic curtain that never kept the water, or the heat, inside. Her new room had a pedestal sink over which hung a medicine cabinet mirror. An entire bathroom to herself.

There was a writing desk with a yellow desk chair in the near left corner. It was fully decked out with all the modern accoutrements. USB plugs as well as regular plugs. There was a desk lamp that also had plugs in the base. There was a post-it note that read, "*Wi-Fi password is 121675.*" Junior made a note. It was the same password as the gate code. Easy enough to remember. The desk seemed out of place in a room that, for the most part, seemed to be decorated at the turn of the century. The 19th century. It was fully stocked with notebooks, pens, and enough office supplies for her to run a small business for a year.

Between the bed and the desk stood an old-fashioned Narnia-style wardrobe. It was not yellow but a dark brown.

It was slightly raised off the floor on legs and stood at least two feet over her head. It was at least four feet wide. On the right side, there was ample space to hang her clothes and the dresser was built into the left.

It took her more time to look around than it did to unpack. She set her electronics up on her desk, her electronic picture frame on the mantle. She made a short video tour of her room and sent it off to Suzy and her mother with promises to video chat later that night. She went to the bathroom with the door open just because she could. She washed her face, pulled her hair back in a ponytail, wrapped a yellow scarf around her neck, and set out to explore.

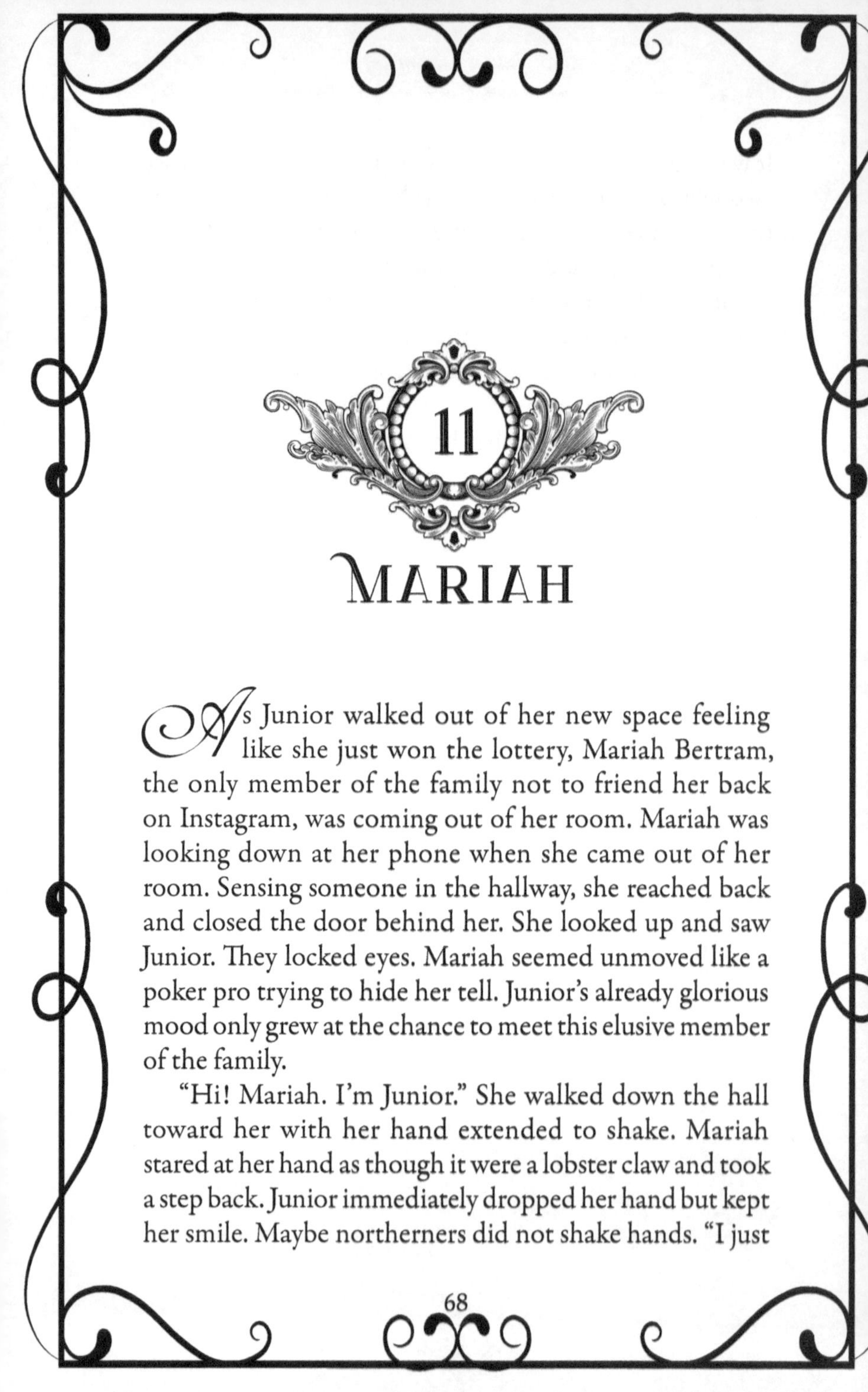

11

MARIAH

As Junior walked out of her new space feeling like she just won the lottery, Mariah Bertram, the only member of the family not to friend her back on Instagram, was coming out of her room. Mariah was looking down at her phone when she came out of her room. Sensing someone in the hallway, she reached back and closed the door behind her. She looked up and saw Junior. They locked eyes. Mariah seemed unmoved like a poker pro trying to hide her tell. Junior's already glorious mood only grew at the chance to meet this elusive member of the family.

"Hi! Mariah. I'm Junior." She walked down the hall toward her with her hand extended to shake. Mariah stared at her hand as though it were a lobster claw and took a step back. Junior immediately dropped her hand but kept her smile. Maybe northerners did not shake hands. "I just wanted to say thank you so much for welcoming me into your home. I just set up my room."

Mariah looked past her to the door out of which she came and back to her smiling face. "The playroom?"

"That's what Portsmouth said it was. He said you don't use it anymore, so your mom had it set up for me."

"Well, sorry you got the shaft on that one." She shrugged her shoulders and curled up her lips into a snarl. "I guess they'd rather have you here with the girls than in the East Wing with the boys where you could be in an actually decent room. Prudes. It's not like there is even anyone over there. Ed lives on campus; he stayed there all summer working for Res Life. He's a resident assistant. A few dorms are open in the summer for summer students and some of the kids' camps they host. He doesn't need the job, but he likes doing lame stuff like that. And then of course Tommy, well, he's just ... Tommy."

Never one to want to start an argument, Junior, who thought the room was perfection and was looking forward to having the Bertram girls in her wing, simply responded, "Well, I certainly appreciate it just the same. It is a lot nicer than what I am used to."

"Don't you have, like, your own house or something?"

Junior was momentarily surprised that Mariah would know that about her as she remained social media distant. "Well, yes, that is true, but it is an old, old house that has not been updated hardly at all since my great-grandfather built it. I have a tiny fridge and a weird shower. My sink in the bathroom is nothing like that one in there."

"Well," Mariah said as she looked down at her phone which buzzed several times while they were talking, "whatever. I would love to have my own house even if it was

janky. Someone is always watching everything you do here. There are all kinds of rules, like lunch at two on the weekends no matter how hungry you are, and they do your laundry on Monday."

She was no longer looking at either her phone or Junior; she was clearly venting some deeper problems she had. "What if I need something washed sooner? What am I supposed to do? And, like, the way they do my sheets and all the pillows. Why do I need so many pillows? I can't even get into bed, and when I finally do, the sheets are so tight. Every night, I get in there and it's like being in a vice. No matter how many times I say I don't want it like that, it doesn't matter because that is 'how it has always been done.' God! It sucks." She stamped her foot down and had a death grip on her phone.

One of Junior's gifts was to know when to say nothing and to be present. It was part of why people didn't notice her but also why people felt totally comfortable being around her. In the same way that no one ever felt strange confessing to his or her favorite cuddly toy from childhood, no one felt strange confessing to Junior. At this point, Mariah could not have known that consciously, but as stated, it was a gift she had, and like some people calm animals and others know how to cook without a recipe card, Junior knew how to put people at ease.

The silence stretched out, and eventually, Mariah's phone buzzed again, and she came out of her rage-filled trance. She remembered where she was and with whom she was standing.

"Well, anyway," she began, not acknowledging anything untoward happened at all, "I'll show you around before lunch, OK?"

Still not wanting to speak, Junior just nodded and smiled.

"Well, this is the West Wing. We live here. You saw my door. That one," she said as she started walking the way Junior came in, "is Julia's. In between our rooms is a living room. We share it. TV, couch, fridge, video games, the usual stuff."

It was most certainly not usual for Junior at all. While she and Suzy shared a home and they did have their own fridge, they did not have a TV, video games, or anything of the sort. They didn't even have wireless internet.

The rest of the tour consisted of Mariah giving little clues about where to turn to find which section of the house. There was a painting of Dr. Mansfield next to the North Wing, one of town on the East Wing, and one of the college near the West Wing. "Essentially, the house has three identical wings all on one floor. The basement has the servant quarters, laundry, kitchen, all that normal domestic stuff. You came in on the south side of the house. That has the foyer and a door to the basement that looks like an entryway closet. The boy's wing is east, we are west, and Mom and Dad are north. Ours is long and skinny; Mom and Dad's is a big rectangle. Don't ever go in there unless invited, but you won't be invited. The center of the house has the Dining Room, The Nook, and The Lounge. We eat most of our meals in The Nook. All the weekday meals are in there. It is pretty low-key, sort of à la carte. We hang out in The Lounge after lunch sometimes. Most of the time, though, Mom lays in there and naps with Pug. Yes, her dog is a pug called Pug. It's embarrassing. Dad and Pug don't get along so he doesn't allow her in the North Wing, so she pretty much lives in the center of the house.

Pug has a bed in The Lounge. It is nicer than most people's beds. Again, pretty embarrassing.

"You don't have to really worry about getting lost because as you saw in our wing, there is just one main hall down each one that ends. There's a door to the outside at the end of each hall. It is an exit only. There is no handle there to let you in, so if you go out that way, like if you sneak out or something, you have to walk of shame back through the front door."

Junior had no idea why anyone would need to sneak out. She certainly wouldn't be doing any sneaking. There was never anywhere to sneak in Unincorporated Nowhere, but even if there were, why would anyone sneak? If she wanted to go somewhere, she just went there.

"It's quicker to go to campus out that door though, so if you are running late, just book it out there. Campus is just a five-minute walk. Have you been there yet?"

"No, I just got here, and Norris picked us up..."

"Us?" Mariah's tone turned from sleepy tour guide to defensive. Clearly, one interloper was enough.

"My brother Bill is here for a bit before he heads out to Texas for basic training. He rode up with me on the train."

Mariah's tone swung right back. "Oh. Right. Mom said something. Anyway, campus... we have orientation Monday, but we will be over there tomorrow. We have to go to church. Norris is insisting. Normally, we just go to the biggies, Easter, Christmas, stuff like that, but she has been making a big stink, and Mom would rather just give in when she makes a stink. We all do really. She's nice and all, but when she has a mission, she is like one of those dogs, you know... um..."

"A terrier?"

"Yeah, that's the one. From that movie about the dog show. You know that one?"

Junior had never seen a movie about a dog show, nor, as far as she could tell, would she be interested in such a thing, but she never bashed what others loved, so she just said, "I don't think so."

The phrase "I don't think so" was one of the greatest weapons in her arsenal. In general, one is rarely verbally assaulted after saying, "I don't think so." It has been known to happen of course, and it will happen later in this story, but before we get there, to the final time we hear Junior say anything in these pages, there are more people to meet and places to see.

"Yeah, well, it's funny. We can watch it sometime. We have a lot of movies, both old-school Blu-Rays and some on the cloud."

"The cloud? You have personal cloud storage?"

"Sure, everyone does. I'm sure Portsmouth set you up with something. I'll bet he left a manual in your desk somewhere. Dig around. There is a cloud for the whole family too. That's where we keep the movies, but you can back up all your stuff to your own location."

"Wow. That is incredible. Thank you," Junior said. It would be wise to stop here and explain that whenever Junior has ever uttered the word "wow" she unironically actually means it just like everything else she has ever said in her life. One never must worry that one will get anything but honesty from Junior. If one is looking for anything remotely involving platitudes or smoke blowing up one's backside, it is best to never ask Junior.

Mariah, not used to hearing such earnestness, was unsure how to respond. So, she said "Whatever" which was her catchall word. It could mean whatever she wanted it to. In this case, it meant, "People do not thank me for things, and I'm not sure if I know how to accept thanks, so I will deflect."

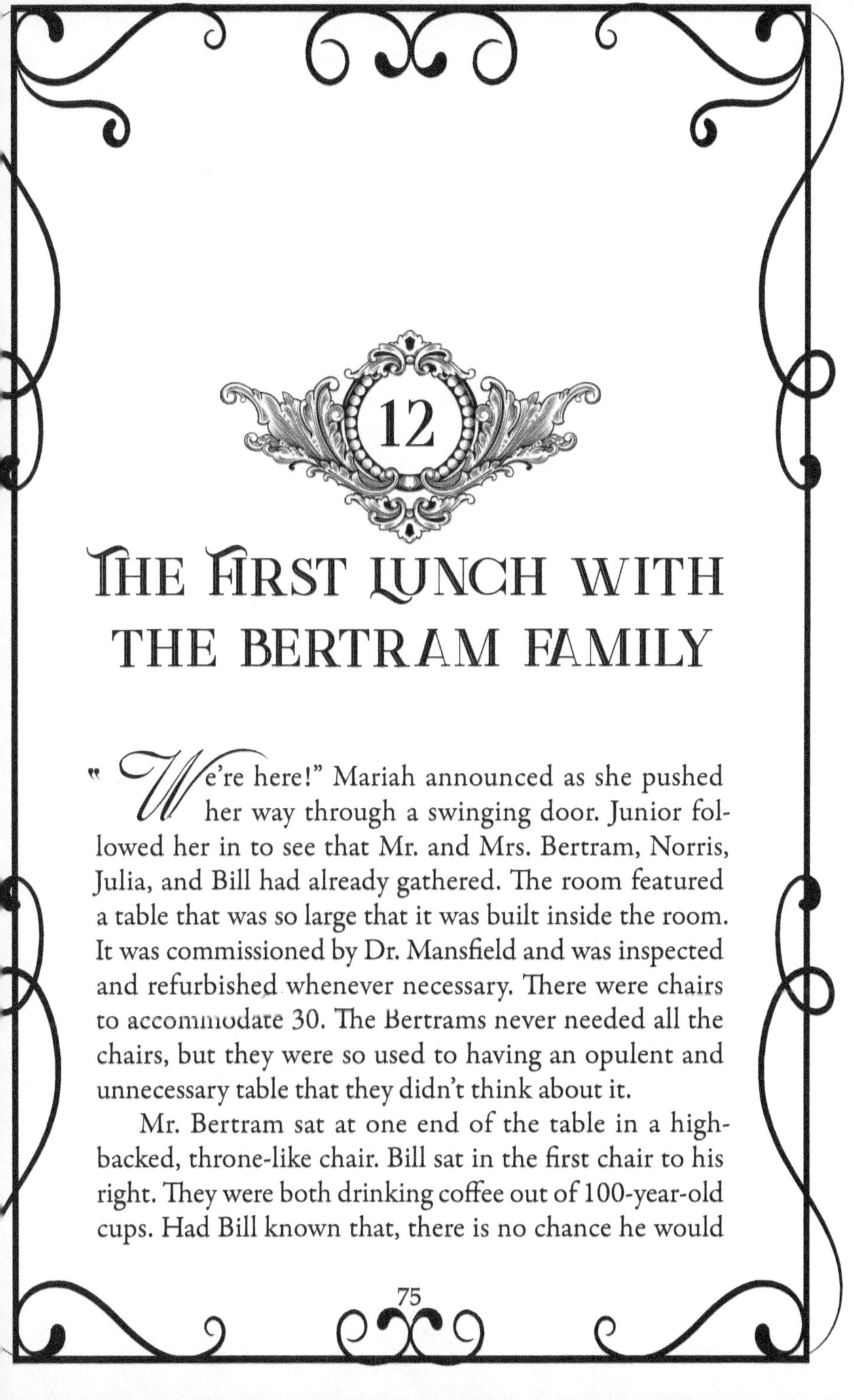

12

The First Lunch with the Bertram Family

"We're here!" Mariah announced as she pushed her way through a swinging door. Junior followed her in to see that Mr. and Mrs. Bertram, Norris, Julia, and Bill had already gathered. The room featured a table that was so large that it was built inside the room. It was commissioned by Dr. Mansfield and was inspected and refurbished whenever necessary. There were chairs to accommodate 30. The Bertrams never needed all the chairs, but they were so used to having an opulent and unnecessary table that they didn't think about it.

Mr. Bertram sat at one end of the table in a high-backed, throne-like chair. Bill sat in the first chair to his right. They were both drinking coffee out of 100-year-old cups. Had Bill known that, there is no chance he would have accepted the drink. They seemed to Junior to be engaged in an enjoyable conversation. Julia was sitting as far away as she could from them on the opposite side corner of the table, looking down at her phone. Norris and Candy were engaged in some sort of secret conversation as Norris' lips were just inches from Candy's ear. She was not actually paying attention but was leaning back looking under the table to see what Pug was doing. The room smelled amazing, yet none of the family was eating.

Directly across from the entrance was the door to the basement. It was propped open. Along the wall sat a serving buffet. Upon the buffet rested stainless containers that one normally sees at major events or at hotels in the breakfast room. Sterno lamps blazed beneath each container. A young woman, dressed like a chef, stood at attention at one of the buffets next to a small gong.

Bill looked up and waved and smiled. Junior, whose eyes were as wide as the saucers upon which the coffee cups sat, did a finger wave back at him and mouthed, "Oh my goodness."

"Julia, this is Junior," Mariah said as she walked over to get a plate, seemingly forgetting that she had taken up the charge of being a guide.

"Um, hi," Julia said. "Wanna sit with me?"

"Sure, that would be great. I should go say thanks to your mom first though."

"Of course." Julia looked over at the woman in the chef's uniform and jerked her head her way. The woman picked up a tray and placed an antique cup and saucer along with two crystal glasses, one short and one tall along with a cloth napkin and full silverware set, and brought them over to the chair next to Julia. She set the place for Junior.

"It is not yet 2, dear," Candy said to Mariah just as she was about to pick up a plate. The clock above the buffet showed 1:54. "You know we don't eat until 2."

Mariah mumbled something under her breath that no one could hear. She stomped past the stack of dishes and went to introduce herself to Bill.

Junior approached Candy and started, "Mrs. Bertram, I just..."

Candy stood and pulled Junior into a hug before she could finish. "Oh dear, you call me Candy. We're so glad to have you."

After the hug was over and Junior could get air back into her lungs, she finished her thought. "I just wanted to say, thank you so much ... Candy. The room you gave me is just amazing. I'll never be able to repay you."

Norris quipped. "You will repay her, girl, by excelling in your studies and not sullying The Park nor the Mansfield Gift legacy."

"Yes, Ma'am," Junior said.

"Don't you worry, dear. No recipient of The Gift has ever done anything but bring honor to the school. You can thank me by being the sweet and wonderful girl your mother tells me you are. We're just so happy to have you. Have you met Pug yet?" She folded herself in half, and her head disappeared under the tablecloth. She came back up, holding Pug, who had grown accustomed to such handling that she almost became limp. "Pug, this is Junior. Junior, this is Pug."

"Well, hello there Pug! Aren't you adorable?"

Pug curled her tongue up and breathed heavily. She looked Junior right in the eyes and licked her own face.

"That means she likes you," Candy said.

"That means she's a dog," Norris snarked.

"EDDIE!" Julia shouted from her side of the room just as the person dressed as a cook hit the small gong.

Both sounds startled Junior. She instinctively wrapped the scarf around her neck a bit tighter.

Junior looked over and saw Julia giving her brother Ed a huge hug. He picked her up and swung her around. The sight of such familial affection made Junior smile broadly. Across the room, Bill was grinning just as widely. Mariah, seeing the scene, turned in disgust and began piling up her plate. She never understood why Julia and Ed were so close, nor did she approve.

"Edmund, quit playing about with that child and come meet your guests," Norris snapped.

Ed set Julia down and whispered something in her ear, which caused her to snort in laughter. "Yes, Reverend." All four of the Bertram children were accustomed to taking orders from Norris. Their parents made it clear that she could get away with pretty much anything. They were not particularly religious themselves, so they felt it was good to have some kind of spiritual oversight, and they left that to Norris. The fact that Ed was majoring in Religious Studies seemed like proof that it was working. They really had no idea what a Religious Studies major actually studied, nor that Ed was really most interested in the mythology and other historical aspects of the subject.

He walked over to where his mother and the reverend were sitting. He kissed Norris on the cheek and bent over to give his mother a hug. Pug, seeing her chance to lick a face besides her own, swiped his face.

"Pug is happy to see you too!" Candy giggled like a little girl which was something she did anytime she thought Pug did something particularly adorable.

"Yes, I'm blessed." He wiped his face on the back of his sleeve with his left hand, while he extended his right hand to Junior. "Hi. You must be Junior. I'm Ed. Lovely to meet you. Welcome to the zoo... Uh, The Park."

"Hi. Yes, I'm Junior." She took his hand, and they shook. Junior had shaken thousands of hands. She was the most polite person ever to come from Unincorporated Nowhere. She had touched hands that felt like dead fish, hands that felt like sandpaper, and everything in between. Most people either tried to shake too hard or were afraid of her small frame and wouldn't reciprocate with just a firm, normal handshake. Most people in her generation, Mariah Bertram included, as we saw, don't even know how to shake hands. Here was a young man who, like Junior, fully understood the message one sends through such a simple gesture.

"Lovely to finally meet you. I look forward to getting to know you and helping you around campus. It has been fun to get to see you and your siblings online. I see you brought one of them with you."

He looked over Junior's shoulder to where Bill stood. He reached out and gave Bill the same firm handshake. "Bill, so glad you're here. Welcome."

The two of them released hands and walked over to the serving counter. Mr. Bertram made eye contact with Norris. His fears of bringing a young, smart, and pretty girl into the house disappeared. Norris, seeing the interaction as well, raised her glass across the table to him. He did the same.

By 2:10, everyone was settled in with plates piled high. While the Price children were used to family meals on the weekends and evenings, and they were used to self-serve buffet style, they were also used to mismatched plastic wear and flying food from the littlies. This event, which had been a tradition at The Park since Dr. Mansfield and his family moved in, was much more subdued, much more expensive, and considerably less fun. The Price family meals for all of their close quarters, messy shirts, and noise, were filled with laughter, voices piling on top of voices until they filled the small space leaving everyone much more full than the meals ever could.

To be sure, Bill, Ed, and Tom had a polite and jovial conversation; Norris constantly whispered in Candy's ear while Candy fed Pug, who remained on her lap. Mariah sat alone on one long side of the table, shoveling food with her left hand while tapping away on her phone with her right. Julia and Junior sat at the far end of the table, closest to the door, and had an amiable chat, part of which we shall see here.

"So, you like your room? I know it kind of sucks."

"I like it very much. I have a bathroom to myself, you know."

"You don't normally?"

"No, I have shared with some member of my family or another my whole life."

"Ugh, even the boys?"

At this Junior could not help but laugh. "Yes, even the boys. Although sharing a bathroom with Bill over there was ten thousand percent more pleasant than sharing one with Suzy. Bill has planned on going into the Air Force for as long as I can remember, so he is very neat in both appearance and the way he lives. Suzy is a huge slob. She leaves everything everywhere. She says it's so she can find it, but I think she's just lazy. I mean, if you put things where they belong, then they're also easy to find."

"I guess if I had to share with Eddie, it wouldn't be so bad, but Tommy is the worst. He's gross on purpose, you know. Like, it's a game for him. It's funny when the stuff isn't directed at me, but when it is... ick."

"Where is he? I thought he might be here. I was excited to meet him too."

"Oh, I'm sure he and Yates will roll in sometime before 3."

"Why before 3?"

"That's when lunch is over."

"Really? It isn't over when we're done eating?"

"We stay in here until 3. No one is excused for any reason. If you have to go to the bathroom, go before you come. You can go if you really need to, but you will get a lecture later, so it is better not to bother. We're supposed to be here before or at 2, but for some reason, Tommy can do whatever he wants. He comes late all the time, and other than a word or two from Norris, which has much more bark than bite, no one says anything to him. I mean, if I came in 20 seconds late, they would make me sit and watch everyone eat for like 20 minutes before I could get to eat."

"Really?"

"Really." Julia made her face into a line. "I'm not sure how much Dad and Mom really care, but since Norris is, like, always here, and it matters very much to her, they go along. They lay right in about tradition and all that. It's happened to all of us."

"Except Tommy?"

"Except Tommy."

On cue, the swinging door kicked in with a bang, and Tommy came in looking as though he just crawled out of bed or stayed up all night. "What up, Fam?" Tommy shouted.

Mariah didn't look up from her phone. She expected him to come late and to make a scene. Had anyone been watching, and no one was, one would have seen her flinch when Tommy kicked in the door. Ed looked up and smiled. He and his brother had an understanding: Ed would smile at the dumb things Tommy did and Tommy would do dumb things.

"Thomas, you know that lunch is served at 2. What caused you to be waylaid this time?"

"Oh Norris, you love me," Tommy said as he blew a kiss to his mother and saluted his father. "And who is this?" he said to Julia while looking at Junior.

"I'm Junior Price. I'm..."

Tommy looked from her to Bill, and back. "Right! Fran's kid. I forgot you were coming. Is that your brother over there?"

"Why, yes, Bill is..."

Tommy, apparently done with that conversation, walked away and headed over to meet Bill. He stopped, kissed his mother on top of the head, let Pug lick his face, directly on the lips, and then he kissed Norris on the cheek.

"Don't take it personally. It isn't about Bill; it's about Dad," Julia said. "They are both good guys, well, Eddie is great, and Tommy is good but spoiled. They just..." She cut herself off and waved at the scene of all three men seemingly shining all their light on Bill. "They just really want

Dad's attention, and if he is giving it to Bill, they know that means they need to as well."

Junior took in the information and nodded. "There are a ton of us too. The littlies all compete for Dad's attention too."

"But not you?"

Junior shrugged. "Bill and I get plenty of attention from him." She didn't bother explaining that the attention she got wasn't always the kind she wanted.

"Must be nice. I mean, we joke around, and we laugh. He's a good dad, but..." She let her thoughts drift off as she considered what she wanted to say next. Deciding that maybe telling everything to this stranger wasn't the best way to make new friends, she shared something a bit more hyperbolic.

"I'm not sure if Dad even knows my middle name. It's Jane, by the way."

"Nice, I like alliterations."

"Me too! I love books. I love words. I love..."

"Shut up!" Mariah shouted from across the table. "No one cares, Julia. Junior certainly doesn't."

The whole room was silenced, and instead of looking at Mariah, who clearly deserved a dirty look or six after her childish outburst, they looked to Junior to confirm or deny the claim. Feeling the eyes on her, she swallowed hard and touched her scarf to make sure it was wound tight as she remembered.

Junior looked right at Julia. "I love books too. Who are some of your favorite writers?"

"You don't have to..."

Junior reached out and placed her hand on top of her arm. "For me, it really depends on what I'm feeling that week. Have you ever read E. Lockhart's stuff? *We Were Liars* is a masterpiece."

Julia wiped a tear from her cheek, and the conversation continued as though the outburst never happened. They talked about books until the gong rang at 3, releasing the family from the confines of the dining room.

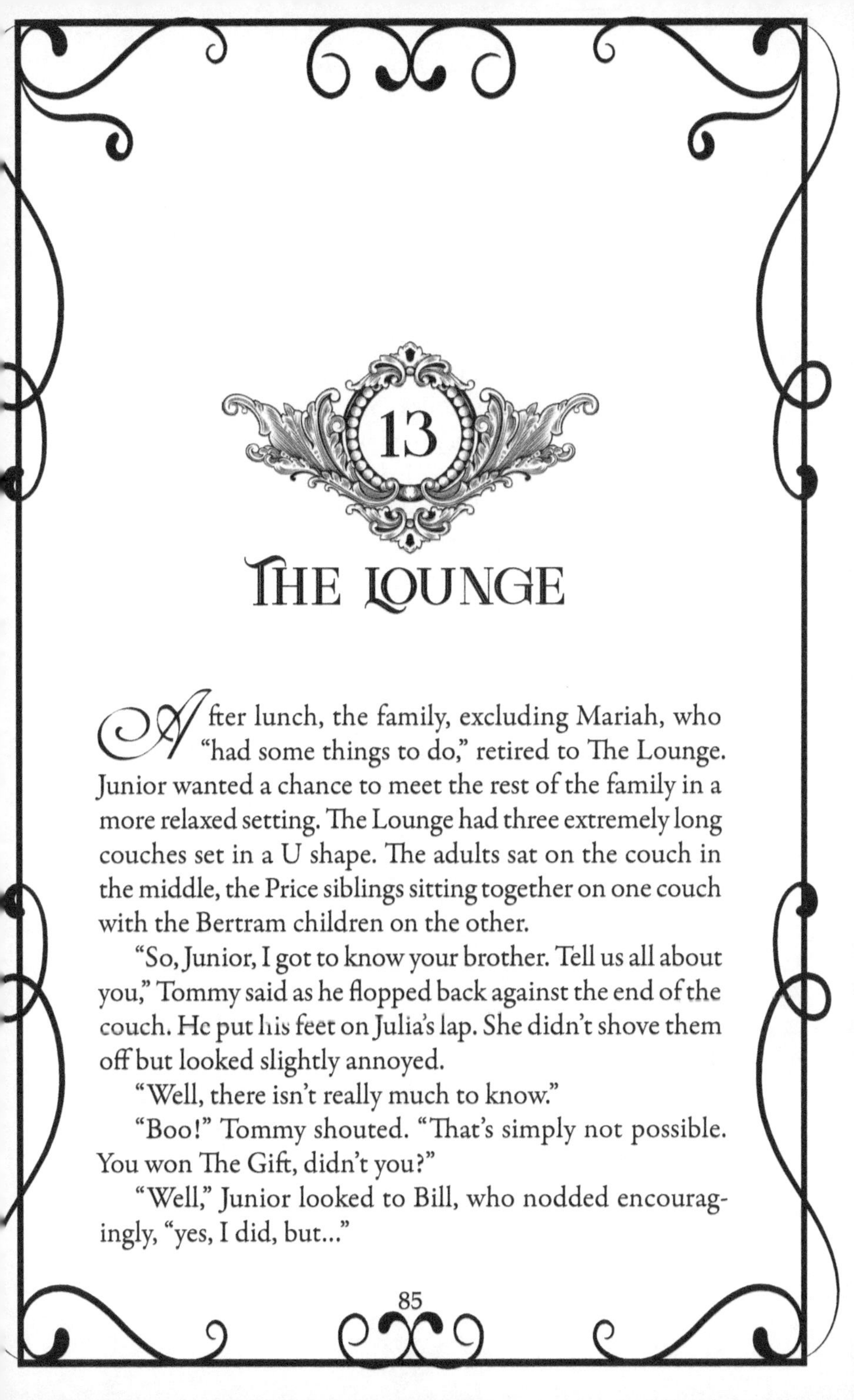

13

THE LOUNGE

After lunch, the family, excluding Mariah, who "had some things to do," retired to The Lounge. Junior wanted a chance to meet the rest of the family in a more relaxed setting. The Lounge had three extremely long couches set in a U shape. The adults sat on the couch in the middle, the Price siblings sitting together on one couch with the Bertram children on the other.

"So, Junior, I got to know your brother. Tell us all about you," Tommy said as he flopped back against the end of the couch. He put his feet on Julia's lap. She didn't shove them off but looked slightly annoyed.

"Well, there isn't really much to know."

"Boo!" Tommy shouted. "That's simply not possible. You won The Gift, didn't you?"

"Well," Junior looked to Bill, who nodded encouragingly, "yes, I did, but..."

"But nothing. What was your essay about?"

One may or may not be surprised to learn that that was the first time anyone had ever thought to ask her this question. As we learned, Junior doesn't share unless asked and so, until that moment, only the selection committee members knew the contents of the essay that most assuredly won Junior the Gift and put this tale in motion.

All eyes turned to Junior. She touched her scarf to make sure she had not loosened it. "Well," she cleared her throat, "I wrote about how I skipped ahead to graduate with Bill and how I thought it might be better for my family if I were out in the world a bit faster. There are just so many of us, as you all know, and while I know it might be easier on Dad to have me around to drive to the store and do those kinds of things, I know it is easier on Mom to have us both there to help out with the littlies, but at the end of the day, it's just better to have two fewer mouths to feed. Obviously, money is tight. Bill and I don't cause any fuss, but fewer people naturally leads to more money in the coffers. They could close up one of the houses and save money there.

"Of course, if I hadn't won The Gift, I would have been going to the community college down there. I was going to use the money I had saved up for my half of room and board for the first year to buy a car. So, I just wrote all about that and how being a young first-year, I would be thrilled to not feel the pressure to choose a major right away as I felt that I had a lot of pressure on me already."

"I hope your essay was more eloquent than that. If not, the standards have dropped considerably," Norris said to everyone and no one. She was notorious for saying the inside things on the outside.

Bill, having heard this for the first time, was too overcome with emotions to take in what Norris said. He was wiping tears off his cheeks. The rest of the family, who was used to Norris' desire to make everything about her while pretending nothing was about her, remained silent.

"Why yes, of course it was, Reverend. I was just paraphrasing for everyone. If you would like to read it, I could email you a copy."

Norris literally waved away the words. "Pffft, that will not be necessary, child. I have the utmost faith in the process."

Desperate to have the attention off of her, Junior asked, "I would love to know more about all of you. It's been cool to get to follow you online, but I know that isn't really everything. I mean, I know it can't be. No one puts all the stuff on there."

Ed and Julia both turned their heads to Tommy. They knew that given the chance to talk about himself, he wouldn't be able to resist.

Tommy swung his feet off Julia's lap, crossed them at the knee, and leaned forward. "Well, my partner, Yates, who couldn't make it for lunch today, but whom you should meet soon, and I live in an old movie theater downtown. Yes, I know, before you ask, it's strange to live in a movie theater. We have turned the employee break room into the living area. There were the right kind of plugs for all the stuff we need, except for the washer and dryer so..."

"They bring their clothes here to have the staff do it on laundry day. Isn't that right, Thomas?"

"Yes, Norris, that's correct. I don't ask you to do it, do I?"

Norris mumbled something that was not polite enough for company.

Tommy continued, "There was already a floor drain in the storage area, so they could wash down any spills for when the syrup for the pop leaked, so we hooked up one of those stand-up basement showers in there. Do you know what that is?"

Junior and Bill both nodded.

"Yeah, it isn't the best. All the heat escapes the top and the room is pretty big, but it does the trick. We've been fixing up the theater itself so we can use it to start showing movies. We ultimately want to start the Mansfield Film Festival for amateur and student films."

"You want to show your abominable films."

Before Tommy could respond to what was Norris' interruption, Bill had already cut in. "You make movies?"

Tommy looked at Norris but answered Bill's question. "I certainly do. Yates writes them, I shoot them and direct them. We edit together. Right now, we use exclusively digital because it is cheaper and easier, but I would like to make a short film on actual film. We have a working projector in the theater, and I think it would be amazing to use."

"It would be amazingly expensive as well and a waste of resources, just like you spending your trust fund buying that damnable theater."

"Save the sermon for tomorrow, Norris. It's my money. I'm trying to start a business. I would think you would appreciate my entrepreneurial spirit. Dad started his own business. It isn't like I was ever going to fly. Besides, now that Bill's around and going to be a pilot, he can take over one day."

"Well, I..." Bill sputtered, finding himself shocked to hear his thoughts coming out of Tommy's mouth. "Well, I don't know anything about business, but once my time in the service is done, it would be an honor to come and work for you, Mr. Bertram, Sir."

"Let's make sure you get your wings first, son." He reached out and patted Bill on the arm. He looked at his watch. "Well, if you will excuse me, I'm going to retire to my office." He stood up, bent back down, and planted a kiss on his wife's cheek.

"Have fun watching the game, dear."

"See you bright and early at the sermon tomorrow," Norris chimed in.

"Of course, Norris. I wouldn't miss it for the world. You kids have a good afternoon. Tommy, why don't you take the Prices down to see your theater?"

Looks exchanged between siblings. Silent conversations were had and agreements were made. "Yes, please!" Junior said.

"I'd love to see what new additions you've made," Ed said.

Julia added, "Who's going to ask Mariah?"

All eyes fell on Tommy. "Oh, let's not and say we did."

With that, the after-lunch conversation was over; the five young people headed for the front door to walk down to the theater. Norris left without saying goodbye. Candy called for Pug, who came scampering in hoping it was naptime, which it most certainly was.

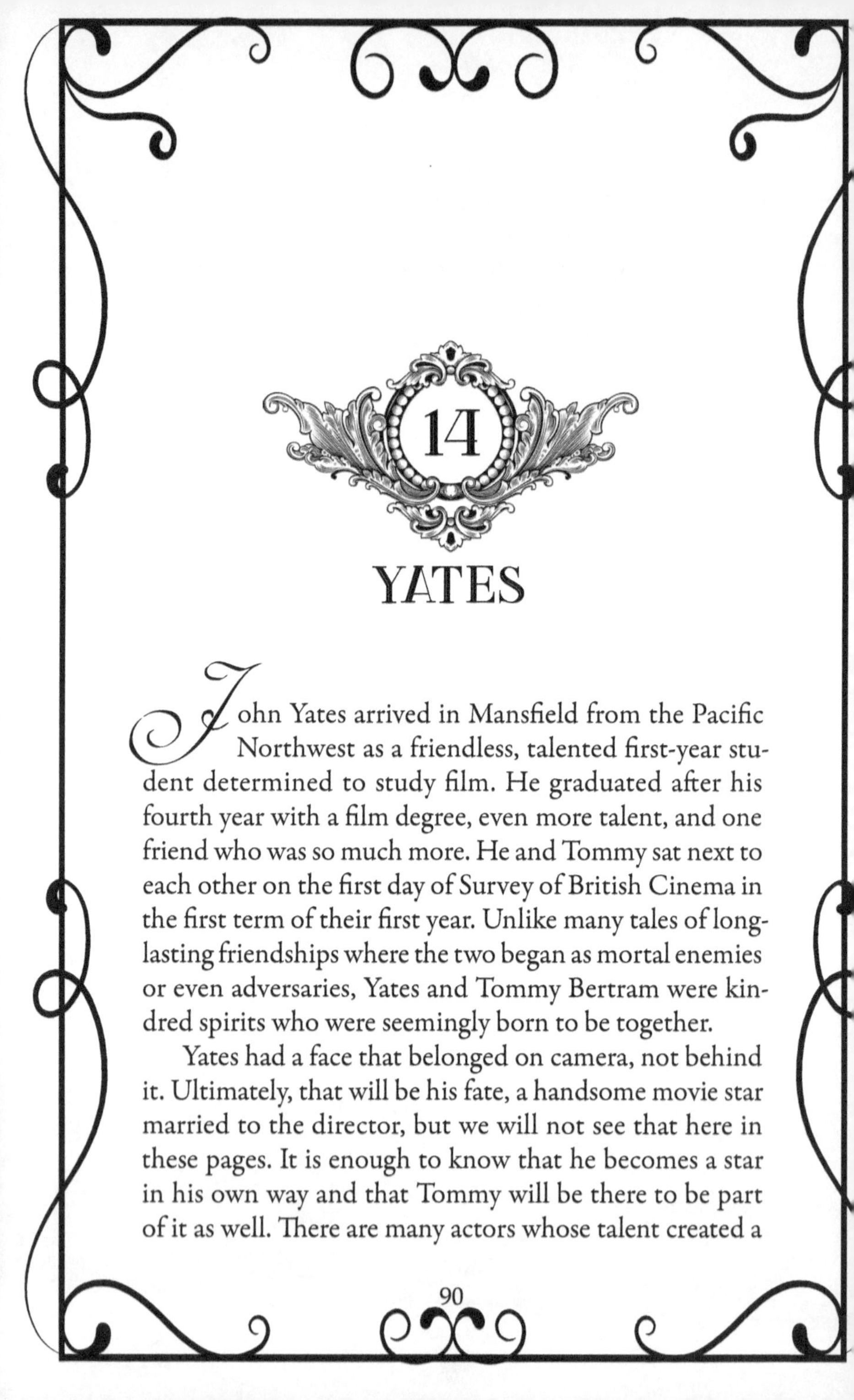

14

YATES

John Yates arrived in Mansfield from the Pacific Northwest as a friendless, talented first-year student determined to study film. He graduated after his fourth year with a film degree, even more talent, and one friend who was so much more. He and Tommy sat next to each other on the first day of Survey of British Cinema in the first term of their first year. Unlike many tales of long-lasting friendships where the two began as mortal enemies or even adversaries, Yates and Tommy Bertram were kindred spirits who were seemingly born to be together.

Yates had a face that belonged on camera, not behind it. Ultimately, that will be his fate, a handsome movie star married to the director, but we will not see that here in these pages. It is enough to know that he becomes a star in his own way and that Tommy will be there to be part of it as well. There are many actors whose talent created a path to stardom, and there are others whose appearance and overall demeanor have given them solid careers even though they lack talent. Then, there are the few unicorns in the acting profession who are pleasant to work with, pleasing to see, and compelling on stage or screen. John Yates was a unicorn.

Yates, like most of the students at Mansfield College, was from a certain class of people who were used to having things and are seldom disappointed. He had a hard time keeping his thoughts to himself. It was this personality quirk that kept him from coming to Bertram's family lunch more often. He and Norris rarely saw eye to eye on anything; people who enjoy being the loudest voice in the room tend to have neither time for, nor patience with, others who share in this affliction. Sometimes people who seem to be exact opposites have the most in common.

Candy loved Yates as though he was another son. He always made her laugh in a way no one else could. Ed and Julia just wanted their big brother to be happy. Thomas found Yates' ambition admirable and said very little more about it. His silence was seen as tacit approval, which for Thomas Bertram was the same as him attaching a banner to the back of one of his planes to announce his feelings. Mariah was openly hostile to both of them all the time. However, since she was openly hostile to everyone and everything all the time, her actions were not considered a good representation of how she felt about them as a couple.

Norris, who also liked almost no one and nothing, most certainly had problems with their relationship. She was convinced that Yates had prevented Tommy from majoring in marketing. Upon graduation, he would be enrolling in an MBA program that would end with him settling down with some nice young person and having a nice, stable boring life. Why it mattered to her was anyone's guess, so readers should feel free to guess, as there shall be no resolution on that issue in these pages.

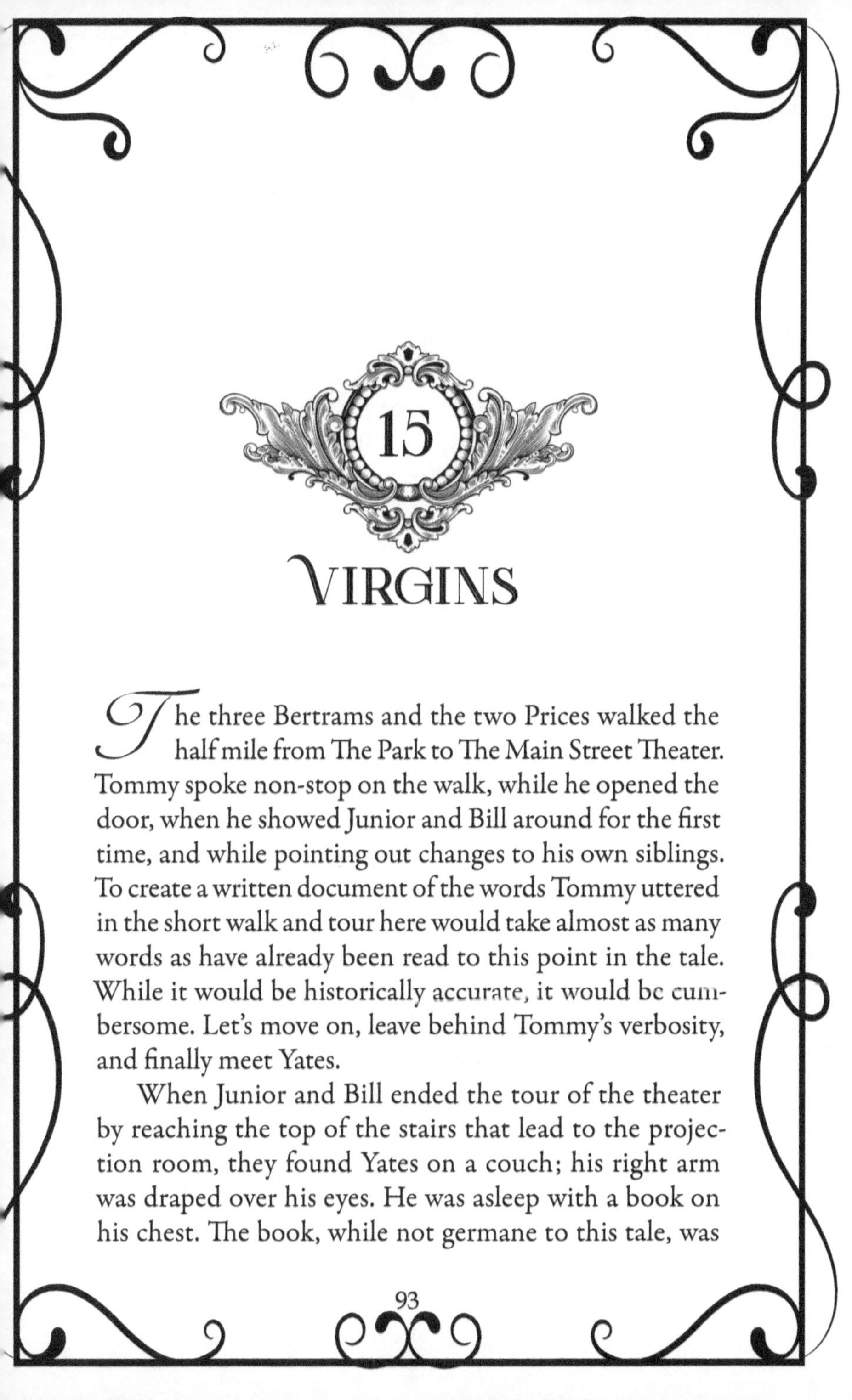

15

VIRGINS

The three Bertrams and the two Prices walked the half mile from The Park to The Main Street Theater. Tommy spoke non-stop on the walk, while he opened the door, when he showed Junior and Bill around for the first time, and while pointing out changes to his own siblings. To create a written document of the words Tommy uttered in the short walk and tour here would take almost as many words as have already been read to this point in the tale. While it would be historically accurate, it would be cumbersome. Let's move on, leave behind Tommy's verbosity, and finally meet Yates.

When Junior and Bill ended the tour of the theater by reaching the top of the stairs that lead to the projection room, they found Yates on a couch; his right arm was draped over his eyes. He was asleep with a book on his chest. The book, while not germane to this tale, was the autobiography of Mary Pickford, entitled *Sunshine and Shadow.*

"Awww," Tommy said in a whisper when they first saw him. "He is so adorable, but he needs to meet you." Tommy clapped his hands. "Wakey, Wakey! We have company!"

Yates' eyes fluttered open. Junior remembered the last time she woke anyone unexpectedly and how poorly that went. She clenched her teeth, waiting for there to be tension. It turns out that, in addition to all of the things learned about Yates in the previous chapter, he does not wake up grumpy. Don't worry; he has flaws. While most of them are not pointed out in this tale, be assured he is human.

"Well," Yates looked at the open page of his book, dog-eared the corner, showing one of his flaws right there, "it's about time. I was getting terribly bored, and I have been in need of some entertainment. Junior and Bill I presume?" He got up and came over and gave them both rib-breaking hugs.

When one is guerrilla-hugged by strangers, one reacts in one of two ways. One either stands, limp-armed, and allows the hug to happen, or one leans into the unexpected physical contact and goes for it. Junior did the former and Bill the latter.

After the hugging was over and they settled down on the couch and theater chairs that had been moved there, Junior said, "Well, I'm not sure we will be very entertaining. I fear that after a day on a train and the biggest lunch of breakfast foods I've ever seen, I'm exhausted."

"Think nothing of it. I'm just excited to finally meet you after stalking you online all this time. I don't have my own account. We share." He patted Tommy on the leg.

Julia and Ed came in just then. "The place looks amazing," Ed said.

"Yeah, the stage looks brand new."

"You think? We've been doing it all ourselves from YouTube tutorials. I think we had sand in our ears for a week," Yates said.

"We did indeed, but it was worth it. I love that these old theaters have stages. It gives us so many more options. In fact..." Tommy took a pause for dramatic effect, "...this Halloween we will be showing..."

"ROCKY HORROR!" Yates shouted and clapped.

Julia and Ed both made sounds of approval that blended together. Bill and Junior looked at each other and had a silent conversation that went something like this:

"What?"

"No clue either."

Yates, seeing the looks, gasped aloud. "Wait! Are you *virgins?*"

"Uh... Um..." Bill stammered.

Junior started wrapping the scarf around her neck, and she spoke into the floor. She didn't want to have this conversation at all but wanted to keep Bill from being even more embarrassed.

"I don't know why it is relevant, but I'm not even turning 17 until next month, and I have never really had a lot of opportunities. There was never really anyone at home who..."

"Stopstop*stop!*" Yates shouted as loudly and quickly as he could so he would be heard over the top of her. "That is soooooo not what I meant."

Bill had sucked in a breath when Junior started talking, and he exhaled it just as Junior sucked one in. She looked up at him, clearly confused.

"People who have never been to a showing of *The Rocky Horror Picture Show* are called virgins. There's a whole thing. I didn't mean for you to..."

"Well," Junior said rubbing the scarf on the front of her neck, "you asked, and well, I..."

Ed, sensing the conversation was about to be stuck in a cul-de-sac, chimed in, "That is awesome, you guys. Are you going to have performers as well as the show, or just the film?"

From there, Tommy and Yates both leaned forward and spoke at the same time, sometimes saying the same thing and other times saying different things.

Ed looked over at Junior, who was looking at him, hoping to catch his eye. She mouthed "Thank you."

He nodded and doffed his fictional cap. They exchanged a smile that went unnoticed by everyone present. Junior turned her attention back to the mix of noise coming out of Yates and Tommy.

As she relaxed, she unwrapped her scarf. Ed, who had not stopped looking at her, noticed.

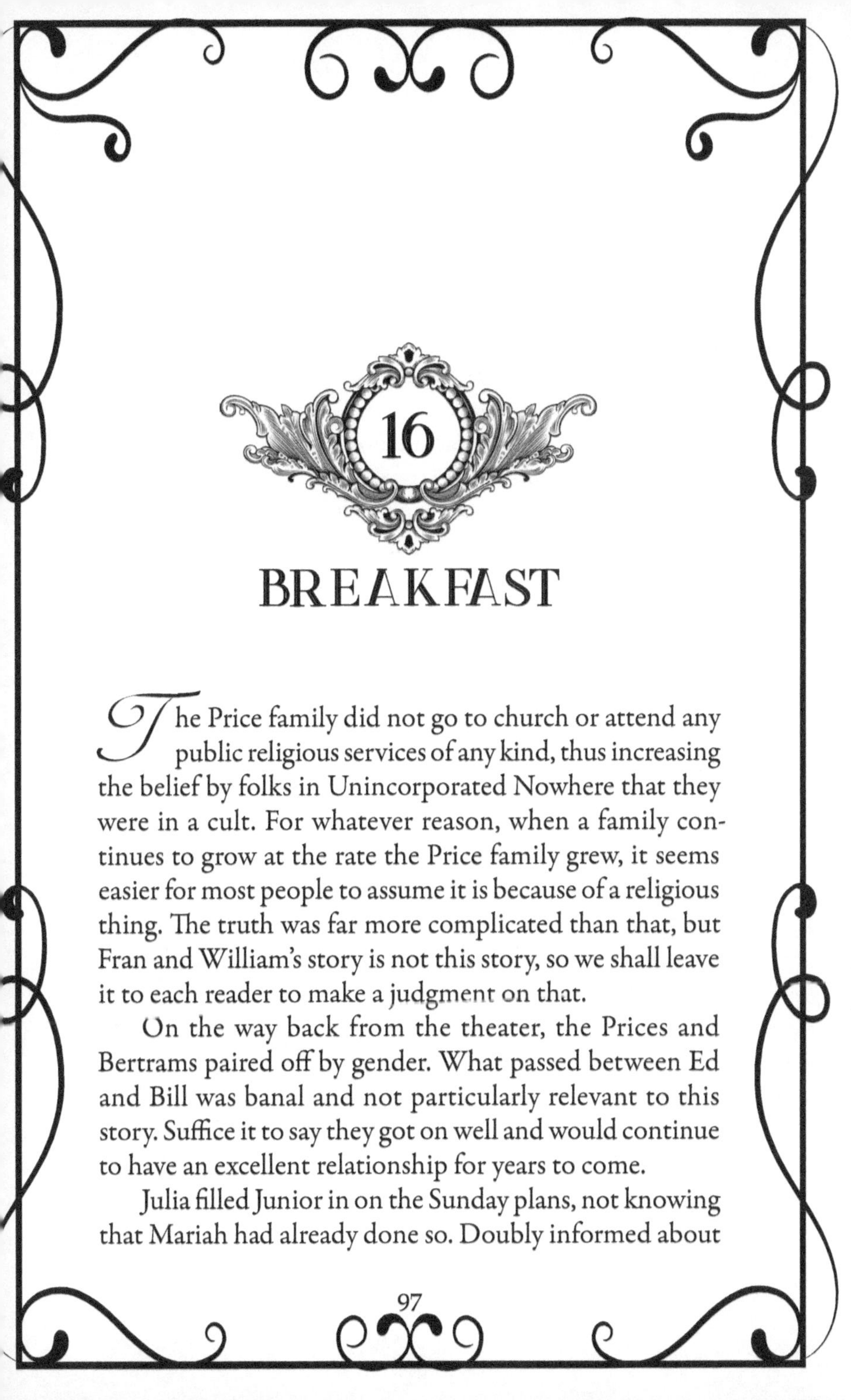

16

BREAKFAST

The Price family did not go to church or attend any public religious services of any kind, thus increasing the belief by folks in Unincorporated Nowhere that they were in a cult. For whatever reason, when a family continues to grow at the rate the Price family grew, it seems easier for most people to assume it is because of a religious thing. The truth was far more complicated than that, but Fran and William's story is not this story, so we shall leave it to each reader to make a judgment on that.

On the way back from the theater, the Prices and Bertrams paired off by gender. What passed between Ed and Bill was banal and not particularly relevant to this story. Suffice it to say they got on well and would continue to have an excellent relationship for years to come.

Julia filled Junior in on the Sunday plans, not knowing that Mariah had already done so. Doubly informed about church and armed with the time the family was to set out for the campus chapel, Junior set her alarm, sent a message to Suzy and her mother, and fell asleep quicker than she ever had in her entire life. While the bed was more comfortable than her bed at home, one can rest assured that if she had instead laid her head on the mantle of her fireplace, she would have slept just as soundly. Exhaustion wins over comfort most of the time.

Junior discovered that the hot water at The Park was seemingly infinite after she took a shower that was so long it would have drained the tank at her house back on The Ranch. She was unaware that the hot water was practically infinite, each wing having its own tankless water heater. Regardless, for the rest of her stay at The Park, she kept her showers to 10 minutes or less out of respect for her host family, none of whom would have noticed or indeed have had any idea of what the monthly utility bills actually were. Naturally, Portsmouth handled all such trivial household matters.

Junior dressed in what she hoped passed for church or at least funeral clothes, which at this point in her experience had meant roughly the same thing. She donned black dress slacks, a black, long-sleeved sheer top with a black tee underneath, and a black scarf, and headed to The Nook.

Julia explained the night before that breakfast was choose your own adventure. The staff prepared a continental breakfast of mostly cold items that could be heated up in the toaster or microwave. Of course, if anyone wished to special order breakfast, the kitchen could be reached through the intercom. No one except Norris and Mariah ever asked for anything special. There were always more than enough choices; some of them were even portable.

She explained that those would be handy for early morning classes. Julia assumed Junior would have mostly morning classes; she knew, based on her older brother's experiences, that first-years get the last choices and Gift winners get no choices.

Most days, Julia grabbed breakfast bars or heated up a breakfast burrito to eat on her way to high school, which began at the ridiculous time of 7:45. Wednesday was her late start day, so she would actually sit and eat like a normal person.

Junior was the second to arrive for breakfast. The room, like the dining room, had a serving table along one wall. There were three bistro tables set up around the room, and there was a padded window seat with a rectangle table in front of it and two chairs on the opposite side.

Bill was already there. He was staring at the cornucopia of breakfast. For lack of options or better ideas, he too had dressed for a funeral. He nodded his approval at her choice of dress.

"Great minds." He held out his fist and she walked over to bump it. "I've been here for five minutes just staring. I have no idea what to do."

Junior patted him on his shoulder. "I saw a TED talk about choice paralysis once. The struggle is real, but the problems are first world. Just have toast. You always end up with toast."

She picked up an orange cranberry muffin that was bigger than her fist. She set it down on the table in the window and went back to pour herself coffee and orange juice.

Junior sat and looked out the window that oversaw the west lawn. The long, skinny West Wing was there. She could see Julia and Mariah's windows. Unlike hers, they had curtains and appeared to be large and clear, not small and frosted. Julia's curtains were open while Mariah's were still closed. Junior looked down at her freshly wound watch and saw it was already nine. Julia said they would take off at 9:45 for the 10:00 service.

Junior could see campus at the edge of the property line. The church steeple stood high in the sky just across the street from The Park. It was over 30 feet tall and the only structure on campus to be that high. The lawn of The Park was perfectly manicured. Several of the bushes were sculpted into walls that were not quite a maze but were clearly designed for privacy. There were several benches and gazebos. Junior imagined herself spending a lot of time out there. Of course, she had yet to experience her first northern winter, so she could imagine all kinds of things before reality would set in.

She absent-mindedly pulled off a piece of her muffin and popped it into her mouth. Until that moment, she thought she understood what muffins were. She thought they were dry, somewhat tasteful breakfast pastries that she occasionally picked up at the Winn Dixie for special occasions. Once her brain caught up with the taste and texture, she closed her eyes and groaned with pleasure. She swallowed the first chunk and resisted the urge to shove the whole thing in her mouth regardless of the fact it would not fit.

"Forget the toast. Get a muffin." She turned to Bill who was still just staring at the offering. "Seriously. Get a chocolate and we'll split them." He was happy to have a choice made for him. He filled up a cup of coffee for himself, put a chocolate muffin on a plate, grabbed a knife to cut it in half, and joined her.

By the time Julia arrived in The Nook, the siblings had unceremoniously licked their fingers clean, not wanting to waste a crumb of their first experience of Proper Muffins. They were also each on a third cup of coffee. Real cups, too, Junior noticed, that being a matched set of traditional cup-sized vessels, with saucers. They were smaller than the chipped, hodge-podge collection of large-to-huge mugs they had back home.

"Hey," Julia said as she entered sporting a blue sweat-shirt with the name of a clothing company emblazoned on the front and jean shorts. She busied herself with the toaster and poured herself a cup of juice.

The Prices exchanged a look that transmitted each of their concerns about being overdressed, but they decided to wait until they saw the rest of the Bertram family before they would get too worried. Julia was, as far as they knew, a rebellious teen. Their worst fears were realized when Tom wandered in wearing tan cargo shorts and a green polo shirt with the Bertram Aviation logo on the right breast pocket. "Morning, kids," he said through a yawn. "How's the coffee?"

"It's excellent, Sir," Bill replied. "I'm on my third cup."

"Is it the dark or the breakfast blend?"

"Um..." Bill replied. He looked at Junior, who shook her head. "How do you know?"

"Don't!" Julia shouted and slid over to put her hand on her father's mouth. "He'll actually tell you," she said, looking over at Bill, "and NOBODY cares." She looked up at her dad as she said it. "AHH! Gross." She pulled her hand away and wiped it on his shirt. "Don't be gross."

"You put your hand on my mouth. Be lucky I didn't bite it." He laughed as he said it. Julia hit him on the chest where she wiped her hand, and she laughed as well. Her toast popped, and she went back to her business.

Tom filled up a cup with coffee, took a sip, and sighed approvingly. "Dark." He took another sip. He winked at Bill. "I'll tell you about it some other time."

Julia shook her head without looking back at her father. "He's just being nice. He doesn't actually care," she said partially with exasperation and partially with jest.

Bill laughed at the light-hearted exchange. Junior could not help but wonder what could have transpired to allow a daughter and her father to be that close. Julia mentioned that she didn't think they were very close and yet, there they were, goofing around and having fun. Maybe Julia's version of close and Junior's version were totally different. Sharing musical tastes is one thing; having a fun, jokey relationship was something else. Her thoughts were interrupted by the sound of clicking nails on the floor followed by a snort and a cough. Pug came in, stood in the entryway, assessed the room, and barked.

"Oh Pug, don't be rude," Candy said as she came right behind her. "Morning, all." Candy wore a black sweater that was stretched down to the middle of her thighs. Underneath were black yoga pants and slip-on shoes. There was a fine layer of dog hair from the bottom of her pants to her mid-calf. "Anything good?" She walked across the room and gave Tom a kiss on the cheek.

"It's always the same, Mom," Mariah said as she walked in the door. She was still wearing what appeared to be pajamas. "It's always the same crappy hotel food. Crappy burritos, crappy bread, crappy fruit, crappy muffins. Crap."

Bill tried to make peace and said, "I thought the muffins were spectacular, myself." He smiled at Mariah, then Candy.

Mariah huffed. "Whatever," she said in his direction and stalked off in the direction of the breakfast buffet's carved fruit area. Under her breath, she mumbled something about hillbillies and bad taste. She grabbed a bowl and somehow overcame her revulsion with the fruit she had just deemed crappy long enough to deign to fill it with fruit.

"Why thank you, Bill," Candy replied. "They are quite delicious. I think I'll have one myself."

Mariah coughed, but it sounded suspiciously like "Carbs!"

"Who has crabs?" Tommy said as he and Yates walked in. "Mariah? I thought you were better than that." Julia covered her mouth to stifle a laugh.

"I hate this family." Mariah slammed her bowl down and stormed out, shoving Tommy out of the way.

"We love you!" Tommy called after her. "Even if you are a crabby carb monster."

Yates wore an outfit that was strikingly similar to Bill's. Apparently, he, too, thought that funerals and church were interchangeable. Tommy was wearing jeans, a white button-down dress shirt, and a tie printed with a picture of Norris with a halo over her head standing in front of a cross.

"Oh, Tommy not again," Candy said when she saw him.

"Oh, you secretly love it, Mommy." He laughed as he said it.

"I openly love it," Tom said. He held up his hand to high-five his namesake. They smacked hands and hugged.

Yates grabbed a cup of coffee and muffin and came over to sit with the Prices. He sat in the window seat. "I always sit over here too. Best to stay out of the splash zone. Don't you just love these?" He took a huge bite off the top of his muffin.

"Is it always like this?" Junior asked.

He held up his finger while he chewed. When he finished he explained, "Not really. Breakfast is often a solitary adventure at The Park, but since it is a church day, they are all here. They seem to, for the most part, like each other. Tom and the boys are pretty tight. He tries with Julia too. No one can get through to Mariah though. She is normally a bit of a hag, but she has been particularly terrible of late. When she and Norris get together, watch out. That is like if Godzilla and Kong teamed up instead of punching each other in the face."

"Yikes," Bill said and looked over at Junior who was rubbing her scarf and looking out the window at Mariah's window.

Junior asked, "Why is she like that? I don't really understand. Everything is so nice here. Mr. and Mrs. Bertram are nice. The rest of the kids seem to like each other and their parents. They like you. They have been nice to us. They don't seem to ask too much of anyone."

Yates considered for a second while he sipped his coffee. "Well, you know how sometimes you open brand new pop, and it is already flat, and you don't really know why?"

They both nodded.

"She's like that."

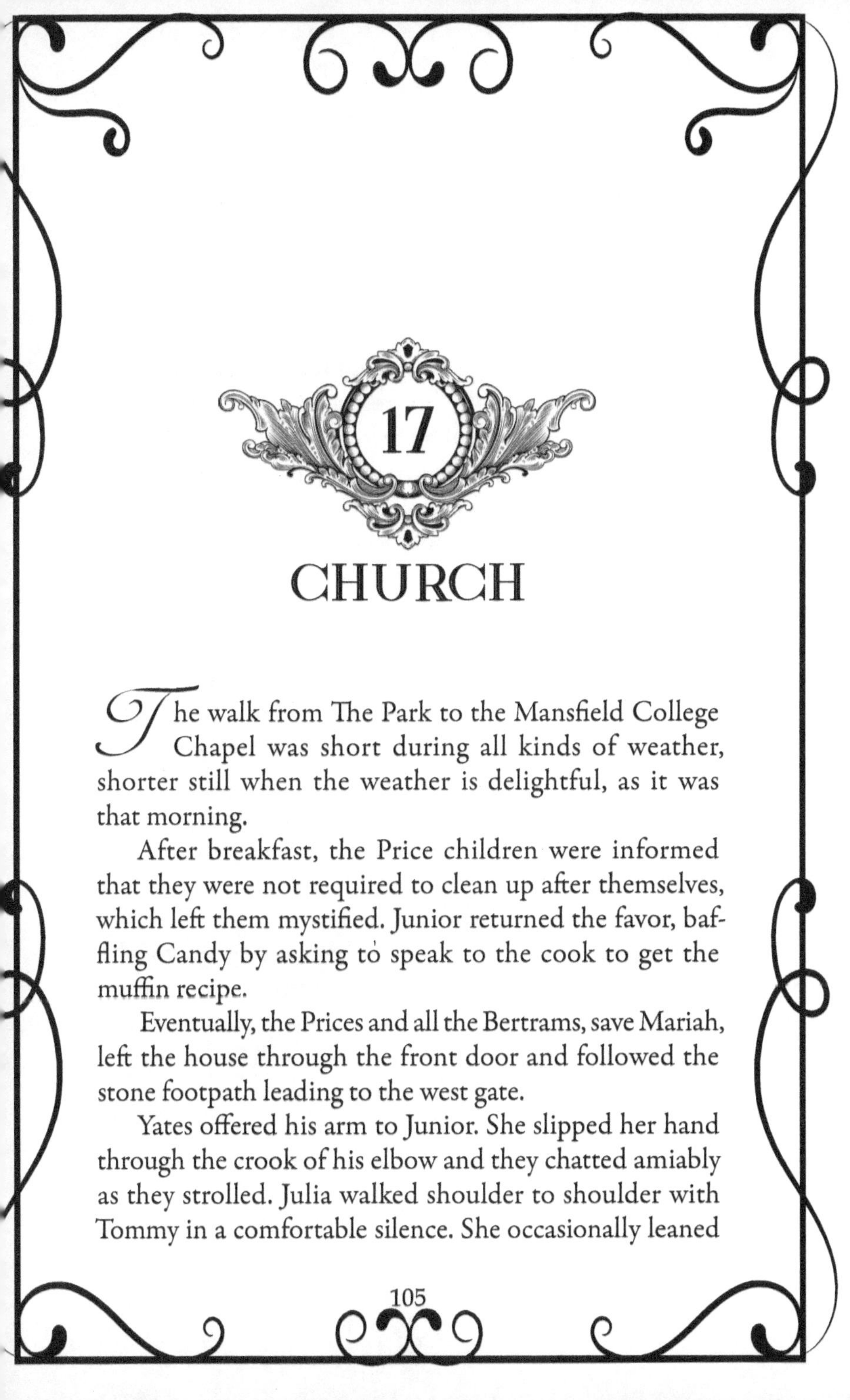

17

CHURCH

The walk from The Park to the Mansfield College Chapel was short during all kinds of weather, shorter still when the weather is delightful, as it was that morning.

After breakfast, the Price children were informed that they were not required to clean up after themselves, which left them mystified. Junior returned the favor, baffling Candy by asking to speak to the cook to get the muffin recipe.

Eventually, the Prices and all the Bertrams, save Mariah, left the house through the front door and followed the stone footpath leading to the west gate.

Yates offered his arm to Junior. She slipped her hand through the crook of his elbow and they chatted amiably as they strolled. Julia walked shoulder to shoulder with Tommy in a comfortable silence. She occasionally leaned into him, and he knocked her back with his hip, reminding them both about the way Julia used to beg Tommy to carry her everywhere.

Tom and Bill discussed something plane-related which holds little interest to the reader and shall thus be left out of the tale. Candy walked and texted increasingly dramatic messages to her eldest daughter. Unbeknownst to her, Mariah had actually not returned to her room after she stormed out. She had, in fact, headed straight for the church in her pajamas and now waited in the nearly empty Mansfield Family Pew next to Ed, who wore a rather more suitable linen suit. What Dr. Mansfield would have had to say about the general chronic occupant paucity in the family pew over the years can of course at best only be imagined. Feel free, once again, to do so.

The family filed in as the campus clock began chiming ten. They sat in stony silence while Reverend Norris gave an extremely ferocious sermon about trust. She began with Psalm 118:8, "It is better to take refuge in the Lord than to trust in man," and it only went downhill from there.

Each occupant of the Mansfield Family pew that day felt the weight of her words in a different way. Junior could not help but feel the words were directed at her. Bill was worried about his ability to blindly follow orders for the next four years. Tommy and Yates were worried about their film distributor. Julia was stressed out about her new year of high school. Ed did not care for the new head of Residence Life, to whom he would be reporting. Tom was worried about the new pilot he hired on a recommendation from his golfing buddy against the advice of his chief pilot. Candy was worried about the new dog groomer. Mariah's list was too long to share here. The phrase "she would rather spit on you than look at you" was not written about Mariah Bertram, but it may as well have been.

After the fire-and-brimstone portion was concluded and the congregation took communion, excluding the Prices, who thought it might be improper for them to participate, Norris came back to the pulpit. She began, "I regret to inform you all that this shall be my final sermon as campus minister." Norris paused for what she thought would be a chorus of gasps. Instead, she was met with muttering. The only gasp flew from the mouth of Candy, who was not upset about the news, but because she had clearly not been told in advance.

She planned on holding her hands up for silence, and since it was rehearsed, she did it anyway. "Dr. Bennet reminded me that my own ancestor created a provision in the position that states one can only hold it for twenty years. Of course, I feel that I have so much to still give to the community that I have agreed, at Dr. Bennet's urging, to stay on as a member of the faculty and as Minister Emeritus. I have moved from the rectory to campus faculty housing, and I look forward to helping your spiritual growth in another way." More muttering from the crowd and a gasp, this time, from President Bennet herself, who was surprised to hear such false versions of events said aloud and in such a public forum.

"I would like to introduce the Reverend Dr. Grant and his niece and nephew, Mary and Henry Crawford, both of whom shall be first-year students and who shall be living with the Reverend in the rectory."

She pointed to the front pew. A small, balding, hunched, seemingly frail man stood and nodded up to the pulpit to Norris. He turned and held his hand up in salutation to the congregants. Two young people, a young man and a young woman, almost his exact opposite in stature, appearance of health, and posture, flanked him on either side. They, like their uncle, raised a hand and waved. Many sets of fraternal twins, especially opposite-gendered twins, must explain that they are actually twins. That was not the case with Mary and Henry Crawford.

"There will be a reception in the congregation room downstairs for those of you who wish to meet Dr. Grant and his family. I urge you all to take the time to meet the man who shall guide Mansfield College's spiritual future." Norris led the congregation in one final hymn as minister of Mansfield College with her teeth clenched together a little tighter than normal.

After the service ended, the Prices and Bertrams circled up to decide if they should go downstairs or not. Aside from Ed, the rest of the family did not intend to return for Sunday services until the next holiday when such an appearance seemed appropriate.

"Well, do you all think we should go down? Norris must be feeling anxiety over the whole situation. It's shocking that she didn't tell us before. Why didn't you tell us, Ed?" Candy scolded.

"Me? I didn't know."

"How can that be? You work for the College."

"Believe it or not, Mother, resident assistants are not privy to all the juicy gossip on campus, nor are we consulted about anything regarding anything as big as replacing the campus minister. You're the highest-ranking member of the Mansfield family; I would have thought you knew. Don't you have a meeting with the president once a semester?"

In fact, Candy Bertram did have a standing meeting with the president. However, because the meeting took place in the President's office and not in her Lounge at The Park and Pug was not invited, she rarely, if ever, attended. Had she attended her meeting in May, she would have been informed of this change. Dr. Bennet also planned to ask Candy to offer living space to Norris at The Park so that one of the faculty houses would not be used up by one person. Candy did not show, and Dr. Bennet was not one to seek out those who did not wish to be sought.

Unwilling to admit this, and now unwilling to go downstairs to be face-to-face with Dr. Bennet, Candy asked Tom, "What do you think we should do?" She knew full well that Tom did not want to be there and would have no interest in going downstairs.

"I think that Norris is coming to lunch, and we wait until then."

"Oh, excellent idea, darling." She patted him on the arm. "Ed, you go down and invite Dr. Grant and those children as well. That will be perfect." Without giving him a chance to respond, she turned and headed for the door. Tom followed her out with a bow and a smile to the circle of young people.

Mariah looked down at herself and, as if she finally realized what she was wearing, chased her parents out the door and squeezed in between them to be shielded from view.

"I'll go!" Tommy said once his parents were out the door. He may have been a man, but he still was their child, and as much as he liked to rabble rouse, he did not like to annoy his mother too much in public, just in private. He knew if he offered while wearing that tie, she would have objected and made them all go, and he knew his father was thrilled to get out of it. He grabbed Yates' hand and headed for the basement door.

"I should too. He'll need a mediator." Ed smiled as he said it.

"Or a bail bondsman," Julia replied. "See you at lunch?"

"You got it, kiddo." He gave her a hug. "You'll still be here?" He directed the question to Bill.

"Yep, my train leaves at five."

"Excellent." He reached out and shook his hand. He took a step back and looked at Junior, who had remained silent and almost invisible during the service and the exchange. "See you there?" he said to her.

"Of course."

"Excellent. I'll see you then. I'm keen to spend some time with you." He wasn't sure if he should hug her or shake her hand or bow his head. He moved forward and stepped back, shadow dancing with himself.

Julia, sensing his awkwardness, chimed in, "No one says keen, dork. You should get down there before he starts a riot. Come on, guys." She grabbed Junior's hand and pulled her away. "I want to show you the rest of The Park before lunch."

Junior waved at Ed as she was being led away.

He smiled and bobbed his head in response. "See you soon."

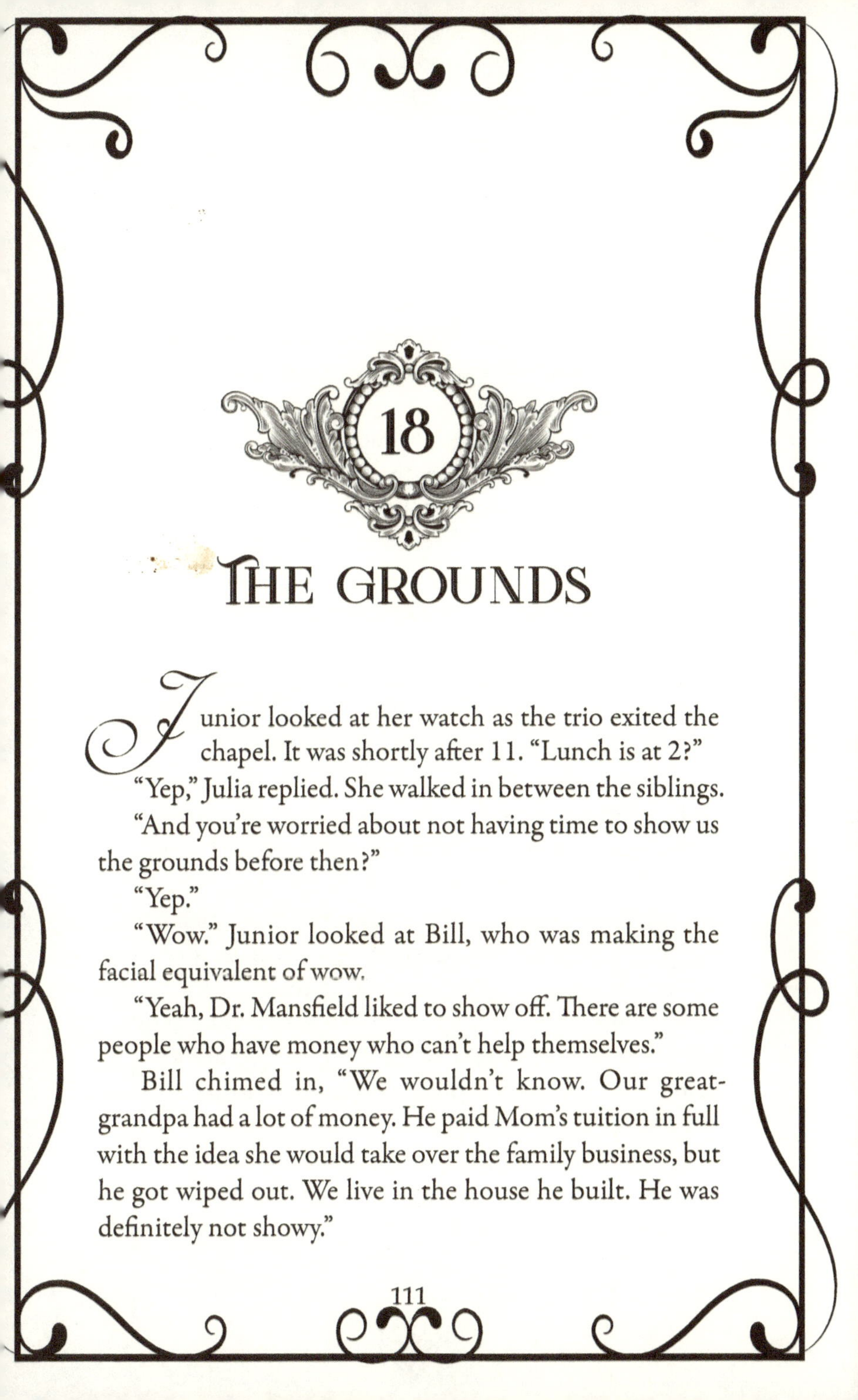

18

THE GROUNDS

Junior looked at her watch as the trio exited the chapel. It was shortly after 11. "Lunch is at 2?"

"Yep," Julia replied. She walked in between the siblings.

"And you're worried about not having time to show us the grounds before then?"

"Yep."

"Wow." Junior looked at Bill, who was making the facial equivalent of wow.

"Yeah, Dr. Mansfield liked to show off. There are some people who have money who can't help themselves."

Bill chimed in, "We wouldn't know. Our great-grandpa had a lot of money. He paid Mom's tuition in full with the idea she would take over the family business, but he got wiped out. We live in the house he built. He was definitely not showy."

Julia nodded. The siblings didn't know if that meant she had heard that story before or if it was just something she did to show people that she was listening. She skipped a few feet ahead of them and turned to face them both. They all stopped. "Can I be honest with you guys?"

They both nodded. "Of course," Junior said. She was always honest, so it would not have occurred to her to need to ask permission first.

"I kind of love it. I mean, I know I shouldn't, but I love living in a mansion and having the huge grounds. I love having someone else do my laundry. I love not knowing how to cook. I love it all so much. It makes me happy to know that I have the option of staying here forever if I want. I'm not like Ed. I don't know if I want to leave it all behind. I know I'm spoiled or whatever, but I love it. I mean, I always say thank you, and I'm super nice to the staff, not like..." She cut herself off as the words caught in her throat as if squeezed by an invisible hand.

"Not like some people, I mean. I know I'm super lucky, and it is all just random. I was born to these people, and that is just a fluke. I wasn't born a girl in Saudi Arabia or some other terrible place, but I am so, so glad that I was. I have a lot of plans to make the world better, and being born me gives me a chance. You know?" She inhaled deeply as though she had expelled something toxic. "So, I totally understand if you don't want me to show you around. I just get super excited about it, and it can come across as being..." She cut herself off again. She looked down, afraid of what the Prices would say.

Junior reached out and touched her arm. "There's nothing wrong with being proud of who you are and where you come from. I sure am. I know we don't have what a lot of people have, but I wouldn't change it for anything. It led me here, didn't it? Bill is going to be an Air Force pilot. Suzy is not yet fifteen, and she can drive a car."

Julia wiped her cheek. She had been hiding the tears. She looked up. "Yeah?"

"Yes," Junior said clearly. Bill nodded along. Junior grabbed Julia by the elbow, swung her around, and locked arms with her. "Let's go see it all."

"OK." Julia wiped her face again. "Let's start by going around the outside. The fence actually circles the whole property..."

For the next few hours, the three circled the outside of the property around Mansfield Circle. Julia pointed out the house where she and her family first lived after her parents were married. Currently, that house, called The Cottage, sat empty, awaiting the time when Norris would eventually retire. There were several other houses that would have towered over any number of the Prices' homes where many of the staff lived. They wandered through the hedges, sat on benches, and ended up spending time in the Carriage House looking over the family car collection.

Julia explained the car situation to them. "Mariah can't drive. She never wanted to. This one," she pointed at a blue crossover SUV, "is Mom's. The truck is Eddie's. The mondo SUV is Dad's. Tommy could have this one," she pointed at a classic yellow sports car, "but he likes to walk."

Bill gasped. "It's a Karmann Ghia." He walked over to it, looking starstruck.

"Is it?" Julia shrugged her shoulders. "Is that a big deal?"

Bill silently nodded and absentmindedly licked his lips. "Can I get in?"

"Knock yourself out. Everyone always wants to."

We shall let Bill have a private moment and follow the rest of the tour with Junior and Julia.

"This one is going to be mine." Julia stopped next to a Jeep. "I wanted something for winter. Dad said this is the one."

"Going to be? You're already sixteen, though."

"Yeah, well..." She shrugged her shoulders and scrunched up her face. I only have my learner's permit, and I don't yet have enough hours. Ed does his best, but he was super busy this summer."

"I have my license, so if you need just a co-pilot, I'm happy to ride around with you."

"Really? That would be great. I will have to check. I don't know if you're old enough. I think you have to be eighteen."

"Well, you know where to find me. I would be happy to help."

"In exchange for your awesomeness, you can drive it anytime you want."

"We should check with Tom and Candy first, shouldn't we?"

"Nope." She opened the passenger door and opened the glove compartment. She pulled out a paper and handed it to Junior. It showed that Julia was the owner of the car.

"Wow." Junior ran her hands over the official paper, slightly disappointed that something which bestowed such significance did not have more weight and texture to it.

"Pretty cool, right? Like I said, I know I'm super lucky or whatever."

Junior nodded. She was overwhelmed by the reminder of the circumstances that brought her there. She wound her scarf tight around her neck.

"All good?" Bill asked as he approached.

"This is Julia's car. Pretty amazing, isn't it?" Junior looked at him and nodded the answer to his question. He knew they could talk about it later.

He nodded back. "Holy crap! Really? Love these. It has wood paneling too. Old school. Nice choice."

"You think? I thought it made it look silly, but Dad said these older ones are built better and are safer. He had an upgraded system put in, so it has Bluetooth for the phone. For safety, he says."

"No doubt. This is a classic. May I?" Bill pointed at the open door.

"Really?"

"Yeah, it's awesome."

"Sure." Julia stood a little taller. Of all the guests she brought to the Carriage House, everyone wanted to get into Tommy's car, but no one wanted to get into hers.

While Bill poked around, Julia showed Junior the bay where the cars were maintained. It looked like an operational auto shop. "One of the ground staff is a mechanic. He changes the oil, rotates the tires, and all that stuff. I don't really know much about it."

"Junior knows all about it," Bill said as he came in from behind them, causing both girls to jump. He laughed a bit at himself. Junior swatted his arm and rubbed her scarf. "We did all that stuff ourselves. It would be a lot easier with a lift though, huh?"

"Really? You can fix a car?"

"Well," Junior, not liking to brag about anything, said, "I haven't fixed everything, but..."

"Yeah. She can if she has to. The only thing she hasn't done is rebuild a transmission, but she could."

"That's amazing!"

"It's not, I mean…"

Bill jumped in. "She doesn't do compliments. It is amazing." Then in a stage whisper, he said, "She would rather burst into flames that let people know that about her, so can you keep it between us?"

Julia crossed her heart and mimed locking her mouth with a key and throwing it over her shoulder.

"Thanks," Junior said. "I just…"

"No explanations needed for me." Julia smiled. She looked up at the clock on the wall of the Carriage House. It was almost 2. "Hungry?"

19

LUNCH GUESTS

Junior, Julia, and Bill arrived in the dining room at five minutes to 2. The food, once again, was arranged on the buffets. This time, instead of breakfast foods for lunch, a more traditional lunch was served. There was a salad, chicken breasts, accoutrements for turning said chicken breasts into sandwiches, French fries, and several kinds of side dishes made with various dressings, cheeses, and noodles.

Tom, Candy, and Mariah were already gathered. Each sat with at least one empty seat between them. Mariah and Tom both scrolled through their phones. Tom was holding a cocktail in his left hand that he occasionally sipped. Candy and Pug appeared to be having a staring contest that Candy was determined to win and for which Pug cared very little.

When the trio walked in, only Tom looked up. He smiled a genuine smile at them. "How was the tour?" He patted the seat next to him, inviting them over.

"It was lovely," Junior said. "I thought…"

"SUP FAM?!" Tommy shouted, drowning out anything she might have said. He came in still wearing the same outfit he wore to church. Yates trailed in. He raised one hand in a wave.

Mariah glanced up over her phone but did not move her head. She mumbled something inappropriate that would prompt someone to ask if she kissed her mother with that mouth. She used to and would again, but at that moment, she did not.

Tommy, on the other hand, regardless of what words came out of his mouth, always kissed his mother and her dog. He bunny hopped over to her and this time kissed her on the cheek before getting a face of Pug tongue. Yates and Bill made the exact same face that silently showed their disgust. Julia rolled her eyes. Tom laughed. No one seemed to realize Junior was answering a question. She sat down next to Tom just in case he eventually wanted to hear the answer. He never asked.

The cook struck the gong just as Norris walked through the door leading Ed, Dr. Grant, and the Crawford twins. "Greetings," Norris said. "Edmund, why don't you make the introductions?" Without waiting for a response, she walked over and sat in the open chair next to Candy, who reached over and patted her leg much like she would Pug.

"Yes, Reverend." He bowed his head a little. "Well, Dr. Grant, Mary, and Hank, please meet the family."

"Not *everyone* is family," Norris said with an emphasis on everyone.

Ignoring her, he pointed around the room, making introductions, beginning with Mariah on the right and ending with his mother.

"Let's eat." Tommy chimed in after it was over. "Guests first, of course." He put his left hand behind his back, splayed his right out in front of him, and waved them over.

Junior and Bill waited patiently as everyone filled their plates and made small talk about how nice it was and how great it smelled, and everything that one expects from this part of the story. It is important to mention, however, where everyone sat, as that has bearing on the future of our tale.

Dr. Grant sat with Norris, Candy, and Pug. He made several subversive comments about dogs in the dining room that went unheeded. The conversation after that was mostly academic, thus making Candy lose interest. She knew when to say "Yes" and "Oh!" and "That's interesting" when necessary. We will not spend much time with them.

Julia sat with Tommy and Yates at the far side of the table near the door so they could be free to speak however they chose without fear of being heard, as they would most assuredly make some playful, but ultimately mean-spirited comments about almost everyone in the room. While some of these remarks are cause for smirking and an occasional belly laugh, we will not spend much time with them either.

Ed and Hank Crawford ended up on Tom's left, while Junior and Bill ended up on his right. Tom loved meeting new people. He liked the look of Hank Crawford. Hank was tall and sturdy, much like Tom himself. He directed a lot of his questions at the new young man in much the same way he did with Bill when he first arrived. Due to the way the five of them sat, both Hank and Ed were not only facing Tom, who was looking back at them; they also faced Junior, who, more often than not, was not looking back at them. Bill, who would look up from his spot at the end of the line, noticed the eyes of the young men as they looked past Tom and to Junior.

Mariah's attitude and demeanor changed quickly once she set her eyes on Hank Crawford. Something inside her shifted. It was not love at first sight, but it was some other biological urge at first sight that also began with an L. She did not invite him to sit with her, however, but she did engage with his sister Mary. Mariah was unsubtle when she disliked someone, but she did know how to play the long game when she liked somebody, or at least felt some other L-word for them.

The conversation was overly polite as the two young women verbally circled each other. Each of these women mined each other for information about the other's brother. Clearly, Mary Crawford felt about Ed the exact same way Mariah felt about Hank. For whatever reason, they both thought the best path forward was to befriend each other. As we know, Ed and Mariah had never been remotely close. While it is true that Hank and Mary were quite close, they knew each other well enough to know that getting entangled in each other's romantic escapades tended to be both troublesome and exhausting.

As the meal progressed and the conversations waxed and waned, Portsmouth entered at 2:20 and whispered into Candy's ear.

"Most certainly not!" Norris responded to the information that was clearly not intended for her. The rest of the conversations abruptly stopped. Tommy leaned over and whispered into Julia's ear, causing her to laugh and choke at the same time. Yates smiled and shook his head while holding in a laugh.

"Oh, don't be that way," Candy replied to the red-faced reverend. She reached over and patted her leg. "See him in, Portsmouth."

"As you wish, Ma'am." Portsmouth nodded. All eyes followed him out of the room and lingered on the door, waiting for his return with the mystery guest who was somehow important enough to be admitted in clear violation of the family rules.

The only sound came from the coughing Julia, accompanied on percussion by Tommy lightly patting her on the back. It has never been officially determined if hitting someone on the back during a coughing fit actually helps, but time-honored traditions hold firm. Just as she finally got it under control and took a sip of water, Portsmouth returned.

"Mr. James Rushworth," Portsmouth stated as he stepped aside, letting the young man in. Had her plate not been piled high, the sound of Mariah's fork falling from her hand in shock would have drawn the attention of everyone in the room, where they would have seen her open-mouthed and beet red. Only Mary Crawford noticed, but as was her way, she stored the reaction away for later use.

"Dreadful etiquette. I apologize," James said as he appeared at the door wearing an outfit that could best be described as a rich boy from a teen movie on a boat. "I had every intention of making it to church, but Daddy and I had some business to discuss." One can but guess and wonder at the fact of a young man of 20, who is not from the Deep South, calling his father "Daddy" with a capital D.

"It's no problem at all, James," Candy said. "We are always happy to have one more. Cook has certainly made plenty." She waved him over to her. "Please, come in and meet everyone."

He came to her and bent over to give what one could only describe as an awkward hug. He reached out his hand to shake Norris' hand. She thought of not taking it to punish him for being so full of himself that he thought it was OK to arrive late to a meal, but the room full of people made her reconsider. She did not make eye contact, however, to make a point that was lost on everyone.

"Well, this is a handsome-looking bunch." He smiled in a way that was practiced. It was empty but reassuring. It was cultivated through years of practicing in the mirror. It was supposed to say, "I'm not a threat, but I'm confident and important." Clearly, if one feels the need to cultivate this and practice in the mirror, confidence issues were likely just the tip of one's problematic iceberg.

Candy went around the room and introduced Dr. Grant, the Crawfords, and the Price siblings while James stood by her side and made empty social intercourse noises such as "excellent," or "my pleasure," or "how do you do." Introductions accomplished, James piled up a plate and joined Mariah and Mary.

He placed his plate on the table in front of the empty chair next to Mariah. He bent over to place a kiss on her cheek, which she accepted with as much joy as she accepted a lick from Pug. Fortunately for her and equally honestly for him, James was unaware of this.

"Hello, darling. You look lovely," James said once he sat down. "It is excellent to meet you, Mary." He nodded to her. He shoved a few fries in his mouth.

"And you," Mary replied, looking more at Mariah's reactions than anything else.

"I thought you said you couldn't come," Mariah said in a tone that could be read as accusatory.

"Yes," he held up his finger to allow himself time to finish chewing, "well, as I said," he pointed to where he stood just moments before as though he were watching a replay, "Daddy and I had business to discuss. It took more time than anticipated, and I missed church. That is what I said: I couldn't come to church. However, since we finished up, I wanted to come see you before I headed back to school."

"What is your business, if you don't mind me asking?" Mary inquired.

"Well," James looked at the inquisitive stranger, at Mariah, and back at his plate, trying to decide which thing was most important, "we mostly do real estate, property management, and construction. Been at it for generations. We actually built the high school where Julia attends."

"His family built it, not him."

"Yes, of course, darling." He looked from Mary to Mariah, who had crossed her arms over her chest and was leaning back against her chair to put as much space between herself and James as possible, making her look more petulant than normal.

"My family built it. Daddy wanted my input on a new golf course project. I'm majoring in landscape architecture. It's a five-year program where I can get a BA and MA. Daddy thinks I can use the new course as my thesis."

"How exciting," Mary said in a tone that absolutely convinced James that she was actually excited. She leaned forward, filling the space vacated by Mariah when she pushed herself back. She did not seem to be practiced at it; it just seemed to come naturally.

Mariah was also convinced that Mary was actually excited and was suddenly much more interested in the conversation. "Where is the course going to be?" She uncrossed her arms and leaned forward, blocking Mary from view. She placed her hand on his arm.

"Yes, well," he took a sip of his water, "that was kind of what I wanted to talk to you about, darling. The land Daddy chose is actually in Florida, so in order to work on this project, Daddy said I will have to spend most of my weekends and holiday breaks down there instead of coming home like normal." He turned from her and shoved food in his face.

This was more for her than for him. James had little to no ability to read people, and so looking away served no apparent purpose except that he had learned over the years that it was best to look away when he told Mariah any big news, so that she would be less likely to storm off. As we have already ascertained, she sure knew how to make an exit.

Mariah looked to Mary, who was either holding the best poker hand or the worst. There was nothing there. She took the fact that James was eating as a sign that she should do the same. Mary Crawford could read almost everyone and rarely overplayed her hand. However, as we will learn later, she could not read Ed Bertram and absolutely overplays her hand. It could be assumed that her desires clouded her judgment. We shall leave it for each

124

reader to decide when that moment arrives later in this story. You will know it when you see it.

Mariah looked around the room at the rest of her family to see if there was anyone in whom she could confide and ask advice. She found them all wanting except perhaps for Norris, who was shooting eye daggers at James. Not because she thought he was breaking Mariah's heart, but because she simply did not like him, thought the Rushworth family were trashy, and considered outsiders at lunch problematic unless she invited them herself. Mariah widened her eyes to get Norris' attention. She shook a little in her seat as well. When Norris finally noticed, Mariah pointed with her eyes out the door. "James. Can you give me a minute alone to think about all of this?"

"Of course." He started to stand.

She put her hand on his shoulder. "Oh no, silly." She had never before, nor would she ever again call him silly in this context. "I'm going to take a turn around The Park. I will be back before the end of lunch." She turned to Mary. "Mary, would you be a dear and keep James company for me?"

Mary was always keen to have people owe her things. "I would be delighted. I know nothing whatsoever about Landscape Architecture."

"Really?" James said with a mouthful of fries.

"It's true. My education is lacking in that department. I'm happy to learn."

Mariah turned her back to James as she stood and mouthed, "Thank you." Mary winked.

She turned back to James. "Thank you for understanding. I shall be back shortly."

"Take your time," Mary said before James could even respond. She leaned in over the empty seat. "So..." That conversation went pretty much exactly how one would expect it to go, so we shall leave it there.

Mariah left the room without looking again at Norris, but she was confident that the signal was received. Norris waited exactly three minutes before she excused herself by saying, "Since the protocols have been absolutely disregarded today, I will follow suit and go powder my nose. Excuse me." She stood and walked out, leaving Candy and Dr. Grant to continue the detailed conversation about Pug's flea bath regimen. One might have been surprised to learn that Dr. Grant was quite interested, as he had a French bulldog called Henri.

The conversation between Norris and Mariah went exactly as one thinks it would have. Norris encouraged Mariah to use this as her way out of the horrible match, and Mariah agreed but would not commit. She had her own reasons for that which will eventually be revealed in these pages. There is no reason to go into depth as they are not deep people. Mariah did not return to lunch as promised, instead leaving it to Norris to inform James that she would speak to him privately later. Norris, who would have preferred to relay an entirely different message to James, dutifully followed Mariah's orders and relayed the message.

James was quite relieved. He felt that a private conversation would allow him to save face when, as he expected would happen, Mariah cut him loose. Much to his surprise, he was not dispatched. In fact, he shows up again later in this story. The conversation that happened between Mariah and James, however, is quite private, so we will discreetly focus our attention elsewhere.

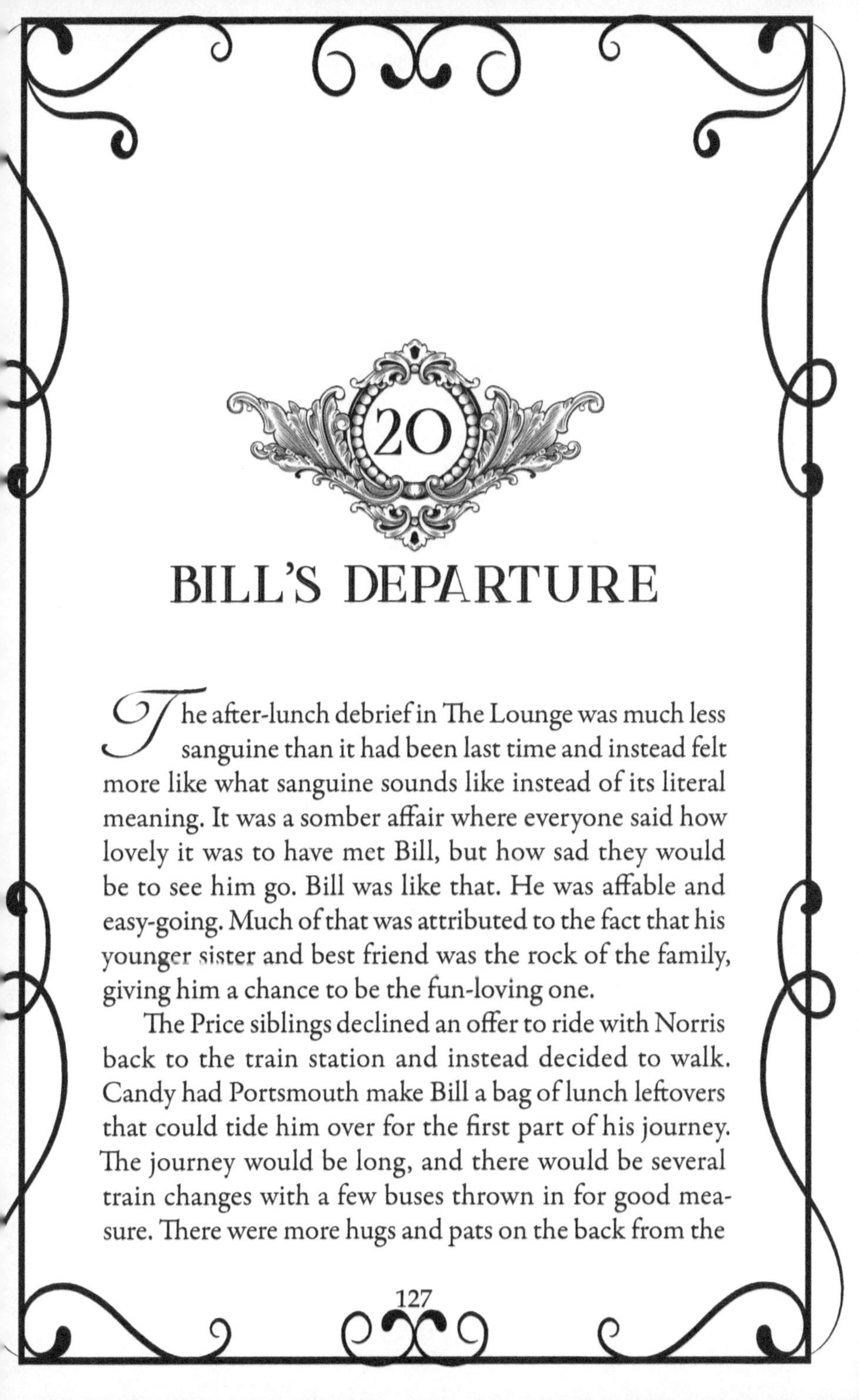

20

BILL'S DEPARTURE

The after-lunch debrief in The Lounge was much less sanguine than it had been last time and instead felt more like what sanguine sounds like instead of its literal meaning. It was a somber affair where everyone said how lovely it was to have met Bill, but how sad they would be to see him go. Bill was like that. He was affable and easy-going. Much of that was attributed to the fact that his younger sister and best friend was the rock of the family, giving him a chance to be the fun-loving one.

The Price siblings declined an offer to ride with Norris back to the train station and instead decided to walk. Candy had Portsmouth make Bill a bag of lunch leftovers that could tide him over for the first part of his journey. The journey would be long, and there would be several train changes with a few buses thrown in for good measure. There were more hugs and pats on the back from the

Bertram family than there were from the Price family. It would give something for both Price siblings to consider for weeks and months to come.

Tommy and Yates joined them for the first half of the short walk. They peppered Bill with questions about what he thought he might expect. He had done plenty of research on Air Force Basic Training and found that while it was challenging, it was often considered much less difficult compared to the other armed services. Neither Tommy nor Yates thought eight weeks of super intensive physical or mental training, where one of the weeks was called BEAST week, was a walk in the park. Tommy often complained, on the walks they did manage to take around The Park, of being on his feet for much too long. Then he would demand they sit on one of the many secluded benches scattered around the property.

The stop-off at the theater was quick. Hugs, back-pats, handshakes, and kisses on the cheeks passed back and forth until eventually, the Price siblings found themselves alone and walking the final few blocks to the train station together.

"They're all pretty great," Bill said. "Except for Mariah. I couldn't get a read on her. I would say it is best to keep your distance."

Junior laughed while she talked. "Yeah, well, we live across the hall, so I don't know about that. Besides, she doesn't seem too interested in me."

"Or anyone."

"Well, not everyone is a people person."

"You aren't a people person, but you're not evil. There's a difference."

"She's not evil."

"Hmmm. Well, we'll see about that."

Junior, not wanting to speak ill of anyone, looked for a solution. "It must be hard to have a new person, some stranger living in your house, and all the attention is always on everyone but her. I suspect that's hard. I'm going to give her a break…"

He interrupted, "Of course you…"

"BUT…" she interrupted back, "I'll give her a wide berth. If she wants to be nice to me, I won't push her away, but I won't go out of my way to become sisterly with her."

Bill nodded. "Perfect."

They arrived at the train station and sat down on the same bench they occupied when they first arrived. While Bill was two years her senior, Junior was his equal in almost every single way. They were essentially twins who would be apart for more than a day or two for the first time in their young lives.

Other families may have used this time to speechify or make a huge public scene as we saw earlier with Suzy, but these two Prices were not those people. They both had so much to say, but neither was sure exactly how to say it.

They sat and leaned on each other in relative silence until the train arrived. They both watched it come to a slow screeching stop, and they exhaled a breath they had been holding for almost seventeen years.

"Send pictures," Junior said as she hugged him hard one last time.

"Will do," Bill said as he wiped away the errant tear.

"I'm proud of you." She stepped back to look up at him without craning her neck.

"Me too." He laughed. "I mean, me too, of you."

She laughed too. "Great English."

"Yeah, Mom would be thrilled."

They laughed and cried and hugged one more time.

He climbed on the train, turned in the door and waved one last time, and disappeared. She didn't want to watch the train pull away, and she knew Bill wouldn't want her to stand there. Junior turned and headed back for The Park, letting her childhood and her brother leave town without her.

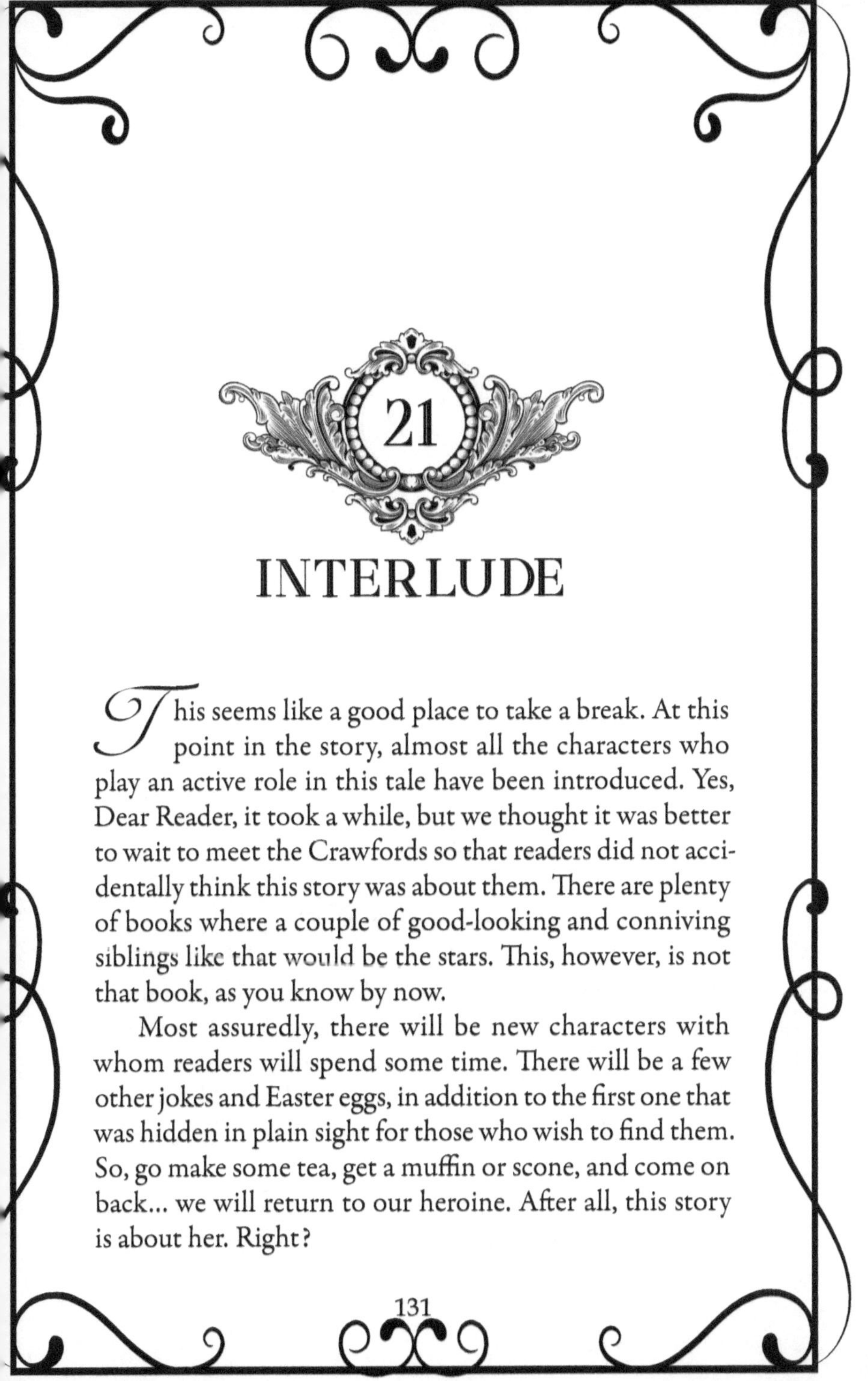

21

INTERLUDE

This seems like a good place to take a break. At this point in the story, almost all the characters who play an active role in this tale have been introduced. Yes, Dear Reader, it took a while, but we thought it was better to wait to meet the Crawfords so that readers did not accidentally think this story was about them. There are plenty of books where a couple of good-looking and conniving siblings like that would be the stars. This, however, is not that book, as you know by now.

Most assuredly, there will be new characters with whom readers will spend some time. There will be a few other jokes and Easter eggs, in addition to the first one that was hidden in plain sight for those who wish to find them. So, go make some tea, get a muffin or scone, and come on back... we will return to our heroine. After all, this story is about her. Right?

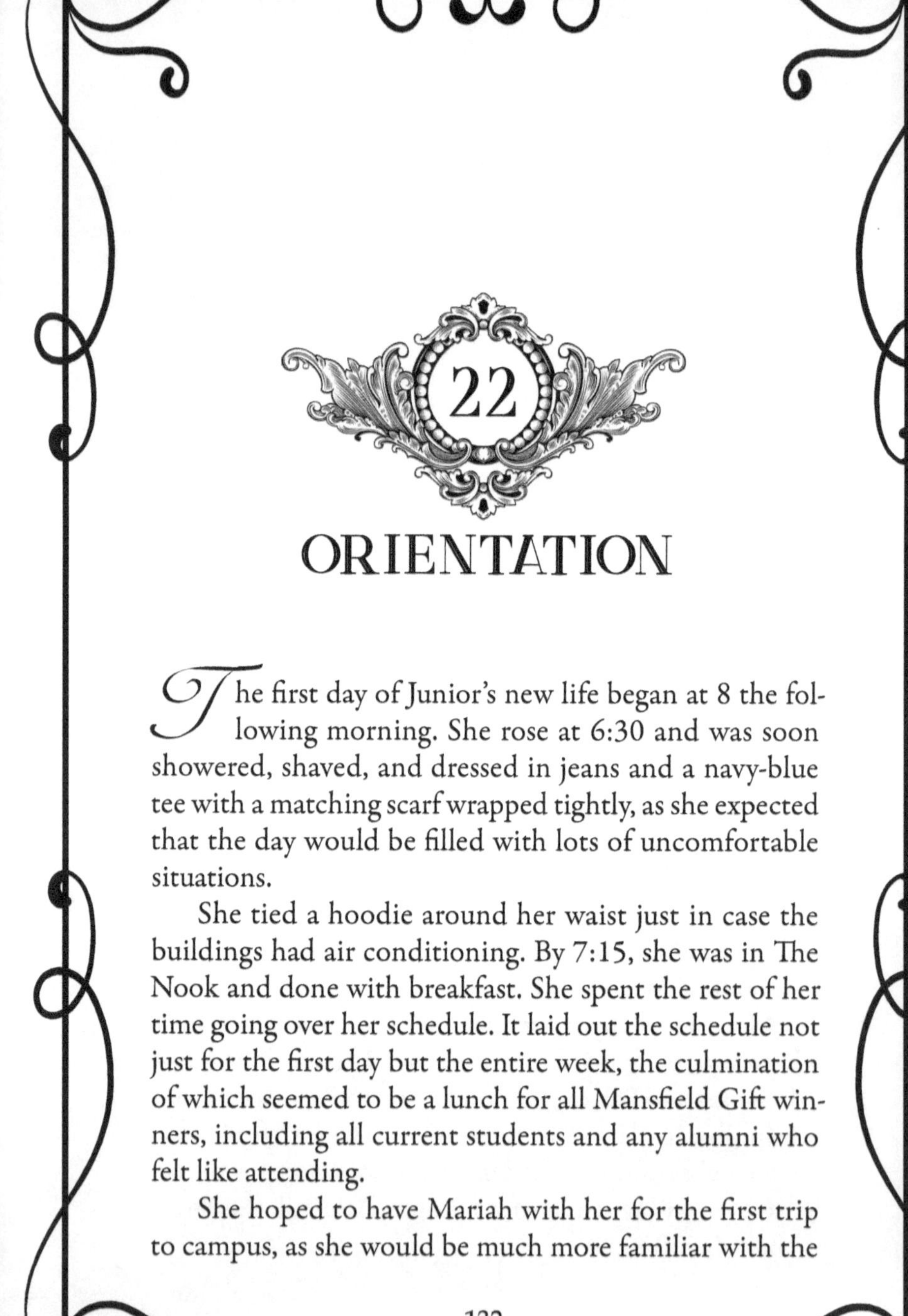

22

ORIENTATION

The first day of Junior's new life began at 8 the following morning. She rose at 6:30 and was soon showered, shaved, and dressed in jeans and a navy-blue tee with a matching scarf wrapped tightly, as she expected that the day would be filled with lots of uncomfortable situations.

She tied a hoodie around her waist just in case the buildings had air conditioning. By 7:15, she was in The Nook and done with breakfast. She spent the rest of her time going over her schedule. It laid out the schedule not just for the first day but the entire week, the culmination of which seemed to be a lunch for all Mansfield Gift winners, including all current students and any alumni who felt like attending.

She hoped to have Mariah with her for the first trip to campus, as she would be much more familiar with the layout, but just to be sure, she studied the small campus map that came with first-year orientation packets. She felt confident that she could make it from The Park to her first stop, Donwell Hall. She was to check in there and meet with her assigned color group. She would, according to the handouts, have a tour guide for the remainder of the day as day one was all about "orienting yourself to campus and your community of learners."

Her phone pinged with a message from Bill. He had just eaten breakfast in Arkansas. He sent a video in the group chat that included Suzy, their mother, Junior, and himself. She plugged in her headphones and listened to him give a full tour of his roomette and view out the tiny window, all done in a terrible British accent.

In her private chat with him, he sent a gif of Obi-Wan Kenobi reminding her about the Force and it being with her always. He wrote, "Good Luck!" beneath it. She replied with a quick "thank you!" GIF, then silenced her phone, plugged her headphones into it, and slid them into her ears. She checked her watch and decided that Mariah must have made other plans. She slipped her bag onto her back and headed for the front door.

Just as she opened the door, she heard, "Have an excellent first day, Miss Frances," echo across the vast foyer.

She spun around and pulled out her headphones. "Thank you, Portsmouth." She bowed to him and smiled.

"Is Miss Bertram walking with you?"

"I thought so, but I don't want to be late on my first day, so I assume she has other plans."

"Yes, Miss. I shall send Mrs. Reynolds to check on her and make sure she did not forget to set her alarm."

"Thanks, Portsmouth."

"No thanks necessary, Miss. I shall see you at dinner."

"See you!" She walked out, closed the door behind her, and plugged her headphones back into her ears. She pulled up a playlist from her favorite rock band, thinking that something new should be accompanied by something old. The opening bass riff from Tesla's "Hang Tough" from *The Great Radio Controversy* came through the headphones. She would indeed hang tough and give it all she had, just as Jeff Keith, the band's lead singer, instructed. She took a deep breath and started to campus.

The Park and Mansfield College are only separated by a narrow road, so Junior was only to the end of the second song on the album by the time she reached her destination. She found the line outside of Donwell Hall where the other first-years stood, quivered, and in one case, managed to give the appearance of lounging without actually leaning against anything at all.

Most of the people were in groups of two or four; having checked into their dorms the day before, they were generally already paired up with roommates or suitemates. She smiled and nodded at folks who dared to make eye contact with her. She kept her headphones in and music on to create some kind of internal armor. The line moved quickly, and within 10 minutes, she was inside the atrium of the building. The line, once through the double doors, quickly fanned out into five lines arranged by alphabet. Junior went over to the M-P line. She pulled out her headphones, wrapped them around her phone, and put them in her bag. In next to no time, she was face to face with Ed Bertram, who stood up when she approached.

"Hi! I wasn't expecting to see you today." She instinctively touched her scarf and gave it a quick rub.

"All Res Life staff are working full time this week." He leaned over, his face much closer to her face than she would have normally been comfortable with, and yet somehow, she managed not to jerk away. He lowered his voice. "I volunteered for this table so I could see how you were doing." He leaned back and stood waiting for a response.

"Well," she was flummoxed, "I, uh, I think I'm OK. I mean, so far, I've walked to campus, listened to music, and stood in a line. I didn't fall down or call anyone a name, so I think I'm doing pretty well."

"Good to have low standards for success." He smiled at her, and he sat down and flipped through the paper boxes that were acting as portable filing drawers. "Well, here's your packet. Looks like you're on the pink team. The teams are all meeting out on the quad. Just go straight through this building and out those doors." He pointed at the stream of first-years going out the other side of the building. "Walt Musgrove is in charge of that group. He's a second-year. He's a good guy. Quiet, almost wouldn't notice him if he weren't right in front of you. His older brother, Chuck, makes a lot of noise around campus. You'll most likely have no choice but to notice him. He breaks stuff. It's a whole thing. Not really sure what the thing is, but he likes the attention. I think Walt signed up for Res Life to try to balance out the dumb stuff his brother does."

Junior just stood quietly, trying to absorb it all. She nodded along as he spoke.

"Well, I think that's all. Your name tag is in there." He tapped the packet. "It says 'Junior' on it. I had them make it special."

She rubbed her scarf again upon hearing that bit of news. "That was really kind of you."

"It's no problem." He looked up at her smiling face. "One more thing." He grabbed her packet back and wrote on the back of it. He stood up again and handed it back to her. He leaned over again and lowered his voice.

She could feel his warm breath on her ear as he said, "That's my number in case you need me for anything. Don't want everyone to know I'm giving that out."

She felt the heat crawl up her neck, and she touched the scarf one last time for good measure. "That's kind of you. Thanks so much. Really. For everything."

"Happy to be of service." He bowed his head a bit. "Have a great day."

"I will. Thanks again." She stepped out of line, and she heard Ed start in with the next person. She paused to watch him sit back down and saw him change his posture and tone to something more formal with the next person. She locked that away into her memory vault to ponder it and headed out onto the quad to find her pink team.

As promised, Walt was a really nice guy. He was shy, unassuming, and incredibly helpful. He subscribed to the theory that if one speaks quietly, those around will quiet down so they can hear what is being said. Unlike the other team leaders, who were acting like carnival barkers, Walt sat quietly under his pink sign, in his pink shirt, on one of several pink sheets he had spread out, in the shade of a tree and greeted each of his charges with a firm handshake and eye contact.

He insisted on everyone wearing their nametags at least for the first day, but he rarely consulted them. He introduced each person to the previous members of the team as though they were old friends. Junior was the tenth person to arrive. After the handshake and introduction, he asked her to take a seat anywhere on one of the sheets, but facing in. Eventually, his full charge of 20 first-years would form a circle for the activities to commence.

That took roughly 30 minutes more. Junior sat and smiled at people and did her best to remain calm. She made small talk as best as she could, which is to say, poorly. She was not a person who asked how one was doing without actually meaning it. Caring was in her nature, but while she may eventually grow to care how these people were feeling, just then she was more worried about herself. She was always used to being younger than everyone in her grade, but for the first time in her life, she felt like a child among her peers.

Many of the young women were dressed in outfits that were so revealing that Junior would have expected to see them in the pages of a Victoria's Secret magazine instead of sitting on a college campus. Some of the young men were bigger than her father, and several of them had full beards. Full beards at age eighteen or nineteen! There was only one person in her class in Unincorporated Nowhere that had a full beard, and he had been held back two times. She tried to see herself the way they must have seen her, but she could not even imagine that a short, plainly dressed girl from the middle of nowhere would even register on their radar.

Before she had a chance to get into a shame spiral, Walt got the team's attention. "Well, the whole gang is here. As you know by now, I'm Walt, and you'll be stuck with me for the next few days. Today's agenda is all about getting acclimated to campus. We will take a tour. I know many of you took one on a campus visit, but I'm going to give you the good tour that we don't give when parents are here. It will take all day and will include a lunch."

There were many polite laughs. Junior had not taken a tour, be it good or bad. She had never actually been on campus until she went to church with the Bertrams, so she was not in on the joke.

"Along the way, we'll stop off at Kellynch Hall to get your student IDs. In case you wonder, the pictures look bad no matter what. We use the same technology they use at the DMV, so you will have to deal with it." More laughs, and this time Junior chimed in. "Before we start, however, we are going to get to know each other just a little bit. I know most people hate icebreakers. I know I hated this part of the first day, but I promise, it'll be good."

The pink team squirmed a bit collectively. It is true that the vast majority of humans hate the idea of icebreakers, but ultimately end up enjoying them. There has yet to be a scientific study on this, but facts are facts.

"Everyone stand up." They all did. "Now, without talking, arrange yourself in order of birthday month and day. The person who has the earliest birthday should be next to me on my left, and then the person who has the latest birthday should be next to me on the right. Got it?" There were nods and non-committal guttural sounds. Junior held up nine fingers and started looking around for folks with eight and ten, hoping other people were on the same page.

In quick succession, the twenty of them silently circled up after flashing all kinds of hand signs using nods and head shakes to clear things up. She and one other person had September birthdays. The two of them next to each other were quite the visual gag. She thought they could be the before and after picture of what happens to people after they were put on the rack during the Inquisition.

Once they were settled in, Walt said, "OK, let's see how we did." He looked at a young woman standing next to him. "Janet, get us started. Say your month and day." They went around the circle, and there was not one mistake. "Excellent work! Now, you all know something about each other, and you didn't have to do anything embarrassing." There was a lot of nodding. "Now, everyone turn to the right." They did. "Let's pat ourselves on the back for a job well done." He reached out and patted the man in front of him on the back." The pink team did as he did. There was nary a scowl and even some genuine laughs. The ice was broken. Facts are facts.

"OK, Pink Team," Walt began, "I have to take the sheets into Donwell before we start our tour. If anyone needs to grab a snack or use the bathroom, you can do both inside. The tables where you registered should have granola bars and drinks. Meet me back here by our tree in ten minutes, and we'll get going."

The rest of the day went pretty much exactly as group leader Walt described it. The ID pictures were not great, although Junior thought hers looked just fine. She did not consider herself particularly photogenic, nor did she think she was repulsive. She really didn't consider herself very much outside of keeping the blotches from becoming a topic of conversation by wearing the scarves.

Lunch was served in Delaford Hall. The campus was small enough that there was only the need for one central dining hall. The large room was divided into two parts, appropriately named Upper Delaford and Lower Delaford. Walt took his charges upstairs because there were long tables enough for his whole team to sit together, whereas downstairs was more of a café style space where people sat in small groups. The food was college cafeteria food. That is to say, it was edible but not exactly good. This is not the fault of the staff. They did their best with what they had. Preparing meals for thousands of people every day means that substance takes precedence over style.

As she was technically an off-campus resident, Junior would probably not spend much time in either Upper or Lower Delaford. For orientation week, however, an exception was made for locals. Many of the Mansfield students used the pejorative term "townie" to refer to folks who lived in Mansfield proper. For some reason, the people who lived in town, even those who attended Mansfield College, were treated with the same disdain. This practice takes place in small college towns in every corner of reality. Junior was not technically a local, nor was she a resident, putting her in a state of limbo to which she was most accustomed.

She spent an amiable lunch chatting with her September birthday buddy, Aaron. His first name turned out to actually be Franklin, but he went by his middle name because he was named after his grandfather, who lived with him and his moms. They joked about having gendered derivatives of the same first name and similar reasons for their respective alternate monikers. Aaron mused that they could always end up being an old married couple in a Roald Dahl book. She laughed. It was overall an excellent time.

The all-day tour ended back where it began. Although there were many complaints about sore feet and aching backs, not one of them came from Junior. Walt promised that there would be more sitting and less walking on day two of orientation as they would be meeting their faculty advisors and getting their schedules. The day would not actually start until lunch.

Walt instructed them to meet at the same table in Upper Delaford at noon. He bid them all farewell and left them to their own devices. Nineteen of the twenty members of the pink team headed for Angeline Hall, the first-year dorm. Aaron offered a salute to Junior. When he asked her what her dorm number was, she told him she was staying off campus with some family friends in order to save money, so he knew she would not be joining them. She returned a salute and smiled.

It was 3:30, and she was in desperate need of a snack. She pulled out her phone for the first time all day; she saw several updates from Bill that she could read through once she had a full stomach. She plugged in her headphones, resumed playback on the Tesla album from her last position, and started back to The Park.

She did not know the snacking protocol at The Park. At home, she had her own kitchen in her own house. She had not even been downstairs to see the kitchen or anything. She wiped her feet after entering the house and upon not seeing Portsmouth right away, she went to the basement door. Before she could open it, the front door opened, and Mariah stepped in. She was dressed in a red top that looked like a sports bra that Junior owned and low-rise Daisy Duke shorts. Her hair was up in a messy bun, and she had giant circle-framed sunglasses that covered most of her face.

"Oh." She pulled her glasses off and stuck them on top of her head, making her bun look like it was wearing sunglasses. "Hey. So, about this morning…" She looked down at her phone and not at Junior.

"No problem. I just hope everything is OK."

Mariah looked up to see whether she was being sincere. Junior only had one gear when it came to sincerity. She was the fixie bike of sincerity. She was always engaged. Seeing this to be true, Mariah kept eye contact. "Yeah, well, I wasn't feeling great last night, and so I forgot to set my alarm. Mrs. Reynolds got me up and out the door on time."

"You feel better now?"

"I do. Actually, I'm starving. How about you?"

"I am. I was just going to find Portsmouth because I didn't know the rules on snacking."

"Well, perfect timing. Follow me." Mariah kicked her flip-flops off and headed toward The Nook. "That door to the basement in The Nook leads to the kitchen. We have a whole cupboard of snacks and a fridge with drinks and stuff. They keep one of the carafes filled with coffee at all times in The Nook, but the rest of the stuff is downstairs."

They entered The Nook and went straight down the stairs. Instead of the stairs ending into a hallway that had rooms, it ended directly into a kitchen that was at least 20 feet wide and 15 feet long. Junior's house back on The Ranch was only a 20 by 20 square. There was a door on the opposite side. It led to the rest of the hallways and rooms for staff. "Over here," Mariah walked over to a pantry door, "is where we have our goodies, and that fridge," she pointed with her head, "is ours too. There is diet and regular pop. Tea. Iced coffee. Bottled water. Whatever. The rest of the stuff is staff only. Don't touch."

Mariah pulled the pantry door open and actually stepped inside. It was a walk-in pantry roughly the size of her bathroom upstairs. The walls were filled with every possible kind of wrapped snack imaginable. "If there is something we don't have that you want, let Portsmouth know and he will get you hooked up." She grabbed a container of Goldfish crackers that were in the shape of a milk carton.

Mariah's phone pinged. She fished it out of her back pocket, smiled, and put it back. "I have to deal with this right now, so I'm gonna leave you to it. The door has a lever, so when you shut the door, the light goes off. By-ee."

Junior was overwhelmed by her choices. She checked her watch; it was almost four. She was hungry but did not want to ruin her dinner. She grabbed a granola bar and some dried fruit. She closed the door slowly just to be sure that Mariah was right about the light going off; she was. The fridge was indeed packed. There was a pitcher of sweet tea. She was happy to have that bit of home with her. She went back upstairs to eat her snack and to check in on her brother.

Before she knew it, an hour had passed, and she was sitting in the window seat, sipping her tea, texting with Bill, who was in Texas and on his final leg of the journey. She told him about her day, and he tried to make being trapped on a train a good thing. The only reason she knew that time had passed was that the cook had appeared from the basement door with the evening's dinner.

"Oh!" Junior said. "Hi. I'm sorry."

"Nothing about which to be sorry, Miss. There is no crime in sitting quietly."

"Still, I don't want to be in your way." She got up and walked over to her, actually putting herself in the way where before she was not. "I'm Junior. I'm going to be staying here."

"Yes, Miss. I know who you are. Portsmouth told me all about your arrival."

"Well, it's nice to meet you..." She left it hanging, hoping she would fill in her name. She extended her hand to really drive the point home.

"Betty." She looked to the door and back down the stairs before she reached out and shook Junior's hand. "Welcome to The Park, Miss Price."

"Junior."

She shook her head. "Miss Frances is the best I can do."

Junior sighed. "Oh. Ok." They released hands, but before Betty could turn away and resume her duties, Junior asked, "Betty? If I wanted to ever, um, I don't know, cook for myself, would that be allowed?'

Betty could not have been more shocked if Junior had declared that she wanted to bite the head off a live chicken. "Has there been a problem with the meals, Miss?"

Junior realized her mistake and felt the hives start to form on her neck. She wrapped her scarf tight. "Oh no! Nothing like that at all. Please. I am so sorry, it's just that, well, where I'm from, I do my own cooking, and I bake quite a lot. I loved the muffins you made, and I just thought I could try to make them myself sometime so when I went home, I could do it for my family."

Once again, Junior's sincerity won the day as Betty could tell this was the truth. She screwed up her lips in thought. "Well, Miss, no one has ever asked before, and while I would love to have some company in the kitchen from time to time, I would have to clear it with Portsmouth, who would most likely have to clear it with Mrs. Bertram."

Junior nodded along as Betty talked. "I totally understand. Thank you so much." She smiled her big smile and shook Betty's hand again. "I'm going to actually get out of your hair now. I'll be back soon. It smells delicious."

"Thank you, Miss. It's nothing special, just some baked chicken and mashed potatoes."

"Perfect. Comfort food is just what I need. Do you know when everyone else comes to dinner? When, say, Ed or Tommy come, do they come at a particular time?"

"It depends on the day. 5:30 is a good time to catch someone."

"Excellent. See you then." With that, Junior went to her room to drop off her bag and to clean up for dinner.

"What an odd girl," Betty said to the empty room once she had gone. "Sweet, but odd."

Junior returned to her room and did a quick video chat with Suzy, who had apparently just realized Junior had orientation, even though Junior mentioned it several times. Junior suspected Bill had something to do with the sudden recollection, but it was nice to be asked.

While the conversation was intended to be about Junior's first day on campus, and how that went, it quickly devolved into Suzy asking for advice about how to handle their father's moods and some of the tricks to getting the littlies to mind.

When it was over, Suzy signed off with, "Glad your first day was awesome!" Junior wondered where she gathered that impression from, as Junior hadn't actually said anything about herself.

When she returned to The Nook, Ed and Julia were there. They both looked up and were obviously genuinely pleased to see her. The three of them spent an hour catching up on their days.

Julia, who had yet to return to school, had spent most of her time practicing her parallel parking. She was overly nervous about it; she knew that if she failed the parking portion of the driver's test, she wouldn't even get out on the road. Ed was the leader of the blue group and told some stories about some of his charges. Junior sat happily listening to the Bertrams; they were really talking more to each other in front of her anyway, not really speaking *with* her. While that might make some people feel ostracized, Junior was aware that she was a guest here and that her place in the overall picture of The Park had yet to be realized.

No other member of the family had arrived for dinner by the time Ed checked his watch and explained that he had some Res Life meetings to attend to prepare for the next day. Julia had plans with a few members of her Field hockey team. They all ran cross country in the fall to stay in shape, and they started conditioning the following week to get a jump on pre-conditioning conditioning. On the way out, Junior thanked Betty by name, causing the two Bertram children to exchange a quizzical look. We can neither confirm nor deny that it was the first time either Ed or Julia had heard their cook's first name.

Junior, who was used to walking and being relatively active, was surprisingly exhausted from the first day. She decided to be bold and not actually set an alarm for the next morning, knowing that she did not have to be on campus until noon. She managed to sleep until eight, which was the equivalent of most teenagers sleeping until ten. She was unsure if pajamas were acceptable in the house proper, so she threw on some jeans and a Tesla band logo t-shirt. She loosely wrapped a black scarf around her neck, grabbed her phone and headphones, and headed to The Nook. She drew her hair into a hair tie as she walked.

The room was empty save for the food. She took a blueberry muffin and some coffee to the window seat. She sat alone listening to Van Halen's *5150* and watched the activity at The Park. The lawns were being mowed, the hedges were being trimmed, and she knew there was a lot of activity going on beneath her feet. There were so many members of the staff that she feared she would never meet them all. She only realized how much time had passed when the final notes of the final song, "Inside," ended.

It wasn't until later, when she was with her pink team at lunch, where Aaron sat right down next to her and called her "Grandma Fran," as though they had been hanging out for years and saw each other all the time, that she realized how infrequently she saw any of the members of the Bertram family.

It was then, too, that she realized that she actually wanted to see them. Even though she and her brood had three houses, they were always in each other's way. While she was extremely grateful for having her own private room and, more importantly, bathroom, she was not accustomed to being totally alone. While it was true that she did not care for large gatherings, she realized that total solitude was not something she really liked either. There was a joke on *Seinfeld* about only having three friends. She laughed at that while binge-watching it with Bill, Suzy, and her mom, not realizing until later that she was in the room with her three friends.

Before she had too much time to consider the implications of all of this, Walt announced that it was time to meet with their advisors after which they were to head to the gym for registration. The meetings with the advisors would take place in each advisor's office. He walked around the table and handed them all the name of the advisor, the department for which that person taught, and the building in which that person's office resided.

Junior's paper read: Allen: History: Pulteney.

"If you don't know where your building is, or if you think you know where your building is, or just because I don't want to be the only team leader who loses his charges, make sure you check with me before you leave. Your appointments are either at 1, 1:30, or 2, so you will have some downtime before registration starts at 2:30. I would recommend you go back to the library. That place is going to be your friend so you should get used to it. Plus, they have a coffee shop, and I just so happen to have gift certificates for one free drink of your choice." He reached into his back pocket and held up a stack of cards. Jubilant sounds from all quarters. "So, the only way you can get your card is to check with me about how to get to your faculty building. Deal?"

A collective "Deal!" blasted back at him.

"Excellent." He wiggled his fingers together like Mr. Burns. "Line up according to your meeting times."

Junior was in the group of one o' clocks. She ended up fourth in line. When she got to the front, she handed Walt her paper, and he handed her a gift card. "Let's see what you got here." He looked down and nodded. "Nice. Dr. Allen is a cool guy. Practically been here since the place was founded but sharp as a tack. History major?"

"Um, no." She leaned in to whisper the next part as she was not sure what the status of Gift winners was on campus writ large. "I'm one of The Mansfield Gift winners."

"Wow. Congratulations. That's amazing." He held up his hand for a high five. She smacked it. "You don't need to whisper. If I won that, I would be wearing a shirt every day that read 'Gift Winner.'"

She squinted at him. She did not believe for a second that he was that kind of guy. "Really?"

He smiled and shook his head. "OK. No. Still, that's awesome. I won't tell."

"Thanks."

"You got it. So, Pulteney is actually right across the street. Go out the front door and down the steps. It is the big three-story red brick monster with white pillars. Allen's office is on the third floor. Take the stairs. The elevator is tiny and slow. Plus, the front stairs are all open-aired. After your meeting, go out the opposite side of the building, the one facing the quad. The gym is directly across the quad. You can't miss it. The building to the right is the library, so head over that way, and you will be all set. That's all we're doing today. Tomorrow we meet here for breakfast at 8. Got it?"

She nodded. "Got it."

"Great. Have a good one. See you in the morning."

Junior arrived outside of Dr. Allen's office with five minutes to spare. The door was open. She peeked in and saw a short, round-faced man sitting at a desk writing longhand on something. He was bald on the top but had a horseshoe of white hair around the side. She knocked on the doorframe. "Dr. Allen?"

He looked up from his writing, looking a little lost as though whatever he was writing had transported him somewhere. Still, he smiled and had a welcoming face. "Yes." He looked over her head above the door where Junior assumed a clock hung, "You must be Frances. Come in."

"Everyone calls me Junior. My mom is also Frances," she said as she walked across the tidy office and reached her arm across the desk to shake his hand.

Not being accustomed to that kind of greeting, he was not prepared. He could not remember the last time a student tried to shake his hand. He recovered quickly and stood to shake. "Very well. Nice to meet you, Junior."

"You as well, Sir. My mother is an alumnus, actually. She was called Fran Ward back then.

"Hmmm." He pointed at one of the high-back seats in front of his desk for her to sit, and he plopped himself back down in his chair. "Doesn't ring a bell."

"It was worth a try. She majored in economics and accounting, so your paths most likely didn't cross."

"Yes, well, that is likely. There are not a lot of students here, but not everyone chooses to take history as part of his or her core. She wasn't a Gift recipient herself, was she?"

"No, Sir. Our family's financial situation has deteriorated quite a bit since my mother was my age."

"Yes, well," he was clearly flustered by her directness and at his own blunder, "I was not making a commentary on your family's financials. I apologize."

"Thank you, Sir." She looked down, sensing his discomfort. She wrapped her scarf a bit tighter just in case the conversation took a turn.

He cleared his throat to get her attention again. "I was just saying that *if* she had been a Gift winner, there was a better chance we would have crossed paths. I'm one of five Gift advisors. We each have one Gift winner per year, and this year, I have been blessed to be your advisor. Of course, since I started by putting my foot directly into my mouth, it is your right to request an advisor swap."

"Oh, no, Sir. I didn't mean to make you uncomfortable; I was just being honest. I'm not ashamed of my family situation. I just believe in being direct and honest." She looked right at him when she said it so he could be sure.

"Well, that is admirable, Junior. I suspect it was one of the key factors in you earning The Gift."

"Thank you, Sir." She smiled. She was rarely given a lot of positive reinforcement regarding her compulsive need to tell the truth at all times. "I appreciate that."

He smiled back at her and felt himself relax. He wanted to steer the conversation back to safer grounds, so he decided to cut the rest of the personal chit-chat he normally included in these first meetings with advisees.

"Well, let's get started then, shall we?" He reached into his desk drawer and pulled out a manila folder. "I have your schedule right here." He opened it and took out the top sheet. He slid it across the desk to her. "You'll see that we have the first two years already mapped out. All of The Gift winners take the same first sixteen courses. You don't all take the same sections, nor do you take them in the same order. Take a moment or two and look it over."

Junior leaned forward and brought the schedule to her. The paper had her name at the top. There were then four squares. Each one had the year and term. The names of the courses were listed there, and next to them was a blank line. She saw that her first four courses would be College

Algebra II, Early Modern Europe, Composition II, and Introduction to Western Religion.

"You'll notice that you begin with College Algebra II and Composition II. Test scores factor into the decision-making process for The Gift winners, so we know what skills you have in Mathematics and English. Your essay was also evaluated as part of the process, and no one wins The Gift without being able to place into these second-level courses. It is essential that you get a full scope of the Liberal Arts here at Mansfield. Questions so far?"

"Does that mean my core is actually sixteen classes as opposed to ten?"

Dr. Allen nodded and smiled. "Very astute. More proof that you were the right choice. It is true. You must complete all sixteen classes, or you forfeit The Gift."

"I assume this has never happened."

"It has not. I will be totally frank with you, as you respect that kind of thing. When you reach the second term of your second year, you will be ready for it to be over. That's going to be the most difficult term of your four years. It is not because the courses will be so hard, but because they will be so simple. Many of your classmates will be taking classes in their majors at that point, and you will just be declaring yours."

"Is this rotation set in stone? I can't, say," she looked down at her page, "swap when I take Psychology with when I take Philosophy?"

He nodded. "It is. The five advisors take care to make sure that we don't have a lot of The Gift students in the same year crossing over into the same classes. It is not strictly possible to keep you from ever having another Gift recipient in a class. It will happen, as some courses have fewer sections. We want each person to have his or her unique experience, however, even though the courses are the same."

She nodded and smiled. "Makes perfect sense."

"Excellent. Now," he reached back into the folder, "here is your schedule." He tapped it with his finger. Before he passed it over to her, he explained more in-depth. "Gift winners do not have to stand in line to register for classes for the first two years."

"That's great. I wasn't looking forward to standing in a hot gym for an hour today."

"Yes, well, there is a caveat. You also have to take specific dates and times. For the first and second-year, Gift recipients take classes Monday and Thursday from 8-10 and then 1-3. Tuesday and Friday you have classes from 10-12 and then 3-5. All courses for everyone are set up as Monday/Thursday and Tuesday/Friday, but you have these specific times for the first two years.

"Wednesdays are off days for all courses on campus. Those are days when clubs and organizations meet while faculty have meetings and make the educational sausage. You can sign up for a physical education course. They are no additional cost and they meet at various times on Wednesdays. You could learn to play tennis, high dive, or fence. There are also many excellent volunteer opportunities if you want to become involved with the community. Those teams do their work on Wednesdays. The first Wednesday of the term is selection day. All the courses, clubs, and groups set up on the quad at tables and try to convince people to join up. First-years are allowed to join two. The longer you stay, the more groups you may join. You are not required to join any, of course. However, these are great opportunities to make new friends outside of your rigid schedule."

"That sounds amazing. Is that new? Mom never mentioned it."

"It was instituted about ten years ago when we realized that third and fourth-years were able to schedule themselves courses from Tuesday through Thursday and have five-day weekends. While we certainly want people to go home and visit their families, we really want the Mansfield experience to be valuable. There was some grumbling when we first started it, but like you, most people think it is a good idea."

"It really is. I'm so excited."

"I'm glad to hear it." He slid the full schedule over. "I recommend you spend some time this afternoon going around campus to find your buildings and classrooms. Since you don't have to stand in line and everyone else does, you and your fellow Gifters should have the run of the place." He stood up. "Now, if you'll excuse me, I need to take a break before my next meeting."

"That's a great idea. Thank you, Sir." She grabbed the schedule and put it, and her two-year rotation paper in her bag. "I have a gift card to the coffee shop in the library. I'm going to go cash that in and then I'll do just that." She shook his hand again. "It was great to meet you."

"You as well, Junior. My office number and email are both on your schedule so reach out if you need anything. I'll see you Friday at The Gift recipient lunch."

"Thank you. See you then, Sir."

It was not until she was firmly seated in another high-back chair in the fiction section of the second floor of the library that she finally took out her schedule and her campus map. She planned on taking Dr. Allen's advice. She found the library on the map and then found The Park as well. She planned on spending a lot of time in the library between classes, but she knew she would most likely be coming directly from The Park for her morning classes.

Monday and Thursday Morning was College Algebra II in Barton Hall with Dr. Steele. Monday and Thursday afternoon was Early Modern Europe with Dr. West back in Pulteney. While technically a history class, the course straddled departments and could count toward Political Science or History. Tuesday and Friday morning was Composition II with Dr. Smith in Sanditon Hall. Finally, Introduction to Western Religion was located in Northanger with Dr. Norris. Had Junior been holding her coffee, she would have dropped it. Had she been in any building other than the library, she may have shouted an expletive.

23

FUN AND GAMES

After Junior had fully recuperated from her shock, she did what she said she would do. She walked around campus for nearly two hours figuring out her best path to and from everything. She listened to the rest of the Van Halen catalog with Sammy Hagar as the lead singer. She and her father had many a row about this. He was a David Lee Roth guy all the way, and she was ride or die for Sammy. She felt that having an extra guitarist in the band made them sound better. He liked the flash and show of "Diamond Dave." She sent him a text reminding him about it. He was unresponsive.

She tried to remember if there were times when she discussed music with him if those times were fun for him, or if he simply responded to her because she almost always had a different opinion than he had. They both liked the music but liked it differently. She felt she was more critical of it, while he just liked what he liked without being able to explain why. It is true that sometimes we like what we like for no good reason, but Junior liked knowing why.

She ended up having dinner totally alone that night as Julia was going out with the team. The rest of the Bertram family was absent again. She sent texts back and forth with Bill, who was staying in a Motel 6 in San Antonio while he waited to report. The whole thing was strange. There were not a lot of rules in the Price family, but that was most certainly one. No phones at dinner was the policy, and they all adhered to it, but sitting alone, she figured the policy could go out the window, and if anyone joined her, she would put it away.

She called it an early night and was up and out the door to meet her team for breakfast without seeing anyone, even Portsmouth. She was not sure if Mariah was actually participating in the events of orientation week or if she used her status as a Mansfield to get out of it. She would have asked if she actually ever saw her.

During breakfast, Walt announced that this was actually the final day of orientation with the pink team and that the next few days were all about building community in Angeline with the RAs and their residents. So, as a final bit of campus-wide fun, the color teams would be competing in a scavenger hunt. The winning team earned fifty dollars each in Bennet Bucks to be spent in any on-campus store or café. The second-place team would get twenty-five dollars each and third place would get ten.

There were flags hidden all around campus. Each team would get ten clues to start off. They would pair up in teams of two, figure out the clue, and then go find the pink flag hidden at that place. They would bring it back to

Delaford, and they would go out again. The first team to have all forty flags back won.

Regardless of success or failure, the game ended at noon with a barbeque on the quad. The winners would be announced. There would be a carnival set up where people could play games and win other items with the Mansfield crest emblazoned upon them.

"Grandpa Frank and Grandma Fran for the win?" Aaron asked Junior after Walt had wrapped up his explanation.

"You got it. I spent most of yesterday afternoon wandering around campus, so I feel pretty good if our questions about our destinations are campus only. Other than the train station and the theater, I haven't been anywhere in town."

"Well, you've been to two more places in town than I have. My moms dropped me off at Angeline. They packed the van to the rafters with everything I could ever need so we didn't even need to go to the store for any last-minute necessities. There was a family pizza party in the basement over there, so they stayed for that, and we didn't even have to go out to eat. I suspect they sat in the van and cried for an hour before they were calm enough to go home."

"Only child?"

"Yep."

"I'm the second oldest of a brood. My older brother and I both left at the same time; he rode up here with me. Only my sister really cared. I suspect the littlies don't know I'm gone. Mom is due to have twins any day now, so there will still be eight of them."

Aaron whistled.

"You said it." They both laughed. In order to change the conversation, Junior pulled out her marked-up map. "So, yesterday, I did this while you were registering. I know, it's a bit OCD, but I hate being late, and I wanted to know the best walking route from the most important buildings for me and my schedule." She color-coded each course and drew lines that represented the best walking path between buildings. On top of each line, she wrote the time it took to walk at a regular pace. She rubbed her scarf as he studied the map, worried that he might think her overzealousness absurd. She was in the habit of wrapping it tight on her walk to campus. There was almost always a chance of being overwhelmed as she figured everything out.

"Wow. This is amazing. I'm totally stealing this idea and doing this tomorrow."

"Thanks. It really helped me. I feel so much better about Monday."

"I'll bet. Plus, this is going to make us an unstoppable force in this game. I mean, you've even figured out how to cut between or through buildings to save time. That's genius."

Before she could find a way to get out of accepting his praise again, Walt saved her. "OK, ramblers, let's get rambling. Dump your trash and huddle up around me."

Within three minutes, the pink team was in a circle with Walt in the middle. He was holding up ten pink note cards fanned out in his hand. "OK, I want you to know that I really don't care if we win or lose. My team came in last place when we did this last year, but I had a blast anyway. I want to remind you all that other teams and team leaders will be a bit more competitive, so beware of folks trying to lead you astray out there. Don't follow another team. None of the flags are in the same place, so when you get to your destination, you'll be the only one looking for your flag. Finally, and I mean this, have fun!"

He held out the note cards. Luckily for Walt, he was not claustrophobic as the team collapsed in on him, temporarily leaving him blocked from the world. Most teams grabbed their cards and ran out. Junior and Aaron sat back down at their breakfast table with Junior's map. Walt, seeing the slow and steady strategy, gave them a smile and a nod before going over to join the rest of the leaders. As she watched him walk away, she saw Ed out of the corner of her eye, going over to join the group. He smiled and waved.

"Conspiring with the competition?"

"No, nothing like that. He's a friend or a potential friend. I'm not really sure. His parents own the house where I'm staying."

"Wait, really? Isn't that Ed Bertram?"

"Yeah."

"You said you were staying with friends of your family."

"I am."

"Your family is friends with the Bertrams? You're staying at The Park?"

She resisted the urge to rub her scarf. The whole point of wearing it tight was to stop drawing attention to it. "I am. Is that... Does that...?"

"Oh, no, it's amazing. I would love to get in there and check it out. I'm studying design so I can go to architecture school after this. Maybe one day you could, you know, bring me over? I'm your first friend and all."

She exhaled a nervous breath. "Of course, yes. I'll check with Candy, but I don't think it should matter. Now that my living arrangements are settled, let's get to it." Junior and Aaron's card had the following printed upon it: "The name of the founder facing the land of the rising sun."

"We have to go to Japan? I don't think we'll be back by lunch," Aaron joked.

Junior looked down at her map. On the eastern border of campus, there was a welcome sign. "I think it's here. The name of the founder facing the land of the rising sun." She tapped the spot. "What do you think?"

He nodded. "Sounds like the best place to start."

She drew a line with her finger around the edge of the map. "If we go out this way and down this street that is on the edge of campus, no one will see us, and it's a straight shot."

"Lead on, Magellan."

They walked out of the front stairs and discovered that they were not really too far behind. Most of the teams were strewn about the steps of Delaford, heads together, trying to figure out their clues. They walked the two blocks to the edge of campus and turned east.

Once they were across the street, Junior said, "So, architecture." She looked up at him to see his expression as he took in her statement. He broke into a toothy grin.

"So, architecture." He nodded and kept smiling. "Yeah. Well, I feel like I was born with a pencil in my hand. I don't remember a time when I wasn't sketching or designing. My moms say that I was about two when I figured out how to use a book as a straight edge. They were not thrilled to have a bunch of marks all over their books, so they got me a protractor. Just a cheap junk thing, but once they showed me what it did, I was captivated. I would sit for hours at the table and draw. My earliest memory is drawing what the kitchen looked like from my point of view. I figured out how to do the angles, so it had depth and everything."

"That's amazing."

"Thanks. Yeah, I mean I was like four or five. Angie, she's my birth mom, had it framed, and Lucy, my other mom, has it on the office wall."

"Do you call them by their first names?"

"Not often. It helps when I explain them to people, but normally I will look at whichever one of them I want to talk to and say 'Mom.' They just always seem to know which one of them I need."

"Like a secret language."

He stopped walking at looked down at her. "Exactly."

"My brother and I can say a lot with a look. There are so many of us that a secret language would be drowned out by the actual language. There is just a constant din of noises that Bill and I had to figure out how to express our-selves across the table or the room." They started walking again. "Sorry, so Lucy has your first memory in her office."

"Right, so yeah. They put me in art classes as my after-school program from the jump. By the time I was in high school, the actual art classes they offered were pointless, but we had some drafting classes both physical and CAD. The teacher was great. She let me work on my own proj-ects. Instead of making me do the basics, she pretty much let me do an advanced directed study while earning credit. She eventually got me to dual enroll at the community college during my junior year. My Prof there told me that Mansfield had a 99 percent acceptance into architecture school from their design program, so that was that. I'm here now as a first-year who should be able to graduate as a third-year, but I may just double major in Art History and stay the whole time. I've heard it can be hard to be a young graduate. People don't take you seriously."

Junior resisted the urge to check her scarf. She knew it was wrapped tight.

He stopped and whacked himself in the forehead. "Oh, man. So stupid. Sorry. I didn't think. You just…"

"It's fine." She waved him off. "I didn't really think much about it until that first day of orientation. In high school, I sort of blended into the background. That's my plan here too. I'm just going to go to classes and learn everything I can, and it should all work out. I made it here at sixteen, and I'll be twenty-one when we graduate, so I'll worry about it then." Looking to change the subject, she pointed. "There's the corner of campus. The sign is just there."

Aaron, thankful for Junior's help in extricating his foot from his mouth, followed her half a block to the sign. The sign itself had a concrete base wrapped in brick. It stood four feet high. The word "College" sat on the bottom and the word "Mansfield" sat on top of that. Both words were cast in some kind of metal that was welded together and braced to the pedestal with hurricane straps. Each letter was roughly two feet tall, making the name of the founder too tall for even Aaron to investigate clearly from the ground.

They circled the base and found nothing. They looked in the nooks and crannies of the word college and found nothing. Junior studied the top of the base. There was enough space around it for her feet to fit. "Boost me up." She nodded, convincing herself it was the right decision.

"Are you sure?"

"Yep, your feet are too big. You couldn't get more than a toe in any of these spaces. You can spot me."

Aaron knelt down on one knee and intertwined his fingers. Junior put her left foot in his palms. She put her left hand on top of his head and extended her right. He asked, "On three?"

"One, two, three then go or one, two, THREEE?"

"Threee."

She nodded. "One."

"Two," he replied.

"THREEEE!" they said together as she pushed off with her right foot and he lifted up. Her right foot landed on the spot between the double Ls and her hands grabbed the top of the F. She pulled her left foot up and allowed herself to find her balance before she spoke.

Aaron stood, arms out, ready to catch her. "You good?"

She tested her footing and found it was firm. "Yep." She nodded but didn't look down at him. She looked to her left and bent down a little, making sure her fingers were still on the F, and scanned the M A N and S. Nothing caught her eye. She looked to the right and saw a bit of pink on the middle line of the E. "There it is. On the E." She calculated that it was within reach, but she didn't want to use one hand and lean over, so she slid her feet along the edge and moved her hands along with it until she was in front of the E. Aaron moved along with her on the ground. She stood up tall, wrapped her left arm all the way over the E, grabbed the flag with her right hand, and dropped it on the ground.

He whooped. "Go team!"

She put both hands on the top of the E and looked down at him. He had his hands up. "I'll grab you by the waist. You let go, and I will bring you down."

"Nah." She urged him back with a flick of her head, and she turned and jumped. She landed on her toes and dipped down into a squat. She stood, and he was applauding, so she held her hands above her head like she was an Olympic gymnast on a dismount.

"Wooo!!!! Tens across the board, but an eight from the Russians."

"Figures." She laughed and bent over to pick up the flag. She stuffed it into her back pocket and checked her watch. "If the next one is as easy as this one, we'll have plenty of time to map your class route before lunch."

They returned to Delaford, and Walt informed them they were the first member of any team to return. He held up both hands for a double high five. After the pleasantries were exchanged, he pointed them over to a table where fifty reusable travel mugs, each emblazoned with the Mansfield crest, waited for the first twenty-five teams who returned. "Your reward awaits."

There was a 51st mug filled with sharpies so they could decorate their mug in some way to differentiate it from the others. Junior pulled out a pink sharpie to commemorate the team and simply wrote "Jr." on the blank side. Aaron pulled out a black one and did a rudimentary outline of the facade of Delaford. It took less than two minutes but was a striking resemblance. Both Junior and Walt applauded. Aaron bowed. They stowed their mugs in Junior's backpack.

Walt pulled out the second pack of ten pink notecards and allowed them to pick. Since Aaron picked last time, he insisted that Junior do so. She pulled the one on the far right out of the pack and flipped it over. It read: "What never? Hardly ever!"

"I am the Captain of the Pinafore: And a right good captain too," Aaron started singing.

"*Pirates of Penzance?*"

"Nope. *HMS Pinafore.* Common misconception. I've been schooled by my moms."

"Well, tell them thanks for the lesson." Junior sat down and pulled out her map. "I'm thinking we either need to go to the library and look at either the sheet music, the soundtrack, the DVD, or the book or to the music building for pretty much all the same reasons."

Aaron looked over her shoulder at the map. The music building, while technically on campus, was off the main quad and on the path back to Angeline. "Well, it makes sense to go to the music center first because there are fewer places to look. Most of it will be locked up, so we can try the doors. If the sheet music library is open, we know we are gold. If not, we hit the library."

"Deal." She held up her hand; he smacked it.

"GO TEAM!" Walt shouted as they left. "I'm such a proud papa. They grow up so fast." He sniffled and dabbed a fake tear from the corner of his eye.

It turned out that the entire music building was locked. They knew because they walked around the whole thing and tried every door twice, just in case. Due to Junior's excellent mapping skills, they took a short cut back to the sign of their first victory and turned left. There was a delivery alley along the side road that took them to the basement entrance of the library.

The basement housed the movie and music collection. The student desk worker seemed genuinely surprised when the door opened. It normally took first-years a while to learn about the other way in, and in the day and age of streaming, most of them never ventured down to the basement, which also housed magazines and the old microfiche. When Fran went to Mansfield, the basement was packed most days.

"CDs or DVDs?" Junior asked.

"Doesn't matter."

"OK, I'll do CDs. DVDs are over there." She pointed.

"I would ask why you know that already, but I'll only be embarrassed when your reasoning makes sense, and I'll feel like a slacker." He wandered away in the direction she pointed. Before she could even make it to the CD aisle, she heard Aaron sing, "I'm a right good Captain too." He came out waving the pink flag. "Well, you're a right good captain."

"You knew the song was from *HMS Pinafore*. I would have been looking into the wrong musical for sure." She checked her watch; it was just past 10. "Looks like we have lots of time to kill."

"Oh, the pains of being geniuses."

"The hardships never end."

They went upstairs and stopped off at the café to fill up their travel mugs. They sipped coffee and strolled across the quad past the ground crew and members of the Resident Life team setting up for the afternoon of food and fun.

"Behold the conquering heroes," Walt said as they walked back in. "This must be some kind of record. Only five other teams are back with their first flags."

"We even stopped and got coffee," Aaron said.

"I wish I could send you back out there, but the rules are the rules. What are you going to do now? You have a while before lunch."

"We're going to wander," Aaron said.

"OK. Have fun. Great work, you guys."

They exchanged a few more pleasantries, and they headed out to map out Aaron's routes. There is little reason to go into too much depth. The conversations they had were mostly geography-based as Junior explained all the tricks she had uncovered the previous day.

By the time they had all of Aaron's routes mapped out, they were starving and ready for whatever they were serving at the campus picnic. It turned out everything was pre-packaged for ease of transport and bug exposure reduction. There were coolers full of sandwiches and drinks and boxes of chips sitting next to plates of cookies. They collected their lunches and headed back to the tree that they would forever call the pink tree, where Walt had once again laid out his pink sheets.

Near the food tables, a small stage had been erected. There were drums, guitars, and a keyboard waiting to be played. Dr. Bennet climbed up and tapped the lead singer's microphone.

"Excuse me, everyone. Excuse me." The talking quickly quieted down. "Thank you all. First, I would like you all to give your group leaders a huge round of applause." Dr. Bennet motioned with her hands for the group leaders to stand. "Please stand up, group leaders." She started the applause and the first-years followed suit. This lasted for a solid thirty seconds before she started speaking again.

"I hope you've all had an excellent few days. It has been a delight to see all these young people on campus.

Summers here are lonely." She reached into her vest pocket and pulled out her glasses and from the other, she pulled out a note card.

"I'm not one for long speeches, and I know all of you just want to find out who won the competition. When I read the winners, I would like the group leader to stand; when I'm done, I will personally deliver your team the Bennet Bucks." A cheer went up at the reminder of the prize. "In third place, team PINK!" Cheers all around. Walt stood and walked around, giving high-fives to the team. "In second place, team RED!" More cheers. A woman popped up wearing a red shirt and took a bow. She, like Walt, walked around her area congratulating her team. "And the winning team, is team... BLUE!" Junior could not help herself, but she joined in the applause. Ed sprang up from his spot. He told his team to stand, and they got in a line, reminiscent of a cast line at the end of a play. They all held hands. Ed counted out three, and they bowed together. The whole crowd applauded.

"Congratulations again to the winners. Have fun today. There are plenty of prizes still to be won at the carnival." She pointed to the center of the quad, where all kinds of games were set up. There was more applause. "Also, while the carnival is going on, you will be treated to a performance from a campus band. I have been assured that they will keep it PG-13." Laughter erupted from someone sitting close to the stage. She looked down at the group sitting there, and she wagged her finger. "If you don't, I'll get up here and play something on the piano, and trust me, none of you want that." More laughter. "Thank you all again. Have fun and enjoy your lunch."

The rest of the day passed by exactly as one would think a day like this would. People ate too many cookies and felt terrible. They won inexpensive plastic items with the name of Mansfield College on them. Some people won actual prizes like sweatshirts, hats, umbrellas and jackets, all adorned with the Mansfield crest.

The band, The Pump Room, was an all-female quintet who played a mashup of covers, including oldies, country, hip-hop, and rock. They only played hits and they kept the energy up. When the keyboardist started the opening riff of Van Halen's "Jump," Junior turned to the stage and woo-hooed. She was playing mini-golf at the time with Aaron and his roommate, TJ. She almost hit Aaron with the club as she lifted it over her head. She apologized profusely. He laughed it off.

The band wrapped up their epic two-hour set by playing "Sweet Caroline" and leading the whole campus in a singalong. Dr. Bennet thanked them for keeping it clean and dismissed everyone. Aaron and Junior exchanged numbers, officially making him her first friend, and headed off in opposite directions.

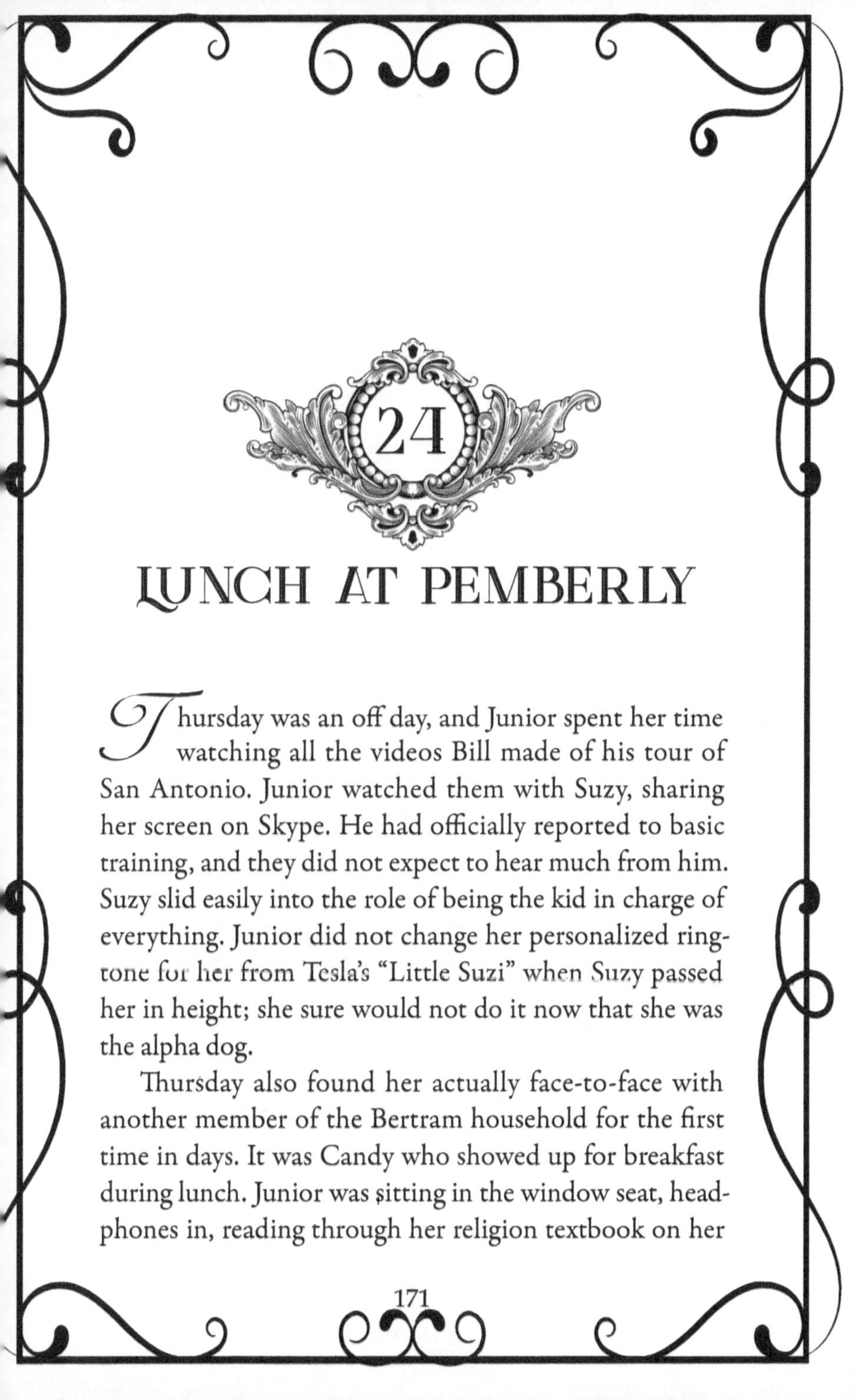

24

LUNCH AT PEMBERLY

Thursday was an off day, and Junior spent her time watching all the videos Bill made of his tour of San Antonio. Junior watched them with Suzy, sharing her screen on Skype. He had officially reported to basic training, and they did not expect to hear much from him. Suzy slid easily into the role of being the kid in charge of everything. Junior did not change her personalized ringtone for her from Tesla's "Little Suzi" when Suzy passed her in height; she sure would not do it now that she was the alpha dog.

Thursday also found her actually face-to-face with another member of the Bertram household for the first time in days. It was Candy who showed up for breakfast during lunch. Junior was sitting in the window seat, headphones in, reading through her religion textbook on her tablet. She opted for digital-only copies of everything to keep herself from having to lug everything around.

They had a pleasant conversation about Pug's grooming appointment, in which Junior nodded and smiled for twenty minutes, and Candy explained the process of sedating Pug before the appointment as she hated having her "nails done." After the information session ended and Candy finally put a piece of food into her own mouth, not in Pug's, Junior asked if she could invite Aaron over sometime, explaining his architectural interest in The Park. Permission was granted, and Junior was reminded she did not need to ask. Candy went on and on about how she was part of the family this was her house too.

On Friday, Junior slept until 7:45, ate alone again, took a long walk around the grounds, showered, and dressed for The Mansfield Gift Lunch at Pemberly. Each year, all of the first-year Gift recipients joined with the rest of the recipients and any alumni recipients who could attend the lunch at the Presidential residence, all mingling and networking.

Junior wore the same clothes she wore to church. All black is generally considered dressy enough in any circumstance. The event began at 11:30. Junior arrived at 11:25 and rang the bell. She was startled when the president herself answered the door. "Hello dear, I'm Mary Bennet."

Junior held out her hand and looked her host right in the eye. Like Junior, she was vertically challenged. "Dr. Bennet," they locked hands, "it is my honor to meet you. Frances Price Jr. Please call me Junior. Everyone does."

"Well, it is lovely to meet you, Junior. Congratulations on making it here."

"Thank you, Ma'am. Receiving the letter from you was the best day of my life."

"Well, let's hope that we can find a few days during your time here that top it."

Junior nodded and smiled. "They will have to be pretty spectacular."

"You're young. There will be so many wonderful days to come. Trust me. I can promise that today will not end up beating that day, but I also promise it will be as fun as lunch with strangers can be. If you'll head that way," she pointed to the hallway on the right, "you'll find the parlor. Please grab a drink and mingle. You're not the first one here. In fact, this party is notorious for having everyone here before the designated time."

Junior shook her hand again, resisted the urge to hug her, and walked down the hallway, following the sound of voices and music until she reached the parlor. Junior stopped as soon as she crossed into the room to take it all in. It was easily as large as the dining room at The Park. There were small, high-back loveseats spread around the room with round end tables on each side. There was a baby grand piano in the corner with an actual piano player dressed in a tuxedo.

There was a bar set up with a bartender, also in a tuxedo. She walked over and asked for a sweet tea. She saw a woman sitting alone but looking eager on one of the loveseats. She was dressed in black pants and a white button-down shirt with a black tie and vest. Junior walked over and asked if she could sit. The woman patted the empty spot.

"I'm Junior." She set her tea on the end table and reached over to shake the woman's hand.

"Maggie." She shook back. "Lovely to meet you. What year are you? Yes, I'm English," she said, acknowledging her accent with a playful smile.

Junior could tell but would never have asked but decided to go along with the conversation. "I'm a first-year. Yes, I'm a southerner."

Maggie laughed. "Yes, I suppose I deserved that. It's just, so far, everyone has guessed something wrong."

"What's your favorite wrong guess?"

Maggie thought about it and reached to the side table to take a sip of her coffee. "Well, I would say the one that made no sense to me was someone who thought I was South African. I mean, English and Afrikaans sound nothing alike!"

Junior laughed. "There are a lot of movies where the baddies are South African, and they are rarely actually played by South Africans."

"I suppose that could be it."

Junior took a sip of her tea. "Tell me more about you. We've established you're a Gift winner and not South African."

Maggie, who was unaccustomed to having friends, or sharing much of herself, felt, as sometimes happens when meeting a complete stranger for the first time, that this person was going to be one of her people. It turned out that she would be right. Junior and Maggie shall be linked for life. If it was because of a feeling or if it was because of her being so open when they first met is up for debate. So, she launched into her unfiltered story. "I'm a first-year. My real name is Margaret. I'm the youngest of four, but my older brother has a different mum, so I'm sort of the youngest of three. While I was not technically a mistake, my parents were so worn out by the middle sister that they pretty much let me raise myself. My dad died. My mom was a mess. We moved out of the family home and into a guest house. I drifted into the background of everyone's life. I did weird stuff. I wear ties. I like art. I like boys and girls. My best friend is an old lady. I was often called 'that other Dashwood girl.' Until I won The Gift, I wasn't even sure I was real."

Junior found herself nodding along. She shared her own story of being invisible. They chatted amicably and realized they had a lot in common. They quickly decided to exchange phone numbers. Maggie used WhatsApp as her primary service so that she didn't need to get an American number. She helped Junior install it and set it up. By the time everything was done, the piano had stopped, and Dr. Bennet appeared at the door, inviting them all to the dining room for lunch.

There were five round tables in the room. Everyone had an assigned seat. Each table had room for eight people. One student from each year's group of Gift recipients with the corresponding advisor, one member of the administration, and two alumni winners. Junior found her seat at Dr. Allen's table. He stood up and shook her hand and told her to sit next to him so he could introduce her around.

Dr. Allen made the introductions. Junior did her best to remember all the names. One seat at her table remained unclaimed. Dr. Allen explained that the missing person was a musical prodigy called Jane Fairfax. She was capricious and so her attendance was not assured. He hoped she would arrive if for no other reason than to treat them all to a concert after lunch.

"She's the keyboardist in The Pump Room, so you already heard her play if you were at the first-year carnival," the third-year said.

"I was there. They were excellent. I loved their cover of 'Jump.' She really nailed that opening riff."

"Yes, well," Dr. Allen chimed in, "there is no doubt of her talent, but it's simply breathtaking hearing her play some of her original compositions. Hopefully, you will have the opportunity."

"I hope so. I'd say that I listen to music more than I do anything else."

That opened the door to a conversation around the table about what kind of music everyone liked and did not like and why. The tastes were vast, and the conversation was lively. It lasted through the salad, the meal, and into dessert. Not once did Junior feel the urge to rub her scarf.

As coffee was being served, Dr. Bennet stood. The room quieted down. "I want to thank you all for a delightful afternoon. Each year that I'm in this position and lucky enough to host this lunch, I feel blessed. I know being the recipient of The Gift can sometimes feel like a heavy burden, but I assure you, it is one worth carrying. The Gift is the exemplification of what a well-rounded person can do in life. While I did not create The Mansfield Gift, I'm blessed to have been the arbiter of it for the past ten years, and I look forward to all the years to come."

Dr. Allen stood and led the group in an ovation. Junior's table rose first, and eventually, the rest of the room did as well. Dr. Bennet was not expecting it and waved it off, but they persisted. She took a bow and then pushed her hands down to make everyone sit. They obliged her.

"Thank you. That was not necessary, but I appreciate it. I would just like to conclude by reminding the students, both current and alumni, that you are the best of us, and we are incredibly proud. Remember, my door is always open. Well, not literally, you should call first or at least knock." Everyone laughed. "Feel free to have your coffee and linger for a while. I would like to extend the time for the first-years and invite you back to the parlor to have your coffee with me there. However, if you have prior engagements," she looked at her watch, "I would understand. I know there are some events going on in Angeline very soon, and I would not want to keep you."

With that, the majority of guests packed up, shook hands, exchanged final pleasantries, and departed from the historic presidential home. The five first-years were herded back to the parlor where the bartender from before still stood as though he was trapped in amber the whole time. The three love seats were moved into a triangle shape in the center of the room, with the end tables dotting each point of the triangle. On each table stood a carafe of coffee.

Junior and Maggie had a conversation with their eyes and heads. They claimed a loveseat. The first-year from Arkansas and the first-year from Seoul sat on one of the love seats, having clearly connected at some point before, as they too spoke without speaking. The young man from Washington arrived last and introduced himself to the group. He took the lead in starting the small talk by asking them all about their roommates.

Before Junior could explain her living arrangements, Dr. Bennet arrived and sat in the remaining seat. "Hello, everyone. I appreciate your time. I know you all have so much to do before your courses begin on Monday, but I wanted to just touch base with you all to make sure you know that one of my favorite presidential duties is to act as a pseudo-secondary advisory role to all The Gift recipients, especially during their first two years."

The five young people were surprised to learn this, and their reactions and body language revealed that surprise. They all leaned forward or shifted in their seats in anticipation of finding out what this would entail.

"I know you are all scheduled within an inch of your lives, this lunch included, but I want you to know, that should you desire it, I'm here to offer the group of you a monthly lunch. This is not required, but I encourage you to attend if possible. The lunches are held here on the first Wednesday of the month. It is a casual, come-as-you-are event. It is a great time for the five of you to bond; as you know, you will have no classes together." She took a sip of her coffee. "Honestly," she looked at all of them in the eyes as she paused for effect, "it is a selfish endeavor on my part. When I was a student here, I was a lonely middle child who, as a Gift recipient, felt isolated. I was not great at making friends and lacked the personal skills that my sisters all seemed to possess. While I loved every minute of my time at Mansfield, and I made some excellent friends, I really did not know my Gift family, and so, when I became President ten years ago, I decided to expand The Gift lunch tradition. It has been the bright spot of my week as I meet with one group per week. I do so hope you will choose to attend."

Dr. Bennet's seatmate spoke up and happily accepted the invitation, and the rest of the group followed suit. "Thank you all so much. Now, with all of that big news out of the way, tell me how you are doing." She sat back and sipped her coffee.

The conversation went on for over an hour longer. The small group broke up only when one of the house staff entered and reminded Dr. Bennet that she had another event starting soon.

Four of them walked together back to Angeline. Junior, full of hope, and with another friend in her contact list, walked back to The Park grinning from ear to ear.

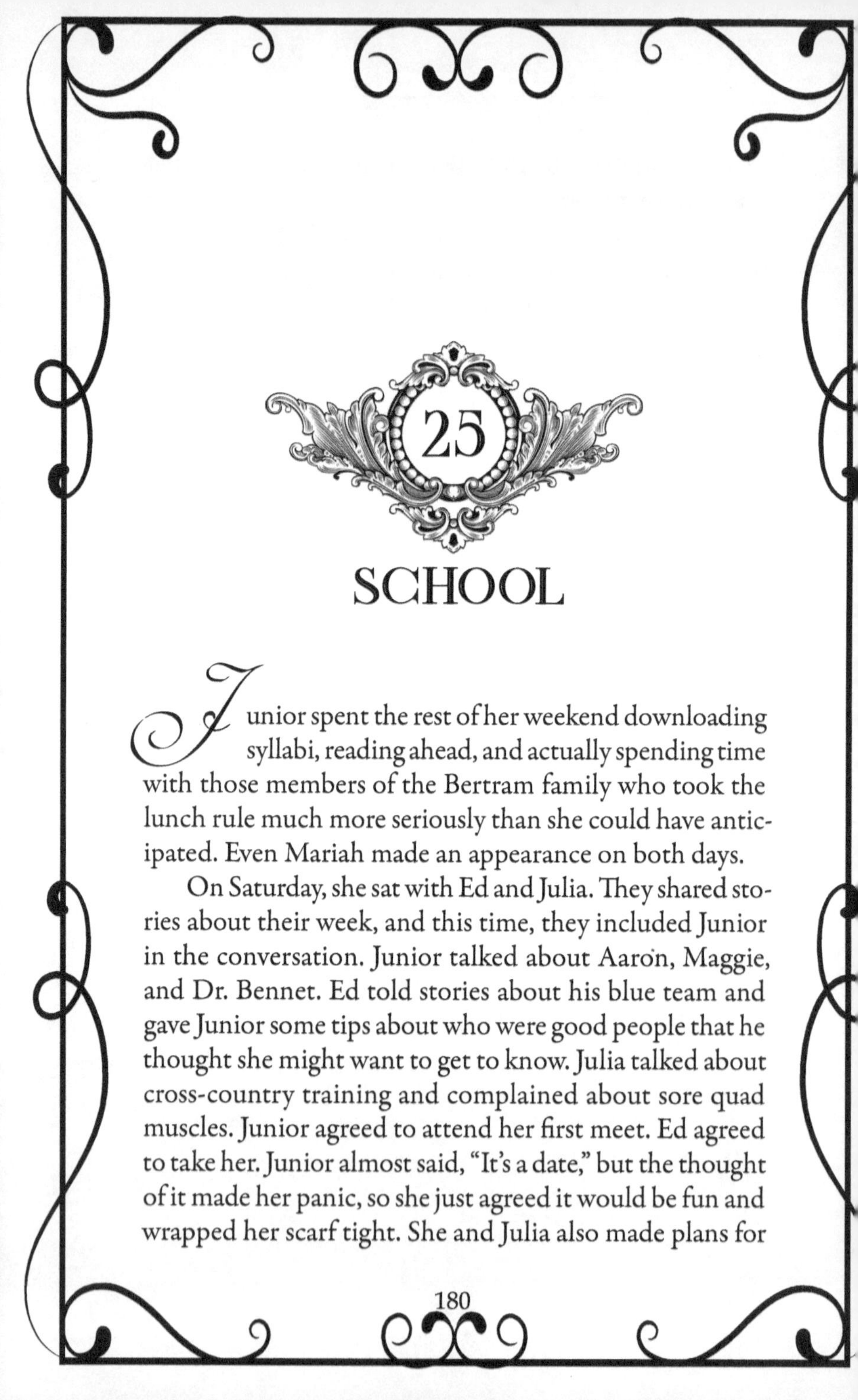

25

SCHOOL

*J*unior spent the rest of her weekend downloading syllabi, reading ahead, and actually spending time with those members of the Bertram family who took the lunch rule much more seriously than she could have anticipated. Even Mariah made an appearance on both days.

On Saturday, she sat with Ed and Julia. They shared stories about their week, and this time, they included Junior in the conversation. Junior talked about Aaron, Maggie, and Dr. Bennet. Ed told stories about his blue team and gave Junior some tips about who were good people that he thought she might want to get to know. Julia talked about cross-country training and complained about sore quad muscles. Junior agreed to attend her first meet. Ed agreed to take her. Junior almost said, "It's a date," but the thought of it made her panic, so she just agreed it would be fun and wrapped her scarf tight. She and Julia also made plans for

Junior to take her driving after Junior's birthday. Ed made a joke about wheels of danger. Julia punched him.

On Sunday, she sat with Tommy and Yates, who pumped her for information about herself as though they were writing her biography. Ultimately, Tommy reminded her that she mentioned she had a birthday coming up, and after finding out when it was, decreed that he and Yates would throw a party in her honor at the theater. She tried to decline until Yates explained that Tommy was going to have the party anyway and pretend it was for her, so she might as well be there. Tommy promptly interrupted everyone else's conversation and told them they would all be invited to Junior's seventeenth birthday party, even Norris.

Monday morning found Junior awake at 5:30. She had been up far too late video chatting with Suzy, who would not start school for another week. One might think that the two spent a lot of time talking about Junior's adventures and the fact that she was starting college the next day, but of course, that was not the conversation. If one listened in, one would not even know Junior was in college. There is no reason to linger there. Junior knew exactly how it would go, which is why she chose to ring her sister. She wanted to take her mind off things.

So, with little sleep and lots of anxiety, Junior found herself dressed and in The Nook by 6:15. Tom was there, sipping his coffee and reading the morning paper on his tablet. If he was surprised to see someone else up at that hour, he didn't show it.

"Morning, kiddo." As a toast, he raised his coffee, which was in a travel mug. "Come sit with me." He patted the tabletop.

She filled her cup and sat across from him. "Good morning. Are you always up this early?"

"Depends on the day. You?"

She took a sip and nodded. "Same."

"Nervous?"

She exhaled a breath she didn't know she had been holding. It was the first time anyone thought to ask her that question. "So much. It's just that I know I'm not the first generation to go to college or anything, but The Gift is such a huge deal, and you and Candy are so nice to let me be here that I just want to make you proud, and I don't want to let my mom down or my Grandpa Ward, I know he isn't alive, but none of this would be possible without him, and Dr. Bennet made a big deal out of it, and Norris makes me feel like I will disgrace everyone I've ever met and..."

He interrupted her as she took a breath. "First, take a deep breath. Don't ever let Norris make you feel any particular way. Her default is to make people feel bad. Trust me. I've had years of experience at disappointing her. Secondly, I know your mom, and I have to say that there is nothing you could do to let her down. I'm only getting to know you, but I'm already proud that you live here with us. You make the whole family better just by being here. Betty told me you took the time to get to know her. I appreciate that. I don't think anyone else here besides me knows her name.

"Mary Bennet sets the bar high because she knows you can reach it. Don't let her scare you. She sees herself in all the other Gift winners. She is a true believer in the idea that the old man had. More so than my wife, who shares his name and has his house." He paused and took a sip of his coffee. "Seriously, you are going to be great. I promise." He held out his fist in the same way he saw Bill do it.

She reached out and bumped it with her own. "Thanks."

"You got it." He looked at his watch. "I've got to hit the road. I'm taking a flight this morning. I'll be back sometime tomorrow night. Have a great first day." He stood up and filled his mug. There was a brown bag sitting there that hadn't been there before. He grabbed it. "Tell Betty thanks for me, will you?"

Junior was amazed. "She's like a ninja."

"She is. If you need her to pack you anything, just ask. You have that weird schedule, so if you don't want to come back here between classes, I'm sure she could make something that will last all day."

"Thanks, I will."

"Don't forget to have fun too, OK?" He tousled her hair on his way out, just as though she was one of his own.

Fully fed, overly caffeinated, and spirits raised from her pep talk and a "Have a Great First Day!!!" text from Ed, Junior jittered her way through her first day. She was surprised to learn that the first days of class were not really full classes. Her Algebra class met for only twenty minutes. Dr. Steele was nothing Junior thought a Math teacher would be. She had created an image of a well-dressed, *Men in Black* type. Instead, he came into class in flip-flops, cargo shorts, and a stained ringer tee. He passed around a sign-in sheet, went through the syllabus, assigned homework for Thursday, and let them go into the late summer morning.

After spending the rest of her morning in the library doing her Thursday homework, she learned that there were lots of hidden spaces around the building. She found the old stacks where bound magazines from years past were housed. Each stack was only six feet tall, so six floors of stacks fit inside the regular three floors of the library. She discovered that there was a stairwell that led to a single bathroom off the fourth stack. There were several study carrels, a few high-back chairs, and the windows opened. She settled in there to text with Suzy and her mother while she ate the lunch Betty packed for her.

Her Early Modern Europe class with Dr. West, a tall woman who wore a top ponytail that made her seem even taller, kept her in class for one of the two allotted hours. Dr. West went around the room and asked each student, twenty-four in all, to give a short introduction which included one's full name, preferred name, place of origin, course of study, preferred pronouns, and European country about which s/he/they knew the least. Junior was the only person to select Malta, which made Dr. West smile. She sent them away with a reading assignment, which Junior had fortunately already done.

After an evening where she once again dined alone, Junior ran into Julia in the hallway on her way back to her room. Julia's running clothes clung to her as she was drenched with sweat. They had a brief chat about her run. They agreed to meet for breakfast the next day, as Junior had a late start and hoped to sleep past 5:30.

She fell asleep sitting in front of her fireplace with her tablet on her lap. It was only when it fell off her lap that she crawled into bed, fully clothed, and slept.

Junior arrived at her Composition II course buzzing with joy as Julia had not only met her for breakfast, but she actually asked her how her first day went. Her day brightened when she discovered Aaron was in her class.

Dr. Smith, a small man who wore a blue polo shirt tucked into his blue jeans, kept them for a mere ten minutes. He handed out the syllabus, told them to sign up on the sign-in sheet on the way out, and gave them an assignment. One thousand words in MLA format explaining what they thought their strengths and weaknesses as writers were and what they hoped to accomplish in his class to improve on both.

Junior showed Aaron the fourth-floor stack, although he had to hunch over to enter. After an hour or so, Aaron moved on to have lunch and head to his next class. They arranged to meet up on the steps at Delaford the next day so they could go check out all the groups together. Junior ate her lunch and texted Suzy. Bill had managed to write an email to her. He was tired, had lost five pounds already, and found that he had made one friend.

She and her classmates filed into their room in Northanger and sat in relative silence. Unlike her other courses where the teachers were already there greeting people as they came in, the professor's desk sat empty.

At exactly three, Norris walked in, dressed in her full ministerial garb, complete with white collar. She said, "That's enough," as though she was expecting the room to be full of noisy first-years as opposed to a relatively sedate and reserved group. Her hair was done up in a tight bun.

She placed her black briefcase on her desk. She wheeled the combination until the latch clicked. She laid it flat, opened it, and pulled out a stack of notecards. She sat them on the desk and closed her briefcase, closed the latches, and wheeled the combination to keep out any would-be religion thieves. She did all of this as the students sat in shocked silence, which she mistook for reverence.

She looked up at them and cleared her throat. "Now then. This is Introduction to Western Religion. I am the Reverend Doctor Norris. You will call me either Reverend or Doctor Norris. Even you, Frances." She looked directly at Junior, who had taken her seat in the back row, hoping to avoid just this kind of confrontation. Eighteen other sets of eyes followed Norris' gaze.

Junior wound up her scarf and sat up ramrod straight and said, "Yes, Reverend." She looked her right back in the eyes and remembered Tom's words of advice.

"I want to disclose to you all Frances and I have a pseudo-familial relationship, and I want to assure you all that she will receive no special treatment in this course. She, like you all, will treat me with the respect I have earned." She let that comment hang there, letting them all ponder what that meant while making no comment about how she would treat them.

"I will not be taking attendance in this course. I am being paid to teach this. You are paying to learn. If you do not wish to attend these lectures, do the work, or put in effort, it matters not a whit to me. I expect each of you has already read the syllabus which I provided online last week. I shall not be providing one to you, so go find it if you do not have one. For those who have not read it yet, I will make it clear here that in my class, you will not take notes on computers. I cannot stand the sound of clacking fingers. You will either take notes the old-fashioned way or you will sit and listen. Those are your only choices."

The uncomfortable silence overtook the room. Norris reached into the side pocket of her jacket and pulled out her reading glasses. "Now then." She cleared her throat, looked down at the first note card, and began her lecture.

The students scrambled to pull out pens and paper, and for the next 110 minutes, Norris read from her note cards. When she finished, she looked back up at her students who were in various states of agitation, frustration, and exhaustion, she asked, "Any questions?"

Junior recognized, early on in the lesson, that Norris was simply reading a truncated version of the first assigned reading. She wondered why Norris would bother doing a lecture on something only to have them read it later, but she kept that question to herself. Being called out for simply existing and having a "pseudo-familial" relationship was enough attention for the day.

Silence screamed back at her as nineteen students collectively held their breath, not wanting to accidentally make a sound that could be construed as a question keeping them in the classroom any longer than necessary. Norris waited for thirty full seconds, trying to make eye contact with each student in turn, before she finally relented, "Excellent. Do the assigned reading for Friday. You are dismissed."

They could not get their papers in their bags quickly enough. Many didn't even bother packing up; they just rushed past Norris, who was unlocking her briefcase again, and headed for the door and the restrooms. Junior surfed out on the flood of students.

She hoped that one of the Bertram children would be there for dinner so she could relate her bizarre Norris story to someone who would understand. She went straight there upon arriving back to The Park to ensure she had maximum time during meal hours. She spent two full hours alone save for Betty. Junior asked her when everyone else normally ate, and she explained that it was not her place to comment on the comings and goings of anyone in the household, as was the requirement of protocol and Portsmouth and good manners.

She returned to her room at 7, wrote Bill a long email, checked in with her mother and Suzy only to confirm that the twins had yet to be born, and collapsed in her bed by nine. Loneliness apparently made her have the sleeping habits of an elementary schooler.

She and Aaron spent Wednesday table hopping around the quad. There were at least one hundred folding tables set up. It turned out that Mansfield had a Trekkie group who were part of the Federation, with a full command structure to boot. There was a club for Mimes of Mansfield, which Aaron *almost* had her convinced he was going to join. "My moms are big into miming." He somehow maintained a straight face.

Ultimately, he joined the poker club. Each Wednesday, they met after lunch in Upper Delaford, and they played until dinner. They bet following the rules set forth by the band of Gen X students who created the club in the 90s called the *Benny and Joon* rules. In that movie, the characters wrote items they owned on post-it notes and used those things to bet. The following week, they brought the items and paid up. Junior had actually seen that movie and thought it was a classic. Aaron, upon hearing that Johnny Depp was in it, thought he would take a pass. Still, he loved poker, so he thought the rules were good regardless of how they had been created.

Junior ended up joining the breakfast book club. They met on the last Wednesday of each month to talk about whatever book the group had selected. Junior explained that she did not have a meal plan. The president seemed to think that it wouldn't be a problem as they were pretty flexible when it came to Wednesday groups, but he promised to check and let her know. They exchanged numbers.

The September book was a graphic novel called *Decelerate Blue*. The club always had a few copies of the monthly book on hold in the library. In a few days, her name would be on the approved list. She could sit and read it in the library, but she couldn't check it out. Considering how much time she planned on spending in the library each week, she was excited to have something else to do.

Aaron had to reluctantly pass on the invitation to The Park for lunch as his RA had a floor activity planned. They made plans for the following Wednesday, and they went their separate ways. Junior returned to The Park, where she was expecting to once again eat lunch alone. She was pleasantly surprised to find Yates in The Nook when she arrived. He had come up to The Park to pick up something for Tommy, who still had a large collection of things in his old room, smelled the food, and decided to stay.

"Hooray!" Yates said when he saw her. "I'm so excited to see you. I wanted to see how your first week was going." He got up and gave her a big hug, lifting her off the ground.

She held on tight as her feet came off the ground. While she was not a fan of being hugged in such a manner, she was a fan of human contact, so she uttered no complaint. Once he set her back down, she said, "It's been really good and really strange. How much time do you have?" She walked over to the serving table and made herself a turkey sandwich, put some chips on her plate, and poured some sweet tea.

"All the time you need. Tommy sent me up here to get some sheet music for your party. He is in the process of laying tile in the lobby. He knows I'm not interested in being handy, so this errand was supposed to take a while. The sheet music is not going to be easy to find, nor do I expect it to really be there. In fact, I think I know right where the songbook is on the shelf at the theatre, but I went along with it because he was being sweet and giving me an 'out.'"

"You don't mind that he's doing it under false pretenses?" she asked as she sat back down.

"Fair question," he said as he took a sip of his drink and thought about how to answer. "Not to get all up in your business, but have you been in a relationship before?"

Surprisingly, she didn't feel the hives starting to form as she shook her head. She made a mental note of it. Was there something about Yates that made her immune, or was it the way he asked? She would ponder it later. We shall see the results of that internal conversation later in this tale.

"Yeah, I figured. You're young, smart, and cute. If memory serves, you only have one of the three things dumb straight boys are looking for."

"Young?" she asked with a mouthful of chips. Leaning into the comfort she felt with him.

"Ding, ding ding." He put his finger on his nose as he made the noise. "Young, dumb, and hot. No offense."

"None taken?" She smiled as she formed her response as a question.

"It's just, most hot girls work hard to be hot. They are cute girls who do themselves up for attention, not because of how it makes them feel. There are people who do themselves up because it makes them feel good. You can tell the difference by how they carry themselves and the desperation stinks. You know, like," he lowered his voice to a whisper and leaned in, "M-A-R-I-A-H."

She snorted out a laugh. "Are you worried she is dumb too? I suspect she can spell her own name."

"I know she can. I just worry it is a *Candyman* situation. I don't want to say her name and have her appear."

Junior choked on a chip. She downed some more tea and regained her composure, feeling guilty for laughing but relieved that she could still do so.

"OK?"

"Right as rain." She opened her mouth and said, "AHHH."

He laughed and continued, "Well, anyway, once you find a person, I assume a young man..." He paused and raised his eyebrows.

She nodded. "I think so. I mean, I've never been kissed, so maybe if the right girl came along, but I'm pretty sure it's boys."

"I figured. Anyway, when the right young man comes along, and you and he move beyond just having the feels, I mean, you still have them, Tommy and I call it 'the tingles,' but you also want to just spend time with the person in the non-tingles moments." He paused, hearing what he was saying. "OK, sorry, I promise this isn't 'The Talk.' I assume you've had that with Senior."

Junior nodded and noticed there were still no hives, even though a conversation like this should have made her neck look like a full map of Indonesia. When she did have "The Talk" with her mother, she was more mortified than she was at that moment.

"Well, anyway, the point is, once you're with the person you want to be with, you learn about him as a person. You know what he likes and dislikes, and you want to do things for him. You want to surprise him and make him happy and make sure he's not miserable. So, today, Tommy wanted to get me out of the house because he loves me. He knows if I was there, I would be on the floor with him laying tiles even though I would hate it." He paused and took a drink. "So, he created a chore for me to do."

"Right." She paused. "But, why not just say, 'Hey Yates, I'm doing the tile. I know you don't want to be here. Have a good day' instead of going through the whole rigmarole of making up a story? Especially if he knows that you know?"

"It's just more fun and romantic this way. You'll see."

Junior couldn't imagine it being more romantic or fun to be dishonest with the person you love, regardless of the reason. She realized that Yates and she were not going to agree completely on this. He was speaking from experience, of course, and as he pointed out, she had none. Still, she saw what it was like to have her parents sit around in uncomfortable silence. She settled for, "We'll see," as a good, generic response.

It seemed to please him. He spent the next hour asking questions about her first few days and offering advice on how to cope with Norris. Granted, he admitted, none of them had ever had her as a professor, so Junior was some kind of pioneer, the Sacagawea of Mansfield, as he put it. They laughed about the idea of her showing up for class Friday in deerskins with a baby but thought cultural appropriation was a bad thing.

She was buoyed by the time and attention from Yates, including an exchange of numbers that came with frequent texts full of images of Sacagawea, that the remainder of her week flew by. While she felt some of the same loneliness each day at mealtime, she pushed through, knowing that her contact list was filling up.

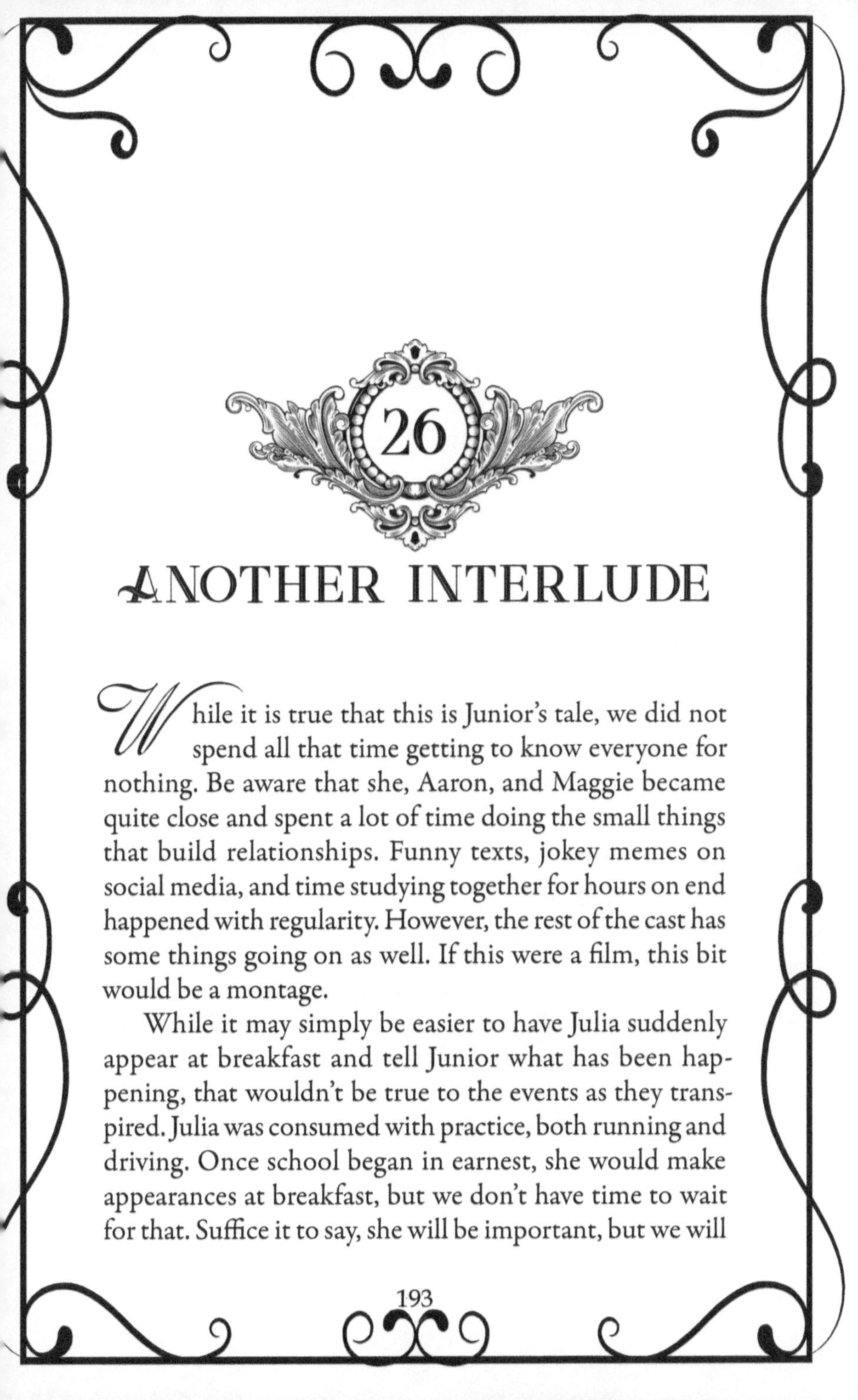

26

ANOTHER INTERLUDE

While it is true that this is Junior's tale, we did not spend all that time getting to know everyone for nothing. Be aware that she, Aaron, and Maggie became quite close and spent a lot of time doing the small things that build relationships. Funny texts, jokey memes on social media, and time studying together for hours on end happened with regularity. However, the rest of the cast has some things going on as well. If this were a film, this bit would be a montage.

While it may simply be easier to have Julia suddenly appear at breakfast and tell Junior what has been happening, that wouldn't be true to the events as they transpired. Julia was consumed with practice, both running and driving. Once school began in earnest, she would make appearances at breakfast, but we don't have time to wait for that. Suffice it to say, she will be important, but we will have to wait to catch up with her during one of those soon-to-be frequent morning chats.

We could also pretend that the first lunch after Junior's first week could come with insight into what everyone had been doing. That would make sense. It is clear that everyone showed up for weekend lunch out of fear of being excommunicated from the family. Of course, the only person who could actually do that, Candy Bertram, would never do such a thing. Still, the fear of it was always enough to make sure Tom was home from a trip, Ed could find a way out of his duties as a Resident Assistant, and Mariah could find her way out of her room that was fully stocked with enough food to keep her away from everyone for months at a time.

There is no real way to squeeze all of that into a conversation, however, without having to dip in and out of multiple conversations over multiple lunches. Instead, we shall give a quick update so we can rejoin the story at Junior's birthday party, where she will once again employ "I don't think so" effectively. It isn't until we reach the final part of this tale where the use of "I don't think so" is followed up by angry shouts and consternation. We do not want you to think that when you see it used coming up, it means what you think it means. Be patient.

Mary Crawford continued to ingratiate herself to Mariah Bertram in an attempt to get closer to Ed, whom she considered worthy of her attention. Ed enjoyed the attention, being not entirely immune to the wiles of a young, attractive woman. He slowly learned, however, that Mary and he had very little in common besides Mariah, and frankly, he didn't like his sister very much.

Hank Crawford similarly had his sights set on gaining the attention of a Bertram. The feelings between him and Mariah were reciprocated but complicated, as we shall see at Junior's party. Just be sure that there is a lot going on there, and Junior will be unintentionally roped into it eventually.

Norris continued her assault on decency and pedagogical practices by reading note cards each day in class and choosing to grade on a curve, thus ensuring that someone would fail every assignment and, ultimately, her course. This new practice resulted in an unprecedented exodus from her classes. The registrar mentioned casually to Dr. Bennet that there had been a new record set for first-week transfers, which led to Dr. Bennet doing a more-than-casual bit of day drinking.

Tommy and Yates were using Junior's party as an excuse to test out the capacity of the theater for their official unveiling at the Rocky Horror Halloween party. The tile floor looked "HGTV-worthy," according to Yates, which made Tommy so happy that they spent some private time breaking it in, which in hindsight turned out to be a terrible idea. Sometimes "the tingles" end in unintentional bruising.

Yates and Junior found themselves together at other meals when Tommy was busy doing handy things around the theater. Their chats were mostly reciprocal. He asked a lot of questions about her; since Junior naturally didn't care to be the only focus, she asked many in return. He never had a little sister but found that maybe he would have been an excellent big brother. He also liked to come up occasionally and check in on Candy. He worried about her loneliness. Junior found his care and attention to his someday mother-in-law even more endearing.

Tom and Candy's lives remained shrouded in mystery. Candy would occasionally be seen napping with Pug in The Lounge, and Tom would be seen occasionally at breakfast, but even when he was not on a flight, he would go into the office. On weekends, he would arrive from his private rooms to eat with the family and participate in post-meal chats in The Lounge before returning to his own world, which consisted of no one knew what.

Bill was doing very well in Basic Training. Air Force life suited him. He made one actual friend and found several people with whom he felt he could spend time. His time there, while rigorous and mentally and physically exhausting, was enjoyable, and he was thriving. Everyone was incredibly proud of him. There is no record of how his father felt about any of this, but as we shall see soon enough, he withdrew more and more from the family.

Suzy adjusted well to her new role as family chauffeur and boss of her own home. It suited her a little too much for Fran's liking, so she arranged for Suzy to head up north for siblings' weekend/Junior's birthday. More on that to follow.

Fran insisted these two babies would be the last of the Price line. Since she knew her husband could not be bothered to have minor surgery, she decided that during the C-section, she would have her tubes tied. It would be her first C-section, but the doctor convinced her that it would be better due to the fact she was having twins. The surgery was planned for the final day of September. They could come sooner, but the 30th was a day on which none of the other Price children were born, and it was within the window the doctor felt comfortable.

Ed and Mariah were lunching with the Crawford twins more often than Ed would have liked, but being a nice guy who was trying to make an effort for his sister's sake, he submitted. Additionally, he had been selected as the first third-year ever to be asked to represent Mansfield College at a conference. He was being asked to turn his paper on examining the Gnostic Gospels through a historical lens into a presentation. It was only after he committed that he found out it was only a poster session. While he, and everyone who attended conferences knew, poster sessions were unappealing, uninformative, and, for the lack of a better word, lame, he still agreed to go; a commitment was a commitment. He was to travel to the big state university where James was a student to do the presentation. So, it was really just an afternoon drive on a Wednesday when he already didn't have class. Still, he tried to think of it as an honor.

Mariah lured Hank into her life while making sure she kept James around just in case. She purposefully cropped Hank out of most of her Instagram photos unless either Ed or Mary was in them as well. It was a tangled web of lies and deception that occasionally involved propping open the back door in the West Wing while locking the adjoining door between her room and the space she and Julia shared. It would be foolish to think this was a practice she invented just for Hank, even though she told him it was true. The truth is, James Rushworth could walk from his estate, through The Park, and through that propped-open door with his eyes closed.

Thus ends the interlude. Junior thrived in all of her classes, even her religion class. While Norris would have been thrilled to discover Junior ended up at the bottom of the curve, it never happened. There is a reason she graduated high school and was awarded The Gift at age sixteen. Of course, as we know, when the calendar turned from August to September, her sixteenth year was wrapping up. She felt much older than her years indicated, and yet, she was fully aware she was, in many ways, much younger. So, with all of that, let us jump to the big day.

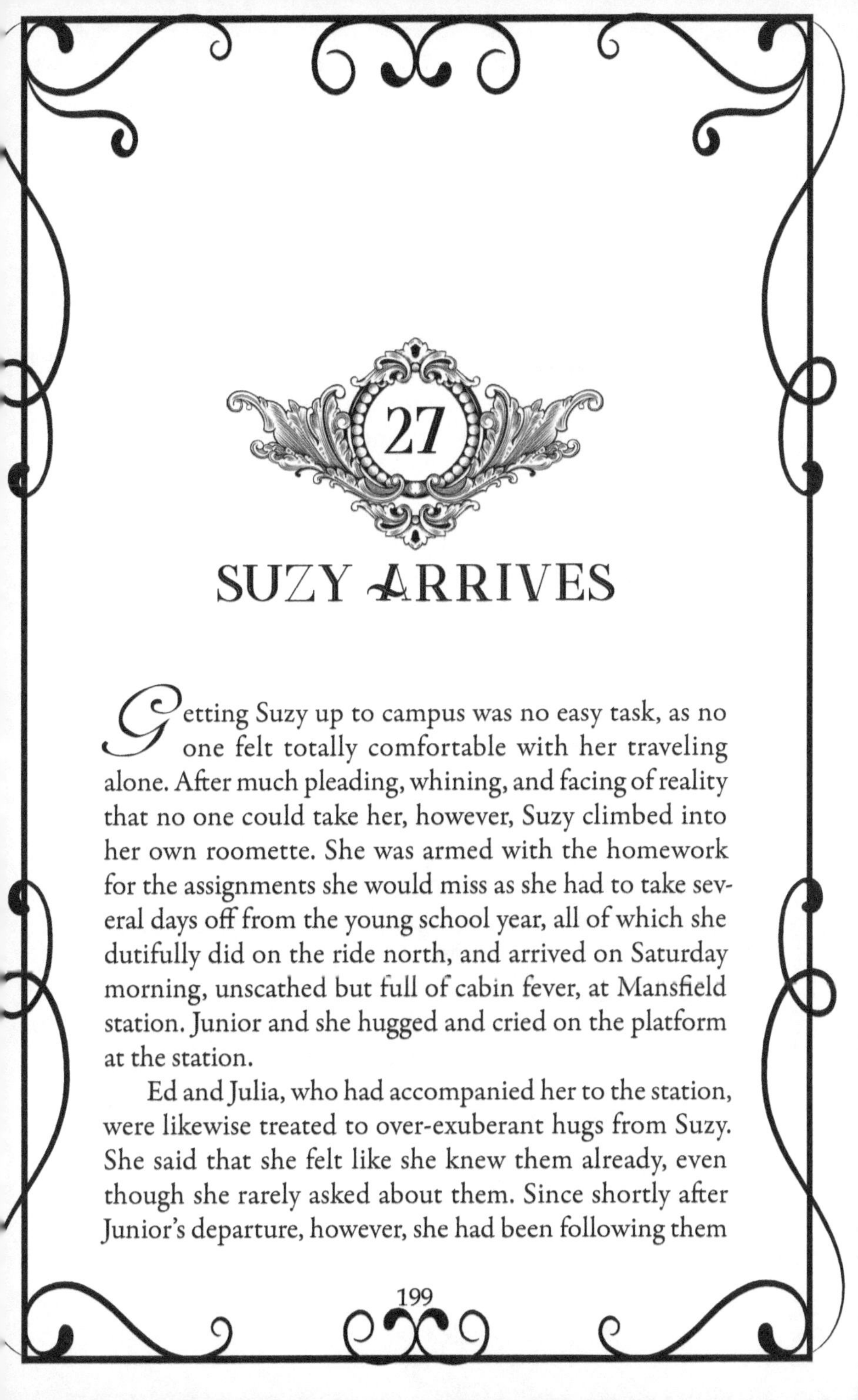

27

SUZY ARRIVES

Getting Suzy up to campus was no easy task, as no one felt totally comfortable with her traveling alone. After much pleading, whining, and facing of reality that no one could take her, however, Suzy climbed into her own roomette. She was armed with the homework for the assignments she would miss as she had to take several days off from the young school year, all of which she dutifully did on the ride north, and arrived on Saturday morning, unscathed but full of cabin fever, at Mansfield station. Junior and she hugged and cried on the platform at the station.

Ed and Julia, who had accompanied her to the station, were likewise treated to over-exuberant hugs from Suzy. She said that she felt like she knew them already, even though she rarely asked about them. Since shortly after Junior's departure, however, she had been following them on Instagram. That can often be more informative for the things a fifteen-year-old could want to know anyway.

The Bertrams peppered Suzy with questions as they walked back to The Park. Being the center of attention was not a thing she could fully understand, but it was a sensation that she could get behind and would never fully feel again until years later when she attended Mansfield; although that is a different story altogether.

After arriving at The Park and collecting snacks from The Nook, the Prices briefly hid away in Junior's room. They had lots to do before lunch. Suzy wanted to see the campus and walk around The Park, but mostly she wanted to see Junior's room in real life. Portsmouth had offered to set up Suzy in a guest room in the East Wing, but they were looking forward to sharing some space again. Junior was small enough, and her bed was big enough that they could share, sleepover style.

"Holy crap-o-la," said Suzy as Junior shut the door behind her. "This is incredible." She dropped her bag on the floor and started twirling around with her arms out. "Do you think there is any room in any of our houses where I could spin like this and not hit a person or a thing?" She sped up her spinning, not expecting an answer to her question as she knew it was rhetorical.

Junior plucked her bag off the ground and set it on her desk so that Suzy wouldn't accidentally trip over it, break something, and end the weekend before it began. Eventually, the spinning ceased, and the sisters settled into the high-back chairs in front of the fireplace. Junior fended off her pleas to start a fire right away by promising they could do one the next morning.

Suzy filled Junior in on all the gossip around the high school. Of course, Junior was never in on any of the gossip when she went there, but she was familiar enough with the names that she could nod and make noises at the right times. Eventually, after Suzy ran out of things to say on the subject and after she spun around in the bathroom, they headed for campus.

Siblings' weekend was a big deal at Mansfield. While it was designed to keep students connected to their families, it mostly served as a two-day commercial for the virtues of attending Mansfield College. It worked as a sort of educational nepotism. It was incredibly successful as well, as we can see from our tale thus far.

The first-year welcome carnival was re-assembled on the quad. Once again, The Pump Room took center stage. Once again, food and fun were plentiful. Junior warned Suzy against overeating as lunch was served at 2, but as everyone knows, 15-year-old girls who have to oversee younger siblings, know how to drive, and have a propensity for spinning invariably also have bottomless pits for stomachs.

They met up with Maggie, who had no one with whom to spend time, as the youngest sibling and a foreigner to boot. They also found and hung out with Aaron, who as an only child, was always interested in seeing how siblings interacted. They played games and ate and danced and sang and laughed and laughed. Before heading their separate ways, Junior once again confirmed they knew where the party was, what time to come, and that they were NOT to bring gifts. They all promised, exchanged sweaty hugs, and went on their separate ways until the evening.

"That Aaron is a cutie," Suzy said as soon as they stepped foot on The Park's property.

"Yeah. I suppose."

"You suppose? What's not to like?"

"Well," Junior thought about it, "there is just something about him that reminds me of Bill and..."

Suzy interrupted. "Don't ruin it for me. I mean, I know I'm too young and I live too far away, and all the reasons it will never be, but don't ruin it for me." She made some gagging and puking noises.

"I'm not saying he reminds YOU of Bill. I'm just saying that I think there are some people with whom we are destined to be just friends. I'm OK with that."

"Fine." Suzy threw her hands up in defeat. "I'm just saying you're not a kid anymore, and you've never had a boyfriend or been kissed or anything. I just was pointing out that an attractive boy in your orbit was there for the kissing."

They sat on a bench near the Carriage House. "And you know all about it, do you?" Junior asked, assuming it would put an end to the inane conversation and would steer them back to other things.

"Well..." Suzy drew out the pause, "since you mentioned it..." Of course, Junior had not mentioned it at all, and she realized all too late that Suzy had set her up by almost making an entire conversation about Junior. "...there is this new guy, Ricardo, and well..." Suzy went on and on about this new boy; while Junior did not know him, nor would ever know him, she listened intently for ten uninterrupted minutes only to discover that Suzy was not any closer to being kissed. Still, she had convinced herself that it would happen any day, and while she was thrilled to be up at Mansfield, she did think missing the home football game at Unincorporated Nowhere High was going to set her back a few weeks. Ricardo was a big sports fan, and while he played soccer, not football, he supported all teams equally. Suzy had an elaborate plan that involved spilled popcorn, but it was quite convoluted and sure to have failed. There is thus no reason to dwell on it all here.

They eventually made it in for lunch which once again put Suzy at the center of attention. She actually sat next to Candy so she could get some close contact with Pug. Suzy loved dogs, but Fran insisted that pets were an unnecessary expense in a family of their size. While Suzy knew it to be true, she resented her mother all the same.

This freed up Junior to have lunch with Ed and Julia. Tommy and Yates decided to skip as they had "last-minute decorating" to do for the big party.

"I really don't know what all the fuss is about. People turn seventeen all the time, and I've only known them for like a month," Junior opined.

"Yeah, it isn't really-really about you. I mean, it is, but it isn't," Julia explained. "I mean, there is going to be a cake and there is going to be singing and jubilation. I suspect your name will be in lights or paper or balloons, but really, it's a reason for them to have a party and show off."

Ed nodded along. "They just love to do grand gestures, and this is one that is equally about you and them."

"So, I'm giving them a gift for my birthday?"

"Great way to think of it. Yes. You're a good person who would totally give out gifts at your own birthday party," Ed said.

"You must have done that at your parties when you were a kid, right?"

Junior looked down and wrapped her scarf tight. "Well, I've never actually had a birthday party with anyone other than my family. We couldn't really afford it, and well, my dad isn't big on company, and my mom is always pregnant or breast-feeding and..." she looked back up, focusing on a spot across the room, "...all the kids are born late August or September, so that time of year is essentially worse than Christmas. Normally, we just have one big combined party with one cake. Mom kept a record so we could alternate on whose birthday the big party was actually held. I'm sure that early on, I had lots of turns, but I don't have any memories of us actually celebrating on the thirteenth. I think this may actually be my first party."

Julia put her hand on her mouth. Ed reached out and put his hand on Junior's arm. "Hey, we're sorry."

Junior waved him off and rubbed her neck. "No, don't be silly. I'm just overreacting. I mean, it isn't as though we needed anything. I mean, I had my own house. I graduated high school early. It was good." She looked at both of them and nodded. "Besides, it was such a big deal for the littlies when it was their day. Mom made sure the cake had a few different flavors. She was the master of the Neapolitan cake. She would even mix up the flavors on the outside, so it would fool us each year. Sometimes it was straight, but most of the time, the frosting and the cake flavor didn't match."

"I'll bet chocolate/strawberry was the best," Julia said.

Junior nodded. "Oh man, yeah. The chocolate cake with strawberry icing was practically perfect."

"Well, I'm going to pig out tonight on whatever it is they have down there." Julia patted her stomach. "I think I lost ten pounds since cross-country started, and I wasn't even trying. I can't seem to stop eating." From there, the conversation drifted as conversations do.

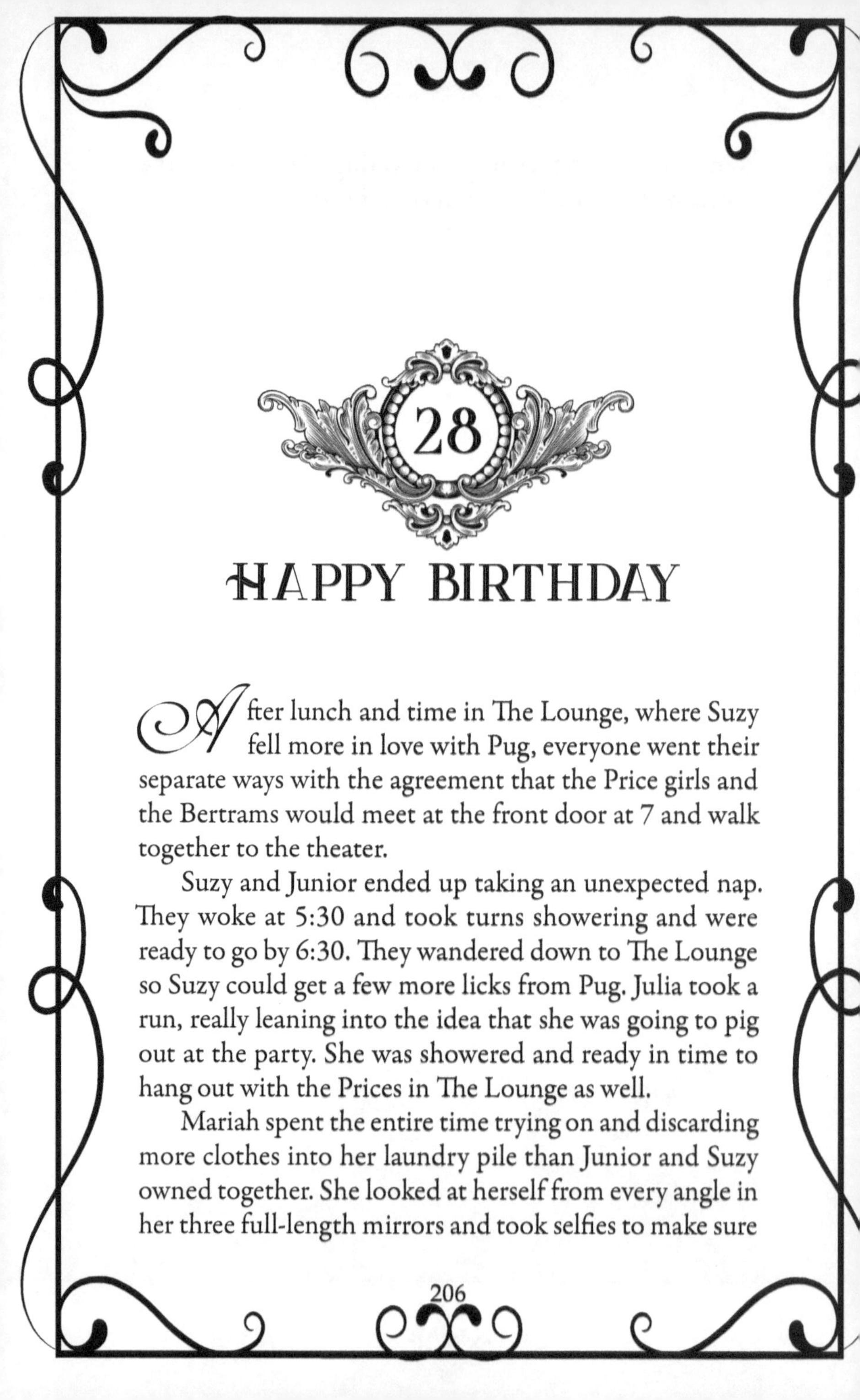

28

HAPPY BIRTHDAY

After lunch and time in The Lounge, where Suzy fell more in love with Pug, everyone went their separate ways with the agreement that the Price girls and the Bertrams would meet at the front door at 7 and walk together to the theater.

Suzy and Junior ended up taking an unexpected nap. They woke at 5:30 and took turns showering and were ready to go by 6:30. They wandered down to The Lounge so Suzy could get a few more licks from Pug. Julia took a run, really leaning into the idea that she was going to pig out at the party. She was showered and ready in time to hang out with the Prices in The Lounge as well.

Mariah spent the entire time trying on and discarding more clothes into her laundry pile than Junior and Suzy owned together. She looked at herself from every angle in her three full-length mirrors and took selfies to make sure she liked what she saw. Never really satisfied, but resigned that she looked "hot enough" in her mini-skirt/cardigan combo, she closed the door to her room at 7:01, determined to make the evening about her.

She was disappointed to discover her sister and the Prices were not standing by the door looking at their watches and tapping their toes as she suspected they would be. Instead, she heard laughter coming from The Lounge. She crept as silently as her stilettoed feet would allow, only to discover that she could have been wearing a bell and the women in the room would not have noticed. Candy was holding court, telling some kind of story using the Pug voice she once promised to only use in front of family. Her mother had never broken a promise, and Mariah did not like what that meant.

She stomped into the room, making as much noise as she could. "So, you want to be late for your own party? Wow. Selfish much?" She turned and walked out.

The four of them watched her walk away. After ten seconds of silence, Julia rolled her eyes and said, "Told you."

"Oh, I hate it when she acts like that," Candy said.

"Mom. Really? Then you must hate her every day."

"I don't hate her, darling. I hate her actions. It's different." She waved them away. "Now go. Have fun. Be safe." She swung her legs onto the couch and rolled onto her back. She patted her chest and Pug crawled up there. "We're very tired and going to nap."

"At 7?"

"Yes, dear. I'm going to nap at 7. It could turn into a whole night of sleep. You'll have to find out what happened when you return." She kissed her hand three times and blew it in the direction of the girls. She did one more. "That one is a special one for you, Junior. Happy Birthday."

Junior reached out, caught it, and placed her hand on her cheek. "Thanks, Candy."

They turned toward the door. "Midnight!" Candy shouted. "Tommy knows you will all turn into pumpkins at midnight and must be back by then."

"Got it, Mom," Julia said as she held up her hand on the way out of the door.

"Goodnight, Candy. Goodnight, Pug," Suzy said.

"Goodnight Moon," Candy replied.

By the time they got to the door, it was wide open. Mariah was waiting outside, looking angry. The girls all slid on their shoes. Junior bent over to tie her All-Stars up. Mariah watched them and assessed their outfits. They all wore jeans and tees. Julia and Suzy had their hair up while Junior had hers down, like always, with a scarf around her neck. Julia wore a little makeup, but the Prices did not. Suzy and Junior started walking toward the access gate.

The Bertrams fell into step about ten feet behind the other two. "I can't believe this is what you are choosing to wear. I mean, with them," Mariah pointed ahead with her chin, "I expect hillbilly chic, but you know better."

Julia stopped, sensing things could get out of hand. She turned and looked at Mariah. "We're going to a birthday party at our brother's house."

"I'm not saying you needed to skank out or anything, but I mean," she twirled around, "a little effort goes a long way. Other people will be there. You could at least try. We already have to spend the whole night explaining why we have some trailer trash charity case living with us, now I'll have to explain why my sister is choosing to dress like a bum."

Julia knotted her right hand into a fist and stepped forward and whispered into her sister's ear. "I'm going to pretend I didn't hear any of this." She looked ahead, making sure the Prices had not stopped walking. They were well out of earshot, but Julia kept her voice to a whisper. "I don't know what kind of demon crawled inside you and makes you act this way, but I swear to god, if you try to embarrass them tonight, I will make the rest of your life miserable. Do you think I don't know about the rigged back door? I wonder what Dad will say about that, or Dr. Grant, or James, or better yet, Nor..."

All the worst-case scenarios that could possibly happen raced through Mariah's mind. She said with gritted teeth, "Fine." She turned and started walking.

Julia came up behind Mariah and draped an arm over her shoulder. "I knew we could find a way to get along." She kissed her sister hard on the cheek and then licked her.

"Gross." Mariah wiped her face and her scowl turned into a smirk.

"You love me."

"Maybe."

"I won't tell."

"You better not."

"Who would believe me anyway?"

They walked in amiable silence until they caught up with the Prices who, upon finally realizing they were alone, waited at the access gate.

"Everything OK?" Junior asked, genuinely concerned.

Mariah plastered on her biggest, brightest smile. "Peachy keen." She walked up to Junior and slid her arm under Junior's, locking them together at the elbow. "Let's party, birthday girl."

Junior, not one to look a gift horse in the mouth, smiled back and nodded. "Yeah, let's party." For the record, Junior had no idea what that actually meant. In the Venn diagram of life experiences, the part where partygoing and being kissed crossed over, there was a giant empty space.

When they arrived at the theater, they discovered that Tommy and Yates had either hired staff, or bribed some college boys with free food and drink, to dress like old-timey ushers and act as servers and docents to give full tours of the fully renovated theater. One of them stood watch outside and spoke into his walkie-talkie as the group approached.

The front panes of the glass doors had the blinds drawn, but the sounds from inside could not be contained. The sound of muffled music came through, and it was clear that the lobby was well lit, and shadows of plenty of guests could be seen through the shade. Junior was sure Yates said not to leave The Park until 7, but she didn't know that meant she would be the last to arrive.

The young man looked right at Junior as though he knew who she was, although she was sure she had never seen him before, and said, "Happy Birthday." He opened the door and stepped aside to let her group in. Suzy and the Bertrams went in first.

Junior had a best-case scenario image in her head based on movies and books and a conflicting worst-case scenario image as well. The first was streamers, balloons, a small cake, and a hanging sign that read "Happy Birthday." The second was dust and junk lying around, as she knew they were renovating the place.

Instead, when they walked into the lobby, she put her hand over her heart and immediately felt tears well in her eyes. Maggie and Aaron were already there smiling impishly, as they were in on this ruse and played along earlier that day. The Crawfords were there. Mariah had already walked over to Hank. Ed was standing next to Mary but had maneuvered Julia in between them. He held up his phone that had Bill's face on the screen. Tommy and Yates, dressed in negative tuxedos, Yates in white with black tie and Tommy in black with white tie, applauded. There were many people she had never met. They formed a semi-circle around the entrance. The music had changed, and the whole room sang "Happy Birthday" with Bill's recorded voice from the video on Ed's phone being slightly off the pace.

Junior reached out with her other hand, and Suzy took it. There were balloons, but they were massive, clear balloons that seemed to have lights inside them, and they were tied down with, or for those that were at the ceiling, had tails that were made from scarves. All kinds of scarves of all kinds of materials and colors.

When the singing ended and hugs were given and Junior wiped away her tears for the seemingly millionth time, Yates came in for a final hug and whispered, "The scarves are all for you when this is over. Happy Birthday." Of course, the tears started flowing again, but he wiped them away and said, "Let me give you the tour."

The cake stood on its own table. It had four tiers. She had been to weddings with smaller cakes. The 1 and 7 that sat atop the smallest tier had sparklers sticking out of them, ready to be lit. There was a buffet-style setup for the food. All the food was finger food or miniature versions of regular-sized foods. They got all the things she loved. The silverware and dinnerware were real. Both of her imaginary versions of this event featured plastic flatware and paper plates, so seeing plates and utensils nicer than what she had at home in Unincorporated Nowhere being used as party favors was a bit overwhelming.

The hallway from the lobby to the main theater had pictures of "famous Juniors" all over it. Robert Downey, Sammy Davis, Dale Earnhardt, O'Shea Jackson, Lucille Ball, and so on down the line until the final picture was of Junior herself. It was a candid shot from just earlier in the day when she, Aaron, Maggie, and Suzy were on campus. She looked up at Yates, who said, "I was in disguise."

"If the theatre business doesn't work out, you can always become a private investigator." Junior laughed.

The doors to the main theater were open. The stage had been converted into a dance floor with a DJ standing by. There were more glowing balloons, and this time they were tied down with ribbons and weighted anchors all around the edge of the stage to try to keep people from falling off.

"We have the public bathrooms working, but you can use ours. You know where it is. We know there isn't really a ton of places for people to sit in big groups and talk, but we decided last minute that we didn't want everyone up in our space, so you and your pals can go up there, and that is it."

"You got it." She nodded as she took it all in. They arrived at the foot of the stage. Yates held out his hand and escorted her up. He led her over to the center of the stage as the guests filed in. He walked over and took the microphone from the DJ. "Thanks, everyone, for coming to celebrate the newest addition to our bizarre little family."

The assembled guests applauded. Junior rubbed her scarf, smiled, and bowed.

"I know that not all of you know our little Junior yet, but by the end of the night, I'm sure you'll all love her as we do." More applause. "Well, let's get this party started. Mr. DJ, if you please."

The opening guitar slide from Tesla's "Heaven's Trail" blasted from the surround sound speakers in the theater. Junior mouthed, "No way" as the sound system was so loud, there was no way her voice would be heard.

"Yes way," he replied. They both bobbed their heads and swayed as the opening lyrics started. By the time the song began in earnest and the drums came in, almost everyone else in attendance was on stage headbanging along to Junior's favorite band, save Hank and Mariah, who had slipped away as the crowd moved from the lobby to the main theater.

Their absence was not noted for some time as the eclectic selection from the DJ kept people happy. Junior, not one to have ever danced with someone to whom she was not related, found that she enjoyed having more than a sibling and her mother present for the event. The DJ kept things going for an hour and a half, music cranked at concert level, whipping people up into a frenzy of dancing. Junior bounced around from group to group, getting hugs and twirls from friends, family, and strangers. She let herself go and danced to songs she had never heard but found that she loved. She reminded herself to get the playlist so she could lock the night into her memory forever. Eventually, just before nine, Tommy grabbed the mic and asked everyone to move back to the lobby for cake. Junior, having been the only one there who never sat down or left the dance floor, actually felt her knees buckle on the stairs. Ed was standing beside the stairs as she was coming down. He reached his hand up and she took it. They locked fingers and eyes.

"You OK?" he asked her once her feet were on solid ground.

"I think so. I've just never danced that long or that hard before."

"Here." He handed her the cup that was in his other hand. "Drink this. You're probably dehydrated and over-heated. It's lemonade. Not ideal, but we can get you some water in the lobby."

She took the drink and drank it slowly, resisting the urge to knock it back. "Thanks." She handed the empty cup back to him and, realizing she was still holding his hand, let go and looked down, rubbing her neck.

At that point, they realized they were the last two people in the theater. "Shall we?" Ed offered his arm.

"Yes, let's." She slipped her hand into the crook of his elbow, and they walked up the aisle toward the lobby.

Mary Crawford had spent the majority of the evening trying to make sure Ed had a full view of her cleavage, only to be constantly disappointed whenever he looked over her head or shimmied away to dance with his brother, or sister, or anyone else. She stood at the exit door and watched the events unfold in the theater. She was not at all pleased by what she saw.

When they arrived, Yates waved Junior over to the cake. The sparklers were lit, the song was sung, and Junior stood behind her cake, looking through the sparklers at a room full of people who were there for her. Even those she didn't know were singing with passion. Tommy and Yates had the best of friends. When it was time to try to blow out the sparklers and make her wish, she realized her wish had already been granted, which was good news. As it turns out, one cannot blow out sparkler candles.

The cake was cut and served. The music started back up but at a lower volume. Folks were encouraged to dance but could sit in the theater and talk at a reasonable volume. Tommy explained that while they were technically in the business district, there were a handful of neighbors who, like them, lived above their shops, and Tommy and Yates promised them that at 9, things would calm down and the noise would be reasonable. The more mellow nature of the party worked as a way to thin the herd a bit, and by 10, only those who actually knew Junior remained.

Julia had taken a shine to Aaron and had spent much of her time on the dance floor, finding ways to dance as near him as possible. While there was no way to talk out there, she found that he was happy to chat when they had cake. His interest in The Park was an open door to a conversation that lasted so long, they found themselves sitting on the floor in the lobby as Julia ate her third piece of cake.

It was only when he had to excuse himself to use the restroom that Julia realized she had not seen Mariah since they arrived. She Nancy Drewed her way into the main theater, where she spied Junior and Ed on the dance floor doing their best version of middle school slow dancing while Mary Crawford, who was dancing with Tommy, glared at them over his shoulder. Yates and Maggie were sitting on the edge of the stage, engrossed in some kind of conversation that involved a lot of nodding from Maggie and hand waving from Yates. Aaron came up behind her as she lurked in the darkness.

He whispered in her ear, "What are we doing?"

She jumped a little and covered her own mouth to stifle a scream, although, while the music was much quieter than before, there was little chance the dancers would have heard anything. "I'm looking for my sister," she whispered back.

"Is it a secret mission?"

"Sort of."

"Can I come with?"

"Sure." She tried to keep the radiant smile that was ready to burst from her face under control, but in truth, she was unable to do so.

The unlikely pair made their way to the private kitchen/former breakroom only to find it empty. "Only one place left to look." She looked up with her eyes.

"Outer space?" Aaron joked.

"Yep. The launch pad is just upstairs."

"Do we want to go up there though? I mean, if they are up there, I don't suspect they are playing Scrabble."

Julia considered this. It is true she knew what her sister was doing with Hank up there, and on the nights he snuck in through the rigged door, but she didn't really want to know *exactly* what she was doing. "Yeah, maybe not. I mean, they could not even be up there. They could have bailed some time ago."

"Right. It's like Schrödinger's bedroom. Right now, they're both there and not there."

"Smart." Julia nodded. "Wanna dance?"

"Let's." He bowed and waved his hand at the door. "After you."

While she hoped he would have offered her his hand, she was thrilled that he hadn't said no. They danced and made merry.

Meanwhile, upstairs, in Schrödinger's bedroom, Mariah was asleep on the bathroom floor, and Hank was getting ready to finally join the party. While the imaginings of Aaron and Julia had not exactly come to pass, there was no way they could have known what happened afterward. Mariah had become violently ill and spent the majority of the evening retching. Hank, not sure exactly what to do, stalked the festivities that were happening just below him on Instagram and sent messages back and forth with his sister who, while sympathetic to his plight, did not want to leave Junior alone with her own attempted conquest.

Between her covert shots and the overt shots on social media, Hank came to the realization that the mousy girl from the south, when she relaxed and had fun, had a glow about her. There was a sense of playful innocence there that he found appealing. In shot after shot, she was dancing with wild abandon. When it wasn't obscured by hair flowing freely, there was a huge, joyous, alluring smile on her face.

"Mariah," Hank said as he stood at the bathroom door. He looked at his paramour, wrapped in a blanket, with a towel as a pillow. "Mariah," he said again, louder this time. He shook his head and mumbled to himself, "Can't hold your booze. How embarrassing." He walked away from her, leaving her just where she was, checked his hair in the mirror, and went downstairs to see if he could help his sister with her problem.

He came down the stairs and headed for the lobby to make it seem as though he was just getting a quick snack, sneaking away from the party. He came into the main theater, where the remaining party-goers were all on stage dancing in a big circle to some 90s boy band. The fact remains that no matter what one's favorite band is, or what kind of music one likes, when a boy band plays at a party or a club, everyone dances and somehow knows the words. Well, almost everyone. Hank thought the talent of the band and the quality of the fun they were having were incongruous. Still, he plastered on a smile and walk/danced his way down the aisle and joined the circle, stepping between Ed and Junior. He lip-synced words approximating the song, making it seem as though he knew more than the chorus of each song, and pretended to have a blast.

Sensing he had a good thing going, the DJ blended one boy band into another, and the group cheered. This went on for a while. Hank took Junior's hand and twirled her around a few times, trying to imprint himself on her memory in some way. Unfortunately for him, Junior liked the spinning and dancing with one person enough that she spun out of one of his twirls into the middle of the circle. She proceeded to dance up to each person and grabbed them and twirled and spun. She laughed and swung and was simply the human embodiment of joy. While he was defeated in that moment, he had to admit, the glow that he saw online was nothing when compared to seeing it in real life.

Later, as the DJ announced it would be the last dance, Hank swaggered over to Junior and held out his hand, "May I have this dance?"

She looked up at him and smiled. She tucked her hair behind her ears and touched her scarf. "I don't think so."

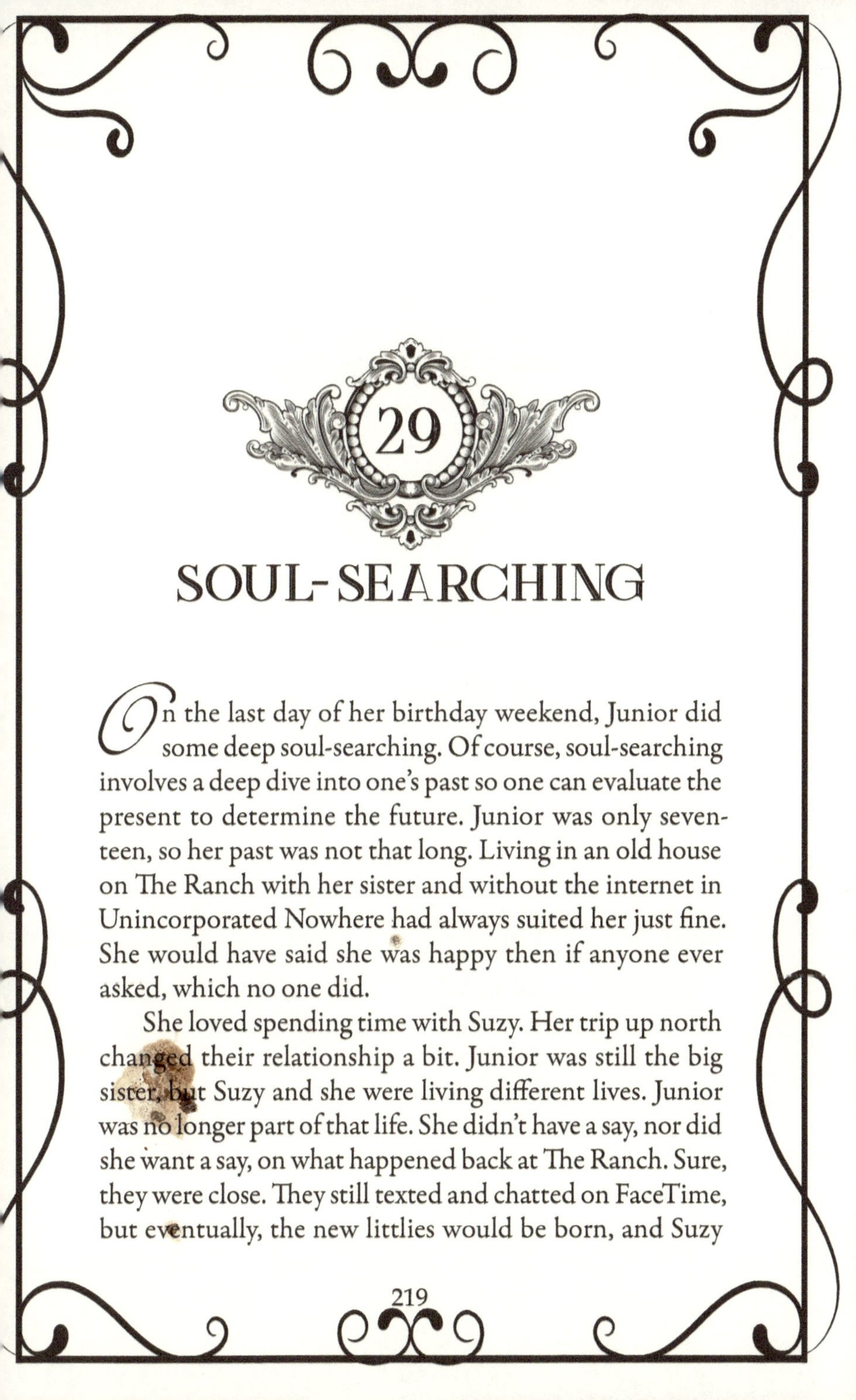

29

SOUL-SEARCHING

On the last day of her birthday weekend, Junior did some deep soul-searching. Of course, soul-searching involves a deep dive into one's past so one can evaluate the present to determine the future. Junior was only seventeen, so her past was not that long. Living in an old house on The Ranch with her sister and without the internet in Unincorporated Nowhere had always suited her just fine. She would have said she was happy then if anyone ever asked, which no one did.

She loved spending time with Suzy. Her trip up north changed their relationship a bit. Junior was still the big sister, but Suzy and she were living different lives. Junior was no longer part of that life. She didn't have a say, nor did she want a say, on what happened back at The Ranch. Sure, they were close. They still texted and chatted on FaceTime, but eventually, the new littlies would be born, and Suzy would be consumed with that and with this Ricardo boy. While Junior couldn't imagine being a Price and having time for romance on The Ranch, she gave Suzy all the support she could.

She missed Bill like a phantom limb. She would have a funny story or an idea to tell him and would be sad when she couldn't. She had taken to actually writing letters on the weekends, giving him weekly updates of what she assumed were silly problems to someone who was learning how to shoot weapons and go to war. Still, she wrote the letters and sent them out every Monday morning when she was on campus.

She loved her family. Of that there was no doubt. However, she had to admit that while she was often surrounded by people and could have company whenever she wished, she was actually, maybe, just a bit lonely. It is true that one can be quite lonely in a room full of people, especially when those people are all blood relatives who think they know everything about everyone else already, and so they have stopped asking any questions.

This long look made her realize that loneliness had become a default setting. She was programmed to think that she deserved to be lonely, and so she was. She liked her privacy, of course. In fact, she sighed with relief when Suzy's train pulled away. While having Suzy there was delightful, she had almost forgotten not only what it was like to have to share a bathroom with anyone in general; she had nearly forgotten that Suzy thought that closets, dressers, and hampers were the natural enemy of clothes and so, to keep them safe, left them strewn about.

She looked through the social media shots of her birthday party. She had been so caught up in everything that she didn't take one picture herself. Thankfully, she was born of a generation who were afraid that a thing didn't actually happen if it was not captured digitally. She downloaded and saved hundreds of pictures and added them to her digital picture frame. She loved watching the images of a life she never thought she would have mixed in with the life she always knew. She sat alone in her room at The Park and realized, for the first time ever, an undeniable truth that many people much older and seemingly wiser than Junior Price never realize: being alone and being lonely do not have to be the same thing.

30

DRIVING MISS JULIA

$\mathcal{A}$s promised, Junior started taking Julia driving after her birthday. Julia did some digging and found that she only needed a licensed driver in her household to ride around with her. Ultimately it would be Candy who signed off on the hours, so Junior insisted that she be given permission to do so.

When Junior approached her during lunch on Sunday and asked, Candy was quick to give her blessing. She said, "That would be wonderful, Junior. Thank you so much, dear." Then she lowered her voice and whispered, "I just barely survived my time in the barrel with Mariah; as you know, we tell everyone she decided she didn't want to drive. I just don't think I can do it again. I know Julia is going to be much better, but still."

Junior started out driving on the first day they practiced. She wanted to be comfortable with the Jeep, and she wanted to know all of the things she should tell Julia to do. Plus, she wanted to feel safe in her surroundings. She had really only seen a few square blocks of town and campus.

"I didn't really expect it to be like this," Junior said after she completed what felt like a full right-hand turn on the road that was technically going straight. She had both hands on the wheel and had insisted that the music be low enough so they could talk through things without having to shout, as Jeeps are notoriously noisy as is.

"Like what?"

"So curvy and hilly. Town is a grid and campus is too. Except for The Park and the quad, everything is on a little square, and getting lost would be impossible."

"Huh? I never really thought about it that way, but yeah. The Mansfields were notoriously rigid and the Rushworths are, let's just say, not."

"James' family owns all of this?" Junior asked as the road made a sharp left-hand turn, making her understand things a bit more.

"Not anymore. Just like we don't own the whole town anymore. In both cases, everything was designed to the specifications of the family who sold the property to the state. I don't think the Rushworths wanted the area surrounding town to become a city or town or whatever, so they sold the land in ways that required the roads to go around it."

"There must be lots of accidents."

Julia nodded. "Yeah, when we were doing our practice out here, the Driver's Ed teacher said that at least once or twice a year, some dumb, drunk college kids miss a turn and go careening into a field or smash into a tree. When Tommy was in school, I think he was a second-year, a few fourth-years died. It made the state news and everything. There was talk about putting rails up on country roads, but when people realized how expensive that would be, it was quickly dropped."

"Yeah, what's the death of youth compared to a few million dollars that could be spent covering a tax cut?" Junior shook her head. "I'll just never understand." She wiped a tear off her cheek and sniffled. "Sorry." She wiped the other cheek. "I just don't get it. I just want people to do the right thing. Why is doing the right thing so hard for some people? It just makes me so angry and hurt. Sorry. I just..."

Julia touched her shoulder and saw, for the first time, why Junior always wore a scarf. The blotches were spreading up her neck. "Oh hey, I'm sorry. Are you OK? There's a little park just around the next curve if you want to..." She trailed off, leaving it for Junior to decide.

She sniffled some more and nodded. "Yeah, that would be good." They drove in silence for just another mile while Junior tried to get herself together and fretted over the fact that she had not wrapped her scarf tight.

They pulled into what could only be described as the country version of a rest stop. Instead of having any modern facilities, there were two outhouses and a hand-operated pump for water. Instead of sturdy, concrete benches or tables, there were old, somewhat shaky, wooden picnic tables. Junior stopped the car, and they got out. Julia pulled a cooler out of the back seat.

"You packed a cooler?"

"Yeah, well, I wasn't sure how long we'd be, and I'm always, always hungry." She sat on the top of the table and put her feet on the seat.

Junior climbed up and did the same. She started to wrap her scarf tighter.

"You don't have to do that," Julia said while rifling through the cooler. She didn't want to look at Junior while she said it. "I saw. I won't tell." She looked up, smiling, and offered Junior a bag of iced animal crackers.

Junior took the crackers and appreciated the directness and the snack. "Thanks." She stopped winding the scarf and let it hang. She ran her fingers over the rash, feeling the small bumps. "It's not really a secret. I wouldn't lie if anyone asked. It's just that..."

"No one asks. I get it. No one asks me anything either." Julia reached back into the cooler and came out with a can of sweet tea. "Here. I know it isn't the same, but it's portable. I don't know how to make the real stuff."

Junior took it and looked at the side. "Wow. Where'd you get this?"

"The fridge downstairs. Dad asked Betty to get them. Didn't you know?"

She shook her head. "No, she's been making me pitchers of it, and I just fill up my bottle before class. I..." She started to get choked up again. She snorted and laughed. "God, I'm a mess." She wiped her cheeks again. "That is just so nice. I'll thank them both when I see them next."

"That'll be novel. I don't think anyone thanks Dad for anything."

"Except you." She popped the top of the can and took a sip. It was not how she would make it, but it wasn't bad. She made an approving face and nodded at Julia, who was watching to see the results.

"Well, except me. Right. I just think... they do so much for us, you know? Like I said before, I know how lucky I am. Dad didn't need to work, Mom is loaded, and yet he does. He created a business and made his own fortune. He even paid Mom back all the seed money. That company is theirs on paper, but it's really his."

Junior chewed and swallowed her first iced elephant. "That is so awesome. Is that where Tommy and Ed get their contrarian attitudes?"

"Probably. I mean, Dad is so proud of them, but Mom is worried that no one is going to live in the big house. They know Ed has bigger academic goals that will take him away. He loves Mansfield, but he doesn't think he will be taken seriously on campus because of nepotism. They think Mariah will end up with James, which is absurd, but I think they are probably right. She has James whipped already, and if she wants it, it'll be so. He's clueless, but he loves her. We can all see it. So that means she is out of the picture too, meaning they think it has to be either Ed or Tommy. I think they want it to be Tommy, him being the oldest and all. I hear Mom and Norris talking all the time about it. I mean. Hello! I'm right here. This isn't 1814. A woman can be the head of the clan. Mom is."

"Is that what you want? You want the big house and all of that?"

"I think I do. I mean, I'm only sixteen, I know, but I can see myself there. I have so many things I would like to do. We have so much money, we could start the Mansfield Charity. Can you believe we don't have one?"

Junior gave a non-committal shrug. The thought of running a private charity was out of the field of her imagination.

Interpreting the shrug how she wanted, Julia plowed ahead. "I have this idea that I'll get out of here for a few years. NOT go to Mansfield but get out. Go to some HUGE school like James did and do an international program. I'm good at languages. I'm already in advanced Spanish, and I just started French I. I want to be in the world. Figure things out and then, after I have made myself into who I know I can be, I want to come back here and bring that stuff with me. I want to bring Mansfield into the twenty-first century. Right now, the only thing I can think of is a charity wing. I don't even know what we would do, but that's why I need to get out there," she waved her arms around at the world, "and see it all so I can make all of this better."

Junior leaned forward as Julia talked. Julia seemed so free at that moment, and Junior was in awe of the freedom she felt there. It was infectious, and she thought that maybe she might be able to try. "That is so awesome. I mean, really. I see it in your eyes. The way you talk about it, I can just tell that you're going to make it all happen."

Julia smiled at her and exhaled a breath she didn't know she was holding. She deflated a bit as she let it out. "You think so?"

Junior nodded. "I know so."

"Thanks. I just need to get Mom to realize it too. I wish I could just tell them both."

"Well, if you don't mind me saying…" Junior waited for permission before she spoke next. Offering up advice was not her forte.

"Of course. Go." Julia leaned in to show she wanted to hear it.

"Well, you said you and Tom aren't close, but I don't think that's quite true. I think you are. I see how you joke around. He is pretty comfortable with you. He likes you. I mean, of course he loves you, but he likes you too. I think, maybe, you think he likes the boys best because maybe, just maybe, someone else has been making you feel that way."

Julia thought about it for a while and let it sink in. They ate and drank and were quiet. Eventually, Julia nodded. "Yeah. I mean, I think that's probably right, and I think we both know who is the one doing it. You know, she hardly talks to me at all, but she talks about me all the time, or she talks about what it means to be a Mansfield all the time. I just want to tell her once, just once, that I'm a Bertram, not a Mansfield. I mean, yeah, I get it, I am, but I'm a Bertram too. It's just so much, you know? It's like, when would I say it all? How do I even start?"

"Like you said, you're only sixteen. You've got time. Besides, I don't think Tommy plans on running the family, and it sounds like Tom is already trying to recruit Bill to take over the freight company despite having just met him."

"Yeah. He really likes Bill."

"Doesn't he just kind of like everyone? I mean, Tom is just nice, isn't he?"

Julia nodded and smiled. "Yeah, but he really, really likes Bill. I can tell."

"Oh well, if he really, really likes him, then fate has written it."

They both laughed at that and sat in comfortable silence as they finished their snacks. Junior looked at her watch and at the sky. "How many hours of night driving do you have to do?"

Julia perked up. "Really?" She looked up at the sky. "Five!"

"OK. It's clear that my idea of getting my bearings around here is fruitless, as I have absolutely no idea where we are or how to get back. So," she tossed Julia the keys, "let's knock out a few of those hours."

They spent the rest of that first night covering much less important topics, but they talked about so many things. Aaron took center stage for a while; Julia was, despite her big, adult, world-changing ideas, still a teenage girl, and so she asked Junior to see if it was even possible for Aaron to be interested in someone two years younger. Junior doubted it, but she promised to ask. At that moment, she knew that her path to being less lonely would be paved by curvy and twisty back roads on the outskirts of Mansfield.

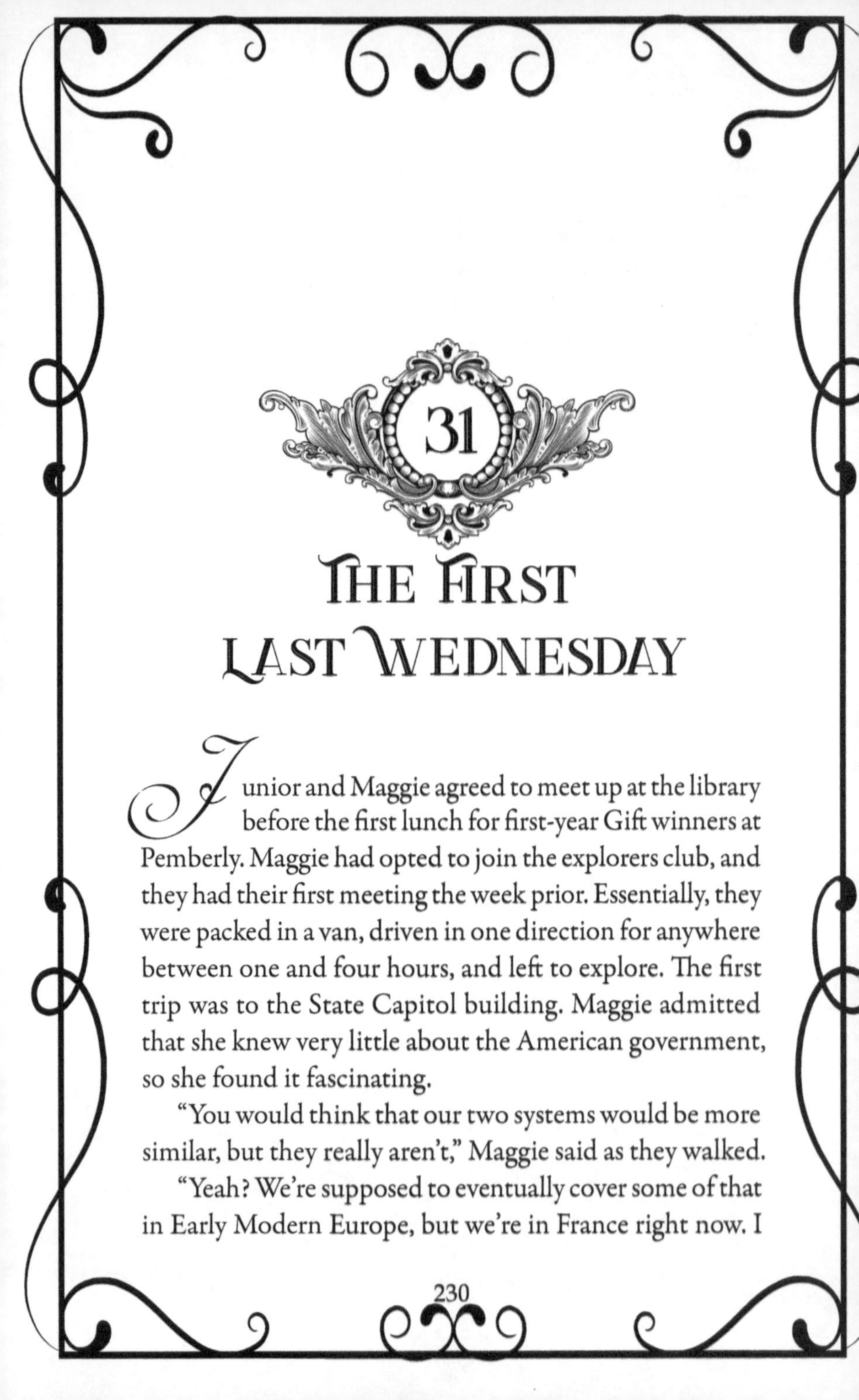

31

The First
Last Wednesday

Junior and Maggie agreed to meet up at the library before the first lunch for first-year Gift winners at Pemberly. Maggie had opted to join the explorers club, and they had their first meeting the week prior. Essentially, they were packed in a van, driven in one direction for anywhere between one and four hours, and left to explore. The first trip was to the State Capitol building. Maggie admitted that she knew very little about the American government, so she found it fascinating.

"You would think that our two systems would be more similar, but they really aren't," Maggie said as they walked.

"Yeah? We're supposed to eventually cover some of that in Early Modern Europe, but we're in France right now. I will be honest and say the only thing I know about the UK government I learned from books and TV shows, so…"

"Actually, surprisingly accurate in many cases."

"Really? Wow. There is nothing here that's remotely accurate. Well, nothing I've seen. A bunch of liars who lie to each other and to everyone so they can raise money to keep the job." She thought about it for a second. "Well, I suppose *The West Wing* is pretty accurate then. That show really kicks the characters who are idealists down until they are just cynics or in jail."

"Cor, pretty grim."

"That's the most British thing I've heard you say." Junior laughed.

"What? Cor?"

"Yeah."

Maggie cranked up her accent to Dick van Dyke campiness levels and said, "Well Guvner, I'll do betta."

"Well, bless your heart," Junior replied in the deepest drawl she could muster.

They went back and forth like that, each of them trying and failing miserably to do the other's accent. By the time they arrived at Pemberly, they were laughing so hard their sides hurt.

Dr. Bennet stood out front greeting students as they arrived. They tried to get their giggles under control as they approached, but that only made them laugh harder. "Hello, ladies. Welcome. Glad to know that you are in fine spirits."

"Hi, Dr. Bennet," they said simultaneously, and while it was not remotely funny, they both burst out into laughter again.

"Well, I can't wait to hear all about it at lunch. Will I need to separate you?"

"No," Maggie said.

"No, Ma'am," Junior said.

"Excellent. Please head into the parlor. We shall dine in there today. I'm sure you both remember the way."

"Yes, Ma'am," they both said and managed to contain their laughter.

Lunch was an entertaining and educational affair. Dr. Bennet asked Gift members to share some information about one of the classes they were taking. Since each of them was in a different rotation, Dr. Bennet thought it could be useful for future terms.

Junior made sure to not go into detail about her Religion course; she remembered the gasp Dr. Bennet let out at Norris' final sermon and was confident that there was no love lost between the two of them. She didn't want to cause any waves as she had a great admiration for Dr. Bennet and an aversion to Norris. Instead, she shared that she admired the way Dr. West approached Early Modern Europe. She asked them all on day one to name a country about which they knew very little and then, she tailored an ongoing research project for each of them that would culminate with a paper and interactive lessons that each student would teach to the rest of the class.

Everyone agreed that was an excellent idea, and hearing about it made them all much more excited about the course. As far as they were all concerned, the description of the course by Junior outshone the vague name of the course. This included Maggie, born when the UK was still in the European Union; it could give her some insider information that could be useful. Even she was reluctant to take that course until Junior let them in on the secret.

Each gift winner illuminated the rest of the group with some amazing tales from each preferred course. The conversation was easy and fun, and before they all knew it, their time was up, and Dr. Bennet had to "return to the real world" as she put it.

As they were filing out, she did call out to Junior. She said, "Junior, if you don't have anything pressing, would you mind staying behind and escorting me back to my office?"

Junior and Maggie gave each other looks that seemed to say, "What?!" and "Why?!" and "Are you in trouble?" and "I hope not" at the same time.

Her mouth said, "Sure. No problem at all." She turned to Maggie, "See you soon." They fist-bumped, and Maggie caught up with the rest of the group who were heading back to Angeline.

"Thank you so much. Just give me a minute, and I'll grab my briefcase."

Junior waited on the front porch as she was trying to soak in the last of the heat. The cool air was already moving in, and for a southern girl from Unincorporated Nowhere, late September felt like what she thought winter would feel like. Of course, she had been warned by her mother that the Mansfield cold was something she couldn't explain, and that she just needed to be prepared. So she stood, her face turned up to face the sun and her eyes closed, when Dr. Bennet closed the door and snapped her out of it.

"Thanks again for waiting."

"It's no problem at all. I just hope everything is all right."

"Why yes, of course, it is." She started walking so they were side by side, and she asked, "I just wondered if I could ask you a few questions about your Religion course."

Junior did everything within her power to keep the groan inside. To this day she wasn't sure if she managed; since there were only two people present, no one can know for sure, but if it did escape, Dr. Bennet chose not to acknowledge it at all because she understood. Junior rubbed her scarf; feeling more secure, she said, "By all means."

"Well, I've been hearing some things about that course. As you know, because you are still in it, a large number of students withdrew after the first week. Based on what I've been told, Dr. Norris is, oh dear, how can I say it..." She made some lip-smacking noises as she thought of the most tactful and appropriate word.

"Dry?" Junior offered.

Dr. Bennet exhaled a sigh of relief. "Yes. Thank you, dear. Dry."

"She really is. We just read, listen to lectures, take tests, and repeat. There isn't much else to it. She's covering everything the syllabus says we will. It isn't exciting at all, but she's thorough. We essentially cover everything twice."

"Hmmm," Dr. Bennet said as she searched for the right thing to ask next. They walked along in silence; Junior was really not trying to get anyone in trouble, least of all Norris. "Well, and I know you are not supposed to really think about this for another year or so, but is there anything about the way that Reverend Norris teaches that would make you feel so inclined to major in theology?"

"Not remotely, Ma'am, but I couldn't say for certain if I would have considered that at all anyway."

"That's fair, but you seemed to take a shine to Early Modern Europe, and you asked the most questions when we brought up Western Political Thought. Did you come here thinking you had an interest in global politics and public policy?"

Junior immediately started shaking her head. "No. Not at all. My high school government teacher was a year from retirement. Mom always said he was just 'holding down his chair' and she would give me other things to read. Novels mostly, some historical fiction or some alternate histories, anything to help me think about the things she thought we should be learning. Then we would talk about them while we were doing things around the house. I always found that interesting, but really, though, it was more about spending time with my mom. I have a lot of siblings, so any one-on-one time was precious."

Dr. Bennet nodded. "I get it. I'm the middle of five. All girls. My dad was quite a reader, and I loved education, so whenever the rest of the girls were at parties or chasing boys, we had our own fun on the weekends talking about educational theories. Boring, I know, but I don't think I would be here if it weren't for those Friday and Saturday nights in the library with Dad."

"You think those talks are what helped you win The Gift?"

"I do." She nodded as she said it. "I suspect the same is true for you."

They walked for a few more steps in silence. Junior took in what she said and turned it over in her mind. Dr. Bennet stopped as they were approaching her office building. "Well, thank you, Junior. I suspected I knew the answer, but I just wanted to hear it from someone who was in the class."

"Norris isn't in any trouble, is she?"

Dr. Bennet was impressed that Junior didn't ask if she was going to be in trouble or if this conversation would get back to Norris. Most people would be more worried about themselves than someone for whom she didn't really care. She shook her head. "No, dear. Not at all. There isn't really anything I can do, I'm afraid. She has the right to teach her courses however she wishes. We call it academic freedom. As long as she meets the outcomes, which it sounds like she does, there is nothing I can do. I think I will have to play the long game with the *good Reverend*." Junior could hear the sarcasm in her voice as she said it. "I just want to know as much as I can know. It's the only way to do my job." She sighed and then smiled. She reached out her hand, and Junior shook it firmly. "Thank you for the walk and talk, Junior."

"You're welcome, Ma'am. I'll see you next month, if not sooner."

"Yes, dear, of course. My door is always open should you need anything." With that, Dr. Bennet went into her office.

Junior stood, looking around campus. Small groups of students had club meetings on the quad. Others were playing catch with a frisbee. Others still just sat and read or listened to music while engrossed in their phones. The chat with Dr. Bennet left her with lots of feelings about lots of things. She wasn't sure what they all meant. She pulled out her phone and sent a text to the one person she could think of who knew the most about navigating all things Mansfield, both the college and the family.

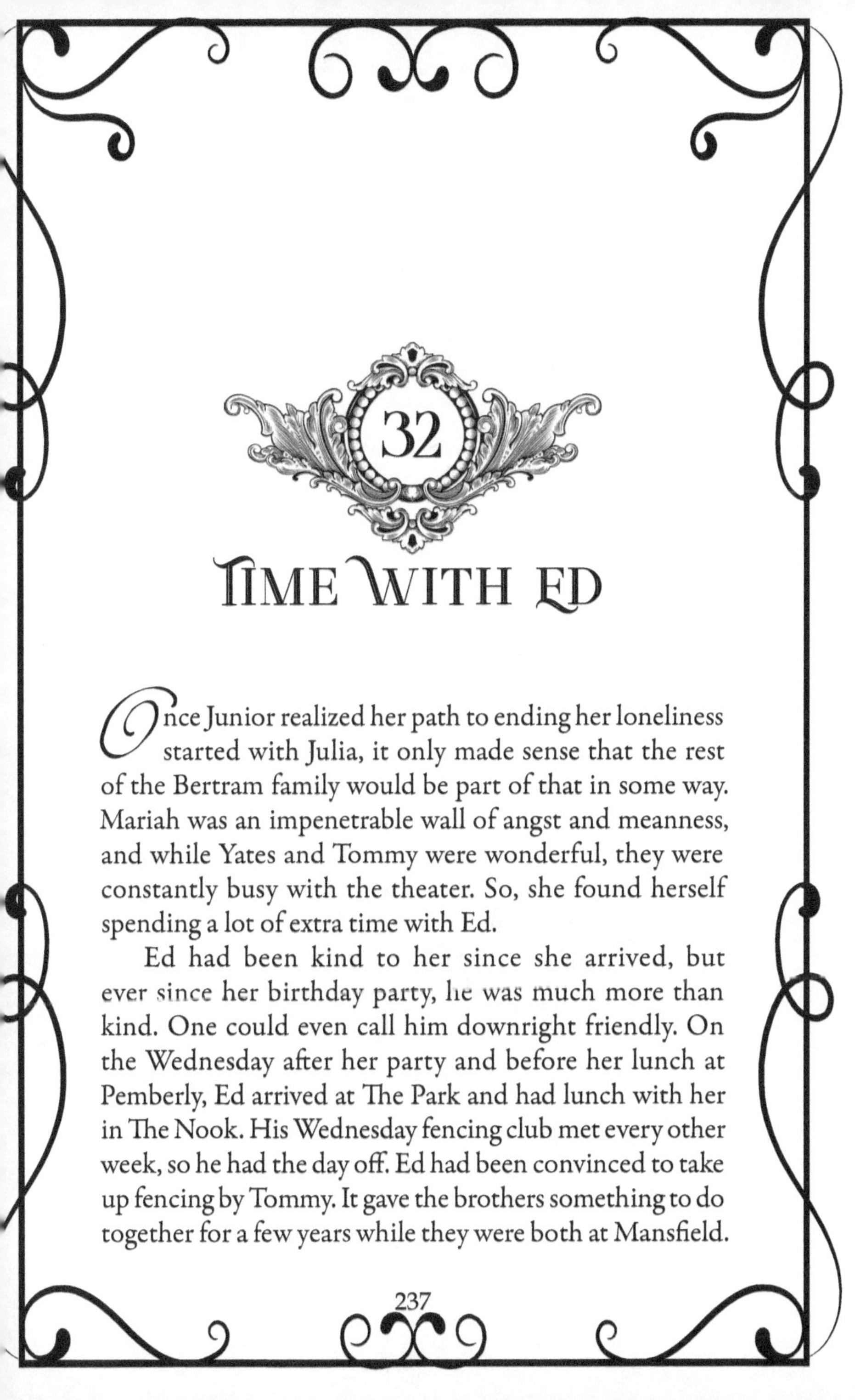

32

Time with Ed

*O*nce Junior realized her path to ending her loneliness started with Julia, it only made sense that the rest of the Bertram family would be part of that in some way. Mariah was an impenetrable wall of angst and meanness, and while Yates and Tommy were wonderful, they were constantly busy with the theater. So, she found herself spending a lot of extra time with Ed.

Ed had been kind to her since she arrived, but ever since her birthday party, he was much more than kind. One could even call him downright friendly. On the Wednesday after her party and before her lunch at Pemberly, Ed arrived at The Park and had lunch with her in The Nook. His Wednesday fencing club met every other week, so he had the day off. Ed had been convinced to take up fencing by Tommy. It gave the brothers something to do together for a few years while they were both at Mansfield.

Tommy took up fencing because everyone who could fence ended up with a part in the yearly Shakespeare play. In fact, during Ed's first year and Tommy's third, Ed was recruited to play a soldier in *Henry IV Part I,* where Tommy's turn as Hotspur resulted in Ed's stage death. Now, as a third-year himself, Ed found that acting did not suit him, but fencing did. He enjoyed it very much.

Junior was quite surprised when she entered The Nook, notebook in hand and ready to spend another lunch alone writing a letter to Bill, only to find Ed sitting with his back to the window across from the seat where she normally sat. He was sipping a drink and reading. The light from the window backlit him in such a way that she might have thought he was a figment of her imagination, but he looked up, said hello, and smiled.

After they ate, they spent the rest of that day walking around The Park, chatting about anything and everything. The time slipped by so quickly that Ed was still on the grounds by the time dinner was served in The Nook. They took the same seats and were joined by Julia, who, having had a big day at practice, where she was named team captain, was thrilled to find them there. They fell into an easy conversation where they both promised to attend her first home meet the following Thursday. The conversation lasted until 7:30 when Ed had to go as he was on call that night for his dorm and had to start his first walk-through by 8.

The following Thursday and for several other days during the fall, Junior and Ed found themselves spending time sitting in collapsible camping chairs on the cross-country course, waiting for Julia to run by. Cross-country is really not a spectator sport, inasmuch as it is a sport where the supporters of the runners sit in one place and entertain themselves for a while with sudden bursts of applause and shouting. They passed many hours sitting, chatting, and falling into such comfort that Junior could occasionally be seen in his presence with her scarf hanging loosely, bare neck exposed, completely hive-free.

For home meets, they would wait until Julia was done, and they would go out to get ice cream or whatever Julia craved. Yes, they have unlimited supplies of everything at The Park, but sometimes, it was nice to just be out and about with friends. When they could attend away meets, which was usually only on the weekends, Julia was required to ride back with the team on the bus. Junior and Ed, therefore, found themselves driving around the winding roads in Ed's truck, with the music on low so they could talk.

They discovered that their musical tastes were quite different. As a historian, he appreciated late twentieth-century rock music; he just didn't love it. He thought the songs were often far too long and had guitar solos for the sake of guitar solos. However, when he just wanted to sing along, he preferred pop music. The bouncier and sillier the better. He read heavy books and thought all the time about the implications of feudalism on the modern European economy, or how religious zealotry actually had some positive effects on the development of modern American thought, and other things like that; when trying to relax, he just liked stuff that wasn't trying too hard to do too much. They found common ground with what Junior called Bubble Gum and what Ed called Power Pop. They agreed that the guitarists were mostly pretty good, and that led them into a rabbit hole of random guitar player-based knowledge that seemed superfluous to everyone in their vicinity.

They never seemed to run out of topics of conversation. Ed was naturally inquisitive, and Junior was clearly academically inclined, thus, they talked and talked until the clock told them it was time to stop. So, because of all of that, Junior texted Ed after her conversation with Dr. Bennet, asking him to meet her in the fourth stack after fencing was over.

She was writing Bill a letter when he arrived. The acoustics in the stacks were such that no one could really sneak up on anyone. Since she knew he would be entering soon, she held up one finger as she finished up her thought. He came in carrying two coffees, saw her upraised finger over her hunched form, and took a seat in one of the high-back chairs without a word.

When she finished up, she looked over at him and smiled. "Coffee? For me? Bless your heart."

"How is one to know when you mean that and when you mean the opposite?" He reached out with the coffee. She took it.

Their fingers touched for less than a second. Junior's mouth immediately went dry, and she felt the heat crawl up from her collar bones. She brushed her scarf, relieved to discover she had kept it tight since lunch. Her mental hard drive stored the information for later. She sipped her coffee to recover her senses.

"Well, I suppose you can't really know since the tone is supposed to sound the same no matter what. Right then, I was just joking around." She sipped again, relieved to have an actual problem to solve. "But why was I joking around? I mean, I do genuinely thank you for getting me the coffee, so why joke about it? Hmmm." She looked past him at the wall and tried to work it out. "I mean, I don't really use it all the time. I think it's because it can mean so many things, and people use it to be mean. I was just kidding, but that could be mean too..." she trailed off. She could feel the heat crawling up her neck.

Ed reached out and touched her knee. "Forget it. Sorry. I was just kidding too. I knew you weren't being mean."

Her eyes moved from the wall to his face, and she saw his concern and sincerity. This look crashed into the feeling of ... something, radiating from his hand on her knee. She knew, too, that he was touching her in a sincere and forthright way, but there was still something there. She wasn't sure how to handle it. She closed her eyes and took a breath. The heat on her neck felt like it was going to leave burn marks. She wiped away a stray tear. He released his hand. "Sorry. It's just," she sniffed, "I don't like to be mean, you know, and I never would want..."

"You could never be mean in a million years. Forget it. I was kidding. I knew you were kidding."

"Yeah, I'm bad at kidding, I guess." She tried to smile.

"Well, maybe you need to practice more?" he suggested.

She shook her head both as an answer to him and as a way to clear her head. "I'm fine. Really. Some people are sarcastic, and some people are not. I'm not. It's OK. I can play to my strengths. You know, being nice and telling the truth. That wins me all the friends."

"See, you have a bit of sarcasm in you."

"I could paint a self-portrait in self-deprecation."

"And a poet."

She blushed. She smiled. "Thank you for understanding."

"Of course. So, I can't imagine you asked me here to talk about your sarcasm abilities."

"I did not." She took a sip of the coffee. Took a breath. Felt her neck cool off. The conversation and her feelings had righted themselves. "So, I saw Dr. Bennet today."

He nodded. "The Gift lunch thing?"

"Yes, indeed. The Gift lunch thing. Well, she had me stay after and had me walk her to her office so she could ask me a bit about Norris' class."

Ed did a bomb drop whistle.

Junior shook her head. "She was just looking for an honest assessment of things. Norris isn't in any trouble or anything."

"Yeah, I know. Academic freedom." Ed did air quotes with his finger. "I've talked to her about it. I have a few students on my floor who know of our family connections and have complained to me."

"You talked to Norris about it? She knows?"

Ed nodded. "She knows. She knew before I even got to her. She said," Ed switched to his best Norris impression, "'Edmund, I know exactly what I'm doing, and I would thank you to mind your own business.' She went on and on about academic freedom and that she couldn't be touched, blah blah. It was pretty frustrating. So, you know, it was like a normal conversation with her."

Junior laughed at that. She was always glad to hear that other people, including those who actually shared blood with Norris and who had grown up around her, also found her problematic. "I wish I could understand her."

Ed shook his head at that. "No. No, you don't. I've spent 19 years trying to understand her. I'm the one in the family who is most like her, and yet, I'm no closer to understanding why she is so mean to me, and to everyone really, except Mariah. Mariah walks on the clouds, and the rest of us wallow around in the filth. The best thing to do is for you to do what you are doing. Just tolerate her. She is only tolerating the rest of us, so turnabout is fair play." Ed's face was turning pink, and he wasn't looking at Junior anymore. He was looking off at the far wall, clearly imagining some indignity she made him suffer.

"Sorry. I didn't mean to upset you."

Ed brought his focus back to Junior, and seeing the concern on her face, he softened. "No. No. I'm sorry. We were talking about you. I didn't mean to hijack it with my own stuff."

"Not at all. It's good. I always want to listen. You just seem really upset, and I wasn't trying to do that, but my thing can wait if you need to get this off your chest."

"There's nothing more I can say. Really. She just drives me nuts, and whenever I get going on her, I can't stop it. So, I'm sorry. Really."

He reached out and placed his hand on her knee again. Once again, she felt a jolt of electricity run through her whole body. She took a sip of coffee and closed her eyes as she did so in an effort to collect herself. He took his hand off her knee. She tried not to exhale when he did so. She opened her eyes. He was sitting back in his chair, attentive, ready to listen.

"Seriously, I didn't actually mean to talk about Norris at all, but she was the reason I was talking to Dr. Bennet, and there was something else she said that I wanted to run past you."

"Shoot."

"Well, it actually started when Julia and I were out driving one day." She told him all about the conversation they had about the guard rails and how upset she got over it. "So, then today, Dr. Bennet pointed out that I really seemed animated when I was talking about the political classes, and she thought it might be something to consider. I know I'm not supposed to pick a major until next year, and I've only been in school for a short time, but it would be silly for me to leave this stone unturned."

"Well, there are quite a few options." Ed leaned forward again and launched into some of the opportunities that Mansfield had for political science majors.

Junior asked a lot of questions. Some of which he could answer and some they had to look up. He asked her questions about different interests and things she thought she might do and what kinds of public policy she was interested in changing. They talked until they ran out of coffee and continued talking as they walked to The Park, where Ed stayed through dinner.

That night, back in her room alone, Junior tried to process everything she was feeling. She called Suzy, who upon hearing that Junior had some confusing feelings about Ed, launched into a thirty-minute diatribe about how Ricardo was giving her mixed messages, which ended abruptly when their father burst into Suzy's room to tell her that it was time. The twins had decided they couldn't wait for the C-section.

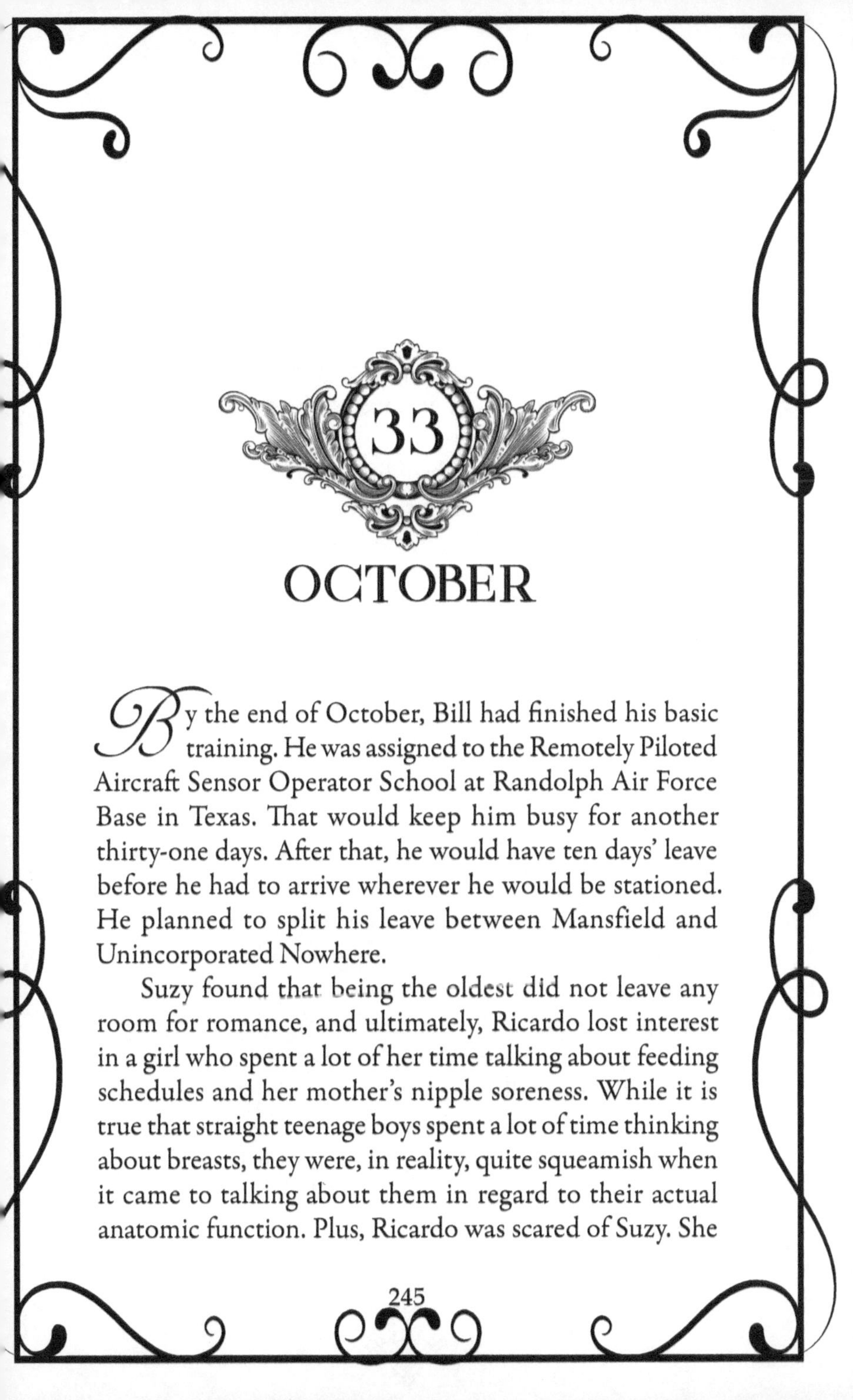

33

OCTOBER

By the end of October, Bill had finished his basic training. He was assigned to the Remotely Piloted Aircraft Sensor Operator School at Randolph Air Force Base in Texas. That would keep him busy for another thirty-one days. After that, he would have ten days' leave before he had to arrive wherever he would be stationed. He planned to split his leave between Mansfield and Unincorporated Nowhere.

Suzy found that being the oldest did not leave any room for romance, and ultimately, Ricardo lost interest in a girl who spent a lot of her time talking about feeding schedules and her mother's nipple soreness. While it is true that straight teenage boys spent a lot of time thinking about breasts, they were, in reality, quite squeamish when it came to talking about them in regard to their actual anatomic function. Plus, Ricardo was scared of Suzy. She already had one foot into womanhood, and he was looking for a girl.

Mr. Price treated the arrival of the newest members of the family with the same sense of urgency that he did with the previous eight children. That is to say, he didn't care much. His nap routine was slightly altered because twins, it turns out, do not always like to sleep at the same time. So, he opened up the other house so he could have some "peace and quiet."

Because Bill was legally obligated to stay where he was, this put pressure on Junior to drop out of school, enroll in the community college, and help. Well, that is to say, Junior put pressure on herself. Fran, knowing this was happening inside her eldest daughter's head, said in no uncertain terms that Junior was not welcome on The Ranch. If she arrived, she would be sent away. This conversation was full of tears for both the Senior and Junior Price, but they agreed it was for the best.

Thus, Fran arranged with Candy to have Junior stay through all of the remaining holiday breaks. Candy was thrilled that she could "help out a dear sister" in such a way. So, in an effort to pay her respects to a matriarch, even if it was not her own mother, Junior took to spending time with Candy and Pug in The Lounge for a few hours a day a few days a week. The conversations swung wildly from a graphic description of Pug's family tree to Junior trying to explain how to turn off the annoying app alerts on Candy's phone. The two fell into an easy friendship. It took a few months for Mariah to realize what was going on, and when she did, she made a very big deal out of it in an attempt to distract everyone from her own bad news. More on that later.

Julia and Junior's driving excursions continued with regularity. They talked about almost anything and everything that came to mind. Julia realized, shortly after Junior's birthday party, that her crush on Aaron was just that, a crush. While she and Junior were close in age, they were miles apart in maturity and experience, which meant she and Aaron were even farther apart. She was sure that nothing could come of it. When she expressed this to Junior, she did so without remorse or sadness.

She said, "You know, there's something special about having short, imaginary relationships. I don't need to make a breakup box, and we can stay friends."

Truthfully, Julia was an excellent driver, and Junior never once had to tell her what to do. Even when they were caught out in a horrific rainstorm while on the highway, Julia knew enough to simply slow down, put her hands at ten and two, and drive carefully with the lights on. By October 30, she had earned enough hours to have her own driver's license. The first thing she did was go for a drive with Junior. When Junior pointed out that she could go alone if she wished, Julia replied by asking, "Where's the fun in that?" They went out for smoothies. It was Julia's treat as a thank-you.

While it sounds like Junior could not possibly have any more free time, what with her pretty full social life, she and Ed still managed to spend at least a few hours together several times a week. Often it was at Julia's meets, but due to the fact that Wednesdays were relatively free, they often spent time in the stacks, on the quad, or just at the theater helping Yates and Tommy get ready for opening night. Those hot flashes she felt when she and Ed were together had neither ceased nor diminished; sometimes, she found that she could even feel her skin prickle when he looked at her a certain way.

It was Yates who finally addressed what he called "the elephant under her scarf" one morning in mid-October. She walked into The Nook one Tuesday morning for a late breakfast to see him sitting across from her normal seat in the window. It was such an unexpected pleasure that she bounded over to him for a hug. While she still didn't like being picked up and swung around, she did like it when he hugged her like a brother. Since he was sitting, she knew she could get one without the other.

"To what do I owe this honor? Did Tommy need something from his room again? At what point is he just going to move it all to the theater?" she asked after they broke apart and she walked over to get a muffin and some coffee.

He waited until she sat down. "Nothing like that at all, although you make an excellent point. One I have made repeatedly, and which maybe you could try to make some time as well. The truth is, I'm here for you."

"Really? What did I do?"

"Well, it's two things, really. The first is that we need to figure out what you're going to wear on Halloween. It's your virgin show, and while most people get super sultry for a show, I know you would never, ever, remotely be comfortable in most of the clothing options, so I wanted to talk you through it. Clothes, actions, the whole deal."

"I watched that video you sent me. The virgin's guide. It made it seem like I just needed to do whatever made me feel comfortable."

"Yes, of course, that's true, but you're a guest of the presenters, and I was hoping that instead of jeans and a flannel, which would be super comfortable, we could still get you in character, but you know, tastefully." He smiled and batted his eyelashes at her.

"I'm listening."

"Early on in the movie, Janet is wearing this pink A-line dress with a cardigan. Totally tasteful and on-brand for you, while being in character. I was thinking to have some fun, we would do your hair in the big Sarandon curls, drop a hat on you, get you all dolled up, and really go for it."

She made a show of thinking about it while she chewed, even though she knew the answer before he even started talking. She knew he would never ask her to do anything that would make her feel uncomfortable. She made what she thought were "thinking faces" and even went so far as to tap her chin. Finally, she said, "Done."

"Excellent! The night of, you'll need to come down to the theater early and help us set up, and then we'll get you all fixed up." He clapped his hands. "I'll have everything we need."

"Makeup too?"

"Oh honey, you have no idea what Tommy and I are going to do. We have all the makeup for this one."

While she had never seen the show, she had seen enough pictures of Tim Curry in his costume to have an idea of what she could expect out of them. They didn't really do halfway on anything. "So, what's the other thing?"

Yates took a sip of his coffee and prepared himself. He looked more serious than she had ever seen him. "Right, well, thing two is about you and Ed."

"What about us?" The word "us" made a litany of images run through her head. Immediately, she felt the heat flicker on her neck. She went to wrap her scarf tighter, but he reached out and stopped her.

"Kiddo, the fact that you have to do that upon hearing his name says everything about it."

She dropped her head onto the table and let her hair fall around her face. Without looking up, she asked, "It's that obvious?"

"Only to the people who have never met you. There are some kids in Ghana who don't know for sure, but they've been busy. I suspect that the lady at the gas station doesn't know, but give it time."

With that, the rash, fully unleashed, crawled up her neck and took hold. She sat up and let him see it. "Yeah. OK. What do I do?"

He smiled and rubbed his hands. "Well, the first thing we need to do is talk it through. Unless something drastic happened since the last time we spoke on this topic, you are, uhhh..." He thought about his words carefully, but she interrupted.

"Woefully inexperienced and totally clueless."

He laughed and nodded. "OK. I was going to say, 'still a budding flower,' but let's go with yours."

"Wait. You said everyone knows. Does Ed know? Does Julia?" She dropped her head back on the table with a bang.

Yates reached out and rubbed her head. "Don't do that, pumpkin. Brain damage and all."

"Well?" she asked, waiting for an answer.

"I'm 100 percent sure Julia knows because, well, she and I talked about it yesterday. As for the boy himself, I think, and this is total conjecture, but I would say the signs point to yes. He gets pretty moony-eyed when he sees you."

She lifted her head up. "Yeah?"

"Is that a good thing?"

"I want it to be...?" she trailed off.

"You don't sound sure."

She pointed at herself. "Inexperienced and clueless."

"Right, well, I can't do anything about the first thing, and honestly, the second thing is not bad. The fun of your first relationship is figuring things out."

"Relationship?"

"Of course, neither of you is the kind of person who would do anything halfway. I'm not saying he has to put a ring on it, but I can't imagine you're looking for a fling."

She scrunched up her face as if she had just smelled sulfur, and she shook her head. "God no. It's just, I'm not sure if I want a relationship either. I'm seventeen. He's nineteen. I don't know what I'm doing. He has a whole life plan. I don't. That's the point of The Gift, you know. No plan. Figure things out as I go. I didn't move across the country to meet a boy. I moved across the country to do something great. Something. I don't know what it is yet. I think I'm figuring it out. He's helping me for sure, and I really do like him so much. He's fun and smart, and he's going places, all the places. I just... I'm seventeen, you know? I just said that. I just... AHHH." She slammed her head back on the table.

Yates reached out and rubbed her head again. "Let's just take it one step at a time, OK? The first step is admitting there are feelings. I mean, I already knew, but admission is important. Now that it's out in the world, you have to deal with it."

"Is this like AA?" she asked as she sat back up. There was a red mark on her head where she had banged her head on the table.

"The second step is to not let the feelings get in the way. That whole rambling mess you just spouted was spot on.

You're young and 'in like.' There is no pressure. I promise you that there's no pressure. You can take it slow or fast..."

"Slow!"

"Yeah, I know, but I just wanted to give you options. The point is you should take it somewhere. Take ... it, whatever it is. Do something. You're right. You didn't come here to meet a boy, but you did. You met that other gangly boy too, and you knew immediately he wasn't the boy for you, but he was important, and that British girl, Maggie, she's there too. Dr. Bennet and me and even," he lowered his voice to a whisper, "M-A-R-I-A-H is important in that you learn how not to be and who to avoid.

"That's part of it all. College isn't just about the education. Sure, it is. I learned a lot, but the most important thing for me was meeting Tommy. Not just because he's my person, I'm not saying Ed is your person, but with Tommy, there is more. There's the theater and the plans and the career we can make together. College is about the people you meet and the experiences you have with them. Love and loss and joy and heartbreak. That's part of it."

"You should really be on the commercials for college."

"Yeah, I should be on all the commercials. They pay really well."

"So," she took a deep breath, "what does doing something look like?"

"I'm so glad you asked." He got up, filled both their coffee mugs, and sat back down. "I know it isn't the most popular thing in the world, but I'm all about the direct approach, and based on what I know about you, so are you. You don't need to bat your eyelids and do some lap dance. You just need to flat-out say how you feel and see what happens. You're not a honey pot, and that nonsense that Mariah does and those of her ilk is beneath you."

"Her ilk, huh?"

"Too much?"

"Just right."

"I thought so too. So, tomorrow Julia has an away meet. You should suggest to Ed that you go. That gets you alone in the car for some hashtag straight talk."

"Too much."

"Yeah, I felt it too."

"So, the direct approach."

"It worked for me. I have faith it will work for you too. Ed is a great guy, and I think he is just too nice to make a move. He's not a guy who has even thought the words make a move in his life, which is why I think you might be perfect for each other."

Junior pulled out her phone and texted Ed right then, seeing if he wanted to take a trip to Julia's meet the next day.

He replied in less than a minute with an enthusiastic "Absolutely!!" He even used two exclamation points, which Yates thought was a good sign.

"So just remember, be yourself. The direct approach only works when you're yourself. If you come in all hot and crazy, then the situation is hot and crazy."

Junior nodded. "Right. Be myself. Choke on my own words and break out in a rash. Got it."

"Right, but you're so adorable when you do that, so yes. Do that. In fact, and this is the part you are not going to like, I think it is important that you don't wrap up tight. Let him see it. If you're really going to be yourself, be your whole self. I know why you wear scarves. I get it. You're a private person with a nervous condition who gets more nervous when talking about her condition and even more nervous when she talks about herself. I don't judge. I get it. I don't wear a rainbow cape, but I'm not ashamed of who I am, and you shouldn't be either. There is a difference between hiding in plain sight and hiding from yourself. If this is something you want, if you want to try this with Ed, then you should not need to hide from him either."

"That's beautiful." She wiped a tear that she hadn't realized had escaped.

"Yeah, I should be in all the commercials," he joked and broke the tension. "So, good plan?" he asked while he nodded his head, trying to convince her to do the same.

She nodded and smiled. "Yeah. Good plan."

She spent the rest of the day in a somewhat distracted fog. She walked right past Maggie in the library, who, while used to being ignored in England, was having none of that in America. She shouted, "Oi!" and gave Junior a hip check, which, in turn, some spilled coffee, luckily on the tiles, and which they both cleaned up while uttering apologies through their laughter. Eventually, they made it to the stacks, where Junior told her all about it.

Maggie, unfazed, said, "Right. You suck at girl stuff."

"I do. I really do."

"Yeah, it's fine, though, because that is what he likes, obviously. That Mary Crawford is constantly heaving cleavage in his face, and he seems uninterested. I mean, I know she's terrible, and I'm interested."

Junior nodded. "She is stunning."

"Right, but what else is there really?"

"Well, she got in here."

"Yeah, yeah, but anyone can get in here, remember? That's the whole thing about Mansfield. Pay in cash, welcome in. We had to try. We had to be more than a bag of money. Ed already has all the bags of all the money he could ever want, yet he, what, wants to be a historian? A religious scholar. He needs someone who gets that. Someone who has some thoughts in her head. You may not be stacked like Mary Crawford, but you have double-D brains for sure."

With that, Junior spit out her coffee laughing and was forced to clean the library floor for the second time in just a few minutes. While she was laughing and wiping and hoping she didn't leave a stain, the meaning behind the joke actually set in. There was no reason to be nervous. There was no reason to care so much. If Ed liked her, it was for what she had already done, not what he thought she could do or would do. With that, the fog cleared, and she headed into the next day clear-eyed and confident.

The next day she felt relaxed and happy throughout the whole ride to the meet, the time during the meet, and the sweaty hugs with Julia after the meet. There was no reason to worry, she told herself. He either liked her in a romantic way or he didn't. That whole adage about romance ruining a good friendship was balderdash anyway. The best couples were good friends. Her parents, who were a terrible couple, were not friends. She never really understood what it was her mother saw in her father, but yet love is often stronger than like. Love sometimes made smart people do stupid things. Like made people do smart things because while we choose to like someone, we don't always choose who we love. Junior thought both were important, and if love was never in the cards with Ed, liking was enough.

So, on their way back to The Park, with the midwestern fall sunset almost over even though it was still mid-evening, the two of them stopped at a coffee shop one town away from Mansfield. They went to a local park and put the tailgate down on the truck. They sat, legs dangling over the side, waiting for the sun to fully set so they could watch the stars. They sat in the comfortable silence they both came to expect when they were just sitting. Sometimes in the stacks, when they were doing homework or reading, they could comfortably sit for hours.

Ed thought about how his parent's silences were never comfortable. They were always tense, almost relieved silences. They were exhausted from having talked for years and years, and they just wanted each other to shut up, or maybe it was that they had almost zero common interests that were not directly tied to the kids. He suspected that was why his dad took as many trips as he did; when he came back, they rediscovered each other. Those return days were the days when The Park was full of laughter and light. He thought about Tommy and Yates and the way they could sit and write or storyboard forever without ever saying one thing and how they would occasionally look up at each other, at the same time, as though they were mind melding, and smile.

He felt content with having spent time with one of his favorite people cheering on one of his other favorite people, and what that could mean for his future, when Junior broke the silence and said, "So, I've been thinking." It made him feel like she had heard his thoughts.

"Yeah? I like that about you."

"Do you?"

"Yep, I'm on team brains. Not in a zombie way, though."

"You're saying zombies wouldn't want my brains?"

"Oh, they totally would! I'm just saying, for me, as a non-zombie, brains are good. Thinking is great. I like it in people. I do it all the time. I think lots of people never really think, so when I suspect people do it, I'm thrilled, but when someone actually admits to it, I'm over the moon."

"Well, remember that feeling for a few minutes, just in case you are not super thrilled with the thoughts I've been thinking."

"Ohhhh-kayyyy," he dragged it out, "but I can't imagine there is anything you could be thinking that would make me crash into the moon instead."

She took a deep breath, exhaled, and said in one long sentence, "Well, Ed, you're great and I'm so happy we are friends and well, I like you really, really, not just as only a friend, I mean, I want to be your friend, but I want to be kissing friends and well, not just that, kissing isn't the only part of it, it is, but it isn't you know, but friends with potential I guess, you know, like in that old movie with John Cusack, like I would like to maybe see what happens if we threw some romance into the pot I'm sorry this is awkward, I don't know what I'm doing."

Ed's feet quit swinging, and he set his cup down next to him on the tailgate. He looked over at her and noticed that she didn't have her scarf tied up tight around her neck. It was hanging loose, and he could see a constellation of red blotches crawling up her neck. He reached out to touch her there, on her bare neck, the place that showed all of her emotions. She let him.

His fingers, still hot from the coffee, felt cool against her neck. She looked at his face and watched as he was processing not only what she said, but what he was seeing. She could see a conversation happening within himself.

He was moving his head around as he considered something. He looked her in the eye and slid his hand behind her neck. He leaned forward, and we shall leave it there. Junior wouldn't want anyone to linger too long on this intimate moment. Suffice to say, that by the time they climbed back into the truck, the coffee was cold, but they were quite warm.

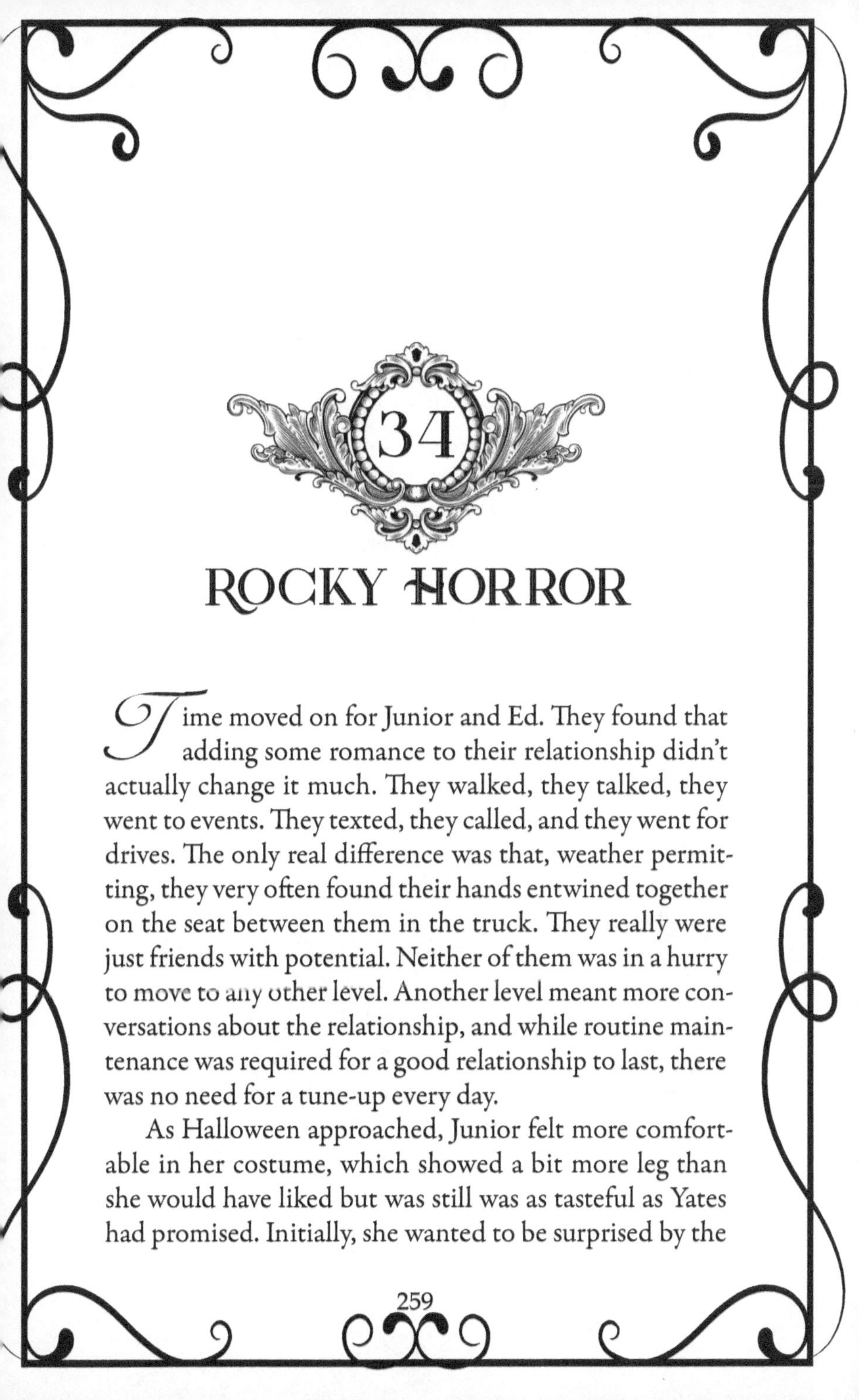

34

ROCKY HORROR

Time moved on for Junior and Ed. They found that adding some romance to their relationship didn't actually change it much. They walked, they talked, they went to events. They texted, they called, and they went for drives. The only real difference was that, weather permitting, they very often found their hands entwined together on the seat between them in the truck. They really were just friends with potential. Neither of them was in a hurry to move to any other level. Another level meant more conversations about the relationship, and while routine maintenance was required for a good relationship to last, there was no need for a tune-up every day.

As Halloween approached, Junior felt more comfortable in her costume, which showed a bit more leg than she would have liked but was still was as tasteful as Yates had promised. Initially, she wanted to be surprised by the costume, but ultimately she decided it was best to try it on beforehand after a long conversation with her mother, who had lost her own Rocky Horror virginity at the same theater over twenty years prior.

She did, however, pass on the opportunity to go to the theater the week before Halloween and watch the movie. Yates and Tommy had to do a trial run to make sure everything worked, and they offered everyone the chance to come. Junior just really wanted her first time to be her first time. Yates had sent her some videos that helped her prepare, and while she was tempted to watch some recorded shows, she just wanted to experience it the way her mother had, albeit with more clothes on than her mother, who had apparently dressed in a way that she felt she shouldn't describe but that Junior would see soon enough.

Due to the current romantic situation, it was decided that it would be best for Ed to dress as Brad. He asked his father if he could raid his wardrobe as apparently Brad, according to Tommy, needed to look like a guy who either sells golf clubs or talks about golf clubs. Reluctantly, Tom agreed, and even then, he made Ed promise that if any of his clothes were irreparably harmed, he would have to pay to replace them.

Julia chimed in, "Yeah, but how would you even know?" This brought laughter from all corners of the room. Tom joined in, although he thought Julia was making fun of the ragged state of his clothes, which were most assuredly not ragged, whereas everyone else knew she was making fun of the fact all of his clothes looked the same.

The night of the show, Junior agreed to have dinner at the theater and help set up final decorations and gift bags that were given out with each paid admission. The bags were filled with a plethora of things she didn't fully understand, including flashlights, bells, toast, newspapers, empty water guns, rubber gloves, noisemakers, cards, confetti, hot dog chew toys for dogs, and toilet paper. Tommy and Yates assured her that it was all necessary. They hung signs that read: **WHILE WE WANT YOU TO ENJOY YOUR TIME IN TRANSYLVANIA, NEITHER WATER NOR RICE WILL BE USED IN THE PERFORMANCE. ANYONE SEEN USING EITHER WILL NOT DO THE TIME WARP AGAIN.** They hired a few extra ushers, including a few members of the Mansfield intramural rugby team, just in case there was a need to physically remove some people.

Once they were done, they ate and left Junior alone to dress. They were changing backstage and didn't want to ruin the surprise for her, nor did they want her to see what they were wearing and run off before the show even started.

They had roped off a VIP section for Junior, Ed, Aaron, Maggie, Mariah, and the Crawfords. Much to her chagrin, Julia was not allowed to come; Candy was at that same show with Fran all those years ago and was not keen on sending her sixteen-year-old daughter to see that show yet, no matter how mature and smart she was for her age. Instead, she stayed at The Park and was forced to listen to Norris give a fire-and-brimstone sermon about the hedonism on display under the family banner.

Ed arrived first and came down front. After exchanging a long hug and a chaste kiss, as they were not yet used to public displays of affection, he told her he had to go backstage to help Tommy get in his costume.

"Yates is back there."

"Yeah, well, turns out it's a two-man job. You'll see." He climbed the stairs and disappeared stage left.

Maggie and Aaron, who were not Rocky Horror virgins, arrived next. Maggie was dressed in a French maid's outfit with fishnet stockings and high heels completing the look. She had painted her face white and put bright red lipstick and dark black eyeliner on to accentuate her features. Aaron, dressed in a black suit, wore a wig that was bald on top and had a long mullet in the back.

"Nice hair," Junior said as she reached up to give him a hug.

"It'll make sense," he said back.

"Will it? None of this makes any sense." She hugged Maggie.

"It will," Maggie replied. "Let's sit up here and watch people come in." She climbed up on the front of the stage across from their seats and dangled her legs over the end.

Aaron decided he would go back and see if they needed any help backstage, leaving the two of them as they watched all manner of people enter. Some people were dressed like Aaron and Maggie. Others had biker jackets. Others had gold corsets and top hats. Some people had doctor scrubs. There were a few other Janets, as well as plenty of Brads. There were a few men just wearing boxer shorts or some other kind of underwear. Most of them were self-conscious and were standing with their hands defensively in front of their crotches. Junior wondered why anyone would dress that way if they were that uncomfortable.

"What are they?" Junior asked Maggie, pointing to a group of women who came in wearing only their bras and underwear. Some of them wore panties, while some wore slips.

"Janets."

"I'm Janet!?" she said defensively. "I'm not going to have to... I'm not going to..." She trailed off and rubbed her scarf.

"No. No. It's fine." Maggie rubbed her back and tried to calm her down. "It's just that..." and before she could explain further, in walked Mary Crawford. Maggie simply choked on her words, and Junior followed her gaze.

Mary's top, if one could call it that, was a white, lacy bustier. Her bottoms, if one could call them that, were white panties and a garter belt with stockings. She stopped at the top of the theater with the purpose of causing a scene. She knew her seats were down front, but she clearly wanted everyone to stop and look. It worked.

Mariah and Hank entered behind her, he as one of the bikers, and she with a gold sequined top hat and matching suit jacket that she had buttoned up around her mid-section, making it look as though she wasn't wearing a shirt underneath. He scanned the crowd, saw Junior and Maggie on the front of the stage, nodded to them, and leaned down to whisper in Mary's ear. Her posture immediately changed. She went from standing as though she was posing for a statue to be made of her, with her back straight, chest out, to a pouty teenager in seconds. The three of them walked down to the front of the theater. Mariah and Hank took their seats and started going through their bags. Mary walked over and stood in front of Junior and Maggie.

"Hey," Junior said when she approached, giving her a smile.

Ignoring the greeting, Mary asked, "Where's Ed? I have to ask him something."

"He's backstage helping Tommy and Yates," Junior replied.

Mary walked up the steps and asked loudly, to get the attention of as many people as possible, "This way?" She pointed to stage left with her arm fully extended, determined to let everyone take a good, long look at her and her outfit.

Junior nodded, and Mary walked off. Maggie elbowed her in the ribs.

"Ow. What'd you do that for?"

"You just sent a stripper backstage to look for your boyfriend."

"Firstly, she's not a stripper." She took a beat and asked, "Is she? Is Janet a stripper?"

"No. Janet's not a stripper. It's just that, well, there are some pretty racy things in this movie, and well, Janet, as you can see," she waved around to the gathering crowd, "she spends time in her underwear as does Brad."

"Those are Brads? Oh, man." Junior smacked her head. "Mary knew Ed was dressing as Brad, so she chose to dress as underwear Janet."

"Right."

Junior took a second to process that. She went through multiple scenarios and ultimately decided that it was all fine. She proceeded to explain it to Maggie. "Secondly..."

"Secondly? Are we doing a list?"

"Yeah, I said firstly a minute ago."

"Right, sorry, I was distracted by all the stripper talk."

"You started the stripper talk and besides, secondly, you were the one who told me I had double-D brains and that was all that mattered. You're right. I do have double-D brains. Ed told me he likes that I think about things. He thinks most people don't, and I'm sure Mary Crawford is most people. I'm not worried. If Ed was interested in Mary, he had plenty of chances before today."

"Fair enough. I did say that, and Ed is a great guy. It's just..." She looked over to the spot where Mary stood. "Wow."

"Yeah, wow indeed."

"I suspect old Grandpa Frank is back there right now, all nine feet of him trying not to look down her top and failing." They both were looking at the space where she disappeared behind the curtain and were laughing at the image of Aaron hovering over Mary Crawford. They were drawn from their giggling by the sound of a cough.

They turned and saw Hank standing there, trying to look charming. He had a fake grin plastered on his face that had always worked for him. "Hi, um," he cleared his throat, "I just wanted to say that I love your costumes. Where'd you get them?"

"Yates got it for me."

"I picked it up at a brothel," Maggie said in a deadpan, emotionless way. She had never really taken to Hank, and after his disappearing/reappearing act at Junior's birthday, she had decided to actively dislike him. "I'm going to go be somewhere else now." She turned to Junior. "You good?"

"Yeah. Could you get me a soda and some popcorn?"

"They say pop here. Can't you acclimate?"

"Not on this one." She reached into the pocket of her cardigan and pulled out a twenty. "Get yourself something nice, too," she said as she patted Maggie on the cheek.

"Oooh. A sugar momma." Maggie kissed Junior on the cheek, leaving a set of lip prints. She hopped off the stage and walked away without another word to Hank.

Hank took her spot on the stage. "She doesn't like me."

"No, she really doesn't."

"What did I do to her? I don't think I've said more than ten words to her in the few months I've known her."

Junior just let that sit there and chose not to comment. Just because she always said the truth, it didn't give her permission to be mean. People often confused honesty for harshness. They're not the same thing. They may be first cousins, but not the same thing.

"What about you? Do you dislike me?"

"I don't dislike you, Hank. I don't dislike most people. I just, well..." She interrupted herself when she realized someone was missing to ask, "Where's Mariah?"

"Oh, she, uh, she said she needed to use the restroom before the show started. I swear, her bladder must be the size of a pea. It takes us three hours to watch a two-hour movie because she has to pause and go all the time. You know what I mean, right?"

"I know what you mean about Mariah's bladder?"

"Yeah, you must notice when you guys hang out and do movie nights. In her and Julia's living room thing that is between their rooms."

As Junior processed what she was hearing, she just stared into Hank's face. He seemed genuinely convinced that the Bertram girls and she spent time together watching movies. Of course, Mariah mentioned it that first day, but the invitation was never made, and Junior would certainly never invite herself.

It was true that she and Julia spent time in that room watching movies, but Mariah was never there. She was either just "out" or locked away in her room. She would even occasionally open the door to her room and ask them, in not the nicest of terms, to keep it down when they were having too much fun.

She had been roped into some sort of lie, and she did not like it. She felt the heat start to crawl up her chest and onto her neck. She rubbed the scarf she had made sure to wrap tight. She took a breath and started, "We…"

"There you are," Mariah said, suddenly appearing next to them. "I've been looking everywhere for you."

"I've been here the whole time," Hank said. "You were the one who left, not me."

"Well, I found you. That's all that matters now. Let's go get some popcorn. I'm starving."

"We just ate."

"Come on." She pulled his hands and he slid off the front of the stage. "I don't want to miss the start."

With that, they were gone, and Junior found herself sitting on the edge of the stage, alone, in a room full of people, thinking hard about what the implications were of what Hank had just told her. She was chewing on her lip, rubbing her neck, staring at the middle distance, her eyes out of focus, when she felt someone sit down next to her.

"Miss me?" It was Ed.

She turned and looked up at him with a glowing smile. "I did actually, but it's been an eventful…" she looked at her watch, "half-hour since we last saw each other. I have something interesting to tell you. Don't let me forget."

"Got it." He knocked his forehead with his fist. "Something interesting from Junior. Locked it in."

She laughed. "Does that work?"

"Not really."

"Well, I can't imagine I'll forget this, so we'll most likely be OK."

Ed looked out at the theater, which was almost totally full. "This is pretty cool. I'm really excited for them. They worked so hard."

"They really have." She turned away from the crowd and looked back up at him. "Did you know about the underwear Janets?"

For once, it was Ed who turned a new shade. He looked away from her and then looked back, not sure how she would take it. "I did. Should I have told you?"

She shook her head. "No, it's OK. It's just, I mean, I'm not a prude. I've seen rated R movies. I've listened to songs. I read books. I get it. I just..." She thought of the best way to say it and once again, opted for the direct approach, "hope you don't expect me to..."

"No!" he interrupted. "No, no, no, no, no, *no,*" he rattled off in quick succession. "I would never expect that of you. That's why I dressed as fully dressed Brad."

"Plus," she said, "it's getting cold. Who would want to walk around dressed like that after the show? Brrr." They both laughed. "Sorry. I know better. I know you would never... it's just, well, Maggie said some things that got in my head and..."

"Hey, I like you. This you. Because you're you." Then he started singing, "Don't go changin' to try to please me..."

"Oi, is this a special moment?" Maggie asked as she shoved the drink in between them.

"And what if it was?" Junior asked as she took the drink.

"I would say... Blech." She made a retching sound as she stuck her finger in her mouth.

"Oh, you're just jealous." Junior leaned over and kissed her on the cheek.

They all laughed and found their way to their seats. The lights flickered, announcing that there were only five minutes to go before the show started. Aaron and Mary came out from opposite ends of the backstage area and walked down the stairs to join the group. Mary sat in the empty seat next to Ed, and Aaron next to Maggie.

Maggie reached over and pulled Aaron's shirt, so he had to bend over so his ear was equal to her mouth. She whispered, "What's that all about then?"

"What's what all about?"

"You and the tart coming out at the same time?"

"You saw the lights flashing, right? Was I supposed to wait back there for a minute so you could think I had to redress or something? Besides, you do know other people are back there, right?"

"Hmmm. Likely story. I've got my eye on you, bruv." She switched from her normal accent to the thickest East-end cockney stereotype she could muster.

"Whatever," he said and sat back up and shoved her in the shoulder. "Tart. This is America, we say..."

The lights dimmed, and people started clapping. Mariah and Hank slipped into their seats next to Mary. The screen turned on and there, for all to see, was a giant set of red lips. The show began.

Junior was immediately transfixed. The show was part movie, part live-action performance. There were characters on the stage dressed like she and Ed. There was a wedding and songs; she used some of the items from her gift bag. Eventually, the characters who were dressed like Aaron and Maggie showed up, and they ran up on stage and led the crowd through the "Time Warp." Aaron had to hunch way over to affect the hump his character had. When the number was over and everyone, including Junior, had danced along, the "Time Warp" being self-instructive, there was raucous applause. They bowed and returned to their seats.

Soon thereafter, Yates appeared, wearing essentially the same outfit Mary was wearing except in black. He had white paint on his face and red, red lips. He sang, he danced, he was magnificent. Junior, who would have been mortified to be dressed the way he was, was in awe of his fearlessness.

Of course, when it was time for Tommy to appear, dressed as the titular character, Rocky, she was floored. He wore nothing but a gold, sequined Speedo, lots and lots of baby oil, and a blonde wig. She finally understood why they didn't want her to see them in their costumes before the show. Had she not actually realized what was happening, she would have freaked out completely, broken out everywhere beyond her neck, and spent the performance watching from the projection booth.

She respected that the film and the performance led the viewers up to the more and more outrageous aspects of the story. Each new thing was sufficiently more bizarre and more boundary-pushing than the thing that came before it, making it seem almost tame by comparison. When the show ended and they were all sweaty and full of joy, the cast took a bow. Tommy and Yates held their hands high and took another bow. They kissed, and the crowd howled and clapped. The stage cleared off except for Yates.

He stood there, still in his high heels and fishnets, turned on the mic, and said, "Thank you all for coming." More applause. He tamped it down with his hands. "We invite you all to stick around for dancing. Makes sure you check out the list in the lobby for our upcoming shows." Even more applause. "Well, I can't promise more full audience participation, but we are pleased to announce that starting next weekend, we will be playing cult classics at nine o'clock on Friday and Saturday. What do you think we have next week?" He paused to let people shout out the names of their favorite movies. It was just noise, and there was no way he could have picked any one movie out of the din. "Yes, all good guesses, and we have a suggestion box on the concession counter. However, next week…"

Tommy came out, dressed in a skintight, purple jumpsuit. He wore bowling shoes and carried a battered bathrobe. He slipped it on Yate's shoulders. He reached into the pocket and pulled out some sunglasses and a long, ratty wig. The crowd erupted. They started shouting, "Dude! Dude! Dude!"

"That's right, Dudes. Please shine your balls and join us for a BIG adventure next weekend as we screen *The Big Lebowski*." The crowd erupted again. "After that, we have *Thelma and Louise* as well as *Waterworld*. We will round out November with the Thanksgiving classic, *Planes, Trains and Automobiles*." The cheers were deafening. Yates took a bow. "Thank you! Enjoy the after-party." The rest of the cast members came out with champagne bottles and they tried to coordinate popping the corks. It didn't actually work well, but corks popped and champagne spilled. Tommy and Yates were each handed a bottle. They kissed, toasted each other, held the bottles up to the roaring crowd, and knocked back huge gulps.

The music started playing as Yates and Tommy climbed down off the stage and tried to talk to their little group but were swarmed by well-wishers and backslappers. Mary grabbed Mariah's hand and pulled her up onto the stage where they started to dance in a way that was comparable to some of the performances in the movie. It wasn't long before a collection of Brads, in various states of dress, climbed onto the stage and tried to make themselves part of the show.

Junior and Ed exited the main theater and found the lobby milling with people. They got drinks and pretzels and sat on the floor against the front window. They eavesdropped on the crowd. All of them were raving about what a great time they had and talked about coming back to the theater for whatever events were next planned. Tommy and Yates, still dressed in their new getups, entered the lobby and were once again swarmed.

Eventually, they extracted themselves from their adoring fans and plopped down on the floor next to Junior and Ed. "Well?" Yates asked.

"It was spectacular," Junior gushed.

"Yeah, I'm so impressed. You guys really made something special happen. I can't believe how many people are still here. You must have made a mint on concessions," Ed said.

"That's the hope, little brother. It wasn't super cheap to get the movie, and of course, we went all-in on the costumes. We did get the theater kids from the college to do the parts without having to pay them, so that worked out, but we did have to feed them and water them during rehearsal. Plus, we did the gift bags."

"Well, I think that's a brilliant piece of marketing. I've noticed a lot of people hanging onto them. There are going to be lots of them out there in the world. I know I'll be carrying mine around proudly," Junior said.

"Fingers crossed," Yates said.

"Sounds like everyone is excited about El Duderino next weekend," Ed said, brevity not being his thing.

"I've seen that one. It was one of the few movies Dad actually watched with us. I remember that more than the actual movie. I kept looking at him to see if he would actually laugh or even smile."

"Well, I hope you grace us with your presence so you can enjoy it the way it was meant to be enjoyed," Tommy said.

"Wild horses," Junior replied. "Besides, weekend movies are just my speed. I don't think I could do this," she waved around, "every weekend. I think once a year is going to be good for me."

"Well, Cinderella, on that note," Yates grabbed her hand, "since this is the one night a year that you're out at the ball, let's get back to it." He pulled her up; she reached out for Ed's hand and he for Tommy's. They took their human chain back to the theater to join the fray.

By the time they arrived back on the stage, the crowd had thinned, but those who were still there were all drinking from plastic cups. Some were dancing and splashing it around, like Mary Crawford, who was still surrounded by a group of men and boys, all of whom clearly had the same thing on their minds. Others, like Aaron and Maggie, were sitting down in small groups, chatting and drinking. There was a lot of champagne to be shared. It turns out that selling alcohol requires a license, but giving it away backstage to guests is a different story.

Seeing that everyone was having some, Junior pulled Ed's head down to meet her mouth and shouted into his ear, "You know that I don't care if you have any, right?"

He nodded and smiled. He mimed himself drinking and then he held his stomach and crossed his eyes. Then he held his hands up in an X shape. He leaned down to her ear. "Tommy and I had an adventure in Dad's liquor cabinet when I was fifteen. That was enough for me. No thank you."

Even though neither of them drank a drop of champagne, both of them ended up wearing plenty of it. A group of "underwear Janets" tried and failed to infiltrate the "protective" circle of Brads, Rockies, Eddies, and the other Riff-Raff that had taken root around Mary, whose cup had remained full for the whole evening. While Hank and Mariah disappeared quickly, Maggie and Aaron were still on stage dancing hard. They bounced around between all the groups and were both sweaty messes, but joy radiated from them.

A slow song started up and Yates came on over the mic, "This is it, everyone. Last song of the night. Thanks for coming. See you next weekend."

Many people groaned and dispersed after coming to the realization that they, like Aaron and Maggie, were sweaty and gross. That left just a few people on the stage. Yates and Tommy grabbed each other and swayed slowly. Maggie and Aaron each paired off with a Janet. Aaron, not sure where to put his hands on his scantily-clad dance partner, had a vice grip on her waist. Maggie and her Janet were much less concerned with appearances. There was almost no daylight between them. Maggie had her arms over her partner's shoulders and her Janet had her arms wrapped around Maggie's ribs.

Mary seemingly selected one of the Brads and was dancing not so much with him, but against him. He seemed rooted in place while she swayed and gyrated against him. A few of the remaining circle sat in the front row and leered at the show.

Junior looked up at Ed who was looking over at the show Mary was putting on. She could see his jaw was clenched.

"Is she going to be OK?" Junior asked.

"I don't think so."

They stopped dancing and held each other as they watched the scene unfold. As the song wound down, Junior said, "You should…"

While at the same time Ed said, "Someone should…"

They looked at each other.

"It has to be you."

"Yeah?"

"I trust Aaron and Maggie, of course, but they've also been drinking. Who else can it be?"

Ed looked around and quickly and quietly assessed the situation. He exhaled a breath he didn't know he was holding. He looked down at Junior who had been watching him the whole time. He nodded and smiled. He bent forward and she lifted up on her toes. Their lips met in the middle.

With that, Ed went over to fill Tommy and Yates in on the idea. They helped him shoo away the remaining guests. Maggie winked at Junior as she and her Janet left holding hands. Aaron waved and grinned stupidly as his dance partner gathered her things from the audience. Junior gave him a thumbs up.

Mary was lying down on the stage, her head on the lap of the Brad with whom she danced. Junior sucked in a breath and went over where they were. "Hi, I'm Junior." She stuck her hand out to the Brad.

"Brad," he said with a growl.

"Really? A Brad called Brad. How funny."

"What do you want, Glinda?" Mary growled.

"Are you calling me Glinda, as in Glinda the Good Witch?"

"Ugh. Yes."

"Well, thank you very much."

"It wasn't supposed to be a compliment."

"Right, well…"

"Go away already."

"Can't you see she doesn't want to talk to you?" asked the Brad called Brad.

Undeterred, Junior pushed on. "Yes, well, I just wanted to let you know that Ed has offered to take you home…"

Mary was up on her feet with ninja-like skills. She started combing her hair with her fingers. "Really?" Her cheeks were flushed, and she wobbled a bit on her feet.

"Good witches never lie," Junior said as she crossed her heart.

"Who's this Ed now?" Brad called Brad asked.

Mary leaned over and kissed him on the cheek. "Well, thank you for a lovely evening, but you should run along now." She waved him away with her hands. "Run along."

"Seriously? I thought…"

"Well, guess you thought wrong," Mary retorted.

"But you said…"

"Well, a girl is entitled to change her mind, isn't she?"

Junior chimed in, "She is, you know, Brad." She smiled a big, toothy smile up at him.

"Whatever." He stormed off mumbling some things that could have been a lot of things men should never say to or about women.

Mary and Junior stood silently and watched him go up the aisle. He shoved his way past Ed, who was coming back into the theater.

"He doesn't seem very pleasant," Junior commented.

"Shut it."

Junior mimicked locking her mouth with a key.

By then, Ed stood at the base of the stage. He looked up quizzically at Junior. She shrugged her shoulders.

"Well, are you ready to go?" he asked Mary.

"Of course, you know, I just appreciate this so much..." She started slurring her words and stumbled a bit walking down the stairs. As Ed moved over to grab her hand, she threw herself onto him. He caught her over his shoulder, which was clearly not what she wanted. He looked up at Junior and shook his head and rolled his eyes. She laughed and blew him a kiss.

Ed squatted down and put Mary on her feet. "Did you bring a jacket?"

"I'm not sure," she said in a baby doll voice. "I just don't wemember."

"Did you just say wemember?" Yates asked as he came up behind them. "Classy. Everyone thinks drunk Elmer Fudd is sexy. Here," he took off his robe, revealing he was still wearing his Frankenfurter outfit, "wear this."

She refused to take it. So, Ed took it and put it on her shoulders. "Thanks."

"You're the hero, man. I just live here." He looked up at Junior. "Did you have fun?"

"I did."

"Good. I'll see you soon. Tommy is out there in the lobby. He's gonna walk you back. I'm off to bed." He blew her a kiss and she caught it. He gave Ed a hug and

whispered something in his ear. They both laughed. "See you, Elmer." He rubbed the top of Mary's head, messing up her hair.

"AHHH," she shrieked and started to try to fix it again.

"Let's go," Ed said as he waved Mary forward. She started up the aisle. Junior descended the stairs and gave him one more hug and peck on the lips.

"You are a hero," she said.

"ED!" Mary shrieked from the top of the theater. She plopped down on the ground. "I need help."

"I'm a hero," he said. "See you tomorrow?"

"I hope so."

They looked up at Yates, who stepped over Mary as though she wasn't even there. He shook his head and kept his murmurs to himself.

"I'm gonna wait down here a few minutes. I don't think she'll make as big of a show if I'm not there. I'll count to thirty and then head up."

"Good plan. See you tomorrow."

"Eddie!"

They both grinned, shook their heads, then he took off.

She watched him go, and instead of counting to thirty, she sang the "Time Warp," which she had to admit was a potent earworm, and assessed the damage in the theater. The stage had puddles of liquid and sticky patches where the liquid had dried. There wasn't one row that didn't have cups or popcorn or wrappers of some sort on the ground. She looked at her watch just as October gave over to November. She nodded and made the decision to return tomorrow to help them clean. It was the least she could do after they had been so kind to her.

She finally made it to the lobby, only to find Tommy curled up on the ground asleep. She bent over and whispered, "Tommy," in his ear. He didn't move at all. She pushed him a bit and he flopped from his side to his back. "Tommy," she said again, to which he replied with a snore.

Where other people would have pushed and kicked Tommy until he woke up, marched upstairs to get Yates, or called Ed and made him come back, Junior Price did no such thing. Instead, she pulled her phone out of her cardigan pocket, unwound her headphones, found the brooms and mops in the storage closet, and went about cleaning up. She felt happy that she had spent the evening with so many people she had grown to love, but she was also content to have a moment to herself where she could be useful.

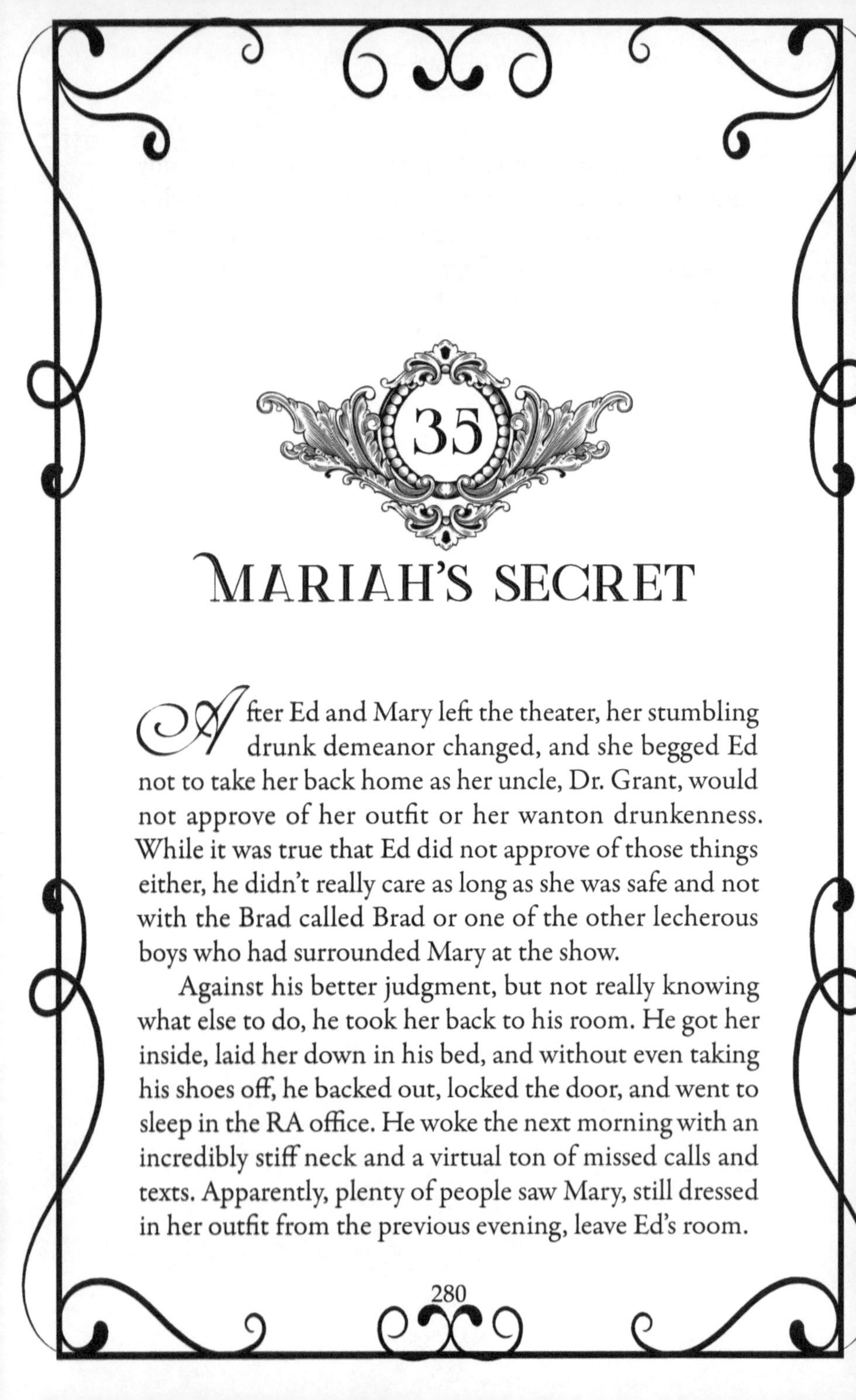

35

MARIAH'S SECRET

After Ed and Mary left the theater, her stumbling drunk demeanor changed, and she begged Ed not to take her back home as her uncle, Dr. Grant, would not approve of her outfit or her wanton drunkenness. While it was true that Ed did not approve of those things either, he didn't really care as long as she was safe and not with the Brad called Brad or one of the other lecherous boys who had surrounded Mary at the show.

Against his better judgment, but not really knowing what else to do, he took her back to his room. He got her inside, laid her down in his bed, and without even taking his shoes off, he backed out, locked the door, and went to sleep in the RA office. He woke the next morning with an incredibly stiff neck and a virtual ton of missed calls and texts. Apparently, plenty of people saw Mary, still dressed in her outfit from the previous evening, leave Ed's room.

There was even some video that circulated on social media because that is just something that has to happen for anything to be real in the time when our story takes place. By the time the video reached Junior's phone, she had already spoken to Ed. He scanned his texts, cracked his neck, and called her immediately.

She was eating breakfast with Mariah when he called. She almost didn't take it as time with Mariah was rare, and she didn't want to be rude. She was still exhausted from staying up all night cleaning. She decided to walk back to The Park at dawn. She took a shower and came down to breakfast with the intention of sleeping until Saturday Lunch.

When her phone, which was sitting face-down with the ringer off, as she normally did at mealtime, started buzzing, Mariah said, "That'll be Ed. You should take it."

She flipped it over, and shocked to see Mariah was right, she answered, "Hi?"

He said in one long breath, "So last night I took Mary back to my room because she was scared her uncle would be mad and I slept in the RA Lounge, but people saw her leave my room and now the rumors are flying and there are videos online."

Before Ed could promise her that nothing happened, Junior was saying, "Oh, poor Mary."

On his end of the phone call and on her end of the table, both Bertrams asked, "Poor Mary?"

Junior looked up at Mariah and spoke into the phone. "She may have bad intentions, but she doesn't deserve to be slandered. Who does?"

Ed said, "I knew you'd understand."

Mariah said, "You've got to be kidding me."

To Ed, Junior said, "Of course. I'm sorry this happened to you too. I'm here with Mariah right now. Can we talk later?"

"Hmmmm. Breakfast with Mariah. I hope her intentions are better."

Mariah froze in place on her way out of the room, having assumed that Junior would stay on the phone with Ed as that's what she would have done in a similar situation. She looked back at Junior.

Junior motioned for her to sit back down. She mouthed the word "Please." To Ed, she replied, "I don't think they are, but I have a few things we need to talk about."

"Really? You and Mariah huh? Well, that's a story I hope to hear. After lunch?"

"Absolutely."

Mariah had not fully committed to sitting back down, but she was standing closer to the table at least. "Something we need to talk about? Look, I didn't encourage Mary to do..."

"No, it's not that. I knew what would happen when I told Ed to take her home. Rumors don't bother me. There's rarely any truth to them, and even when there is, they aren't my business."

Mariah came closer and stood with her hands on the back of the chair. "Are you for real? I mean, how can you be like this?"

"I don't know how else to be. This is just me."

Mariah flopped down in the seat. "Yeah, well, it's creepy."

"Hmmm. Mary called me Glinda. Do people think Glinda is creepy?"

"No... Maybe... It doesn't matter. It's weird. You're weird. There is no way I would have gotten that call you

just got about my boyfriend and worried about the reputation of the other girl."

Junior nodded at that and took a sip of her coffee.
"Well, I'm glad you brought up reputations because, as you
stated, I'm weird, and as Mary stated, I'm the good witch,
and so, I found it troublesome that I was wrapped up in a
lie you told about me."

"I didn't..." Mariah started instinctively at first, ready to
defend herself regardless of the situation, but she stopped
herself short when she realized what it was. "What did
you say to him?"

"Well, I didn't have a chance to say anything. You
showed up and took him off to get snacks."

"What would you have said?"

Junior shook her head. "We both know what I would
have said."

"Well, what are you going to say now?" She squirmed
a bit in her seat.

"I'm not going to say anything unless he asks. There is
a difference between being honest and being a tattletale.
Your business is your business. I don't care why you lied. I
don't care what you want to do. I just want to know why
you felt the need to drag me into it. I didn't do anything
to you. I didn't push my way into your business. I'm sorry
if you're mad that Candy let me live here or whatever, but
I think I have been more than respectful. You're not interested in being my friend, and I'm OK with that. We don't
need to be friends. If you want me out of your way, I'll get
a job and find an apartment. I just don't understand."

"Oh. My. God. Really? You think this is that? You
think I don't want you here? I don't even care one way or
the other. You're right. If I didn't know you were here, I

wouldn't know. You don't do anything. That was it. The fact that you don't do anything was perfect. If I told Hank I was watching movies with Julia, he might believe it, I mean, Julia's always busy and she's always posting about it. But she's always posting about you too, so when I said we all were watching movies, he totally bought it."

"Ohhhh-kayyyy. That explains why you used me in your deception, but it doesn't explain why you needed to lie in the first place."

Mariah shook her head. "Seriously?"

"Seriously. I don't get it. What's the secret? What is such a big deal that you have to lie to Hank? I mean, I know I'm new to the girlfriend thing, but sometimes, I just want to be alone, and I don't want to see anyone, even Ed."

"And you say that out loud, to Ed?"

"Of course. What would I say?"

Mariah gasped and shook her head. "AHHHH!" she shouted.

"What?"

"I mean, I don't even have time for this right now." She waved her hands all around the room. "Look, it wasn't for alone time OK. I'm still seeing James. I was with him. He comes over sometimes at night. He drives down from school and sneaks in. He is away on the weekends, so he comes down during the week. It's the same thing Hank does, and I didn't want him to think he could come over. If it was a girls' night with you and Julia, he wouldn't dare. He thinks you're, like, totally pure and good, which you totally are. It's super annoying." Mariah inhaled loudly as though having to say all of that was so exhausting.

"So, you're cheating on James with Hank and on Hank with James?"

"It sounds so bad when you say it like that."

"Why didn't you just break up with James? He is away. It would make sense, wouldn't it? You could both have just seen other people or whatever, and have an open relationship. Why the sneaking?"

"It's just complicated, OK," she shouted. Then she whispered, "It is so, so complicated. I'm..." Mariah burst into tears and dropped her head onto the table. She sobbed and sobbed. She convulsed and shook. Not sure what to do, Junior scooted closer and rubbed Mariah's back until she cried herself out.

36

BORN TO RUN

Well, Dear Reader, it doesn't take a genius to figure out what Mariah was going to say before she burst into tears. Even Junior, a sheltered southern girl from Unincorporated Nowhere, understood what came next. That is not to say she knew what to do next, but she knew what Mariah was trying to say.

Of course, as Junior established, she was not a tattletale, and if someone had asked directly, "Is Mariah pregnant?" she would have answered, "That isn't my business to tell." Which to the trained ear, and let's face it, the untrained ear as well, that means "yes."

The rest of the Bertrams would later have private conversations about whether Mariah confessed to Junior first because she knew that doing so would force her to tell the rest of the family. Others suggested she spilled the beans because she knew that Junior was not keen to judge others, whereas everyone else in the family would have had something incredibly snarky to say. Another theory was that she was so exhausted from the stress of keeping the secret, hiding all the food she was eating, her evening sickness as we have seen, it was never morning sickness, and her changing body in baggy clothes, that she would have confessed to Portsmouth had he been there that morning. We shall leave it for each reader to determine which of these is true, and to consider what Portsmouth knew without being told.

Tommy and Yates' *Rocky Horror Picture Show* triumph might reasonably have been expected to be the topic on everyone's lips the next day at Saturday Lunch. Perhaps this is why everyone's focus was immediately grabbed when a seemingly unusually scared and yet somehow still belligerent Mariah Bertram, even as she stood, and before she opened her mouth, once everyone was seated and had their mouths full about ten minutes past 2, to say "Excuse me, everyone. I have something I would like to say."

She looked over at Junior who, realizing what was happening, tried to give her a reassuring look. She smiled and nodded. She mouthed, "It will be OK."

"Well, as you know, I've been acting strange lately and dressing differently. I've been missing out on lunches and other meals. I've been moody and staying locked in my room."

"So, like when you were twelve," Tommy chimed in.

Tom laughed. Candy nodded. Pug licked her own face. Norris said, "It wasn't so bad."

"Well," Mariah took a pause. Everyone, Tommy included, expected her to verbally eviscerate him. "Sort of. It is a hormonal... I mean... it has to do with hormones..."

She took a breath to say the line that she could not bring herself to say earlier in the day. Hoping someone else would interrupt her and fill in the blank on her behalf. As the whole family realized what was going on, they each had their own thought.

Tom: "I'm going to be a grandpa?"

Candy: "I'm going to be a grandma!"

Julia: "Is our shared room going to be a nursery?"

Yates: "Duh."

Tommy: "Babies are so ugly."

Ed: "..." He was genuinely stunned.

Junior: "She's being so brave."

Norris didn't keep it to herself. She said aloud, "I will ruin his life."

"No, no, no, no no!" Mariah said. She waved her hands in front of her. "There will be no life-ruining, Norris. This is on me. This is all on me."

"Well, just because I'm a woman of the cloth that does not mean I believe this has been an immaculate conception, dear."

"Of course not. It's just, well, I haven't said anything to him yet."

Tommy chimed in and said, "How is it possible he hasn't noticed?" He made general hand gestures in her general direction. "You look..."

"If you say fat, I will stick this in your eye," she said as she picked up a fork.

"Different," Yates interjected. "You said so yourself."

"Yes, honey, thank you. Different. I was going to say different." Tommy patted Yates' arm.

"Sure you were," Mariah said as she squinted her eyes.

"The question does stand though," Julia remarked.

"Yes, well..." Mariah cleared her throat and looked at her parents, who had somehow remained silent for proceedings thus far. "Mom? Dad? James is the father."

Norris shouted. "NO!" Everyone turned to look at her. "It's Henry Crawford. The father is Henry Crawford. It must be. The way he follows you around. I would understand why you would fall victim to his charms. That Mary throws herself at Edmund, and even I hear the talk on campus. Young people can't help it sometimes. Lust is the devil's business. I was there when your mother met your father and when Fran succumbed to that sailor."

Both Ed and Junior shouted, "Hey," at the same time.

"Nothing happened with Mary," Ed assured everyone.

"Don't talk about my mother," Junior demanded. Only later in our tale would she realize that she didn't say anything to defend her own father being referred to as "that sailor" when Tom was called "your father."

Norris continued on without acknowledging that anyone else had even spoken. "You would never allow a Rushworth to..." She made a sour face as if she was imagining the things, she could not say.

"It's James. I promise."

"Right, but how can you be sure?" Julia asked.

"It can ONLY be James," she said again.

"What about the..." Julia cut herself off when she realized what she was about to say in front of everyone. While she had no intentions of ever using the back door trick, she didn't want to rule it out just in case.

"It isn't Hank. It really isn't. I wish it was him. I so desperately wish it was him, but by the time I met him, I was already... you know... so I just didn't think it would be right to, you know... so we haven't... you know."

If anyone was bothered by the fact that a pregnant teenager was unable to name the act that got her pregnant, they didn't let on in that moment. However, it is safe to assume that Yates and Tommy had a long talk about it on the walk home.

"Well, clearly the only thing to do is to keep the secret for now, and then we can take Mariah out of the country for a term abroad. I can chaperone her, and we can return in the summer with none being any wiser," Norris stated, as though there had already been a long conversation, and it was decided fact.

With that, the flood gates opened, and almost everyone started offering opinions on what should happen next. There was a collective murmur that made the voices indistinguishable. While we could discern them all here for the reader, it will be made clear shortly that none of those ideas would ever come to fruition.

"ENOUGH!" Tom shouted, and the room went silent. They all looked over at him. He was standing, palms face down on the table, the sound of them slapping down covered by his booming voice. Tears were streaming down his face. "None of what any of you want matters, does it? What I want, what Candy wants and most definitely what you want, Norris, is all irrelevant."

Norris tried to start talking, but Tom just ran right over the top of her with his speech that would later be so important in the Bertram family that it became used as other parts of speech. Tommy would often say, "Don't go all Tom on me" to Yates. Julia would utter, "My professor totally Tom-ed us today" when describing a powerful lecture. Ed would later refer to it in a birthday speech as his dad's "Born to Run" speech, referring to Tom's favorite song that he often called so epic it changed the course of history for the next generation.

"What matters here is that we clearly failed as parents, and the rest of you, Junior notwithstanding, failed as a family. This is not a family possession. First and foremost, she is a human being. This young woman is going to give birth to a child, out of wedlock to be sure, and that may end up harming the *precious* Mansfield name, but to me, the biggest issue is that you are thinking about everything but Mariah, expectant young mother-to-be. No matter what happens, *regardless of her choices*, her life is going to be irrevocably different than she thought it would be." He flashed Norris a look that quelled the protest already rising in her throat.

"*Obviously*, she is quite far along and plans on having the baby, so whether she keeps it, or she gives it up for adoption, whether she stays here with us or moves out, whether she gets married, runs off to Europe with Norris, whatever happens, her life is going to be different. Think further than your privileged egos for once in your bloody lives and put yourself in her shoes.

"Mariah. I am forced on behalf of the *whole* family," another glare at Norris, "to apologize for letting you down. Yes, you took the risks when you made the choices you made, and here you are facing the music. Clearly, we don't know all the circumstances here..."

Norris finally interjected. "She obviously didn't really know enough or care enough to be careful enough..."

Tom straightened up and Norris fell silent. "Might it have been avoided if she felt like she could trust even one of us a little more? Maybe, maybe not. Maybe it was an accident. Maybe it was a fluke. All those things are possible, but I don't care about any of those things. If she chooses to share that with any of you, that is her choice, but I beg you all, give her the space to talk to you. Otherwise, don't ask."

"The Bertram family is about to be one person bigger, regardless of the decision that Mariah makes. Until then, I want you all to keep your suggestions to yourself unless asked directly. You all have opinions. I'm sure you all have hot takes. I don't care. Mariah does not care. Only two people in this room know what it means to be a parent, and only one knows what it is like to give birth.

"And so, today of all days, I am breaking with tradition. I am walking out of this dining room before 3 I implore you all to follow me, so that the one woman who can actually offer any advice has the room, without any distractions, to speak to the other woman whose life is about to change."

He walked over to Mariah, who was openly sobbing for the second time that day, hugged her, whispered something private in her ear, and kissed her on the cheek. With that, Tom Bertram walked out of the dining room and into the history books. Tommy and Yates started a slow clap as he left. Junior, Julia, and Ed chimed in as they followed him out the door. Tommy took Norris by the hand and tried to pull her out of the room. She refused to stand, so Yates and he picked up her chair and carried her out while she sat, arms crossed, in protest.

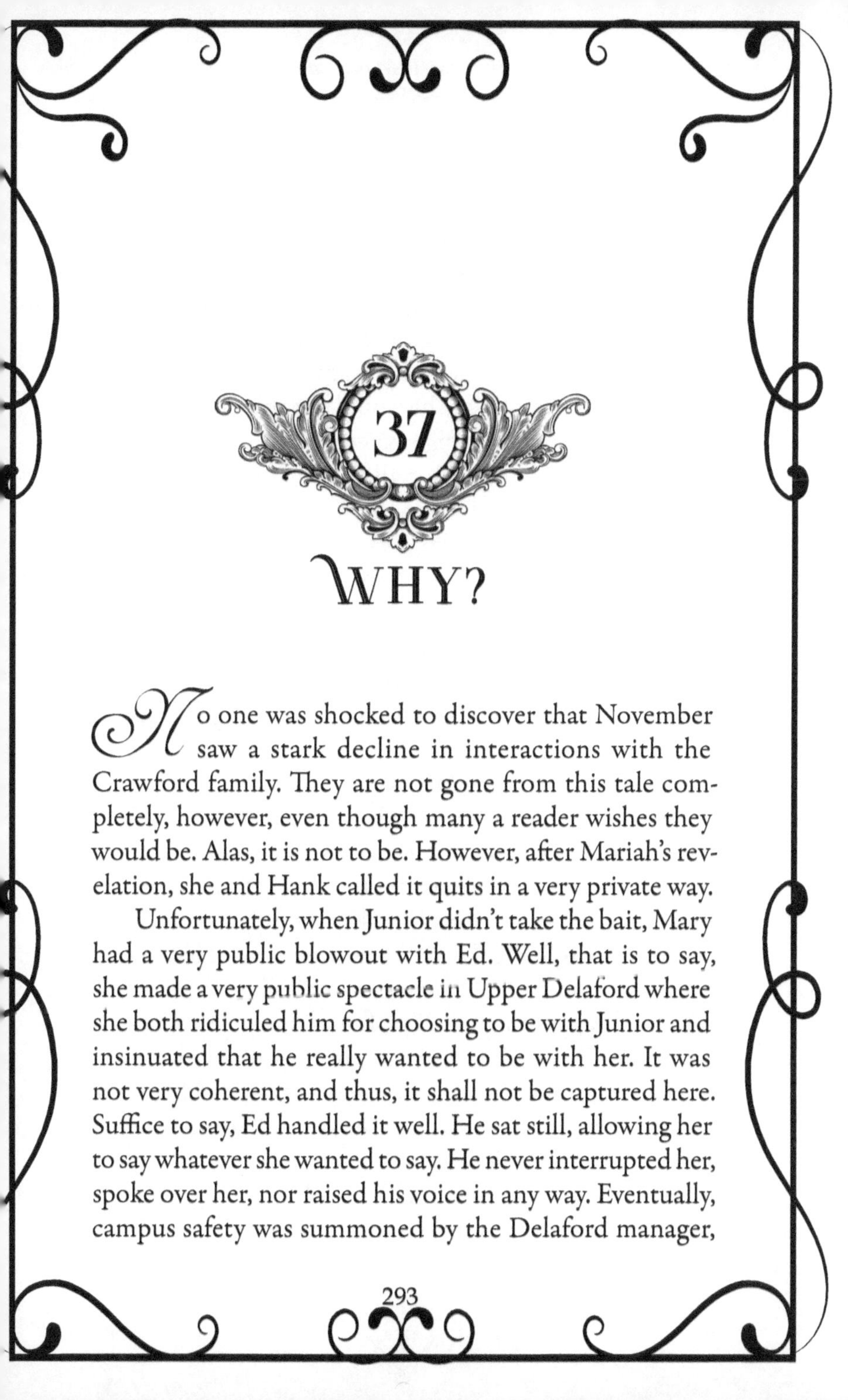

37

WHY?

No one was shocked to discover that November saw a stark decline in interactions with the Crawford family. They are not gone from this tale completely, however, even though many a reader wishes they would be. Alas, it is not to be. However, after Mariah's revelation, she and Hank called it quits in a very private way.

Unfortunately, when Junior didn't take the bait, Mary had a very public blowout with Ed. Well, that is to say, she made a very public spectacle in Upper Delaford where she both ridiculed him for choosing to be with Junior and insinuated that he really wanted to be with her. It was not very coherent, and thus, it shall not be captured here. Suffice to say, Ed handled it well. He sat still, allowing her to say whatever she wanted to say. He never interrupted her, spoke over her, nor raised his voice in any way. Eventually, campus safety was summoned by the Delaford manager, and she was escorted out. When the situation was relayed to Junior, she simply said, "Poor Mary."

In better news, Bill graduated from what Junior had been calling "the drone academy" and arrived the Sunday before Thanksgiving. He stayed with her and the Bertrams for a few days before he headed back down to Unincorporated Nowhere. He wanted to see the family and meet the twins before he would start his assignment in the Nevada desert applying his newly acquired flight skills.

Junior was elated. She walked down to the train station far too soon, and while the winter coat her mother bought her was quite warm, a southern girl on an exposed train platform for an hour in the November chill of the northern Mid-West of the United States felt the chill for the rest of the day. So much so, that after the lengthy hug and brisk walk back to The Park, they spent a lot of the first few hours back in each other's company sitting in front of the fire in her room.

"Tell me everything," Bill said.

So she did. There is no need to recount it all here, Dear Reader, as you've read the previous pages, so all is clear. This is not one of those stories that insults the reader by reprinting entire sections in a slightly different way. No one likes that. Suffice to say, there were several bathroom breaks with some replenishing of snacks and drinks. Bill, who was always hungry before, found that physical fitness in the world and physical fitness in the military were different things, and thus, his stomach was essentially a monster that occasionally woke him in the middle of the night demanding to be filled.

Lunch that day was all about Bill. He was greeted as a conquering hero. Even Mariah, who had previously not spoken a word to him, asked a few questions. After the "Born to Run" speech, she had finally started trying to be nicer. She failed most of the time. Only Tommy had the nerve to call her out when she was being awful. Norris chastised Tommy for doing so; he in turn would make rude sounds or hand gestures. To Tom and Candy, this all meant things were back to normal and all was well. Pregnant or not, no one liked to cross Mariah. Norris thought, even though she was pregnant with a Rushworth, that Mariah hung the moon and treated her as though she did.

Tom had taken the whole week off, so while Junior had classes on Monday and Tuesday, and of course, Norris kept her students until the last possible minute on the final day before break, Bill and Tom spent time in Tom's private office. It was quite an honor. The four Bertram children had only ever been in the private office for what Candy termed, "Wait until your father gets home" time. Tom's bark and his bite were quite mild, so those moments often devolved into "I'm not mad, I'm just disappointed" speeches with variable effect depending on just how disappointed he was.

No one had just been invited in as an equal until Bill arrived. It was, however, evident to everyone that seeing Bill in his dress blues demanded attention and respect. Thus, no one was upset or jealous. They all agreed they would have been upset if Tom hadn't done so. Also, they spent most of their time talking about drones and planes. No one else was interested anyway.

The time he spent there went far too fast. Junior considered buying a train ticket to come with him, but knowing her like he did, he told her point-blank that he had been told by their mother not to allow such a thing under any circumstance and that she was not allowed to come back until Spring Break at the earliest. They both knew what would happen if she went home and saw what was going on down there. The only reason he was allowed to come home was that he was legally obligated to leave. So, he was gone on Wednesday, and Junior wore his absence like a chain that night.

Of course, it wasn't really his absence that wore her down as much as what his absence represented. She wanted so very badly to be there for her mother and the family. The guilt of it all, which she had managed to fend off by being busy with school and happy with her new experiences, crashed on her when she had five straight days with nothing to do.

Fortunately, she had arranged with Candy and Tom to let Maggie spend the holiday at The Park. She could have stayed in a hotel or in the dorm where many non-English speaking international students stayed, but if she was packing up and living out of a suitcase for five days, and since she planned on spending a lot of time with Junior anyway, it just made sense.

They set her up to sleep in the guest room in the East Wing where Bill stayed, but she spent Wednesday night in Junior's room where she and Julia did their best to cheer her up. However, they knew that before any cheer could be had, the elephant in the room had to be acknowledged. Julia brought a chair in from the shared room so they all sat in front of the fire sipping hot beverages.

"Look, I know Mom is just looking out for me, but I don't think it's OK to forbid me. I mean, yes, I'm technically still a minor in the eyes of the law and all that, but I'm out here, doing my best to adult. She's the one who set this up for me to live here. I was going to get an apartment and a job."

"I hear that," Maggie said, "but it isn't that she is concerned with you not being an adult. She's concerned with you adulting too much."

Julia nodded. "Yeah, it's about how she wants you to be a normal kid... Uhhh... young adult, college-type person."

"Good save, Jules," Maggie said. Normally Julia hated it when people called her Jules, but Maggie's accent was pleasing to her ear, and so she let it go.

"No, I know. I know. I really do. But she raised me this way. It's like asking me to suddenly write with my other hand for no reason."

"BUUUZZZZZ!" Maggie shouted. "Wrong answer. There IS a reason. A good, good reason. It's like that time in *Rocky II* where Mickey makes him switch to fighting right-handed to trip up Apollo. Eventually, he makes him..."

"Right!" Julia interrupted. "Mickey thinks it is the key to actually winning."

Maggie raised one eyebrow at her. "Impressive."

"Dad and I did a full Rocky marathon before the *Creed* movie came out and then again when the second one came out."

"Nice. That is some quality parenting. So..."

"Is that the one with 'Eye of the Tiger'?" Junior chimed in.

"*Rocky III,*" they said at the same time.

"I've never seen any of them."

"Well, we should rectify that, but AFTER I make my point."

"How about you make your point, and we don't watch grown men punch each other, but do something more fun instead?"

"There isn't as much punching as you might think," Julia said.

Junior made an incredulous face.

"No, she's right. There is a lot of punching for sure, but they are mostly montages with uplifting songs and hot, sweaty people."

"Hot as in hot, or hot as in *hot?*"

"Is it cheeky to say both?"

"Is it both?" Junior looked to Julia for an answer.

"It is. I mean, Stallone is kind of gross, but the new ones have Michael B. Jordan."

"And Tessa Thompson. Total smoke show," Maggie replied.

"As alluring as they both are, and I thought she looked fantastic in a suit in that *Men in Black* movie, I'll pass."

"Whatever. Your loss. So, my point is... What were we talking about?"

"Switching hands," Julia and Junior both said in a deadpan.

"Right. Switching hands. So, there was a reason for it. It was important. He fought with his other hand, gained the advantage, but then switched back to win. Your mom only wants you to do this for now. She isn't banning you from home forever, she just needs you to fight with your other hand for a while until you feel like you can make the choice to switch back."

"Hmmm," Junior said aloud as she thought about it. "You make some sort of twisted sense, but that doesn't make me feel less guilty."

"Well, in *Rocky IV*..."

"Enough Rocky wisdom." She laughed and reached over to put her hand over Maggie's mouth. "I get it. I get it. She's doing this for my own good. She loves me. It's just, I wish..." Junior trailed off when she realized what she was going to say.

"What?" Julia leaned forward in her chair. "It's just what?"

"You wish what?"

"Well, it's just that I wish..." She put her hands over her face embarrassed to say the next thing. The other two, sensing that silence was the right move, held their tongues. When Junior realized they were not going to bail her out, she wiped away the tears that squirted out and said in a whisper, "I wish she would explain to me why."

"Why what?" Maggie asked.

"Why she loves him more than she loves us." She started crying hard then.

They both jumped up and scrambled over to her. Maggie stood, and Julia knelt. They wrapped their arms around her, Maggie at her shoulders and Julia at her waist, and just let her cry. Sometimes that is the sign of the best kinds of friends. The ones who just let you do what you need to do without getting in the way.

After the crying was over, Junior just couldn't bring herself to talk about it anymore. Fear not, Dear Reader, she will. The three of them spent the rest of the night gossiping and speculating about how they thought Thanksgiving dinner would go, considering it was the first time Norris and James would be in the same room since the big announcement.

38

Thanksgiving at The Ranch

Holidays at The Park are epic in nature and hectic for the staff. They are all technically given the long weekend off, but they are still required to have everything ready before they go. So, the few days leading up to any holiday means they must do their regular duties as well as prepare the meal for the holiday itself.

Essentially, on the morning of any major holiday that revolved around food, Portsmouth arrived early to put the turkey or ham, depending on the holiday, into the oven to slow cook. He then placed the side dishes into their own ovens and set the timers. It was then up to the Bertrams to remember the food was cooking downstairs and to take it out before it burned or there was a fire.

Fortunately for the family who lived upstairs and unfortunately for the staff who worked downstairs, Norris and this tradition were inextricably linked, so she too arrived at The Park uncomfortably early to "oversee" Portsmouth. Each year, in quiet pockets of The Park, conversations happened about how Portsmouth felt about this. No one believed he welcomed the "help." Of course, he would never speak anything of the sort.

Thanksgiving, and all holidays at The Park, were treated with weekend food rules. There was "do it yourself breakfast," but nothing else would be served until 2. This suited Tom quite nicely as he felt holidays, in general, and Thanksgiving, in particular, were all about bonus days to watch sports. He was thankful that multi-millionaires wanted to put themselves at risk for his entertainment, and multi-billionaires were happy to pay them to do so. 2:00 was generally a perfect time for a break in the action. Had he been "allowed," he would have installed a TV in the dining room for these special occasions, but since he didn't own the house, he did not. His favorite invention that was not aviation-related was the DVR. He recorded the games when he came to the meal and then caught up when he got back. The halftime break allowed him to skip ahead quite a bit so he could be back to live by the time the second game of the day started. He always took dinner alone so he could watch into the night.

Junior, Julia, and Maggie all poured out of Junior's room around 8 a.m., having stayed up until around 4. They lurched and stumbled, bed-headed and wrinkly, to The Nook. They had no particular plans for the day, and so they took their time drinking coffee after stuffing themselves on bagels and muffins. They took "bonus" muffins back to their rooms to make sure they wouldn't be hangry before lunch.

Junior saw a text from her mother that read, "Happy Thanksgiving, baby." She then wrote the words "Turkey emoji" in parentheses, not knowing how to include a turkey emoji. "Talk tonight. I love you."

Julia went back to her room and said she was just going to nap for as long as she could. Junior and Maggie crawled back into Junior's bed as well. Maggie fell asleep almost immediately. Junior was unable to follow suit, so after an hour of trying, at around 10, she quietly took some clothes into the bathroom, got dressed, and grabbed her phone and heavy jacket as she slipped out of the door while silently letting Maggie sleep.

She opened the back door to the West Wing and was pushed back by a gust of wind. She had not zipped her coat up yet, and she berated herself. She had yet to see snow, but she was convinced, with temperatures this low, that it would come any day. Of course, southerners think anything below fifty is arctic. She would learn what real cold was during her time at Mansfield, but in that moment, she couldn't imagine anything more primed for snow.

She walked across the yard and entered the Carriage House, which was thankfully heated. It was a luxury most northerners do not afford their cars, but because they had a full-service auto shop, which included oil, heat was a necessity. Plus, Candy just wanted it heated in there for the rare times she had to walk out to get her car.

Junior climbed into the front seat of Julia's Jeep, the only car she was expressly given permission to use, set her phone on the steering wheel, and pressed the button to FaceTime Suzy. She knew her mom wanted to talk later, but she just wanted to check in. She could imagine the crazy scene in the kitchen, a scene in which she had always been in the picture.

She knew that the Thanksgiving meal was served at noon on The Ranch, so their dad could be done by 12:30 when the Lions game started. Of course, the big house's dining room and the living room were all one big space, so the TV was on the whole time, regardless of what time the food was served. He did relent to Fran's request that it at least be on mute until after dessert was served.

Betsy answered the phone. The camera was pointed at the ground, and she was on the move, making Junior a bit motion sick. "JUNIOR! IT SAYS JUNIOR'S NAME." She was shouting. "JUNIOR'S CALLING, MAMA!"

"It's me, sweetie," Junior said, but her little sister couldn't hear her.

"Here, Little Bit, give it to me." She heard Bill's voice.

"No!" She giggled, clearly thinking it was a game. She started running, making Junior feel like she was in a terrible point-of-view horror movie. She saw little feet, stained carpet, the TV, and eventually, it all went dark. She could still hear her sister's heavy breathing.

"Junior?" the voice said from the dark.

"Yes, baby, where are you?"

She laughed again. "Shhhh, don't tell. Under Mama's bed."

"OK. I won't tell. Can you flip the phone over so I can see you?" The phone spun around, and there was a quick glimpse of the inside of her mouth filled with baby teeth and giggles, and then it went back, face down. "I meant just part way, honey. Not all the way around."

"Junior?" The joy dropped from her voice.

"Yes?"

"Where are you hiding?"

Tears welled up in her eyes, and a lump formed in her throat, making it hard to talk. She croaked, "I'm at college. Remember? We talked about it."

"Yeah?"

"Yeah. It's big-person school."

"Do I go?"

She sniffed and wiped her face with the palm of her hand. "You most certainly will go. Just not for a while."

"Suzy goes next?"

She laughed through the tears. "That's right baby, Suzy goes next. We take turns. You have ten years yet until it is your turn."

She sighed and grunted, "That is longer than me."

"I know it's longer than you, but don't worry. You just worry about going to little person school. You go now."

"I do. I don't like it."

"No? Oh, that's too bad. Why don't you like it, baby?"

"My teacher smells weird, and there is a mean girl, and the lunch is yucky, and I don't like shoes all day, and the potty is big, and the carpet is itchy, and I get tired, and my hand hurts and..." She seemed to run out of steam. "I just don't like it."

"Well, that is sure a lot of things to not like."

"Yeah. It is." They sat in silence for a while. "Junior?"

"Yeah?"

"Do you like big person school?"

"I do like it very much. Even though one of my teachers smells weird, and the potty is big, and I don't like shoes all day, and I get tired, and there is a mean girl."

"Really? You like it still?"

"I do, baby."

"But why?"

"Well, there is a teacher who doesn't smell weird, and lots of boys and girls who are nice, and I take my shoes off when I come back to my room, and I like to learn things."

"What kind of things?"

"Oh my! All kinds of things. I learn about other countries and kings and queens…"

"There's really queens?"

"There most certainly are. One of the nice girls I met here is from a country that had a queen."

"Nuh uh."

"It's true."

"What's her name?"

"My friend or the queen?"

She scoffed. "The queen a'course."

"She was called Elizabeth."

"Like me?"

"Yes, like you, but nobody calls her Betsy or Little Bit. They used to call her Lillibet, though."

"That's almost the same."

"It is. Almost. Mostly, they called her 'Your Majesty.' She was Queen for longer than anyone had ever been queen."

"What happened to her?"

"She just got very old, sweetie. She passed away not long ago."

"Was she a thousand?"

Junior laughed. "No, she was almost one hundred."

Silence for a few moments. "I don't know no one who's a one hundred."

"Me neither, but I get to learn about her and a whole bunch of other stuff too."

"Yeah, that sounds good. Can I come learn with you?"

The tears made a sudden reappearance. "Maybe, but not until you finish little kid school."

She sighed. "Fine. But that is so long."

"I know it is, Little Bit." Junior thought for a second and wiped her face. "Tell you what."

"What?"

"You and I will be pen pals."

"What's pen pals?"

"Well, I'm going to write you a letter and put it in the mail today. In a few days, it will show up at the post office…"

"Who brings it?"

"There are a lot of people. They pass it from hand to hand and car to car until, eventually, it arrives down there, and Suzy or Mom will bring it from the post office and…"

"Suzy does mail."

"OK. So, Suzy will bring it to you from there, and then you will open it and read what I wrote you, and then you will get a new piece of paper and write me a note back. Suzy will take it back to the post office, and I will get it up here."

"I can't read all the words, though."

"Right, but if you keep going to little person school, you will learn all the words."

"Yeah?"

"Yep. That's how I got so good at words and was able to come to college."

"OK!" Junior heard scrambling sounds and heard her little sister's voice fade away as she was out to tell the rest of the house the whole story.

"Hello!" she shouted, hoping someone would hear her voice.

There was suddenly light as the phone flipped over, and she saw Bill's face wet with tears. "Happy Thanksgiving!"

"Hey, it's rude to eavesdrop." She smiled big at him.

"Yeah, well…" He was sitting on the edge of the bed in their parent's room in almost the same spot she sat when her entire odyssey began. He realized she was sitting in the Jeep. "Why are you in a car?"

"Oh, yeah, Maggie is asleep in my bed, and I just wanted to talk to you guys without bothering her."

"So, you went out to the garage?"

"Um, it's Carriage House, thank you very much," she said in her poshest northern aristocratic accent.

"Well." He mimicked clasping his pearls. "Excuse me. My faux pas." He pronounced it "Fox Pass."

"Don't let it happen again."

"Isn't it cold?"

"You will not believe this, but it's heated out here."

Bill nodded. "That checks out."

"Yeah, well, believe it or not, I didn't call to talk about heated garages."

"Really? Hmmm. Seems like you did. That and to convince Little Bit to stay in school."

"About that…"

"Hold on." Bill set the phone on the bed. This time, instead of utter darkness, the camera was facing directly into the light. She had to look away. She could hear some mumbling in the distance, which she assumed was actual talking, and eventually, she heard a door close, and the phone leveled back out to show both Bill and Suzy.

"Hi!" She started to tear up again.

"Happy Thanksgiving!" Suzy said with a big happy voice that belied the look on her face.

"What's wrong?" She sat up straighter in the seat and leaned forward. "Don't you dare say nothing." She pointed her finger at the camera.

"It's not one thing really. It's just, Mom is not, well…" Suzy looked over at Bill as though having him home gave her permission to not be in charge for a minute.

"Mom is what?" Junior knew where the keys were for the Jeep and started doing the math in her head on how long it would take to drive home.

Bill could see the look on her face. "No! It's not that. Don't you dare. She is fine. She's just run down."

"Suzy said Mom is not well," Junior said.

"No, I didn't."

"You did, though."

"I said, Mom is not…" pause, pause, pause "…well…"

"Argh."

"Just stop for a second," Bill ordered, his military voice coming through. "Both of you."

They both clamped their mouths shut. "Now. I've only been here a day, but Mom and I have been in touch while I was at the drone academy," he said, using her vernacular, "but it is clear Mom is worn out. Dad has moved into the old house and comes around during meals. Not that he did much before, but this is a different level of negligence. At least when he was sitting in the chair, he could yell at someone to shut up or glare at someone until she or he picked something up or minded Mom."

"You're not making this better," Junior said with her teeth clenched.

"I'm getting there." He looked up, and Suzy looked over at the door. They both held their breath, waiting to see if it would open. Junior found herself holding hers as well.

When twenty seconds passed and the door hadn't opened, they all let it out, and Bill continued. "So, I finally convinced Mom to get on government assistance. Suzy helped too, of course, and filled out most of the paperwork, but essentially, everyone is on free lunch, and the potty-trained littlies are in daycare, so she's home with just the twins and the toddler."

"What? Really? Why didn't anyone tell me?"

"We're telling you now?" Suzy said as a question.

"It just happened a few weeks ago. It took a while. We weren't sure it was going to go through. Dad is already on disability and all."

"That's why she said the food is yucky."

"Yeah. Mom doesn't make lunches anymore. It saves so much time," Suzy said. "She is right, though. The lunches are pretty bad." She made a lemon face.

"So, now, just after she is used to having some time to breathe during the day, everyone is here, and she has to do Thanksgiving."

"And I called, and you are both in here talking to me."

"Right," they said together.

"Oh, man," she said. "I'm so sorry. I didn't know."

"Right. You didn't know. Just, she's frazzled. She wanted to wait to talk to you until after it was over, and your day was over. She knows the rules up there that you won't even start eating until 2."

"She left me a text this morning saying we could talk tonight, but I just missed you all and..." She trailed off and fought back some tears. She hunched over and wiped her face. She took a deep breath. "Right, well, this is good. It's all good. You shouldn't be in here with me. Get out there. Tell her I love her."

"We will," they said together.

"Love you both."

"Love you," they said together.

"Bye!" they all said at the same time.

The screen went blank. The clock read 10:35.

Thirty-five minutes and everything she thought she knew had changed. Her mother's mantra of "we have enough help right here" was no longer valid. Junior knew she should feel good that her mother finally realized she couldn't do it all, and that asking so much of her children was too much, but she couldn't help but wonder what could have been had she changed her tune about that ten years sooner.

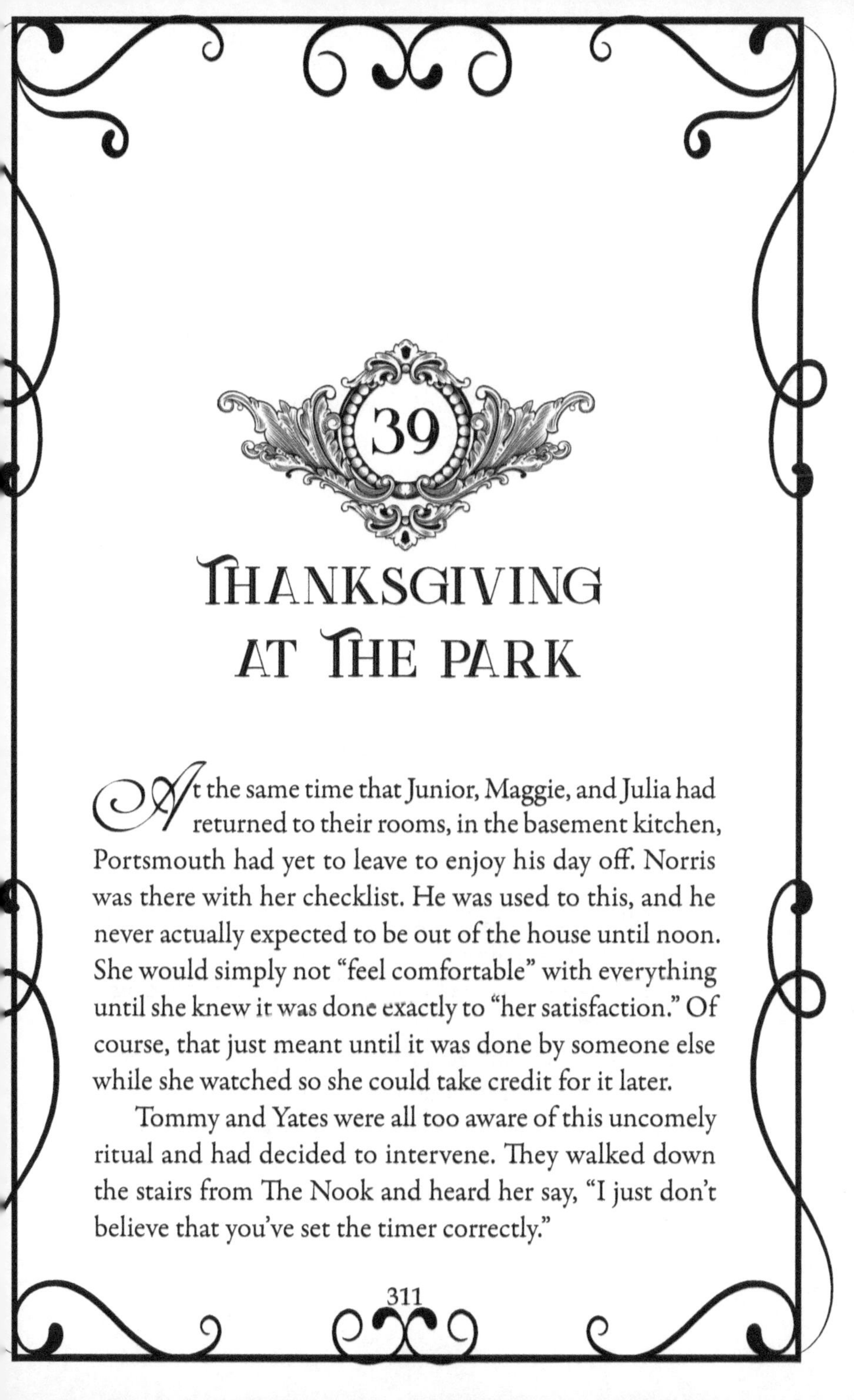

39

THANKSGIVING AT THE PARK

At the same time that Junior, Maggie, and Julia had returned to their rooms, in the basement kitchen, Portsmouth had yet to leave to enjoy his day off. Norris was there with her checklist. He was used to this, and he never actually expected to be out of the house until noon. She would simply not "feel comfortable" with everything until she knew it was done exactly to "her satisfaction." Of course, that just meant until it was done by someone else while she watched so she could take credit for it later.

Tommy and Yates were all too aware of this uncomely ritual and had decided to intervene. They walked down the stairs from The Nook and heard her say, "I just don't believe that you've set the timer correctly."

"Norris," Tommy said in a sing-song voice as he turned the corner from the hallway to the kitchen, "Portsmouth has never done anything wrong in my entire life. If you think he didn't set the timer correctly, you must have sprinkled some hallucinogens on your bran flakes."

"Pfft. Thomas, this does not concern you, nor you, Johnathan."

"You see, this is a holiday. Mom and Dad want Portsmouth to be thankful that he works here, not miserable. Besides, you don't actually live here, you know."

Portsmouth, to his credit, stood stock still and made no facial expressions, nor did he make a sound. Whether this display on his behalf was welcomed or embarrassing would never be discovered. He would, however, find himself back in his residence by nine on every holiday following that one. Take from that what you will.

"You don't live here either, Thomas."

"That is pretty weak tea," Yates chimed in. "I'm rubber and you're glue. Really?"

"I would expect so much more from you," Tommy said.

Norris' fists were clenched. "I don't have to stand here and be insulted."

"Well, we have a rather comfortable sofa if you'd rather sit," Tommy deadpanned.

"This isn't over, Thomas," she said through clenched teeth.

"Promise?" He smiled a full-toothed grin back at her.

"Fine." She crumpled up her checklist and threw the wadded paper at them, turned on her heel, and stormed out.

"It's too bad there aren't doors down here. It would have been better if she could slam one on the way," Yates said laughing.

"So true." Tommy laughed too. He turned to Portsmouth. "Portsmouth, my friend. I would like to officially relieve you of kitchen duty. Please, go enjoy your weekend." He held out his hand.

Portsmouth bowed his head, refusing to shake hands as that, to him, was a bit too familiar. "Thank you, Mister Bertram. I shall." He looked to Yates. "Mr. Yates." He bowed his head again.

Yates replied in kind, "You're a good man, Portsmouth."

"Thank you, Sir." He took two steps backward, turned and exited the kitchen, and disappeared down the hallway to the back cellar entrance the staff used.

They watched him go. When he was out of sight, Yates asked, "Where does that back door come out?"

"There's a tunnel that goes out past the Carriage House. It's near his cottage. The staff who don't live here park out there."

"I learn something new every day."

"Yeah well, today you get to learn how to sit upstairs in The Nook while watching the clock."

"Well, I think I can handle that. There's coffee, snacks, and you. What else could I want?"

"I totally agree that I come in third on that list," Tommy said as he started walking toward the stairs.

Yates smacked him on the backside as he passed by. "Well, it all depends on the day where you rank."

"Totally fair."

They settled into the window seat in The Nook. They ate, drank, and worked on a screenplay until the timer went off, and they were required to go down to the kitchen to move the food to serving trays.

Norris stormed off to the front Lounge where she sat angrily pretending to read, clearly hoping someone would come by to ask her why she wasn't downstairs supervising the meal. No one asked, and when Tommy and Yates wheeled the meal into the dining room later in the day with much pomp and circumstance, no one asked her then either.

She could only keep quiet for so long. She was stoic when Candy stood and welcomed James with a hug welcoming him officially to the family. When Tommy and Yates served the meal, she said nothing. After it was eaten and after Junior and Maggie offered to clear the dishes and take them downstairs, she kept her thoughts to herself. Even after Ed and Julia served dessert, her lips remained zipped.

However, when Tom, who wore a Honolulu blue polo shirt in support of his team, started edging toward the door so he could go watch the second half of the Lions game, Norris stood up and cleared her throat. "I have been quiet long enough."

"Oh, come on!" Tom shouted. "Can't you just keep whatever thing you are mad about to yourself for thirty more seconds?"

She shot daggers at him with her eyes. "I cannot, Thomas. This concerns you. It concerns you all." She looked over at Junior and Maggie. "Well, not you. You may go. This is family business."

"Hey!" Ed shouted.

Julia shook her head.

"Why?" Tommy asked.

Junior, who had chosen to leave the scarf loose the whole meal, started to wrap it tight as she stood up. "I understand." She reached her hand out and Maggie took it. "We'll just…"

There was the sound of a smacking hand on the table followed by a loud, "NO!" Everyone was surprised the booming voice came from Candy.

They all turned to look at her. She was standing up and had placed Pug, who was on her lap the whole meal, right on the table. She stood still, and feeling the tension in the room and the attention on her, the little dog hunched down and growled, ready to defend Candy at any cost. The fact that she licked her face in the middle of the growl did take some of the power out of the moment, but she didn't know that.

"You don't go anywhere. Junior is part of this family. She has spent more time with me and has learned more about Pug than you ever have. Maggie is her guest, and guests of family are like family. She can stay. Everyone sit! You too, Tom."

Tom plopped into the chair nearest him at the same time Pug, hearing the command, sat right on the tabletop. Junior and Maggie followed suit, albeit much slower and gingerly. They kept their legs tense in case they needed to spring up and bolt.

"Now, what is so important, Ethel?"

"Ooohhhhh, no you di-ent," Tommy howled.

Everyone else in the room took a collective breath at the sound of Norris' first name. It was the first time any of them had heard anyone use it with her in the room. She hated the first name because it was the name that her mother gave her. The name that signified to her that her mother tried to take being a Mansfield away from her. Even though going by Norris waved it about for everyone to see, no one could fault a woman for having her father's name. However, to her mother, who hated being a Mansfield, who hated everything it stood for, all the pomp and circumstance that came with the family name was too much for her. So she married the first man she found who was willing to have her and left town. To add insult to injury, she named her only child, a daughter, not after one of the many Mansfield women, but after the matriarch of the Rushworth family.

To her credit, Norris let it bounce off her as though no shot had been fired. "I'm making it known that after the semester ends, I shall be taking a leave from teaching to do some traveling, and when I return, I shall expect my residence in The Park to be ready for me. I shall be claiming my birthright. Young Thomas reminded me today that my place here is limited. He is correct. The Mansfield name in general, and The Park in particular, are falling into disrepair, and it is my duty to rectify this. I will admit to having my pride hurt when that horrible woman, Dr. Bennet, took away my livelihood. I should not have been so desperate to find a way to stay on the staff. I should have moved here and taken my rightful place in my cottage. Maybe if I had, everything this year would have gone much differently."

The room was utterly silent as they processed what that meant for each of them and what she was insinuating about the past year. Ed was mouthing, "What did you do?" to Tommy, who was trying to figure out how it was his fault. He wasn't denying it, but he was trying to replay his conversation with her that morning. What could he have said that made her do this? Norris looked around the room at each of them individually, daring them to make eye contact.

"This is about me, isn't it?" Mariah asked, breaking the silence just before her mother could say anything. "Me and James." She reached out and took his hand. "You're just so mad that…"

"As much as I am put off by your unfortunate circumstances, dear, it is not about you. Not just about you. Look at you all. You are all so desperate to get away from this place. Thomas, you are always flying away doing God knows what. Why? You don't need the money. You married a Mansfield." He opened his mouth to speak but Norris plowed on. "Young Thomas and Johnathan are the talk of the town with that grotesque burlesque show they put on. Everyone knows you're a Mansfield son, and yet you treat the name like it is trash.

"Yes, you Mariah, not only having unprotected intercourse, but to do so with a Rushworth. What could be worse? You have literally added insult to injury. Julia, I suppose we have hopes for you, but know I saw you and your team running past my residence without your shirts."

Everyone turned and looked at Julia with shock. "We had our sports bras on. You can't run topless! Hello?"

"It is uncouth, darling. With your sister in the family way, you cement the impression that the Mansfield girls are, she held up her fingers to do air quotes, 'open for business.'"

"Bertram. Our last name is Bertram, not Mansfield," Julia growled.

"Yes, well, that is evident, isn't it?"

"And you, Edmund. You were the one. You were the one who was going to take my place. You were going to be the second member of the family to minister to the souls of Mansfield College. You were the best hope to save the family name, and yet you choose to publicly run around with..."

Ed stood up, but before he could say anything, Candy interjected, "Stop right there. Stop. Right. There. We have had enough of you. I let you go on because I wanted you to have your say. I wanted you to have your big show. What better day than on a holiday where we all have nowhere else to go, right? You can lean into the tradition. The Mansfield way. I saw you wait until Tom was almost out the door. I saw how you looked at James during the whole meal. I know how you feel about Yates, but we love him. We can take it. We deal with it because we are all used to your vitriol."

Norris gasped and grabbed her chest.

"Oh, that's enough of that. This is all my fault, you know that, right? I'm the reason Norris is like this. I created this monster. Everyone, Junior, I'm sorry, dear."

Tom tried to stop her, "Stop. Candy, you're not to blame..."

"No, Tom. I am. When Daddy got the letter from Norris notifying him that she had won The Gift, I begged him to pay for her room and board. I had always thought it was so horrible that she was ostracized from the family simply because her mom didn't want to be part of it. I'm the one who got her back in."

"I won The Gift, Candy! I won it. I earned my way back."

"Yeah, but without Daddy's money, where would you have been?"

"I would have... I could have..."

"What? You could have what? You wouldn't have gone to Mansfield. You wouldn't have been back here. You wouldn't have made your way back into the family.

Your 'Birthright,' as you call it, would have been lost to you and maybe..."

"You won The Gift?" Junior interrupted before Candy could say something she couldn't take back. "Why didn't you say something? We're the same."

They could see her face change as though she was physically slapped. "We are most certainly not the same, child. I deserved it. The Gift was made for people like me and your friend Margaret there. People who are from good families who have fallen on hard times. It was made to give people a Mansfield College degree to lift themselves up or to make themselves even more special than they already were. Not for dirty little nobodies who will do nothing with their degree and breed more little nobodies.

"The Gift was made for people to lift themselves back to where they belong. It was because of The Gift that I showed my uncle that I was worthy of the family name. That I was a person of whom the Mansfields could be proud. I did everything I could do to bend myself, to mold myself into the perfect person. The sterling image of what it meant to be a Mansfield. I scraped and clawed and did whatever I could do.

"Yet here you all sit born into luxury, born with a place in the world and you all, every one of you has fallen under the spell of this ... charlatan." She waved her hands at Junior, whose rash had escaped her scarf and was crawling its way up her face and onto her cheeks. "I knew just what would happen. I was foolish to insist she live here after I couldn't stop you from allowing her to come in the first place. I thought she would be underfoot and in your way, Candy, and the girls would hate her, and Edmund would only see her as a sister. I just wanted to save you all, save this family from allowing another Ward to ruin your lives. Just like her mother, she would worm her way into the family only to let us down later. She would find a way to manipulate you all and make you love her... make you love her so deeply only to leave you for some, some, poor, broken down sailor because that is what those Ward women do. They waste every opportunity. They spit in the face of greatness. They turn their back on you. They lead you on and then they..." She clamped her hand over her mouth. Tears were streaming down her face. She hadn't meant to say it all. Not aloud. She hadn't expected anyone to let her get that far. Someone always interrupted her.

Save for Pug's panting, there was not a sound. Without realizing it, everyone held their collective breath. They all felt trapped in time. Frozen in the moment of realization. It was Junior who broke the spell the way that only Junior could. "Oh, Norris, I'm so, so sorry."

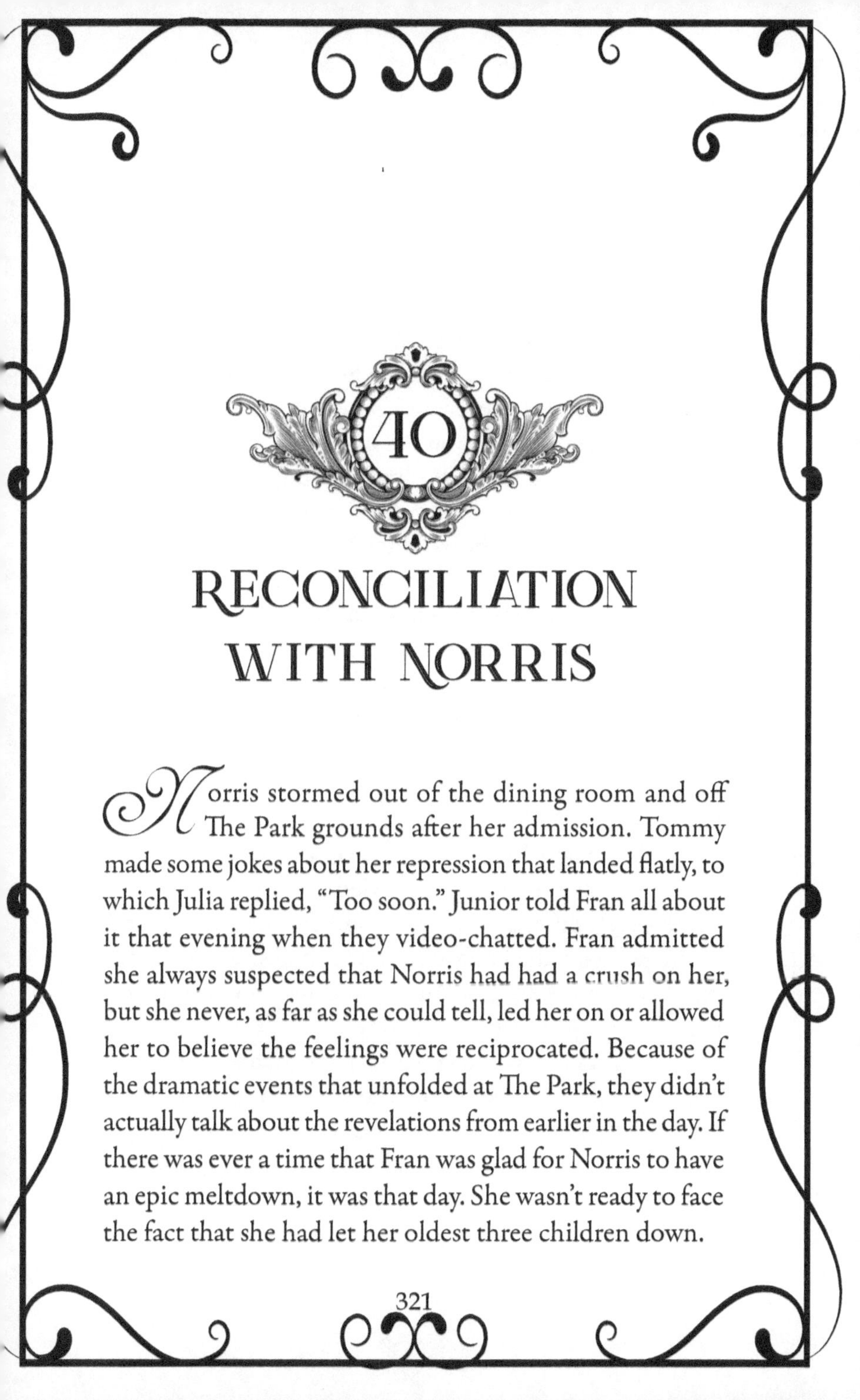

40

RECONCILIATION WITH NORRIS

Norris stormed out of the dining room and off The Park grounds after her admission. Tommy made some jokes about her repression that landed flatly, to which Julia replied, "Too soon." Junior told Fran all about it that evening when they video-chatted. Fran admitted she always suspected that Norris had had a crush on her, but she never, as far as she could tell, led her on or allowed her to believe the feelings were reciprocated. Because of the dramatic events that unfolded at The Park, they didn't actually talk about the revelations from earlier in the day. If there was ever a time that Fran was glad for Norris to have an epic meltdown, it was that day. She wasn't ready to face the fact that she had let her oldest three children down.

Candy tried several times to speak to her cousin, but to no avail. Fran was enlisted to try to have a heart-to-heart, but Norris had disconnected her phone and was not opening her door to anyone. Every blind was drawn on her house. Occasionally, a sliver of light would appear in the cracks of the shades, but no one saw her outside of class. Ed walked next to her one day on her way from her house to class, but she didn't even look at him to acknowledge he was there. She didn't respond to anything he said, making him feel as though he was losing his mind.

She submitted her letter of resignation to Dr. Bennet, effective at the end of the semester, and cancelled her office hours. Dr. Bennet, who had hoped for this day, was taken aback by the timing. Knowing that finding a permanent Religious Studies professor mid-year would be a challenge, she called her cousin, Reverend Collins, and asked him to take the job for one semester. His wife, Charlotte, who was a Bennet family friend, encouraged him to take the position, insisting that being apart for just four months wouldn't be so bad.

Even though Junior saw Norris several more times during class, there was no acknowledgement that anything was remotely different between them. Norris was cold and calculated with the handful of remaining students in her class. She showed up, lectured, and left. She no longer asked if anyone had any questions.

Tommy delivered flowers and a note of apology to her front door. He waited across the street to see what happened. Patience and Tommy Bertram were not words people often used in the same sentence, and so, after an hour, he wandered back to the theater. He came back the next day to check, and they had not moved. He came back every day for a week, and they never moved, even though it was clear she must have seen them. Eventually, he went back up on the porch to take them away. He found that on the back of his note, the words "Apology not accepted" in angry, childish script.

Julia couldn't be bothered to try to connect to Norris. They had never been close. Norris had doted on Mariah so much, it often felt to Julia as though Norris didn't know she existed except to remind her that she wasn't good enough or male enough or anything enough. Until the day of the great Thanksgiving meltdown, she and Norris had rarely spoken. She offered advice in her general direction and would espouse wisdom to the room that was clearly directed at Julia, but for some reason, Norris rarely used her name or looked at her.

Tom did nothing to try to rectify the situation. He had long since believed that the Mansfield traditions were held in place by Norris and her desire to keep the name pristine in some way or other. It was an open secret that she had begged Candy, on the day of the wedding, to keep her name so that the children could be named Mansfield.

She openly lobbied to have Tommy's first name be Mansfield as Tom wasn't one of those men that would have ever demanded his wife take his last name, and had she really cared, he would have been fine with splitting last names on the kids as well. Two Mansfields and two Bertrams, but he was against naming a child Mansfield Bertram. Norris took that personally. When Tom asked her why she didn't just change her name to Norris Mansfield, she responded with, "Don't be foolish, Thomas. Norris isn't a first name."

It was Mariah, of course, who finally broke the log jam. Ed drove her over, and they sat in his truck, parked directly in front of the house, waiting for their chance. Once Norris arrived, she made sure to waddle up on the porch, making a scene. She wore a tight-fitting hoodie as a jacket so that everyone could see that there was a cold, pregnant woman banging on the door. The neighborhood was full of other faculty members and students who lived in off-campus housing. There are still some things that will bring people of all backgrounds together. One of them is being terrible to a pregnant woman. While Norris cared very little for what the rest of the faculty, student body, or Mansfield locals thought of her teaching style or her Sunday sermons, both of which she felt were more than adequate, she did not want them to think she was the kind of person who could ignore a cold, pregnant woman.

After five minutes of pounding and general scene-making that included phrases such as, "Oh, it's so, so cold, and my back hurts so much. If only my own family would let me in so I can warm up and sit down," the door was pulled open from the inside. Mariah turned and flashed a thumbs up at Ed, who peeled away from the curb, forcing Norris not only to have to take her in but also to drive her home later.

The words that passed between Mariah and Norris are lost to history. Neither of them has ever shared the contents of that conversation. All Mariah would say is that Norris still felt she had done nothing wrong, and that the fault lay entirely with Fran. She did, however, forgive everyone else, Tommy included, although she said she was going to go forward with her plan to travel for a time. She would not visit The Park again, however, as she felt Junior's presence was too much of a reminder of "all she had lost."

Junior, once again, offered to get her own place in town; once more, Tom and Candy would not have it. They expected that Norris would return from her self-imposed exile in the fall, pretend nothing ever happened, and move into The Cottage as planned. That is not what happened at all. While no one knows what they said that day, it was later clear that they hatched a plan that involved Hank Crawford and a rectory posting in Northampton, England, to be enacted sometime after the birth of the child. While everyone would be shocked by the scandal of it all, those events have no more bearing on what happens in the following pages, and so, we shall take our leave of Norris for the remainder of this tale.

41

FINALS

While all of that was happening, Junior was both excited and sick to her stomach that her finals were fast approaching. She was excited in that these finals represented college credits that were hers forever. No matter what else happened in her life, Mansfield College would forever be part of her "permanent record," as they say. She was nervous for all the same reasons. She did not want to face-plant and put herself in a hole. As a Gift winner, she had high standards she was required to hold.

Dr. Bennet opened up her home to all The Gift winners for the first two weeks of December. Finals week was the third week of December, and then they were off until the second Monday in January. She knew all too well the pressures associated with The Gift, and she also knew that during the final few weeks of every term, the library was suddenly the most popular place on campus. She wanted to give them space to study, blow off steam, and just support each other. Her formal dining room was set up for snacks and commiserating, while the parlor had twenty small tables, each with one chair, set up around the room. Each Gift winner had a nameplate on their own table. The place was open to them from sunup until midnight for the final two weeks of the term. The elusive Jane Fairfax made an appearance. She said few words to anyone, but she did thank Dr. Bennet, which was a first, and Dr. Bennet faked a swoon. Jane smiled.

Junior took full advantage of the space. While she had a room to herself and could be sure to be left alone most of the time in the breakfast nook, there was something to making the effort to go study. She assigned one album per subject, and that would be the album she would listen to during the test. Of course, while Norris said that the practice of listening to music while testing was prohibited, all the other professors allowed headphones. Besides, she wanted her room to be a place for relaxing, not a place to worry about work. It was the first time in her life where she had her own space, and she respected it. It was why she spent so much time in the stacks, but even her hidden sanctuary was overrun by what Maggie called "tourists."

She also met with Dr. Allen to discuss her second leg of the four-leg rotation. Of course, she had no choice as to what courses she would take, but he wanted to talk her through them, check in and see how her first term went, and generally be as supportive as possible. Her new rotation featured Political Science, Chemistry, Survey of American Literature, and Music Appreciation.

It was the last one that had her stressed out the most. She assumed it would not be about classic rock, but classical music. She tried that joke out on Dr. Allen, who informed her that the course was wider-ranging than she might think, and that Dr. Schlesinger liked to give students the opportunity to write papers and do presentations about musicians that made music in the past fifty years.

She left his office envisioning herself standing in front of the class, wearing a Tesla shirt, explaining the difference between the man, the car, and the band while the opening riff of "Paradise," guitar mixed with piano, played behind her.

While she was busy with all of this, she and Ed spent as much time together as they could. Ed didn't have any finals, but he had papers and projects due during finals week, and thus, he could stop working whenever he needed a break. He had been working on his assignments since the semester began, and so he was very nearly done. She found him to be an excellent distraction from the rigors of studying.

She wished she had a load of papers to write instead of taking tests. Save for Composition II, which had a full written-in-longhand essay final, she had to prepare for three random multiple-choice and fill-in-the-blank tests. She didn't like tests. She didn't think they reflected the hard work and dedication one put toward the whole semester, but since grades were due for the professors just a few days after the end of finals week, many of them opted for machine-graded tests, especially in the 100 and 200 level courses where the courses had a lot of students.

Still, she felt that she was on the right track, so much so that she and Ed attended the showing of *Serenity* at the theater the weekend between the end of the term and finals week. The movie was a sequel to a show that was cancelled back in the early aughts, before she was born, but it was something both her parents actually liked and watched together, so she had seen the show and the film multiple times. Yates and Tommy still dressed up like characters as they introduced the films each week, and so, when they could, Ed and Junior dressed up as well.

For that showing, Ed dressed in a sharp suit and Junior dressed in overalls and a ratty long-sleeved shirt she found at the local thrift shop. While the two characters they played, the doctor Simon Tam and the mechanic Kaylee Frye, never officially got together, nearly everyone shipped them, Ed and Junior included. Neither Aaron nor Maggie could join them, but Julia was allowed to go to this screening, so she picked up a pair of combat boots from the thrift shop. She paired them with a summer dress and leggings, and thus, she was River Tam, sister of the doctor, super-genius expert fighter, and the most powerful character in the 'verse.

Junior had not grown accustomed to the cold, no matter how many times everyone told her she would. She wore the thick, polar-rated jacket her mother gave her every time she stepped foot outside. When she had to walk to class, she wore mittens and earmuffs that Candy gave her, and she doubled her scarves to try to block any air from getting in. She pulled the hood up at all times, not caring about the state of her hair afterward. So it was, that on the walk to the theater to see the movie, she looked like she was heading onto the ice while Ed looked like he was off to work in an office, as his suit jacket was his only protection from the cold and Julia threw on a hoodie to cover her bare arms.

They warned her that it was only going to get worse in February. She found that impossible to believe, but she tried to make light of it as best she could, although she was terrified. She thought thirty degrees was unreasonable, and yet, she knew it would occasionally reach temperatures near or below zero with wind chills even lower still. She joked that maybe she could convince Dr. Allen to register her for all online classes each winter.

Ed tried to make the whole thing sound like fun with promises of making snow angels and snowmen. Even time with Ed was not appealing enough for her to get remotely excited about a future of frostbite. While in the near future, she would indeed play in the snow, she never, ever grew accustomed to the cold, and while her time up north was always remembered with fondness, in the distant future, she only spent time there, if she could help it, when the weather was mild.

Some colleges and universities like to come up with a unique finals schedule, but Mansfield College never subscribed to that methodology. They felt that learning and testing should happen at the same time. To that end, each student had one final per day, per week. Courses that met on Mondays and Thursdays did finals on Monday and Thursdays. Classes that met before noon had the exam on the early day in the week; classes that met after noon had them on the later day in the week. The same thing happened for Tuesday-Friday courses. On Wednesday, Delaford was open for twenty-four hours for all students, regardless of where they lived, on or off campus. The menu was all comfort food all the time. What that meant for Junior was that the last final she had to take, of the first term of her first year, was with Norris. She felt as though that was some sort of test in and of itself. She was not looking forward to that, but she did not let it get in her way.

So, bright and early Monday morning, she found herself in The Nook before the sun came up, quizzing herself on Algebraic formulas. She was never bad at math. Still, she studied and did all the practice assignments in the book, even if they were not assigned. She arrived at her classroom early to find others had the same idea. Fortunately, Dr. Steele had also arrived early and placed a test packet, face down, on each desk. It was decided that all students who arrived early, especially at 8 on a Monday, were afforded extra time to start.

Junior plugged in her headphones, pulled up Van Halen's *5150*, took a deep breath, and flipped over her test just as Sammy shouted, "Hello, baby," on the first track. She closed her eyes and let the music take her. Since the album was so short, she assumed she would listen to the whole thing at least three times through before she finished, but she was pleasantly surprised to be halfway through the second listen when she filled in the final answer. She looked back over her test answers until she reached the end of the second run-through. She didn't find any flaws in her logic or math skills, and so, before 9 in the morning, she was done with her first college exam. Dr. Steele wrote a note on the board that grades would be posted later in the day and wished them all an excellent break.

Since there was really nothing she could do to study for her Composition final the next day, she returned to The Park with the idea she would crank up her fire and take a nap, but she couldn't relax. That was how she found herself spending the rest of the day with Candy and Yates, who were dressing Pug up in different outfits and posing her for pictures that would be used for the family Christmas cards.

When Junior's Algebra grades were posted, she was on a break with Yates in The Nook. She had earned her first A at Mansfield. There was dancing. He swung her around, and she found that she minded even less each time he did it.

The next day, she arrived for her Composition II final early, but Dr. Smith was not as accommodating as Dr. Steele. She had her album of choice, Joan Jett and the Blackhearts, *I Love Rock and Roll,* cued up and ready to play. While it too was short, there wasn't a slow song on the whole album, and she really wanted to keep her energy up.

When the class began, Dr. Smith explained that they would be asked to come up to the desk, pull a topic out of the fishbowl, grab a blue exam book, and then go back to their desks and wait ever so patiently for him to start their time. When the time was right, they would open their papers and write their personal narratives. She and Aaron grabbed their books and slips of folded paper and sat down next to each other. They reached out and fist-bumped.

"Good luck, Grandpa Frank."

"Back at you, Grandma Fran."

Once everyone was seated, they opened their folded slips of paper. Her slip had the following question: "What was the most formative moment for you OUTSIDE the classroom during your first term at Mansfield?"

She nodded, closed her eyes, and tried to decide on one thing. So much has happened in these three months, she wasn't sure what would count as most formative. What did formative even mean? She looked over at Aaron, who was already hunched over, pen flying. About half of the class followed suit and were already writing, while the other half were either looking terrified or, like her, lost in thought.

She waved at Dr. Smith to get his attention. She pointed at herself, made her fingers walk across her palm, and raised her shoulders in a shrug. He nodded and then pointed at his watch and pointed at her with a stern look. She gave him a thumbs-up and got up. She left her coat behind so that he knew she wasn't venturing too far. She went into the bathroom and looked at herself in the mirror. She tried to imagine the person she was when she first arrived and compared her to this person who looked back at her.

She looked the same as far as she could tell; turning seventeen hadn't really changed her looks much. She hadn't grown an inch since she was fifteen, but maybe there was a curve to her face that wasn't there before. She certainly had eaten better up here than she ever had at home. She walked the same amount, though, and while she hadn't put on the "freshman fifteen," she might admit to the first-year "five to ten." She didn't have a scale to know for sure, but she felt fuller.

She unwound her scarf and looked at her neck. There wasn't a blemish anywhere. She was clearly keyed up and nervous about this essay, and yet her skin showed no sign of it. She thought back to Thanksgiving, when the rash crawled out of its hiding place and went up her face. What was the time before that when she felt the burning in her neck? She couldn't actually remember.

She ran her fingers over her smooth neck and knew that she couldn't just write about one thing. She had to write about how all the things came together to form this new person she saw. It all started that day, all those months ago at the post office and the months before that when she applied for The Gift, and all those years before that when her mom came to Mansfield. She smiled at her reflection and fist-bumped herself. She had the answer.

She hit play as she walked into the room. The opening drumbeats of the titular song of the album drove her forward. She picked up two more blue books off the desk and smiled at Dr. Smith, who nodded at her confidence. She sat, cracked her neck and her knuckles, and started.

She was the last person to finish. She handed Dr. Smith the five full bluebooks and apologized for giving him so much to read. He joked that next term, he would put a word limit on the finals, and he would call it the Price rule. He told her grades would be posted by Friday. She hadn't realized how hungry she was until she actually heard her stomach growl as she was wrapping herself in frigid-weather gear. Aaron was waiting for her in the hallway. He went back to The Park with her for lunch.

All of that sitting in silence had them both bursting, so they talked the whole way back, all through lunch and right up until it was time for him to go to dinner with his poker buddies. They hugged tight just in case they didn't see each other again until January, and they promised to text and talk throughout the break.

She woke up early on Wednesday and trudged through the snow that had fallen, while she cursed the cold, to go spend the morning studying at Pemberly. She headed into the dining room first to eat breakfast with Maggie. When she arrived, only Dr. Bennet was there. They had coffee while they debriefed on the term. Junior shared how Dr. Bennet was featured in her final essay for Composition, and while she was an unflappable woman, Junior was sure Dr. Bennet blushed.

When Maggie arrived, they ate Danish pastries while Maggie talked about how her finals had gone up to that point. As they chatted, the room filled up with more Gift winners of various ages, and Dr. Bennet got up and mingled, catching up with them all and reassuring those who needed it.

After a morning of eating, studying, and eating some more, Junior returned to The Park for a lazy afternoon with Ed. They curled up on a couch in The Lounge and ended up taking an unexpected nap that was abruptly ended when Pug found them in her space and gave them a good dressing down. Candy came running into the room and scolded Pug for waking them, but Pug was unrepentant and would most assuredly do it again.

Wednesday dinner in The Nook was much more crowded than normal as Tommy and Yates arrived not only to get a free meal but also to scout the property for a film they planned on shooting there. Tom had reluctantly agreed to let them use his private office for one scene, and he was going to give them a supervised visit after dinner. While Junior had seen them excited by many things, she had, up to that point, not seen them this thrilled about anything. Clearly, Bill's time in the office was a much bigger deal than any of them had let on.

On Thursday, after lunch, armed with a full stomach and Queen's *The Game*, she headed to take her Early Modern Europe final. She was admittedly disappointed that Dr. West was going the fill-in-the-blank and multiple-choice route for the final. Considering the amount of creativity and energy Dr. West put into the course, Junior expected the same for the final. However, it made sense that she wanted to put her feet up at the end, having given it her all for fifteen weeks.

The test was more geography than anything, and Junior zipped through it. The fill-in-the-blank questions were still multiple-choice, and they were all about the kind of government in each European country. There, too, she felt confident. She finished before she even rolled back around to the first song on the album. She went back through and checked her answers. She was confident on the first run-through, but she wanted to spend a few more minutes reflecting on what was her favorite class. Wistfully, she returned the form to Dr. West, and she headed out into the hallway to get all her layers on to face the cold December afternoon.

Dr. West followed her out and mimed to have Junior follow her away from the door. She left her coat unzipped and followed her.

"Junior, I just wanted to say that I hope I see you again in one of my classes. Your passion for the subject was, well, frankly unrivaled by anyone this term."

"Thank you. Wow." She took a minute to gather herself. She was not expecting that to be the conversation. "I was just thinking about how sad I was that class was over. It was really my favorite."

Dr. West put her hand over her heart. "That means a lot to me."

"Well, I won The Gift, so I won't be able to take anything else until my third year."

Dr. West nodded. "I totally understand." She was quiet for a second, and it was clear she was lost in thought. Junior stood and waited, not wanting to distract her. "Would you maybe be interested in working for me in the meantime?"

"What now?" It was Junior's turn to put her hand over her heart.

"Well, I'm the department chair in Poli-Sci, and we could use a student worker. It doesn't pay a lot, but..."

"I'll do it!" Junior shouted and slapped her hands over her mouth and looked over at the open door. She saw one of her classmates look up, annoyed. She mouthed "Sorry" to her. She looked back at Dr. West and whispered, "I'll do it."

"Don't you want to know what the job entails?"

Junior shook her head. "I didn't realize how much I wanted it until you offered, but now that you have, well..."

"Fair enough." Dr. West reached out her hand and Junior shook it. "Come by my office in the first week of the next term, and we can get you started. I'll fill out all the paperwork over break, so everything will just need a signature, and we will be good to go."

"Oh my goodness. Thank you, Dr. West. I won't let you down."

"I know, Junior. You have a good break, OK?"

"Oh man. I will. Thank you again."

With that, they parted ways, and Junior, who was so excited and overwhelmed, stepped out into the cold without zipping up her jacket or putting on her mittens. After three seconds, she was back in the building mumbling curses at herself as she bundled up and raced for The Park.

She called, FaceTimed, or texted everyone she knew to tell them the news about the job offer. The responses were all positive and encouraging, save for her dad, who ignored it completely. The message showed up unread. She tried to imagine where he was and what he could be doing that would stop him from even opening the message but failed to figure out what could be going on. Faced with taking her last final with Norris in the morning, she opted to push it out of her mind and focus on that.

After lunch on Friday, she headed to Pemberly for one final study session. The other first-years, except for Maggie, were all there. She felt confident in herself for her last final, and she opted to spend the time packing as she was heading back to England for the holiday after spending the weekend at The Park. She wanted to drop everything off at The Park before her final. They arranged everything with Portsmouth, who, as always, was more than accommodating. She and Junior agreed to meet in the lobby of Northanger and walk back together as they expected Junior to need more time to finish whatever madness Norris had planned.

Junior, feeling fully caffeinated and ready as she would ever be, wrapped herself up and headed out into the cold winter afternoon only to discover that Dr. Bennet was leaving at the same time. They walked together, and Junior told her about the job offer from Dr. West. Dr. Bennet smiled brightly.

When they reached Northanger, Dr. Bennet came in with her. When they reached her classroom door, Dr. Bennet came in as well. The front desk sat empty, and Dr. Bennet hung her coat on the back of the chair. She set her briefcase on the desk and snapped it open. Junior stood still, looking perplexed. She looked at the handful of other students who had made it to the end of the term who were also confused as to why the president was there.

Dr. Bennet looked at her watch, and seeing it was 3 on the nose, said, "Well, class, I'm afraid that the good Reverend Norris will not be here to administer your final. She apparently booked her travel arrangements for today, and somehow was unaware that international travel requires more time at the airport preparing to leave, and thus, in order to make her trip less stressful, I have agreed to proctor this exam."

Junior thought that was a bit below Dr. Bennet's pay grade, but clearly, there was a reason she chose to do it. Maybe she was there just to make sure Norris was actually gone. Regardless, the relief she felt that she did not have to see Norris one last time and that she would not be grading the finals, washed over her, and she felt the weight of it slide off of her.

However, once Dr. Bennet placed the packet on her desk, she felt it all over again. The final had the following written on the front:

This final is worth half of your final grade. It consists of 500 questions. There are five answer sheets, each one consisting of 100 questions. Make sure you label each sheet with your last name and the corresponding numbers. You must have it completed within the two-hour time limit. If the two hours are up and you are not completed, the work you have completed shall be graded as is. In order to ensure there is no cheating, headphones, talking, or trips to the bathroom will not be allowed. So, if you must go, go before you open the packet. If you leave the room, speak or look anywhere other than the test, you will forfeit any opportunity to finish.

Rev. Norris. PhD.

"Good luck," Dr. Bennet said with the most reassuring smile she could muster.

Junior weakly smiled back. She closed her eyes, took a breath to try to center herself, and then opened the packet. Each question was three to six sentences long and had five options for answers. She wrote, "Price, 1-100" at the top of one of the answer sheets, and she began.

Of the ten students who remained until the end of the term, one of them actually finished the test. One of them stood up about thirty minutes in, swore loudly, and stormed out, leaving his test on his desk. Another, with twenty minutes to go, ran out, leaving everything behind, and went straight to the bathrooms. She waited in the hall until the time was up, and she came in to collect her things. When Dr. Bennet announced there were five minutes remaining, Junior still had fifty questions to answer. She spent four minutes skimming and scanning the remaining questions looking for "easy" answers. She managed to get twenty more filled in that way. She spent the last minute filling in E for each answer, assuming Norris would think they would all guess C.

After the tests were submitted, Junior moved over to the side of the room and did some stretches as her legs were cramped and her back was tight. Dr. Bennet informed them that she would submit the grades no later than 8 that evening. She told them all she was proud of them for getting through the course, and told them they all would have some special Mansfield swag waiting for them when they returned back from break. Not that a messenger bag could make up for the fifteen weeks they spent with Norris, she just wanted to help them feel like they were seen.

Junior took her time getting her winter gear on. They had reached that part of December in the Midwest when the sun started to set near 5. Through the windows, it looked hazy out, and she watched the literal sunset on her first term at Mansfield come to an end. She was glad she could walk back with Maggie so she could have someone to lean on and from whom she could steal some heat.

Dr. Bennet was all packed up by the time Junior was done, and so they walked out of the classroom together. Dr. Bennet shut the light off on the way out. Maggie was sitting on a bench in the hall, scrolling through her phone. She looked up from her phone with her tongue out and eyes crossed, making both of them laugh.

"You ladies have excellent breaks. Safe travels to you, Maggie. See you next term." She patted her briefcase. "I'm off to go have a glass of wine while I watch a machine grade these tests."

"Have a good holiday," Maggie said.

"Thanks. You too," Junior said.

Junior slid her arm under Maggie's, and they headed out into the cold.

"How'd it go?" Maggie asked.

"Let's just say, I'm glad it was my last final. If it had been first, I would've dropped out."

"Yikes. Wanna talk about it?"

"I don't. I just want to get back to The Park and eat and be warm. How was your last one?"

"I feel kind of bad, actually. It was a breeze. I was done in half an hour."

"That's awesome. Don't feel bad."

"Good. I won't. It was great. It was Art History. I loved it. My teacher was amazing. We talked a bit after, and she teaches some visual art and filmmaking courses that I want to take when I can. She is like, my spirit animal or something. I've just sort of sat on it because I wasn't supposed to think this way. I kept saying to myself, 'I know, I know, we're not supposed to know already,' but, like you knew about Poli-Sci, I just sort of knew with Art. I've always wanted to do it. My whole life, but like, being here made me consider it could be real. Now I know there isn't much of a job for artists, like old-timey artists, but there is so much I could do with an Art degree, you know?"

"Yeah, you could teach, or restore classics, or work for an animation studio, or do comics or storyboards for movies, or a million other things. You don't have to know, but if you do know, that's brilliant."

"Exactly." She leaned her head down on Junior's shoulder, relieved to have finally said it out loud to someone who understood and just took it in without judgment. With that, they arrived at The Park. They headed straight to The Nook, where Ed and Julia were waiting to hear all about everything they had to say. They matriculated from The Nook to The Lounge. There they shared stories with Candy and Pug, who was not thrilled by the company at that time of night, but allowed it because Candy was having such a good time, and Maggie was always extra affectionate where belly rubs were concerned.

At 8:00, Ed, Junior, and Maggie pulled out their phones to check their final grades. Ed, once again, earned four As. He tamped down the excitement by claiming that it was easier to get better grades in the third and fourth years, as they were all subject-specific. Maggie earned two As and two Bs. She was so excited that she did a swing dance number with Pug, who did not appreciate it even though everyone clapped.

Junior earned an A in Early Modern Europe, earning an A on the final. She already knew she earned an A in

Algebra. She pulled off an A- in Composition II. She was sure that Dr. Smith was going to mark her way down for her insanely long essay, but he seemed to have either given up or been impressed as he gave her a B on the final. In Religion, she managed to earn a B- overall, having somehow pulled a C+ on her final. Never in her life had she been more excited to earn a C+ on a test. Swept up in the joy and excitement, Candy demanded they all make their way back to The Nook for some celebratory junk food, and for the first time since she arrived at The Park, Candy Bertram joined them for a late meal in The Nook.

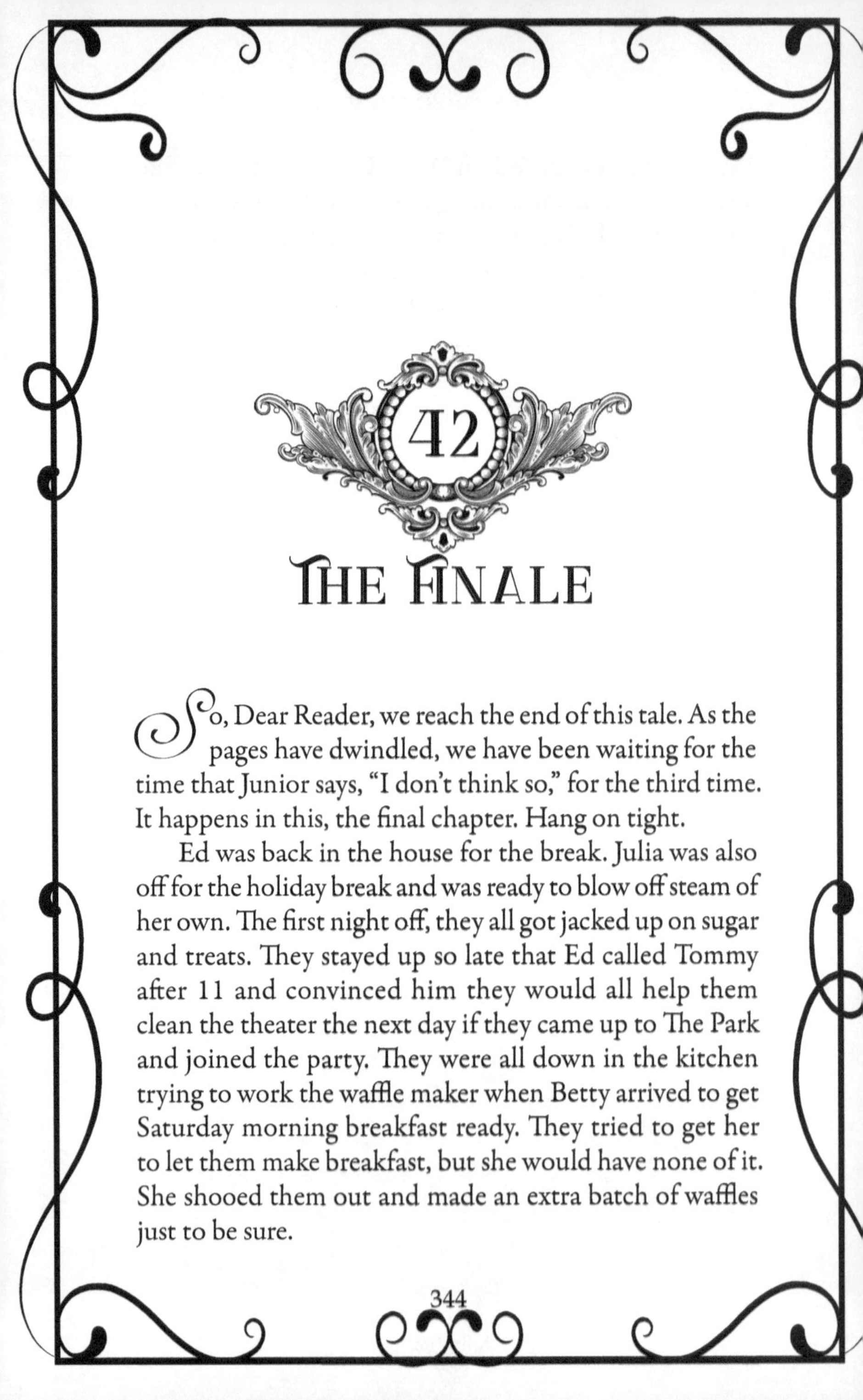

42

THE FINALE

So, Dear Reader, we reach the end of this tale. As the pages have dwindled, we have been waiting for the time that Junior says, "I don't think so," for the third time. It happens in this, the final chapter. Hang on tight.

Ed was back in the house for the break. Julia was also off for the holiday break and was ready to blow off steam of her own. The first night off, they all got jacked up on sugar and treats. They stayed up so late that Ed called Tommy after 11 and convinced him they would all help them clean the theater the next day if they came up to The Park and joined the party. They were all down in the kitchen trying to work the waffle maker when Betty arrived to get Saturday morning breakfast ready. They tried to get her to let them make breakfast, but she would have none of it. She shooed them out and made an extra batch of waffles just to be sure.

Fully fed and totally slap-happy, they bundled up and made their way down to the theater to help clean up. They were showing holiday classics, and that weekend's show was *Elf*. There were plenty of syrup bottles strewn around the theater. They placed them at the end of each row so people could pour it on their popcorn. Tommy convinced them that it was better than it sounded. They all agreed they would find out for themselves as they planned on going later that night.

They slept until 2:00 when they all arrived, still in their sleeping clothes for Lunch. Ed, Julia, and Maggie passed on time in The Lounge for more sleep, but Junior felt rested enough, so she took her coffee into The Lounge.

"It's been quite a first term, hasn't it, dear?" Candy asked after they were settled on the same couch, Pug between them.

"I can't believe it's over already. I mean, it feels like I just got here, but that I've always been here too. That's stupid."

"No, not at all. It makes perfect sense. I try to remember that time when I was first meeting your mother and when Norris came back into my life, and you know, sometimes it feels like it was just yesterday, and then Julia walks by, and I realize she's almost an adult and I'm old."

"You're not old."

"Oh, that's sweet of you, dear, but regardless of how old you are, once you have four grown children, you feel old."

"Well, Mom must feel like she's ancient then."

"Maybe, but you know, she still has babies. I think babies keep you young."

"Good thing there will be one here soon."

"No, no. I meant your own babies keep you young. Grandchildren make you older than the hills." The meaning of the words and the look on Candy's face were incongruous.

"Oh, come on. You're totally excited."

She smiled and nodded. "I really am. It's strange because when we had that whole ugly announcement lunch, I never once thought, 'why me?' or 'I'm too young to be a grandma.' I just felt a sense of calm come over me. It was like," she paused and looked at Junior for a second, "now don't take this the wrong way."

"OK?"

"It was like when I got that message from Fran asking us if you could stay. I just felt like it was right. Like the universe, or God, or whatever you believe, just whispered in my ear and said, 'Yes.'"

Junior threw herself, tears flowing, across the couch and wrapped Candy in a hug. Pug grumbled and tried to move out of the way, but Junior scooped her up and brought her into the embrace. "Thank you." She whispered it over and over, but it didn't feel like it was enough.

Eventually, after Pug tried to lick the tears and after they dried, Junior returned to her room to leave Candy and Pug to take their afternoon nap. She and Maggie spent the day watching a few bad action movies, for which Maggie had an affinity, on Junior's laptop. They eventually went to see *Elf*, this time without costumes, and discovered that syrup on popcorn was as bad as they thought.

The next morning, before the sun even rose, Maggie and Junior piled into Julia's Jeep so Junior could take her to catch her plane. Maggie was not looking forward to spending three hours alone in the airport, but she was happy that Junior offered to drive her. She took a bus when she arrived in the fall, and it wasn't until she arrived at

Angeline to check in that anyone ever spoke to her. She expected her trip back home to be filled with long silences, so she and Junior filled the 90-minute drive with all the words they could say.

They yammered on about nothing important and everything in the world. The conversation dipped and dove with occasional sips of coffee. When they were about twenty minutes from the airport, Maggie felt a sense of dread in her chest. She reached out her hand to Junior.

She glanced over at the movement and saw Maggie's open hand. She took it. "What's up?"

"I just..." She trailed off and tried to find the words. "I just know I should be thrilled to be going back home, to see my mum and sisters, but I'm just..."

Junior waited, giving Maggie a chance to find the word for what she was just, but when nothing came, she offered, "Scared?"

Maggie squeezed her hand. "Scared. That's it."

"What of?"

"Of everything. You know. I've said it all before."

"No, say it again. Say it all. I'll always listen. As many times as you have to say it. Sometimes, you just have to get it out."

The encouragement of a real friend is all often most of us need, Dear Reader, so it was for young Maggie Dashwood. "I was a bit of a mistake baby, you know. I said I wasn't technically one, I'm only three years younger than Marianne, but I totally was, and so my whole life was different than my siblings. I hardly know my brother and his wife. I have a nephew called Harry. I mean, I don't think he even knows I exist. That's OK. He isn't that much younger than me, maybe like eight years, so it's weird to have an aunt that is so close in age, although, I guess that's going to be you and your family, isn't it?"

"I suppose it could be. I sure hope not, though. I mean, I suppose I could have a kid in eight years, but I don't even want to think of it at all right now."

"Yeah, no. Let's not. Ick. It's going to be so weird around The Park with a baby as it is. Let's not have it be yours."

"Agreed." She squeezed her hand.

"Anyway, when I applied for The Gift, I didn't tell anyone because no one ever asked what I wanted to do. No one in my house once said, 'Hey, Margaret, what are your plans for the future? Hey Mags, did I see you snogging a girl last week and a boy the week before? What's up with that? Maggie, I heard you won an art prize in school.' My brother-in-law Edward used to ask, but then they had kids and so got busy, and Mum switched into Nan mode, and I was just Auntie Maggie. I've told you about Gran Jennings, who is like my best friend, and it was nice to have her. I wouldn't have made it without her, but it shouldn't have been her job to care, you know? So, yeah, I'm scared to go back. I feel seen by people for the first time, really." She exhaled when she finished. Even though she didn't say it in a rush, it felt to her like it came out as one long breath.

"Oh, Maggie. I'm so sorry you feel that way. You are seen here." She dragged Maggie's hand over and touched her heart. "No matter what happens when you go home, you know that you will come back and your people will be here waiting for you. We will see you."

"Can we video chat now and again while I'm gone just so I won't become invisible?"

"Of course. You'll never be invisible to me." She pulled her hand up to her mouth and kissed the back of it. "You know, and not to be a me-monster..."

"You could never be a me-monster, girl."

"Yeah, well, hang on and see." She let go of Maggie's hand and took a sip of her coffee. Maggie followed suit. They grasped hands again and Junior continued, "I know what it's like not to be seen, but for me, it was like I was so visible that I wasn't really there. Does that make any sense?"

"Maybe? Do you mean they all had a vision of what you were, so that is all they saw?"

"Right! See, we totally see each other. It's like, I was the oldest girl, the family mechanic, the babysitter, the mail bringer, the chauffeur, and on and on. When I skipped a grade, it was like they saw it as a step closer to adulthood so I could do more adult things for them. They let Suzy get her driver's license at fifteen. I mean, really?"

"Well, she is totally responsible."

"She is. For sure she is, but should she have to be? I mean, being fifteen should be all about crushes and kisses and being stupid, not driving your dad home from the bar." She clenched her left hand over the top of the steering wheel, and the Jeep wiggled a bit on the road. She took a breath. She pulled her hand from Maggie's and gripped the wheel at ten and two. "Sorry. I promise I'm not trying to Thelma and Louise us."

"I know, but to be fair, if it came to that, you would totally be my Thelma."

"Yeah, I think it's more that you'd be my Louise. Thelma needs her more."

"Agree to disagree on that."

"How about agree to debate it later?"

"Deal."

They let the silence sit there as they could see the bright lights of the airport ahead of them. Junior turned on the right turn signal, and she got off the interstate. They followed the signs to International Departures.

"Do you need to..." Maggie started.

Junior shook her head. "No. Not right now. I didn't mean to. It's just, you got me thinking, you know, and well, I guess, I need to think about it more, but I don't think I have the words right now. I know we've talked about our families and stuff before. It's just, when you get ready to see them, it all feels like fresh wounds."

"I get it. I have hours in an airport and more on a plane to let those wounds fester. I get it. I do. But I know when you find the words, you'll tell me, and when I find mine, I'll tell you."

They pulled up in front of the terminal and stopped in an unloading zone. "I know. Thank you." She leaned over to hug her. "Love you, Louise," she whispered in her ear.

"Love you too, Thelma." Maggie pulled back and wiped her face. "OK. Enough. I'll be back in three weeks."

"Right, we spent seventeen years without each other before."

"So, three weeks is nothing." They leaned in and hugged again. A horn blared. They jumped away, laughing. Maggie opened the door and gave the car behind her the two-fingered salute. She went around to the back of the Jeep and grabbed her bags. They locked eyes in the rearview mirror. Maggie winked and Junior smiled. She smiled back and slammed the back door. Junior pulled out. She rolled her window down and stuck her left hand out above the roof and waved as she pulled out of the airport and back to the interstate.

Over and over, she replayed in her head what Maggie had said about being seen and how she felt when she talked about it. She pulled off at the first exit, drove through a fast-food place, and ordered breakfast. She sat in the parking lot and ate her egg sandwich and had a think. The clock on the dashboard read 5:30. She knew that Julia always slept with her phone charging next to her bed. She hated to do it, but she couldn't make the next decision without Julia's permission. She was not an "ask for forgiveness rather than permission" kind of person.

She pushed the contact icon and pulled up Julia. The phone rang three times. "Hello?" Her voice was partial panic and partial confusion. Few people ever called Julia. She was a texting girl all the way.

"I'm sorry. I know this is terrible but..." and she explained herself to Julia, who, even with the shock of being dragged from slumber by a ringing phone before the sun rose, was coherent and compassionate. After ten minutes of conversation and three "are you totally sures?" from Junior, and three assurances from Julia, they hung up. She had already connected her phone with Julia's Bluetooth, plugged into the charger she left in the car so she wouldn't ever be without power, turned her music library to random, and hit play. The opening keyboard riff from Europe's "The Final Countdown" blared from the speakers. She thought it was quite appropriate. Junior got back on the highway, heading away from Mansfield, but to the interchange that would take her due south to Unincorporated Nowhere.

According to her GPS, the trip would take fifteen hours. She knew that was if she drove straight through, without breaks, and obeyed the speed limits. Since Junior was a "set the cruise at two miles per hour over the limit" kind of person, she knew fifteen hours really meant sixteen or more. Still, she figured she could pull into The Ranch later that evening. Of course, having spent hardly any money in her first term, she could easily stop along the way, get a room, sleep it off, and arrive midday on Monday. She figured she would let her body make that decision, considering she let her heart make the decision to head south, even though it meant, for the first time in her life, she was going against her mother's wishes.

Ed called at 8. "Hi!" she answered, genuinely excited to hear his voice, for him to keep her company for a while.

"Hi?" He said it as a question. "Are you OK?"

"I am. I promise."

"Julia tried to explain it to me, but she admitted to thinking it might have been a dream as well. She knocked on your door, and when you didn't answer, she went in to check. When she saw you were gone, we knew it was real."

"Oh, man. Tell her I'm sorry again and thank you again for letting me take the Jeep and..."

"I will, I promise," he interrupted. "Listen, I'm not worried about Julia; I'm worried about you. I'm not worried about you being out on the road or anything. I know you're smart and will stop if you need to and get a hotel before dark if you need to, but I'm just worried because this seems like a big deal, and I want to know how you are. How's your heart? How's your head?"

She smiled big even though he couldn't see. It meant so much to her that he didn't see her as a damsel in distress. "I appreciate that. I'm not sure, actually. I think that is why I just feel like I need to do this. Maggie said some things while I was taking her to the airport about meeting her family for the first time and not being seen, and well, it broke some things open in me I wasn't expecting. I considered just coming back and working through it with you all, and while I knew you would help and make me feel better, you always do, the other stuff, the stuff I'm feeling that I haven't even named yet, wouldn't be named. It wouldn't be fixed." She took a beat and thought. Ed waited for her. "Sorry, that's all. I don't have anything else right now, but no, I don't think I'm totally OK, but this is my way to make it OK. It might not, but there's only one way to find out."

Ed was quiet for a few seconds as he processed it all. "Makes perfect sense to me."

She smiled even bigger. She didn't know that was possible. "Thank you."

"So, where are you now?"

They talked for two hours about everything and nothing. Julia popped into the conversation, accepted the apologies, and assured her that everything was fine. By the time she stopped for gas, food, and a break, and before she entered the mountains, she saw texts from Tommy, Yates, and Candy, all giving her words of encouragement and support. They all offered an ear to keep her company as she drove. She felt buoyed even more than she already did.

Five hours later, her trek almost to the two-thirds mark, she stopped again and sent Maggie a message telling her what she did and thanking her for the inspiration. She sent Bill a message too. She just said, "On a road trip. Call me when you can." She never knew when she could speak to him, but she wanted him to be aware of what was coming. She was past the point of no return so he couldn't talk her out of it, but she wanted to get some perspective from the only person who could sort of understand.

Two hours later, shortly after she crossed into her home state, he called.

"Hey, Bill!" she said as brightly as possible.

"Hi! How's the trip going?"

"It's going pretty well. I just passed Thornton Lacey, actually," she said, naming the small village in the northern part of their state.

He was quiet as he placed it. "Frances," he said in the sternest voice he could muster.

"William," she mimicked back.

"What are you doing? Mom said..."

"Yeah, I know what Mom said, but I don't think she's right."

"You don't think?"

"I don't know for sure. How can I know? I mean, if the whole point is that if I come home, I'll feel too guilty to leave, then that means I'll never be able to see her or any of the littlies, ever. I won't come home for Suzy's graduation or for any of the boys or Little Bit. You heard her, Bill. She thinks I'm hiding."

"She's a kid. She doesn't mean..."

"No!" she shouted more forcefully than she thought she would. "I mean, yes, she's just a kid, but that's exactly why she means what she says. She thinks I'm hiding from her. Can you imagine what she thinks of me? I didn't come see the babies. I didn't even show up for that."

"I didn't either. We have our own lives now."

"You do, Bill. You do. You're living your dream. She could see you in your uniform. She understands that. I'm just..."

"You're living your dream too."

"Am I? How do I know? Am I just following in Mom's footsteps? Like, literally? If I'm really living a life that I'm choosing, that means I can choose to come and go as I see fit. It means I can leave when I want to. It means that I won't end up with a degree from a world-class college only to what? Move back to The Ranch and play nanny to my siblings and take care of enough things so Dad moves back into the big house? Is that my fate?"

He was silent on his end of the phone. She didn't give him an out. Eventually, after minutes passed, he said, "It could be, but I don't want it to be, and I'm just worried that if..."

"Well, I'm worried too." She finally said it out loud and it didn't make her cry like she thought hearing the words aloud would. Like they did for Maggie. Instead, she straightened her back and said it again. "I'm worried too, but you know what? I'm ready to face it. I'm ready."

"Well then, little sister," Bill said, hearing the way her voice changed, as though he, too, was expecting tears. "I think you are."

She allowed her back to relax back into the seat, and they talked until the sun was totally set, and she was at the edge of Unincorporated Nowhere. He wished her luck and told her he wanted her to tell him all about it, even if that meant she had to send a million texts in the middle of the night.

She stopped at the only gas station in the area and filled up. She texted everyone, telling them where she was. The replies came in relentlessly. Even Tom sent her a message. It was just a thumbs-up emoji, but it was something. She stretched and popped her back. She wished she had stopped to get some clothes along the way. She felt gross and sticky. The heat and humidity she missed so much was thick in the air. It was one of those early winter nights in the fall that feels like summer everywhere else.

She ran her hands through her hair, took her scarf off, and felt her neck. She couldn't feel any of the internal heat that gave her warnings of a coming outbreak. She climbed in and pulled down the visor to look at herself. There she was, disheveled but calm. She fist-bumped herself, flipped up the mirror, started the Jeep, and headed home.

It is a truth universally acknowledged that when a child returns from college for the first time, the child regresses. It is not the child's fault. It just happens. It is that truth that burned deep in Fran's heart that made her push so hard to keep Junior away. So, when she saw a Jeep pull down the long drive of The Ranch and park, she wasn't too concerned. She thought it would drive past the big house and go back to the first house, where her husband had been holding regular card games with some of his acquaintances. However, when it stopped in front of the big house and she saw her eldest daughter climb out, she burst into tears.

Junior stood for a few moments in the drive, looking around The Ranch. She was trying to see it with new eyes, but it was dark and her evaluation would have to wait. She climbed the stairs on the front deck and opened the kiddie gate that kept the littlies from falling or wandering off too far. The motion lights clicked on, and the front door swung open. There stood her mother, tears running down her cheeks, arms straight down, not sure if Junior would want a hug or if she would come over and slap her. Seeing her mother there, crying and unsure, crashed down on her.

She ran toward Fran, who opened her arms and took her in. They hugged and cried for some time.

Eventually, they silently went into the house. After 9, silence in the big house was mandatory to make sure all the kids stayed asleep through the night. Junior, wordlessly pressed toward her mother's room to see the twins in real life. She held her mouth as she cried over them. She kissed her hand and touched it softly to each of their heads. She backed out of the room and closed the door. She saw that the light was on in the laundry room. Fran was in there, on the floor, her back to the wall. She had two glasses of tea sitting next to her. Junior closed the door and then sat with her back to the washing machine. She took the tea and drank a big gulp. She felt the sugar and caffeine rush through her. She exhaled.

"Hi, Mom," she said, and the tears started up again.

"Hello, my sweet girl." She leaned forward and held out her hand. Junior took it. "I'm so glad to see you."

"I'm glad to see you too. We have a lot to talk about, and I thought maybe we would do it in person."

Fran exhaled and deflated back against the wall. "You're right. We do."

"We don't have to do it right now. Not right this second, but soon. While I'm here. After Christmas. Definitely before I go back, because Mom, and I need you to hear me on this: I'm going back. OK?"

Fran looked down and let her hair drape in front of her face. She started crying again. She nodded. "OK. Yes." She looked up and smiled at her. "I promise."

"Thank you."

She stood up and reached her hands down to pull her mother up. They stood and hugged again. Fran squeezed

and squeezed until Junior tapped her on the back and whispered, "Can't breathe." The tension broken and the conditions of the visit settled, Fran went off to bed and Junior collapsed on the couch. She was asleep in seconds.

She woke to the feeling of the air being forced from her lungs. "JUNIOR!" Little Bit was screaming her name as she bounced on her chest. "You're home. Yay!"

"Hey, sweetie. I am."

"Forever?"

"You need to get off, baby. I can't breathe, and you're so big, I can't lift you." She scrambled off and stood right next to the couch, not giving her any room to swing her legs. Junior pulled herself into a sitting position with her legs pulled close to her chest. She patted the empty spot on the couch so her sister would sit down. "Well, the first thing I need to do is use the potty. Then we can talk. I want to hear all about how school is going now. I meant what I said about you being my pen pal, but I haven't heard back from you yet. So, we need to talk."

"So not forever then?"

"No baby, not forever. For a little while. We'll talk, OK?"

She exhaled and frowned. "OK."

"Can you go make us some cereal? I'll meet you at the table."

Feeling important, she perked right up. "Yep!" She sprang off the couch and buzzed into the kitchen.

Junior spent the morning being swarmed by the pack of littlies, who were overly excited to see her. She held each twin as long as she could, trying to make each of them get a sense of her, knowing full well they wouldn't really ever know her. Abstractly, she knew that was the case, but it wasn't until she was in the room with them that it hit her. It was compounded by the fact that the three-year-old wasn't totally sure who she was, and it was only after the others started playing with her and climbing on her that he joined in. She smiled her way through it all and soaked in all of the kisses, hugs, and knees in the back. She hadn't missed those.

When the twins went down for their morning nap, and the newness of her being there wore off on the rest of the pack, she wandered back to her old house to shower and get some of her old clothes that she had left behind. She saw Suzy sitting on one of the Adirondack chairs, coffee steaming next to her on the table, head bent over her phone, seemingly oblivious to everything.

She stopped and picked up a rock and threw it so that it skipped across the ground and banged against the porch. Suzy looked up, ready to do battle with whichever sibling dared. When she saw who it was, she dropped her phone and ran toward her big sister. Much like the embrace Junior and her mother shared, this one ended when Junior begged for breath.

"What are you doing here?" Suzy asked finally.

"Well, that's a long story. Actually, it's a short story about a long drive. Can I persuade you to make me a cup of coffee while I shower, and then I'll tell you all about it?"

"Sure, yeah. Of course."

"The boys in there?"

"Nope, they are at some ... thing. I don't know. I didn't pay attention. I just knew I'd have the house to myself for a few days."

"That sounds awesome. I'm staying up front, so you don't have to worry."

"Well, you don't have to. You can stay. You aren't a gross boy. I mean. Was I that gross at eleven and thirteen?"

"Well..." Junior said.

"Never mind. I don't want to know. Just go shower. You smell like toddler farts and baby puke."

"I know." Junior made a face. "I kind of missed it, though."

"I know you did, you big dummy. That's why you weren't supposed to come back."

"Right, well..."

"No!" Suzy held up her hands. "Shower, change, coffee, then talk."

They spent the afternoon catching up. While the intention was for Junior to give a big speech about why she drove fifteen hours on a whim, without any clothes, when she sat down in the chair, wet hair hanging down to air dry, Suzy launched into some tirade about some girl from school who had a bad attitude. That dominated most of the conversation as clearly Suzy had been storing it all up, and it was going to burst forth no matter what.

Eventually, they got to Junior's stuff, where they fell into an easy routine again. By the time they headed up to the big house for dinner, they felt as though no time had passed. Their father didn't join them. Apparently, after Thanksgiving, he simply stopped coming up for meals without any explanation. It was another secret they kept from her. While that was strange, and despite the fact that Bill wasn't there, dinner felt familiar and good. Fran did the cooking. Junior did the serving. Suzy did the clearing. Junior washed, Fran dried, and Suzy put the dishes away.

Junior did hide away for a few minutes in the laundry room to video chat with Maggie, who was having a better time than she thought she would, but she still complained that it felt all superficial. She said it felt like they were all being extra nice, and it was creeping her out. They kept it light and did their best to encourage each other, all while making promises to do a long sleepover-style catch-up after Junior picked Maggie up from the airport the Friday before the next term began.

For the rest of the evening, the three of them sat out on the deck while the littlies played in the yard. Junior and Fran talked about the cold and how unbearable it was up there. Suzy called them both soft and assured them that when she went to college somewhere up north, she would be fine. They knew better than to tell her she was wrong.

After the kids were scrubbed, snacked, and tucked away in bed, Suzy headed back to her house. She asked if Junior wanted to come, but everyone knew it was just her saying the thing that was expected of her. Junior declined. She snuck into the laundry room each night to talk to Ed and catch each other up on the day.

The next two days were essentially a repeat of the first, and before Junior knew it, Christmas had arrived. Children don't know what holidays are like for other people until they are older, and so the littlies had no idea that in other parts of Unincorporated Nowhere, there were much bigger celebrations. The older kids, the two boys having returned from wherever they were on Christmas Eve, knew all too well what was going on in other homes, but not wanting to ruin any of it, they smiled and laughed. Their father even made an appearance, making the kids even more excited. He and Junior exchanged few words. He was still mad at her, but she smiled at him and said Merry Christmas, not wanting to ruin anything for the kids. They treated him as though he was an extra present, so the day was, for lack of a better term, jolly.

That morning after, instead of being woken by screaming kids or kicks to the head, the smell of brewed coffee jolted her from her slumber. She looked out the window and saw it was still dark. Not exactly sure what was going on, she stumbled to and from the bathroom. When she returned, she saw the light on in the laundry room. She went in and found her mother on the floor with two cups of coffee.

Junior came in and shut the door behind her.

"It's time," Fran said.

"Yeah. I know. It's been time. I've just been waiting. I told you. After Christmas."

Fran exhaled. She was relieved. She was worried that Junior had, without intending it, and against all of her mother's wishes, become part of the fabric of The Ranch again. "Really?"

"Really. I was planning on it later today. I can even show you the message I sent to Maggie yesterday. It says, 'Happy Christmas. Going to ruin everything tomorrow. Love you.'"

Fran couldn't help herself. She laughed. "You won't ruin everything."

"I might."

"Well then, let me go first."

Junior reached her mug out, and they toasted. "OK."

"First, I want to say that I was so shocked and scared when you first got here that those tears you saw were not of joy but of fear. Fear that you would let me keep ruining your life."

"You didn't..."

"No, I know. You got out, and Bill got out, but I tried. Unwillingly at first, but ultimately, I tried. I made that saying up about having everything we needed. I brainwashed you all. I turned our family into the cult that everyone thinks it is. It's why I didn't want you to come back. I knew, I just knew you would fall right back into things, and you'd never leave."

"But you're wrong, Mom. I told you on the first night. We'd talk about it later. I said, after Christmas. I said that. I said, I'm going back."

"Kids say things and they forget. How many times has Suzy said she hates me?"

"I'm not Suzy. I'm not other kids. I'm me. When have I ever said I would do something and then not follow through? Name one time."

They sat in silence. Fran knew she was right, of course. Junior didn't lie. Junior didn't back down. She may change her mind, but even then, she would have an entire explanation as to how and why she changed her mind. "I can't."

"You can't. That's right. So, what hurts most here is not really that you willingly didn't look out for us because I can sort of understand that. You love Dad. He has always been your person. Above us. That's OK. I wish he weren't your person, but he is. What kills me is that you thought I was so weak. I'm not fragile just because I'm small.

"You know why I came down here? I came here to show you that getting out is possible. Sure, you can make the excuse that Bill has no choice but to leave or he is breaking the law. That is true, but that isn't why he could come and go at will. It's because he's strong too. He's been gone for years. Once he made a plan for the Air Force, he was gone. You know it. I know it. I wanted to show you that I'm strong too. I know you think I'm weak. I know you think that if you hadn't set me up with the Bertrams, I wouldn't have gone to Mansfield, but that's not true. Just because dad blew the money, it didn't matter. I was going. I would have found a way."

"Oh, honey, I don't think that. I just, I know how big your heart is, and I thought you'd come back and see the state of things and just…"

"The state of things is better, right? Bill says you applied for assistance. You send the kids to daycare. You have them on free breakfast and lunch. That's good, Mom. That's a good thing. You can't keep this up. You can't…"

"I know. It's just… I'm embarrassed."

"People are on assistance. More than half the kids who live down here are on it. That isn't embarrassing. That's what it's for."

"No. I know. I'm not embarrassed about that. I'm ashamed that I didn't do it sooner. I'm sick that I put all of this on you. The others too, but mostly on you. I'm sorry that I love your dad so much that I can't get out of it."

"That's it though, Mom. You can. I love you so much it breaks me. I love Suzy and the boys and Little Bit so much. I mean, the twins are never even going to know me, but I love them. I would give them a kidney, but I'm going back. I'm showing them how much I love them by going. The easy thing to do would be to stay. The hard thing, the right thing, is to go, and I'm going.

"I'm not here to fight. I'm here to do what I have always done. I do what's right. I used to think there was something wrong with me. You know? Like, why can't I just sneak out? Why don't I skip out on the mailbox rental? Why don't I just say whatever anyone wants to hear so they will like me? There's this girl at school who called me Glinda, and she thought it was an insult, but it isn't. I am Glinda. I am good. I do what's right no matter what. Even when it's hard and unpopular. I'm proud of that. I just thought, if I said it, you wouldn't hear it, but if I showed you, well, you'd know it could be done.

"You know, at Thanksgiving, when I found out about the assistance, I actually thought about how my life would have been different if you had done that years ago. I thought about Bill and Suzy too. I thought that everything would have been better for all of us. Mostly, better for you, but all of us. We could have all had a chance at a," she made finger quotes, "'normal life.' Whatever that means. I'm not proud of it, but I'll admit to thinking all of that for a while."

"Oh, baby, I know. I'm so..."

"No, that's just it though, Mom. I'm not asking you to be sorry. You didn't ruin my life. You didn't ruin Bill's life. You gave us our lives. The pressure was huge, and I'm glad that the rest of them won't have to feel it, but the pressure, the weight of it all, didn't crush us. It's like we carried around a backpack full of emotional weight for years, and when we took it off, we were so much stronger than everyone. So, while there is a lot to say, and there is a lot you did wrong, I'm not denying that, but you did what you did, and you made us who we are."

They sat in silence. Fran was in awe of the child she had made who was such an inspiration. Finally, Fran said, "Listen, I know..."

"Mama?" Betsy's voice came through the closed door. "I think the twins is up. I tried to sing to them, but that didn't work."

"Coming, sweetie," Fran said. She stood up, reached out to Junior, and pulled her up. Fran went about changing and feeding the twins while Junior set the table for Betsy and the littlies.

After breakfast, Junior dressed in an old ratty pair of jeans she had left behind and one of her dad's t-shirts he had left in the big house. It was huge on her, but it would serve the purpose. She hugged everyone and gave them kisses and promises of letters and video chats. She climbed into the Jeep, and instead of backing down the driveway, she drove deeper into The Ranch and pulled up next to the first house. The one where her dad was sleeping.

Before she could go in, she went to her old house and snuck into Suzy's room. She knelt down next to the bed and kissed her on the cheek. "Love you, silly girl." Suzy didn't budge. Like their father, she slept like the dead. She left a note on top of Suzy's phone, ensuring she would see it. She stopped in the kitchen on her way out and grabbed a few supplies from under the sink.

She went back over to the original house, the one her great-great-grandfather had built, and she walked in like she owned it. The smell of staleness hit her. She could not imagine that the windows or doors had been opened for months. She turned on all the lights on the main floor. The room was cluttered with empty bottles. The sink was full of dishes. The garbage was overflowing. She pulled out her phone, turned on *Mechanical Resonance*, the first Tesla album her dad ever played for her, and got to work.

She opened every window, letting the breeze flow through. She poured the garbage into one of the bags she got from her house. She brought the whole box of lawn bags over. She filled two more with trash from around the house and set all three bags on the porch. She washed all the dishes, dried them, and put them away. She found several of the plates and mugs were chipped and broken. She threw those in the garbage can that she had lined with a new bag.

She sprayed down and cleaned every surface in the place. It was clear no one had cleaned it since she and Bill had moved out. She went to the storage closet in the bathroom and got the broom and mop. Once she was totally done, and she felt the whole ground floor was as clean as it could be, she went out to the Jeep and got the clothes she wore on the drive down. She went back into the house. The fresh air that flowed through had blown away not only the stale odor but the bleach smell, too. She closed up all the windows, set about making a pot of coffee, and went into the bathroom to change.

She shut her music off and just listened to the sounds of the house. She hadn't realized how quiet things were back here in the old houses. She was on her second cup, sitting at the kitchen table, a full hour after she had first entered the house when she heard her father's movement upstairs. She felt the heat start to creep up her neck, but she resisted the urge to get her scarf. She rubbed her neck and willed her heart to quit hammering. She got up and poured him a cup of coffee.

He came in, seemingly unsurprised by the state of things, and sat down across from her. He took a long sip of his coffee and smacked his lips. "What's all this then?"

"It's a metaphor, Dad."

"Is it?" He looked at her with dead eyes.

"It is." She felt her anxiety rise and the heat climbing up her chest around her collarbone.

"For?"

"Come on." She felt anger rise and it seemed to fight back the anxiety. "You've tried to fool everyone your whole life, but I know that you're not stupid. Mean. Cold-hearted. Lazy. Manipulative. Sure. Not stupid."

"Well, I never did any of that fancy school learning like you and your mother. I'm not smart enough to get into the Air Force like your brother. I'm just some lowly swabby. So why don't you tell me? Tell me what you came to say. Say it to my face." He was pounding the table at that point. "Tell me all the horrible things I've done. How I've ruined your life, and your mom's life. Tell me all about it. Go ahead. Say whatever you want to say. I'm a loser, is that it? I don't deserve your mother? She's too good for me? Say it! Let's have it out. Tell me how you're cleaning things up and taking out the trash and how I'm the trash." He was shouting. He stood up and was looking down at her. His neck was red and blotchy. Hers was clear and smooth. He leaned forward on his forearms so that his face was just inches from hers. He dropped his voice to a low growl. "Come on. You know you want to."

She looked up at him and was not scared. She stood up slowly, not breaking eye contact with him. She shook her head and said, "I don't think so." She turned and walked out of the house, letting his shouts and insults bounce off her back. She climbed into the Jeep and ignored him as he ran out onto the porch, shouting and waving his arms around. She started the ignition and drove past the big house. She waved at her mother, who was standing on the porch and who could clearly hear her husband's shouts and wails. Junior didn't look back, though. She turned right out of the driveway and headed north, toward home.

The Austen Chronicles will return with
That Other Dashwood Girl.

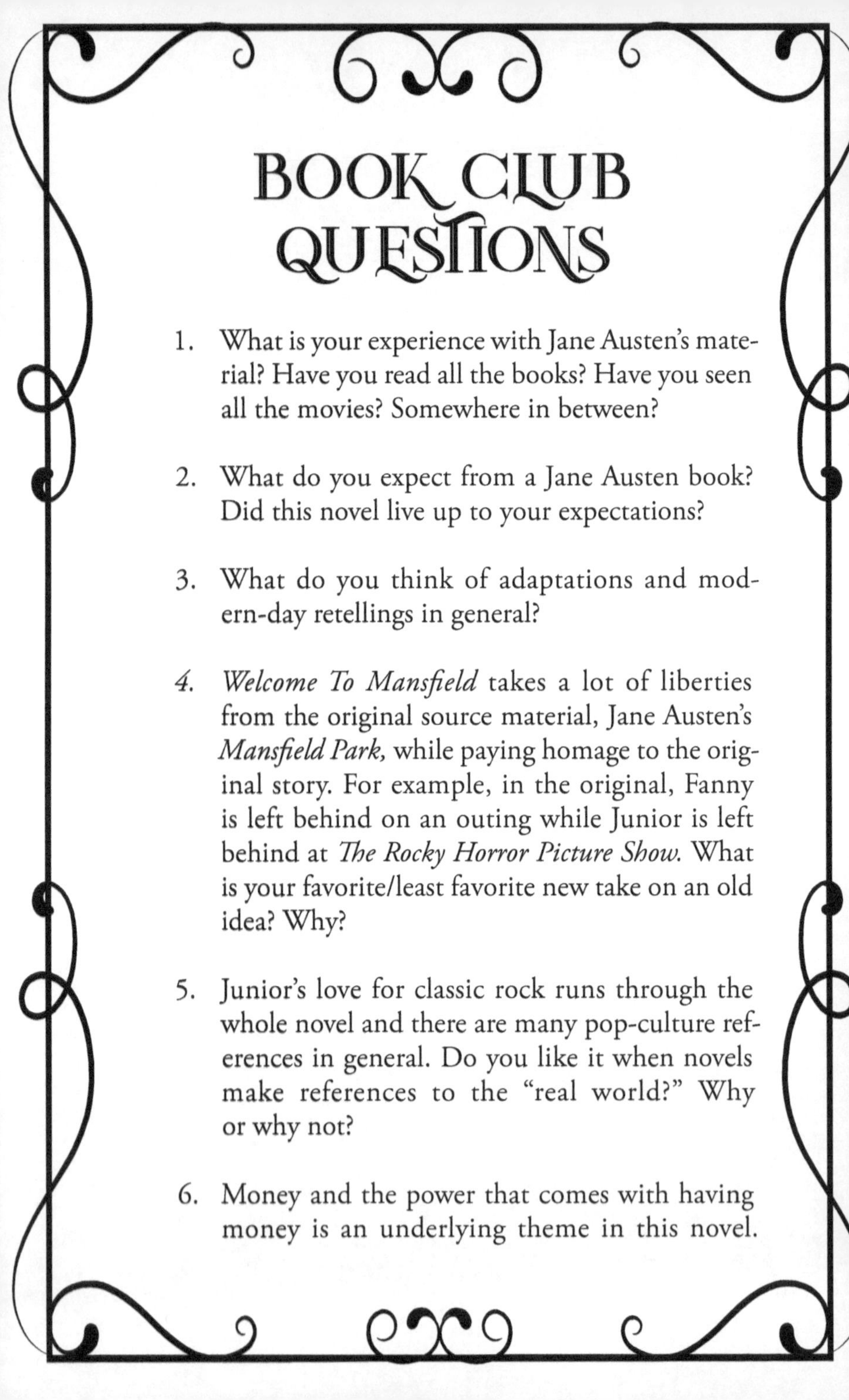

BOOK CLUB QUESTIONS

1. What is your experience with Jane Austen's material? Have you read all the books? Have you seen all the movies? Somewhere in between?

2. What do you expect from a Jane Austen book? Did this novel live up to your expectations?

3. What do you think of adaptations and modern-day retellings in general?

4. *Welcome To Mansfield* takes a lot of liberties from the original source material, Jane Austen's *Mansfield Park,* while paying homage to the original story. For example, in the original, Fanny is left behind on an outing while Junior is left behind at *The Rocky Horror Picture Show.* What is your favorite/least favorite new take on an old idea? Why?

5. Junior's love for classic rock runs through the whole novel and there are many pop-culture references in general. Do you like it when novels make references to the "real world?" Why or why not?

6. Money and the power that comes with having money is an underlying theme in this novel.

What are some examples from the book that ring true in your life or community?

7. Norris is very concerned with her family name and family legacy. Can you relate to that pressure of having to live up to your family name?

8. Junior shows no jealousy and never takes the bait when Mary acts the way she does. Why do you think that is? Would you react the same way?

9. Junior is asked to keep several secrets in this book. How does that conflict with the fact that she always likes to be honest at all costs?

10. Found family is at the heart of this novel. Do you think that found family can be just as important to someone as their blood family?

11. There is no real "villain" in this novel, but there are several characters who have nefarious motives. Which of those characters is the most sympathetic? Which is the least sympathetic?

12. What do you think about the final chapter? Does Junior earn her catharsis? What will happen with her parents after what she did? Has she set them on a new trajectory?

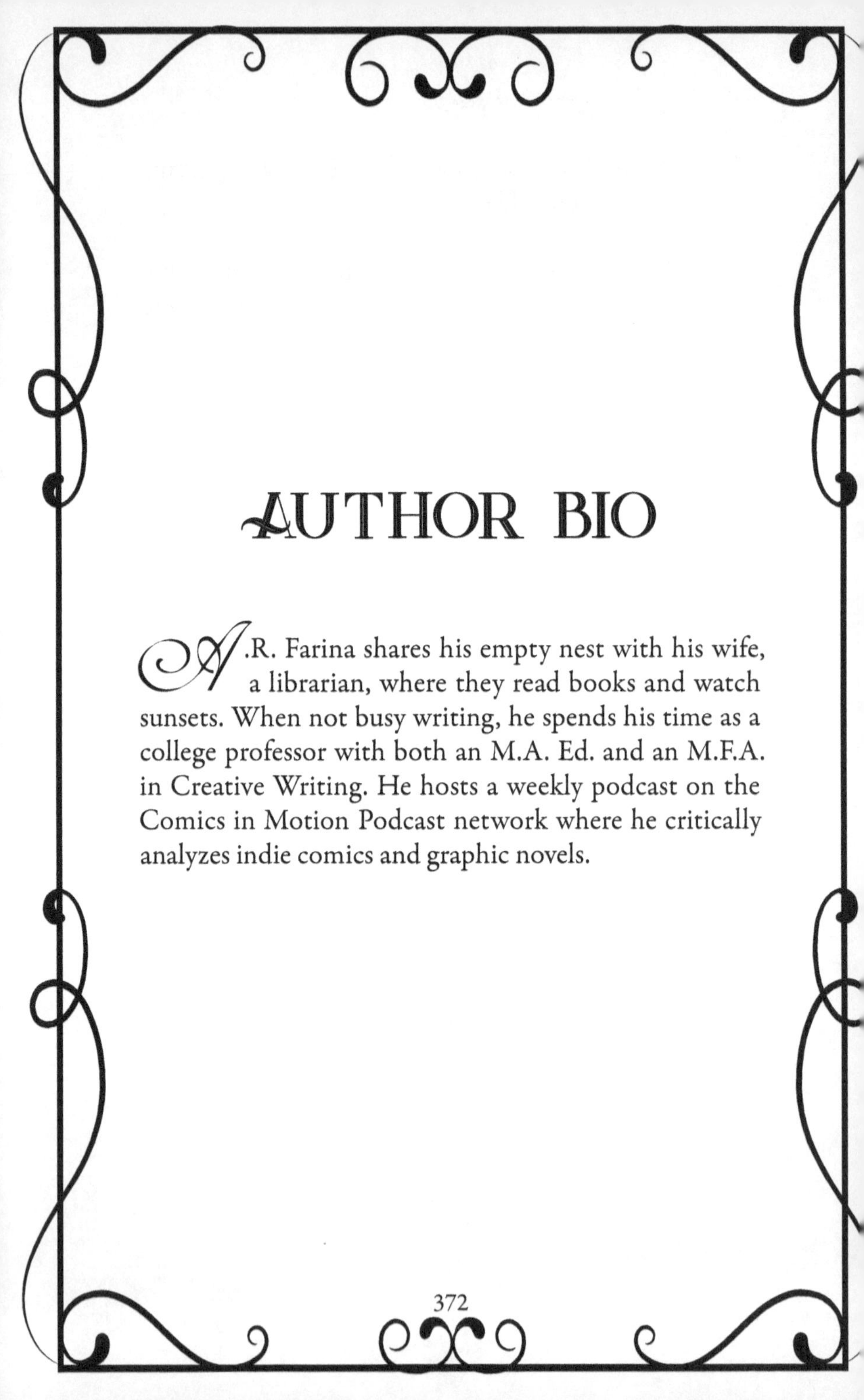

AUTHOR BIO

A.R. Farina shares his empty nest with his wife, a librarian, where they read books and watch sunsets. When not busy writing, he spends his time as a college professor with both an M.A. Ed. and an M.F.A. in Creative Writing. He hosts a weekly podcast on the Comics in Motion Podcast network where he critically analyzes indie comics and graphic novels.